BLOOD SISTERS

VAMPIRE STORIES BY WOMEN

Other Anthologies Edited by
Paula Guran

BLOOD SISTERS

VAMPIRE STORIES BY W⦾MEN

Edited by Paula Guran

Night Shade Books
New York

Night Shade books may be purchased in bulk at special discounts for sales promotion, corporate gifts, fund-raising, or educational purposes. Special editions can also be created to specifications. For details, contact the Special Sales Department, Night Shade Books, 307 West 36th Street, 11th Floor, New York, NY 10018 or info@skyhorsepublishing.com.

Night Shade Books® is a registered trademark of Skyhorse Publishing, Inc.®, a Delaware corporation.

Visit our website at www.nightshadebooks.com.

10 9 8 7 6 5 4 3 2 1

Library of Congress Cataloging-in-Publication Data

Blood sisters : vampire stories by women / edited by Paula Guran.
    pages cm
  ISBN 978-1-59780-818-7 (paperback)
1. Vampires--Fiction. 2. American fiction--Women authors. 3. Paranormal fiction, American.
I. Guran, Paula, editor.
 PS648.V35B64 2015
 813'.0873808375--dc 3
                        2015006845

ISBN: 978-1-59780-818-7

Cover design by Claudia Noble

An extension of this copyright page can be found on page 472.

Printed in the United States of America

CONTENTS

INTRODUCTION:
Welcome to My House!
Enter Freely and of Your
Own Free Will!

Paula Guran

There are many great reference books and essays about vampire literature. This is not one of them. It's only an extremely brief, overly simplistic, and far from complete history of vampire fiction that is (meaning no disrespect to the innumerable fine and hugely important male authors of such fiction) intentionally shaped to highlight women's authorial role in such. It is based, in part, on the introduction to *Vampires: The Recent Undead* (Prime Books, 2011), an anthology I edited that focused on short vampire fiction published 2000–2010. (You can read the entire essay from which I am recycling some bits here at paulaguran.com/vampires-the-recent-undead-intro.)

***

The idea of the vampire has probably been around since humanity first began to ponder death. In Western culture the vampire has been a pervasive icon for more than two centuries now, but the image of the vampire as something other than a disgusting reanimated corpse was profoundly reshaped in the early nineteenth century by a group of British aristocrats.

Mary Wollstonecraft Godwin, Percy Shelley, Matthew Lewis, Lord Byron, and Byron's physician, Dr. John Polidori, decided to amuse themselves one damp summer 1816 evening in a villa on Lake Geneva by writing ghost stories. Mary Godwin (who later married Shelley) created a modern myth (and science fiction) with *Frankenstein, or Prometheus Unbound*. Polidori picked up a fragment of vampire fiction written by Byron on that fateful night and eventually produced a novelette based on it: "The Vampyre." It featured the charismatic Lord Ruthven: a seductive refined noble as well as a blood-sucking monster who preyed on others. Ruthven was obviously based on the already notorious "bad boy" Byron.

"The Vampyre" became wildly popular, particularly in Germany and France. The theatres of Paris were filled by the early 1820s with vampire-themed plays. Some of these returned to England in translated form. As for fiction: "The Vampyre," Brian Stableford has written, was the "most widely read vampire story of its era . . . To say that it was influential is something of an understatement; there was probably no one in England or France who attempted to write a vampire story in the nineteenth century who was not familiar with it, one way or another."

Polidori's story was certainly the inspiration for the serialized "penny dreadful" *Varney the Vampire or, The Feast of Blood* (1845-47) by (most likely) James Malcolm Rhymer. *Varney* appealed to the masses, but was of even less literary merit than the short story to which it owed so much.

It took Sheridan le Fanu to craft a true literary gem with his novella "Carmilla," published in 1872. The tale of a lonely girl and a beautiful aristocratic female vampire in an isolated castle also brought steamy sub-textual lesbian sexuality into the vampire mythos.

But it was Bram Stoker's novel *Dracula* (1897) that became the basis of modern vampire lore: Dracula was a vampire "king" of indefinite lifespan who could not be seen in mirrors, had an affinity to bats and aversions to crucifixes and garlic. He had superhuman strength, could shapeshift and control human minds. Stoker's vampires needed their native soil and the best way to kill one was with a stake through the heart followed by decapitation. There were humans who, like Abraham Van Helsing, hunted vampires . . . etc.

Of course, *Dracula* did not leap solely from Stoker's imagination to the page, nor did le Fanu's "Carmilla" or Polidori's earlier vampire. Their influences were many, but all were also products of the Gothic genre—the first truly popular literature . . . and the first genre to be written mostly by women.

The Gothic mode originated with Horace Walpole's *The Castle of Otranto* (1764). Walpole, at first, published the novel as the translation of a medieval manuscript. This deception made the work critically acceptable. Once Walpole admitted authorship, however, the literati generally spurned it as superstitious romantic trash.

Clara Reeve made the Gothic somewhat more tolerable to the pundits by introducing eighteenth-century "realism" and downplaying the more fantastic elements used by Walpole in her novel *The Old English Barron* (1798).

Ann Radcliffe, used the technique of the "explained supernatural"— all sorts of scary uncanny things might occur, but most were ultimately revealed to have natural causes (rather like *Scooby-Doo* plots)—to write Gothic novels. With her fourth work, Radcliffe produced the first bestselling novel: *The Mysteries of Udolpho* (1794).

As with popular novels today, a flood of imitative novels followed and most of them were written by women. These may not have been vampiric, or even very good, but they still bit into the same public vein.

As for the vamps—before Stoker (and possibly before le Fanu), there were vampire stories written by women as well as men. Some are lost due to pseudonyms and intentional anonymity, but known examples include:

- Eliza Lynn Linton's "The Fate of Madame Cabanel," published in 1880. It portrays provincials who label a stranger among them—the innocent Fanny Cabanel—as a vampire due to their superstition, bigotry, and ignorance (of, among many other things, proper drainage and sanitation).
- "Let Loose" (1890) by Mary Chomondeley is an odd, but effective, story of a man who wears high collars looking for a crypt in which there is a fresco painted by his father. Deaths coincide with his appearance and scars on his neck do not match those of the dog he claims bit him.
- "Good Lady Ducayne," published in 1896 by Mary Elizabeth Braddon is a "scientific" variant on the legend of Elizabeth Báthory, a Hungarian countess who allegedly killed hundreds of girls between 1585 and 1610 to obtain their virginal blood believing she would retain her youth if she bathed in the vital fluid. In Braddon's novella, the wealthy aristocratic Lady Ducayne's sinister doctor, Parravicini, performs "experimental surgery" on girls in her employ to obtain blood he then injects into her ladyship to prolong her already long life.

- In "A Mystery of the Campagna" (1886) by Anne Crawford (Baroness von Rabe) the bloodless corpse of the narrator's friend is found after being seen with a lovely woman. A sarcophagus is found in an ancient vault in which the remarkably healthy-looking occupant is the same woman. Helpfully, among the Latin inscriptions naming her as Vespertilia, is one in Greek that translates as "The blood-drinker, the vampire woman." A wooden stake to the heart is inevitably employed.

Stoker also acknowledged an 1885 essay by Emily Gerard on "Transylvanian Superstitions"—later part of her 1888 book *The Land Beyond the Forest*—as important to his research. He "borrowed" some elements: the term *nosferatu* and information about a "Devil's school, the *Scholomance*, where the members of the Dracula family learned the secrets of the 'Evil One.'"

[Note: The claim that "The Skeleton Count, or The Vampire Mistress," allegedly written by Elizabeth Caroline Grey and published in 1825 or 1828—thus supposedly making it the first known published story by a woman—has been, at best, debunked as unproven and, at worst, a complete hoax.]

Having acknowledged some of the influence eighteenth- and nineteenth-century women had on Bram Stoker, we must now admit that the Dracula-type vampire popularized by the novel, as well as stage productions and films that followed, heavily dominated authors' and readers' minds for many years.

Fantasy, the "weird," and science fiction in the first half of the twentieth century was primarily written in the short form, so the vampire appeared in stories rather than novels. In those days genre writing of that type was produced predominately by men. But women managed to be published, and a few wrote vampiric prose.

One of the most notable vampiric works by a woman in the early twentieth century is the ambiguous but eerie "Luella Miller" (1902) by Mary E. Wilkins Freeman. Freeman's character was a type of "psychic vampire," a schoolteacher who seemingly draws the life out of anyone close to her. No one, including Luella, is really sure this deadly effect is either intentional or evil.

Whether C. L. (Catherine Lucille) Moore's "Shambleau" (1933) is a vampire story may be open to question, but one can make a good argument that the alien Shambleau is a form of vampire. At first assumed by the hero to be an attractive human women unjustly victimized by a Martian mob, she turns out to be a creature who sucks the life-force out of others with her wormlike "hair" while placing her victims in an addictive ecstatic state.

Various vampiric attributes and powers were added or subtracted in films and short stories produced during the first five decades of the last century. The vampire thrived in those two media, but no notable vampire novels were published until 1954 when Richard Matheson contributed the idea of vampirism as an infectious disease with apocalyptic consequence in his novel *I Am Legend*.

By the 1960s, short form vampirism was also mixed with other science fiction tropes such as being an inherited genetic condition. Vampires were even rendered in a sympathetic light—as long as it was acknowledged they were, by nature, evil and chose (as humans could) to resist their monstrosity and to be "good."

Evelyn E. Smith's vampire, Mr. Varri, in "Softly While You're Sleeping" (1961) is courtly and gentle. Unlike her human beaus (and earlier fictional vampires) Varri neither attempts to force or compel Anna, the young woman in the story. However, she knows the vampire's love will still destroy her, so she chooses to reject him.

The early 1970s brought an onslaught of novel-length vampirism. Men wrote most of these novels but, again—in that era—the preponderance of *any* type of science fiction, fantasy, or what became the horror genre was authored by men.

In one landmark work, Stephen King's 1975 *'Salem's Lot*, the author downplayed vampiric eroticism, upped the level of terror, and focused on the vampire as a metaphor of corrupt power. King also updated vampirism by placing his vampires in small-town America.

Fred Saberhagen's novel *The Dracula Tape* was published the same year as *'Salem's Lot*. The Count himself narrated Saberhagen's far more obscure, but still significant, novel. He relates *his* side of Bram Stoker's story and, naturally, portrayed himself in a favorable light.

About six months later, in May 1976, Anne Rice's *Interview with the Vampire* was published. Rice radically revised the icon of the vampire, albeit more fully with the second of what became her Vampire Chronicles, *Lestat*, which didn't come along until 1985. The first novel was set among vampires of varying characters—who, unlike Dracula, sought out others of their kind to form communal and even "family" groups. The aristocratic Lestat de Lioncourt echoed Lord Ruthven more than the comparatively dreary Count Dracula; the middle-class Louis de Pointe du Lac clings to his bourgeois morality: a vampire with a conscience (and considerable angst).

Interview was not an immediate success. It attained bestseller status a year after its first publication when Ballantine released a paperback edition.

The second Vampire Chronicle novel, *Lestat,* proved how the audience for *Interview* had grown when it became an instant bestseller. In it, the character of Lestat refuted Louis's claims and characterization presented in the initial novel; more of the vampire universe is revealed. The formerly androgynous characters became more sexualized and earlier subtler homoeroticism more overt. Lestat is not exactly evil, but rather a complex personality—even a rebellious antihero—whose complexity has grown over the course of (currently) eleven novels.

Rice's two New Tales of the Vampire novels (*Pandora,* 1998, and *Vittorio the Vampire,* 1999) and the six Lives of the Mayfair Witches novels also share and expand the vampire universe of the Chronicles.

Interview with the Vampire revitalized interest in vampire fiction; *Lestat* did much to revise the archetype itself. Some have suggested that Rice has even supplanted Bram Stoker as the most important author of vampire fiction.

Chelsea Quinn Yarbro is not as well known as Rice, but her vampire, the Count Saint-Germain, has had a profound influence on vampire fiction.

Hôtel Transylvania (1978) introduced the character of Le Comte de Saint-Germain. Cultured, well traveled, articulate, elegant, and mysterious, he first appears in the court of France's King Louis XV. Since then, Yarbro has presented—in a non-chronological manner and with name variations suitable to language, era, locale, and circumstance—the Count's life and undeath from 2119 BC and (as with the novella included here) into the twenty-first century. (Roger, his "servant" in "Renewal," became the vampire's right-hand ghoul in Rome in AD 71.) The books and stories of the Saint-Germain Cycle—currently twenty-seven novels and shorter fiction enough to fill two collections—combine well-researched and detailed historical fiction, romance, and horror.

Saint-Germain was the first genuinely romantic and heroic vampire. Although he must take blood to survive, it is an erotic experience for his partners and does no harm. And, though immortal, he seeks out the company of humans and assists them. During his long publishing life, Saint-Germain has been portrayed in many historical periods and settings; in each, it is humankind, its actions and prejudices, that provides the horror.

In the 1980s and 1990s vampires appeared in all varieties in literature (and other media) as traditional monsters, heroes, detectives, aliens, rock stars, psychic predators, loners, tribal, erotic, sexless, violent, placed in alternate histories, present in contemporary settings . . . the vampire became a malleable metaphor of great diversity in many forms, even—first in Lori Herter's *Obsession* (1991)—in the romance marketing category.

A number of outstanding vampiric novels were published in the eighties and nineties, but Anne Rice continued to make the firmest impression on the masses as the bestselling queen of vampire novelists.

Works by other women during this period may not have been as widely read as Rice's, but they contributed a great deal to the expansion of the vampire mythos.

Tanith Lee's *Sabella or The Blood Stone* (1980) is a short but powerful—and often overlooked—science fiction vampire novel. The titular character is a "vampire" who lives on a future colonized planet. Sabella is unknowingly taken over by a member of an extinct alien race of bloodsuckers as a child. In Lee's signature poetic and sensual style, Sabella gains knowledge of herself while the author metaphorically explores a number of issues including post-colonialism, religion, and ecology.

Since Suzy Charnas McKee's Nebula award-winning novella, "The Unicorn Tapestry" (1981), is re-published in this anthology, I'll only note that it became part of an episodic novel, *The Vampire Tapestry*, featuring the unique vampire Dr. Edward Lewis Weyland, a vampire of biologic rather than supernatural genesis. This, coupled with Weyland's social behavior, has led some critics to consider *The Vampire Tapestry* as a major work of feminist science fiction.

Also in a science fictional vein: the alien vampire species explored in Jacqueline Lichtenberg's *Those of My Blood* (1988) and Elaine Bergstrom's vampires of alien origin in her six-book saga of the Austra family that began with *Shattered Glass* (1988). Bergstrom's story, however, is modern Gothic and the Austras have been part of human history for thousands of years.

Lee Killough's *Blood Hunt* (1987) played a part in the establishment of the vampire detection novel. In it, Gareth Mikaelian, an honorable police detective, is transformed into a vampire—and retains his human personality. P. N. Elrod introduced Jack Fleming, a hard-boiled 1930 private investigator, who—transformed into a vampire with his "murder"—seeks his own killer in *Bloodlist* (1990), the first of twelve novels.

Married Victorian-era investigators James and Lydia Asher are involved—at the instigation of the vampire aristocrat Don Simon Ysidro—in solving a vampiric crime in *Those Who Hunt the Night* (1988) by Barbara Hambly. In its sequel, *Traveling With the Dead* (1995), Ysidro joins forces with James Asher.

Victoria "Vicki" Nelson (also known as "Victory Nelson," for her success in solving crimes), a Toronto police officer forced to turn PI due to a degenerative eye disease, teamed up with Henry Fitzroy—a vampire born as the illegitimate son of Henry VIII—in *Blood Price* (1991), the first of Tanya Huff's five Blood Books. (A 2007 Canadian TV series, *Blood Ties*, was based on the books.)

Nancy A. Collins's debut novel, the award-winning *Sunglasses After Dark* (1989), introduced punk vampire/vampire slayer Sonja Blue. The character begins as Denise Thorne, a human raped and left for dead by the vampire Morgan. Denise awakes in a mental hospital. As Collins has explained: ". . . her identity had fragmented during the trauma, wiping out her memories and creating the persona of Sonja. Although Denise died in the operating room, she had been revived via modern medicine—but not before the vampire 'seed' planted in her took hold. Sonja is technically a living vampire, meaning she has their powers/attributes, but still possesses a soul. Unfortunately, the vampire side of her personality—called The Other—is constantly fighting for control of their shared body, and has a tendency to go on horrific rampages, killing foe and friend alike. . . . The world Sonja Blue inhabits can best be described as Vampire Noir. She lives on the fringes of society, hunting the supernatural creatures that pose as humans while preying on them—such as vampires, werewolves, ogres, and demons—known collectively as Pretenders. She uses her own unique Pretender abilities to identify them and hunt them down, as they are 'invisible' to average humans. Sonja views herself as a one-woman hit squad, determined to rid the world of those who prey on humanity—especially vampires." There is also a element of detection involved in the plotlines as Sonja seeks the truth about herself and the world and the vampire who unintentionally made her. Graphic and violent, Collins's vampire fiction is action oriented. Although the now-influential character may return someday, the last Sonja Blue novel, *Darkest Heart*, was published in 2002.

Lost Souls (1992), a debut novel by Poppy Z. Brite, may deserve a better description than its author has given it: "... lush and passionate and energetic as hell ... Basically, it's about a bunch of kids: fifteen-year-old babygoth Nothing, who runs away from his suburban home to seek his ... favorite band; the band members themselves, Steve and Ghost, a redneck and a psychic from Missing Mile, North Carolina; and Molochai, Twig, and Zillah, a roving band of freaks [vampires] who end up being Nothing's real family. There's a plot in there somewhere, involving trips to New Orleans during which the noxious green liqueur Chartreuse is consumed, love and betrayal, babies who eat their way out of the womb, and lots and lots of blood, sex, drugs, cheap wine, and Twinkies." But that's also a pretty accurate description of what became a cult classic for a generation of alienated youth. The sex is bi- or homosexual, occasionally incestuous and usually graphic; the use of drugs may well have established a new metaphor for vampirism. Brite's vampires were a separate species who do not turn humans into vampires, although they can interbreed with them. (Vampiric infants kill their mothers of either species at their gory births.) Most fed on blood, but some found sustenance otherwise. The oldest (close to four hundred years old) is fanged, is sensitive to sunlight, and cannot imbibe in human food or drink. Younger (only about a century old) vampires filed their otherwise normal teeth to points, could tolerate the sun, and eat and drink. Like more traditional vampires, they healed easily, were very strong, and had superhuman senses. They evidently lack other commonly portrayed paranormal powers. Destroying the heart or brain (or giving birth) could kill Brite's vampires.

In another debut novel, *AfterAge* (1993) by Yvonne Navarro, vampires took over the world and wiped out most of humanity. Running low on their food supply, the vamps started capturing and breeding people like cattle. Although the tropes of vampirism having a scientific basis and bloodsuckers conquering Earth echoed Matheson's *I Am Legend*, Navarro played the plot more like a war novel with a stalwart band of survivors defeating conquering invaders with savvy, spunk, and science.

Toward the end of the last century—sometime after the release of Laurell K. Hamilton's fourth Anita Blake Vampire Hunter fantasy novel,

The Lunatic Café (1996), perhaps during the second (1997-1998) or third (1998-1999) season of television series *Buffy the Vampire Slayer*, and just before Christine Feehan's romance *Dark Prince* (1999)—the first of her Dark series—was published, vampires started getting "hot."

The "good guy" vampire—usually sexy, often romantic, sometimes redeemed or redeemable, sometimes ever-heroic—started to dominate pop culture. So did sexy-but-empowered female vamps and kick-ass vampire hunters.

Paranormal romance and "urban fantasy"—the terms and their applications were not always clearly delineated—became extremely popular for about a decade. The demand for these types of books gave many women new opportunities to offer their versions of the vampire mythos to the public in both novels and short fiction.

The romance genre is not really this anthology's territory. One practical reason is that romance does not lend itself to short fiction well; another is that I intentionally wanted a diverse mix of stories. Yes, the romantic is definitely an element in some of these tales of speculative fiction, but it is not the central theme. And a romance is a romance— that *is* its theme.

Novels—like those pioneered by Lee Killough and Tanya Huff—that mixed the supernatural with detection/mystery and romantic relationships are, however, our turf. Primarily fantasies, these plots are set in alternate versions of a contemporary or near-future world much like our own in which the supernatural (including vampires) is present either publicly or hidden from most of humankind. And, for practical purposes, you frequently find this type of fiction (often as extensions of or additions to novel series) in the short form.

Anita Blake's adventures, related in Laurel K. Hamilton's series, assume a world in which vampires and were-creatures have gained legal rights. Beginning with *Guilty Pleasures* in 1993, the twenty-first Anita Blake novel will be published in 2015.

Charlaine Harris's Southern Vampire Mystery series (now usually referred to as the Sookie Stackhouse novels) also posits a world in which vampires have "come out of the casket" and established themselves legally. The central character, a psychic waitress, solves mysteries in each outing. Starting with *Dead Until Dark* (2001) and ending in 2013 with the thirteenth Sookie Stackhouse novel, *Dead Ever After*, the series gained even more widespread popularity when *True Blood* premiered on HBO in

2008. The television show, both a critical and financial success, ran seven seasons, ending in 2014.

In the first decade of the twenty-first century, numerous series featuring vampires—both good and evil—became bestsellers. But *Twilight* (2005)—a vampire fantasy/romance for teens by Stephanie Meyer—its three sequels and consequent films, propelled the blandly romantic, pretty boy/man vampire hero to stratospheric levels of popularity.

Although generally disdained critically and considered more of a romance than a fantasy, *Twilight*'s "sparkly vampires"—so named because her immortal bloodsuckers can live in sunlight; they avoid it because their cold, hard bodies sparkle "like thousands of tiny diamonds" in bright sunshine—may have served a vampiric purpose beyond the commercial. Meyerpires had a keen emotional affect on its multitude of fans. For better or worse, few vamps since Lord Ruthven have done that.

The vampire archetype is immortal *because* it is so variable. Despite the sparklers, nasty vampires still survive here and there in all media. The occasional highly metaphorical vampire (like *The Historian* by Elizabeth Kostova, 2005) rooted in Count Dracula is still part of our literary psyche, as are viral/apocalyptic vamps, the comedic vampire, the "science-based," and the science fictional/sociological vampire (*The Fledgling*, Octavia Butler, 2007).

And there are still adult vampire novels: Robin McKinley, long known for her children and teen fantasies, moved into the adult market with the witty *Sunshine*, in which the heroine must overcome the terrifying memories of being captured by vampires, and help defeat her fanged foes. The winner of the Mythopoeic Fantasy Award for Adult Literature when first published in 2003, it was reissued in 2008. Gail Carringer's Parasol Protectorate series—*Soulless* (2009), *Changeless* (2010), *Blameless* (2010), *Heartless* (2011), and *Timeless* (2012)—mixed a "novel of manners," steampunk, vampire hunting, and madcap adventuring, while poking a bit of fun at paranormal romance.

There is also a large amount of *really* adult vampire erotica around these days. Explicit and not always romantic, this vamp fiction has a wide audience.

But, yes, the latest wave of vampire fiction has been fuelled by the "young adult/teen" market, which—although written for teens—is also read by preteens and adults. [The Twilight books/movies are not the sole impetus; fertile ground was laid by TV series *Buffy the Vampire Slayer*

(1997–2003) and its spin-off *Angel* (1999–2004); both mixed vampire fantasy with romance and horrific elements and were aimed at younger audiences. Other fantasy films and television series have added fecundity.] Although the majority of these works are either blandly romantic or center on a school milieu, some provide broader metaphors and much deeper meaning. Many writers of adult fiction have transferred their skills, at least for now, to this market. Older YA "classics" like *The Silver Kiss* by Annette Curtis Krause (originally published: 1990) have found new blood. Less classic, but entertaining, L.J. Smith's The Vampire Diaries series (first four novels published 1991–1992) has not only returned from the grave, but become a television series (renewed, in 2014, for its sixth season.)

As for short vampire fiction—which is, after all, why this anthology exists—2000–2010 brought opportunities for original urban and paranormal romance stories and both types of fiction written for the young adult market. Vamps also crept into many urban fantasy, paranormal romance, supernatural mystery, and cross-genre original anthologies without a specifically fanged theme. Even funny vampires found their way into anthologies in the oughts. There were fewer occasions, however, for writers with other vampiric ideas to show their talents.

For *Vampires: The Recent Undead*, I compiled a list of two dozen selected anthologies from the first ten years of the twenty-first century. Four years later I can't really think of any more to add other than *Blood and Other Cravings*, edited by Ellen Datlow; *Evolve 2: Vampire Stories of the Future Undead*, edited by Nancy Kilpatrick; and *Teeth: Vampire Tales,* edited by Ellen Datlow and Terri Windling—all published in 2011. There are, of course, still venues for a great vampire story—often, these days, in online magazines.

Vampire fiction may return to its coffin at times, but it always seems to rise from the grave with renewed strength. After all, Anne Rice—who once stated she'd never return to writing her Vampire Chronicles—published the novel *Prince Lestat* in 2014 and *Blood Paradise* is expected in 2015. That Universal Pictures and Imagine Entertainment acquired the motion picture rights to the entire Vampire Chronicles series in August 2014 is another indication there is future life for Rice's version of the icon.

Where are we now circa 2015? Who knows? One way or another, you can bet fresh blood will be found.

If you are an avid vampirist, you are sure to have come across some of these previously published stories before, but I think you'll also make some new discoveries. You will find a wide variety of vampire stories, each written by a woman. In fact, the stories are so diverse, it was difficult to decide what order in which to present them. I opted to place them in, as closely as I could, in chronological order *by the period in which each story is set*, from the sixteenth century to the near future. It is an unusual editorial choice that, of course, can be completely disregarded by the reader. Feel free to bite into any story you please; you can even start at the end.

As I noted back in 2011, such diversity is to be expected. Our times are marked more by division than cohesion. That new threats and new terrors have arisen seems to be even truer for 2015. How we face those fears—or escape them—has a lot to do with our preferences in vampires.

As Nina Auerbach once stated: "Every age embraces the vampire it needs, and gets the vampire it deserves."

Only now, I think we need to make "vampire" plural.

Paula Guran
December 2014

A PRINCESS OF SPAIN

Carrie Vaughn

Carrie Vaughn is the author of the *New York Times* bestselling series of novels about a werewolf named Kitty, the most recent installment of which is *Low Midnight*. She's written several other contemporary fantasy and young adult novels, as well as upwards of seventy short stories. She's a contributor to the Wild Cards series of shared world superhero books edited by George R. R. Martin. An Air Force brat, she survived her nomadic childhood and managed to put down roots in Boulder, Colorado. Visit her at www.carrievaughn.com.

Vaughn's most famous character, Kitty Norville, may not be a vampire, but they are part of her fictional world. "A Princess of Spain," however, has nothing to do with supernatural "modern life." The story instead offers an explanation for a key moment in sixteenth-century English history—the consequences of which changed the world forever . . .

November 14, 1501, Baynard's Castle

Catherine of Aragon, sixteen years old, danced a pavane in the Spanish style before the royal court of England. Lutes, horns, and tabors played a slow, stately tempo, to which she stepped in time. The ladies of her court, who had traveled with her from Spain, danced with her, treading circles around one another—floating, graceful, without a wasted movement. Her body must have seemed like air, drifting with the heavy gown of velvet and gold. She did not even tip her head, framed within its gem-encrusted hood. She was a piece of artwork, a prize for the usurper of the English throne, so that his son's succession would not be questioned. King Henry had the backing of Spain now.

Henry VII watched with a quiet, smug smile on his creased face. Elizabeth of York, his wife, sat nearby, more demonstrative in her pride, smiling and laughing. At a nearby table sat their two sons and two daughters—an impressive household. All made legitimate by Catherine's presence here, for she had been sent by Spain to marry the eldest son: Arthur, Prince of Wales, heir to the throne—thin and pale at fifteen years of age.

All these English were pale past the point of fairness and well toward ill, for their skies were always laden with clouds. Arthur slouched in his chair and occasionally coughed into his sleeve. He had declined to dance with her, claiming that he preferred to gaze upon her beauty while he may, before he claimed it later that evening.

Catherine's heart ached, torn between anticipation and foreboding. But she must dance her best, as befitted an infanta of Spain. "You must show the English what we Spanish are . . . superior," her mother, Reina Isabella, told her before Catherine departed. She would most likely never see her parents again.

Arthur did not look at her. Catherine saw his gaze turn to the side of the hall, where one of the foreign envoys sat at a table. There, a woman gazed back at the prince. She was fair skinned with dark eyes and a lock of dark, curling hair hanging outside her hood. Her high-necked gown was elegant without being ostentatious, both modest and fashionable, calculated to not upstage the prince and princess on their wedding day. But it was she who drew the prince's eye.

Catherine saw this; long practice kept her steps in time until the music finished at last.

The musicians struck up a livelier tune, and Prince Henry, the king's younger son, grabbed his sister Margaret's arm and pulled her to the middle of the hall, laughing. All of ten years old, he showed the promise of cutting a fine figure when he came of age—strong limbed, lanky, with a head of unruly ruddy hair. Already he was as tall as any of his siblings, including his elder brother Arthur. At this rate he would become a giant of a man. Word at court said he loved hunting, fighting, dancing, learning— all the pursuits worthy of any prince of Europe. But at this moment he was a boy.

He said something—Catherine only had a few words of English, and did not understand. A moment later he pulled off his fine court coat, leaving only his bare shirt. The room was hot with torches and bodies. He must have been stifled in the finely wrought garment. Because he was a boy, the court thought the gesture amusing rather than immodest; everyone smiled indulgently.

Catherine took her seat again, the place of honor at the king's right hand. She gazed, though, at Arthur. She did not even know him. She did not know if she wanted to. Tonight would be better. Tonight, all would be well.

He continued staring at the foreign woman.

The evening drew on, and soon the momentous occasion would be upon them: Arthur and Catherine would be put to bed to consummate their marriage. To seal the alliance between England and Spain with their bodies. Her ladies fluttered, preparing to spirit her off to her chambers to prepare her.

In the confusion, the lanky figure of a very tall boy slipped beside her. The young prince, Henry.

He smiled at her, like a child would, earnestly wanting to be friends.

"You've seen it, too," he said in Latin. She could understand him. "My brother, staring at that woman."

"*Sí*. Yes. Do you know her?"

"She's from the Low Countries," he said. "Or so it's put out at court, though it's also well known that she speaks French with no accent. She's a lady-in-waiting to the daughter of the Dutch ambassador. But the daughter kept to her apartments tonight, and the lady isn't with her, which seems strange, doesn't it?"

"But she must have some reason to be here." And that reason might very well be the young groom who could not take his gaze from her.

"Certainly. Perhaps I'll order someone to spy on her." Henry's eyes gleamed.

Catherine pressed her lips together but didn't manage a smile. "It is no matter. A passing fancy. It will mean nothing tomorrow."

Arthur was *her* husband. Tonight would make that a fact and not simply a legality. With a sudden burning in her gut, she longed for that moment.

"In nomine Patris, Filii, et Spiritus Sancti."

The bishop sprinkled holy water over the bed, where Catherine and Arthur were tucked, dressed in costly nightclothes, put to bed in a most formal manner for their wedding night, so that all might know that the marriage was made complete. At last, the witnesses left them, and for the first time, Catherine was alone with her husband.

All she could do was stare at him, his white face and lank ruddy hair, as her heart raced in her chest. He stared back, until she felt she should say something, but her voice failed. Words failed, when she couldn't decide whether to speak French, Latin, or attempt a phrase in her still halting English. *Why can he not understand Spanish?*

"You are quite pretty," he said in Latin, and leaned forward on shaking arms to kiss her on the lips.

She flushed with relief. Perhaps all would be well. He was her husband, she was his wife. She even *felt* married, lying here with him. Warm from her scalp to her toes—pleasant, illicit, yet sanctioned by God and Church. This was her wedding night, a most glorious night—

Before she could kiss him back, before she could hold him as her body told her to do, he pulled away. Unbidden, her arm rose to reach for him. Quickly, she drew it back and folded her hands on her lap. Must she maintain her princess's decorum, even here?

Arthur coughed. He bent double with coughing, putting his fist to his mouth. His thin body shook.

She left the bed and retrieved a goblet of wine from the table. Returning, she sat beside him and touched his hand, urging him to take a drink. His skin was cold, damp as the English winter she'd found herself in.

"*Por Dios,*" she whispered. What had God brought her to? She said in Latin, "I'll send for a physician."

Arthur shook his head. "It is nothing. It will pass. It always does." He took a drink of wine, swallowing loudly, as if his throat were closing.

But he had been this pale and sickly every time she'd seen him. This would not pass.

If they could have a child, if he would live long enough for them to have a child, a son, a new heir, her place in this country would be assured.

The wine would revive him. She touched his cheek. When he looked up, she hoped to see some fire in his eyes, some desire there to match her own. She hoped he would touch her back. But she only saw exhaustion from the day's activities. He was a child on the verge of sleep.

She was a princess of Spain, not made for seduction.

He gave the goblet back to her. With a sigh, he settled back against the pillows. By his next breath, he was asleep.

Catherine set the goblet on the table. The room was chilled. Every room in this country was chilled. Yet at this moment, while her skin burned, the cool tiles of the floor felt good against her bare feet.

She knelt by the bed, clasped her hands tightly together, and prayed.

December 15, 1501, Richmond

Another feast lay spread before her. King Henry displayed his wealth in calculated presentations of food, music, entertainment. However much the politics and finances of his realm were strained, he would give no other appearance than that of a successful, stable monarch.

Catherine did not dance, though the musicians played a pavane. She sat at the table, beside her husband, watching. Husband in name only. He had not once come to her chamber. He had not once summoned her to his. But appearances must be maintained.

He slouched in his chair, leaning on one carved wooden arm, clutching a goblet in both hands. He had grown even more wan, even more sickly, if possible. Did no one else see it?

She touched the arm of his chair. "My husband, have you eaten enough? Should I call for more food?"

He shook his head and waved her off. It was not natural, to treat one's wife so. He was in danger of failing his duty as a prince, and as a Christian husband.

But what could she do? A princess was meant to serve her husband, not command or judge him.

"Your husband will take mistresses," her mother told her, in her final instructions before Catherine set sail. She told her that it was the way of things and she could not fight it. But Isabella also said that her husband would do his duty toward her, so that she might do *her* duty and bear him many children.

Her duty was turning to dust in her hands, through no fault of her own.

In the tiled space in the center of the hall, the young Prince Henry danced with the strange foreign woman. Catherine had no evidence that this woman was her husband's mistress, except for the way Arthur watched her, desperately, with too bright eyes.

The woman danced gracefully. She must have been a dozen years older than her partner, but she tolerated him with an air of amusement, wearing the thin and placid smile, as though sitting for a portrait. Henry was a lively enough partner that he made every step a joy. His father was training him for the clergy, it was said. He might be the greatest bishop in England someday—the crown's voice in the Church.

Catherine begged leave to retire early, before the music and dancing had finished. She claimed fatigue and a sensitive stomach. People nodded knowingly at the information and offered each other winks. They thought she was with child, as any young bride ought to be.

But she wasn't. Never would be, if things kept on in this manner.

It was difficult to spy in the king's house unless one had command of the guards and could order them to stay, or leave, or watch. She did not have command of anything except her own household, which the English court treated as the foreigners they were. Really, though, her duenna and stewards commanded her household—Catherine was too young for it, they said. Her parents had sent able guardians to look after her.

Nevertheless, against all her instincts, after dark—well after the candles and lanterns had been snuffed—Catherine donned a black traveling cloak over her shift and set out, stepping quietly past her ladies-in-waiting who slept in the outer chamber. Very quietly she opened the heavy door, giving herself barely enough space to slip through. The iron hinges squeaked, but only once, softly, like a woman sighing in her sleep.

Two more chambers, sitting rooms, lay between her and Arthur. The spaces were dark, chill. Thick windows let in very little of the already faint moonlight. Her slippered feet made no sound on the wood floors. She kept to the paneled walls and felt her way around, step by careful step.

Guards walked their rounds. They passed from room to room, pikes resting on their shoulders. England had finished its wars of succession relatively recently; for the royal family, there was always danger.

If she were very quiet, and moved very carefully, they would not see her. She hoped. If they found her, most likely nothing would happen to her, but she didn't want to have to explain herself. This was very improper for a woman of her rank. She should go back to her own room and pray to God to make this right.

Her knees were worn out with praying.

She listened for booted footsteps and the rattle of armor. Heard nothing.

She reached the chamber outside Arthur's bedroom. A light shone under the door, faint, buttery—candlelight. A step away from the door she paused, listening. What did she think she might hear? Conversation? Laughter? Deep sighs? She had no idea.

She touched the door. Surely it would be locked. It would be a relief to have to walk away, still ignorant. She touched the latch—

It wasn't locked.

Softly, she pushed open the door and looked in.

Looking like an ill child far younger than his years, Arthur lay propped up in bed, limp, his eyes half-closed, senseless. Beside him crouched the foreign woman, fully clothed, her hands on his shoulders, clutching his linen nightclothes. Her mouth was open, and her teeth shone dark with blood. A gash on Arthur's neck bled.

"You're killing him!" Catherine cried. She stood, too shocked to scream—she ought to scream, to call for the guards. Even if they could not understand her Spanish, they would come at the sound of panic.

In a moment, a scant heartbeat, the foreign woman appeared before Catherine. She might as well have flown; the princess didn't see her move. This was some dream, some vision. Some devil had crept into her mind.

The woman pressed her to the wall, closing Catherine's mouth with one hand. Catherine kicked and writhed, trying to break away, but the woman was strong. Fantastically strong. Catherine swatted at her, pulled at a strand of her dark hair that had come loose from her hood. She might as well have been a fly in the woman's grasp. With her free hand she grabbed Catherine's wrists and held her arms still.

Then she caught Catherine's gaze.

Her eyes were blue, the dark, clear blue of the twilight sky over Spain.

"I am not killing him. Be silent, say nothing of what you have seen, and you will keep your husband." Her voice was subdued, but clear. Later, Catherine could not recall what language she had spoken.

Catherine nearly laughed. What husband? She might as well have chosen the convent. But she couldn't speak, couldn't move.

The woman's touch was cold. The fingers curled over Catherine's face felt like marble.

"You are so young to be in this position. Poor girl."

The woman smiled, kindly it seemed. For a moment, Catherine wanted to cling to her, to spill all her worries before this woman—she seemed to understand.

Then she said, "Sleep. You've had a dream. Go back to sleep."

Catherine's vision faded. She struggled again, tried to keep the woman's face in sight, but she felt herself falling. Then, nothing.

She awoke on the floor. She had fainted and lay curled at the foot of her own bed, wrapped in her cloak. Pale morning light shone through the window. It was a cold light, full of winter.

She tried to recall last night—she had left her bed, obviously. But for what reason? If she'd wanted wine she could have called for one of her ladies.

Her ladies would be mortified to find her like this. They would think her ill, keep her to bed, and send for physicians. Catherine quickly stood, collected herself, arranged her shift and untangled her hair. She was a princess. She ought to behave like one, despite her strange dreams of women with rich blue eyes.

An ache in her belly made her pause. It was not like her to be so indecorous as to leave her bed before morning. As she smoothed the wrinkles from her dressing gown, her fingers tickled. She raised her hand, looked at it.

A few silken black fibers—long, shining, so thin they were almost invisible—clung to her skin. Hair—but how had it come here? Her own hair was like honey, Arthur's was colored amber—

She had seen a dark-haired woman with Arthur. It was not a dream. The memory of what she had seen had not faded after all.

That day, Catherine and Arthur attended Mass together. She studied him so intently that he raised his brow at her, inquiring. She couldn't explain. He wore a high-necked doublet. She couldn't see his neck to tell if he had a wound there. Perhaps he did, perhaps not. He made no mention of what had happened last night, made no recognition that he had even seen her. Could he not remember?

Say nothing of what you have seen, and you will keep your husband. Catherine dared not speak at all. She would be called mad.

This country was cursed, overrun with rain and plague. This king was cursed, haunted by all those who had died so he might have his crown, and so was his heir. Catherine could tell her parents, but what would that accomplish? She was not here for herself, but for the alliance between their kingdoms.

She prayed, while the priest chanted. His words were Latin, which was familiar and comforting. The Church was constant. In that she could take comfort. Perhaps if she confessed, told her priest what she had seen, he would have counsel. Perhaps he could say what demon this was that was taking Arthur.

A slip of paper, very small, as if it had been torn from the margin of a letter, fell out of her prayer book. She glanced quickly around—no one had seen it. Her ladies either stared ahead at the altar or bowed over their clasped hands. She was kneeling; the paper had landed on the velvet folds of her skirt. She picked it up.

"*Convene me horto.* Henricus," written in a boy's careful hand. Meet me in the garden.

Catherine crumpled the paper and tucked it in her sleeve. She'd burn it later.

She told her ladies she wished to walk in the air, to stretch her legs after the long Mass. They accompanied her—she could not go anywhere without them, but she was able to find a place where she might sit a little ways off. Henry would have to find her then.

Here she was, in this country only two months and already playing at spying.

Gravel paths wound around the lawn outside Richmond, the King's favorite palace. Never had Catherine seen grass of such jewel-like green. Even in winter, the lawn stayed green. The dampness made it thrive. Her mother-in-law Elizabeth assured her that in the summer, flowers grew in glorious tangles. Around back, boxes outside the kitchens held forests of herbs. England was fertile, the queen said knowingly.

Catherine and her ladies walked to where the path turned around a hedge. Some stone benches offered a place to rest.

"Doña Elvira, you and the ladies sit here. I wish to walk on a little. Do not worry, I will call if I need you." The concerned expression on her duenna's face was not appeased, but Catherine was resolute.

Doña Elvira sat and directed the others to do likewise.

Catherine strolled on, carefully, slowly, not rushing. Around the shrubs and out of sight from her ladies, Henry arrived, stepping out from behind the other end of the hedge.

"*Buenos días, hermana.*"

She smiled in spite of herself. "You learn my language."

Henry blushed and looked at his feet. "Only a little. Hello and thank you and the like."

"Still, *gracias.* For the little."

"I have learned something of the foreign woman. I told the guards to watch her and listen."

"We should tell your father. It is not for us to command the guards—"

"She is not from the Low Countries. Her name is Angeline. She is French, which means she is a spy," he said.

Catherine wasn't sure that one so naturally followed the other. It was too simple an explanation. The alliance between England and Spain presented far too strong an enemy for France. Of course they would send spies. But that was no spy she'd seen with Arthur.

She shook her head. "She is more than that."

"She hopes to break the alliance between England and Spain by distracting my brother. If you have no children, the succession will pass to another."

"To you and your children, yes? And perhaps a French queen for England, if they find one for you to marry?"

He pursed boyish lips. "I am Duke of York. Why would I want to be king?"

But there was a light in his eyes, intelligent, glittering. He would not shy away from being king, if, God forbid, events came to that.

He said, "There is more. I touched her hand when we danced. It was cold. Colder than stone. Colder than anything."

Catherine paced, just a little circle beside her brother-in-law. She ought to tell a priest. But he knew. So she told him.

"I have been spying as well," she said. "I went to Arthur's chamber last night. If she is his mistress—I had to see. I had to know."

"What did you see? *Is* she his mistress?"

Catherine wrung her hands. She did not have the words for this in any language. "I do not know. She was there, yes. But Arthur was senseless. It was as if she had put a spell on him."

Eagerly, Henry said, "Then she is a witch?"

Catherine's throat ached, but she would not cry. "I do not know. I do not know of such things. She said strange things to me; that I must not interfere if I wish to keep Arthur alive. She—she cast a spell on me, I think. I fainted, then I awoke in my chamber—"

Henry considered thoughtfully, a serious expression that looked almost amusing on the face of a boy. "So. A demon is trying to sink its claws into the throne of England through its heir. Perhaps it will possess him. Or devour him. We must kill it, of course."

"We must tell a priest!" Catherine said, pleading. "We must tell the archbishop!"

"If we did, would they believe us? I, a boy, and you, a foreigner? They'll say we are mad, or playing at games."

She couldn't argue because she'd thought the same. She said, "This woman made me sleep with a glance. How would we kill such a thing?"

Even if they *wanted* to kill her. What if the woman was right, and if they acted against her she would find some way to kill Arthur? Perhaps they should bide their time.

"Highness? Are you there?" Doña Elvira called to her.

"I must away," Catherine said, and curtsied to her brother-in-law. "We must think on what to do. We must not be rash."

He returned the respect with a bow. "Surely. Farewell."

She hoped he would not be rash. She feared he looked upon all this as a game.

"His Highness is not seeing visitors," the gentleman of Arthur's chamber told her. He spoke apologetically and bowed respectfully, but he would not let her through the doors to see Arthur. She wanted to scream.

"You will tell him that I was here?"

"Yes, Your Highness," the man said and bowed again.

Catherine could do nothing more than turn around and walk away, trailed by her own attending ladies.

What they must think of her. She caught the whispers among them, when they thought she couldn't hear. *Pobre Catalina.* Poor Catherine, whose husband would not see her, who spent every night alone.

That evening, she sent Doña Elvira and her ladies on an errand for wine. Once again, she crept from her chambers alone, furtive as a mouse.

I will see my husband, Catherine thought. *It is my right.* It should not have been so difficult for her to see him alone. But as it was the palace swarmed with courtiers.

She wanted to reach him before the woman arrived to work her spells on him.

Quietly, she slipped through Arthur's door and closed it behind her.

The bed curtains were open. Arthur, in his nightclothes, sat on the edge of the bed, hunched over. She could hear his wheezing breaths across the room.

"Your Highness," she said, curtsying.

"Catherine?" He looked up—and did he smile? Just a little? "Why are you here?"

She said, "Who is the woman who comes to you at night?"

"No one comes to me at night." He said this flatly, as if she were to blame for his loneliness.

She shook her head, fighting tears. She would keep her wits and not cry. "Three nights ago I came, and she was here. You were bleeding, Arthur. She hurt you. She's killing you!"

"That isn't true. No one has been here. And—what business is it of yours if a woman has been here?"

"I am your wife. You have a duty to me."

"Catherine, I am so tired."

She knelt at his side and dared to put her hand on his knee. "Then you must grow strong. So that we may have children. Your heirs."

He touched her hand. A thrill went through her flesh, like fire. So much feeling in a simple touch! But his skin was ice cold.

"I am telling the truth," said the boy who was her husband. "I remember nothing of any woman coming here. I come to bed every night and fall into such a deep sleep that nothing rouses me but my own coughing. I do not know of what you speak."

This woman had put a spell on them all.

"Your father is sending your household to Ludlow Castle, in Wales," she said.

He set his lips in a thin, pale line. "Then we shall go to Ludlow."

"You cannot travel so far," she said. "The journey will kill you."

"If I were really so weak my father would not send me."

"His pride blinds him!"

"You should not speak so of the king, my lady." He gave a tired sigh. What would have been an accusation of treason from fiery young Henry's lips was weary observation from Arthur's. "Now please, Catherine. Let me sleep. If I sleep well tonight, perhaps I'll be strong enough to see you tomorrow."

It was an empty promise and they both knew it. He was as pale and wasted as he had ever been. She kissed his hand with as much passion as she had ever been allowed to show. She pressed her cheek to it, let tears fall on it. She would pray every day for him. Every hour.

She stood, curtsied, and left him alone in the chamber.

Outside, however, she waited, sitting on a chair in the corner normally reserved for pages or stewards. Doña Elvira would be scandalized to see her there.

In an hour, the woman Angeline came. She moved like smoke. Catherine had been staring ahead so intently she thought her eyes played a trick on her. A shadow flickered where there was no flame. A draft blew where no window was open.

Angeline did not approach, but all the same she appeared. She stood before the doors of Arthur's bedchamber as regal as any queen.

Catherine was still gathering the courage to stand when Angeline looked at her. Her face was alabaster, a statue draped with a gown of black velvet. She might as well have been stone, her gaze was so hard.

Finally, Catherine stood.

"*Es la novia niña*," Angeline said.

The princess would not be cowed by a commoner. "By the laws of Church and country I am not a child, I am a woman."

"By one very important consideration, you are not." She turned a pointed smile.

Catherine blushed; her gaze fell. She was still a maid. That was certainly not *her* fault.

"I demand that you leave here," Catherine said. "Leave here, and leave my husband alone."

"Oh, child, you don't want me to do that."

"I insist. You are some witch, some demon. That much I know. You have worked a spell on him that sickens him to death—"

"Oh no, I'll not let my puppet die. I could keep your Arthur alive forever, if I wished. I hold that secret."

"You . . . you are an abomination against the Church. Against God!"

She smiled thinly. "Perhaps."

"Why?" Catherine said. "Why him? Why this?"

"He'll be a weak king. At best, an indifferent king. He won't be leading any troops to war against France. He will keep England a quiet, unimportant country."

"You do not know that. You cannot see the future. He will be a great king—"

"One need not see the future to guess such things, dear Catherine."

"You will address me as Your Highness, as is proper."

"Of course, Your Highness. You must trust me—I will not kill Arthur. If his brother were to become king—you have seen the kind of boy he is: fierce, competitive, strong. You can imagine the kind of king he will be. No one in Europe wishes for a strong king of England."

"My father King Ferdinand—"

"Not even King Ferdinand. From the first, he wanted a son-in-law he could control."

Catherine knew it was true, all of it, the chess-like machinations of politics that had ruled her life. Her marriage to Arthur had given Spain another playing piece, that was all.

There was no room for love in any of this.

She was descended from two royal houses. Her ancestors were the oldest and most noble in all of Europe. Dignity was bred into the sinews of her flesh. She stood tall, did not collapse, did not cry, however much the little girl inside of her was trembling.

"And what of children?" she said. "What of the children I'm meant to bear?"

"It may be possible. Or it may not."

"I do not believe you. I do not believe anything that you say."

"Yes, you do," she said. "But more importantly, you cannot stop me. You'll go to sleep, now. You will not remember."

She wanted to fling herself at the woman, strangle her with her own hands. Tiny hands that couldn't strangle a kitten, alas.

"Catherine. Move away. I know what she is." The command came in the incongruous voice of a boy.

Prince Henry stood blocking the chamber's other doorway. He had a spear, which seemed overlarge and unwieldy in his hands. Nevertheless, he held it at the ready, feet braced, pointed at the woman. It was a mockery of battle. A child playing at hunting boar.

"What am I, boy?" the woman said in a soft, mocking voice.

This only drove Henry to greater rage. "Succubus. A demon who feeds on the souls of men. You will not have my brother, devil!"

Her smile fell, darkening her expression. "You have just enough intelligence to do harm. And more than enough ignorance."

"I'll kill you. I can kill you where you stand."

"You will not kill me. Arthur is so much mine that without me he will die."

She'd made Arthur weak and subsumed him under her power. If that tie between them was severed—

Catherine's heart pounded. She could not stop them both. They would not listen. No one ever listened to her. "Henry, you must not, she is keeping Arthur alive."

"She lies."

The woman laughed, a bitter sound. "If Arthur dies, Henry becomes heir. That reason will not stay his hand."

But Henry didn't want to be king. He'd said so . . .

Catherine caught his gaze. She saw something dark in his eyes.

Then she tried to forget that she'd seen it. "My lord, wait—"

The woman lived in shadow—was made of shadow. She started to flow back into the hidden ways by which she came, moving within the stillness of night. Catherine saw nothing but a shudder, the light of a sputtering candle. But Henry saw more, and like a great hunter he anticipated what the flinch of movement meant.

With a shout he lunged forward, driving the spear before him.

The woman flew. Catherine would swear that she flew, up and over, toward the ceiling to avoid Henry. Henry followed with his spear, jumping, swinging the weapon upward. He missed. With a sigh, the woman twisted away from him. Henry stumbled, thrown off balance by his wayward thrust, and Angeline stood behind him.

"You're a boy playing at being warrior," she said, carrying herself as calmly as if she had not moved.

Henry snarled an angry cry and tried again. The woman stepped aside and took hold of the back of Henry's neck. With no effort at all, she pushed him down, so that he was kneeling. He still held the spear, but she was behind him, pressing down on him, and he couldn't use it.

"I could make you as much my puppet as your brother is."

"No! You won't! I'll never be anyone's puppet!" He struggled, his whole body straining against her grip, but he couldn't move.

Catherine knelt and began to pray, *Pater Noster* and *Ave Maria*, and her lips stumbled trying to get out all the words at once.

The prayers were for her own comfort. Catherine had little faith in her own power; she didn't expect the unholy creature to hear her words and pause. She didn't consider that her own words, her own prayer, would cause Angeline to loosen her grip on Henry.

But Angeline did loosen her grip. Her body seemed to freeze for a moment. She became more solid, as if the prayer had made her substantial.

Henry didn't hesitate. He threw himself forward, away from Angeline, then spun to put the spear between them. Then, while she was still seemingly entranced, he drove it home.

The point slipped into her breast. She cried out, fell, and as she did Henry drove the wooden shaft deep into her chest.

The next moment she lay on the floor, clutching the shaft of the spear. Henry still held the end of it. He stared down at her, iconic, like England's beloved Saint George and his vanquished dragon.

There was no blood.

A strangeness happened—as strange as anything else Catherine had seen since coming to England. With the scent of a crypt rising from her, the woman faded in color, then dried and crumbled like a corpse that had been rotting for a dozen years. The body became unrecognizable in a moment. In another, only ash and dust remained.

Henry kicked a little at the mound of debris.

Catherine spoke, her voice shaking. "She said she was keeping Arthur alive. What if it's true? What if he dies? I'll be a widow in a strange country. I'll be lost." Lost, when she was meant to be a queen. Her life was slipping away.

Henry touched her arm. She nearly screamed, but her innate dignity controlled her. She only flinched.

He gazed at her with utmost gravity. "I'll take care of you. If Arthur dies, then I'll take care of you, when I am king after my father."

Arthur died in the spring. And so it came to pass that Henry, who had been born to be Duke of York and nothing else, a younger brother, a mere afterthought in the chronicles of history, would succeed his father as King of England, become Henry VIII, and marry Catherine of Aragon. He would take care of her, as he had promised.

He was sixteen at their wedding, a year older than Arthur had been. But so different. Like day and night, summer and winter. Henry was tall, flushed, hearty, laughed all the time, danced, hunted, jousted, argued, commanded. Their wedding night would be nothing like Catherine's first, she knew. *He is the greatest prince in all Europe,* people at court said of him. *He will make England a nation to be reckoned with.*

Catherine considered her new husband—now taller than she by a head. Part of her would always remember the boy. She could still picture him the way he stood outside Arthur's chamber, spear in his hands, fury in his eyes, ready to do battle. Ready to sacrifice his own brother. Catherine would never forget that this was a man willing to do what he believed must be done, whatever the cost.

She wanted to be happy, but England's chill air remained locked in her bones.

SHIPWRECKS ABOVE

Caitlín R. Kiernan

The *New York Times* recently hailed Caitlín R. Kiernan as "one of our essential writers of dark fiction." Her novels include *The Red Tree* (nominated for the Shirley Jackson and World Fantasy awards) and *The Drowning Girl: A Memoir* (winner of the James Tiptree, Jr. Award and the Bram Stoker Award, nominated for the Nebula, Locus, Shirley Jackson, World Fantasy, British Fantasy, and Mythopoeic awards). To date, her short fiction has been collected in thirteen volumes, most recently *Confessions of a Five-Chambered Heart, Two Worlds and In Between: The Best of Caitlín R. Kiernan (Volume One)*, the World Fantasy Award-winning *The Ape's Wife and Other Stories*, and, soon, a second "best of" volume. Currently, she's writing the graphic novel series Alabaster for Dark Horse and working on other projects.

Kiernan rarely delves into the vampiric, but when she does, the result is—as with "Shipwrecks Above"—both darkly poetic and highly original . . .

This one, she rides the tides. She has been hardly more than a shade drifting between undulating stalks of kelp, and she has worn flickering diadems of jellyfish, anemones, and brittle stars. The mackerel and tautog swap their careless yarns of her. For instance, that she was once a dryad, but then fell from Artemis' favor. Weighted about the ankles, so was she drowned and whored out to the sea, cast down from all sylvan terrestrial spheres, from all pastures and forests that have *not* been drowned. But this is no more than the bitter fancies that fish whisper to one another, tales told *in* school, and such stories have even less substance than what has been left of her. She was never a dryad. She was only a woman, very long ago, though not so far back as the tautog and mackerel might have you suppose. The imagination of fish knows no bounds.

She was once only a woman, as I've said, and a woman who had the great misfortune to attract the attentions of something that was *not* only a man. He loved her, or at least he *named* it love, knowing no other word for his desires and insatiable appetites. He loved her, and so must she not, by right, be his? After all, she was the daughter of *his* sister, and had he not *loved* his sister and shown to her all the ruthless dedication of that love, before she ungratefully fled from him? Hence, might not this fatherless Székely child—christened Eõrsebet Soffia by some mangy Calvinist priest—be reasonably considered flesh of his own flesh? Yet, when the noble boyar claimed her, his impertinent sister dared protest the allegation. So he had her killed, and István Vadas, hero of the Thirteen Year's War and cherished ally to the Wallachian Prince Michael the Brave, did take the girl away from her village in the year 1624.

On that day, Eõrsebet was sixteen and seven months, and had never yet looked upon the sea.

Her father and lover, her self-appointed Lord in *all* matters of this world and in any to come hereafter, ferried her high into the Carpathian wilderness, up to some crumbling ancestral fortress, its towers and curtain walls falling steadily into decrepitude. It was no less a wreck than the whalers and doggers, the schooners and trawlers, she has since sung to their graves on jagged reefs of stone and coral. And it was there, in the rat-haunted corridors of István's moldering castle, that she did refuse this dæmonic paramour. All his titles, battlefield conquests, and wealth were proved unequal to the will of a frightened girl. When he had raped her and beaten her, he had her bound and, for a while, cast into a deep pit where she believed that the Archangel Michael, bringer of merciful Death, might find her and bear her away from this perdition unto the gilded clouds of Heaven.

"You have chosen to spurn the Light of my devotion," István told Eõrsebet Soffia, his dry lips pressed to the hagioscopic squint of her cell door, murmuring through that "leper's window" rather than allow her to glimpse even the flickering of torchlight. "Therefore, it seems more than just that I should *aid* thee in seeking out the lightless realms." István went away, leaving her with no further explanation of intent, but at the dawn of the next day, upon the crowing of the cock, his jailer blinded the girl with an iron poker heated in glowing coals. The wounds were bound with the finest Chinese silk, taken from ravaged Ottoman caravans.

Her screams were nothing new to the rats, or to the mortar, the spiders, or the limestone blocks of the keep, for her Lord knew well the worth of torture, just as he knew the worth of a good warhorse or a Karabelá sabre.

In a greater darkness than she had ever imagined, and in greater pain than she'd had cause even to suppose could exist, Eõrsebet wept and prayed her delirious, fevered prayers to St. Michael. She knelt in filthy straw and dirt and offal, beseeching *any* angel or saint to intervene on her behalf. But, as before, all her supplications went unanswered.

And when another Transylvanian night had crept across the mountainside, the sun abandoning the steep Bârgu forests to the wolves, István Vadas came to her again. Her father told her, solemnly, that she might serve him still, for what need had he of a bride who could see? "You are not diminished," he assured her, his voice as smooth as honey and cold as a serpent's blood. "You may yet attend and obey me in matrimony, and know my mercy. Merely assent, and you will be set free, and never again know pain or the humiliation of imprisonment."

But, straightaway, she named him a liar, and worse things, too, and István made a grand show of having been stung through and through by her words.

"You murdered my mother, your own sister," Eõrsebet whispered, her voice raw from tears and the wasted prayers. "I shall *follow* her, rather than submit and willingly permit thy seed to enter me. I shall make for thee a *happy* corpse, before I call thee husband or bear fresh imps to assume the strangling yoke of thy name.

"Only show me to the well," she said, "for gladly will I go down into that gullet and be drowned. It would be a kinder fate than what you offer."

"If this is as my belov'd wishes," he replied, pretending to crushing disappointment. "If this is her last word on the matter, so be it. I will demonstrate to thee my complete adulation, in due course, and hold you here no more. I will break the shackles and throw open the door to this cell, and none shall risk my judgment by blocking thy retreat from me."

Even in her agony and bewilderment, Eõrsebet was a girl wise beyond her ten and six years, and she saw through the boyar's promises. Or, more precisely, she saw how it was that he said one thing and meant quite another, how it could be he would hold true to every syllable of these oaths he'd spoken, and *still* ensure her doom. It was only sport to him, a grim diversion which he would win even if he lost.

An old lobster once came near to guessing the truth of her, so she devoured him, leaving nothing but an empty shell to settle amongst the sausage weed and sea lettuce.

While Eōrsebet sat in her cell, awaiting whatever form her undoing would assume, the boyar called upon the dark gods to whom he'd always paid tribute. The true deities to which the *Sárkány Lovagrend*, King Sigismund's *Societas Draconistrarum*, had long ago pledged itself, all the while hiding behind a proper papal mask. And by these agencies was the warlord and sorcerer István Vadas granted the power to rain down upon his daughter a terrible curse. He spoke it in her nightmares, as she managed to doze fitfully in that decrepit oubliette. He whispered in some unhallowed grove, and the winds brought his words into her dreams.

"Daughter," he said, and "Dear heart," and "Beloved." Immediately, her dreaming mind did recognize that voice, but Eōrsebet found herself poisoned by some sedative potion and unable to awaken.

"Thou wouldst have darkness, which I have already gifted to thee, rather than look upon my face. Thou wouldst be drowned, against our marriage, and this request will I also honor. You shall be drowned, my sweet Eōrsebet, and so set free. But, in good conscience, I cannot commit thy soul to this garrison's well, no. I will see thee to far more majestic waters."

This is the secret that doomed the old lobster, and if it is known to any others within Poseidon's mansions, they have wisely kept it to themselves.

"Now, my *second* gift to thee, Eōrsebet," the boyar spoke within the confines of her dream. "For all eternity wilt thou wander the deep places of the world, carried to and fro by the whims of the tides. Thou wilt be of the water, and the water will be thy womb. But thou shalt hunger, as do those *strigoi* who must feed from off the living. Yet only once in every year may thee leave the sustaining waters to slake thine thirst on the blood you will ever more crave. And, even then, you may not wander far from the shore. This is my gift, daughter, in lieu of matrimony, though I fancy it makes of thee another sort of wife."

So Eōrsebet's prison was opened, and a coach made ready to receive her. But, before her departure, the jailer branded the girl's back with such unnameable symbols as the dark gods had insisted to István she should hereafter wear, if the curse were to be lasting and irrevocable. She was dressed in a fine gown of golden threads, and driven away from the boyar's keep, down from the mountains and into Wallachia. The coach saw her through to gates of Bucharest and to a bridge spanning the Dâmbovia River. Shackled in irons, she was cast upon the waters.

She has long since forgotten the drowning, the short fall from the bridge and the shock of hitting the icy torrent below. She cannot now recall the fire as her lungs filled, or the brief panic before her dissolution and rebirth. The Dâmbovia carried her to the Arge at Oltenia, which bore her forth to the Danube, her wide, rolling road towards the Black Sea, just south of the ancient city of Constana.

This small inland sea was her first tomb, and for many decades it seemed to her a boundless vault of wonders, as tombs go. She found a voice she'd not had in life, and with it she trilled raging storms and canted days when the waters grew so becalmed all sails hung limp upon their masts. She sang to sailors and to fishermen from Sevastopol to Varna, from the coasts of Georgia to the port of Odessa. She appeared, sometimes, to suicides, inviting them, and with her melodies she did draw to their deaths men and woman and children, and even cattle and wild beasts, when the mood found her.

Sometimes, she would feel István's eyes upon her again, for his evil doings and services had earned him strange powers and another sort of undeath. From broken minarets, where he now had only rats and beetles and quick green lizards for company, he watched her with eyes turned black as coal. And finding that gaze intolerable, his siren would seek out some convenient undertow and sink down and down, passing into silty, anoxic nights so dense that not even his eyes could penetrate them.

Once a year, and only once a year, she stepped from the waves and walked waterfronts and streets and alleyways, as any woman would. She chose her victims carefully, and stole away the salty crimson oceans locked up inside each and every one.

And this was the round and rut of her existence, until the thing that death and István's spite and sorcery had fashioned of Eörsebet found her way to the narrow straits of the Bosphorous. By this route, she came, slowly, to the Turkish Sea of Marmara and, finally, past Gallipoli and through the Dardanelles into the Aegean. But this was all so very long ago, as I have said, in the days and nights *before* she became a shade drifting through the perpetual Atlantic twilight, an oceanic phantom of kelp and driftwood.

She followed dolphins and mercurial shoals of fish to the stony shores of Crete, then into the Ionian Sea, where it is said the body of the son of Dyrrhachus was tossed, after his accidental murder at the hands of

Heracles. She came to know the affection of whales, who also sang, though to other ends than her own. She followed pods of spermaceti from one end of the Mediterranean to the other, skirting the northern capes of African deserts, and was delivered, finally, to Gibraltar.

Perhaps it was only a matter of time (and she has no end of time, surely, excepting that one day the world might conclude and she with it) before storm waves and abyssal currents carried her north to the mouth of the Thames, and then west to London. In the year 1891, during the gloaming of Victoria's England and more than three full centuries after the boyar's men had shoved her from a bridge in Bucharest, Eōrsebet Soffia raised her head above the stinking, tainted waters of that river befouled by industry and sewage, and gazed sightlessly upon its fetid, teeming banks.

One day, a poet will write: "The river sweats/oil and tar." But this day, it also sweats *her*, the boyar's daughter, the sea's prostitute. She wends her all-but silent way between the close-packed clipper hulls, and no one notices when she slips from the water and onto the noisome squalor of Saint Katherine's Docks. Amid the bustle, there in the shadows of the ships and warehouses, who's to take exception at the spectacle of one more bedraggled doxy? Who will look closely enough to note the scars where her eyes were, or a few barnacles dappling her gaunt cheeks or the backs of her hands? The docks are a riot of "…solid carters and porters; the dapper clerks, carrying pen and book; the Customs' men moving slowly; the slouching sailors in gaudy holiday clothes; the skipper in shiny black that fits him uneasily, convoying parties of wondering ladies; negroes, Lascars, Portuguese, Frenchmen; grimy firemen, and (shadows in the throng) hungry-looking day-laborers…" Or so Doré and Jerrold described it nineteen years prior to the day of Eōrsebet's arrival. She moves, barefoot, between baskets and crates, wagons and hogshead casks, "through bales and bundles and grass-bags, over skins and rags and antlers, ores and dye-woods: now through pungent air, and now through a tallowy atmosphere, to the quay…" (once more quoting from the published memoir of Doré and Jerrold's pilgrimage).

She crosses a narrow canal bridge, which carries her from the docks, away from the anchored fleets and (to steal from the narrative of Doré and Jerrold one last time, I do promise) into "…shabby, slatternly places, by low and poor houses, amid shiftless riverside loungers…on to the eastern dock between Wapping and down Shadwell. Streets of poverty-marked tenements, gaudy public-houses and beer-shops, door-steps packed with lolling, heavy-eyed, half-naked children; low-browed and bare-armed women greasing the walls with their backs, and gossiping the while such gossip as scorches the ears; bullies of every kind walking as masters of the pavement, all sprinkled with drunkenness…"

There is almost in her a regret that the city has not made more of a challenge from this day, her one and only shore leave of the year. There are so many here who can be taken with the smallest bit of effort, the least premeditated and most lackadaisical of seductions, and how few among them would ever be missed? She could easily feast, slaughtering a dozen without any especial effort. She could forget her predator's instinctual cautions and play the glutton; the hollow created by her plunder would be no more than that made when lifting a single grain of sand from off a dune.

Concealing herself within the stinking gloom of a side lane, she watches and breathes in all the heady, disorienting odors and tastes and sounds of these Citizens of the Crown. Eōrsebet's senses are assailed, as though she's come upon a single gigantic organism stranded by the river's tidal retreat, stranded and rotting, though it is still very much alive; something too concerned with petty squabbles and daydreams and debauchery to even notice how near at hand it is to perishing.

But she'll take only one. István made of her many sorts of demons, but all are creatures of habit. And habit dictates that only one in London shall die this day by her hand. Habit reminds her that taking *more* than one might have dire consequences. A mere scrap of the frightened Székely girl she once was asks if the consequences would truly be so unfortunate, discovery and her subsequent undoing. *What sort of life is this?* it asks. Sometimes, Eōrsebet listens to this voice. Sometimes, she allows it to speak at length, but only sometimes, as it inevitably fills her with melancholy and anger and memories she's no longer sure are even her own. Today, she bids it be silent, if ever it wishes to be heard again. She shows it the outskirts of hellish regions of the mind, to which she might so easily banish that voice, were it her fancy to do so. Eōrsebet replies (speaking aloud, though not above whisper) that this is the sort of life for which she has been *shaped*. And there are too many lighthouses and sea caves remaining that she has not yet harrowed, too many ships she has not foundered, countless beating hearts not yet stilled by drowning, entire oceans left unexplored. But, also, there is the unending hunger, István's hunger and her truest master, pulling her along like a cod hooked on an angler's taut line.

"I am not finished," she says, and her English is better now than when she came ashore at Dover the year before, or at Brighton, the year before that. She repeats the words, delivering them with more finality, "I am not finished." Hearing this, both the meaning and the tone, that small ghost in her withdraws, and will not be heard again for very many months.

In short order, Eōrsebet Soffia espies a dingy young Irishman with eyes the color of the sky on a clear November day and hair like soot. He will do. He will be more than sufficient, and as the young man is somewhat worldly, and possessed of a famishment all his own, it is a simple enough matter to lure him into the side lane and to her. She knows ten times ten thousand songs, and each one is more beautiful that the last. She sings, in a voice pitched so that none but he will hear the melody, and he thinks this must be an angel's voice. And so, as he draws near, what he sees is angelic beauty, not the ruin of her, not the demon. The concealing glamour is another facet of her father's gift, though she may choose whether or not to don the mask. But it is easier to seduce a man to a warm embrace, and to lost brown eyes and lips that do not stink of estuary muck. Later, in the aftermost instant left to him, when she has been bedded and fucked and he is, for the moment, spent, she will cast aside the charade. He may see the truth of her at the end, and she has always thought this her *own* singular gift. Clarity at the brink of oblivion, largesse before the void. It is no manner of kindness, however, for what unimpeachable gift in this world may *be* kind? It is one honest breath, before her sharp yellow teeth and the saltwater flood that flows out of her from every pore and orifice.

Whoever finds the broken, oddly shriveled body, may wonder at the mattress and sheets drenched and reeking, at the gaping hole in the Irishman's throat. That unlucky innkeeper may cross him- or herself, may mutter a prayer before calling upon a constabulary beadle or policeman. More likely, the corpse will be disposed of in a less sensational and less public fashion. Regardless, she has never been hunted, and has begun to doubt she ever shall be.

By sunset, she has slipped back into the muddy river, regretting only that another year must past before she can again step foot on dry land and take her prey from amongst the breathing multitudes. But this one rides the tides, hardly more than a shade, and her mistress is the sea, as her father was a devil. Her belly full, she finds a wreck and coils herself in between the limpets and mussels, the oysters and thick growths of sponges. She will sleep for a few hours, or a day, or, more rarely, a fortnight. She will dream of the sun and high mountain villages, of meadows dotted with goats and sheep. Of rain. And then she will awaken, and slip away, unnoticed, except by the crabs and eels that wreath her like a winding shroud. The white, wheeling gulls may glance down to perceive her silhouette moving swiftly past just beneath the waves, and knowing what they see, sail higher.

THE FALL OF THE HOUSE OF BLACKWATER

Freda Warrington

Freda Warrington is the author of twenty-one fantasy novels including the Blood Wine series (Titan Books): *A Taste of Blood Wine*, *A Dance in Blood Velvet*, *The Dark Blood of Poppies*, and *The Dark Arts of Blood*. She has spent most of her life in Leicestershire, UK, where the atmospheric landscape inspired her to write otherworldly fiction, such as *Elfland* (winner of the 2009 Romantic Times award for Best Fantasy Novel). Her 1997 Dracula sequel *Dracula the Undead*—which views Stoker's count from an entirely different perspective, while staying true to its Victorian forebear—won the Dracula Society's award for Best Gothic Novel.

Vampires have fascinated her since childhood. (To learn more about the author, visit www.fredawarrington.com.) Her dark, gothic Blood Wine books began to evolve in the 1980s, long before the most recent explosion of vampire fiction. The main character in the story below, Sebastian, is also a major player in *The Dark Blood of Poppies*, and his experience here takes place before the novel begins—setting the scene, in a way . . .

She enters the room, luminous by the light of the candle she carries. In the darkness beyond her curtained bed, I wait unseen. No one ever sees me until I want them to; I'm less than a whisper, a dream. The bedroom is cavernous. Its heart glows orange from the fire banked in the grate, but this weak radiance cannot reach the massed black shadows around it.

She is luscious, barely eighteen. Her hair falls like honey over the white shoulders of her nightdress. She's quite short, slightly plump; completely desirable. Her eyes are darkest violet, her mouth so deep a red it looks almost purple, like a ripe plum. Her name is Elizabeth.

She's the only surviving child of her parents and they've arranged a marriage for her, so I've learned, to some cousin who will come here to live and thus secure the future of the family estate and fortune . . . A respectable Christian marriage, designed to provide mutual wealth, a place in society, a new dynasty . . . all that stuff. I don't care for the dry details.

She's a virgin, trembling on the chasm lip of marriage. That's all we need to know.

She sets down the candle beside her bed and climbs in.

Clutching the sheets around her chin, she stares with those enormous pansy-petal eyes at her future. A pulse ticks in her temple. Can she sense me watching?

A maid bustles in, causing me to draw back with a faint hiss of annoyance. This young, freckly intruder chatters as she pokes the fire, then wipes her hands on her apron and fusses with the bedcovers even as my prey sits prettily against the pillows, waiting for her to leave. The maid brushes dangerously close to me as I draw back behind the heavy bed-curtains. She has no idea I'm there, inches from her. She says things like, "Ah, it's soon you'll be married! You look like a child still. Before you know it, your own children will be running around the place, and you a grand lady!"

The girl smiles enigmatically.

At last the maid is gone, taking her bustling energy with her. The fire fades to a red sulk. Elizabeth bends towards the candle, her lips pouting to blow it out—then she hesitates. Looking over her shoulder, she asks, "Who's there?" She speaks lightly, as if she feels foolish at her own sudden fear.

If ever someone introduces himself to you by saying, "Don't be afraid," my advice is to run, run like the wind! Why would a stranger anticipate fear, unless it was they who posed a danger? Yet that is what I say. I even speak her name.

"Elizabeth. Don't be afraid."

She startles, clutching the bed covers to her chin. Her eyes are pools of astonished innocence. I catch her warm scent; soap and rosewater, with a hint of smooth female musk beneath. She's terrified—not in a make-a-screaming-rush-for-the-door sense, but in the deeper way that turns the victim deathly still. Yet there's fascination in her gaze. Before she acts, she needs to know what I am. And that's the space I have to work in.

"How did you get in?" she whispers. "Who are you?"

"A ghost," I reply. I move just enough to let her see me. Her lips open. I glimpse myself in the looking-glass on her dressing table—it's a myth that we cast no reflection—and I see what she must see; a high, curved cheekbone, shapely nose and jaw, long black lashes. Pallid features a sculptor might have chiseled with idealistic fingers, shaded by hair that is dark, formless and too long. My eyes are deceptive; they're the green-brown of hazel nuts and they look gentle, pensive. They tell you nothing about my character.

"Just a shade, fair child," I tell her gently. "I need your help. Would you help me?"

There's so much history in this house, Blackwater Hall. I should know, for I built it.

Eight years the construction took me, and in 1704 the Hall was finished, standing magnificent beside the River Blackwater amid the rich landscape of County Waterford. My wife Mary was weeks from giving birth. Years, it had taken us to conceive a child! Now all my dreams were close to fruition. Soon we would be leaving the decrepit tower of my Norman and Anglo-Irish ancestors and moving into the new mansion, a place grand enough to befit our heirs. Such struggles I'd had to keep my estate from the hands of the conquering English! I even changed faith from Catholic to Protestant to save it from confiscation—and yet it slipped from my hands anyway. All gone in one terrible night.

Perhaps this was divine punishment. To me, it meant little to betray my religion, since I never was devout. All I cared about was keeping my lands—not out of greed, but passion. I loved my birthright so deeply, I valued it even above my immortal soul. Some say Irish Catholicism is only one step away from paganism, that the faerie folk were never destroyed, only assimilated into the new faith and given the names of saints so the people could still worship without heresy. I believe in those darker, older gods: devouring black mother Callee and her ilk. They never went away, only vanished into sea and stone, tree and sky. And that dreadful night, three of them came to wreak vengeance. Three ancient gods with burnished skins and writhing hair and terrible golden eyes.

They took me, and reforged me into what I am.

The trinity who chose me personified that very peculiar delusion some vampires have—that they have become mythological personalities, demi-gods. And who's to say they are wrong? We slip into another reality when we change, a soup of dreams and nightmares that some call the Crystal Ring. It swarms with archetypes born from the human subconscious (and from the subconscious of other beings, too, I don't doubt). Who is to say that the thought-form of a god or an archangel can't take over a newly made vampire, fusing with a soul that has been broken apart like a raw egg?

I digress.

When I recall my human self, I peer through a veil. I recall Mary as beautiful, a tall fine woman. We loved each other, I thought . . . I'd been patient with the long time it took her to conceive, as I had with the long construction of the house. Wasn't that enough to prove my devotion? Apparently not, by her standards. Mere days before the house was ready for us, it came to pass that I discovered her in the old tower house in the company of some stuttering, milkweed clerk from Dublin. She was packing, ready to run away with him.

Each time I return to Blackwater Hall and stand once again in the courtyard, the grey walls rising like thunderclouds above me, I relive that night. The yellow ropes of Mary's hair hanging over her breasts, the swell of her belly beneath her clothes as she made her confession. "*The child is not yours, Sebastian. In ten years, you could not give me a child. You care nothing for me—all you love is the house! My lover has come for me and we're leaving.*"

She shrank away then as if I would strike her, but I didn't. Instead, I ran into the courtyard of the new house and screamed my rage at the heavens. The black sky split open, and the deluge of rain sent me skidding to the door of a cellar. Somehow I'd gashed my arm in my anguish and blood was dripping from me.

In a few fatal minutes I'd lost everything. I had no wife, no child, so what now was the use of a grand hall? There was wood stacked inside and I meant to set light to it, to burn my dream to its foundations.

The darkness inside the cellar was absolute, but I knew its shape: a long chamber with racks set ready for storage. Only a store-room . . . yet it felt in that moment like an ancient torture chamber, silent but for the drip of water and the sobbing of the damned. I remember sinking down against the wall in my despair, my last moments of being human…

Then someone shut the door.

They'd been shadowing me for months, years. In retrospect, I felt they'd been watching me all my life. They had marked me as "special" in some way, prime raw material for vampire-hood. Who knows why they chose this moment? Perhaps it was my anguish that drew them. Or merely the scent of my rain-watered blood.

They were vampires and yet they were angels. I mean that they *believed* they were angels, messengers from a punishing God, something more than mere demons. Simon, a magnificent golden man with extraordinary deep yellow eyes like a cat's. Fyodor, an attenuated male with silvery flesh and snow-white hair. Rasmila (Callee?), a woman with dark brown skin, her hair a fall of blue-black silk.

In that annihilating moment, all my human concerns fell away in a blast of lightning from heaven.

"Sebastian," they said, their voices as mellifluous, amused, and coldly sonorous as bells. "Don't be afraid. We have come only for your blood and your soul."

Only.

I remember how different the world looked, afterwards. Nets of light webbed a clear deep sky; I'd never before seen with such clarity, never dreamed that such crystalline beauty was hidden from mortal eyes. I could see for miles; northwards to the Galtee and Knockmealdown mountains, to the towers of Cahir Castle, the Golden Vale of Tipperary and Cashel of the Kings; closer at hand, my own beloved estate. The stump of the old stone tower was a shadow behind the new house, which appeared a great, pristine mansion like a gold casket swathed in deep blue twilight. Three storeys it has, with tall imposing windows, a pillared portico that soars the height of the frontage. All was wrapped in night-colors I'd never seen before. The air was sweet and icy, like wine.

How unutterably beautiful it was, the home that I built for myself. For us.

And then I walked away.

I left, only because of what I became. What need had I for anything of the mortal world? I needed no wife or child, no home, no land or wealth, none of that. All I needed was blood, and the wonder of my new senses.

I had no intention ever of coming back. And yet…

Here I am again, unseen in the shadows, a ghost haunting the ruins of my own life.

There are two ways I might proceed with Elizabeth. The road of instant violation and swift death; or the slower path of enthrallment, followed by a wasting decline into madness. Each has its own pleasures, so I am undecided. I live in the moment, watching how the warm light gilds the swell and dip of her breasts, the way her tongue flicks out to make her lips glisten.

"A spirit?" she whispers. And then, "I know you. I've seen you before."

This shocks me. No one is meant to see me! Her parents never have, nor their servants nor any of their numerous visitors and relatives. They're aware of me; I am the guilty secret that no one mentions. They shiver and start at shadows, but they don't see me. "When have you seen me, fair one?" I ask very gently.

"When I was a child. You never spoke to me before."

When last I was here, Elizabeth had indeed been a small child. Her older brother lay dying of a mysterious wasting disease, so crazed by strange ecstatic nightmares that they called the priest to exorcise him... Ah, memories. She doesn't know that I was responsible. Obviously she glimpsed me, yet never connected my appearance to his death.

"What did you think, when you saw me?"

"I don't know. You were just a face in the shadows. A sad and restless soul with such beautiful eyes."

"You weren't afraid, then?" I smile in relief. "You know I'm a friend."

"Yes," she murmurs. So, she has some dim memory of me, which has imprinted itself favorably upon her. And thanks to that—after her initial alarm—she's receptive. She sees me, not as a threat, but as someone familiar, fascinating. A lonely, mysterious phantom!

The idea of killing her, swiftly or slowly, loses its appeal. Instead—to win her trust! Her love. There's a novelty.

"You are the ghost of Blackwater Hall," she says, speaking as decisively as a child.

"Yes." I laugh softly at that. "I suppose I am."

Her eyes grow more intense. "You're him, aren't you? You're Sebastian Pierse, who murdered his wife and her lover, and then disappeared."

"And been in torment over it ever since," I concur. "She betrayed me most sorely, but I wronged her the more. Now I seek atonement."

"My parents and grandparents have always feared you," she whispers. "They are always looking over their shoulders in the dark. They brought in priests to cleanse the place—but it didn't work, did it?"

I try not to laugh at this, since she's so sincere. I speak with quiet, desperate need. "Elizabeth, it is the dearest wish of my heart to trouble the household no longer. But I'll never be at peace unless you help me."

"Help you, how?" She is trembling. We're half in love already. The warm weight of her body so close is driving me mad.

"Should I pray for you?"

"Yes. Let me come to you at night like this, and we'll pray together. A link with the living…"

"I can't have a man in my room!" she says in a panic. "I'm to be married."

"But I'm not a man, I'm a soul in torment. Connection with a living being, that's all I need."

"All?"

"And a sip of your life-blood."

She blinks. It doesn't sound much, put like that. She touches my hand, doesn't flinch when I sit beside her. "You're very solid, for a ghost," she says.

We talk like this for a long time, a game of thrust and parry that grows ever more intense. There are soft touches between us; my fingertips on her hand, hers on my sleeve. Confidences are shared. She holds nothing back.

I gather she is dreading this marriage to a man older than herself. It is no love match, clearly. As our dialogue strays into more intimate areas, she confesses that she fears the wedding night. "George will expect me like this—all pure, untried and nervous. But I . . . I don't see why I should be lying here ignorant and frightened!"

"You deserve pleasure," I tell her. "He will not give you pleasure; you are just a possession to him."

"How do you know?"

"I can tell, from your words, exactly the sort of man he is. Domineering, certain of his rights. He will have despoiled a hundred women in his time and yet expect his wife to be a perfect innocent. He will use you brutishly." My outrage is genuine. "I can't bear to think of him hurting you."

She chafes her lip with her teeth. I want to bite that rose-pink pillow. I see in her eyes a violet fire of rebellion. At last she asks, "Will you show me, then? So that when the time comes, I'll know what to expect and I won't be afraid. Will you, Sebastian?"

"Nothing would please me more." I speak with complete sincerity.

"But he must never know!"

"He won't," I reassure her. "It will be our secret. After all, with a ghost, it doesn't count."

At last I lean in and feel the sweet, fresh warmth of her neck against my mouth. She sighs. I am lost.

When I became a vampire I walked away from Blackwater Hall. I left others to find my wife and her lover in the old stone tower, where I had left them marinating in pools of their own blood. I took ship to America, like the long wave of Irish emigrants after me, thinking never to return. I put an ocean between myself and the old country; I wanted no more of its shadowy magic, its religions and superstitions, its wars and the endless struggle I'd had just to hold onto what was mine.

In those early years of my new existence, I was savage and bitter. Yet as time passed, as bitterness faded and I brought the bloodthirst under control, I began to think of the house again.

Some sixty years after I left, I came back. Just curiosity, you understand. I discovered that the scandal of Sebastian Pierse—who'd murdered his wife, her lover, and her unborn infant before vanishing—was local legend; a folk-tale told by old men in their cups. My estate had been claimed by the British and awarded to a family of English Protestant settlers. They were decent enough folk, I concede, who looked after the estate well and were fair to the tenants. I'd no argument with the way they ran my affairs.

And yet, they had no right to be there. I owed it to the house and to myself to haunt them a little, to frighten the old men, to feed on the young and strong. To turn a capable wife into a crazed neurotic, to kill a first-born son here, a beloved daughter there. Just to darken their lives once in a while, as the generations came and went.

So every few years I return to Ireland for old times' sake, and listen with pleasure when people say, "That Blackwater Hall is haunted; it's cursed the family are!" And I slip silently into the house and torment the hapless inhabitants a little more. I could have killed them all, but I let them stay and survive. Why?

If I were of a more violent disposition, I would have ousted the usurpers long ago. I prefer to play a long and subtle game.

How much more sense it makes to let them stay, to enjoy the slow burn of revenge over a century or three. I tolerate them for the pure pleasure of haunting them.

"Just a sip, just a drop of your lifeblood," I whisper to Elizabeth in the darkness. "It must be freely given. Without it, I'll fade from Earth and be dragged into hell." In the euphoric convulsions of our lovemaking I draw on her neck as she groans with delight and pain. I resist the urge to take too much; she's too delightful to me, alive. And so she thinks she's saving a poor damned soul from the abyss!

For a while, anyway. By the time she realizes the falsehood, she no longer cares.

It helps that I have this supernatural glow of beauty—the honey in the trap—that her new husband lacks. And she has the darkness in her soul that welcomes me, loving the danger and deception of it, loving the sheer sin.

I was right about the husband. He's some remote cousin of hers and his name is George. He's an older man, experienced in the ways of the world to the point of debauchery. He's handsome enough in his way; tall and strong, with a ruggedly arrogant face, thick brown hair, an overpowering sense of arrogant masculine entitlement. (Probably I would have been just like him, had my human life progressed as planned). George has made a fortune from trade in Dublin. He's been everywhere and done everything, and yet he expects as his due a shimmering, untouched maiden on his wedding night! To me, he seems coarse and charmless. There can be no love in this match. Society has shackled her to him, but her hidden self writhes and lashes against it like a serpent.

Elizabeth acts well the part of his new bride. How innocently she glides from church to bridal chamber, trembling and virginal, God-fearing and full of nervous anticipation. How flawlessly she feigns pain and inexperience! Attentive to detail, she even covertly pricks her finger on a pin to fake a few drops of virgin blood (ah, her sweet blood) on the sheets. Drunk on wine, blind in his triumphal lust, the husband suspects nothing.

As he takes her, grunting and oblivious, she looks at me over his shoulder. Her lips part and her eyes shine as she smiles at me, her secret lover in the shadows.

Every girl should have one.

I am standing once again in the courtyard, which still seems to echo with the screams of Mary and her pallid weed of a lover as I tear them apart, feasting on their blood, ripping the still-moving fetus from her womb to suck the tender fluids from it as if from an unborn lamb...

I write about all this as if I still cared, but in truth, I don't. When the unholy trinity of vampires came to feed on my blood and grief in the rain—golden Simon, dark Rasmila and pale Fyodor, as white as ectoplasm—I entered a clearer state of consciousness in which human pain no longer tore me. Since I was determined to burn down Blackwater Hall at the time, you could say that they saved the house, my three demon-angels. Should I thank them?

Whenever Elizabeth and George are absent, I walk through the salons as if I own the place. It has an eerie grandeur. There are high ceilings with elaborate plaster decoration, impressive fireplaces surmounted by coats of arms, rows of long windows hung with gorgeous curtains. Exotic rugs sprawl on polished floorboards. Along the walls are the antlered heads of stags, staring out with black marble eyes. And countless dark portraits of ancestors, fixing their painted gazes on mine.

Double doors lead from one great room to the next; here a drawing room that is insistently golden; wallpaper, frames, curtains, the scrolled woodwork of chairs, all gold. There are chairs lush with needlepoint roses, tapestry stools and firescreens. Too many ornaments; clocks, statuettes, vases, elephants carved of onyx and jade. More paintings, huge mirrors rimmed with gilt.

None of this stuff is mine. Only the shell matters.

These great rooms—which feel so alien to me, even though I commissioned them—fill me with delicious, creeping awe. This place has the feel of a theatre, each room a lavish set waiting endlessly for the actors to arrive. The house creaks. Speaks. Upstairs there are nurseries and playrooms where expensive toys have been played with too little. Alas, the mortality rate of children has been tragically high over the decades—and not all my fault, far from it.

Feeding upon infants is a dull game, after all. True pleasure lies in toying with the adult inhabitants. I goad them, rather as a dog scratches at fleas, to remind them they should not be here.

Some regard the house as ugly. All things decay, of course. Each time I come I see further hints of weathering, paint peeling, rust-marks streaking the render. Perhaps Blackwater Hall is, as some claim, a brute of a place, as desolate as a prison fortress. Well, I don't ask anyone to admire it. It's the mirror of my soul. It is my soul.

In truth, I've no need to reclaim it, because it was never truly taken from me. It can't be taken; it's as if it exists partly in the Crystal Ring, an etheric house that transcends its earthly form. It transcends beauty itself.

If I speak of my house like a lover, it is because I regard it as a lover.

On the surface, Elizabeth is the good wife, attending church, managing her household, pretending to be thrilled when her husband brings her some trinket. She affects ignorance of his gambling, drinking and whoring when he's away in Dublin or in London. Like the dutiful wife she is, she turns a blind eye. But she has a secret.

Me.

Our limbs twine like snow in the moonlight, blood streaking darkly down her throat. Blood on snow. She knows by now that I'm no ghost, that my needs are nothing to do with saving my poor tormented soul— but she's beyond caring. We are both too addicted to this sensual game. When she feels faint, I hold her up and give her dark stout to drink, to strengthen the blood.

She knows that if we keep doing this, it will kill her, yet she cannot stop. Neither of us can. Urgently she welcomes me to her bed, whenever the husband is absent.

Then one night, panting in the aftermath of passion, she cries, "You must leave me alone, Sebastian." She pushes me away into the wreckage of bed sheets, her essence still sweet on my tongue. "I need to have children. Can you give me children?"

I laugh and reply, "I hardly think so. We both know that I can't."

Even in life, as I've mentioned, I failed to impregnate my wife. Whatever cold essence now spurts from my member, it is as clear as ice water and as sterile as *poteen*. There is no life-force in it.

"Then you have to go, and leave me to my husband!"

So I do as she asks—out of curiosity, not compassion. I let her alone for a few years, and children she has. Three rosy daughters and two sons, who suck as greedily upon her breast as ever I have feasted on her neck. The beating urgency of life will always win out against the vampire.

Why did I indulge her? Well, I have patience. Of course the temptation was there, to guzzle the life from those rosy children, from mother and father too, all in one debauched night—but I didn't. What am I, a fox in a flapping hencoop, to go on killing and killing until nothing moves anymore? No.

I was too soft on Elizabeth but, you see, if I'd destroyed her—and it would have been so easy, done in a moment—I'd have destroyed the very conditions that made my existence worthwhile. I was in love, a little. If not with her, then with the situation.

I still had to feed, of course, and so I went away for a while, a fair few years in fact, and found entertainment elsewhere. I might even have lost interest and never gone back at all—but by coincidence, nearly twenty years on, we meet at a ball in Dublin.

Elizabeth greets me with the same sly smile of recognition and, as I bow gallantly, we both know—the game is on again. She is tangibly older of course—flesh thickening, her stiff layers of corsetry and clothes giving her the grandeur of a duchess. Still a desirable woman, though. She still has the gleam in her violet eyes, once so innocent, now full of shrewdness; knowing and sultry. I still desire her—how not? Her flesh is as plump with blood as ever and the blood as sweet in its promise.

Later, at Blackwater Hall once more, we face each other in her bedchamber, but something is different. The first thing she says to me is, "Make me a vampire."

I only look at her. Somewhere deep inside me, dreary horror wells, a kind of tired revulsion.

"That's what I want," she insists. She clasps my arms, imploring me with luminous eyes. "Look at you, forever young and powerful, fearing nothing! I want that too!"

"Never." I tear myself from her. Surely my contempt must pierce her to the heart. "I couldn't do it, even if I wanted to. It's not a simple process. It takes three vampires to create a new one." And I explain a little about Rasmila, Fyodor, and Simon.

"Then find two others to help you," she persists, addressing me as if I were some inept boot-boy.

"Don't you understand?" I say patiently. "The gathering of three means that the change can't happen by accident. It must be planned. Which means that it must be desirable."

"But it is. I desire it."

"Desirable to *them*. To me."

She looks at me as if I've lost my mind. The look makes me angry.

"Who do you think you are, Elizabeth?" I say with cold spite. "You were never anything to me but blood-filled flesh. What, you think you're worthy of immortality? No, you are not so special. You are no different from any other mortal. A lump of ageing flesh."

Strangely, she doesn't appear to react much. Her eyes narrow a little, but she keeps her burning, wounded anger contained inside her. She doesn't scream or beg. I'm too dismayed at her tiresome request to care about the feelings she is hiding.

Eventually she says, in a surprisingly cutting tone, "What you're telling me is that you, alone, lack the power to transform me. You can't do it without help. Poor Sebastian."

I should have killed her for that. Should have done so long before now. I hate it when I let them reach this stage.

I go away then, leaving her standing ghost-like in the centre of the large and shadowy bedroom that, so often, had witnessed our convulsions of ecstasy.

Unbelievable as it may seem, I almost entirely forget she ever made this request. It passed from my mind in the manner of a lover's tiff. Some months later I arrive at the house again, as jaunty as a young suitor who's gone off, got drunk, and returned later utterly oblivious to the fact that his lady friend has been seething with rage all this time.

I can't altogether have forgotten, though, because I feel wary. I don't approach her at once. Instead I haunt stairwells and alcoves for a time, watching the family from a distance. It amuses me to do this, but I'm sure Elizabeth knows I'm around. She's uneasy and over-sensitive, just as she used to be in the old days when I would look at the pale peach column of her neck with such delicious longing.

Actually, I have some vague intention of starting on one of the daughters now. Or maybe a son, for a change. Or all of them. They must be of an age to make it fun.

Alas, it seems I'm too late. Where did the time go? All but one of the offspring appear to have left—farmed out to schools or to relatives in order to become ladies and gentlemen, ready to marry money and enter society—they're out there in the world, but Elizabeth and her husband are still here. Their youngest is about eight, a plain bookish boy who doesn't interest me.

Still, I'm a patient man. I can wait for the son to grow up and come home with a trembling, fresh young wife, or even wait for grandchildren… After all, the house is mine. Generations will come and go but I will always be here, like a curse.

Only something is wrong.

I start to notice changes in Elizabeth. She's lost weight; she looks younger, more slender, her hair restored to its lustrous gold. She's languorous, pleased with herself—as she used to be in the early days with me. The changes aren't just in her, but in her husband George, too. It's as if his coarseness has been fine-polished away, and he no longer strides around like a drunken officer, slapping the furniture with a riding crop. Instead there's a thoughtful quality about him, a shine to his hair and a pale bloom to his skin.

Have I been blind? Isn't it strange, how we don't see what we don't *expect* to see? Some ghastly trick has been played upon me, here in my own house. Voices seem to be whispering and laughing at me from the corners of ceilings. Stags stare at me from black glass eyes. Something is pulling at me, an unseen current whirling me along, rendering me as wide-eyed and vulnerable as Elisabeth on that first night. As if in a trance, I walk into the drawing room and they are sitting in chairs on either side of the fireplace, George and Elizabeth, just as if they have been waiting for me to arrive. They sit perfectly composed, like brother and sister, hands lightly clasped in their laps. They are gazing at me with liquid eyes and their skin glows like candle-flames shining through the thinnest possible shell of wax.

"How did you do it?" My voice almost fails as I speak, emerging hoarse as an old man's.

"We met your angels," she answers simply. "Your three angels. They came back. I knew what they were and I persuaded them to transform us."

I should have remembered. The vampire's kiss, when it does not kill, brings madness. Not always in the form of wilting terror, but sometimes as a kind of megalomania.

"Why? They can't be persuaded. They take only those who are special, chosen. That is what they told me."

"And it's what they told us, too," she answers serenely. "You take yourself too seriously, Sebastian. Perhaps they changed us simply to annoy you."

"But him?" I point at the husband, who looks back at me. He sits motionless as only vampires can, fixing me with his all-knowing, pitiless gaze. "That—that coarse, arrogant, drink-raddled *merchant*?"

"Why would I want to be immortal, without my husband at my side?" she replies, genuinely surprised.

"You hate him, and all he represents!"

"No, I don't. It was your idea that I hated him, that he maltreated me. Your perception, not reality. I love my husband. Have you no idea of the wonders I've shown him? We are one soul, George and I."

So, all the arts she learned from me, she has taught him in turn! And far from being suspicious at her knowledge, it turns out he was delighted with it, enthralled! Unbelievable.

And now they are holding hands, and he lifts hers to his mouth, pressing her knuckles to his lips. She laughs, showing the tips of her new fangs. "What, did you think you alone were the custodian of this delicious dark secret? Selfish Sebastian. You wouldn't share, so we found another way, and now we don't need you anymore." And she laughs again. Laughs at me!

So this is what I did.

I went away and dressed myself up as a priest, and I arrived in the nearest village all disheveled, with a crusading fire in my eye; a man of the cloth, on a mission from God. First I found the local priest and plied him with whisky as I told my story. Despite his unpromising appearance, he was soon full of holy ardor. He was a fiery fellow, eager to make his mark on the world, to impress his bishop and win the undying admiration of his congregation, or something on those lines. I wound him up and set him spinning.

He gathered the populace, and I spun my story; that Elizabeth and George were undead, that they'd sold their souls to the Devil in exchange for immortality, that I'd been hunting such creatures down across Europe, Britain and Ireland for years in order to bring them the mercy of death. Oh, a rare tale I wove.

I'd come to warn them, to help them purge the evil. Were they with me? Oh yes, by God, they were!

The priest fell in eagerly behind me like a captain behind a general. He took me for the scholar and holy man I purported to be and he wanted to play the hero, scrambling for his share of my glory. Turned out I'd walked into a community already possessed by rumor and fear. Elizabeth and George were young vampires, you see, not yet adept at hiding their tracks. There had been deaths, injuries that set a fair old fire of stories blazing. I'd walked in at the perfect time to become the savior of the community.

All I had to do was to point and say, "They're the guilty ones," and the entire town became a mob, ablaze with righteous vengeance.

They will fight like tigers, I warned, so we'll go in a big band like an army. Some of us will probably die, but that's the risk we must take to be free of this curse.

They don't sleep in coffins, I told them, but they are more dangerous by night and more apt to be off their guard during the day, from the necessity of pretending to be human. Don't bother with a stake to the heart, I said—that will only make them mad. No crosses, either, you'll only waste time while they laugh. Simply hack off their heads, I instructed. Hack the heads and the bodies into pieces, then throw the pieces onto a bonfire.

That should do the trick.

And so it happened that I led a vast, inflamed army to Blackwater Hall—priests and farmers, blacksmiths, washerwomen and their big daughters, stomping along with rolled-up sleeves, everyone—and they took Elizabeth and her husband by surprise and overwhelmed them.

Too inexperienced to vanish into the shadows of the Crystal Ring, they fought for their lives with fangs and nails. They fought with all the desperation of mortals—and thus they fell, hacked to pieces.

The mob spared the little boy, who watched as his parents were cut down before his terrified eyes. Had he known what they'd become? How could he not? And yet, I still believe he didn't know. His parents had kept up a front of humanity for his sake, ensuring that he only saw what they wanted him to see.

I still wonder what nightmares haunted him down the rest of his years. At one time I would have been eager to know… would have sought him out wherever he was, and hidden in the shadows watching the liquid shine of his gaze questing for me in the darkness…

Strange, I never did. I lost my taste for it, somehow.

In the midst of this carnage, I slipped away.

A column of smoke rose behind me, turning the air bitterly fragrant like autumn—but it was a pyre that burned, not the house itself.

Their children survived. The older ones, I understand, never set foot in Blackwater Hall again. The youngest son, however—once he'd reached an age to make his own choice—lived there until his death; a bachelor. Quite eccentric, quite mad. He never threw anything away, it seems. He filled the place with collections; with animals stuffed rigid under glass domes, with drawers full of fossils and coins, with butterflies pinned in glass cases and huge, ugly beetles impaled on cards. As if, by heaping talismans around himself, he built a great nest in which to hide from the darkness outside.

A grand job he did of tormenting himself; he didn't need any help from me at all.

Some years ago, he died and since then Blackwater Hall has lain empty, a shell loved by no one. And here it remains, falling into slow decline.

Sometimes I still come back.

I view the familiar sweeps of grass, magnificent lone trees, copses, the river gleaming like milk in the vaporous gloom. In the distance, the mountains are soaked in layers of folk tale and myth, haunted forever by the black goddess Callee. And there it stands, Blackwater Hall; a great mansion, broodingly desolate. The walls are mottled and flaking, as if the place is shedding its skin with age. The windows, fogged like cataracts with dirt, stare indifferently at long-neglected gardens and stables.

I stand outside and gaze at it for hours, watching it decay by slow degrees. I'm filled with the sensation that it was not I who built the house after all, but some greater power acting through me. In darker moments I feel that I have simply been used in order to create a theatre for some great drama that has yet to unfold. In my mind the house is a sighing black tomb, and in place of antlered stags along the walls, there are horned demon heads.

Thus the house remains to this day—its walls gray with neglect, paint cracking, windows netted with cobwebs and dust. Somehow it withstands the vigorous, mindless invasion of life—the nesting of birds and bats, vegetation trying to drag it down with green tendrils. I wander the grand salons and bedrooms, corridors and attic nurseries, where rocking horses stand motionless under the soft, endless fall of dust. The edifice endures like an ancient castle fortress, tired yet impervious to time.

Was it I who sucked the life from this house? Will it ever be done with its revenge? I wanted the family gone and yet, without them, it is nothing. The house is dead yet here it stands, undead. Blackwater Hall draws me back, I swear, like a jealous lover. I know it is not done with me yet.

One day it may yet spring to life again. Some rich and enterprising young family might take on the Hall and restore it to glory, filling the rooms with fresh colors, with the chat and bustle of their lives, with scents of flowers and cooking; with the vigor of their own throbbing, blood-filled bodies. Children will run laughing and screaming along the endless corridors. Doll's house doors will be opened, gigantic child-faces staring in awe through the windows. Rocking horses will creak into life.

And on that day I will be here, waiting to claim my own.

IN MEMORY OF . . .

Nancy Kilpatrick

Award-winning author and editor Nancy Kilpatrick has published eighteen novels, one nonfiction book, and has edited thirteen anthologies. Of those, eight of the novels are vampiric, including her popular Power of the Blood world. Two additional volumes collect some of her vampire short fiction: *The Vampire Stories of Nancy Kilpatrick* and *Vampyric Variations*. Three of the anthologies she's edited are *Love Bites; Evolve: Vampire Stories of the New Undead; Evolve 2: Vampire Stories of the Future Undead*. A goodly number of her two hundred and twenty published short stories fall into the undead realm. She writes on other themes, but vampires are still near and dear to her heart. This has propelled her to acquire, over the years, a vast book collection of vampire fiction and nonfiction that now totals well over 2,200 titles. Look for her upcoming (non-vampire) anthologies: *Expiration Date* (spring 2015) and *Nevermore! Murder, Mystery and the Macabre* (fall 2015). Check nancykilpatrick.com for updates, and join her on Facebook.

In the following story, Kilpatrick weaves real historical characters and a few facts into an unusual tale of psychic vampirism . . .

If memory serves, yellow marigolds and blue narcissus clotted the flowerbeds of my father's estate in Clontarf that August. The gardener had outdone himself, and it was as though at every turn, life itself permeated the grounds—short-lived life. But 1875 was the spring of my years. Barely seventeen and dreamy, the way Irish girls were then, my future stretched before me like an endless bare canvas, awaiting whichever colors and brush strokes I deigned to paint upon it. Had I but known the outcome of that fateful afternoon, surely I would have fled to the bluffs, hurled my young body over the cliffs and onto the jagged rocks below.

The lawn party my parents hosted was not as large as some, but the *crème de la crème* was in attendance. I recall gazing from the terrace, across the clipped lawn, at the finely attired men in their frockcoats, and the women in soft silks hidden beneath frilly parasols to ward off the sun's rays. Suddenly, for some unknown reason, I gazed upward. A flock of ravens swarmed overhead, so thick that they shrouded the sun's rays, darkening the sky temporarily, sucking up all the light from it. The sight sent a chill down my spine, as if this were a terrible omen of some sort. Just as quickly, that gloomy manifestation evaporated, like a nightmare on awakening, leaving behind only a wisp, a remnant. Immediately the sky brightened.

"May I present my daughter." My father's voice startled me, and I turned. "Florence, this is Mister Oscar Wilde. Mister Wilde is a writer, in his first year at Oxford."

"How very nice to meet you." The words caught in my throat, and I extended my gloved hand.

His face was almost an anachronism. Long, large-featured, flesh pale yet ruddy, with emotion-laden eyes and a peculiar twist at the corners of his full lips. The exact nature of the crooked line between those lips was, for some time, a mystery to me. And what I often felt then to be a grimace, I have now come to understand to be something entirely more sinister.

Mister Wilde took my hand in his and kissed it, in the continental fashion. "Lieutenant-Colonel Balcombe, your daughter is both remarkably beautiful and, I can see already, utterly charming in a way which will shatter many hearts, all of which, no doubt, will be exceedingly eager to be broken."

I, of course, blushed at such a forthright yet backhanded compliment from this man so startlingly overdressed in a lilac-colored shirt with a large ascot clinging to his throat. If truth be known, more than anyone else, he resembled George the Fourth, which made me smile secretly—what the French would have called *joli-laid*. His countenance was singularly mild yet his expression ardent. He spoke rapidly, in a low voice, and enunciated distinctly, like a man accustomed to being listened to. Yet beyond all that, his eyes arrested me. I'd never seen such wild intensity, juxtaposed with fragile sensitivity. To this day, try as I might, I simply cannot recall their color, which makes no sense, considering how strongly they held me. What I do recall is that they seemed to capture my very essence, as surely as if my dear soul were a butterfly, suddenly enslaved in a net. A delicate creature destined to be pinned to a board.

My father was called to greet another arriving friend, leaving me to the mercy of this peculiarly enticing stranger.

"There is nothing like youth," he said, in a theatrical manner, gesturing lavishly, speaking loudly, attracting the attention of those standing nearby, yet holding my eye as if it were me alone to whom he spoke. "Youth has a kingdom waiting for it. To win back my youth . . . there is nothing I wouldn't do . . ."

I, of course, laughed at such melodrama. "Surely you know nothing of wanting your youth back. My guess, from your appearance, is that you are all of two and twenty."

"From appearances, your guess is nearly correct, less the two. Youth is not merely a chronological order of years, but more a state of mind. The life that makes the soul, mars the body."

"How strange you are!" I blurted, then felt my face flame. After all, I hardly knew this man, and had not the familiarity with which to taunt him. But he took it in good humor.

"More peculiar than you at present can know. However, Florence, may I call you Florrie?"

"Well, yes, if you like—"

"I do like! Florrie, you must permit me to escort you to church this coming Sunday for the afternoon service."

Flustered, flattered, I could only stumble over my words. "Well . . . of course. I would be delighted to have you attend our simple country chapel—"

"Excellent! The day is too bright, not the proper setting for a man to offer attention to a woman."

"And church is?"

"One's virtues either shine or dim when the virtuous speak."

With that he kissed my hand again and was gone.

I recall standing, looking down at my hand, which felt as if burning ice had dropped onto it. Then I looked up. My eyes scanned the crowd of my parents' friends. Oscar Wilde had disappeared.

"Tell me about your work, Mister Wilde." We walked, his hand cupping my elbow, guiding me through the tall rock-strewn grass down the hill toward the rectory, and the chapel beyond, my parents not far ahead of us. I admit that this contact proved thrilling to my girlish body. My affections had already begun swaying in his direction, which, of course, both of us knew.

"My name is Oscar Fingal O'Flahertie Wills Wilde, but you may call me Oscar."

So formal a response made me laugh.

This caused him to glance down at me and frown slightly. "Is that mockery I hear?"

"Mockery, no. Amusement, Oscar. You are so serious. How do you get on in society?"

"I suppose society is wonderfully delightful. To be in it is merely a bore. But to be out of it simply a tragedy. But you were inquiring as to my work."

"Unfortunately, I have not had the chance to read you as yet, although I'm certain you must be a fine poet and will go on to be an excellent writer of prose."

"You are either foolish or perceptive, but, of course, I favor the latter. And what do you know of poetry?"

"I know that it is a taste of God's passion."

"Poets know how useful passion is. Nowadays a broken heart will run to many editions."

"You speak of broken hearts on such a beautiful summer's day? Have you survived one?"

"A poet can survive everything but a misprint."

"You're not very forthcoming, are you, Oscar?"

He stopped walking and turned toward me. I felt my heart flutter. The air seemed to encase the two of us.

"Florrie, all art is quite useless. Before you stands a shallow man, make no mistake about that. One in need of a muse who will inspire him beyond mere banality. More, nourish him."

Words escaped me. I knew not what to answer, or if an answer was at all required. I only knew that we seemed to stand there for an eternity. And as we stood together, locked in an embrace, his eyes drew me until I felt myself dimming, willingly. I knew in those moments I would offer up to him whatever he needed, whatever he wanted.

"Miss Balcombe. It is so nice to see you. And may I enquire, who is your friend?"

The voice of the Reverend Sean Manchester broke the moment. Suddenly it was as though I'd been under a spell. I felt stunned, aware that I'd not heard the birds or felt the intense heat for some time. But rather than perceiving the good Reverend's voice as a lifeline, cast toward a drowning swimmer, I felt it an intrusion. With some effort, I forced myself back to the surface of the waters known as reality.

"Reverend Manchester, may I introduce Mister Oscar Wilde. You will have heard of him, no doubt. He is an aspiring poet, who has already had work published."

"Indeed. I have heard much."

"And I'm certain you shall hear more in future. There is only one thing in the world worse than being talked about," Oscar said, "and that is not being talked about."

The two men shook hands, but perfunctorily. I was dismayed at this adversarial climate between them. I knew it could not be me, for after all, Reverend Manchester was an older gentleman, married a number of years, with several nearly grown children. I could not have known at the time the entirety of this wedge, but I soon had an inkling of its nature.

"You are a young man and already famous throughout the British Isles."

"Don't you mean *infamous*?"

"Infamy implies sin."

"There is no sin except stupidity."

"If you believe not in sin, I presume then that you also give no credence to conscience."

"Conscience and cowardice are really the same things."

"Then, sir, in your opinion, why do men go astray?"

"Simply, temptation. The only way to get rid of a temptation is to give in to it, it seems to me."

"Oscar!" I felt compelled to interject a note of sanity, for things had got out of hand. Even a poet should respect a man of the cloth. "Surely you believe in salvation! You were raised a Christian, were you not?"

At this, he turned to me again. A small, crooked smile played over those lips, and his eyes again compelled me to focus on him exclusively. That same potent pull threatened to overwhelm me, although his words kept me from sinking. "Florrie, dearest, we are all in the gutter, but some of us are looking at the stars."

"Heaven might be a better destination," Reverend Manchester said, "although there is an alternative."

"And that, I presume, is Hell. Well, Reverend, I have visited that place and not, I suspect, for the last time. I have found it wanting."

Reverend Manchester said nothing more, but the look in his eyes spoke volumes. The church bells were tolling madly, the service about to begin. "I must attend to my parishioners," he said perfunctorily, and, almost as an afterthought, "It is good we have met, Mister Wilde."

"Yes. A man cannot be too careful in the choice of his enemies."

Reverend Manchester looked startled by this blatant statement. But in my eyes, Oscar had merely said what was evident—the two men did not see eye to eye, although I should have thought 'enemy' too strong a word.

Reverend Manchester excused himself. Oscar turned to me. Before I had the chance to collect my thoughts, he grasped my shoulders and quickly pressed his lips to mine. I was shocked. Embarrassed. Titillated. I scanned the small group of parishioners; none had seen this outrageous act, including my parents, thank God!

When I looked again at Oscar, all of this evident on my face, no doubt, something strange occurred. The contrast between us struck me. His face had become ruddy, while I felt light-headed and pale. He seemed sure of himself, whilst I, on the other hand, had been knocked entirely off balance. As I stared at him, time became irrelevant. The importance of my life seemed to diminish in my mind. The call of my soul's high longings became faint to my ears. A peculiar image came to me: I was composed of tiny particles which normally adhere together as a solid but were now being separated by some invisible dark force. And then, there was only Oscar.

"I must be off, Florrie," he said.

"What? You're not attending the service?" I heard my voice as if from a distance. Who is asking this question? I wondered. And who pretends to care for the answer?

"I have other plans. Permit me, though, to call on you this week."

It wasn't exactly a question, but more of a statement he made. And before I could respond, he turned and was gone.

I know that Reverend Manchester's sermon focused on the devil, finding him here and there, and being on guard, but I could only concentrate on snatches of what was said. You see, I was already in love. At least, I called it love then, but I have since learned to identify it as indenture. Bits of my soul were siphoned from me that day and what would occur afterwards would make a normal woman grieve for a lifetime. But already I had ceased to be normal and even my gender became inconsequential to me. And I was incapable of grief.

Oscar visited my home twice a week for two weeks. After that, he became a permanent fixture in our parlor. Nightly, mother or my auntie chaperoned, as was the custom then. Neither approved of him—Oscar was not an ordinary man. I was only too eager to assure them that he was, in fact, a genius, destined for great things. They would have none of it.

"You can't be serious!" Auntie chided me. "What kind of a husband do you think a man wearing a purple great coat would make!"

"Style," I informed her, "is not a paramount concern, although his dress is *avant garde*, in my opinion."

"Your opinion," Mother said, "hardly matters here. You're but seventeen years of age. Need I remind you that your father and I make your decisions as long as you reside under our roof? This is not a match made in heaven."

"But it is not made in that other place either, Mother. Were you never young once? Did your heart not rule you when Father was near?"

"My head superseded my heart, or at least the heads of your maternal grandparents. Fortunately, their clearer minds prevailed. You are seeing entirely too much of Mister Wilde."

"You're young, child," Auntie declared. "There are other suitors, more worthy."

In the way of youth, I created a scene, as they say, and left them both standing there speechless. But it was as though I watched my antics, disconnected. Then, of course, I interpreted my reaction to being overly intimidated at vexing my elders with my disrespectful behavior.

Time has proven auntie's word both right and wrong—incorrect in the context of her meaning, but correct in a broader meaning, for I have been loved by at least one other man, much to his detriment.

Mother remained adamant, but Father, however, admired Oscar, and could see that his name would be remembered through the ages. Although, being my father, and concerned with my interests, he was not particularly comfortable with Oscar's financial situation. Unfortunately our family fortunes had taken a turn for the worse—I was dowerless and, in Mother's words, must count on a "strong pecuniary match." Oscar, you see, was a spendthrift. His inheritances and endowments were few and far between, and his wants exceeded his resources throughout his life. He spent much too freely, on both himself and his friends. And on me. At Christmas of that year, Oscar presented me with a token of his affections.

Inside the exquisite sculpted shell box of ivory I found a tiny cross. I held it up by the chain and the illumination from the gas lamp seemed to make the gold sparkle. I became mesmerized by that sparkle, and only Oscar's voice returned me to the room.

"Wear this in memory of me," he said, as though he were dying.

On one side was an inscription, uniting our names. My eyes must have shown what was in my heart.

"Florrie," he said ardently, grasping both my hands, falling to one knee before me, in the presence of Auntie, who instantly paused in her needlework.

"I am too happy to speak," I told him. "You must speak for both of us."

I expected a proposal of marriage, although I knew that while he was still a student, marriage was forbidden him. I would have been satisfied with a profession of undying love. But Oscar, in his theatrical manner, while Auntie gazed on, said something entirely unexpected.

"The worst of having a romance of any kind is that it leaves one so . . . unromantic. You have, of course, won my heart."

And that was that.

Father and Mother, though, on hearing of this incident, took it seriously, although there had been no commitment elicited. They proceeded to check more deeply into Oscar's fiscal and also personal affairs. Unsavory rumors were alluded to, but my parents refused to provide to me the details.

"Then they are only rumors," I said stubbornly, "whatever their nature. I believe it is unchristian-like to lower oneself to pay credence to mere hearsay."

Mother looked angry. "Now you're beginning to speak as rudely as he."

Father merely raised an eyebrow.

I took a deep breath. "I intend to marry Oscar Wilde!"

"Nonsense!" Mother laughed.

"And has he proposed?" Father wanted to know. "Because he has not as yet spoken with me."

"I know he will," I assured them, although I did not feel completely certain of this. I felt in my heart that Oscar loved me—for he said he did, or so I thought—and what I felt with him erased that horrible feeling of disconnection which became stronger and stronger each day. But the actual words which lead to a vow went missing.

My persistence forced my parents' hand.

"Then you will wish to know, Miss," Mother said in her crispest voice, "that your intended has been seen in Dublin."

"Well, of course. He was in Dublin just last month, which you know as well as I do."

"How impertinent you have become! What I know, which you are about to discover, is that Oscar Wilde was spotted dangling on his knee a woman known as Fidelia."

"Scandalous lies!"

"And further, Mrs. Edith Kingsford of Brighton has offered to intercede on his behalf with the mother of her niece Eva in arranging a match."

I'm certain that the look on my face betrayed my heart. Disassociated though I was, a feeling of being crushed overcame me. That after one year together, Oscar saw fit to toy with my affections seemed impossible, and yet . . .

Without apology or excuse, I raced from the room. I could not bear to hear more. I tried to deny to myself what my parents told me, and yet when I went over details, little incidents rose from memory. Despite his attentions toward me, I was not blind. Oscar flirted outrageously with every young woman in his sphere. And, since I was facing fact, I had also to acknowledge to myself that he paid equal attention to young men.

When next he visited over the holidays, I was cool to him. His inquiries as to my emotional state brought evasion on my part. "I shan't argue with you," I assured him.

"It is only the intellectually lost who ever argue," he declared.

"Must you always speak as if these are lines from your writings?"

"But they are, Florrie. What can life provide but the raw materials for art."

"I should think that life might be a bit more serious to you."

"Life is too serious already. Too normal. Don't you find it so?"

"And what's wrong with normal? God. Family. Work. Those are what life is all about."

He paused at that. "Fate has a way of intervening in what otherwise would be normal."

I looked at him seriously. "Oscar, I refuse to engage in a battle of witty repartee with you. You have broken my heart."

I waited, but his reply at first was silence. His eyes seemed to sparkle yet were, at the same time, imbedded with impotent sorrow, the latter catching me off guard.

Auntie was, of course, in the parlor with us, although the hour was late and she must have been exhausted—when I glanced across the room, she was dozing by the window.

Oscar, it seems, had observed this also. We sat side by side on the loveseat before the fire. He moved closer and his arms encircled me. I cannot express the apprehension laced with arousal that filled my being. The silence in the room felt like a vise, holding me tightly in its grip, as tightly as Oscar's arms held me. Heat blazed through my body, as if I'd fallen into the fireplace; incineration threatened.

I recall noticing his lips as they came toward mine, twisted into a shape I can only describe as portraying cynicism. I felt both horrified and kindled, but I could not turn away. As his mouth found mine, I experienced a peculiar sensation, as if the breath from my body were being sucked from me. I know I began to panic, arms attempting to flail, legs kicking, noises coming from me. And then I watched helpless as blackness rushed toward me. In a moment of some hellish truth, I recognized that the universe itself was simply empty, Godless, friendless, a place so hollow that love had no reason to exist. And then, I remembered nothing more until I stood at the door, saying farewell to Oscar.

"So, this is goodbye," he said cheerfully, as though it were a happy occasion. I struggled to feel something, and yet I felt numb.

"Have a good trip back to England," I managed. "And be well. You will always be in my heart." The last was not something I felt, but something that came to me, like words on a piece of paper, as though they had no connection to either myself or the situation.

"Ah, but Florrie, you have no heart," Oscar laughed. "At least not anymore." His voice was cold. And while the emotional impact escaped me, my dear body felt the attack and shuddered. In that moment, I recognized my fate. My essence had been taken from me and I would forever be vacant.

I did not hear from Oscar for two years. My parents had finally found a match for me of which they approved. He was an Irishman, of good breeding, a civil servant with ambitions to be a writer. Oscar, in his theatrical manner, sent a letter on hearing of my engagement. He declared that he was leaving Ireland, "probably for good," so that we might never have need to set eyes on one another again. He demanded that I return the golden cross, since, he stated, I could never wear it again. He would keep it in memory of our time together, "the sweetest of all my youth," he said. I could not help but picture that cynical twist to his lips as I read without passion this melodramatic epistle. I kept the cross.

The man I married was a giant, handsome enough, an athlete, an avid storyteller, but was never the good provider Mother had hoped for. In that way he was like Oscar. And in one other. His literary aspirations drove him to write for both the theater, and for print. Since I'd always entertained the notion of acting, once he discovered this, he endeavored to win me over; I enjoyed a short career on the stage and made my theatrical debut in a play written by my husband. On opening night, I received an anonymous crown of flowers, death-white lilies—I knew they had been sent by Oscar. That was just his style.

I need not reiterate my own marital history. Because my husband obtained a modicum of fame in his lifetime, all of the "facts" of our life together are a matter of record. The birth of our son Noel. The various tragedies of my husband's professional life, and a scattering of successes. His illnesses, one of which led to his death. The fact that he left me exactly £4,723. Suffice it to say that outwardly our lives appeared normal, at least for those who travel in theatrical and literary circles. But a part of me went missing, and my husband was keenly aware of this lack. And, he knew the source. I told him. It consumed his spirit as surely as my own had been swallowed.

As to Oscar Wilde, over the years I watched him ingest the souls of others—the poor woman he eventually married, Constance Lloyd, and Lord Alfred Douglas, the man with whom he had a lifetime affair, but two of the many whose lives were altered irrevocably. Indeed, Oscar portrayed himself accurately enough in *The Picture of Dorian Grey*. You have likely read the accounts of his life. As always, he sums himself up best: "I was made for destruction. My cradle was rocked by the Fates." Had I but the fortitude, I might have felt some compassion for his trials and tribulations. And in the end, when Robert Ross wrote that macabre account of Oscar's death, describing how "blood and other fluids erupted from every orifice of his body," I could view the words with but a scientific interest. Oscar had left me incapable of compassion. Nay, incapable of all feeling.

Try as he might, my loving husband could not overcome the damage caused by Oscar Wilde. And although I failed as a wife, still, in at least one regard I inspired my husband; his greatest work will live on, of that I am convinced, even as the works of Oscar Wilde seem to cling to life from beyond the grave. I have sworn it to myself that I will preserve my husband's memory and protect his works to the end of my life—it is the very least I can do.

My husband was more than an insightful man, he was intuitive. If you have not as yet, perhaps you will eventually hear of him and the dark novel which depicts, in metaphor, the agony of the hollow existence of the woman whom he held dear, whose very soul had been absorbed for the refreshment of a psychic vampire.

A Personal Reminiscence,
by Florence Balcombe Stoker
Widow of Irish Writer Bram Stoker
1925

Author's note: Many of the "facts" in this story are true, howbeit spun by the author into a work of fiction. Oscar Wilde did court the beautiful Florence Balcombe. He presented her with a gold cross necklace, which he asked her to return—she refused. He was known for his dalliances, including with the women mentioned in this story. Florence Balcombe went on to marry Irish writer Bram Stoker, by most accounts neither the happiest nor the saddest of marriages, and gave birth to one child, a son. She enjoyed a very brief career as an actress on the London stage. Stoker, of course, penned Dracula *for which, after his death, she fought and won a lawsuit against Germany filmmaker Murnau for copyright infringement. Part of her compensation was that all copies of the silent film* Nosferatu *were turned over to her for destruction although, somehow, a few reels managed to survive the fires. It is this lawsuit and its consequences for which Florence Balcombe is best known.*

WHERE THE VAMPIRES LIVE

Storm Constantine

Storm Constantine has written over twenty books, both fiction and nonfiction and more than fifty short stories. Her novels span several genres, from literary fantasy, to science fiction, to dark fantasy. She is most well known for her Wraeththu Chronicles—*The Enchantments of Flesh and Spirit* (1987), *The Bewitchments of Love and Hate* (1988), *The Fulfillments of Fate and Desire* (1989)—and the Wraeththu Histories, *The Wraiths of Will and Pleasure* (2003), *The Shades of Time and Memory* (2004), *The Ghosts of Blood and Innocence* (2005). Although not vampires, the post-human Wraeththu are magical and sensual hermaphroditic beings who, when their story first began almost thirty years ago, broke new ground in speculative fiction. In her single vampire novel, *Burying the Shadow* (1992), humankind meets its collective end and a highly eroticized universe of vampires takes its place.

In "Where the Vampires Live," Constantine asks: How can you love someone who is so beyond all that is real it is impossible even to give them a name?

Zenna knew where the vampires gathered after sundown. She could climb out of the attic window, jump onto a limb of the ironwood tree outside and be free of the house, unheard and unseen, in minutes. She would run like a white hind between the dappled shadows of night, perhaps shape-shifting as she ran; hind to girl to hind. Her feet would seem barely to touch the ground. Her hair would be full of moths, drawn to it as if to a white flame.

Ariel would watch secretly from her own window, further down the house, full of envy, wistfulness and other aches she could not identify.

Ariel was Zenna's cousin, and she had come to live in the Green House in the spring, right at the edge of the forest, far from town. Ariel's father had died many years before and recently her mother had suffered some kind of disgrace that had affected her ability to be a mother—apparently. Ariel did not know what had happened; all she knew was that her mother had seemed to become someone else, a stranger in familiar skin. This troubled her so much she couldn't bear to think about it, so it came as rather a relief when her uncle and aunt had offered to take her in for a while.

It quickly became clear to Ariel, who was well-mannered and prudent, that she was the kind of daughter that Maeve and Darn would have liked to have had. They tried very hard not to show it, but Ariel was aware of the irrepressible leaps in their spirit when she asked for things politely, or did chores without being asked. Zenna was a wild creature; wilful, often bad-tempered, but seductively fascinating. When she turned on her light, none could fail to be blinded by it, hypnotized into adoration. Getting her own way was a trait inbuilt into her being. She had magic in her that made it happen. No one could dislike her, because it is impossible to dislike a beautiful wild thing, a rare spirit of nature, just because it is naturally wild. But sometimes, watching her cousin, Ariel could not help but remember something her maternal grandmother had once said. "Some people are cursed in life, darlin'. Watch out for them. When a soul touches you on the inside, so that the whole world goes black but for them, take care. For they can take you to a doom."

There had been more to this conversation, one of many lectures Granny gave on the potential horrors of life, but Ariel had forgotten the rest now. All she could think about, remembering those words, was what it would be like to be black on the inside, as if a hooked finger had poked through your skin and bone and had touched your heart, leaving a dark spot that grew and grew.

"Do you believe in vampires?" Zenna asked Ariel that one summer afternoon, as the girls sat by the pond in the garden. The day was hot. The air smelled green.

Ariel laughed politely. She always did that when she didn't have an answer.

"Well, do you?"

"I don't know . . . Do you?"

Now it was Zenna's turn to laugh, and this was a very different sound from Ariel's. "Do you know," she said, "people always say 'you can't be too careful.' But the fact is: you can." She jumped to her feet. "Come on," she said.

Come where? Down to the greenwood, where the shadows are brown and gold. Down to where the earth breathes so loudly you can hear it with human ears. Step through a barrier from here to there. It's where otherness comes alive.

Zenna took Ariel to a place deep in the forest. They passed a tumbledown wooden shack covered in ivy. Zenna said the body of the woman who had lived there was still lying on the floor behind the door. No one knew that she had died. She had become mostly ivy. Ariel shuddered and ran on. When she held Zenna's hand it was as if her feet too barely touched the ground. If they ran fast enough the world became a blur and it was possible to see another world beyond this one—always there, but you can't see it normally.

Zenna's destination was a dragonbark grove. The trees there were ancient; they were tall yet they stooped beneath the weight of their own age. Five of these trees were still alive; three dead, lying on the ground and riddled with insect nests. Zenna sat down on the spongy wood of one of the dead trees. There was a dampness to this grove, even though the sun was hot and high summer reigned in the greenwood. It was the breath of the earth, oozing out through mulch and mold. The canopies of the living trees were immense, the wings of dragons. Despite the absence of breeze, the leaves fluttered high overhead as if impulses from the roots shivered through them; impulses to fly.

Zenna swung her legs, leaning back on stiff arms.

"Are they *here*?" Ariel whispered. She wondered whether this was a game, and whether she was playing it right.

"At this time of day? Are you kidding?" Zenna sighed. "I wonder if they sleep beneath the dead leaves, but of course you'd never find them, even if they did. They would just become part of the soil, or would look like soil anyway. They are not what you think."

Ariel wasn't sure what she thought vampires to be. In her mind, all she saw was a flash of red eyes, some fangs glinting, a hiss of silk. "What are they?" she dared to ask.

"Very much creatures of earth," Zenna replied. "They are not about death, nor come from death. They are the greatest example of life. They live on life itself."

"Blood . . ."

"Well yes, everyone knows that." Zenna stood up.

"Have you actually *seen* them?" Ariel asked.

Zenna glanced at her cousin over her shoulder. "It is actually very difficult to see them. They are camouflaged. At night they must be clustered on the roofs of houses, standing beneath the trees in gardens, watching and waiting for a place of entry."

"That's horrible."

"Why?" Zenna pulled a scornful face. "They don't kill people, you know. That's just made up, because people are scared of what they don't understand. But if you are bitten, you are never the same again."

"You become like them?"

Zenna paused. "No. You are never the same again because you *don't* become like them."

"But have you *seen* them?" Ariel persisted.

Behind Zenna's silence, Ariel could hear the cracklings and rustlings of the forest. It was never silent. It seemed to be quiet but was full of noise. Things moved unseen.

At last Zenna said, "You can only see them for yourself. This isn't something that can be told."

Perhaps it was just a game, the wild fancy of a girl at the cusp of womanhood, seeking romance and danger in the breathing forest. If Zenna had come across a strange creature in this place, it might not be a vampire, but something else, far less mysterious and far more dangerous.

"I would like to see for myself," Ariel said.

"Then wish for it," Zenna said. She held out her arms and turned slowly in a circle, head thrown back. "Wish for it with all your might. But you will never know when it might come true." She was clearly in love: with the place, with an idea, with life itself.

Ariel did what she thought people were supposed to do when making a wish. She closed her eyes, very tight, and thought hard. *I want to see the vampires.* Even as she thought this, half of her was playing a girlish game, but the other half was standing at the brink of fear, holding out a tiny flickering candle into the dark. This half was actually a very old part of herself, who was wise enough to know even the most outlandish wishes can come true.

Two days later, Zenna shook her cousin awake in her bed, in the dead hours of the night. Ariel awoke from a dream of red flowers, something to do with a white dog, a star that could speak. She blinked at the pale vision of Zenna, whose eyes were wide and dark. "What? What?" she hissed, suddenly afraid. Was the house on fire?

"I need you to come with me," Zenna said.

"Why? Where?"

Zenna pursed her lips, screwed up her eyes and shook her head briefly. "It's your wish," was all she'd say. "Please hurry."

Ariel got out of bed and put on her clothes. Were there vampires on the roof now? If she listened carefully enough, would she hear them scratching at the slates? Part of her was lecturing the rest of her many parts with a quiet and patient voice. *Don't go with her. Whatever she's found, whatever she wants to show you, it won't be what she thinks it is. A good girl now would say "no". Why are you putting on your shoes?*

"Don't put on your shoes," Zenna said. Perhaps she could read minds and could hear the measured voice of Ariel's inner good girl. But her reasons were different. "We must go barefoot. It's quicker that way."

At night, the forest dares to speak aloud. As Ariel ran with her cousin, she could hear the immense cracks and groans of the trees, as if they were flexing their stiff ancient spines, pulling painfully their twisted roots from the possessive soil. The breath of the forest was now loud in Ariel's ears. All manner of creatures might lurk in the darkness; humans were interlopers in this particular time and space. But when Ariel held Zenna's hand and ran so fast, she felt she became something other than human and that this would protect her. She would not let go of Zenna's hand, whatever happened.

The dragonbark grove felt as if something had just finished there; it had the air of a room where twenty people had just walked out of the door. All that is left is the smoke of their conversations, wisps that will eventually fade away. The bright moonlight made it possible to see almost as clearly as if the sun were in the sky.

"The vampires were here," Ariel whispered. It was clear to her now that Zenna had wanted to share this experience and had come for her quickly. A pang of affection went through Ariel's heart. It felt like a long, white-hot pin.

"It's not just that," Zenna said. She let go of Ariel's hand and immediately Ariel felt fear, not affection. The pin was cold in her heart, making her breathless. Zenna was already walking away through the dappled moonlight; she was like a white hind again, lifting her feet delicately. Ariel blinked. She ran after her cousin.

Zenna had come to a halt before the greatest of the dragonbark trees; it must be their queen. "Here," she said. "Look." A pause, and then, with the slightest tremor of doubt: "Can you see?"

Ariel came to stand beside her cousin, and Zenna took her hand again, lacing their fingers lightly. With her free hand, Zenna pointed gracefully at the foot of the queen tree.

For a time Ariel could see nothing. She realised she didn't believe, and that in itself was quite shocking to her. But then she *could* see: there was someone curled up among the knuckles of the roots. As she looked closer, she could see that this someone was trembling. They were half covered with leaves, perhaps their shadowy garments were actually made from leaves. Zenna dragged Ariel nearer, her fingers had closed tightly about Ariel's own.

"It's a boy," Ariel said, half relieved, half disappointed.

Zenna glanced at her, said nothing. Again she let go of her cousin's hand and hunkered down. "He's hurt," she said. "They left him behind."

"He's a boy," Ariel said, in a voice that sounded to her like her aunt's. Maybe she was shattering magic, but if the boy really was hurt, fairy tales were no good for him.

You can't be too careful . . . you can . . .

Ariel went to the boy and touched him. He uttered a sigh and shuddered. He reminded her of a wounded dog, but it was too dark here to look for injuries. "We should take him back," she said.

"Into our house?" Zenna sounded afraid, and for once Ariel felt older and more confident and capable than her cousin.

"We can't just leave him here. He needs to be looked at . . . a doctor . . ."

"We shouldn't do that. They'll come back for him. It would be stealing . . ."

"Zenna!" Ariel sighed heavily. "Stop it. I don't know what he's doing here, but this lad is very much flesh and blood like us. Help me get him to his feet."

Ariel put her arms about the boy and tried to lift him. It surprised her how light he was, almost insubstantial. "He's half starved," she said.

With clear reluctance, Zenna came to help. He didn't resist them. He uttered soft whines, like a puppy. All the other sounds of the forest had faded away. For the briefest moment, Ariel thought how they might just have dragged this boy into the mundane world. Perhaps he didn't belong in it. But this was just a fleeting thought.

Maeve and Darn, and the doctor who came to inspect the boy, decided he must be a traveller lad, somehow separated from his people. He did have an injury, yes. He'd been shot in the thigh.

"No doubt caught stealing from some farm," the doctor said as she put away her things.

Everyone was gathered in the small spare room at the top of the house; an attic full of light that remained golden-brown even when the sun shone right through the window. The boy lay on a narrow bed. He was dark of skin and hair, slight of form, more like an elf than a boy. No wonder Ariel and Zenna had been able to carry him home as if he were no more than a handful of leaves.

"We'll call the police," Darn said.

But Maeve said, "No." She was Zenna's mother after all, and perhaps the sight of this fey, dark creature affected parts of her that had been asleep for many years. "There's no need for that. Not yet. Let him speak first."

The doctor had cleaned the boy's wound and stitched him up. There was no bullet. It had gone right through him. No one spoke again of official things, such as hospitals and authorities. They lived right on the edge of the forest and things were different here.

The boy slept for two whole days, and Maeve stayed with him, sitting by the narrow bed reading a book, or else curled up on the mattress that Darn had carried to the attic room. Zenna was often there too, frowning at the boy on the bed. No one really spoke about things, not even Zenna, although Ariel guessed her cousin's head was full of unspoken thoughts. It was as if they were all waiting for something. The weather became hotter and all around the Green House was a narcotic humid atmosphere that slowed movement, that stilled voices.

Ariel found sleep difficult during that time. At night, she lay awake breathing quickly, listening to the soft pound of her heart, her ears straining for other sounds. In particular, her senses extended upwards, out through wood and slate, to the roof. *I am too many people,* she thought. She wasn't sure what was real; the sort of world where common sense held sway or the sort where you could run so fast you could flash into another world. She sensed nothing on the roof, and in some ways that worried her more than if she'd felt the opposite.

On the morning of the third day, the boy opened his dark eyes and for some time lay staring at the ceiling. Maeve heard him sigh and put down her book. It was as if an invisible call shuddered through the Green House and everyone who lived there was drawn to the attic so that by the time Maeve murmured softly, "Who are you?" Zenna, Ariel and Darn were in the room also.

The boy looked at Maeve and there was no expression in his eyes that Ariel could interpret. If anything, he just looked resigned.

"Water," Maeve said and Darn brought a cup of it to the boy. They held his head so that he could drink, and he did so.

Zenna flicked a glance at her cousin, and Ariel was able interpret what it meant. *Maybe we shouldn't be giving him that.* But both girls remained silent. He was drinking. Perhaps he needed it after all.

"Can you remember anything?" Maeve asked the boy.

He shook his head very slightly, still looking at her.

Maeve smiled at her husband. At least the boy could understand them. "You were hurt," she said. "Everything will be all right. Don't worry. We'll help you."

"What's your name?" Darn asked.

The boy shook his head.

"Where are your people?" Darn continued, voice firm. "We'll need to find them."

Now the boy looked cornered, eyes wider, gaze flicking from the window to the door.

"Stop that," Maeve said. "He's only just woken up. Give him time, Darn." She stroked the boy's hair, hushed him as you would a baby. "It's all right. Nothing to fear. I'll bring you some soup." She stood up. "Help me, Zenna."

The family left the room, leaving only Ariel behind. No one had noticed she'd stayed back or that she hadn't been given a job to do. She wanted to tell the boy she was only a visitor too, but what was the point of speaking? She could sense it displeased him. So she sat down on the chair where Maeve had sat for the past few days and began to hum a tune. She closed her eyes and made the tune green and cool, like the forest depths.

She heard a soft sound, like water running over stones. It was the boy's laugh. "We *can* speak," he said, hardly more than whisper, "but only when it's needed. And we rarely answer questions."

Ariel opened her eyes and stared at him. "This is a question you must answer," she said. "Will your people come for you?"

"I'm not lost," he replied. He would not speak again that day.

Everyone knows that if you bring a changeling child into your home, or some creature of the otherworld, the otherness rubs off. It drifts like pollen through the still, summer rooms, and what were once just shadows take on feet and walk.

It was inevitable that Zenna was most affected by what had happened. Ariel felt she was destined only to be a witness to whatever transpired, nor would she affect the inevitable outcome in any way. She told herself firmly not to lie awake listening for sounds on the roof, because there wouldn't be any. She must not be infected by Zenna's feyness. The boy himself was like the summer light of the forest, sometimes green-gold sunlight, sometimes almost invisible in shadow. They named him Jack, because he would not tell them any other name. Most of the time it was easy to believe he was just a boy, separated from his family, but then his wound healed so quickly. After only a couple more days he was back on his feet. He did the chores that Maeve asked him to do without hesitation. He whistled to the geese that strutted around the pond, and they came to him, wings held out like arms. Maeve watched him from the kitchen window, smiling.

Jack was quiet, inhumanly so, but no trouble. He kept himself busy, and did not interact with the girls particularly, other than to nod his head in greeting should he come across them. Zenna could not keep her eyes off him. She speculated about him continually; it was naturally the topic that consumed her, and Ariel mostly played along because Jack interested her also. She just didn't want to think he was anything but a stray, albeit an intriguing one.

Every afternoon, they would sit by the pond and Zenna would talk about Jack. "He walks in daylight, he eats the food we eat," she said one day, clearly perplexed. "I had thought they would be white as ghosts, like moon people, but he is dark like the trees."

"Maybe that's because he isn't a vampire," Ariel had to say.

Zenna tossed her an annoyed glance. "I don't know why I bother telling you things. You just strip the magic out of everything, so the world will never be like that for you. How can you possibly think he's just a normal boy? Look at him."

Jack was stacking logs he had just chopped in the shadow of a shed attached to the house. Ariel could see nothing abnormal in his behavior or movements. "He's a gypsy boy," she said.

"But what does he want with us?" Zenna continued, ignoring that response. "He's not spoken of his people or even questioned what he's doing here. He simply *is*, part of our lives now, living here amongst us. I wonder if we're foolish."

"He's fed well, he's got new clothes, and probably has a better life," Ariel said. "If he was thieving when he got shot, he's not going to tell us about that, is he?"

"He could steal from us, but he hasn't," Zenna said. "He could take everything we own and run away and sell it. But he stays, and chops logs, and does what Ma asks him."

"Then it's because that's what he wants. Perhaps he likes it here."

"No, he's just waiting," Zenna said firmly.

"Then why don't you just ask him what for?" Ariel asked, somewhat tartly, because she was feeling impatient with her cousin. She didn't think Zenna would do any such thing because Jack had an air about him that turned questions to stones in your throat. Even if you wanted to speak to him, and imagined it vividly, actually doing so was another matter.

Zenna gave her cousin an arch glance and jumped to her feet. The geese were startled and bustled off, honking. Ariel watched Zenna walk to the shadow of the shed. She was a girl in a fairytale about to reach out to a wolf, about to prick herself on a deadly thorn, about to change the future. Ariel also got to her feet. She didn't want to miss what might be said.

She was still some feet away from the shed when Zenna said to Jack, "What are you waiting for?"

Jack didn't pause in his work; there wasn't the slightest hesitation.

"Well?" Zenna persisted. "It's not that you can't speak, it's that you won't. But you're living here in our house, eating our food, sleeping in our attic, and I demand that you answer me."

Still there was no response. Zenna grabbed hold of Jack's right arm and shook him. Ariel fully expected him to retaliate then, to bare his teeth in a snarl, to show a darker nature. All he did was cease working. He let Zenna shake him and when she had finished he turned to face her. He reached out with the arm she had grabbed and touched her, very lightly, with one finger just above the heart.

Zenna shot backwards a couple of feet as if he had punched her. She staggered a little then fell on her back.

Ariel couldn't help uttering a cry. Jack looked at her for a moment, then carried on stacking the logs. "Tell her she cannot come," he said.

"What?" Ariel had heard the words very clearly. She didn't know why she queried them.

He walked away, round the side of the house.

Zenna had scrambled to her feet. She ran past Ariel in the direction Jack had taken, but presently returned. "He's gone," she said. "What did he say to you?"

"Are you all right, Zenna?" Ariel felt light-headed. The day no longer seemed quite so real.

"Never mind that. What did he say?" Zenna rubbed her chest in the place where Jack had touched her.

"He said to tell you that you cannot come. I don't know what he meant."

Zenna frowned and pulled down the neck of her dress. "Did he mark me?" she asked.

Ariel leaned forward. "Yes," she said. There was a small mark on Zenna's pale skin, in the shape of a crescent moon. He must have dug his fingernail into her, and yet the touch had appeared to be so light. "It's just a scratch, I think. Not even that. What did it feel like?"

"I can't remember. I simply found myself on the ground." Zenna shook her head. She didn't appear to be upset about the incident, just puzzled. "Tell me now you think he's just a boy," she said.

That night, very late, a wind came up from the east. The moon was nearly full, but the clouds rushed past her, didn't pause to carry her like they sometimes did, edged in silver. The Green House creaked in the arms of the wind.

Sitting sleepless by her bedroom window, looking out, Ariel realized that everything had a voice; houses, forests, wind, even, impossibly enough, silence. The wind was singing and Ariel knew what it meant. A song of searching, for the wind never stops, always going forward, asking: Who?

Where? When? There were feathers in the wind, glowing white. It had its own wings. And in that moment, Ariel realized her true nature. Stubbornly refusing to believe in something did not make it go away. The world had a secret life and some people could see it. Perhaps her mother had.

Then she saw them. Four of them. Down in the garden, among the rhododendrons, shapes in the dark. There were no glowing eyes, no vivid flash of white teeth, just shapes. They looked like beasts, crouched and waiting. They had come for Jack. He would leave now.

In an instant, Ariel was on her feet. She ran out of her room and down the stairs and her feet made no sound. They didn't even touch the stairs. Sure enough, Jack was in the kitchen and no one else was there. She had to ask a question. She couldn't help herself. "Who are they?"

"My father and his brothers," Jack said. He opened the door to the garden, where the wind was hurrying past. "Will you come?"

"Yes," Ariel said. She took the hand he offered her.

"It will be just this once," Jack said. "Do you understand that?"

"Yes."

Walking across the wind was difficult because it wanted them to go the way it was going. It seemed to take a long time to reach the other side of the garden. Jack's hand was hot and dry. He was speaking in a language Ariel did not know, a constant sibilant murmur: "Ah kaya, hala, hala, mah kah nay."

Jack's kin came out from the foliage, huge and sinuous. They were cats and yet not. They had golden hoops in their tufted ears, and manes that were plaited with feathers and beads. They stretched and groaned and rubbed around Jack. One of them looked at Ariel, and breathed upon her. Its breath was hot and moist. Ariel reached out and laid a hand upon the enormous dark head. It smelled of the earth. The animal raised a paw and then, with a swift and unexpected movement, slashed Ariel with its claws across the chest, above the heart, tearing right through her shirt. Ariel did not stagger back, nor felt any pain, but saw she was bleeding. Her blood looked black. She looked at the beast and let the questions fall from her eyes: Why? Had she not trusted? Had she not believed and so allowed the true sight to come to her?

The cat reared up and then it was a man standing before her, dark and wild, a creature of the hidden places. "You can't be too careful," he said.

Jack put a hand upon her shoulder. "It's all right," he said. "Let me, not him. His tongue is too rough."

So Ariel let him lick up her blood, which he did neatly, as a cat would savor a saucer of cream. These things were really happening to her, there might be no future, but she didn't care. She was dreaming on her feet. Jack's voice brought her out of her reverie.

"You see, you're fine. Now we can run." He took her hand again.

"Where?"

"With the wind."

When she awoke in her bed, Ariel knew she was supposed to believe it had been all a dream. Then she would get out of bed and her feet would have soil between the toes, her legs would be scratched from brambles, there would be a wound above her heart from where a vampire had supped her blood. She lay in bed, breathing quickly. Above her, the ceiling was covered in sparkling motes that did not disappear when she blinked. She heard Maeve call her name. So she slipped from between the white sheets and looked down at her feet. They were clean. Perhaps he had licked them clean after he'd carried her to her bed, exhausted. It hadn't been a dream. There were her clothes, thrown over a chair, and the shirt was torn and bloody. Ariel picked the shirt up and stuffed it into the back of the wardrobe, among dozens of pairs of old shoes that perhaps Maeve had worn, many years before. Ariel looked at her wounds; they were nearly healed. She hoped the scars would not vanish.

The first words Maeve said to her downstairs were: "Have you seen Jack?"

This was ridiculous. How could she? She'd been in bed. Ariel shook her head.

Zenna came in from outside. She looked like someone lost. "He's gone," she said. "I know. They came for him."

Ariel could not look at her cousin. She was thinking of fast paws, galloping along the wind, of hot moist breath, of the time when true sight came to her and made it so that she could never be the same again.

"You must be glad," Zenna said to her. "Everything can be all normal again now."

"Stop it," Maeve said. "He might be taking a walk." But the tone in her voice showed she didn't really believe that.

How can you love someone who is so beyond all that is real it is impossible even to give them a name? If a person stands up in his real skin and shows you his real self, and you see it is not human, but something more beautiful and wondrous, even though it is potentially deadly, is that enough to change a life forever? But it is a fairy-tale, just words in the dark. How can you feel grief when that is taken from you?

The women of the Green House were struck down by grief. Even the geese by the pond lay down and stretched out their necks, spread out their white wings in the grass.

For a week Ariel was not entirely in the real world. The east wind had brought rain, dark and heavy, so that every day felt as if it was weeping. Ariel didn't think about whether Jack and his people might come back for her or not. It was impossible to think about anything. She lived in memory alone, like walking through a gallery of pictures, studying each one, experiencing it, but without having any opinion. Her memories brought her great pleasure; her secrets. No one knew. No one suspected. Ariel was the sensible one. It was Zenna who would have strange things happen to her; be taken under the hill by the faery folk, and be allowed home for only six months of the year.

Ariel drifted through the weeping days, while Maeve and Zenna comforted each other. They drew closer in a way they never had before. They were changed too. But the spell over Ariel eventually began to melt away. She could feel the real world coming back. She could not turn into a beast and walk the wind. She could not drink blood and become "other." That was the tragedy of it. She would never be the same again because she *couldn't* be like them. Zenna had been right about that. But at the same time she was not how she'd used to be. She was marked, lines down her torso the color of mulberries.

On the night of the next full moon, Ariel climbed onto the roof of the house. Summer was ending, already the air smelled of decaying fruit and smoke. Autumn air would always smell that way, even if there were no fires, no fruit trees. There were no vampires on the roof, or down in the garden. How cruel they were. And how stupid was she to have believed that once would be enough. Of course it wouldn't, but even so she had consented.

It was no surprise to her that Zenna wriggled out of her window and used the limbs of the ironwood tree to reach the roof. She did not speak to Ariel at first, but just stood beside her, hands on hips, gazing at the forest behind the house. Eventually she said, "Are you going to tell me or not?"

There seemed no point in being arch and saying, "What do you mean?" Ariel sighed. "I will show you," she said.

Zenna turned round. Ariel could see she was full of pain and jealousy. She had guessed, no doubt, because Ariel's secrets were written all over her; she smelled of them. Ariel took off her shirt. In the moonlight her skin was parchment and the claw marks looked like burns.

"Claws, not teeth," Zenna said.

Ariel nodded. "When they take your blood, perhaps it is something in their saliva that makes things happen. But it doesn't last. You were right about that. It does change you, though; enough to feel a stranger in this world, but not enough to belong in theirs."

"Tell me what happened," Zenna said. "Please."

Ariel did so. She spoke the words of a story so unlikely, she could hardly believe it herself, yet it had happened.

"I should hate you," Zenna said, "because it feels like you took something that was mine. But I'm glad it changed you. We are similar now."

Ariel tried to smile. "We can outrun time."

"For now." Zenna held out her hand. "Come on. Maybe we are not as stupid as they think."

Hand in hand, two girls run through the moonlit forest. They run so fast they are merely blurs of light. They run so fast they cause cracks in the bark of trees that leak a green-yellow radiance. It is the were-light of seeing.

LA DAME

Tanith Lee

Tanith Lee was born in the UK in 1947. After school she worked at a number of jobs, and at age twenty-five had one year at art college. Then DAW Books published her novel *The Birthgrave*. Since then she has been a professional full-time writer. Publications so far total approximately ninety novels and collections and well over three hundred short stories. She has also written for television and radio. Lee has been honored with several awards: in 2009 she was made a Grand Master of Horror and honored with the World Fantasy Convention Lifetime Achievement Award in 2013. She is married to the writer/artist John Kaiine.

Lee's fictional vampires are truly too numerous—and too diverse—to cover here. They range from the fairly conventional ancient female vampire of "Nunc Dimittis" (1983) to the "alien vampire" Sabella (mentioned in the introduction) to the surreal story-within-a-story "The Isle is Full of Noises" (2000). While *"La Dame"* is one of Lee's most original vampire variants, it also harkens back to some of our most primal beliefs about the sea and ships . . .

> "The game is done! I've won! I've won!"
> Quoth she, and whistles thrice.
> *The Rime of the Ancient Mariner*
> Samuel Taylor Coleridge

Of the land, and what the land gave you—war, pestilence, hunger, pain—he had had enough. It was the sea he wanted. The sea he went looking for. His grandfather had been a fisherman, and he had been taken on the ships in his boyhood. He remembered enough. He had never been afraid. Not of water, still or stormy. It was the ground he had done with, full of graves and mud.

His name was Jeluc, and he had been a soldier fourteen of his twenty-eight years. He looked a soldier as he walked into the village above the sea.

Some ragged children playing with sticks called out foul names after him. And one ran up and said, "Give us a coin."

"Go to hell," he answered, and the child let him alone. It was not a rich village.

The houses huddled one against another. But at the end of the struggling, straggling street, a long stone pier went out and over the beach, out into the water. On the beach there were boats lying in the slick sand, but at the end of the pier was a ship, tied fast, dipping slightly, like a swan.

She was pale as ashes, and graceful, pointed and slender, with a single mast, the yard across it with a sail the color of turned milk bound up. She would take a crew of three, but one man could handle her. She had a little cabin with a hollow window and door.

Birds flew scavenging round and round the beach; they sat on the house roofs between, or on the boats. But none alighted on the ship.

Jeluc knocked on the first door. No one came. He tried the second and third doors, and at the fourth a woman appeared, sour and scrawny.

"What is it?" She eyed him like the Devil. He was a stranger.

"Who owns the pale ship?"

"The ship? Is Fatty's ship."

"And where would I find Fatty?"

"From the wars, are you?" she asked. He said nothing. "I have a boy to the wars. He never came back."

Jeluc thought, Poor bitch. Your son's making flowers in the muck. But then, the thought, What would he have done here?

He said again, "Where will I find Fatty?"

"Up at the drinking-house," she said, and pointed.

He thanked her and she stared. Probably she was not often thanked.

The drinking-house was out of the village and up the hill, where sometimes you found the church. There seemed to be no church here.

It was a building of wood and bits of stone, with a sloping roof, and inside there was the smell of staleness and ale.

They all looked up, the ten or so fellows in the house, from their benches.

He stood just inside the door and said, "Who owns the pale ship?"

"I do," said the one the woman had called Fatty. He was gaunt as a rope. He said, "What's it to you?"

"You don't use her much."

"Nor I do. How do you know?"

"She has no proper smell of fish, or the birds would be at her."

"There you're wrong," said Fatty. He slurped some ale. He did have a fat mouth, perhaps that was the reason for his name. "She's respected, my lady. Even the birds respect her."

"I'll buy your ship," said Jeluc. "How much?"

All the men murmured.

Fatty said, "Not for sale."

Jeluc had expected that. He said, "I've been paid off from my regiment. I've got money here, look." And he took out some pieces of silver.

The men came round like beasts to be fed, and Jeluc wondered if they would set on him, and got ready to knock them down. But they knew him for a soldier. He was dangerous beside them, poor drunken sods.

"I'll give you this," said Jeluc to Fatty.

Fatty pulled at his big lips.

"She's worth more, my lady."

"Is that her name?" said Jeluc. "That's what men call the sea. *La Dame.* She's not worth so much, but I won't worry about that."

Fatty was sullen. He did not know what to do.

Then one of the other men said to him. "You could take that to the town. You could spend two whole nights with a whore, and drink the place dry."

"Or," said another, "you could buy the makings to mend your old house."

Fatty said, "I don't know. Is my ship. Was my dad's."

"Let her go," said another man. "She's not lucky for you. Nor for him."

Jeluc said, "Not lucky, eh? Shall I lower my price?"

"Some daft tale," said Fatty. "She's all right. I've kept her trim."

"He has," the others agreed.

"I could see," said Jeluc. He put the money on a table. "There it is."

Fatty gave him a long, bended look. "Take her, then. She's the lady."

"I'll want provisions," he said. "I mean to sail over to the islands."

A gray little man bobbed forward. "You got more silver? My wife'll see to you. Come with me."

The gray man's wife left the sack of meal, and the dried pork and apples, and the cask of water, at the village end of the pier, and Jeluc carried them out to the ship.

Her beauty impressed him as he walked towards her. To another maybe she would only have been a vessel. But he saw her lines. She was shapely. And the mast was slender and strong.

He stored the food and water, and the extra things, the ale and rope and blankets, the pan for hot coals, in the cabin. It was bare, but for its cupboard and the wooden bunk. He lay here a moment, trying it. It felt familiar as his own skin.

The deck was clean and scrubbed, and above the tied sail was bundled on the creaking yard, whiter than the sky. He checked her over. Nothing amiss.

The feel of her, dipping and bobbing as the tide turned, gave him a wonderful sensation of escape.

He would cast off before sunset, get out on to the sea, in case the oafs of the village had any amusing plans. They were superstitious of the ship, would not use her but possibly did not like to see her go. She was their one elegant thing, like a Madonna in the church, if they had had one.

Her name was on her side, written dark.

The wind rose as the leaden sun began to sink.

He let down her sail, and it spread like a swan's wing. It was after all discolored, of course, yet from a distance it would look very white. Like a woman's arm that had freckles when you saw it close.

The darkness came, and by then the land was out of sight. All the stars swarmed up, brilliant, as the clouds melted away. A glow was on the tips of the waves, such as he remembered. Tomorrow he would set lines for fish, baiting them with scraps of pork.

He cooked his supper of meal cakes on the coals, then lit a pipe of tobacco. He watched the smoke go up against the stars, and listened to the sail, turning a little to the wind.

The sea made noises, rushes and stirrings, and sometimes far away would come some sound, a soft booming or a slender cry, such as were never heard on land. He did not know what made these voices, if it were wind or water, or some creature. Perhaps he had known in his boyhood, for it seemed he recalled them.

When he went to the cabin, leaving the ship on her course, with the rope from the tiller tied to his waist, he knew that he would sleep as he had not slept on the beds of the earth.

The sea too was full of the dead, but they were a long way down. Theirs was a clean finish among the mouths of fishes.

He thought of mermaids swimming alongside, revealing their breasts, and laughing at him that he did not get up and look at them.

He slept.

Jeluc dreamed he was walking down the stone pier out of the village. It was starlight, night, and the pale ship was tied there at the pier's end as she had been. But between him and the ship stood a tall gaunt figure. It was not Fatty or the gray man, for as Jeluc came near, he saw it wore a black robe, like a priest's, and a hood concealed all its skull face but for a broad white forehead.

As he got closer, Jeluc tried to see the being's face, but could not. Instead a white thin hand came up and plucked from him a silver coin.

It was Charon, the Ferryman of the Dead, taking his fee.

Jeluc opened his eyes.

He was in the cabin of the ship called *La Dame,* and all was still, only the music of the water and the wind, and through the window he saw the stars sprinkle by.

The rope at his waist gave its little tug, now this way, now that, as it should. All was well.

Jeluc shut his eyes.

He imagined his lids weighted by silver coins.

He heard a soft voice singing, a woman's voice. It was very high and sweet, not kind, no lullaby.

In the morning he was tired, although his sleep had gone very deep. But it had been a long walk he had had to the village.

He saw to the lines, baiting them carefully, and went over the ship, but she was as she should be. He cooked some more cakes, and ate a little of the greasy pork. The ale was flat and bitter, but he had tasted far worse.

He stood all morning by the tiller.

The weather was brisk but calm enough, and at this rate he would sight the first of the islands by the day after tomorrow. He might be sorry at that, but then he need not linger longer. He could be off again.

In the afternoon he drowsed. And when he woke, the sun was over to the west like a bullet in a dull dark rent in the sky.

Jeluc glimpsed something. He turned, and saw three thin men with ragged dripping hair, who stood on the far side of the cabin on the afterdeck. They were quite still, colourless and dumb. Then they were gone.

Perhaps it had been some formation of the clouds, some shadow cast for a moment by the sail. Or his eyes, playing tricks.

But he said aloud to the ship, "Are you haunted, my dear? Is that your secret?"

When he checked his lines, he had caught nothing, but there was no law that said he must.

The wind dropped low and, as yesterday, the clouds dissolved when the darkness fell, and he saw the stars blaze out like diamonds, but no moon.

It seemed to him he should have seen her, the moon, but maybe some little overcast had remained, or he had made a mistake.

He concocted a stew with the pork and some garlic and apple, ate, smoked his pipe, listened to the noises of the sea.

He might be anywhere. A hundred miles from any land. He had seen no birds all day.

Jeluc went to the cabin, tied the rope, and lay down. He slept at once. He was on the ship, and at his side sat one of his old comrades, a man who had died from a cannon shot two years before. He kept his hat over the wound shyly, and said to Jeluc, "Where are you bound? The islands? Do you think you'll get there?"

"This lady'll take me there," said Jeluc.

"Oh, she'll take you somewhere."

Then the old soldier showed him the compass, and the needle had gone mad, reared up and poked down, right down, as if indicating hell.

Jeluc opened his eyes and the rope twitched at his waist, this way, that.

He got up, and walked out on to the deck.

The stars were bright as white flames, and the shadow of the mast fell hard as iron on the deck. But it was all wrong.

Jeluc looked up, and on the mast of the ship hung a wiry man, with his long gray hair all tangled round the yard and trailing down the sail, crawling on it, like the limbs of a spider.

This man Jeluc did not know, but the man grinned, and he began to pull off silver rings from his fingers and cast them at Jeluc. They fell with loud cold notes. A huge round moon, white as snow, rose behind the apparition. Its hand tugged and tugged, and Jeluc heard it curse. The finger had come off with the ring, and fell on his boot.

"What do you want with me?" said Jeluc, but the man on the mast faded, and the severed finger was only a drop of spray.

Opening his eyes again, Jeluc lay on the bunk, and he smelled a soft warm perfume. It was like flowers on a summer day. It was the aroma of a woman.

"Am I awake now?"

Jeluc got up, and stood on the bobbing floor, then he went outside. There was no moon, and only the sail moved on the yard.

One of the lines was jerking, and he went to it slowly. But when he tested it, nothing was there.

The smell of heat and plants was still faintly about him, and now he took it for the foretaste of the islands, blown out to him.

He returned to the cabin and lay wakeful, until near dawn he slept and dreamed a mermaid had come over the ship's rail. She was pale as pale, with ash blond hair, and he wondered if it would be feasible to make love to her, for she had a fish's tail, and no woman's parts at all that he could see.

Dawn was so pale it seemed the ship had grown darker. She had a sort of flush, her sides and deck, her smooth mast, her outspread sail.

He could not scent the islands anymore.

Rain fell, and he went into the cabin, and there examined his possessions, as once or twice he had done before a battle. His knife, his neckscarf of silk, which a girl had given him years beore, a lucky coin he had kept without believing in it, a bullet that had missed him and gone into a tree. His money, his boots, his pipe. Not much.

Then he thought that the ship was now his possession, too, *his* lady.

He went and stood in the rain and looked at her.

There was nothing on the lines.

He ate pork for supper.

The rain eased, and in the cabin, he slept.

The woman stood at the tiller.

She rested her hand on it, quietly.

She was very pale, her hair long and blond, and her old-fashioned dress the shade of good paper.

He stood and watched her for some time, but she did not respond, although he knew she was aware of him, and that he watched. Finally he walked up to her, and she turned her head.

She was very thin, her face all bones, and she had great glowing pale gleaming eyes, and these stared now right through him.

She took her hand off the tiller and put it on his shoulder, and he felt her touch go through him like her look, straight down his body, through his heart, belly and loins, and out at his feet.

He thought, She'll want to go into the cabin with me.

So he gave her his arm.

They walked, along the deck, and he let her pass into the cabin first.

She turned about, as she had turned her head, slowly, looking at everything, the food and the pan of coals, which did not burn now, the blankets on the bunk.

Then she moved to the bunk and lay down, on her back, calm as any woman who had done such a thing a thousand times.

Jeluc went to her at once, but he did not wait to undo his clothing. He found, surprising himself, that he lay down on top of her, straight down, letting her frail body have all his weight, his chest on her bosom, his loins on her loins, but separated by their garments, legs on her legs. And last of all, his face on her face, his lips against hers.

Rather than lust it was the sensuality of a dream he felt, for of course it was a dream. His whole body sweetly ached, and the center of joy seemed at his lips rather than anywhere else, his lips that touched her lips, quite closed, not even moist nor very warm.

Light delicious spasms passed through him, one after another, ebbing, flowing, resonant, and ceaseless.

He did not want to change it, did not want it to end. And it did not end.

But eventually, he seemed to drift away from it, back into sleep. And this was so comfortable that, although he regretted the sensation's loss, he did not mind so much.

When he woke, he heard them laughing at him. Many men, laughing, low voices and higher ones, coarse and rough as if torn from tin throats and voice boxes of rust. "He's going the same way."

"So he is too."

Going the way that they had gone. The three he had seen on the deck, the one above the sail.

It was the ship. The ship had him.

He got up slowly, for he was giddy and chilled. Wrapping one of the blankets about him, he stepped out into the daylight.

The sky was white with hammerheads of black. The sea had a dull yet oily glitter.

He checked his lines. They were empty. No fish had come to the bait, as no birds had come to the mast.

He gazed back over the ship.

She was no longer pale. No, she was rosy now. She had a dainty blush to her, as if of pleasure. Even the sail was like the petal of a rose.

An old man stood on the afterdeck and shook his head and vanished.

Jeluc thought of lying on the bunk, facedown, and his vital juices or their essence draining into the wood. He could not avoid it. Everywhere here he must touch her. He could not lie to sleep in the sea.

He raised his head. No smell of land.

By now, surely, the islands should be in view, up against those clouds there—But there was nothing. Only the water on all sides and below, and the cold sky above, and over that, the void.

During the afternoon, as he watched by the tiller for the land, Jeluc slept.

He found that he lay with his head on her lap, and she was lovely now, prettier than any woman he had ever known. Her hair was honey, and her dress like a rose. Her white skin flushed with health and in her cheeks and lips three flames. Her eyes were dark now, very fine. They shone on him.

She leaned down, and covered his mouth with hers.

Such bliss—

He woke.

He was lying on his back, he had rolled, and the sail tilted over his face.

He got up, staggering, and trimmed the sail.

Jeluc attended to the ship.

The sunset came and a ghost slipped round the cabin, hiding its sneering mouth with its hand.

Jeluc tried to cook a meal, but he was clumsy and scorched his fingers. As he sucked them, he thought of her kisses. If kisses were what they were.

No land.

The sun set. It was a dull grim sky, with a hole of whiteness that turned gray, yet the ship flared up.

She was red now, *La Dame,* her cabin like a live coal, her sides like wine, her sail like blood.

Of course, he could keep awake through the night. He had done so before. And tomorrow he would sight the land.

He paced the deck, and the stars came out, white as ice. Or knives. There was no moon.

He marked the compass, saw to the sail, set fresh meat on the lines that he knew no fish would touch.

Jeluc sang old songs of his campaigns, but hours after he heard himself sing, over and over:

"She the ship
"She the sea
"She the she."

His grandfather had told him stories of the ocean, of how it was a woman, a female thing, and that the ships that went out upon it were female also, for it would not stand any human male to go about on it unless something were between him and—her. But the sea was jealous too. She did not like women, true human women, to travel on ships. She must be reverenced, and now and then demanded sacrifice.

His grandfather had told him how, once, they had had to throw a man overboard, because he spat into the sea. It seemed he had spat a certain way, or at the wrong season. He had had, too, the temerity to learn to swim, which few sailors were fool enough to do. It had taken a long while for him to go down. They had told the widow the water washed him overboard.

Later, Jeluc believed that the ship had eyes painted on her prow, and these saw her way, but now they closed. She did not care where she went. And then too he thought she had a figurehead, like a great vessel of her kind, and this was a woman who clawed at the ship's sides, howling.

But he woke up, in time.

He kept awake all night.

In the morning the sun rose, lax and pallid as an ember, while the ship burned red as fire.

Jeluc looked over and saw her red reflection in the dark water.

There was no land on any side.

He made a breakfast of undercooked meal cakes, and ate a little. He felt her tingling through the soles of his boots.

He tested the sail and the lines, her tiller, and her compass. There was something odd with its needle.

No fish gave evidence of themselves in the water, and no birds flew overhead.

The sea rolled in vast glaucous swells.

He could not help himself. He slept.

There were birds!

He heard them calling, and looked up.

The sky, pale gray, a cinder, was full of them, against a sea of stars that were too faint for night.

And the birds, so black, were gulls. And yet, they were gulls of bone. Their beaks were shut like needles. They wheeled and soared, never alighting on the mast or yard or rails of the ship.

I'm dreaming, God help me. God wake me—

The gulls swooped over and on, and now, against the distant diluted dark, he saw the tower of a lighthouse rising. It was the land, at last, and he was saved.

But oh, the lighthouse sent out its ray, and from the opposing side there came another, the lamp flashing out. And then another, and another. They were before him and behind him, and all round. The lit points of them crossed each other on the blank somber sparkle of the sea. A hundred lighthouses, sending their signals to hell.

Jeluc stared around him. And then he heard the deep roaring in the ocean bed, a million miles below.

And one by one, the houses of the light sank, they went into the water, their long necks like Leviathan's, and vanished in a cream of foam.

All light was gone. The birds were gone.

She came, then.

She was beautiful now. He had never, maybe, seen a beautiful woman.

Her skin was white, but her lips were red. And her hair was the red of gold. Her gown was the red of winter berries. She walked with a little gliding step.

"Lady," he said, "you don't want me."

But she smiled.

Then he looked beyond the ship, for it felt not right to him, and the sea was all lying down. It was like the tide going from the shore, or, perhaps, water from a basin. It ran away, and the ship dropped after it.

And then they were still in a pale nothingness, a sort of beach of sand that stretched in all directions. Utterly becalmed.

"But I don't want the land."

He remembered what the land had given him. Old hurts, drear pains. Comrades dead. Wars lost. Youth gone.

"Not the land," he said.

But she smiled.

And over the waste of it, that sea of salt, came a shrill high whistling, once and twice and three times. Some sound of the ocean he had never heard.

Then she had reached him. Jeluc felt her smooth hands on his neck. He said, "Woman, let me go into the water, at least." But it was no use. Her lips were soft as roses on his throat.

He saw the sun rise, and it was red as red could be. But then, like the ship in his dream, he closed his eyes. He thought, But there was no land.

There never is.

The ship stood fiery crimson on the rising sun that lit her like a bonfire. Her sides, her deck, her cabin, her mast and sail, like fresh pure blood.

Presently the sea, which moved under her in dark silk, began to lip this blood away.

At first, it was only a reflection in the water, but next it was a stain, like heavy dye.

The sea drank from the color of the ship, for the sea too was feminine and a devourer of men.

The sea drained *La Dame* of every drop, so gradually she turned back paler and paler into a vessel like ashes.

And when the sea had sucked everything out of her, it let her go, the ship, white as a bone, to drift away down the morning.

CHICAGO 1927

Jewelle Gomez

Jewelle Gomez's writing—fiction, poetry, essays, and cultural criticism—has appeared in a wide variety of venues, both feminist and mainstream. A social activist with careers in theatre, public television, the arts, and philanthropy, she is best known for her novel *The Gilda Stories* (1991). The vampire, Gilda, is an escaped slave who comes of age over a span of more than two hundred years. Vampirism itself is a gentle and mutually beneficial exchange: Gilda delves into a human mind and, in exchange for the blood taken, she leaves a belief the individual can achieve something very important to them. Taking a lesbian/feminist perspective, Gomez places her protagonist in a series of adventures in different eras and communities that exist at the edge of white middle-class America. Gilda herself—black and lesbian—is an outsider among the ultimate outsiders: vampires. Gomez also authored a theatrical adaptation of *The Gilda Stories*, retitled *Bones and Ash*, which toured thirteen U.S. cities in 1996.

"Chicago 1927" gives us a slice of Gilda's immortal life as she experienced it during the Roaring Twenties . . .

High and light, the rich notes of her song lifted from the singer like a bird leaving a familiar tree. The drummer stopped and only a bass player snuck up behind her voice, laying out deep tones that matched hers. Gilda stood at the back of the dimly lit room, letting the soothing sound of music ripple through the air and fall gently around her. Her gaze was fixed on the woman singing on the tiny stage, whose body was coiled around the sound of her own voice. Gilda had come to the Evergreen each weekend for a month to hear the woman sing. LYDIA REDMOND, INDIAN LOVE CALL the window card read outside underneath her picture. On her first night walking through the streets of Chicago, Gilda had seen the sign and been drawn by the gleaming beauty of the face.

The sheer simplicity of Lydia's voice rang persistently inside Gilda's head.

The smoky air and clink of glasses crowded around Gilda, filling the room almost as much as the attentive audience. Black and brown faces bobbed and nodded as they sat at the tiny tables on mismatched chairs.

Others stood at the short bar watching the set along with the tall, light-skinned bartender, Morris. Some stood in the back near the entrance transfixed, as did Gilda.

She had finally created the opportunity to meet Lydia Redmond through the club's owner Benny Green. It had taken only a slight glance held a moment longer than necessary to plant the idea, and Benny treated Gilda like she was a long-missed relative. Lydia had been full of playfulness when they'd sat together at Benny's table after her show one night. The luminescence in the photograph that had drawn Gilda shimmered around Lydia when she laughed. The sorrow that cloaked so many club singers had only a small place within Lydia. When she looked into Gilda's eyes, she'd read her so intently that Gilda had to turn away.

The last note of a sweet, bluesy number wavered in the air, then was enveloped in unrestrained applause and shouts. Gilda smiled as she slipped out of the door of the club's entrance into the short alley and was startled to see Benny holding a young boy by the collar.

"I ain't jivin' you, Lester. You get home to your sister right now. You want me stoppin' by to have a talk to her?"

"Naw."

"Naw what?"

"Naw sir."

"I done told you don't hang in this alley. You ain't heard they shootin' people this side of town?"

"Yes sir," the boy said blankly as if he'd been told he was standing in a loading dock.

"I'm tellin' you there's been shootin' here, boy! Don't crap out on me."

"Yes sir." Lester let himself show the surprise he felt,

"Here," Benny said as he handed the boy a folded bill. He looked about seven years old and was dressed in pants and a jacket much too large for him, like many children Gilda had seen.

"Take that to your sister." Benny's thin mustache curved up as his lips could no longer resist a smile. "Tell her come by my office tomorrow . . . no, not tomorrow. Make it the next day, tell her come at noontime. Ya hear?"

"Yes . . . yes sir." The child's face lost its stiff fear and as Benny shoved him toward the mouth of the alley, he almost smiled.

"Damn."

"A colleague?" Gilda said lightly.

"He'd like to be. How in hell can you keep 'em out the game if you can't keep 'em in the house?" Benny's voice was raw with anger.

Gilda didn't have to listen to his thoughts to sense the anxiety and concern swirling around underneath his hard tone.

"I already got two laundry women. Looks like I'ma have to hire me another one. She lost her job." Benny jerked his thumb in the direction of the darkness where the boy had disappeared. "His sister, she takes care of a passel of them."

Maybe you should open a laundry house. Gilda let the thought slip from her mind into his.

"Maybe . . . you know I got the back end of the joint, facing off North Street . . . Maybe I'll set them girls up in there. Get us a laundry going! Damn. That's it."

"You have a good heart, Benny."

"What else I'ma do?"

"That's what I mean," Gilda said.

"Lester's okay, he just ain't got nothin' to do but hang around trying to grab some pennies. Morris had to snatch him up out some trouble last week."

"You and Morris need to be on the city council," Gilda said with a laugh as she started toward the mouth of the alley.

"Hey, you comin' by the party later? We got a fine spread." His smooth brown skin was like velvet in the light of the alley. He pulled at the cuffs of each sleeve under his jacket and smoothed his hand across his short-cut hair, readying himself to return to the bar.

"I'll be there."

"You know, cousin, you need to be careful walking these streets by yourself in the middle of the night."

"Thanks, Benny, I'm just going up to the corner. I'll be right back."

"Umph." Benny grunted his disapproval, then said with a smile, "You know I can't handle it when a good-lookin' woman stands me up." Gilda waved as she turned and walked swiftly out to the street. She looked north, then south before she picked her direction. The air felt brisk and fresh on her smooth skin, untouched by the decades that had led her to this place. The deep brown of her eyes was still clear, sparkling with questions just as they had when she was truly a girl. Her full mouth was firm, tilted more toward a smile than a frown, and inviting, even without the faint trace of lipstick she occasionally applied.

The fragrance of fall was in the trees just as it had been every season for many years. Gilda marveled at how different each part of the country smelled; and over time, the scent of everything—grass, wood, even people—altered subtly. Nothing in her face revealed that eighty years had passed since Gilda had taken her first breath on a plantation in Mississippi. After journeying through most of the countryside and small towns west of the Rocky Mountains, this was her first stop in a major city in some years.

As she strode through the streets, Gilda was self-conscious about her clothes. Although some women had worn pants for almost fifty years, she was still frequently among a select few wherever she went. It had caused ripples of talk since her arrival in town, but she would not relent or be forced to maneuver in the skimpy skirts that were currently the rage. Her solid body was firm with muscles that were concealed beneath the full-cut slacks and jacket. The dark purple and black weave of her coat hid the preternatural strength of her arms. Her hair was pulled away from her face, in a single, thick braid woven from the crown of her head to her neck. There was nothing about Gilda that any of the men who frequented the Evergreen would call elegant, yet the way she moved through the room left most of them curious, attentive.

Gilda removed the matching beret she wore and tucked it inside a deep pocket in the lining of her jacket. Tonight, few would notice her as she passed. She turned off of the downtown street and walked toward the river. Here the noise was louder, lower. The echo of Lydia Redmond's voice receded as Gilda's body succumbed to its need. She remembered the first time she'd gone out into the night for the blood that kept her alive. Running through the hot, damp night in Louisiana with the woman, Bird, who'd first given her the gift, Gilda had been astonished at the ease of movement. They'd passed plantation fields as if they rode in carriages. She'd barely felt the ground beneath her feet as the wind seemed to lift them through the night. They'd found sleeping farmhands, sunk deeply into their dreams, and Bird, always the teacher, had allayed Gilda's fears.

Whatever horror there might be in the act of taking blood was not part of this for them. Bird taught Gilda how to reach inside their thoughts, find the dream that meant the most while taking her share of the blood. In exchange for the blood Gilda learned to leave something of help behind for them and in this way remained part of the process of life.

Later, Gilda heard of those who did not believe in exchange. Murder was as much a part of their hunger as the blood. The fire of fear in the blood of others was addictive to some who became weak with need for the power of killing. Or, even worse, they snared mortals in their life of blood without seeking permission. The eyes of these killers glistened with the same malevolence she'd seen in the eyes of overseers on the plantation when she was a girl. The thud of their boot on the flesh of a slave lit an evil light inside them. Gilda avoided those with such eyes. To have escaped slavery only to take on the mantle of the slaveholders would have shamed Gilda and her mentor, Bird, more than either would have been able to bear. Instead, she thrived on the worlds of imagination that she shared with others.

We take blood, not life. Leave something in exchange. The words of that lesson pulsed through Gilda with the blood. In the exchange, it was usually easy to provide an answer to the simple needs she discovered as she took her share of the blood. In one situation a lonely woman needed to find the courage to speak aloud in order to find companionship; in another a frightened thief required only the slightest encouragement to seek another profession. Gilda enjoyed the sense of completion when she drew back and saw the understanding on their faces, even in sleep.

Gilda had lived this way for more than eighty years—traveling the country, seeking the company of mortals, leaving small seeds among those whose blood she shared. But recently, with each new town, Gilda had begun to lose her connection with mortals. She had little confidence in her ability to live in such close proximity with them and maintain her equilibrium. In the last town, she'd settled comfortably, remote enough from neighbors to avoid suspicion. Yet she'd enjoyed the life of the small black community in Missouri and been inspired by them. Their scrubbed-clean church, the farmers who distributed food from their land to people who were hungry, the women who nursed any who needed it. The burden of insults and deprivation they faced each day was only a small part of what they shared. Gilda had found herself deeply enmeshed with someone whose life was so rooted in that town, it was clear she was meant for the age in which she lived. The companionship had renewed Gilda in ways that were as important as the blood. Despite the temptation to bring someone into her life, Gilda saw that to disrupt another's would have been disaster. Again, Bird's lessons had helped her find her way through the confusion of power and desire.

Gilda had moved on, leaving her cherished companion behind, finding her way onto the road alone once more. In her isolation, she'd begun to feel the weight of her years.

A sound drew her back to the moment; footsteps were approaching her quickly from behind. This was a neighborhood in which the men who worked on the railroads and in the meatpacking plants often drank hard and followed their impulses. Her caution hardened into defense when she saw two white men barreling toward her. Gilda had recently read in one of the newspapers that the Ku Klux Klan was having a large resurgence across the country and these two exuded that same kind of agitation. The larger man, dark curly hair falling in his eyes, threw his arms out to envelop her in an embrace; the other was close behind. Gilda stepped aside quickly and left him empty-handed and bewildered. She realized that both were drunk, but her evasion seemed to anger the curly-haired one. The short man, more inebriated than his companion, fell to his knees laughing at the sight of his off-balance friend.

"Come on, darlin'. A little kiss, that's what we want," he said from his kneeling position in a thick Irish brogue.

"It'll be more'n a kiss when I'm done," Curly said with a nasty edge.

Gilda glanced over her shoulder at the lights of the low building from which they'd emerged. No one else seemed to be exiting; only the distant music of a stride piano punctuated the night.

"Commere." Curly grabbed at Gilda as she easily ducked his grip.

The one on his knees found it all so funny he couldn't get up. Gilda tried to back up to create enough room to turn away, planning to move so swiftly that they would never see the path she'd taken. Curly, now enraged by the failure to capture his prey, drew back his fist. His arm was broad under the heavy work jacket and his fist was massive as he struck out with the force of a wrecking ball.

Gilda stopped the man's fist in the air before it reached her face and squeezed until she heard one bone break. The man on the ground sat contentedly, still laughing as if he were listening to Fibber McGee and Molly on the radio. Rage filled Curly's face; then was replaced by fear as he saw first the anger and then the swirling orange flecks in Gilda's eyes. To come all this way and still be faced with the past made Gilda dizzy with outrage. She listened to the bones snapping in Curly's hand and in her mind saw the man who'd tracked her down when she'd escaped the plantation. A simple overseer who did not see her as human. The memory of the ease with which he'd enjoyed trapping her and his excitement as he'd anticipated raping her blazed inside Gilda's head. The hard crackle of barn hay sticking the flesh of her back as she'd prayed not to be discovered; that light in his eyes that burned everything around him; the stink of his sweat as he'd hulked above her. The feel of the knife in her hand as it had entered his body. A sound of crying. Gilda shook her head to free herself from the images of her past that crowded in.

She held the curly-haired man with her gaze, leading his mind into a foggy place where he would rest until she was done. She let his broken hand drop, sliced the thick skin on his neck with the long nail of her small finger, and watched the blood rise rapidly. A ferrous scent filled the air and she pressed her lips to the dark red line, drawing his blood inside her. A kiss had not been all he'd had in mind. Any woman alone by the stockyards was fair game to him. And no one would ever hear a colored woman's accusation of rape.

She pushed into his thoughts to find something she might fulfill rather than let herself enjoy his terror as she drained him of life. Inside, his insecurities flooded him like a mud broth; her rape would not have been the first. Only his camaraderie with his friend, the short one on the ground, still drunk and laughing, held any importance. As she started to pull away and leave him with his life, she probed further and saw the image of a young girl, the daughter of the woman who ran the boardinghouse where he lived. A parasitic lust clouded the space around her in his thoughts. Gilda pushed them aside and inserted a new idea: *This child could be your friend*, just like the short man who sat oblivious beside them. He'd never imagined women as anything other than prey, but his investment in this girl's safety—her nurturance—might provide a renewed connection to the world around him. Gilda wiped her mouth clean and released him. He fell to the ground beside his friend, who only then looked up, puzzled. The short one who laughed almost toppled over when he tried to stand and better assess the situation.

"Hey . . . you . . . what'sa matter?" He blinked and as he swayed Gilda stepped backward away from the two, leaving them frozen in their comic tableau as she sped away.

The blood that would carry her through centuries burst inside her veins. A flush of heat rose in her body and suffused her face and neck with deepening color. Her dark skin glowed with the renewed life flowing inside her. The definition of her arms and shoulders sharpened imperceptibly with each step. Yet, even as she sighed with enjoyment of the fresh blood, she wondered why she would want all the years that lay ahead. Men of this type, of all races, filled the roads and towns wherever she went. A woman had as much chance of survival on a city street as an antelope wandering into a pride of lions. Gilda shook the image from her mind and moved away from the raw smells and animal fear.

When she was back on a main street she slowed her pace and turned to look in the shop windows, hoping to supplant the images that tried to take root. The city was growing so fast merchants barely had time to keep up with it. Elegant gowns were hung next to daytime dresses; divans reclined beside kitchen stoves. The whole city felt as if it were bursting with life.

Gilda stopped in front of a store that held tools and looked at the saws and lawn mowers, then pulled back to catch her image in the glass. According to superstition, she had no soul; therefore, she could cast no reflection. But those of her kind had lived long before Christian mythology permeated contemporary society. In the glass, Gilda recognized the face she'd always known. Almond-shaped eyes, never quite ordinary, even without the orange flecks of hunger, dark eyebrows that gave her face a grave intensity, full lips now firm with thought—the same West African features that she'd seen in many other faces as she'd traveled the country. Gilda smiled at her reflection, set her beret at an alluring angle, straightened her jacket, then hurried back toward the Evergreen.

Benny Green had bought the corner building where his club was located almost as soon as he saw the sign EVERGREEN. It was fate; the place was almost named for him. He'd been saving for years with one idea in mind—to own something, a place where colored people could be comfortable, some people would get work, and he'd be an easy part of the world because he'd created it. He didn't know how long he could keep his ownership hidden from his employees and friends, but in the months since he'd opened up he'd dodged all questions. With Prohibition it was hard enough: police looking for a handout, enforcers, who seemed to work all sides of the street, demanding their cut. Rivals were always looking for an opening so they might take over the prosperous business that the Evergreen had become. Sometimes they tried to push—causing trouble in the club, harassing patrons outside. It was simpler for Benny to let everyone think he was somebody he wasn't. He paid for protection, kept a low profile, never let his joint get in the papers, and pretended he was just a manager who reported to someone else.

The door into Benny's flat was at the top of the stairs that led up from the street behind the club. Gilda stood on the landing in a moment of anticipation. She would be in a room full of people, her people, for the first time in decades. The colored people of Chicago liked being invited to Benny's parties. She tapped on the door and a small woman in a maid's apron opened it almost immediately. Her face was suffused with a smile, which she worked very hard to maintain as she examined Gilda's austere pants and matching jacket.

"May I take your . . . wrap?" she said, barely belying her confusion.

"No, thank you. The ensemble wouldn't work without it, wouldn't you say?"

The maid laughed easily. "You can sure say that, ma'am." She swept the door open wider to usher Gilda in as she continued to chuckle.

"Kinda cute, though. Kinda cute," she repeated as she waved Gilda toward the living room and walked away.

His apartment above the bar was a rambling affair that Gilda had visited only once before. She'd heard how he'd hired an out-of-work friend to repaint it. Then he'd hired another club patron, who'd just lost his job, to decorate the parlor, and when one of his waitresses needed extra money, he'd hired her to redo his dining room. Eventually one friend or another had tended to the whole place. Morris always teased, "That man'll never give you a free drink. But he always got a job for ya." The result of Benny's fragmented approach to decoration was a flashy blend of opulence and primitivism, each of which seemed to be evolving. An African mask was hung amid chiffon draping in the entry hall. Through the door, Gilda saw the clean, curving lines of the period in the sideboard and divan. And everywhere were stacks of books and other things that had never found their proper places. The sound of someone plunking out Bix Beiderbecke's "In the Mist" on the piano had reached Gilda long before she entered the rooms. The pianist halted repeatedly, trying to get a grip on the snaking melody. Laughter and voices almost swallowed the sound of the effort.

In the first parlor, a long table was barely visible beneath platters of chicken, sweet potatoes, and cole slaw. Bowls overflowed with pickles and other things Gilda didn't recognize. She did recognize Hilda, the tall, slender natural redhead who waited tables at the Evergreen. Her hair and tawny skin were shown to best advantage by her crisply tailored black silk dress, cinched at the waist with a three-inch-wide belt that matched her hair perfectly. She waved at Gilda and continued on her way toward the piano where Emory, who usually played drums, was still attacking the Beiderbecke tune. His circle of wavy, mixed gray hair had receded far back on his head but he still appeared youthful as he concentrated on the tune. Gilda walked past them, wading into the scent of perfume that hung in the air. The click of high heels and deep male voices filled the room, mingling with the piano as if orchestrated by Ellington.

Through a door, in the smaller parlor she saw Benny in the dining room playing bartender behind a short, highly polished version of the mahogany bar in the Evergreen. He'd changed into a light-colored silk jacket that hung softly on him. Morris, in a reversal of his nightly routine behind the bar, relaxed on a leather and chrome barstool, his tall frame barely contained. They appeared to be intent on their conversation as Benny served him a drink, but he glanced up and noticed Gilda among the half dozen other guests mingling near the doorway.

"Come on over here, cousin," Benny shouted.

"Harlem ain't got nothin' on Chicago," Morris was saying as she approached. "Tell this man, Gilda. What Harlem got we ain't got?" Morris's light brown eyes sparkled with challenge, more playful than he'd ever appeared downstairs. His ever-present white shirt was, as usual, fresh and firm across his broad shoulders.

"I ain't sayin' nothin' against Chicago, man," Benny answered in a soft teasing voice she'd heard often when the two men were together.

"You think we ain't got no colored writers?" Morris went on. "We got colored writers here. And we got the music. Shit, you know that yourself!" Morris took a drink as if that ended the discussion. "What about Richard Wright? He got his chops here. And you ain't heard of Katherine Dunham, man?" Indignation was building like a balloon over Morris's head. "Where you think King Oliver been playing for the last five years? Same with Alberta Hunter—"

"Lemme get you something," Benny interrupted Morris, "'fore this man starts trying to run for mayor."

Gilda asked for champagne and he laughed. "Girl, you need something more'n that on a night like this."

"They may go to Harlem, but they find themselves here. In Chicago!"

"That'll do me, Benny. Honest." Gilda had no luck trying to appear demure and was relieved when she heard Lydia's voice behind her.

"Aw, Benny, stop annoying the chick. Give her what she wants. You trying to get the woman drunk?" Lydia leaned in closer to the bar.

Benny, faking villainy, twirled an imaginary mustache, much larger than his own.

Gilda inhaled Lydia's scent deeply before she turned. A light blend of cinnamon and magnolia wafted from her hair, making Gilda's heart beat faster. She was startled to see that Lydia wore bronze satin pants that clung to her narrow hips. On top she wore a pale golden chiffon blouse that highlighted her copper skin, which shone through the filmy fabric.

"You like it?" Lydia asked as she watched Gilda, who seemed unable to catch her breath.

Gilda finally found her smile. "You look quite . . . chic. I believe that's the word."

Benny prepared another drink and held the short rock glass as if he didn't want to let it go.

"Come on, give," Lydia said, then took the drink.

"Lyd's kinda handy with the sewing machine," Morris said. "She even made them curtains that run 'cross the stage."

"Hey, why should you get all the gab?" Lydia teased Gilda. "Half the town's talking about your outfits. Hell, when you walk in the club I gotta turn the lights up so they stop lookin' at ya." Her laughter was totally unladylike and flew into the room, compelling others to join her. It was the same sound that filtered through her singing.

She grabbed Gilda's arm and drew her away from the bar. "Lemme show you the joint before they eject Emory and plunk me down at the piano." Gilda followed her through the kitchen to what looked like a comfortable office. Gilda stepped inside and leaned against a narrow desk, watching as Lydia crossed the room sipping from her drink. Her wavy dark hair was loose around her shoulders and the vibrant red polish on her nails gleamed in the dim light. Gilda was fascinated by the way she filled the room.

"So, uh, what do you think? About me, my singing, stuff like that." She almost sounded like a child; her enthusiasm and curiosity were unconscious and genuine.

"Your voice carries almost all the joy in the world."

"Um." She stopped and leaned against a bookcase to think for a moment.

"Benny likes you a lot," Gilda said, pausing. So many thoughts were swirling in her head, she couldn't easily choose one. Gilda felt ripples of desire expanding inside. She put her drink down and pressed her hands to the desk.

"How can you tell that?"

"He can't take his eyes off you. If you're anywhere in the room his body is turned in your direction as if you were the sun."

"Ain't you the poet?"

Gilda felt embarrassed, but there was no sign of it. Her skin remained the rich dark color it had always been.

"Ben's like my brother."

Gilda's skepticism was obvious.

"No, really. He took good care of me when I needed it and I do the same."

"Have you been friends long?"

"I was traveling with a show. 'Blue Heaven.' You ever see it?" Gilda shook her head.

"About a year ago we're doing the gig and I got sick. Him and Morris got me to the hospital when the troupe moved on. Made sure I had everything. Then give me the job singing at the Evergreen. They are two right guys. Benny's always helping somebody with something. The colored school, this church or that one. He's gotta buck for everybody." The description fit easily with the impression that Gilda had formed since arriving in town.

"So what's your game?" Lydia made the question sound soft, not an accusation.

Gilda thought a moment. She could easily have diverted the question, but she didn't want to, at least not right away.

"I'm trying to decide what to do next," Gilda said, knowing Lydia could never understand how big a question it was.

"Stick around this burg for a while." Lydia's voice carried the same invitation to joy that Gilda had heard in her singing.

"I think I will."

"Good. Benny's gonna need someone like you."

"Someone like me?"

"Smart, figuring on the future. That's his one . . . kinda flaw, you know. Colored folks in this town need this, they need that." Lydia's eyes were unwavering as she watched Gilda listening to her. She spoke and examined Gilda at the same time. "He's always thinkin' about it, but he's got no sense of a plan. You a woman who knows somethin' about planning for the future. And he don't know how to handle those mugs that keep edging up on him." Lydia's confidence in her words and in Gilda surprised her.

Gilda looked around her at the books and ledgers. It felt like a room bursting with ideas and with life; Benny's presence was as strong here as it was downstairs in the Evergreen. Gilda wouldn't let herself listen to Lydia's thoughts. That was another lesson from Bird she'd embraced: intruding on another's thoughts simply for personal gain was the height of rudeness. So, the reasons for Lydia's certainty remained unclear. Lydia watched Gilda watching her, as if she awaited Gilda's assent. The memory of Lydia's scent unfurled like an unexpected fog in Gilda's head and she tried to clear her mind.

"Why does the billboard say 'Indian Love Call'?" Gilda asked.

"My father was Wampanoag. Back East, you know, the Indians they named Massachusetts for. They were Wampanoag."

Gilda looked again at Lydia and recognized the bone structure. The blending of African and Indian lines was so common in this country, yet Gilda had forgotten. She'd seen many women who looked like they might be Lydia's relatives.

"Of course," she said.

"That was Benny's idea, not mine. My mother would be fit to be tied." She sipped from her glass, then set it down on a shelf and moved closer to Gilda. This time the cinnamon and flowers were real, not a memory. "She's not much for people pretending not to be colored."

"But you're not."

"Naw. Everybody likes a bit of mystery. So this year I'm it."

"What about next year?" Gilda kept her breath shallow, trying not to take in too much.

"I'll be Lebanese!"

The room was filled first with Lydia's laughter, then Gilda's. Deep inside an image blossomed for her, a tiny glimpse of her past. Inside she held a precious moment of laughter between her and one of her sisters as they'd toiled among the rows of cotton. The reason for mirth had quickly faded then. In the expansive dining room with Lydia, Gilda recaptured that forgotten joy and savored it as fully as if her sisters were still alive and in the room beside her.

This was what Gilda found so entrancing in Lydia's voice. It was rich with the happiness she'd had; very little sorrow or bitterness weighted her songs. The melodies Lydia sang each night might be mournful when delivered by someone else, but Lydia sang with the light of what was coming, not merely what had been done in the past.

They both stopped laughing, comfortable with the recognition of the feeling growing between them.

"And what's your mystery, lady?" Lydia asked as if she already knew the answer.

Gilda pressed her hand to Lydia's cheek lightly, letting herself enjoy the softness around Lydia's smile. She didn't want to pull away from the question, even though she knew she couldn't answer. Lydia stepped in closer, the full length of her body pressing its aura of heat against Gilda.

The air wavered around them, intoxicated by mist and cinnamon.

Then the unnatural silence in the rest of the flat crashed around them.

No piano, voices, or glasses. The ominous silence was broken by a shout and the explosion of a gun.

"Stay here!" Gilda said in a low voice, and bolted through the door.

She moved quickly but without sound. When she entered the dining room, everybody was huddled on the floor, satin dresses and silk jackets askew. Through the parlor, she could see the front door forced open, almost off its hinges. The maid's face was barely visible thorough a crack in the bathroom door and Gilda waved her back.

"Shit." Gilda heard Morris.

"Everybody stay down," Gilda shouted as she listened to the entire flat—the attackers seemed to have fled. She hurried to the bar. Behind it, Benny lay on the floor. Morris held his hand to the wound in Benny's chest. His fair skin had paled as if the blood were draining from him as well.

"I told him we had to give them the joint. They been wanting in for months." Tears filled Morris's voice. "We got other stuff, we don't need this shit." Morris spoke as if his words could bind the wound.

"Quick, let me." Gilda edged Morris out of the way and knelt beside Benny. "Get them out of here." The floor around Benny was awash in his blood. The moments moved in rapid flashes for Gilda. She looked into his eyes as she tried to find his pulse. He was there and not there.

Morris's apologetic voice was a low murmur as he helped people to their feet and kept the exit orderly. The woman in the maid's apron came out of the bathroom and helped Morris find people's coats.

As Benny's blood cooled around her, Gilda thought of the little boy, Lester, arriving tomorrow at noon with his sister for a job. She could feel Lydia reaching out, begging her to make everything all right as if she knew Gilda was able to hear her. All the connections Benny had with those around him in this room had created a family, and in turn he aided others holding their families together. He was able to help give life in ways different from Gilda. She fought the urge to save Benny with the power only she possessed.

Blood should not be given as an unexpected gift. Bird's admonition rang in her mind, Gilda knew of those who'd not chosen wisely, giving the gift of blood to those unable to manage the powers. She'd seen the results: deadly tyrants, intoxicated by their powers, unable to care about the havoc they created around them.

The explicit wish for the gift must be stated. How can you know who is capable of carrying such a burden? Gilda accepted all the reasons for letting Benny die. She turned to see Lydia standing at the bar looking down at them, her mouth open in horror.

"I know you can save him."

Lydia's eyes were full of that knowing. Gilda didn't understand how that could be, and at the same time knew she could not let Benny's life slip away from him, to be soaked into the hard wooden floor. But to give the blood without his direct request was against all she'd been taught.

Which would be the worse transgression?

Gilda put her lips to the wound in Benny's chest, where the blood had pooled. She took his blood into her mouth and listened for his needs. His mind was full of many people he wanted to help. Pictures of people, of towns, of the Evergreen were lit inside Gilda like reflections from a mirror ball. A fascinating dizziness pulled Gilda closer to Benny's mind. Lydia was deep inside his dreams, too, and it was as she'd said: as a sister.

The most urgent image inside Benny was his love of Morris. Gilda was startled that she hadn't realized it earlier. Their bond had grown out of a mutual care for the colored people of their town. Without the guarded protection they both maintained in public, the kinship and desire between them was unmistakable. The two men were partners in business and in life. There was little time left, but Benny's thoughts kaleidoscoped through her mind like spokes on a wheel. This was a family. They had work to do. Benny's thoughts were filled with an array of faces, although his body was almost still under her hands. She could not ignore the tie that held so many together.

Gilda let herself feel rather than think about what was coming. She would give him her blood and he would survive. Benny, Morris, and Lydia would know what she was. She would have to explain the life of the blood. If he desired it, Benny could go on with his life, fully recovered, and reject that preternatural life. When the hunger came on him, he could fight as if it were a drug, until it subsided, then dissipated completely.

But Benny might also decide to live with the blood. He would have the right to ask Gilda to share with him twice again until he was strong, and she would teach him about their life as Bird had taught her. She could not guess which path he would choose. Only in the moments and years to come would Gilda know the meaning of her decision.

She could feel Lydia staring down at her. With the hard nail of her small finger, Gilda cut the skin on her wrist smoothly and held it to Benny's mouth. At first, the blood just washed down his face. She tilted his head back so his mouth would open. He began to take the blood in and Gilda felt life slowly return to his body. His eyes fluttered, then filled with confusion and relief.

Lydia's eyes showed both her gratefulness and bewilderment when Gilda looked up, Benny's warm blood staining her face and clothes. The door to the flat slammed shut and they heard Morris running.

"Benny," he bellowed as he came. Their life together had seemed about to end when he'd gone to the front of the flat to help the shocked guests leave. His anguish was carried in the tears that ran down his face onto his blood-splattered shirt. He stopped abruptly when he saw Lydia smiling. Incredulous, he looked down at Benny, whose eyes were open and had regained their focus.

A familiar vitality pulsed through Benny's body as Gilda cradled him in her arms. She sensed they would be spending much time together in the coming months.

"He's all right, Morris," Lydia said, as if she knew it was true even though she wasn't exactly sure why. Her voice was full of joy like her songs.

RENEWAL

Chelsea Quinn Yarbro

Chelsea Quinn Yarbro was honored with a Lifetime Achievement Award by the World Fantasy Convention in 2014. She received a Bram Stoker Lifetime Achievement Award in 2009, and was the first woman to be named a Living Legend by the International Horror Guild (2006). Yarbro was named as Grand Master of the World Horror Convention in 2003. She is the recipient of the Fine Foundation Award for Literary Achievement (1993) and (along with Fred Saberhagen) was awarded the Knightly Order of the Brasov Citadel by the Transylvanian Society of Dracula in 1997. She has been nominated for the Edgar, World Fantasy, and Bram Stoker awards and was the first female president of the Horror Writers Association. The author of scores of novels in many genres, her manuscripts are being archived at Bowling Green University.

As noted in the introduction, Yarbro's contribution to the vampire genre—the creation of the character of le Comte Saint-Germain and his still continuing adventures—is immense. The twenty-seventh novel of her Saint-Germain series was published in December 2014. From her two collections of short fiction featuring Saint-Germain, I chose this novella set during World War II. It provides a great deal of information about the form vampirism takes in the universe Yarbro has created . . .

With bloodied hands, James pulled the ornate iron gates open and staggered onto the long drive that led to the chateau. Although he was dazed, he made sure the gates were properly shut before starting up the tree-lined road. How long ago he had made his first journey here, and how it drew him now. He stared ahead, willing the ancient building to appear out of the night as he kept up his dogged progress toward the one place that might provide him the shelter he so desperately needed.

When at last the stone walls came into view, James was puzzled to hear the sound of a violin, played expertly but fragmentally, as if the music were wholly personal. James stopped and listened, his cognac-colored eyes warming for the first time in three days. Until that moment, the only sound he had remembered was the grind and pound of guns. His bleary thoughts sharpened minimally and he reached up to push his hair from his brow. Vaguely he wondered who was playing, and why, for Montalia had an oddly deserted look to it: the grounds were overgrown and only two of the windows showed lights. This was more than war-time precaution, James realized, and shambled toward the side door he had used so many times in the past, the first twinges of real fear giving him a chill that the weather had not been able to exert.

The stables smelled more of motor oil than horses, but James recognized the shape of the building, and limped into its shadow with relief. Two lights, he realized, might mean nothing more than most of the servants had retired for the night, or that shortages of fuel and other supplies forced the household to stringent economies. He leaned against the wall of the stable and gathered his courage to try the door. At least, he told himself, it did not appear that the chateau was full of Germans. He waited until the violin was pouring out long cascades of sound before he reached for the latch, praying that if the hinges squeaked, the music would cover it.

In the small sitting room, Saint-Germain heard the distant whine of an opening door, and his bow hesitated on the strings. He listened, his expanded senses acute, then sat back and continued the Capriccio he had been playing, letting the sound guide the solitary intruder. He gave a small part of his attention to the unsteady footfalls in the corridor, but for the most part, he concentrated on the long pattern of descending thirds of the cadenza. Some few minutes later, when he had begun one of the Beethoven Romanzas, a ragged figure clutching a kitchen knife appeared in the doorway and emerged uncertainly from the darkness into the warmth of the hearthlight and the single kerosene lantern. Saint-Germain lowered his violin and gave the newcomer an appraising stare. His dark eyes narrowed briefly, then his brows raised a fraction as he recognized the man. "You will not need that knife, Mister Tree."

He had expected many things, but not this lone, elegant man. James shook his head, his expression becoming more dazed than ever. "I . . ."

He brought a grimy, bruised hand to his eyes and made a shaky attempt at laughter which did not come off. He coughed once, to clear his voice. "When I got here, and heard music . . . I thought that . . . I don't know what." As he spoke he reached out to steady himself against the back of one of the three overstuffed chairs in the fine stone room, which was chilly in spite of the fire. "Excuse me . . . I'm not . . . myself."

"Yes, I can see that," Saint-Germain said with gentleness, knowing more surely than James how unlike himself he was. He stood to put his violin into its velvet-lined case, then tucked the loosened bow into its holder before closing the top. This done, he set the case on the occasional table beside his chair and turned to James. "Sit down, Mister Tree. Please." It was definitely a command but one so kindly given that the other man complied at once, dropping gratefully into the chair which had been supporting him. The knife clattered to the floor, but neither paid any attention to it.

"It's been . . . a while," James said distantly, looking up at the painting over the fireplace. Then his gaze fell on Saint-Germain, and he saw the man properly for the first time.

Le Comte was casually dressed by his own exacting standards: a black hacking jacket, a white shirt and black sweater under it, and black trousers. There were black, ankle-high jodhpur boots on his small feet, the heels and soles unusually thick. Aside from a silver signet ring, he wore no jewelry. "Since you have been here? More than a decade, I would suppose."

"Yes. "James shifted in the chair, his movements those of utter exhaustion. "This place . . . I don't know why." Only now that he had actually arrived at his goal did he wonder what had driven him to seek it out. Indistinct images filtered through his mind, most of them senseless, one or two of them frightening.

"On Madelaine's behalf, I'm pleased to welcome you back. I hope you will stay as long as you wish to." He said this sincerely, and watched James for his response.

"Thanks. I don't know what . . . thanks." In this light, and with the abuses of the last few days, it was not possible to see how much the last ten years had favored James Emmerson Tree. His hair had turned from glossy chestnut to silver without loss of abundance; the lines of his face had deepened but had not become lost in fretwork or pouches, so that his character was cleanly incised, delineated in strong, sharp lines. Now, with smudges of dirt and dried blood on him, it was not apparent that while at thirty he had been good looking, at fifty he was superbly hand-some. He fingered the tear on his collar where his press tag had been. "I thought . . . Madelaine might have been . . ."

"Been here?" Saint-Germain suggested as he drew one of the other chairs closer to where James sat. "I am sorry, Mister Tree. Madelaine is currently in South America."

"Another expedition?" James asked, more forlorn than he knew.

"Of course. It's more circumspect to stay there than go to Greece or Africa just now, or wouldn't you agree?" He spoke slowly, deliberately, and in English for the first time. "I would rather be assured of her safety than her nearness, Mister Tree."

James nodded absently, then seemed at last to understand what Saint-Germain had said, for he looked up sharply and said in a different voice, "God, yes. Oh, God, yes."

"I had a letter from her not long ago. Perhaps you would care to read it later this evening?" He did not, in fact, want to share the contents of Madelaine's letter with James; it was too privately loving for any eyes but his, yet he knew that this man loved her with an intensity that was only exceeded by his own.

"No," James said after a brief hesitation. "So long as she's okay, that's all that matters. If anything happened to her, after this, I think I'd walk into the path of a German tank." His mouth turned up at the corners, quivered, and fell again into the harsh downward curve that had become characteristic in the last month. He looked down at his ruined jacket and plucked at one of the frayed tears.

Saint-Germain watched this closely, then asked, "Has the fighting been very bad?"

"What's very bad? Some days we kill more than they do, and some days they kill more. It sickens me." He turned toward the fire and for a little time said nothing; Saint-Germain respected his silence. Finally James sighed. "Is there anyone else here at Montalia?"

"My manservant Roger, but no one other than he." Again Saint-Germain waited, then inquired, "Is there something you require, Mister Tree? I would recommend a bath and rest to begin with."

This time James faltered noticeably. "It's funny; I really don't know what I want." He gave Saint-Germain a quick, baffled look. "I wanted to be here. But now that I am, I'm too tired to care." His eyes met Saint-Germain's once, then fell away. "It doesn't make much sense."

"It makes admirable sense," Saint-Germain told him, shaking his head as he studied James.

"I'm probably hungry and sore, too, but, I don't know . . ." He leaned back in the chair, and after a few minutes while Saint-Germain built up the fire, he began to talk in a quiet, remote ramble. "I went home in thirty-one; Madelaine might have mentioned it."

"Yes," Saint-Germain said as he poked at the pine log; it crackled and its sap ran and popped on the dry bark.

"It was supposed to be earlier, but what with the Crash, they weren't in any hurry to bring one more hungry reporter back to Saint Louis. So Crandell—he was my boss then—extended my assignment and when he died. Sonderson, who replaced him, gave me another eighteen months before asking me to come back. It was strange, being back in the States after more than thirteen years in Europe. You think you know how you'll feel, but you don't. You think it will be familiar and cozy, but it isn't. I felt damn-all odd, I can tell you. People on the street looked so—out of place. Of course the Depression was wrecking everything in the cities, but it was not only that. What worried me was hearing the same old platitudes everyone had been using in 1916. I couldn't believe it. With everything that had happened there was no comprehension that the world had changed. It was so different, in a way that was so complete that there was nothing the change did not touch. People kept talking about getting back to the old ways without understanding that they could not do that ever again . . ."

"They never can," Saint-Germain interjected softly. He was seated once again in the high-backed overstuffed chair.

". . . no matter what." He broke off. "Maybe you're right," he concluded lamely, and stared at the fire. "I've been cold."

"In time you will be warm again, Mister Tree," Saint-Germain said, and rose to pick up a silver bell lying on the table beside his violin case. "Would you like to lie down? You could use rest, Mister Tree." His manner was impeccably polite but James sensed that he would do well to cooperate with the suggestion.

"Sure," was James' quiet response. "Sure, why not."

"Excellent, Mister Tree." He rang the bell, and within two minutes a sandy-haired man of middle height, middle build, and middle age came into the room. "Roger, this is Madelaine's great good friend, James Emmerson Tree. He has gone through an . . . ordeal." One of Saint-Germain's brows rose sharply and Roger recognized it for the signal it was.

"How difficult for him," Roger said in a neutral voice. "Mister Tree, if you will let me attend to you . . ."

James shook his head. "I can manage for myself," he said, not at all sure that he could.

"Nonetheless, you will permit Roger to assist you. And when you have somewhat recovered, we will attend to the rest of it."

"The rest of it?" James echoed as he got out of the chair, feeling horribly grateful for Roger's proffered arm.

"Yes, Mister Tree, the rest of it." He smiled his encouragement but there was little amusement in his countenance.

"Yeah, I guess," James responded vaguely, and allowed himself to be guided into the dark hallway.

The bathroom was as he remembered it—large, white tiled and old fashioned. The tub stood on gilt crocodile feet and featured elaborate fixtures of the sort that had been in vogue eighty years before. James regarded it affectionately while Roger helped take off his damaged clothing. "I've always liked that tub," he said when he was almost naked. "It is something of a museum piece," Roger said, and James was free to assume he agreed.

The water billowed out of the taps steaming, but James looked at it with an unexpected disquiet. He was filthy, his muscles were stiff and sore, and there were other hurts on his body he thought would welcome the water, but at the last moment he hesitated, suppressing a kind of vertigo. With care, he steadied himself with one hand and said to Roger, who was leaving the room, "I'm worn out, that's what it is."

"Very likely," the manservant said in a neutral tone before closing the door.

As he stretched out in the tub, the anticipated relaxation did not quite happen. James felt his stiff back relax, but not to the point of letting him doze. He dismissed this as part of the aches and hurts that racked him. When he had washed away the worst of the grime, he looked over the damage he had sustained when he was thrown from the jeep. There was a deep weal down the inside of his arm. "Christ!" James muttered when he saw it, thinking he must have bled more than he had thought. Another deep cut on his thigh was red but healing, and other lacerations showed no sign of infection. "Which is lucky," James remarked to the ceiling, knowing that he could never have come the long miles to Montalia if he had been more badly hurt. The other two reporters had not been so fortunate: one had been shot in the crossfire that wrecked the jeep and the other had been crushed as the jeep overturned.

This was the first time James had been able to remember the incident clearly, and it chilled him. How easy it would have been to have died with them. One random factor different and he would have been the one who was shot or crushed. With an oath he got out of the tub, and stood shaking on the cold tiles as the water drained away.

"I have brought you a robe," Roger said a few minutes later as he returned. "Your other garments are not much use any longer. I believe that there is a change of clothes in the armoire of the room you used to occupy."

"Hope I can still get into them," James said lightly in an attempt to control the fright that had got hold of him.

"You will discover that later, Mister Tree." He helped the American into the bathrobe he held, saying in a steady manner, "It's very late, Mister Tree. The sun will be up soon, in fact. Why don't you rest for now, and my master will see you when you have risen."

"Sounds good," James answered as he tied the sash. He wanted to sleep more than he could admit, more than he ever remembered wanting to. "I . . . I'll probably not get up until, oh, five or six o'clock."

"No matter, Mister Tree," Roger said, and went to hold the door for James.

James woke from fidgety sleep not long after sunset. He looked blankly around the room Madelaine had given him so many years before, and for several minutes could not recall how he had got there, or where he was. Slowly, as if emerging from a drugged stupor he brought back the events of the previous night. There at the foot of the bed was the robe, its soft heavy wool familiar to his touch. Memories returned in a torrent as he sat up in bed: how many times he had held Madelaine beside him through the night and loved her with all his body and all his soul. He felt her absence keenly. At that, he remembered that Saint-Germain was at Montalia, and for the first time, James felt awkward about it. It was not simply that he was jealous, although that was a factor, but that he had never properly understood the man's importance in Madelaine's life.

He got out of bed and began to pace restlessly, feeling very hungry now, but oddly repulsed at the thought of food. "Rations," he said to the walls in a half-joking tone, "that's what's done it." Telling himself that he was becoming morbid, he threw off the robe, letting it lie in a heap in the nearest chair, and dressed in the slightly old-fashioned suit he had left here before returning to America. The trousers, he noticed, were a little loose on him now, and he hitched them up uneasily. He had neither belt nor suspenders for it, and might have to ask for one or the other. The jacket hung on him, and he reflected that he had not gone in for much exercise in the last few years until he had come back to Europe four months ago. He looked in vain for a tie and recollected that he had disdained them for a time. He would have to find something else.

At last he found a roll-top pullover at the bottom of one of the drawers, and he gratefully stripped off jacket and shirt to put it on. It was of soft tan wool, with one or two small holes on the right sleeve where moths had reached it, and it felt lovely next to his skin. With shirt and jacket once more donned, James felt that he presented a good enough appearance to venture down into the main rooms of the chateau.

He found his way easily enough, although the halls were dark. His eyes adjusted readily to this, and he told himself that after all the nights when he and Madelaine had sought each other in the dim rooms and corridors, he should be able to find his way blindfolded. For the first time in several days, he chuckled.

"Something amuses you, Mister Tree?" said Saint-Germain from behind him, his tone lightly remote as he approached. "I heard you come down the stairs a few minutes ago. I'm pleased you're up. I thought you might be . . . hungry."

"I was. I am," James said, turning to face the other man. "But there's . . ." He could not continue and was not certain why.

"For whatever consolation it may be to you, I do sympathize, Mister Tree," le Comte said slowly, looking up at the tall American. "It may surprise you to learn that it will be a while before you become used to your . . . transition." As he said this, his dark eyes met James' uncompromisingly. "Transition?" James repeated with a bewildered smile. "I don't understand."

"Don't you?" Le Comte de Saint-Germain gave James another steady look and said cautiously, "Mister Tree, are you aware of what has happened to you?"

James laughed uneasily. "I think I've been hurt. I know I have. There are cuts on my arms and legs, a couple pretty serious." He cleared his throat nervously. "There were three of us in the jeep, and there was an ambush. No one bothered to find out if we were press, but I don't blame them for that. I don't know which side did it, really." He shook himself self-consciously. "Someone must have walked over my grave."

"Very astute, Mister Tree," Saint-Germain said compassionately.

"I don't remember much more than that. It does sound lame, doesn't it? But I don't."

"You recall being injured." He motioned toward the tall, studded doors that led to the small sitting room where James had found him the night before. "That is a start."

James fell into step beside the smaller man and was mildly startled to find that he had to walk briskly to keep up with Saint-Germain. "Actually, it's all muddled. I remember the crossfire, and the jeep turning over, and being tossed into the air, but the rest is all . . . jumbled. I must have passed out, and didn't come to until after dark. I can't tell you what made me come here. I guess when you're hurt, you look for a safe place, and I've been here before, so . . ." He heard Saint-Germain close the door behind them and stopped to look about the sitting room.

"It seems eminently reasonable, Mister Tree," Saint-Germain told him as he indicated the chair James had occupied before.

"Good," James responded uneasily.

Saint-Germain drew up his chair; the firelight played on his face, casting sudden shadows along his brow, the line of his straight, aslant nose, the wry, sad curve of his mouth. Though his expression remained attentive, his eyes now had a sad light in them. "Mister Tree, how badly were you hurt?"

James was more disquieted now than ever and he tugged at the cuffs of his jacket before he answered. "It must have been pretty bad. But I walked here, and I figure it's more than forty, maybe fifty miles from . . . where it happened." He ran one large hand through his silver hair. "Those cuts, though. Jesus! And I felt so . . . detached. Bleeding does that, when it's bad, or so the medics told me. But I got up . . ."

"Yes," Saint-Germain agreed. "You got up."

"And I made it here . . ." With a sudden shudder, which embarrassed him, he turned away.

Saint-Germain waited until James was more composed, then said, "Mister Tree, you've had a shock, a very great shock, and you are not yet recovered from it. It will take more than a few minutes and well-chosen words of explanation to make you realize precisely what has occurred, and what it will require of you."

"That sounds ominous," James said, forcing himself to look at Saint-Germain again.

"Not ominous," Saint-Germain corrected him kindly. "Demanding, perhaps, but not ominous." He stretched out his legs and crossed his ankles. "Mister Tree, Madelaine led me to understand that you were told about her true nature. Is this so?" Privately, he knew it was, for Madelaine had confided all her difficulties with James over the years, and Saint-Germain was aware of the American's stubborn disbelief in what he had been told.

"A little. I heard about the aristocratic family, and looked them up." His square chin went up a degree or two. "She made some pretty wild claims . . ."

Saint-Germain cut him short "Did you bother to investigate her claims?"

"Yes," James admitted, sighing. "I had to. When she told me . . . those things, I had to find out if she had been making it up out of whole cloth." He rubbed his hands together, his nervousness returning.

"And what did you discover?" Saint-Germain's inquiry was polite, almost disinterested, but there was something in his dark eyes that held James' attention as he answered.

"Well, there was a Madelaine de Montalia born here in the eighteenth century. That was true. And she did . . . die in Paris in 1744. She was only twenty, and I read that she was considered pretty." He paused. "The way Madelaine is pretty, in fact."

"Does that surprise you?" Saint-Germain asked.

"Well, the same family . . ." James began weakly, then broke off. "The portrait looked just like her, and she kept saying it was her." These words were spoken quickly and in an undervoice, as if James feared to let them have too much importance.

"But you did not believe her," Saint-Germain prompted him when he could not go on. "Why was that?"

"Well, you should have heard what she said!" James burst out, rising from the chair and starting to pace in front of the fireplace. "She told me . . . Look, I know that you were her lover once. She didn't kid me about that. And you might not know the kinds of things she said about herself . . ." He stopped and stared down at the fire, thinking that he was becoming more famished by the minute. If he could eat, then he would not have to speak. Unbidden, the memories of the long evenings with Madelaine returned with full force to his thoughts. He pictured her dining room with its tall, bright windows, Madelaine sitting across from him, or at the corner, watching him with delighted eyes as he ate. She never took a meal with him, and he had not been able to accept her explanation for this. As he tried to recall the taste of the sauce Claude had served with the fish, he nearly gagged.

"I know what she told you," Saint-Germain said calmly, as if from a distance. "She told you almost twenty years ago that she is a vampire. You did not accept this, although you continued to love her. She warned you what would happen when you died, and you did not choose to believe her. Yet she told you the truth, Mister Tree."

James turned around so abruptly that for a moment he swayed on his feet. "Oh, sure! Fangs and capes and graveyards and all the rest of it. Madelaine isn't any of those things."

"Of course not."

"And," James continued rather breathlessly now that he was started, "she said that you were . . . and that you were the one who changed her!" He had expected some reaction to this announcement, but had not antic-ipated that it would be a nod and a stern smile. "She said . . ." he began again, as if to explain more to Saint-Germain.

"I'm aware of that. She had my permission, but that was merely a formality." He sat a bit straighter in his chair as the significance of his words began to penetrate James' indignation. "She and I are alike in that way, now. It is correct: I did bring about her change, as she brought about yours." His steady dark eyes were unfaltering as they held James'.

"Come on," James persisted, his voice growing higher with tension. "You can't want her to say that about you. You can't."

"Well, in a general way I prefer to keep that aspect of myself private, yes," Saint-Germain agreed urbanely, "but it is the truth, nonetheless."

James wanted to yell so that he would not have to listen to those sensible words, so that he could shut out the quiet, contained man who spoke so reasonably about such completely irrational things. "Don't joke," he growled, his jaw tightening.

"Mister Tree," Saint-Germain said, and something in the tone of his voice insisted that James hear him out: the American journalist reluc-tantly fell silent. "Mister Tree, self-deception is not a luxury that we can afford. I realize that you have been ill prepared for . . . recent events, and so I have restrained my sense of urgency in the hope that you would ask the questions for yourself. But you have not, and it isn't wise or desirable for you to continue in this way. No," he went on, not permitting James to interrupt, "you must listen to me for the time being. When I have done, I will answer any questions you have, as forth-rightly as possible; until then, be good enough to remain attentive and resist your understandable inclination to argue."

James was oddly daunted by the air of command that had come over le Comte, but he had many years' experience in concealing any awe he might feel, and so he clasped his hands behind his back and took a few steps away from the fire as if to compensate for the strength he sensed in Saint-Germain. "Okay; okay. Go on."

Saint-Germain's smile was so swift that it might not have occurred at all—there was a lift at the corners of his mouth and his expression was once again somber. "Madelaine took you as her lover sometime around 1920, as I recall, and it was in 1925 that she tried to explain to you what would become of you after you died." He saw James flinch at the last few words, but did not soften them. "Like Madelaine, you would rise from death and walk again, vampiric. As long as your nervous system is intact, you will have a kind of life in you, one that exerts a few unusual demands. You have some experience of them already. You are hungry, are you not? And yet you cannot bring yourself to eat. The notion of food is repulsive. We're very . . . specific in our nourishment, Mister Tree, and you must become accustomed to the new requirements . . ."

"You're as bad as she is," James muttered, looking once toward the door as if he wanted to bolt from the room. He wanted to convince himself that the other man was a dangerous lunatic, or a charlatan enjoying himself at James' expense, but there was undoubted sincerity in Saint-Germain's manner, and a pragmatic attitude that was terribly convincing.

"Oh, I am much worse than Madelaine, Mister Tree. It was I who made her a vampire, back in the autumn of 1743." He frowned as James turned swiftly, violently away. "Your change was assured possibly as early as 1922, but Madelaine was so fearful of your hatred that it took her over two years to gather her courage to explain the hazard to you. You see, she loves you, and the thought of your detestation was agony for her. She could not leave you unprepared, however, and eventually revealed . . ."

"This is crazy," James insisted to the ceiling; he could not bring himself to look at Saint-Germain. "Crazy."

"Do you appreciate the depth of her love?" Saint-Germain went on as if he had not heard James' outburst. "Your protection was more important to her than your good opinion. She risked being loathed so that you would not have to face your change in ignorance." He folded his arms. "And you make a paltry thing of her gift by refusing to admit that the change has happened."

James threw up his hands and strode away from the fireplace toward the farthest corner of the room. "This doesn't make any sense. Not any of it. You're talking like a madman." He could hear the unsteadiness of his voice and with an effort of will lowered and calmed it. "I remember what she told me about being a vampire. I didn't believe it then, you're right. I don't believe it now. And you keep talking as if something has happened to me. True enough. My jeep was shot out from under me, I've lost a lot of blood and I've been wandering without food for over three days. No wonder I feel so . . . peculiar."

Slowly Saint-Germain got out of the chair and crossed the room toward James. His compelling eyes never left James' face, and the quiet command of his well-modulated voice was the more authoritative for its lack of emotion. "Mister Tree, stop deluding yourself. When that jeep turned over, when you were thrown through the air, you suffered fatal injuries. You lay on the ground and bled to death. But death is a disease to which we are, in part, immune. When the sun set, you woke into . . . Madelaine's life, if you will." He stopped less than two strides from James. "Whether you wish to believe it or not, you are a vampire, Mister Tree."

"Hey, no . . ." James began, taking an awkward step back from Saint-Germain.

"And you must learn to . . . survive."

"NO!" He flung himself away from le Comte, bringing his arms up to shield his face as if from blows.

"Mister Tree . . ."

"It's crazy!" With an inarticulate cry, he rushed toward the door.

Before he could reach it, Saint-Germain had moved with remarkable speed and blocked James' path. "Sit down, Mister Tree."

"I . . ." James said, raising one hand to threaten the smaller man.

"I would advise against it, Mister Tree," Saint-Germain warned him gently, with a trace of humor in his expression that baffled James anew. "Sit down."

The impetus which had driven James to action left him as quickly as it had possessed him, and he permitted himself to be pointed in the direction of the chair he had just vacated. He told himself that he was in the presence of a lunatic, and that he ought to go along with him; but deeper in his mind was the gnawing fear that against all reason, Saint-Germain might be right. He moved stiffly, and as he sat down, he drew back into the chair, as if to protect himself. "You're . . ."

"I'm not going to hurt you, if that is what concerns you," Saint-Germain sighed. When James did not deny his fear, Saint-Germain crossed the room away from him, and regarded him for two intolerably long minutes. "Madelaine loves you, Mister Tree, and for that alone, I would offer you my assistance."

"You were her lover once, if you're who I think you are." He had summoned a little defiance into his accusation.

"I have told you so. Yes, she and I were lovers, as you and she were." There was an eighteenth century lowboy against the wall, and Saint-Germain braced himself against it, studying James as he did.

"And you're not jealous?" James fairly pounced on the words.

"In time, we learn to bow to the inevitable. My love for Madelaine has not diminished, Mister Tree, but for those of our nature, such contact is . . . shall we say nonproductive?" His tone was sardonic; his face was sad. "No, I am not jealous."

James heard this out in disbelief. "You want me to believe that?"

"I would prefer that you did," Saint-Germain said, then shrugged. "You will discover it for yourself, in time."

"Because I'm a vampire, like you two, right?" The sarcasm James had intended to convey was not entirely successful.

"Yes."

"Christ." James scowled, then looked up. "I said *Christ*. If I'm a vampire, how come I can do that? I thought all vampires were supposed to blanch and cringe at holy words and symbols." He was not enjoying himself, but asking this question made him feel more comfortable, as if the world were sane again.

"You will find that there are a great many misconceptions about us, Mister Tree. One of them is that we are diabolic. Would you be reassured if I could not say God, or Jesus, or Holy Mary, Mother of God? Give me a crucifix and I will kiss it, or a rosary and I will recite the prayers. I will read from the Torah, the Koran, the Vedas, or any other sacred literature you prefer. There is a Bible in the library—shall I fetch it, so that you may put your mind at rest?" He did not conceal his exasperation, but he mitigated his outburst with a brief crack of laughter.

"This is absurd," James said uncertainly.

Saint-Germain came a few steps closer. "Mister Tree, when you accepted Madelaine as your mistress, you knew that she was not entirely like other women. At the time, I would imagine that lent a thrill to what you did. No, don't bristle at me. I'm not implying that your passion was not genuine: if it was not, you would not have been given her love as you have." He fingered the lapel of his jacket. "This is rather awkward for me."

"I can see why," James said, feeling a greater degree of confidence. "If you keep telling me about . . ."

"It's awkward because I know how you love Madelaine, and she you. And how I love her, and she me." He read the puzzled look that James banished swiftly. "You will not want to relinquish what you have had, but . . ."

"Because you're back, is that it?" James challenged, sitting straight in the overstuffed chair.

"No. After all, Madelaine is on a dig, so her choice, if one were possible, is a moot point at best. I am afraid that it is more far-reaching than that." He came back to his chair, but though he rested one arm across the back, he did not sit. "For the sake of argument, Mister Tree, accept for the moment that you have been killed and are now a vampire."

James chuckled. "All right: I'm a vampire. But according to you, so is Madelaine, as well as you."

"Among vampires," Saint-Germain went on, not responding to James' provocation, "there is a most abiding love. Think of how the change was accomplished, and you will perceive why this is so. But once we come into our life, the expression of that love . . . changes, as well. We hunger for life, Mister Tree. And that is the one thing we cannot offer one another."

"Oh, shit," James burst out. "I don't know how much of this I can listen to."

Saint-Germain's manner became more steely. "You will listen to it all, Mister Tree, or you will come to regret it." He waited until James settled back into the chair once again. "As I have told you," he resumed in the same even tone, "you will have to learn to seek out those who will respond to . . . what you can offer. For we do offer a great deal to those we love, Mister Tree. You know how profoundly intimate your love is for Madelaine. That is what you will have to learn to give to others if you are to survive."

"Life through sex?" James scoffed feebly. "Freud would love it."

Though Saint-Germain's fine brows flicked together in annoyance, he went on with hardly a pause. "Yes, through, if you take that to mean a route. Sex is not what you must strive for, but true intimacy. Sex is often a means to avoid intimacy—hardly more than the scratching of an itch. But when the act is truly intimate, there is no more intense experience, and that, Mister Tree, is what you must achieve." He cocked his head to the side. "Tell me: when you were with Madelaine, how did you feel?"

The skepticism went out of James' eyes and his face softened. "I wish I could tell you. I can't begin to express it. No one else ever . . ."

"Yes," Saint-Germain agreed rather sadly. "You will do well to remember it, in future."

On the hearth one of the logs crackled and burst, filling the room with the heavy scent of pine resin. A cascade of sparks flew onto the stone flooring and died as they landed.

James swallowed and turned away from Saint-Germain. He wanted to find a rational, logical objection to throw back at the black-clad man, to dispel the dread that was filling him, the gnawing certainty that he was being told the truth. "I don't believe it," he whispered.

Saint-Germain had seen this shock so many times that he was no longer distressed by it, but merely saddened. He approached James and looked down at him. "You will have to accept it, Mister Tree, or you will have to die the true death. Madelaine would mourn for you terribly, if you did that."

"'Die the true death.'" James bit his lower lip. "How . . ."

"Anything that destroys the nervous system destroys us: fire, crushing, beheading, or the traditional stake through the heart, for that matter, which breaks the spine. If you choose to die, there are many ways to do it." He said it matter-of-factly enough, but there was something at the back of his eyes that made James wonder how many times Saint-Germain had found himself regretting losses of those who had not learned to live as he claimed they must.

"And drowning? Isn't water supposed to . . ." James was amazed to hear his own question. He had tried to keep from giving the man any credence, and now he was reacting as if everything he heard was sensible.

"You will learn to line the heels and soles of your shoes with your native earth, and will cross water, walk in sunlight, in fact live a fairly normal life. We are creatures of the earth, Mister Tree. That which interrupts our contact with it is debilitating. Water is the worst, of course, but flying in an airplane is . . . unnerving." He had traveled by air several times, but had not been able to forget the huge distance between him and the treasured earth. "It will be more and more the way we travel—Madelaine says that she had got used to it but does not enjoy it—but I must be old-fashioned; I don't like it. Although it is preferable to sailing, for brevity if nothing else."

"You make it sound so mundane," James said in the silence that fell. That alone was persuading him, and for that reason, he tried to mock it.

"Most of life is mundane, even our life." He smiled, and for the first time there was warmth in it. "We are not excused from the obligations of living, unless we live as total outcasts. Some of us have, but such tactics are . . . unrewarding."

"Maybe not death, but taxes?" James suggested with an unhappy chuckle.

Saint-Germain gave James a sharp look. "If you wish to think of it in that way, it will answer fairly well," he said after a second or two. "If you live in the world, there are accommodations that must be made."

"This is bizarre," James said, convincing himself he was amused while the unsettling apprehension grew in him steadily.

"When you came here," Saint-Germain continued, taking another line of argument, "when did you travel?"

"What?" James made an abrupt gesture with his hand, as if to push something away. "I didn't look about for public transportation, so I can't tell you what time . . ."

"Day or night will do," Saint-Germain said.

"Why, it was da . . ." His face paled. "No. I . . . passed out during the day. I decided it was safer at night, in any case. There are fewer patrols, and . . ."

"When did you decide this? Before or after you had walked the better part of one night?" He let James have all the time he wanted to answer the question.

"I walked at night," James said in a strange tone. "The first night it was . . . easier. And I was so exhausted that I wasn't able to move until sundown. That night, with the moon so full, and seeing so well, I figured I might as well take advantage of it . . ."

"Mister Tree, the moon is not full, nor was it two nights ago. It is in its first quarter." He was prepared to defend this, but he read James' troubled face, and did not press his argument. "Those who have changed see very well at night. You may, in fact, want to avoid bright sunlight, for our eyes are sensitive. We also gain strength and stamina. How else do you suppose you covered the distance you did with the sorts of wounds you sustained to slow you down?"

"I . . . I didn't think about it," he answered softly. "It was . . . natural."

"For those . . ."

". . . who have changed, don't tell me!" James burst out, and lurched out of the chair. "If you keep this up, you'll have me believing it, and then I'll start looking for a padded cell and the latest thing in straight jackets." He paced the length of the room once, coming back to stand near Saint-Germain. "You're a smooth-tongued bastard, I'll give you that, Saint-Germain. You *are* Saint-Germain, aren't you?"

"Of course. I thought you remembered me from that banquet in Paris," came the unperturbed answer.

"I did. But I thought you'd look . . ."

"Older?" Saint-Germain suggested. "When has Madelaine looked older than twenty? True, you have not seen her for more than six years, but when she came to America, did she strike you as being older than the day you met her?"

"No," James admitted.

"And she looks very little older now than she did the day I met her in 1743. You are fortunate that age has been kind to you, Mister Tree. That is one of the few things the change cannot alter." Abruptly he crossed the room and opened the door. "I trust you will give me an hour of your time later this evening. Roger should be back by then, and then you will have a chance to . . ."

"Has he gone for food?" James demanded, not wanting to admit he was famished.

"Something like that," le Comte answered, then stepped into the hall and pulled the door closed behind him.

The Bugatti pulled into the court behind the stables and in a moment, Roger had turned off the foglights and the ignition. He motioned to the woman beside him, saying, "I will get your bag, Madame, and then assist you."

"Thank you," the woman answered distantly. She was not French, though she spoke the language well. Her clothes, which were excellent quality, hung on her shapelessly, and the heavy circles under her eyes and the hollows at her throat showed that she had recently suffered more than the usual privations of war. Automatically she put her hand to her forehead, as if to still an ache there.

"Are you all right, Madame?" Roger asked as he opened the passenger door for her. In his left hand he held a single worn leather valise.

"I will be in a short time," she responded, unable to smile, but knowing that good manners required something of the sort from her.

Roger offered her his arm. "You need not feel compelled, Madame. If, on reflection, the matter we discussed is distasteful to you, tell me at once, and I . . ." He turned in relief as he saw Saint-Germain approaching through the night.

"You're back sooner than I expected," Saint-Germain said, with an inquiring lift to his brows.

"I had an unexpected opportunity," was the answer. "Just as well, too, because there are Resistance fighters gathering further down the mountain, and they do not take kindly to travelers."

"I see," Saint-Germain responded.

"A number of them wished to . . . detain Madame Kunst, hearing her speak . . . and . . ." Roger chose his words carefully.

"I am Austrian," the woman announced, a bit too loudly. "I am. I fled." Without warning, she started to cry with the hopelessness of an abandoned child. "They took my mother and my father and shot them," she said through her tears. "And then they killed my uncle and his three children. They wanted me, but I was shopping. A neighbor warned me. It wasn't enough that Gunther died for defending his friends, oh, no."

Saint-Germain motioned Roger aside, then held out his small, beautiful hand to Madame Kunst. "Come inside, Madame Kunst. There is a fire and food."

She sat passively while her tears stopped, then obediently took his hand, and for the first time looked into Saint-Germain's penetrating eyes. "*Danke, Mein Herr.*"

"It would be wiser to say *merci*, here," Saint-Germain reminded her kindly. "My experience with the Resistance in this area says they are not very forgiving."

"Yes. I was stupid," she said as she got out of the Bugatti and allowed Saint-Germain to close the door. In an effort to recapture her poise, she said, "Your manservant made a request of me as he brought me here."

Roger and Saint-Germain exchanged quick glances, and Saint-Germain hesitated before saying, "You must understand, this is not precisely the situation I had anticipated. Did my manservant explain the situation to you clearly? I do not want to ask you to do anything you think you would not wish to do."

She shrugged, shaking her head once or twice. "It doesn't matter to me. Or it does, but it makes no sense."

"How do you mean?" Saint-Germain had seen this lethargic shock many times in the past, but long familiarity did not make it easier to bear. He would have to make other arrangements for James, he thought: this woman clearly needed quiet and time to restore herself. She had had more than enough impositions on her.

"It's all so . . ." She sighed as Saint-Germain opened the side door for her and indicated the way into the chateau. "No man has touched me since Gunther, and I was content to be in my father's house, where the worst seemed so far away. When I thought those men might force me, I screamed, but there was no reason for it any more."

"You have nothing to fear from anyone at Montalia," Saint-Germain told her quietly.

She nodded and let Roger escort her into the breakfast room off the kitchen. There was a low fire in the grate and though the striped wallpaper was faded, in the flickering light it was pleasant and cozy. As Saint-Germain closed the door, she sat in the chair Roger held for her and folded her hands in her lap. Her age was no more than thirty, but the gesture was that of a much younger person. "Gunther died six months ago. I didn't find out about it at first. They don't tell you what's happened. The SS comes and people go out with them and don't come home again, and no one dares ask where they have gone, or when they will return, or then the SS might return. It was the local judge who told me, and he was drunk when he did."

Roger bowed and excused himself to prepare a simple meal for Madame Kunst.

"When did you leave Austria, Madame?" Saint-Germain asked her as he added another log to the fire.

"Not many days ago. Eight or nine, I think. It could be ten." She yawned and apologized.

"There is no need," Saint-Germain assured her. "The fare here is adequate but not luxurious. If you are able to wait half an hour, there will be soup and cheese and sausage. Perhaps you would like to nap in the meantime?"

She thought about this, then shook her head. "I would sleep like the dead. I must stay awake. There are too many dead already." She fiddled with the fold of her skirt across her lap, but her mind was most certainly drifting. "I ate yesterday."

Saint-Germain said nothing but he could not repress an ironic smile, and was relieved that he had attended to his own hunger a few days before. The matter of nourishment, he thought, was becoming ridiculously complex.

"You did what?" James exclaimed, outraged. He had come back to the sitting room some ten minutes before and had tried to listen in reserved silence to what Saint-Germain was telling him.

"I saw that she was fed and given a room. I'm sorry that this adds so many complications. Had Roger been able to reach Mirelle, the problem would not have arisen." He was unruffled by James' outburst.

"First, you send your valet out to get a cooperative widow for me, and when that doesn't work because he can't get through to the village, he brings a half-starved Austrian refugee here as a weird kind of substitute, never mind what the poor woman thinks, being half kidnapped. Second, you think I'll go along with this impossible scheme. Third, you're telling me that you bring women here the way some cooks rustle up a half a dozen eggs, and I'm supposed to be grateful?" His voice had risen to a shout, as much to conceal the guilty pleasure he felt at the prospect of so tantalizing a meeting.

"Mister Tree, if there were not a war going on, all this would be handled differently. It may surprise you to know that I am not in the habit of 'rustling up,' as you say, cooperative widows or anyone else, for that matter. However, your situation will be critical soon, if something is not done, and I had hoped to find as undisruptive a solution as possible."

"Well, you sure as hell botched it," James said, taking secret pleasure in seeing this elegant stranger at a loss.

"Lamentably, I must concur." He thrust his hands into his pockets and started toward the door.

James could not resist a parting shot. "You mean you were going to lay out a woman for me, like a smorgasbord, so I could . . ."

Saint-Germain's mobile lips turned down in disgust "What do you take me for, Mister Tree? Mirelle knows what I am and finds it most satisfying. She would enjoy the . . . variety you would offer her. Good God, you don't believe that I would expose a woman like Madame Kunst to what we are, do you? She understands there is a man here suffering from battle fatigue, and is prepared to make allowances. It is dangerous and unwise to spend time with those who are repelled by us. If you are to survive in this life, you must learn to be circumspect." He reached for the door, then added, "Roger found the two boxes of earth from Denver, and that will afford you some relief, but not, I fear, a great deal."

"Earth from Denver?" James echoed.

"Of course. When Madelaine knew that you would walk after death, she arranged to have two cartons of your native earth shipped here, in case it was needed." It was said lightly, but the significance did not escape James. "She had stored it in the stables, and Roger did not find it until late afternoon."

"Earth from Denver. I can't believe it." There would have been comfort and denial in laughter, but James could not summon any.

"She cares what happens to you, Mister Tree. It was not whim but concern for your welfare that made her get those two boxes." He opened the door wide and stepped into the hall. His face was clouded with thought and he made his way slowly to the kitchen.

Roger looked up as Saint-Germain came quietly through the door. "She's bathed and gone to bed."

"Good. Did you learn anything more?" He was frowning slightly; there was an indefinable restlessness about him.

"Nothing significant. She's twenty-nine, comes from Salzburg. She used to teach school, her husband . . ."

"Gunther?"

"Yes. He was an attorney, I gather." He finished tidying the clutter in the kitchen and turned to bank the coals in the huge, wood-burning stove.

"Do you believe her?" Saint-Germain asked quietly.

"That she was a teacher and her husband an attorney, yes. The rest, I don't know." Roger closed the fuelbox and wiped his hands on a rag, leaving blackened smudges on the worn cloth.

"Nor do I," Saint-Germain admitted. "It may only be shock, but. But."

Roger blew out one of the kerosene lanterns. "Is she what she seems?"

"Superficially, no doubt," Saint-Germain said measuredly. "And everything she has told us may be true. If that's the case, she might be blackmailed. If she has children, and they are held by the SS, she might undertake almost anything to save them. Because if she is what she claims to be, and wants to be out of Austria and away from the war, why didn't she stop in Switzerland? That's a neutral country."

"She might not feel safe there," Roger suggested.

"And instead she feels safe in France?" Saint-Germain countered in disbelief. "You know what the French want to do to the Germans these days. Why should she leave the comparative haven Switzerland offers for this?"

"It is espionage?" Roger asked, taking the other lantern and starting toward the door.

"We will doubtless soon find out. But we must be very cautious. All the Resistance would need is an excuse to come here hunting German spies and matters might suddenly become unpleasant for us." He accompanied Roger out of the kitchen and toward the tower, the oldest part of the chateau. "I'm afraid I've scandalized Mister Tree again," Saint-Germain remarked as the reverberations of their footsteps clattered away into the eerie darkness. "He's accused me of pimping."

Roger gave a snort of amusement. "How charming. Did he say it directly?"

"Not quite. That would mean he would have to see too clearly what has become of him. It is unfortunate that you did not reach Mirelle. She would have put an end to all this nonsense, and the worst of his anxiety would be over by now. He's badly frightened; the thing that could not possibly happen to him has happened. Mirelle would tease him out of it. It's a pity she does not want to be one of my blood in the end. She would do well." They reached a narrow, uneven stairway that led into the upper rooms of the tower, and Saint-Germain stood aside for Roger so that he could light his way. The lantern was unnecessary for Saint-Germain, but his manservant required more illumination.

"It's best that she should know her mind now," Roger said, picking his way up the hazardous stairs. "Later, it might be inconvenient."

"True enough," Saint-Germain murmured. "Which room are the boxes in?"

"The second, where the trunks are stored. I stumbled on them by chance." They were halfway up the stairs now, and Roger paid particular attention to this stretch, for he knew that the one short trip stair was located here.

"To hide a box, put it with other boxes," Saint-Germain said, paraphrasing the maxim. "I have always applauded Madelaine's cleverness."

Roger got past the trip stair and moved faster. "Both boxes are unmarked, but there is the stencil design of an oak on both of them, which was what alerted me."

"How very like her," le Comte chuckled. They were almost at the landing, and he smiled his anticipation. "He'll be more at ease with this."

"Perhaps, perhaps not," Roger responded with a shrug. On the landing, he pointed to the door. "That one. There's a stack of boxes in the north corner. They're on the top of it."

As he opened the door and stepped into the room, Saint-Germain said over his shoulder, "You know, it is inconvenient that our scars can't be altered. Plastic surgery might change any number of things. Mister Tree is going to have some distinctive marks on his arms and thighs which will make identification simple. If there were a way to remove them, it might be easier to go from alias to alias. Well, that time may come." He looked around for the stack Roger had described. "Ah. There. If you'll give me a hand getting them down, I will take them to Mister Tree's room."

James woke at sunset feeling more restored than he had since his accident. He stretched slowly, oddly pleased that there were no aches to hamper his movements. He was healing, he insisted to himself. When he rose from the bed, there was the first hint of an energetic spring in his step. He dressed carefully, noticing that his clothes had been pressed some time during the day. The only things that he could not find were his shoes. After a brief hunt for them, he shrugged and settled for a pair of heavy boots he had worn years before when he and Madelaine had gone tramping over the rough hillsides together. As he laced them up, he thought how comfortable they were, and hoped that le Comte would not be too offended by them.

When at last he ventured down to the sitting room, he found Madame Kunst finishing the last of her tea, a few crumbs left on the Limoges plate beside her cup and saucer. He hesitated, then came into the room. "Good afternoon."

She looked up suddenly, guiltily, then smiled as best she could. "Good afternoon, though it is more evening, I think. You are . . ."

"The American suffering from battle fatigue, yes," he said with the same directness he had used to disarm politicians and industrialists for more than two decades. "You needn't worry, Madame. I am not precisely out of control, as you can see." To demonstrate this, he took a chair and arranged himself casually in it.

"I'm glad you're feeling . . . better?" This last change of inflection caught his attention and he leaned forward to speak to her.

"Yes. I'm much revived, thanks." He had deliberately chosen a chair that was far enough away from her that she would not be too much disturbed by his presence.

"You're an officer?" she asked when she had poured herself another cup of tea. She pointed to the pot in mute invitation, saying, "If you like, I could ring for another cup."

"That would be . . ." He broke off, finding the thought of tea distasteful. "Very good of you, but it would be wasted on me," he finished, frowning a bit.

"Is anything the matter?" she inquired apprehensively.

"No, not really." He decided to answer her question. "I'm not an officer, or a soldier, I'm afraid. I'm a journalist. I've been covering the action toward Lyon, but it hasn't been what I expected."

Madame Kunst smiled politely. "I'd think not." She sipped her tea. "What is your impression? Or would you rather not discuss it?"

"You must know the answer to that better than I," James suggested blandly, the habits of caution exerting themselves.

"Only what we are told," she said with a degree of sadness.

"But there must be raids and . . ." he said, hoping she would take up his drift.

"We hear about them, naturally, but Salzburg is not as important as other places. It is not important to shipping or the offensive, so we do not know how the rest of the country is going on." She finished the tea and reluctantly set the cup aside. "They have real butter here, and the milk is fresh."

The mention of food made James queasy, but he was able to nod. "Yes. There are shortages everywhere. Back home, there are ration cards used for meat and other necessary items. The government encourages everyone to grow their own vegetables." He knew it was safe to mention this, because it was common knowledge and there were articles in the newspapers which any enemy spy who wished to could read.

"There isn't much opportunity to grow vegetables in a city flat," she said.

"True enough. I have a cousin who always sends me canned goods at Christmas. She has quite a garden and thinks I need her food." He wanted to get off the subject, but did not quite know how.

Madame Kunst spared him the trouble. "How long have you been in France, Herr . . . I believe I was not told your name."

This time he could not avoid giving his name. "Tree, Madame Kunst. You see, I have been told who you are. I'm James Emmerson Tree. I've been in France a little more than a year."

"So long, with the war and all." She waited patiently for him to answer.

"Reporters go where the story is, and this is the biggest story around," he said with a shrug that did not completely conceal his disillusion with his work. "I'd been in France before, in the Twenties, and it made me the logical candidate to come back to cover this." He ran his hand through his hair. "You'll have to forgive me, Madame Kunst. I must be disconcerting company. These clothes aren't the latest, I haven't done anything much about my hair or shaving, but don't be alarmed." He touched his chin tentatively and felt a slight roughness, as if he had shaved the evening before.

"We do what we can in these times," she said, trying to appear at her best. "I have two dresses, and the other is worse than this one."

There was a tap at the door, and then Roger entered. "Excuse me, Madame Kunst, but if you are finished with your tea, I will remove the tray for you."

"Yes, I am, thank you," she replied, a trifle more grandly than she had addressed James. "It was very good."

"There will be a supper in two or three hours. Served in the breakfast room, as it is easiest to heat." He picked up the tray and started toward the door. "Mister Tree, le Comte would appreciate it if you could spare him a moment of your time."

James scowled. "When?"

"At your convenience. In the next two hours, perhaps?" He gave a little bow and left the room.

"My aunt had a butler like that, years ago," Madame Kunst said wistfully when Roger had gone.

"He's very efficient," James admitted grudgingly, deciding that Roger was a bit too efficient.

"Servants aren't like that any more." She smoothed the skirt of her dress and looked over at James. "How did you find the situation in France? When you arrived?"

"Chaotic," James answered. "It's apparent that this war has taken a dreadful toll on the country."

"On all Europe," Madame Kunst corrected him.

"Sure. But I've been covering France, and this is where I've had to look for the damage, the ruin and the destruction. I've heard about conditions in Russia, and I'm appalled. Italy is supposed to be having very bad troubles, and the Netherlands and Scandinavia are suffering, too, but France, in many ways, is taking the brunt of it. When I was in London, I was shocked, but when I came to France, I was horrified." He sensed that he was talking too much, but was no longer able to stop himself. "The First World War was ruinous, but this is something a lot worse. And the rumors we keep hearing make it all sound more awful than we think it is. There's nothing as bad as trench warfare going on, and no mounted cavalry against tanks, as there was before, but the cities are burning, and the country is laid waste, and there doesn't seem to be any end in sight. What can anyone think? It can't go on endlessly, but there is no way to end it."

"At home, we all pray that it will end," she said softly, her large brown eyes turned appealingly toward him. "Don't you think the Americans could do something? If your president would insist that we stop, all of us, at once, then it could not go on. Without the Americans, the British and the French could not continue this insanity."

"The Americans don't see it that way, Madame Kunst," James said rather stiffly, feeling disturbed by her afresh.

"But what are we to do, if it goes on and on? Everyone in my family is dead but myself, and no one cares that this is the case. Down the street from where my family lived, there is a widow who has lost four sons, all of them flyers, killed in air battles. She is like a ghost in her house. And there are hundreds, thousands like her."

"As there are in France and Italy and England and Holland, Madame Kunst. As there are in Chicago and Montreal and Honolulu." He got up. "Excuse me, but it might be best if I talk to le Comte now, rather than later."

Her face changed. "Have I offended you? Please, don't think me heartless, or uncaring of the sufferings of others. That is why I spoke to you about a resolution to this terrible war, so that there need not be such women ever again."

"I'm not offended," James said, knowing that he was and was uncertain why. As he left the room, he passed near her chair, and for one moment, he was caught and held by the sound of her pulse.

"She gave me a lecture on pacifism," James said at last when Saint-Germain had asked him for a third time what he and Madame Kunst had found to talk about. "She wants me to end the war so no more widows will lose sons. God knows, I don't want to see any more deaths, but what's the alternative?"

"Capitulation?" Saint-Germain suggested.

"Oh, no. You've seen the way the Germans have treated every foot of land they've taken. And they say there's worse things going on. One of the Dutch reporters said that there were cattle cars full of people being taken away. If they're doing that in Germany to Germans, what would they do to the rest of us?" He gestured once. "That could be propaganda about the cattle cars, but if it isn't . . ."

"I do see your point, Mister Tree. I am not convinced that you see mine. Montalia is isolated and splendidly defensible. A person here, or in one of the houses in, shall we say, a ten-kilometer radius, with a radio receiver and a reasonable amount of prudence, might provide the Germans with extremely useful information." He watched James as he said this, expecting an argument.

"But what good would it be?" James objected, taking his favorite role of Devil's Advocate. "You said yourself that the chateau is isolated, and God knows, this part of Provence is damned remote. What could anyone find out here? There's nothing very strategic in your ten-kilometer radius unless you think that they're going to start last-ditch battles for the smaller passes."

"We're very close to Switzerland. As many secrets as gold are brokered through Geneva and Zurich. With a listening post here, a great deal could be learned." Saint-Germain raised one shoulder. "I may be feinting at shadows, but it worries me."

"If they want a listening post for Switzerland, why not in Switzerland?" James asked.

"The Swiss take a dim view of the abuse of their neutrality. Certainly there are monitoring posts in Bavaria and Austria, but it is not as easy to watch Geneva and Lausanne. The Resistance have found men and women doing espionage work in these mountains before. Last year, it was a gentleman claiming to be a naturalist hoping to preserve a particular bird; he climbed all over the mountains, and stayed in the old monastery on the next ridge. He might have accomplished his task, whatever it was, if one of the Resistance men did not become suspicious when he saw the supposed naturalist walk by a nest of the bird in question without a second look. It may be that Madame Kunst is nothing more than an Austrian refugee in a panic, but I am not going to assume anything until she has shown me I have no reason to be concerned."

James chuckled. "And where do you fit into this?"

"I don't want to fit into it at all," was Saint-Germain's short rejoinder. "War ceased to amuse me millen . . . years ago." He shook his head. "Apparently you haven't considered our position. We are both foreigners in a country at war. If we are imprisoned, which could happen—it has happened before—our particular needs would make a prolonged stay . . . difficult." He recalled several of the times he had been confined, and each brought its own burden of revulsion. "You would not like prison, Mister Tree."

"I wouldn't like it in any case," James said at once. "I knew a reporter who was shot by the Spanish for trying to file an uncensored story. He'd done it before, and they caught him trying the same thing again."

Saint-Germain lifted his head, and listened. "Ah. That will be Mirelle. We will continue this at a later time, Mister Tree."

"What?" James cried, remembering the woman's name all too clearly. Now he, too, could hear an approaching automobile.

"You do have need of her, Mister Tree," Saint-Germain said quietly. "More than you know now."

James came off the sofa to round on le Comte. "It's monstrous. I've gone along with some of what you've told me, but I draw the line at this!"

"Perhaps you should wait until you have a better idea of what 'this' is," Saint-Germain said, a touch of his wry humor returning. "She is looking forward to this evening. It would be sad if you were to disappoint her."

"Come on," James protested.

This time, when Saint-Germain spoke, his voice was low and his eyes compassionate. "Mister Tree, you will have to learn sometime, and we haven't the luxury of leisure. Mirelle wants to have the pleasure of taking your vampiric virginity, and you would do well to agree. We are rarely so fortunate in our first . . . experiences. You will spare yourself a great deal of unpleasantness if you will set aside your worry and pride long enough to lie with her. Believe this."

"But . . ." James began, then stopped. He could feel his hunger coiled within him, and he knew without doubt that it was hearing the beat of Madame Kunst's heart that had sharpened it. "Okay, I'll try. If nothing else," he went on with a poor attempt at jauntiness, "I'll get a good lay."

Saint-Germain's brows rose. "It is essential that she have the . . . good lay. Otherwise you will have nothing, Mister Tree. Males of our blood are like this." He was about to go on when there was a quick, emphatic step in the hall and the door was flung open.

Mirelle Bec was thirty-four, firm-bodied and comfortably voluptuous. She did not so much enter the room as burst into it with profligate vitality. Drab clothes and lack of cosmetics could not disguise her sensuality. Her hair was a dark cloud around a pert face that was more exciting than pretty, and when she spoke, it was in rapid, enthusiastic bursts. "Comte!" she called out and hastened across the room to fling her arms around him. "You've kept away so long, I ought to be annoyed with you, but I could never do that."

Saint-Germain kissed her cheek affectionately. "I have missed seeing you too, Mirelle."

As she disengaged herself from his embrace, she pointed dramatically at James. "Is this the baby? Comte, you are a bad, bad man: you did not tell me he was so beautiful." To James' embarrassment, Mirelle gave him a thorough and very appraising looking-over. "Oh, this is very promising," she declared as she approached him. "I do like the white hair. It is distinguished, is it not?" As James tried not to squirm, she laughed aloud and reached for his hand. "You are shy? But how delightful." Over her shoulder she added to Saint-Germain, "How good of you to offer him to me. I am going to enjoy myself tremendously."

"But, Madame, we . . ." James said in confusion, trying to find some way to deal with her.

"Have not been introduced, is that what concerns you? I am Mirelle, and you, I have been told, are James. So. We are introduced now. It remains only for you to show me which room is yours."

James had had experience with many women, but this one took him wholly aback. Yet even as he tried to separate himself from her, he felt the draw of her, and his much-denied hunger responded to her. "Madame . . ."

"No, no, no. *Mirelle*. You are James. I am Mirelle. It is more friendly that way, is it not?" She drew his arm through hers. "You will tell me how you come to be here as we walk to your room."

"I am not sure that . . ." James began with a look of mute appeal to Saint-Germain which he studiously avoided.

"But I am. Let us go, James." She waved to le Comte and went quickly to the door, taking the ambivalent James with her.

"Christ, I'm sorry," James muttered some time later. They were in a glorious tangle on his bed with the covers in complete disarray. "If you give me a little time, Mirelle. I must be more worn out than I knew."

Mirelle gave a sympathetic laugh. "It is not fatigue, James, it is what you are." She trailed her fingers over his chest. "Weren't you told?"

"I've been told all kinds of things the last couple days," he sighed in disgust.

"But this, this is different," Mirelle said generously. "For a man, this is more important, is it not?" She snuggled closer to him, pressing her body to his. "It is not the same when one changes. But there are compensations."

"For this? I've never been impotent before," James said, a note of distress creeping into his voice.

"It is not impotent," Mirelle assured him. "You are more than ready to make love to me, yes? And you are not repelled by me. So this is another matter."

"You don't know what it is that I . . . almost did." He felt suddenly miserable; he wanted to shut out the drumming of her heart that was loud as heavy machinery in his ears.

Mirelle laughed deeply. "But of course I know what you almost did. You are the same as le Comte. You wanted to put your lips to my neck and taste . . ."

"For God's sake!" James interrupted her, trying to move away from her but not succeeding.

"Well," Mirelle said reasonably, "it is what I expected of you. But you have not entirely got the way of it. You are judging yourself by your earlier standards, and they do not apply, my cabbage."

James rolled onto his side and rested his hand on the rise of Mirelle's hip. "Look, you're being very nice about this, and I appreciate it, but . . ." He wanted to shrug the incident off, to promise her another hour when he was feeling a bit better, but he could not find a gracious way to do so. He loved the feel of her skin under his hand and her nearness was oddly intoxicating, so that he could not bring himself to leave the bed or ask her to leave it.

"You are discouraged, but you need not be, James. You have not got used to your new ways. You don't have to worry. Let me show you. I love showing." Her hazel eyes took on a greenish shine of mischief. "You must learn how to satisfy me. It is not too difficult, *ami*, and when it is done, you will do well enough for yourself." She wriggled expertly. "Now, your hand there, if you please. That is a good beginning."

Dazed, James did as he was told, letting her instruct him as if he were a boy of fourteen. At first he could not get the memory of the long nights with Madelaine out of his thoughts, but then, as his passion grew in answer to Mirelle's, he responded to her, and only to her, and this time, though he did not love her as he had supposed he would, he had no reason to apologize.

Roger escorted Madame Kunst to her room, and listened quietly to her protestations that she was reluctant to remain at Montalia. "I have those I wish to meet. It isn't wise for me to remain here."

"But there is fighting, Madame, and you would not be safe, should you venture out into the world as it is now." Roger had received Saint-Germain's instructions several hours before to be solicitous of the Austrian woman.

"They said that there would be a boat at Nice that would take me to Scotland. I must reach that boat. I must."

"My master will make inquiries on your behalf, Madame. It would not be pleasant for you to suffer any more mishaps." Roger was unfailingly polite and slightly deferent, but gave no indication that he would accommodate her.

"He has some influence, this Comte? Could he help me?" Her voice pleaded but her wary eyes were hard.

"That is for him to decide, Madame Kunst. I will mention what you have told me." The hallway was dark where the glow of the lantern did not shine. "You have enough candles in your room?"

"There are plenty, thank you," she answered abruptly. Again she grasped the handle. "I must leave. I must go to Scotland. Can you explain that?"

"I will tell my master what you have said."

Her hands came up to her chin in fists. "Oh, you stupid man!" she shouted in her frustration, and then was at once quiet and restrained. "Forgive me. I must be more . . . tired than I realize."

"Of course, Madame Kunst." He lifted the lantern higher. "You can see your way?"

She did not entirely take the hint. "That woman," she said as she paused on the threshold. "I suppose she is necessary?"

Roger gave her no response whatever and there was a subtle sternness about his mouth that indicated he would not indulge in speculation about his master or Mirelle Bec.

"Well, such things happen, I suppose." She gave a polite shrug to show it made no difference to her if those in the house wanted to be immoral. "The highborn live by their own rules, do they not?"

"Good night, Madame Kunst," Roger said, and stepped back from her doorway. When he was satisfied that the door was firmly closed, he turned away from it and made his way back toward the sitting room where he knew that Saint-Germain waited for him. His sandy head was bent in thought and his face was not readable.

Shortly before sunrise, Saint-Germain found James walking in the overgrown garden. He came up to the American silently and fell into step beside him, letting James choose the path they were to take.

"She showed me," James said after a long while.

"Ah."

Their feet as they walked crunched on the unraked gravel that led between the abandoned flower beds. James reached out and pulled a cluster of dried, faded blossoms off a trailing branch as it brushed his shoulder. "It wasn't what I expected." The paper-crisp husks of the flowers ran between his fingers and fell.

"But tolerable?" Saint-Germain inquired as if they were discussing nothing more important than the temperature of bath water.

"Oh, yeah. Tolerable." He laughed once, self-consciously. "Tolerable."

Saint-Germain continued his unhurried stroll, but pointed out that the sun would be up in half an hour. "You are not used to the sun yet, Mister Tree. Until you are, it might be wisest to spend the day indoors, if not asleep."

"Unhuh." He turned back toward the chateau, saying with some awkwardness, "Mirelle told me she'd be back in three or four days. But she didn't . . . Oh, Christ! This is difficult."

"She will be here for you, Mister Tree. My need is not great just now." He answered the unasked question easily, and sensed James' relief.

"That's what she hinted." James looked sharply at the shorter man. "Why? Is it because you're after that Austrian woman?"

"What an appalling notion! No, of course I'm not." He expressed his indignation lightly, but decided he had better explain. "Oh, if I were determined to . . . use her, I could wait until she was asleep and visit her then, and she would remember little more than a very pleasant dream. It is something we all learn to do in time, and it has its advantages upon occasion. But Madame Kunst is a bit of a puzzle. Her purpose for being here is not known to me, and it would not be sensible or wise to . . . be close to her. If she learned or guessed what I am, and wished me ill, she would have me at a distinct disadvantage. The Resistance might not mind taking off time from hunting Nazis and Nazi sympathizers to hunt a more old-fashioned menace. You must not forget that is how most of the world sees us—as menaces. I would not like to have to leave Montalia precipitately just now." There had been many times in the past when he had had to take sudden flight in order to save himself: it was not a thing he wished to do again. "We must be circumspect, James."

This was the first time Saint-Germain had addressed him by his Christian name, and it startled him. "Why do you call me James? Is it because of Mirelle?"

"Don't be absurd." Saint-Germain's wry smile was clear in the advancing light.

"You've been calling me Mister Tree since I arrived here." The tone of his statement was stubborn and James was plainly waiting for an answer.

"And you have not been calling me anything at all," was Saint-Germain's mild reply.

James faltered. "It's that . . . I don't know what to call you."

"Is it?" Saint-Germain gestured toward the side door that led into the pantry. "This is the quickest way."

As James was about to go in, there came the drone of planes overhead. He looked up, searching the sky, and at last, off to the north, saw a formation of shapes headed west. "I can't tell whose they are," he said quietly.

"American or British bombers back from their nighttime raids. They keep to the south of Paris for reasons of caution." He held the door for James.

"This far south?" James wondered aloud, already stepping into the shadow of the doorway.

"It is possible, James. They have done it before. You have been here very little time and until last night, you were not paying much attention to the world around you." There was no rebuke in what he said, and he felt none.

"True enough," James allowed, and waited while Saint-Germain closed the door behind them and latched it. "Why bother?"

"The crofters around here are very insular, careful folk, like all French peasants. They respect and admire Madelaine because she is the Seigneur. Don't look so surprised, Mister Tree. Surely you can understand this. The peasants are proud of their estate and they are protective of Montalia. Most of them think it is a great misfortune that the lines have passed through females for so long, but that makes them all the more determined to guard Madelaine. They know what she does—or part of it. They would beat their daughters senseless for taking lovers, but the Seigneurs are different, and her adventures provide them endless entertainment."

They had come into the kitchen where Roger was cutting up a freshly killed chicken. He looked up from his task and regarded the two men quizzically. "I didn't know you were outside."

"James was taking the air, and I was coming back from checking the gatehouse," Saint-Germain said. "You might want to purchase some eggs from the Widow Saejean. Her boy told Mirelle that times are hard for them just now."

Roger nodded. "This afternoon." He bent and sniffed the chicken. "They're not able to feed them as well as they did."

"We could purchase a few of our own, if that would help," Saint-Germain suggested, but Roger shook his head.

"Better to buy them. If we bring chickens here, we won't be able to feed them much better than the rest do, and they would resent it. We are still the foreigners, and it would not take much to have them remember it." He began to cut up the bird with a long chef's knife, letting the weight of the blade do much of the work.

"About Madame Kunst . . ." Saint-Germain prompted.

"Nothing more, my master. I have not been able to touch her valise, which is locked in any case. But I do know that it is heavy, heavier than it ought to be, considering her story." Roger looked down at the chicken parts and smiled.

"Very good." Saint-Germain motioned to the American. "Come, James. Let's permit Roger to enjoy his breakfast in peace." He indicated the passage toward the main hall and waited for James to accompany him.

Once they were out of the kitchen, James said, "I don't mean to sound stupid, but I thought Roger was . . ."

"A vampire?" Saint-Germain finished for him. "No."

Apparently needing to explain himself, James went on. "It's only that you seem to be so . . . used to each other."

Saint-Germain turned toward the front reception room where tall windows gave a view of the rising mountains behind the promontory where Montalia sat. "I did not say that he is . . . unchanged, simply that he is not a vampire. Do sit down, if you wish, and be at ease. No," Saint-Germain said, resuming his topic, "Roger is not like us, but he has died and recovered from it. You were right; we are old friends. We met some time ago in Rome."

"If he's died and . . . what is he?" James knew that he ought to be bothered by these revelations, or to admit he was in the company of madmen, but after his night with Mirelle, he could not bring himself to accuse Saint-Germain of anything.

"He is a ghoul," Saint-Germain responded matter-of-factly. He saw James blink. "Don't imagine him back there tearing that poor fowl's carcass to bits with his teeth. There is no reason for it. He eats neatly because it is easier and more pleasant. The only restriction his state imposes on him is that the meat—for he only eats meat—be fresh-killed and raw."

James shuddered and looked away. "I see."

"I'm not certain of that," Saint-Germain said quietly.

Eager to change the subject, James asked, "Why was he trying to look at Madame Kunst's valise?"

"Because she guards it so zealously," he answered at once. "I am curious about a woman who says that she avoided arrest by being out shopping when the rest of her family were taken, and yet carries a large valise. Did she take it shopping with her? Then for what was she shopping? If she picked it up later, why that bag, rather than another? She says that she has three changes of clothes. Good. But where did they come from? Did she buy a dress while shopping, and take it with her when she fled? Did she buy it later? If Roger says that the valise is heavy, then you may believe him. In that case, what is in it?"

"Maybe she went back to her house and grabbed the only valise she could find, stuffed clothes into it, and something of value, say, silver candlesticks, so that she could pay for her passage. She wants to go to Scotland, and I don't know if it would be safe to pay for her trip in marks." James turned the questions over in his mind as he answered, enjoying the process. "What if she got as far as Zurich, had to buy some clothes, but could only afford to buy a cheap valise? If she'd gone to the train . . ."

"And where did she get her travel permit?" Saint-Germain inquired evenly. "Whether she is going to Scotland or Poland, she would have to have the proper papers, or she would not be able to get a ticket, let alone come this far."

"But if she didn't come by train? If she had a car . . ." He thought this over. "She would require proper documents to get over the border, that's true, and if her family was arrested, her name would probably be on a detain list."

"Yes. And where does that leave Madame Kunst?" With a shake of his head, Saint-Germain drew up a chair. "You are a journalist, James, and you are used to examining persons and facts. If the occasion should arise, and you are able to draw out Madame Kunst, I would appreciate your evaluation. Don't force the issue, of course, because I don't want her alarmed. If she is truly nothing more than a refugee determined, for reasons best known to herself, to get to Scotland, it would be a shame to cause her any more anguish. If she is not that, it would be foolish to put her on her guard."

"Are you always such a suspicious bastard?" James asked with increased respect.

"I am not suspicious at all. If I were, I should not have allowed her to come here. But I have seen enough treachery in my . . . life to wish to avoid it." He studied the tall American. "You would do well to develop a similar attitude, James. It spares us much inconvenience."

James gave this a reserved acceptance, then inquired, "What if she is an agent? What will you do then?"

"Inform the Resistance leaders. Yes, there are ways I can do this, and I will if it is necessary. I hope that it is not; I do not want to live under constant surveillance, as I have told you before." He got up. "I have a few tasks to attend to. If you will excuse me?"

As he started toward the door, James called after him. "What tasks?"

Saint-Germain paused. "I like to spend some time in my laboratory each day. It's a bit makeshift, but better than nothing."

"Laboratory? What do you do there?" James was somewhat intrigued, for although he had no great interest in scientific experimentation, he was curious about how Saint-Germain occupied his time.

"I make gold, of course." With James' indulgent laughter ringing in his ears, Saint-Germain left the reception room.

That afternoon James discovered Madame Kunst to be a fairly good, if impatient, card player. They had begun with cribbage and had graduated to whist. As Madame Kunst put down her cards, she said, "After I have my supper, let us play another rubber. You have some skill, it seems."

James, who was used to thinking of himself as a very good card player, was piqued by her comment. "Perhaps, after you have your meal, I will have forgotten my good manners, Madame."

She smiled widely and insincerely. "I do not believe that you have been deliberately allowing me to win—you aren't that shrewd in your bidding, for one thing." She looked around the room. "It is getting dark. How unfortunate that there are no electric lights here."

"But there are," James said impulsively, remembering Madelaine's pride at having them. "There is not enough gas to run the generator to power them. If the cars are going to be driven, it must be kerosene and candles here."

"But there is a generator? Curious." She smiled at James. "Have you seen this chateau when it is alight?"

"Yes," James said, not entirely sure now that he should have told her about the generator. But where was the harm, he asked himself, when a quick inspection of the old stables would reveal the generator, and the allotted fuel for Montalia?

"It must be quite impressive," Madame Kunst said quietly. She was wearing one of her two dresses, an elegantly knitted creation of salmon pink with a scalloped hem and long full sleeves. There were travel stains on the skirt and it would have been the better for cleaning and blocking. Madame Kunst fidgeted with the belt, putting her fingers through the two loops at either side of the waist. It was much more a nervous than a provocative gesture, but James could comprehend that in a lanky, high-strung way she might be attractive.

"It is," he said, taking the deck and shuffling it methodically. "After your meal, we can try again."

"Are you not going to join me?" she asked him.

"No, thank you." Then he recalled what Madelaine had said to him the first time he had dined at Montalia, and he paraphrased her words. "I have a condition which severely restricts my diet. It's simpler for me to make private arrangements for my meals."

"This is the oddest household. Roger tells me that le Comte dines privately in his rooms; you have a . . . condition. If it were fitting, I would suggest to Roger that we both eat in the kitchen, but he won't hear of it." She gave a tittery laugh, then left the room.

James shuffled the cards two more times, taking time and care, then put them back in their ivory box. That done, he rose and sauntered out into the hallway, pleased to see that no one was about. Five careful minutes later, he was in Madame Kunst's room, tugging the valise from under her bed. He knelt on the floor, holding the leather case between his knees while he inspected the lock that held it closed. The valise was not unlike a large briefcase, with accordion sides and a metal reinforced opening. The lock most certainly required a special key, but James thought he might be able to make some progress against it with a bent hairpin, if he could find one. He was so preoccupied that he did not hear the door open.

"You arrant fool," Saint-Germain said quietly but with intense feeling.

James started up, and the valise fell heavily onto its side. "You said . . ."

"I said that you might try to draw her out when talking with her: I did not recommend you do this." He shook his head. "I might as well scribble all over the walls that we have our doubts about her. Good God, if I had wanted the lock picked, I could do that myself. Use a little sense, James."

James' indignation was all the greater for the disquieting suspicion that Saint-Germain was right. "I thought I was taking your hint."

"After all I told you about prudence? Truly?" He bent down and very carefully put the valise back under the bed. "If it reassures you. James, I have examined the lock already, but under less questionable circumstances. It is not as simple as it looks. Not only is there the lock you see, there is a second lock under it, and it is a good deal more complex."

"How complex?" James inquired acidly.

"It takes two keys. I am not sure why, but it does give me pause." He was already crossing the room. "We should leave. Madame Kunst sat down to her supper not long ago, but there is no reason for her to linger over the food. She may come back here shortly, and I doubt either of us could adequately explain what we are doing here."

Grudgingly, James permitted Saint-Germain to take him from the room, but as they started down the long stairs, he made one protest. "Why don't you just break into the valise and tell her that you were required to do it?"

"James, for an intelligent man, you suffer from curious lapses. Why would I do that? What excuse would she believe? And where would be the benefit?" His brows arched and he let James take whatever time he needed to answer the questions.

"Well," James said lamely as they reached the main floor again, "you would know what is in the valise."

"True enough. But do you know, I would rather find out some less compromising way." He frowned, then the frown faded. "I don't fault you for wanting the question resolved: so do I."

James accepted this with ill grace. "You aren't willing to do the obvious, so . . ."

"Do the obvious? It is not quite my style," he said sardonically. "James, play cards with the woman, listen to her, and make note of what she asks you. Tomorrow morning, I will tell her I have arranged for her transportation down the mountain so that she can reach Nice and the boat she says she wishes to take to Scotland. That should precipitate matters."

"And what if that is what she wants, and all she wants?" James asked.

"Then Roger will do it. He has arranged with the authorities in Saint-Jacques-sur-Crete to have a travel pass when it is necessary. In these matters the local officials are strangely flexible." He put one hand on James' arm. "Try to restrain your impulses until then, if you will. Should it turn out that we come through this with nothing more than a touch of war-time paranoia, we may count ourselves fortunate."

James had nothing to say in response, and knew he was not very much looking forward to another round of losing at whist, but he offered no protest as he went back into the room to wait for Madame Kunst.

"Oh, thank you, Herr Comte," Madame Kunst said listlessly over a cup of weak tea the following morning.

"It was nothing, Madame. You told me that this was your wish. I only regret that it took so long to arrange the details. But surely you understand."

"Yes, of course I do." She paused to cough delicately. "I am surprised that you were able to accomplish this so quickly. After what I have been through, I expected I would have to intrude on your hospitality"—again a quiet, emphatic cough—"for a much longer time."

"It is best to act quickly in cases such as yours," Saint-Germain said ambiguously.

"How kind," she murmured, and achieved another cough.

"Is something the matter, Madame Kunst?" le Comte inquired politely, giving in.

"A slight indisposition, nothing more, I am sure." She smiled apologetically.

"Good. I would not like to think that you were ill." He rose from the chair he had taken across from her.

"Oh, I don't believe I'm that. My throat, you know. And it has been chilly." She said this last in a tone a bit more hoarse than when she had begun.

"It is often the case in the mountains," Saint-Germain said by way of courteous commiseration. "I believe there is aspirin in the chateau, but little else. If you like, I will ask Roger to bring you some."

Her hand fluttered up to her throat, lingered there artistically, then dropped once more. "I don't think it will be necessary. If I am troubled by it still this afternoon, then I might ask for one or two tablets."

"Very good. You may want to rest an hour or so. The drive to the coast is long and fatiguing." He left the room to the dry sound of her cough.

"She claims to be feeling poorly," Roger explained to Saint-Germain later that morning. "I brought her the tea she asked for and said that I was looking forward to taking her down to Nice. She claimed to be enthusiastic, but said she did not think she was entirely well, and did not know how easily she would travel."

"She coughed for me," Saint-Germain said. "Apparently she is not as eager as she claimed to be."

"Give her a break," James protested, watching the other two. "Maybe she's got a cold. She's been through enough."

"No matter what she has done, it's possible, of course, that she has caught a cold," Saint-Germain allowed. "But if you were as anxious as she has professed to be out of this country and on your way to Scotland, would you permit a cold to keep you from completing your journey?"

"She might be worn out," James said, determined to discount anything Saint-Germain suggested. "If she's tired enough, she might not be able to fight off a cold or any other bug that happens to be around."

Saint-Germain's dark eyes were wryly amused. "Is that what you thought when you tried to search her valise? Never mind, James. We'll find out shortly what the case truly is."

"How're you planning to do that?" He was a little belligerent and huffy.

"Why, I want to find out if she is really ill. I will offer her a remedy. If she takes it, I'll give her the benefit of the doubt. If she doesn't, then I will be extremely careful with her. As you should be." He turned away toward the old wing where he had set up his laboratory. "And James, if you would not mind, I would like to begin this myself. You may talk to her later, if you choose, but just at first, let me."

"You sound like you think I'd warn her . . ." James shot back. "I didn't get to be good at my job by shooting off my mouth."

"I am aware of that," Saint-Germain said. "But you have gallantry, my American friend, and there are those who have a way of turning that virtue to their advantage. All I ask is that you remember that."

Roger intervened before James could say anything more. "Should I get the Bugatti ready?"

"Yes. Whether Madame Kunst uses it, or one of us, it doesn't matter: the car should be fueled, and ready."

"You're anticipating some difficulty other than this?" James asked, looking about him involuntarily.

"Nothing specific, but in as unsettled a situation as we are in, it might be best." Saint-Germain gave James a penetrating, amused glance. "Do you wish to visit our patient in half an hour or so, to wish her godspeed?"

"Do you want me to?" James sounded irritable, but it was more from frustration at his own inactivity than genuine anger.

"Let us see how she responds to Roger." He motioned toward his manservant. "And to me."

James accepted this with a shrug, and went off to the old library to pass the better part of the morning in trying to decipher the medieval French of the oldest volumes there. He found it intriguing and it kept him from pacing the halls like a stalking tiger.

"How are you doing, Madame Kunst?" Saint-Germain inquired of his guest as he went into her room twenty minutes after his conversation with Roger and James.

"Very well," she said listlessly.

"I trust so; the travel permit I have been able to secure for you is dated only for the next twenty-four hours. It would not be easy to get another one." He came to stand at the foot of her bed. "I can arrange for you to stop at the physician's, perhaps, but you might not wish to be subjected to the questions he is required to ask."

Madame Kunst turned blush rather than pale. "I want to keep away from officials."

"And so you shall. It is better for me, as well, to come as little to their attention as possible. Then, if it is satisfactory to you, I will make sure you have aspirin and brandy and plenty of lap rugs in the Bugatti. It will not make you entirely comfortable, but you probably will not be so until you are in Scotland." He gave her a sympathetic half-smile, and watched her face.

"Yes," Madame Kunst said, her brows twitching into an expression of impatience and dissatisfaction.

Saint-Germain assumed an expression of diffidence. "My manservant has reminded me that there is another medication in the chateau. It is . . . an herbal remedy, and very efficacious, or so I have been told. I would be pleased to bring some to you." He had made that particular elixir for more than three thousand years: it was a clear distillate that began with a solution prepared from moldy bread. The recent discovery of penicillin had amused him.

Madame Kunst looked flustered. "A peasant remedy? I don't know . . . peasants are so superstitious and some of their practices are . . . well, unpleasant."

Very gently, Saint-Germain said, "In your position, Madame Kunst, I would think you would take that chance, if only to make your ship. Brandy is a help, but you will not be clearheaded. With the herbal remedy, you need not be fuddled."

She slapped her hands down on the comforter. "But what if the remedy is worse? Some of those remedies the monks made were mostly pure spirits with a little herbal additive. This is probably more of the same thing."

"I assure you, it is not," Saint-Germain said.

"Oh, I don't know. I will have to think about it." She remembered to cough. "I have to have time to recruit my strength, Herr Comte. I will tell you in an hour or so what I have decided." With a degree of quiet malice, she added, "It was so good of you to offer this to me." Saint-Germain bowed and left the room.

Slightly less than an hour after this, James came bursting out of Madame Kunst's room, running down the corridor, calling for Saint-Germain.

The response was almost immediate. Saint-Germain hastened from his laboratory as he tugged his lab coat off, wishing there were a way he could curb some of James' impetuosity. "A moment!" he cried as he reached the foot of the main staircase.

"We don't have a moment!" James shouted as he came into view on the upper floor. "It's urgent."

"So I gather," Saint-Germain said as he flung his wadded-up lab coat away from him. "But if it is, it might be best not to announce it to the world."

"Jesus! I forgot." He paused at the top of the stairs, then raced down them. "I don't know why it didn't occur to me. It should have."

"We will discuss it later," Saint-Germain said. "Now, what has you so up in arms?"

"Madame Kunst." He opened up his hands. "She's not in her room and her valise is gone."

"Indeed." Saint-Germain's brows rose and he nodded grimly.

"I went to her room, as you instructed, and it was empty. The bed was still a bit warm, so she can't have gone far, or have left too long ago. If we hurry, we can find her." Now that he had forced himself to be calm, all his old journalistic habits came back. "If she's carrying that thing, she'll have to stay on the road, and that means someone will see her, if only a farmer or a shepherd."

"You're assuming she's left Montalia," Saint-Germain said. "I doubt that she has."

"Why?" James demanded.

"Because Roger is down at the gatehouse and he has not signaled me that he has seen her. Not that that makes it simpler," he added dryly. "This place is a rabbit warren and it is not easily searched."

"Especially since we don't know what we're looking for, right?" James said, running one hand through his silver hair.

"That is a factor." Saint-Germain looked up toward the ceiling. "But we also know what we are not looking for, which is a minor advantage." He turned away from James, his eyes on the heavy, metal-banded door to the old wing of the chateau. "I think she may be armed, James. Be cautious with her. Bullet wounds are painful, and if they damage the spine or skull, they are as fatal to us as anyone else. No heroics, if you please. Madelaine would never forgive me."

James did not quite know how to take this, but he shrugged. "If that's how you want it, that's how I'll do it."

"Very good," Saint-Germain said crisply. "And we might as well begin now. First the kitchens and pantry, and then the old wing. With this precaution." He went and dropped the heavy bolt into place on the iron-banded door, effectively locking that part of the chateau.

"Why the kitchens first?" James asked.

"Because of the weapons it offers," Saint-Germain answered. "Knives, cleavers, forks, skewers, pokers. A kitchen is an armory on a smaller scale. If she has gone there, it will be touchy for us."

They completed their search in fifteen minutes and were satisfied that wherever Madame Kunst was, she had not been there.

"This might not bode well. If she has panicked—which isn't likely—it is merely a matter of finding her. But if she is acting with deliberation, it means she is already prepared and we must keep that in mind."

"Does she know we're looking for her, do you think?"

"Quite possibly. That is something else to keep in mind." He was walking back toward the main hall and the barred door. "This may be somewhat more difficult. We can close off the wing, but it provides endless places to hide, to ambush."

"Great," James said with hearty sarcasm.

"Although some of the same advantages apply to us. I wish I knew what it was she is trying to do. If I did, then I could counteract it more effectively." His hand was resting on the heavy bolt.

"And you won't call the authorities," James said.

"We've had this discussion already. You know the answer. We must settle this for ourselves. And for Madelaine, since she is the one who will have to live here when this is over." He let James consider this. "You and I are transient. This is her native earth."

"Okay, okay," James said, then waved a hand at the door. "What do we do, once we get in there?"

"To begin with, we move very quietly. And we make every effort not to frighten her. Frightened people do foolish and dangerous things." He lifted the bolt and drew back the door. "For the moment, keep behind me, James. If you see or hear anything, tap my shoulder. Don't speak."

"Right," James said, feeling a bit silly. He had seen war and knew how great the risks were for those caught up in the deadly game, but skulking around the halls of an old chateau after a woman with a worn leather valise seemed like acting out a Grade-B movie from Universal. When the door was pulled closed behind him, he was disturbed by it. The hall was very dark, with five narrow shafts of light coming from the high, notched windows. James watched Saint-Germain start toward the muniment room, and for the first time noticed the power and grace of his movements—he was controlled and feral at once, beautiful and awesome.

At the entrance to the muniment room, Saint-Germain held up his hand to motion James to stillness. He slipped through the narrow opening, then returned several long moments later. "She is not here now, but has been here," Saint-Germain told James in a whisper that was so quiet it was almost wholly inaudible. "One of the old plans of Montalia is missing."

The two rooms below the muniment room were empty and apparently untouched. James was becoming strangely nervous, as if unknown wings had brushed the back of his neck. He found it difficult to be self-contained and was all for hurrying up the search so that he could bring his restlessness back under control. "She's in the upper rooms if she's anywhere in this part of the chateau," James murmured, wanting to speak at a more normal level.

"Patience, James. You and I have much more time than she does." He made a last check around the small salon, then gestured to James to follow him. "We'll try the tower rooms next. Be careful of the steps."

The narrow, circular stairwell was dark at all times, but Saint-Germain carried no light. James was growing accustomed to his improved dark vision, but was still not entirely confident of this to climb without watching his feet. For once, he was the one who lagged.

The first storeroom proved empty, but Saint-Germain indicated that he wanted to make a warning trap. "Nothing complicated; a few things that will make noise if knocked over. Should she be behind us, we will have a little time," he whispered, and set about his work.

James stood on the landing, experiencing the same unpleasant sensation he had had in the lower room. On impulse, he decided to investigate the next room himself, thereby saving them time as well as giving himself the satisfaction of doing something worthwhile. He moved close to the door, as he had seen Saint-Germain do, and then opened the door just wide enough to be able to slip inside. He was dumbfounded at the sight of the valise sitting on the floor amid the other trunks and broken chairs stored there, and was about to call out when he sensed more than felt another presence in the room.

"Not a sound, Herr Tree," Madame Kunst said softly as she brought up a Smith & Wesson .38 pistol. Her hands were expertly steady as she took aim at his head. "I will use this if I must."

Saint-Germain's warning flashed through James' mind—if his nervous system were damaged, if his spine or skull were broken, he would die the true death, and his resurrection would have lasted merely a week—and he stood without moving. He began to dread what might happen if Saint-Germain should come into the room.

"You have been curious about the valise, haven't you? You have all been curious." She no longer looked high-strung and helpless; that part of her had been peeled away, leaving a determined woman of well-honed ruthlessness. "I have promised to see that it is left in working order, and you will not interfere." She nodded toward the valise, her aim never wavering. "Open the valise, Herr Tree."

Slowly, James did as she ordered. He dropped to his knees and pulled open the top of the old leather bag. He stared down at the contraption in it.

"It is a *beacon*, Herr Tree. Take it out—very, very gently—and put it on that brass trunk by the wall, the one under the window. If you trip or jolt the beacon, I will shoot you. Do you understand?"

With more care than he had ever known he possessed, James lifted the beacon. As he carried it toward the trunk she had indicated, he thought to himself that she had told him. Trip or jolt? Not with Madame Kunst's close observation; he put the beacon in place and hoped it was well-balanced.

"Turn around, Herr Tree," she said, softly, venomously.

James obeyed, hoping that she would not shoot in this little narrow room. "I'm not alone."

"Herr Comte?" she asked quickly.

"Yes."

She walked up to him, just far enough to be out of reach. "And the servant?"

"I don't know," James lied, praying she would believe him. "He . . . he was told to get the car ready." He forced himself to speak in an undervoice though he wanted to shout.

"How helpful," she muttered. She glared at him, apparently wanting to make up her mind, and finally, she cocked her head toward the door. "You will have to come with me, I think. You and I."

James all but ground his teeth. He wanted to rush at her, to yell so loudly that she would drop the .38 and flee from him. "Where are we going?" he forced himself to ask.

"Out. After that, we'll see." She was wearing her salmon-colored knit dress that in the muted light of the room looked more the shade of diseased roses. "Walk past me, Herr Tree. Hands joined behind your head." She came nearer to him. "What you feel at the base of your skull is the barrel of my pistol. If you move suddenly or try to grapple with me in any way, I will shoot. If you move your hands, I will shoot. Do I make myself clear?"

"Very."

"You will reach with your left hand, slowly and deliberately, for the door. You will open it as wide as possible and you will release it."

James did as she ordered, and when she told him to walk out onto the landing, he did that, too, as the muzzle of the .38 lay like a cold kiss on the nape of his neck.

"Now, down the stairs. One at a time. Carefully." She was speaking softly still, but the sound of her voice rang down the stones, mocking her.

On the fourth step down, James heard a sound behind him that did not come from Madame Kunst's steps. Apparently she was unaware of it, for she never faltered nor turned. He wondered if she were so confident of her mastery of the situation that she paid no attention to such things. He moved a little faster, trying to remember where the trip stair was.

"Not so fast," Madame Kunst insisted. "It's dark in here."

Obediently, James slowed. He heard the whisper-light tread behind her, and wished he dared to turn. The trip stair was only a few treads below him. He made his way carefully.

Then, just as he passed the trip stair, something tremendously strong swept by him on the narrow curving stair, knocking him to the side and catching Madame Kunst on the most unstable footing in the tower.

She screamed, twisted. She fired once, twice, and the bullets ricocheted off the stone walls, singing and striking sparks where they touched. One of the bullets struck her in the shoulder and she fell, slid and slid, screaming at first and then whimpering. Her descent stopped only when Saint-Germain reached her.

"You may get up, James," he said as he lifted Madame Kunst into his arms.

Moving as if he were tenanted in a body that was unfamiliar to him, James rose, testing his legs like an invalid. When he was shakily on his feet again, he looked down at the other man. "Thank you."

"Thank you, James. Your methods were reckless but your motive laudable." He looked down at Madame Kunst, who was half conscious and moaning. "I should bandage her and get her to a physician. There must be a plausible story we can tell him."

James had not the strength to laugh at this as he came down the stairs.

"But it will arrange itself," Mirelle said confidently with a nonchalant French shrug. "A refugee woman, she says, came to my farmhouse, and I, what could I do but take her in? I did not know that she was carrying valuables, and when there was a commotion, I investigated." Her minx's eyes danced as she looked up at James. "It was very nice of you to give me the pistol, Mister Tree. I would not have been able to defend her if you had not been so generous." She held out her hand for the pistol.

"How do you explain the rest? The beacon and her wound?" Saint-Germain asked, not quite smiling, but with the corners of his mouth starting to lift.

Mirelle gave this her consideration. "I don't think I will explain the beacon. I think I will present it to a few of my friends in the Resistance and they will see what kind of game it attracts. For the rest, the thief was holding Madame . . . Kunst, isn't it? so tightly that I was not in a position to get a clean shot." She sat back in the high-backed chair that was the best in her parlor. "The physician in Saint-Jacques-sur-Crete will not ask me too many questions, because he likes me and he hates the Germans and the war. Beyond that—who knows? The Germans may take her back, the Resistance may kill her. It does not matter so much, does it?" She folded her hands.

"Mirelle," Saint-Germain said, with more sadness than she had ever heard in his voice, "you cannot simply abandon her like so much refuse."

"You say that, after she tried to kill James and would have killed you?" Mirelle shot back at him. "You defend her?"

"Yes," was the quiet answer.

Mirelle got out of her chair and turned her helpless eyes on James, then looked away from them both. "Perhaps you can afford to feel this way, you who live so long and so closely with others. But I am not going to live long, and I have very few years to do all that I must. Extend her your charity, if you must, but do not expect it of me. My time is too brief for that." She folded her arms and stared defiantly at Saint-Germain.

"You have chosen it," Saint-Germain reminded her compassionately; he took her hand and kissed it.

"So I have," she agreed with her impish smile returning. "For the time, I have the best of both, and when that is done, well, we shall see." She turned toward James. "Would you like to remain here for the evening, James?"

"Thank you, Mirelle, but no." He glanced out the window to the parked Bugatti.

"Another time then. I will be at Montalia tomorrow night?" Her eyes went flirtatiously from Saint-Germain's to James' face. "You would like that, yes?"

"Of course," Saint-Germain said, answering for James.

"Then, good afternoon, gentlemen, and I will see you later. I have a few old friends who will want to hear from me, and the physician to mollify." Without any lack of courtesy, she escorted them to the door, and stood waving as the Bugatti pulled away.

James returned the wave, then looked at Saint-Germain. "What will happen to Madame Kunst?"

"I don't know," he said quietly.

"Does it concern you at all?" James was beginning to feel a twinge of guilt.

"Yes. But it is out of my hands now." He drove in silence.

"Just that easy, is it?" James demanded some minutes later when he had been alone with his thoughts.

Saint-Germain's small hands tightened on the steering wheel. "No, James—and it never becomes easy."

BLOOD FREAK

Nancy Holder

New York Times bestselling author Nancy Holder is a five-time winner of the Bram Stoker Award who has also received accolades from the American Library Association, the American Reading Association, the New York Public Library, and *Romantic Times*. She and Debbie Viguié coauthored the witchy Wicked series for Simon and Schuster. They have continued their collaboration with the Crusade (about a worldwide war against vampires) and the Wolf Springs Chronicles werewolf series. Holder is the solo author of the young adult horror series, *Possessions*, for Razorbill. She has also written many novels and book projects tied to various television series—most significantly, in our context, *Buffy the Vampire Slayer* and *Angel*. Among her approximately two hundred short stories, she's written a few featuring vampires. Holder lives in San Diego with her daughter, Belle, and their growing assortment of pets. Visit her at nancyholder.com.

"Blood Freak" takes us back to the psychedelic era of the 1960s when even Dracula got groovy ...

Captain Blood. The Bat Man. He lived in a real castle, that is to say, someone built it to live in, not to film it, in the middle of the Borrego Desert. That is to say, east of San Diego, that Republican bastion of the Military Industrial Complex of Amerika, north of the Mexican border, where you could score lids of grass for five bucks a pop. His craggy, Scottish castle had been in some John Carradine movie, which some people found more trippy than the rumor that the current owner was a vampire.

Blood was his freak. No surprise, Pranksters: because if you traveled the rippling sidewinder desiccation to that *Shock!* Theater on the mesa, you had to have resources, interior (that is to say, gray matter) and exterior (that is to say, eyes and ears) that the average headfeeder either did not have or use very well. So you synthesized; that is to say, you took things in. You figured things out.

You were observant. You grokked the fullness of the situation.

Going to the castle was the Great Bloodfreak Trek, the GBT, and you did it straight enough to drive, stoned enough to take the edge off, beating on the dashboard to the arrhythmic spasms of your carotid artery and the great good muscle that pumped it all together now. You and whatever merry band you had banded with could not help but hear the stories at the gas stations where you copped a pee and the bars where you guzzled whatever was cheapest ("We don't serve no hippies." "Right on, man, we don't eat 'em.") The bourgeoisie crossing themselves like flipped-out movie extras, and cops warning you off the rumble-crunching dirtrock road. Go back, go back, go back, you stupid kids; he really is a fuckin' bloodsucker.

So are mosquitoes, baby. It's all one big mandala. He was out front with it; *he liked to suck people's blood*, and if you pretended not to grok his trip and showed up on his doorstep anyway, that was your bullshit, not his.

Vlad Dracula was no longer certain if he was mesmerized or bored to tears by the antic dances of the counterculture. In the fifties—Kerouac and the beats, bongos, and a fascination with Italy—he had moved from San Francisco with his servants and his Brides and sought refuge in the desert. In San Francisco there had been too much scrutiny, too many questions, and then a woman he had entertained a number of times began writing poetry that she read in coffee shops:

> *He is my biterman, Daddy-o,*
> *he ramthroats my red trickle*
> *down.*

Thus identified, he had fled.

In the desert, he had hibernated for a time, missing the chill and the rain of San Francisco, the cold and the snow of Europe. But he had existed undetected, and kept himself fed, enjoying his homesickness as only someone who is very old can enjoy the sublime delicacy of emotions less intense than grief or despair—wistfulness, nostalgia, the watercolor washes of faint regret. But for him this was a game; he could leave any time he wanted.

Then came the changeling children, with their psychedelica and their excesses that reminded him of the oldest of his old days. The pageantry and drama of his Transylvanian court, the blood baths and virgins and the joy of opulence and extremity. Somehow one confused flower child stumbled to his castle, and then another, and another, until he was the source of a pilgrimage.

His servants begged him to leave, or at least to halt the flow of half-baked mortality. But he found he enjoyed the little hippies not so much for the quality of their company as the fact that they sought him out. They capered and gyrated for his amusement, ate his banquets, made up terrible, overwrought poetry that they loved to recite to him after dinner, and dared one another, in hushed tones, to bare their necks for him, even though he never asked them to. Was he or wasn't he? He never revealed himself, keeping his own counsel and instructing the Brides and his servants to do likewise.

Gradually he came to trust his admirers as he had once trusted his Gypsies. They proved worthy of that trust, if only because no one who could do anything about him listened to their conjectures about the Court of the Crimson King. His most ardent groupies were ineffectual and inarticulate, and therefore, harmless.

For that harmlessness, Dracula pitied them. In their bearded costumes and banshee hair, they whirled and swirled and postured. *I'm so . . . so much, man!* He wondered if they were actually more controlled and controlling than their middle-class comrades who had gotten Beatle cuts and stayed home with their families. Among the scruffy little vagabonds, each stunt, each pronouncement, each thought was scrutinized, analyzed, compared against an unfathomable standard of intellectual prowess they didn't possess and karmic serendipity that did not exit:

I said "red," man, and the Captain walked into the room!

Whoa, heavy! Check it out! You just told me that and he left the room!

He was sorry that there was no such thing as karmic serendipity. It would have made his long life more interesting.

So, like the hundreds of thousands of this time, he turned to drugs. The children took an astonishing variety of drugs: hashish, marijuana, Thai sticks, peyote, mushrooms, and pills of all shapes and sizes. They popped the pills as one might vitamins; they smoked their hemp and hashish like cigarettes, and the rest they cooked with butter and honey and nibbled like Turkish Delight.

But none of it worked on Dracula. He tried everything, smoking and popping and even shooting up as well as sucking the blood of some child who was high or tripping or strung out. Nothing worked.

Nor could they explain to him what it felt like. Mostly they lay on the cold castle floors with the same vacant delirium that accompanied one of his feedings, making trails with their hands and quoting song lyrics. It was a terrible waste to him that the expansion of these inarticulate, unformed minds yielded nothing more than an increased capacity for vacuousness. Whereas he, with his supernatural lifespan and deep connection to the very mythos of this race, possessed a mind worth expanding, and he couldn't do it.

He kept hoping one of them would rise like cream to the top, someone with whom he could explore and converse, that from this one he could learn the secrets of the drug-taker's universe. He continued to encourage their pilgrimages to his castle, their whisperings and invasions of his privacy. (Is he or isn't he? It's so trippy, the man's so *white*!) The young men all wanted to have sexual intercourse with the Brides, and the young girls wanted to have sexual intercourse with him. That was all right; he was into their scene of promiscuity. Breasts and thighs and hips and sex organs, so much writhing flesh brimming with ramthroat red; it was groovy, as they said.

But after a while, it was all only a series of repeat performances, endlessly repeatable. There was not a one among them he would consider Changing. He had not Changed anyone in almost a century. The hippie children became tiresome and he considered impaling them all. But someone on the outside was bound to find out and then there would be hell to pay. The authorities in America were currently as repressive and autocratic as he had been in his prime. They didn't torture their victims physically, as he had; instead they lied about them to the press and threw them in prisons on trumped-up charges. Had he possessed the same means of mass communication in his day back in Carpathia, he might have done the same thing. It certainly was effective.

Then his lieutenant, Alexsandru, came to him one day with excellent news: Dr. Timothy Leary wanted to pay him a visit. The famous Dr. Leary, father of this entire movement of tuning in and turning on, of dropping acid and exploring alternative realities.

The standard bearer of the deeper life.

Dracula didn't realize at the time that Dr. Leary had just broken out of jail in San Luis Obispo, a town up the coast. He hadn't known Dr. Leary in the first place. But word of his imminent arrival swept through the castle like the sharp wail of a wolf.

Tim Leary, Dr. Leary. The mortal's name was a mantra among the hippie children. Despite his anxiety about the local authorities, Captain Blood found it within himself to chuckle at his own jealousy of their anticipation of the visit. He was used to being the princely topic of discussion. Perhaps a legend should never try to compete with an icon.

He only hoped that Dr. Leary would bring rain to the desert.

He waited like a schoolgirl for the visit, laying in food—the hippies were happy with brown rice and *miso* soup, but one noble must entertain another suitably. He went over his wardrobe—fringed jacket and tie-dyed shirt? Black turtleneck sweater and sports jacket? He presided over the castle preparations—rooms cleaned, linens washed and pressed—until one sunset, Alexsandru's rap sounded on the door of Dracula's inner sanctum and the lieutenant announced, "They've arrived!"

Dracula finally decided on a Nehru jacket and black trousers—he was not a hippie child, he was a grown man—and descended the staircase with an unhurried air although his unbeating heart contracted once or twice.

Leary came to him with both arms extended and took Dracula's hands in his. Dracula looked into his large, deep eyes and knew that at last he had found his mortal counterpart: a man who had lived the depth and breadth of experience. Hopeful, Dracula embraced him.

"Ah," said the mass of counterculture lounging in the great hall. The cavernous room thick with scented marijuana smoke, clove cigarettes, astringent red wine, and sweat. The yeast of sex.

"Welcome," Dracula said.

Leary winked at him and presented his wife, Rosemary. Dracula gaped. She was astonishingly beautiful. His attraction to her was immediate and intense. To mask it, he ignored her.

"We'll dine," he added, sounding to himself old-fashioned and silly, a movie version of Dracula. Lugosi the Drug Addict, not Vlad the Impaler, in whose presence the fathers of daughters trembled and the daughters fainted. In those days, his favor was like a comet tail: either a beautiful radiance or a harbinger of disaster.

How he had fallen in the New World! Plummeted!

The servants prepared an exquisite table, which the hippie children devoured with no hesitation or delicacy whatsoever while Leary spoke of the movements toward universal truth and inner peace. He revealed to

Dracula that many prominent psychiatrists in Los Angeles were using LSD in their practices. They were giving LSD to movie stars like Cary Grant and Jack Nicholson. Cary Grant had wanted to make a movie about LSD. So had Otto Preminger. He spoke of all the brilliant thinkers who had moved to Los Angeles, attracted by the climate of intellectual freedom: Thomas Mann, Aldous Huxley. As he talked, his wife listened as if she had never heard any of this before. Excellent woman! Intriguing man! Dracula was overjoyed that they had come.

So were the flower children, who sprang up in the castle hothouse like so many celestial poppies. In microvans and magic buses, caravans and myriad groups of simpleton singletons. Across the Great Desert on the GBT, to sit at the feet of the great and mysterious Leary.

Who talked faster than a speeding bullet.

Who leaped through chasms in a single bound.

"If we charged admission, you'd be rich," Leary told Dracula one night, as they kicked back with some Panama Red. Rosemary was nowhere to be found, but a few addled braless girls lounged about, perhaps angling to become Brides. Dracula contented himself with caressing them idly, if only to feel the heat of the pulses beneath their skin. It was a pleasant habit, like biting one's nails.

He was more interested in discovering what pulsed inside Leary's brain. The stories the man told! The adventures he had had, inspired by the drugs he had taken! Taking psilocybin in Tangier with William S. Burroughs! Discussing with Allen Ginsberg the politics of ecstasy. Arguing with Jack Kerouac, who disdained him. Leary's life was one vast experimental, highly responsive moment in the now. Dracula came to look upon him as a counterculture Scheherazade, a mortal who could tempt him to stay up all night and look upon the fatal sun.

"Let's go in the hot tub," Leary said suddenly one evening, shedding his clothes. The girls threw theirs off as well.

Dracula had once been warned that he couldn't immerse himself in water, but he had found this to be untrue. The hot tub almost warmed his cold flesh. So he took off his clothes—the king of the undead!—and joined Leary and the young virgins in the water.

"Admission," Leary said. "We'd make enough money to fund the film."

"I'm a nobleman," Dracula replied. "I have obligations of hospitality."

"Vladimir, you've got to shed these outmoded thought patterns," Leary chided him. Though the girls bobbed and grinned, Leary ignored them, talking only to Dracula. It was apparent that the man was faithful to his wife and would continue to be so. Dracula found that admirable, if somewhat stifling. He would like very much for his wife to have a reason to retaliate against ill treatment. She was that stunning.

The girls got tired and left. Leary leaned forward and whispered, "Bite me. I want to know what it feels like."

"So you believe I'm really a vampire?" Dracula asked. "I'm not just another acid trip for the little kiddies?"

Leary looked surprised. "I believed in you before I got here, man. Why do you think I came?"

Dracula was momentarily embarrassed. He had assumed the sophisticated Leary believed that he, Dracula, was simply another guru of the times, a charismatic leader who attracted rootless, searching kids. Dracula had taken pride in the notion that there was something intrinsically fascinating about him besides the fact that he was a supernatural being.

But over the course of the days and weeks, it became apparent that that was the only thing Leary found fascinating about him. Leary interrupted Dracula's musings, both when they were alone and in front of his hippie children of the night. He debated him, and handily won, as Dracula didn't have many facts and figures to pull from his head, while the well-read, well-connected Leary did.

He revitalized many of the young hippies who came to the castle, as a decent guru should. In their quest for coolness, they had become radicalized: they were leftist, cynical, and unhappy.

But Leary lambasted them: "You can't do good unless you feel good," he told them. It became the phrase of the day on the GBT.

The goal became to be happy, to feel good, to grow and learn. And it became obvious to Dracula that his groupies believed Leary could teach them how.

Leary, and not he.

They ate his food and slept in his rooms and barns and outbuildings and bothered his horses and hit on his servants, all the while discussing What Tim Said, What Tim Meant, What Tim Did. They lost sight of the fact that they were guests and became squatters; that they were visitors who had become denizens. They stopped cleaning up after themselves, because Leary didn't. They stopped saying "thank you," because Leary never did.

But worst of all, they stopped being afraid of Dracula. Was he or wasn't he? No one cared. Their minds dwelled now on all the confounding possibilities Leary presented them with so much charm and enthusiasm that they didn't appear to realize he was casting pearls before swine. At least, that was how Dracula saw it all.

One day Alexsandru came to him, bowed deeply, and told him with all deference that the great lord must reassert his position, and that His Grace the Count must tell Leary to leave. Dracula promised to do both.

But it was difficult. In this modern country, he possessed no authority to compel the hippie children to do anything, least of all respect him because he had once been more ruthless than any of the leaders they distrusted. And he didn't want Leary to leave, because as dominating as Leary was, he was the most interesting person Dracula had ever met.

"I sense you have cognitive dissonance about something," Leary ventured one night in the hot tub. "How about this?"

Then he suggested a wild plan: that on the next full moon, when the forces of night were strongest, he, Leary, would ingest terrific quantities of LSD and other drugs, he would then hypnotize Dracula into a receptive state, and then *he* would bite Dracula.

"It will Change you," Dracula told him.

Leary smiled. "It'll Change you, too."

So, Leary tempted Dracula into making him a vampire by promising him an acid trip. That was what it boiled down to, when Dracula examined the offer from all sides. Was it worth it? He imagined Leary moving through the centuries, gathering acolytes, spreading the word. Not about vampirism, surely. Either he would agree to silence on that score, or Dracula would refuse him.

The moon moved through her courses. Dracula watched its progress and Leary watched him, eager to die.

Finally Dracula decided that as much as he wanted the gift of great consciousness, he could not share his powers with Leary. The man was already too strong. His powers of persuasion were admirable and awe-inspiring. If ever they found themselves in disagreement, Dracula would have created his own worst enemy.

He put off telling the charismatic mortal, hoping Leary would understand his reticence and give up the idea himself.

Then Alexasandru informed him the FBI were coming. They had been pursuing Leary, a fugitive from justice, ever since his jailbreak, and they had just picked up on the scent.

Dracula was alarmed. This did not bode well for a blood freak. *The blood freak of all time.*

He told Leary, who apologized profusely.

"The best thing you can do now," Dracula told him, "is to leave as soon as possible."

"Yes," Leary agreed, and Dracula was relieved. He ordered his servants to prepare a marvelous feast for the great man's last night among them. Rosemary dressed for the occasion in a stunning black dress embroidered with jet beads, a costume Dracula's mother might have worn. He wanted her more than ever, and he was sorry he would never have her.

There was wine and revelry and though neither Leary nor Dracula had told the hippie children that Leary was leaving, they seemed to know. Some were packing with the idea of following him wherever he went. At dinner he rose and begged them not to, pointing out that the FBI would surely find him with so many little bloodhounds trailing after. Dracula, jealous, wished the disloyal ones would leave: he would cull his herd that way, swooping down in the dead of night as they made their way across the vast expanses of Leary's flight to Egypt.

"One last glass together?" Leary asked after they finished the magnificent dinner.

"Yes," Dracula agreed.

Dracula led him to the turret room where the already-bubbling hot tub was. They got in, sighing with the heat. Leary poured two glasses of deep, rich Hungarian wine from a bottle on the deck. He handed one to Dracula—who *could* drink it, contrary to folk myth—and they toasted.

"To the incredible possibilities of existence," Leary said, and Dracula found tears in his eyes for that which was not to be, a long and enduring friendship with this extraordinary man.

They drank. Above them, in the skylight, the full moon glowed. Dracula leaned back in the hot water, to discover the beautiful hands of Rosemary kneading his shoulders. He smiled at her and closed his eyes while Leary spoke of something: of what he was not sure, the religion Leary had founded or the beauty of LSD or any of a number of topics. He muscles relaxed, releasing the tension of centuries. He drank more wine, unable, as mortals were, to get drunk.

Words in Leary's soft voice of change and optimism for the future, and the unfolding of mankind, and the need to fly out of oneself and change

and Rosemary melted the furrows out of Dracula's brow

and change

and the next thing of which Dracula was aware was a sharp, deep penetration in his neck, and sucking. Slowly he opened his eyes and said, "You tricked me," but he didn't know how.

Yet, as the blood seeped out of him, the room melted down itself and became a stunning, incandescent forest. Beatific women smiled down on him like the Madonnas of Russian Orthodox icons. His muscles were completely gone, his veins, his arteries, his princely blood. That was okay, that was, as they said, groovy.

He saw the melodies of his homeland—blood red, crimson, scarlet, vermilion; he heard the colors of his life—Gothic chants and Gregorian chants, the keening of lonely wolves and the sweet, ethereal voices of his Brides. The sweeping gales of the children of the night. The laughter of the bat; the plaintive whispers of rodents.

Beautiful, beautiful—chimes in the back of his mind, promising him midnight: one, two, three, in the depths of the black night in Carpathia. The splendor that he was—more magnificent than ever he had remembered. The miracle that he was—and the endless possibilities for expression given to him.

"I can catch my soul," he whispered. "It's so beautiful."

Leary said, "You made it, Vladimir. You're tripping."

And Dracula immediately crashed.

No longer tripping, no longer mesmerized, no longer relaxed. His eyes flew open and he said, "Bastard. Out of my sight. Betrayer. Thief."

"But, Vlad—" Leary began.

Dracula flung himself at him, teeth bared, preparing for the kill, when Leary flew out of reach.

Flew.

Rosemary looked frightened, and backed away from them both.

"I've been Changed," Leary said, settling back into the tub. He opened his mouth and showed Dracula his teeth.

"There's only one way to settle this," Dracula said, rising from the water in all his majesty. He was the King of the Vampires; he would not let this usurper survive another minute.

"Settle it?" Leary asked, perplexed.

"Yes, you idiot." Dracula advanced, sneering at him. The King of Peace and Love. He had no idea what violence he would commit as a vampire.

Leary backed away, ran up against the side of the tub, and crawled out. "Wait a minute. Wait." Perhaps he was beginning to understand he had made a terrible miscalculation.

Then Alexsandru rushed in. "The FBI! They're at the gates!"

Suddenly everyone was scrambling. Into clothes and coats, stuffing passports and money into pockets, the fugitives sneaking through the dungeon to the unguarded rear of the castle. The flower children, rising to the occasion, harassing and teasing the authorities.

The Learys took flight, and were safe.

The FBI were too stupid to see what Dracula was, and left after stern warnings about harboring criminals.

Dracula was alone with his motley crew, and as he looked up at the setting moon, he wept.

Years later, after the flowers and the pharmacopoeial paraphernalia and the dog-eared copies of *The Tibetan Book of the Dead* were locked in attic trunks, it was said that Leary died. It was said that his head was severed from his body and frozen. It was said that he had requested this action in the hope that he could be revived in a more advanced time and brought back to life.

When Alexsandru told Dracula of this, Captain Blood laughed. No one knew exactly why. Some claimed it was because he remembered Leary so fondly. Others, that he found Leary's hope for a second chance as a disembodied head typically Leary, and very amusing.

And still others, that he had ordered the beheading, because that was one way to kill a vampire.

But everyone agreed that of a night, he took the hand of his best beloved Bride, who looked very much like Rosemary Leary, and they flew together over the rippling sidewinder desiccation, shadows like condors against the full and glowing desert moon.

THE POWER AND THE PASSION

Pat Cadigan

Pat Cadigan is the author of numerous acclaimed short stories and five novels. Her first novel, *Mindplayers*, was nominated for the Philip K. Dick Memorial Award; her second and third novels—*Synners* and *Fools*—both won the Arthur C. Clarke Award. Her collection, *Patterns*, was honored with the Locus Award. Cadigan's work has also been nominated for both the Hugo and Nebula awards. The author lived in Kansas City for many years, but has resided in London, England since 1996.

"The Power and the Passion" posits that it may well take a human monster to truly know an inhuman one . . .

The voice on the phone says, "We need to talk to you, Mr. Soames," so I know to pick the place up. Company coming. I don't like for Company to come into no pigsty, but one of the reasons the place is such a mess all the time is, it's so small, I got nowhere to keep shit except around, you know. But I shove both the dirty laundry and the dirty dishes in the oven—my mattress is right on the floor so I can't shove stuff under the bed, and what won't fit in the oven I put in the tub and just before I pull the curtain, I think, well, shit, I shoulda just put it all in the tub and filled it and got it all washed at once. Or, well, just the dishes, because I can take the clothes over to the laundromat easier than washing them in the tub.

So, hell, I just pull the shower curtain, stack the newspapers and the magazines—newspapers on top of the magazines, because most people don't take too well to my taste in magazines, and they wouldn't like a lot of the newspapers much either, but I got the Sunday paper to stick on top and hide it all, so it's okay. Company'll damned well know what's under them Sunday funnies because they know me, but as long as they don't have to have it staring them in the face, it's like they can pretend it don't exist.

I'm still puttering and fussing around when the knock on the door comes and I'm crossing the room (the only room unless you count the bathroom, which I do when I'm in it) when it comes to me I ain't done dick about myself. I'm still in my undershirt and shorts, for chrissakes.

"Hold on," I call out, "I ain't decent, quite," and I drag a pair of pants outa the closet. But all my shirts are either in the oven or the tub and Company'll get fanny-antsy standing in the hall—this is not the wat-chamacallit, the place where Lennon bought it, the Dakota, yeah. Anyway, I answer the door in my one-hundred-percent cotton undershirt, but at least I got my fly zipped.

Company's a little different this time. The two guys as usual, but today they got a woman with them. Not a broad, not a bitch, not a bimbo. She's standing between and a little behind them, looking at me the way women always look at me when I happen to cross their path—chin lifted up a little, one hand holding her coat together at the neck in a fist, eyes real cold, like, "Touch me and die horribly, I wish," standing straight-fuckin-up, like they're Superman, and the fear coming off them like heat waves from an open furnace.

They all come in and stand around and I wish I'd straightened the sheets out on the mattress so it wouldn't look so messy, but then they'd see the sheets ain't clean, so six-of-one, you know. And I got nothing for anyone to sit on, except that mattress, so they just keep standing around.

The one guy, Steener, says, "Are you feeling all right, Mr. Soames," looking around like there's puke and snot all over the floor. Steener don't bother me. He's a pretty man who probably was a pretty boy and a pretty baby before that, and thinks the world oughta be a pretty place. Or he wants to prove pretty guys are really tougher and better and more man than guys like me, because he's afraid it's vice versa, you know. Maybe even both, depending on how he got up this morning.

The other guy, Villanueva, I could almost respect him. He didn't put on no face to look at me, and he didn't have no power fantasies about who he was to me or vice versa. I think Villanueva probably knows me better than anyone in the world. But then, he was the one took my statement when they caught up with me. He was a cop then. If he'd still been a cop, I'd probably respect him.

So I look right at the woman and I say, "So, what's this, you brought me a date?" I know this will get them because they know what I do to dates.

"You speak when spoken to, Mr. Soames," Steener says, kinda barking like a dog that wishes it were bigger.

"You spoke to me," I point out.

Villanueva takes a few steps in the direction of the bathroom—he knows what I got in there and how I don't want Company to see it, so this is supposed to distract me, and it does a little. The woman steps back, clutching her light coat tighter around her throat, not sure who to hide behind. Villanueva's the better bet, but she doesn't want to get any further into my stinky little apartment, so she edges toward Steener.

And it comes to me in a two-second flash-movie just how to do it. Steener'd be easy to take out. He's a rusher, doesn't know dick about fighting. He'd just go for me and I'd just whip my hand up between his arms and crunch goes the windpipe. Villanueva'd be trouble, but I'd probably end up doing him, too. Villanueva's smart enough to know that. First, though, I'd bop the woman, just bop her to keep her right there—punch in the stomach does it for most people, man or woman—and then I'd do Villanueva, break his neck.

Then the woman. I'd do it all, pound one end, pound the other, switching off before either one of us got too used to one thing or the other. Most people, man or woman, blank out about then. Can't face it, you know, so after that, it's free-for-fuckin-all. You can do just any old thing you want to a person in shock, they just don't believe it's happening by then. This one I would rip up sloppy, I would send her to hell and then kill her. I can see how it would look, the way her body would be moving, how her flesh would jounce flabby—

But I won't. I can't look at a woman without the flash-movie kicking in, but it's only a movie, you know. This is Company, they got something else for me.

"Do you feel like working?" Villanueva asks. He's caught it just now, what I was thinking about, he knows, because I told him how it was when I gave him my statement after I got caught.

"Sure," I say, "what else have I got to do?"

He nods to Steener, who passes me a little slip of paper. The name and address. "It's nothing you haven't done before," he says. "There are two of them. You do as you like, but you *must* follow the procedure as it has been described to you—"

I give a great big nod. "I know how to do it. I've studied on it, got it all right up here." I tap my head. "Second nature to me now."

"I don't want to hear the word 'nature' out of *you*," Steener sneers. "You've got nothing to do with nature."

"That's right," I agree. I'm mild-mannered because it's just come to me what is Steener's problem here. It is that he is like me. He enjoys doing to me what he does the way I enjoy doing what I do, and the fact that he's wearing a white hat and I'm not is just a watchamacallit, a technicality. Deep down at heart, it's the same fuckin-feeling and he's going between loving it and refusing to admit he's like me, boing-boing, boing-boing. And if he ever gets stuck on the loving-it side, well, son-of-a-bitch will there be trouble.

I look over at Villanueva and point at the woman, raising my eyebrows. I don't know exactly what words to use for a question about her and anything I say is gonna upset everybody.

"This person is with us as an observer," Villanueva says quietly, which means I can just mind my own fuckin business and don't ask questions unless it's about the job. I look back at the woman and she looks me right in the face. The hand clenched high up on her coat relaxes just a little and I see the purple-black bruises on the side of her neck before she clutches up again real fast. She's still holding herself the same way, but it's like she spoke to me. The lines of communication, like the shrinks say, are open, which is not the safest thing to do with me. She's gotta be a nurse or a teacher or a social worker, I think, because those are the ones that can't help opening up to someone. It's what they're trained to do, reach out. Or hell, maybe she's just somebody's mother. She don't look too motherly, but that don't mean dick these days.

"When?" I say to Steener.

"As soon as you can pack your stuff and get to the airport. There's a cab downstairs and your ticket is waiting at the airline counter, in your name."

"You mean the Soames name," I say, because Soames is not my name for real.

"Just get ready, get going, get it done, and get back here," Steener says. "No side-trips, or it's finished. Don't even *attempt* a side-trip or it's finished." He starts to turn toward the door and then stops. "And you know that if you're caught in or after the act—"

"Yeah, yeah, I'm on my own and you don't know dick about squat, and nobody ever hearda me, case closed." I keep myself from smiling; he watched too much *Mission Impossible* when he was a kid. Like everyone else in his outfit. I think it's where they got the idea, kind of, some of it anyway.

Villanueva tosses me a fat roll of bills in a rubber band just as he's following Steener and the woman out the door. "Expenses," he says. "You have a rental car on the other end, which you'll have to use cash for. Buy whatever else you need, don't get mugged and robbed, you know the drill."

"Drill?" I say, acting perked-up, like I'm thinking, *Wow, what a good idea.*

Villanueva refuses to turn green for me, but he shuts the door behind him a little too hard.

I don't waste no time; I go to the closet and pull out my traveling bag. Everything's in it, but I always take a little inventory anyway, just to be on the safe side. Hell of a thing to come up empty-handed at the wrong moment, you know. Really, though, I just like to handle the stuff: hacksaw, mallet, boning blade, iodized salt, lighter fluid, matches, spray bottle of holy water, four pieces of wood pointed sharp on one end, half a dozen rosaries, all blessed, and two full place settings of silverware, not stainless, mind you, but real silver. And the shirts I don't never put in the tub. What do they make of this at airport security? Not a fuckin thing. Ain't no gun. Guns don't work for this. Anyway, this bag's always checked.

The flight is fine. It's always fine because they always put me in first class and nobody next to me if possible. On the night flights, it's generally possible and tonight, I have the whole first class section to myself, hot and cold running stews, who are (I can tell) forcing themselves to be nice to me. I don't know what it is, and I don't mind it, but it makes me wonder all the same: is it a smell, or just the way my eyes look? Villanueva told me once, it was just something about me gave everyone the creeps. I lean back, watch the flash-movies, don't bother nobody, and everybody's happy to see me go when the plane finally lands.

I get my car, nice midsize job with a phone, and head right into the city. I know this city real good, I been here before for them, but it ain't the only one they send me to when they need to TCB.

Do an easy fifty-five into the city and go to the address on the paper. Midtown, two blocks east of dead center, medium-sized Victorian. I can see the area's starting to get a watchamacallit, like a facelift, the rich ones coming in and fixing up the houses because the magazines and the TV told them it's time to love old houses and fix them up.

I think about the other houses all up and down the street of the one I got to go to, what's in them, what I could do. I sure feel like it, and it would be a lot less trouble, but I made me a deal of my own free will and I will stick to it as long as they do, Steener and Villanueva and the people behind them. But if they bust it up somehow, if they fuck me, that will be real different, and they will be real sorry.

I call the house; nobody home. That's about right. I got to wait, which don't bother me none, because there's the flash-movies to watch. I can think on what I want to do after I get through what I have to do, and those things are not so different from each other. What Steener calls "the procedure" I just call a new way to play. Only not so new, because I thought of some of those things all on my own when I was watchamacallit, freelance so to say, and done some of them, kind of, which I guess is what made them take me on for this stuff, instead of letting me take a quick shot in a quiet room and no funeral after.

So, it gets to be four in the morning and here we come. Somehow, I know as soon as I see the figure coming up the sidewalk across the street that this is the one in the house. I can always tell them, and I don't know what it is, except maybe it takes a human monster to know an inhuman monster. And I don't feel nothing except a little nervous about getting into the house, which is always easier than you'd think it would be, but I get nervous on it anyway.

Figure comes into the light and I see it's a man, and I see it's not alone, and then I get pissed, because that fucking Steener, that fucking Villanueva, they didn't say nothing about no kid. And then I settle some, because I can tell the kid is one, too. Ten, maybe twelve from the way he walks. I take the razor and I give myself a little one just inside my hairline, squeeze the blood out to get it running down my face, and then I get out of the car just as they put their feet on the first step up to the house.

"Please, you gotta help me," I call, not too loud, just so they can hear, "they robbed me, they took everything but my clothes, all my ID, my credit cards, my cash—"

They stop and look at me running across the street at them and the first thing they see is the blood, of course. This would scare anybody but them (or me, naturally). I trip myself on the curb and collapse practically at their feet. "Can I use your phone? Please? I'm scared to stay out here, my car won't start, they might be still around—"

The man leans down and pulls me up under my arm. "Of course. Come in, we'll call the police. I'm a doctor."

I have to bite my lip to keep from laughing at that one. He's an operator maybe but no fucking doctor. Then I taste blood, so I let it run out of my mouth and the two of them, the man and the kid get so hot they can't get me in the house fast enough.

Nice house. All the Victorian shit restored, even the fuzzy stuff on the wallpaper, watchamacallit, flocked wallpaper. I get a glimpse of the living room before the guy's rushing me upstairs, saying he's got his medical bag up there. I just bet he does, and I got mine right in my hand, which they do not bother wondering about what with all this blood and this guy with no ID and out at four in the morning, must be a criminal anyway. I used to ask Villanueva, don't they ever get full, like they can't drink another drop, but Villanueva told me no, they always had room for one more, it was time they were pressed for. Dawn. I'd be through long before then, but even if I wasn't, dawn would take care of the rest of it for me.

They're getting so excited it's getting me even more excited. I look at the kid and man, if I'd been anyone else, I woulda started screaming and trying to get away, because he's all gone. I mean, the kid part is all gone and just this fucking hungry thing from hell. So I stop feeling funny about there being a kid, because like I said, there ain't no kid, just a short one along with the tall one.

And shit if he don't twig, right there on the stairs. I musta looked like I recognized him.

"We're burned! We're burned!" he yells and tries to elbow me in the face. I dip and he goes right the fuck over my head and down, ka-boom, ka-boom. Guess what, they can't fly. It don't do him, but they can feel pain, and if you break their legs, they can't walk for a while until they can get extra blood to heal them up. The kid's fucking neck is broke, you can see it plain as anything.

But I don't get no chance to study on it because the big one growls like a fucking attack dog and grabs me up from behind around the waist. They really are stronger than normal and you better believe it hurt like a motherfucker. He squeezes and there go two ribs and the soft drinks I had on the plane, like a fucking fountain.

"You'll go slow for that," he says, "you'll go for days, and you'll beg to die."

Obviously, he don't know me. I'm hurting all right, but it takes a lot more than a couple of ribs to put me down and I never had to beg for nothing, but these guys get all their dialog off the late show anyway and they ain't thinking of nothing except sticking it to you and drinking you dry. Fucking undead got a, a watchamacallit, a narrow perspective and they think everyone's scared of them.

That's why they send me, because I don't see no undead and I don't see no human being, I just see something to play with. I gotta narrow perspective, too, I guess.

But then everything is not so good because he tears the bag outa my hand and flings it away up in the hallway. Then he carries me the rest of the way upstairs and down the opposite end and tosses me into a dark room and slams the door and locks it.

I hold still until I can figure out how to move and cause myself the least pain, and I start taking off my shirts. I'm wearing a corduroy shirt with a pure linen lining sewn into the front and two heavy one-hundred-percent cotton T-shirts underneath. I have to tear one of the T-shirts off, biting through the neck, and I bite through the neck of the other one but leave it on (thinking about the guy biting through necks while I do it), and put the corduroy shirt back on, keeping it open. Ready to go.

The guy has gone downstairs. I hear the kid scream and then muffle it, and I hear footsteps coming back up the stairs. There's a pause, and then I see his feet at the bottom of the door in the light, and he unlocks the door and opens it.

"Whoever you think you are," he says, "you're about to find out what you really are."

I give a little whimper, which makes him sure enough to grab me by one leg and start dragging me out into the hallway, where the kid is lying on his back. When we're out in the light, he stops and stands over me, one leg on each side, and looks down at my crotch. I know what he's thinking, because I'm looking up at his and thinking something not too different.

He squats on my thighs, and I rip my shirts open.

It's like an invisible giant hand hit him in the face; he goes backwards with a scream, still bent at the knees, on top of my legs. I heave him off quick. He's so fucked I have time to get to him, roll him over on his back and give him a nice full frontal while I sit on his stomach.

It is a truly def tattoo. This is not like bragging, because I didn't do it, though I did name it: The Power and The Passion. A madwoman with a mean needle in Coney did it, one-handed with her hair standing on end, counting her rosary beads with the other hand, and when I saw it finished, with the name I had given it on a banner above it, I knew she was the best tattoo artist in the whole world and so I did not do her, I did *not*. It was some very ignorant asshole who musta come in after I did that split her open and nailed her to the wall with a stud gun, but I caught the beef on it, and the tattoo that saved her from me saved me from the quick shot and gave me to Steener's people, courtesy of Villanueva who is, I should mention, also Catholic.

So it's a tattoo that means a lot to me in many ways, you see, but mostly I love it because it is so perfect. It runs from just below where my shirt collars are to my navel, and full across my chest, and if you saw it, you would swear it had been done by someone who had been there to see what happened.

The cross is not just two boards, but a tree trunk and a crossbar, and the spikes are driven into the forearms where the two bones make a natural holder for that kind of thing—you couldn't hang on a cross from spikes driven through your palms, they'd rip through. The crown of thorns has driven into the flesh to the bone, and the blood drips from the matted beard *distinctly*—the madwoman was careful and skilled so that the different shades of red didn't muddy up. Nothing muddied up; you can see the face clear as you can see where the whips came down, as clear as the wound in his side, (which is not some pussy slit but the best watchamacallit, rendering of a stab wound I have seen outside of real life), as clear as you can see how the arms have pulled out of the sockets, and how the legs are broken.

You just can't find no better picture of slow murder. I know; I seen photos of all kinds, I seen some righteous private art, and I seen the inside of plenty of churches, and ain't nobody done justice to nothing anybody ever done to someone, including the Crucifixion. Especially the Crucifixion, I guess.

Because, you see, you cannot take a vamp out with a cross, that don't mean dick to them, a fucking plus-sign, that's all. It's the Crucifixion that gets them, you gotta have a good crucifix, or some other representation of the Crucifixion, and it has to be blessed in some way, to inflict the agony of the real thing on them. Mine was blessed—that madwoman mumbling her rosary all the way through the work, don't it just figure that she was a runaway nun? I wouldn't a thought it would matter, but I guess when you take them vows, you can't give them back. Sorta like a tattoo.

Well, that's what that madwoman believed, anyway, and I believe it, too, because I like believing that picture happened, and the vamp I'm sitting on, it don't mean shit if he believes or not, because I got him and he don't understand how I could even get close to him. So while I go get my bag (giving a good flash to the kid, who goes into shock), I explain about pure fibers found in nature like the linen they say they wrapped that man on the cross in (I think that's horseshit myself, but it's all in it being natural and not watchamacallit, synthetic, so that don't matter), and how it keeps the power from getting out till I need it to.

And then it's showtime.

I have a little fun with the silver for a while, just laying it against his skin here and there, and it crosses my mind not for the first time how a doctor could do some interesting research on burns, before I start getting serious. Like a hot knife through butter, you can put it that way and be dead on. Or undead on, ha, ha.

You know what they got for insides? Me neither, but it's as bad for them as anyone. And I wouldn't call *that* a heart, but if you drive a pure wood stake through it, it's lights out.

It lasts forever for him, but not half long enough for me. Come dawn, it's pretty much over. Them watchamacallits, UV rays, they're all over the place. Skin cancer on fast-forward, you can put it that way. I leave myself half an hour for the kid, who is not really a kid because if he was, he'd be the first kid I ever killed, and I ain't no fucking kid killer, because I seen what *they* get in prison and I said, whoa, not *my* ass.

I stake both hearts at the same time, a stake in each hand, sending them to hell together. Call me sentimental. Set their two heads to burning in the cellar and hang in just long enough to make sure we got a good fire going before I'm outa there. House all closed up the way it is, it'll be awhile before it's time to call the fire department.

I'm halfway to the airport when I realize my ribs ain't bothered me for a long time. Healed up, just like that.

Hallelujah, gimme that old-time religion.

"As usual," Steener says, snotty as all get-out, "the bulk of the fee has been divided up among your victims' families, with a percentage to the mission downtown. Your share this time is three hundred." Nasty grin. "The check's in the mail."

"Yeah," I say, "you're from the government and you're here to help me. Well, don't worry, Steener, I won't come in your *mouth*."

He actually cocks a fist and Villanueva steps in front of him. The woman with them gives Steener a really sharp look, like she's gonna come to my defense, which don't make sense. Villanueva starts to rag my ass about pushing Steener's hot button but I'm feeling important enough to wave a hand at him.

"Fuck that," I say, "it's time to tell me who *she* is."

Villanueva looks to the woman like he's asking her permission, but she steps forward and lets go of her coat, and I see the marks on her neck are all gone. "I'm the mother. And the wife. They tried to—" she bites her lips together and makes a stiff little motion at her throat. "I got away. I tried to go to church, but I was . . . tainted." She takes a breath. "The priest told me about—" she dips her head at Villanueva and Steener, who still wants a piece of me. "You really . . . put them away?"

The way she says it, it's like she's talking about a couple of rabid dogs. "Yeah," I tell her, smiling. "They're all gone."

"I want to see the picture," she says, and for a moment, I can't figure out what she's talking about. And then I get it.

"Sure," I say, and start to raise my undershirt.

Villanueva starts up. "I don't think you *really* want—"

"Yeah, she does," I say. "It's the only way she can tell she's all right now."

"The marks disappeared," Villanueva snaps. "She's fine. You're fine," he adds to her, almost polite.

She feels the side of her neck. "No, he's right. It *is* the only way I'll know for sure."

I'm shaking my head as I raise the shirt slowly. "You guys didn't think to sprinkle any holy water on her or nothing?"

"I wouldn't take the chance," she says, "it might have—"

But that's as far as she gets, because she's looking at my chest now and her face—oh, man, I start thinking I'm in love, because that's the look, that's the look you oughta have when you see The Power and The Passion. I know, because it's the look on my own face when I stand before the mirror and stare, and stare, and stare. It's so fucking *there*.

Villanueva and Steener are looking off in the opposite direction. I give it a full two-minute count before I lower my shirt. The look on her face goes away and she's just another character for a flash-movie again.

Easy come, easy go. But now I know why she was so scared when she was here before. Guess they didn't think to tell her about pure natural fibers.

"You're perfect," she says and turns to Steener and Villanueva. "He's perfect, isn't he? They can't tempt him into joining them, because he can't. He couldn't if he wanted to."

"Fuckin A," I tell her.

Villanueva says, "Shut up," to me and looks at her like he's kinda sick. "You don't know what you're talking to. You don't know what's standing in this room with us. I couldn't bring myself to tell you, and I was a cop for sixteen years—"

"You told me what would have to be done with my husband and son," she says, looking him straight in the eye and I start thinking maybe I'm in love after all. "You spelled that out easily enough. The agony of the Crucifixion, the burning and the cutting open of the bodies with silver knives, the stakes through the hearts, the beheadings, the burning. That didn't bother you, telling me what was going to happen to my family—"

"That's because they're the white hats," I say to her, and I can't help smiling, smiling, smiling. "If they had to do it, they'd do it because they're on the side of Good and Right."

Suddenly Steener and Villanueva are falling all over each other to hustle her out and she don't resist, but she don't cooperate either. The last thing I see before the door closes is her face looking at me, and what I see in that face is not understanding, because she couldn't go that far, but acceptance. Which is one fucking hell of a lot more than I'll ever get from Steener or Villanueva or anybody-the-fuck-else.

And Steener and Villanueva, they don't even get it, I know it just went right by them, what I told her. They'd do it because they're on the side of Good and Right.

I do it because I like to.

And I don't pretend like I ain't no monster, not for Good and Right, and not for Bad and Wrong. I know what I am, and the madwoman who put The Power and The Passion on my chest, she knew, too, and I think now she did it so the vamps would never get me, because God help you all if they had.

Just a coincidence, I guess, that it's my kind of picture.

THE UNICORN
TAPESTRY

Suzy McKee Charnas

Suzy McKee Charnas has won the Hugo, Nebula, Mythopoeic, and James Tiptree, Jr. awards. Her Holdfast series, a tetralogy written over the course of almost thirty years (the first novel, *Walk to the End of the World* was published in 1974; the last, *The Conqueror's Child* in 1999) is considered to be a germinal work of feminist science fiction. Perhaps even better known is *The Vampire Tapestry*, a book that grew out of the following novella, "The Unicorn Tapestry." [*The Vampire Tapestry* has also been adapted (by Charnas herself) into the play *Vampire Dreams*.] Considered a classic ever since its publication, the *Oxford Times* called *The Vampire Tapestry*: "Probably the best vampire novel ever written." As "Rebecca Brand" Charnas wrote the considerably more traditional vampire romance *The Ruby Tear*. Many of her stories are collected in *Stagestruck Vampires and Other Phantasms* (2006). She lives in New Mexico.

Now, please meet Dr. Edward Weyland, a vampire unlike any other you are likely to encounter . . .

"Hold on," Floria said. "I know what you're going to say: I agreed not to take any new clients for a while. But wait till I tell you—you're not going to believe this—first phone call, setting up an initial appointment, he comes out with what his problem is: 'I seem to have fallen victim to a delusion of being a vampire.'"

"Christ H. God!" cried Lucille delightedly. "Just like that, over the telephone?"

"When I recovered my aplomb, so to speak, I told him that I prefer to wait with the details until our first meeting, which is tomorrow."

They were sitting on the tiny terrace outside the staff room of the clinic, a converted town house on the upper West Side. Floria spent three days a week here and the remaining two in her office on Central Park South where she saw private clients like this new one. Lucille, always gratifyingly responsive, was Floria's most valued professional friend. Clearly enchanted with Floria's news, she sat eagerly forward in her chair, eyes wide behind Coke-bottle lenses.

She said, "Do you suppose he thinks he's a revivified corpse?"

Below, down at the end of the street, Floria could see two kids skidding their skateboards near a man who wore a woolen cap and a heavy coat despite the May warmth. He was leaning against a wall. He had been there when Floria had arrived at the clinic this morning. If corpses walked, some, not nearly revivified enough, stood in plain view in New York.

"I'll have to think of a delicate way to ask," she said.

"How did he come to you, this 'vampire'?"

"He was working in an upstate college, teaching and doing research, and all of a sudden he just disappeared—vanished, literally, without a trace. A month later he turned up here in the city. The faculty dean at the school knows me and sent him to see me."

Lucille gave her a sly look. "So you thought, aha, do a little favor for a friend, this looks classic and easy to transfer if need be: repressed intellectual blows stack and runs off with spacey chick, something like that."

"You know me too well," Floria said with a rueful smile.

"Huh," grunted Lucille. She sipped ginger ale from a chipped white mug. "I don't take panicky middle-aged men anymore; they're too depressing. And you shouldn't be taking this one, intriguing as he sounds."

Here comes the lecture, Floria told herself.

Lucille got up. She was short, heavy, prone to wearing loose garments that swung about her like ceremonial robes. As she paced, her hem brushed at the flowers starting up in the planting boxes that rimmed the little terrace. "You know damn well this is just more overwork you're loading on. Don't take this guy; refer him."

Floria sighed. "I know, I know. I promised everybody I'd slow down. But you said it yourself just a minute ago—it looked like a simple favor. So what do I get? Count Dracula, for God's sake! Would you give that up?"

Fishing around in one capacious pocket, Lucille brought out a dented package of cigarettes and lit up, scowling. "You know, when you give me advice I try to take it seriously. Joking aside, Floria, what am I supposed to say? I've listened to you moaning for months now, and I thought we'd figured out that what you need is to shed some pressure, to start saying no—and here you are insisting on a new case. You know what I think: you're hiding in other people's problems from a lot of your own stuff that you should be working on.

"Okay, okay, don't glare at me. Be pigheaded. Have you gotten rid of Chubs, at least?" This was Floria's code name for a troublesome client named Kenny whom she'd been trying to unload for some time.

Floria shook her head.

"What gives with you? It's weeks since you swore you'd dump him! Trying to do everything for everybody is wearing you out. I bet you're still dropping weight. Judging by the very unbecoming circles under your eyes, sleeping isn't going too well, either. Still no dreams you can remember?"

"Lucille, don't nag. I don't want to talk about my health."

"Well, what about his health—Dracula's? Did you suggest that he have a physical before seeing you? There might be something physiological—"

"You're not going to be able to whisk him off to an M.D. and out of my hands," Floria said wryly. "He told me on the phone that he wouldn't consider either medication or hospitalization."

Involuntarily, she glanced down at the end of the street. The woolen-capped man had curled up on the sidewalk at the foot of the building, sleeping or passed out or dead. The city was tottering with sickness. Compared with that wreck down there and others like him, how sick could this "vampire" be, with his cultured baritone voice, his self-possessed approach?

"And you won't consider handing him off to somebody else," Lucille said.

"Well, not until I know a little more. Come on, Luce—wouldn't you want at least to know what he looks like?"

Lucille stubbed out her cigarette against the low parapet. Down below a policeman strolled along the street ticketing the parked cars. He didn't even look at the man lying at the corner of the building. They watched his progress without comment. Finally Lucille said, "Well, if you won't drop Dracula, keep me posted on him, will you?"

He entered the office on the dot of the hour, a gaunt but graceful figure. He was impressive. Wiry gray hair, worn short, emphasized the massiveness of his face with its long jaw, high cheekbones, and granite cheeks grooved as if by winters of hard weather. His name, typed in caps on the initial information sheet that Floria proceeded to fill out with him, was Edward Lewis Weyland.

Crisply, he told her about the background of the vampire incident, describing in caustic terms his life at Cayslin College: the pressures of collegial competition, interdepartmental squabbles, student indifference, administrative bungling. History has limited use, she knew, since memory distorts; still, if he felt most comfortable establishing the setting for his illness, that was as good a way to start off as any.

At length his energy faltered. His angular body sank into a slump, his voice became flat and tired as he haltingly worked up to the crucial event: night work at the sleep lab, fantasies of blood-drinking as he watched the youthful subjects of his dream research slumbering, finally an attempt to act out the fantasy with a staff member at the college. He had been repulsed; then panic had assailed him. Word would get out, he'd be fired, blacklisted forever. He'd bolted. A nightmare period had followed—he offered no details. When he had come to his senses he'd seen that just what he feared, the ruin of his career, would come from his running away. So he'd phoned the dean, and now here he was.

Throughout this recital she watched him diminish from the dignified academic who had entered her office to a shamed and frightened man hunched in his chair, his hands pulling fitfully at each other.

"What are your hands doing?" she said gently. He looked blank. She repeated the question.

He looked down at his hands. "Struggling," he said.

"With what?"

"The worst," he muttered. "I haven't told you the worst." She had never grown hardened to this sort of transformation. His long fingers busied themselves fiddling with a button on his jacket while he explained painfully that the object of his "attack" at Cayslin had been a woman. Not young but handsome and vital, she had first caught his attention earlier in the year during a *festschrift*—an honorary seminar—for a retiring professor.

A picture emerged of an awkward Weyland, lifelong bachelor, seeking this woman's warmth and suffering her refusal. Floria knew she should bring him out of his past and into his here-and-now, but he was doing so beautifully on his own that she was loath to interrupt.

"Did I tell you there was a rapist active on the campus at this time?" he said bitterly. "I borrowed a leaf from his book: I tried to take from this woman, since she wouldn't give. I tried to take some of her blood." He stared at the floor. "What does that mean—to take someone's blood?"

"What do you think it means?"

The button, pulled and twisted by his fretful fingers, came off. He put it into his pocket, the impulse, she guessed, of a fastidious nature. "Her energy," he murmured, "stolen to warm the aging scholar, the walking corpse, the vampire—myself."

His silence, his downcast eyes, his bent shoulders, all signaled a man brought to bay by a life crisis. Perhaps he was going to be the kind of client therapists dream of and she needed so badly these days: a client intelligent and sensitive enough, given the companionship of a professional listener, to swiftly unravel his own mental tangles. Exhilarated by his promising start, Floria restrained herself from trying to build on it too soon. She made herself tolerate the silence, which lasted until he said suddenly, "I notice that you make no notes as we speak. Do you record these sessions on tape?"

A hint of paranoia, she thought, *not unusual.* "Not without your knowledge and consent, just as I won't send for your personnel file from Cayslin without your knowledge and consent. I do, however, write notes after each session as a guide to myself and in order to have a record in case of any confusion about anything we do or say here. I can promise you that I won't show my notes or speak of you by name to anyone—except Dean Sharpe at Cayslin, of course, and even then only as much as is strictly necessary—without your written permission. Does that satisfy you?"

"I apologize for my question," he said. "The . . . incident has left me . . . very nervous; a condition that I hope to get over with your help."

The time was up. When he had gone, she stepped outside to check with Hilda, the receptionist she shared with four other therapists here at the Central Park South office. Hilda always sized up new clients in the waiting room.

Of this one she said, "Are you sure there's anything wrong with that guy? I think I'm in love."

Waiting at the office for a group of clients to assemble Wednesday evening, Floria dashed off some notes on the "vampire."

> Client described incident, background. No history of mental illness, no previous experience of therapy. Personal history

so ordinary you almost don't notice how bare it is: only child of German immigrants, schooling normal, field work in anthropology, academic posts leading to Cayslin College professorship. Health good, finances adequate, occupation satisfactory, housing pleasant (though presently installed in a N.Y. hotel); never married, no kids, no family, no religion, social life strictly job-related; leisure—says he likes to drive. Reaction to question about drinking, but no signs of alcohol problems. Physically very smooth-moving for his age (over fifty) and height; catlike, alert. Some apparent stiffness in the midsection—slight protective stoop—tightening up of middle age? Paranoiac defensiveness? Voice pleasant, faint accent (German-speaking childhood at home). Entering therapy condition of consideration for return to job.

What a relief: his situation looked workable with a minimum of strain on herself. Now she could defend to Lucille her decision to do therapy with the "vampire."

After all, Lucille was right. Floria did have problems of her own that needed attention, primarily her anxiety and exhaustion since her mother's death more than a year before. The breakup of Floria's marriage had caused misery, but not this sort of endless depression. Intellectually the problem was clear: with both her parents dead she was left exposed. No one stood any longer between herself and the inevitability of her own death. Knowing the source of her feelings didn't help: she couldn't seem to mobilize the nerve to work on them.

The Wednesday group went badly again. Lisa lived once more her experiences in the European death camps and everyone cried. Floria wanted to stop Lisa, turn her, extinguish the droning horror of her voice in illumination and release, but she couldn't see how to do it. She found nothing in herself to offer except some clever ploy out of the professional bag of tricks—dance your anger, have a dialog with yourself of those days—useful techniques when they flowed organically as part of a living process in which the therapist participated. But thinking out responses that should have been intuitive wouldn't work. The group and its collective pain paralyzed her. She was a dancer without a choreographer, knowing all the moves but unable to match them to the music these people made.

Rather than act with mechanical clumsiness she held back, did nothing, and suffered guilt. *Oh God, the smart, experienced people in the group must know how useless she was here.*

Going home on the bus she thought about calling up one of the therapists who shared the downtown office. He had expressed an interest in doing co-therapy with her under student observation. The Wednesday group might respond well to that. Suggest it to them next time? Having a partner might take pressure off Floria and revitalize the group, and if she felt she must withdraw he would be available to take over. Of course, he might take over anyway and walk off with some of her clients.

Oh boy, terrific, who's paranoid now? Wonderful way to think about a good colleague. God, she hadn't even known she was considering chucking the group.

Had the new client, running from his "vampirism," exposed her own impulse to retreat? This wouldn't be the first time that Floria had obtained help from a client while attempting to give help. Her old supervisor, Rigby, said that such mutual aid was the only true therapy—the rest was fraud. What a perfectionist, old Rigby, and what a bunch of young idealists he'd turned out, all eager to save the world.

Eager, but not necessarily able. Jane Fennerman had once lived in the world, and Floria had been incompetent to save her. Jane, an absent member of tonight's group, was back in the safety of a locked ward, hazily gliding on whatever tranquilizers they used there.

Why still mull over Jane? she asked herself severely, bracing against the bus's lurching halt. Any client was entitled to drop out of therapy and commit herself. Nor was this the first time that sort of thing had happened in the course of Floria's career. Only this time she couldn't seem to shake free of the resulting depression and guilt.

But how could she have helped Jane more? How could you offer reassurance that life was not as dreadful as Jane felt it to be, that her fears were insubstantial, that each day was not a pit of pain and danger?

She was taking time during a client's canceled hour to work on notes for the new book. The writing, an analysis of the vicissitudes of salaried versus private practice, balked her at every turn. She longed for an interruption to distract her circling mind.

Hilda put through a call from Cayslin College. It was Doug Sharpe, who had sent Dr. Weyland to her.

"Now that he's in your capable hands, I can tell people plainly that he's on what we call 'compassionate leave' and make them swallow it." Doug's voice seemed thinned by the long-distance connection. "Can you give me a preliminary opinion?"

"I need time to get a feel for the situation."

He said, "Try not to take too long. At the moment I'm holding off pressure to appoint someone in his place. His enemies up here—and a sharp-tongued bastard like him acquires plenty of those—are trying to get a search committee authorized to find someone else for the directorship of the Cayslin Center for the Study of Man."

"Of *People*," she corrected automatically, as she always did. "What do you mean, 'bastard'? I thought you liked him, Doug. 'Do you want me to have to throw a smart, courtly, old-school gent to Finney or MacGill?' Those were your very words." Finney was a Freudian with a mouth like a pursed-up little asshole and a mind to match, and MacGill was a primal yowler in a padded gym of an office.

She heard Doug tapping at his teeth with a pen or pencil. "Well," he said, "I have a lot of respect for him, and sometimes I could cheer him for mowing down some pompous moron up here. I can't deny, though, that he's earned a reputation for being an accomplished son-of-a-bitch and tough to work with. Too damn cold and self-sufficient, you know?"

"Mmm," she said. "I haven't seen that yet."

He said, "You will. How about yourself? How's the rest of your life?"

"Well, offhand, what would you say if I told you I was thinking of going back to art school?"

"What would I say? I'd say bullshit, that's what I'd say. You've had fifteen years of doing something you're good at, and now you want to throw all that out and start over in an area you haven't touched since Studio 101 in college? If God had meant you to be a painter, She'd have sent you to art school in the first place."

"I did think about art school at the time."

"The point is that you're good at what you do. I've been at the receiving end of your work and I know what I'm talking about. By the way, did you see that piece in the paper about Annie Barnes, from the group I was in? That's an important appointment. I always knew she'd wind up in Washington. What I'm trying to make clear to you is that your 'graduates' do too well for you to be talking about quitting. What's Morton say about that idea, by the way?"

Mort, a pathologist, was Floria's lover. She hadn't discussed this with him, and she told Doug so.

"You're not on the outs with Morton, are you?"

"Come on, Douglas, cut it out. There's nothing wrong with my sex life, believe me. It's everyplace else that's giving me trouble."

"Just sticking my nose into your business," he replied. "What are friends for?"

They turned to lighter matters, but when she hung up Floria felt glum. If her friends were moved to this sort of probing and kindly advice-giving, she must be inviting help more openly and more urgently than she'd realized.

The work on the book went no better. It was as if, afraid to expose her thoughts, she must disarm criticism by meeting all possible objections beforehand. The book was well and truly stalled—like everything else. She sat sweating over it, wondering what the devil was wrong with her that she was writing mush. She had two good books to her name already. What was this bottleneck with the third?

"But what do you think?" Kenny insisted anxiously. "Does it sound like my kind of job?"

"How do you feel about it?"

"I'm all confused, I told you."

"Try speaking for me. Give me the advice I would give you."

He glowered. "That's a real cop-out, you know? One part of me talks like you, and then I have a dialog with myself like a TV show about a split personality. It's all me that way; you just sit there while I do all the work. I want something from you."

She looked for the twentieth time at the clock on the file cabinet. This time it freed her. "Kenny, the hour's over."

Kenny heaved his plump, sulky body up out of his chair. "You don't care. Oh, you pretend to, but you don't really—"

"Next time, Kenny."

He stumped out of the office. She imagined him towing in his wake the raft of decisions he was trying to inveigle her into making for him. Sighing, she went to the window and looked out over the park, filling her eyes and her mind with the full, fresh green of late spring. She felt dismal. In two years of treatment the situation with Kenny had remained a stalemate. He wouldn't go to someone else who might be able to help him, and she couldn't bring herself to kick him out, though she knew she must eventually. His puny tyranny couldn't conceal how soft and vulnerable he was . . .

Dr. Weyland had the next appointment. Floria found herself pleased to see him. She could hardly have asked for a greater contrast to Kenny: tall, lean, that august head that made her want to draw him, good clothes, nice big hands—altogether, a distinguished-looking man. Though he was informally dressed in slacks, light jacket, and tieless shirt, the impression he conveyed was one of impeccable leisure and reserve. He took not the padded chair preferred by most clients but the wooden one with the cane seat.

"Good afternoon, Dr. Landauer," he said gravely. "May I ask your judgment of my case?"

"I don't regard myself as a judge," she said. She decided to try to shift their discussion onto a first-name basis if possible. Calling this old-fashioned man by his first name so soon might seem artificial, but how could they get familiar enough to do therapy while addressing each other as "Dr. Landauer" and "Dr. Weyland" like two characters out of a vaudeville sketch?

"This is what I think, Edward," she continued. "We need to find out about this vampire incident—how it tied into your feelings about yourself, good and bad, at the time; what it did for you that led you to try to 'be' a vampire even though that was bound to complicate your life terrifically. The more we know, the closer we can come to figuring out how to insure that this vampire construct won't be necessary to you again."

"Does this mean that you accept me formally as a client?" he said.

Comes right out and says what's on his mind, she noted, *no problem there.* "Yes."

"Good. I too have a treatment goal in mind. I will need at some point a testimonial from you that my mental health is sound enough for me to resume work at Cayslin."

Floria shook her head. "I can't guarantee that. I can commit myself to work toward it, of course, since your improved mental health is the aim of what we do here together."

"I suppose that answers the purpose for the time being," he said. "We can discuss it again later on. Frankly, I find myself eager to continue our work today. I've been feeling very much better since I spoke with you, and I thought last night about what I might tell you today."

She had the distinct feeling of being steered by him; *how important was it to him,* she wondered, *to feel in control?* She said, "Edward, my own feeling is that we started out with a good deal of very useful verbal work, and that now is a time to try something a little different."

He said nothing. He watched her. When she asked whether he remembered his dreams he shook his head, no.

She said, "I'd like you to try to do a dream for me now, a waking dream. Can you close your eyes and daydream, and tell me about it?"

He closed his eyes. Strangely, he now struck her as less vulnerable rather than more, as if strengthened by increased vigilance.

"How do you feel now?" she said.

"Uneasy." His eyelids fluttered. "I dislike closing my eyes. What I don't see can hurt me."

"Who wants to hurt you?"

"A vampire's enemies, of course—mobs of screaming peasants with torches."

Translating into what, she wondered—*young PhDs pouring out of the graduate schools panting for the jobs of older men like Weyland?* "Peasants, these days?"

"Whatever their daily work, there is still a majority of the stupid, the violent, and the credulous, putting their featherbrained faith in astrology, in this cult or that, in various branches of psychology."

His sneer at her was unmistakable. Considering her refusal to let him fill the hour his own way, this desire to take a swipe at her was healthy. But it required immediate and straightforward handling.

"Edward, open your eyes and tell me what you see."

He obeyed. "I see a woman in her early forties," he said, "clever-looking face, dark hair showing gray; flesh too thin for her bones, indicating either vanity or illness; wearing slacks and a rather creased batik blouse—describable, I think, by the term 'peasant style'—with a food stain on the left side."

Damn! Don't blush. "Does anything besides my blouse suggest a peasant to you?"

"Nothing concrete, but with regard to me, my vampire self, a peasant with a torch is what you could easily become."

"I hear you saying that my task is to help you get rid of your delusion, though this process may be painful and frightening for you."

Something flashed in his expression—surprise, perhaps alarm, something she wanted to get in touch with before it could sink away out of reach again. Quickly she said, "How do you experience your face at this moment?"

He frowned. "As being on the front of my head. Why?"

With a rush of anger at herself she saw that she had chosen the wrong technique for reaching that hidden feeling: she had provoked hostility instead. She said, "Your face looked to me just now like a mask for concealing what you feel rather than an instrument of expression."

He moved restlessly in the chair, his whole physical attitude tense and guarded. "I don't know what you mean."

"Will you let me touch you?" she said, rising.

His hands tightened on the arms of his chair, which protested in a sharp creak. He snapped, "I thought this was a talking cure."

Strong resistance to body work—ease up. "If you won't let me massage some of the tension out of your facial muscles, will you try to do it yourself?"

"I don't enjoy being made ridiculous," he said, standing and heading for the door, which clapped smartly to behind him.

She sagged back in her seat; she had mishandled him. Clearly her initial estimation of this as a relatively easy job had been wrong and had led her to move far too quickly with him. Certainly it was much too early to try body work. She should have developed a firmer level of trust first by letting him do more of what he did so easily and so well—talk.

The door opened. Weyland came back in and shut it quietly. He did not sit again but paced about the room, coming to rest at the window.

"Please excuse my rather childish behavior just now," he said. "Playing these games of yours brought it on."

"It's frustrating, playing games that are unfamiliar and that you can't control," she said. As he made no reply, she went on in a conciliatory tone, "I'm not trying to belittle you, Edward. I just need to get us off whatever track you were taking us down so briskly. My feeling is that you're trying hard to regain your old stability.

"But that's the goal, not the starting point. The only way to reach your goal is through the process, and you don't drive the therapy process like a train. You can only help the process happen, as though you were helping a tree grow."

"These games are part of the process?"

"Yes."

"And neither you nor I control the games?"

"That's right."

He considered. "Suppose I agree to try this process of yours; what would you want of me?"

Observing him carefully, she no longer saw the anxious scholar bravely struggling back from madness. Here was a different sort of man—armored, calculating. She didn't know just what the change signaled, but she felt her own excitement stirring, and that meant she was on the track of—something.

"I have a hunch," she said slowly, "that this vampirism extends further back into your past than you've told me and possibly right up into the present as well. I think it's still with you. My style of therapy stresses dealing with the now at least as much as the then; if the vampirism is part of the present, dealing with it on that basis is crucial."

Silence.

"Can you talk about being a vampire: being one now?"

"You won't like knowing," he said.

"Edward, try."

He said, "I hunt."

"Where? How? What sort of victims?"

He folded his arms and leaned his back against the window frame. "Very well, since you insist. There are a number of possibilities here in the city in summer. Those too poor to own air-conditioners sleep out on rooftops and fire escapes. But often, I've found, their blood is sour with drugs or liquor. The same is true of prostitutes. Bars are full of accessible people but also full of smoke and noise, and there too the blood is fouled. I must choose my hunting grounds carefully. Often I go to openings of galleries or evening museum shows or department stores on their late nights—places where women may be approached."

And take pleasure in it, she thought, *if they're out hunting also—for acceptable male companionship. Yet he said he's never married. Explore where this is going.* "Only women?"

He gave her a sardonic glance, as if she were a slightly brighter student than he had at first assumed.

"Hunting women is liable to be time-consuming and expensive. The best hunting is in the part of Central Park they call the Ramble, where homosexual men seek encounters with others of their kind. I walk there too, at night."

Floria caught a faint sound of conversation and laughter from the waiting room; her next client had probably arrived, she realized, looking reluctantly at the clock. "I'm sorry, Edward, but our time seems to be—"

"Only a moment more," he said coldly. "You asked; permit me to finish my answer. In the Ramble I find someone who doesn't reek of alcohol or drugs, who seems healthy, and who is not insistent on 'hooking up' right there among the bushes. I invite such a man to my hotel. He judges me safe, at least: older, weaker than he is, unlikely to turn out to be a dangerous maniac. So he comes to my room. I feed on his blood.

"Now, I think, our time is up."

He walked out.

She sat torn between rejoicing at his admission of the delusion's persistence and dismay that his condition was so much worse than she had first thought. Her hope of having an easy time with him vanished. His initial presentation had been just that—a performance, an act. Forced to abandon it, he had dumped on her this lump of material, too much—and too strange—to take in all at once.

Her next client liked the padded chair, not the wooden one that Weyland had sat in during the first part of the hour. Floria started to move the wooden one back. The armrests came away in her hands.

She remembered him starting up in protest against her proposal of touching him. The grip of his fingers had fractured the joints, and the shafts now lay in splinters on the floor.

Floria wandered into Lucille's room at the clinic after the staff meeting. Lucille was lying on the couch with a wet cloth over her eyes.

"I thought you looked green around the gills today," Floria said. "What's wrong?"

"Big bash last night," said Lucille in sepulchral tones. "I think I feel about the way you do after a session with Chubs. You haven't gotten rid of him yet, have you?"

"No. I had him lined up to see Marty instead of me last week, but damned if he didn't show up at my door at his usual time. It's a lost cause. What I wanted to talk to you about was Dracula."

"What about him?"

"He's smarter, tougher, and sicker than I thought, and maybe I'm even less competent than I thought, too. He's already walked out on me once—I almost lost him. I never took a course in treating monsters."

Lucille groaned. "Some days they're all monsters." This from Lucille, who worked longer hours than anyone else at the clinic, to the despair of her husband. She lifted the cloth, refolded it, and placed it carefully across her forehead. "And if I had ten dollars for every client who's walked out on me . . . Tell you what: I'll trade you Madame X for him, how's that? Remember Madame X, with the jangling bracelets and the parakeet eye makeup and the phobia about dogs? Now she's phobic about things dropping on her out of the sky. Just wait—it'll turn out that one day when she was three a dog trotted by and pissed on her leg just as an over-passing pigeon shat on her head. What are we doing in this business?"

"God knows." Floria laughed. "But am I in this business these days—I mean, in the sense of practicing my so-called skills? Blocked with my group work, beating my brains out on a book that won't go, and doing something—I'm not sure it's therapy—with a vampire . . . You know, once I had this sort of natural choreographer inside myself that hardly let me put a foot wrong and always knew how to correct a mistake if I did. Now that's gone. I feel as if I'm just going through a lot of mechanical motions. Whatever I had once that made me useful as a therapist, I've lost it."

Ugh, she thought, hearing the descent of her voice into a tone of gloomy self-pity.

"Well, don't complain about Dracula," Lucille said. "You were the one who insisted on taking him on. At least he's got you concentrating on his problem instead of just wringing your hands. As long as you've started, stay with it—illumination may come. And now I'd better change the ribbon in my typewriter and get back to reviewing Silverman's latest bestseller on self-shrinking while I'm feeling mean enough to do it justice." She got up gingerly. "Stick around in case I faint and fall into the wastebasket."

"Luce, this case is what I'd like to try to write about."

"Dracula?" Lucille pawed through a desk drawer full of paper clips, pens, rubber bands, and old lipsticks.

"Dracula. A monograph . . ."

"Oh, I know that game: you scribble down everything you can and then read what you wrote to find out what's going on with the client, and with luck you end up publishing. Great! But if you are going to publish, don't piddle this away on a dinky paper. Do a book. Here's your subject, instead of those depressing statistics you've been killing yourself over. This one is really exciting—a case study to put on the shelf next to Freud's own wolf-man, have you thought of that?"

Floria liked it. "What a book that could be—fame if not fortune. Notoriety, most likely. How in the world could I convince our colleagues that it's legit? There's a lot of vampire stuff around right now—plays on Broadway and TV, books all over the place, movies. They'll say I'm just trying to ride the coattails of a fad."

"No, no, what you do is show how this guy's delusion is related to the fad. Fascinating." Lucille, having found a ribbon, prodded doubtfully at the exposed innards of her typewriter.

"Suppose I fictionalize it," Floria said, "under a pseudonym. Why not ride the popular wave and be free in what I can say?"

"Listen, you've never written a word of fiction in your life, have you?" Lucille fixed her with a bloodshot gaze. "There's no evidence that you could turn out a bestselling novel. On the other hand, by this time you have a trained memory for accurately reporting therapeutic transactions. That's a strength you'd be foolish to waste. A solid professional book would be terrific—and a feather in the cap of every woman in the field. Just make sure you get good legal advice on disguising your Dracula's identity well enough to avoid libel."

The cane-seated chair wasn't worth repairing, so she got its twin out of the bedroom to put in the office in its place. Puzzling: by his history Weyland was fifty-two, and by his appearance no muscle man. She should have asked Doug—but how, exactly? "By the way, Doug, was Weyland ever a circus strong man? or a blacksmith? Does he secretly pump iron?" Ask the client himself—but not yet.

She invited some of the younger staff from the clinic over for a small party with a few of her outside friends. It was a good evening; they were not a heavy-drinking crowd, which meant the conversation stayed intelligent. The guests drifted about the long living room or stood in twos and threes at the windows looking down on West End Avenue as they talked.

Mort came, warming the room. Fresh from a session with some amateur chamber-music friends, he still glowed with the pleasure of making his cello sing. His own voice was unexpectedly light for so large a man. Sometimes Floria thought that the deep throb of the cello was his true voice.

He stood beside her talking with some others. There was no need to lean against his comfortable bulk or to have him put his arm around her waist. Their intimacy was long-standing, an effortless pleasure in each other that required neither demonstration nor concealment.

He was easily diverted from music to his next favorite topic, the strengths and skills of athletes.

"Here's a question for a paper I'm thinking of writing," Floria said. "Could a tall, lean man be exceptionally strong?"

Mort rambled on in his thoughtful way. His answer seemed to be no.

"But what about chimpanzees?" put in a young clinician. "I went with a guy once who was an animal handler for TV, and he said a three-month-old chimp could demolish a strong man."

"It's all physical conditioning," somebody else said. "Modern people are soft."

Mort nodded. "Human beings in general are weakly made compared to other animals. It's a question of muscle insertions—the angles of how the muscles are attached to the bones. Some angles give better leverage than others. That's how a leopard can bring down a much bigger animal than itself. It has a muscular structure that gives it tremendous strength for its streamlined build."

Floria said, "If a man were built with muscle insertions like a leopard's, he'd look pretty odd, wouldn't he?"

"Not to an untrained eye," Mort said, sounding bemused by an inner vision. "And my God, what an athlete he'd make—can you imagine a guy in the decathlon who's as strong as a leopard?"

When everyone else had gone Mort stayed, as he often did. Jokes about insertions, muscular and otherwise, soon led to sounds more expressive and more animal, but afterward Floria didn't feel like resting snuggled together with Mort and talking. When her body stopped racing, her mind turned to her new client. She didn't want to discuss him with Mort, so she ushered Mort out as gently as she could and sat down by herself at the kitchen table with a glass of orange juice.

How to approach the reintegration of Weyland the eminent, gray-haired academic with the rebellious vampire-self that had smashed his life out of shape?

She thought of the broken chair, of Weyland's big hands crushing the wood. Old wood and dried-out glue, of course, or he never could have done that. He was a man, after all, not a leopard.

The day before the third session Weyland phoned and left a message with Hilda: he would not be coming to the office tomorrow for his appointment, but if Dr. Landauer were agreeable she would find him at their usual hour at the Central Park Zoo.

Am I going to let him move me around from here to there? she thought. *I shouldn't—but why fight it? Give him some leeway, see what opens up in a different setting.* Besides, it was a beautiful day, probably the last of the sweet May weather before the summer stickiness descended. She gladly cut Kenny short so that she would have time to walk over to the zoo.

There was a fair crowd there for a weekday. Well-groomed young matrons pushed clean, floppy babies in strollers. Weyland she spotted at once.

He was leaning against the railing that enclosed the seals' shelter and their murky green pool. His jacket, slung over his shoulder, draped elegantly down his long back. Floria thought him rather dashing and faintly foreign-looking. Women who passed him, she noticed, tended to glance back.

He looked at everyone. She had the impression that he knew quite well that she was walking up behind him.

"Outdoors makes a nice change from the office, Edward," she said, coming to the rail beside him. "But there must be more to this than a longing for fresh air." A fat seal lay in sculptural grace on the concrete, eyes blissfully shut, fur drying in the sun to a translucent watercolor umber.

Weyland straightened from the rail. They walked. He did not look at the animals; his eyes moved continually over the crowd. He said, "Someone has been watching for me at your office building."

"Who?"

"There are several possibilities. Pah, what a stench—though humans caged in similar circumstances smell as bad." He sidestepped a couple of shrieking children who were fighting over a balloon and headed out of the zoo under the musical clock.

They walked the uphill path northward through the park. By extending her own stride a little Floria found that she could comfortably keep pace with him.

"Is it peasants with torches?" she said. "Following you?"

He said, "What a childish idea."

All right, try another tack, then: "You were telling me last time about hunting in the Ramble. Can we return to that?"

"If you wish." He sounded bored—a defense? Surely—she was certain this must be the right reading—surely his problem was a transmutation into "vampire" fantasy of an unacceptable aspect of himself. For men of his generation the confrontation with homosexual drives could be devastating.

"When you pick up someone in the Ramble, is it a paid encounter?"

"Usually."

"How do you feel about having to pay?" She expected resentment.

He gave a faint shrug. "Why not? Others work to earn their bread. I work, too, very hard, in fact. Why shouldn't I use my earnings to pay for my sustenance?"

Why did he never play the expected card? Baffled, she paused to drink from a fountain. They walked on.

"Once you've got your quarry, how do you . . ." She fumbled for a word.

"Attack?" he supplied, unperturbed. "There's a place on the neck, here, where pressure can interrupt the blood flow to the brain and cause unconsciousness. Getting close enough to apply that pressure isn't difficult."

"You do this before, or after any sexual activity?"

"Before, if possible," he said aridly, "and instead of." He turned aside to stalk up a slope to a granite outcrop that overlooked the path they had been following. There he settled on his haunches, looking back the way they had come. Floria, glad she'd worn slacks today, sat down near him.

He didn't seem devastated—anything but. *Press him, don't let him get by on cool.* "Do you often prey on men in preference to women?"

"Certainly. I take what is easiest. Men have always been more accessible because women have been walled away like prizes or so physically impoverished by repeated childbearing as to be unhealthy prey for me. All this has begun to change recently, but gay men are still the simplest quarry." While she was recovering from her surprise at his unforeseen and weirdly skewed awareness of female history, he added suavely, "How carefully you control your expression, Dr. Landauer—no trace of disapproval."

She did disapprove, she realized. She would prefer him not to be committed sexually to men. *Oh, hell.*

He went on, "Yet no doubt you see me as one who victimizes the already victimized. This is the world's way. A wolf brings down the stragglers at the edges of the herd. Gay men are denied the full protection of the human herd and are at the same time emboldened to make themselves known and available.

"On the other hand, unlike the wolf I can feed without killing, and these particular victims pose no threat to me that would cause me to kill. Outcasts themselves, even if they comprehend my true purpose among them they cannot effectively accuse me."

God, how neatly, completely, and ruthlessly he distanced the homosexual community from himself! "And how do you feel, Edward, about their purposes—their sexual expectations of you?"

"The same way I feel about the sexual expectations of women whom I choose to pursue: they don't interest me. Besides, once my hunger is active, sexual arousal is impossible. My physical unresponsiveness seems to surprise no one. Apparently impotence is expected in a gray-haired man, which suits my intention."

Some kids carrying radios swung past below, trailing a jumble of amplified thump, wail, and jabber.

Floria gazed after them unseeingly, thinking, astonished again, that she had never heard a man speak of his own impotence with such cool indifference. She had induced him to talk about his problem all right.

He was speaking as freely as he had in the first session, only this time it was no act. He was drowning her in more than she had ever expected or for that matter wanted to know about vampirism. What the hell: she was listening, she thought she understood—what was it all good for? *Time for some cold reality*, she thought; *see how far he can carry all this incredible detail. Give the whole structure a shove.*

She said, "You realize, I'm sure, that people of either sex who make themselves so easily available are also liable to be carriers of disease. When was your last medical checkup?"

"My dear Dr. Landauer, my first medical checkup will be my last. Fortunately, I have no great need of one. Most serious illnesses—hepatitis, for example—reveal themselves to me by a quality in the odor of the victim's skin. Warned, I abstain. When I do fall ill, as occasionally happens, I withdraw to some place where I can heal undisturbed. A doctor's attentions would be more dangerous to me than any disease."

Eyes on the path below, he continued calmly, "You can see by looking at me that there are no obvious clues to my unique nature. But believe me, an examination of any depth by even a half-sleeping medical practitioner would reveal some alarming deviations from the norm. I take pains to stay healthy, and I seem to be gifted with an exceptionally hardy constitution."

Fantasies of being unique and physically superior; take him to the other pole. "I'd like you to try something now. Will you put yourself into the mind of a man you contact in the Ramble and describe your encounter with him from his point of view?"

He turned toward her and for some moments regarded her without expression. Then he resumed his surveillance of the path. "I will not. Though I do have enough empathy with my quarry to enable me to hunt efficiently, I must draw the line at erasing the necessary distance that keeps prey and predator distinct.

"And now I think our ways part for today." He stood up, descended the hillside, and walked beneath some low-canopied trees, his tall back stooped, toward the Seventy-Second Street entrance of the park.

Floria arose more slowly, aware suddenly of her shallow breathing and the sweat on her face. Back to reality or what remained of it. She looked at her watch. She was late for her next client.

Floria couldn't sleep that night. Barefoot in her bathrobe she paced the living room by lamplight. They had sat together on that hill as isolated as in her office—more so, because there was no Hilda and no phone. He was, she knew, very strong, and he had sat close enough to her to reach out for that paralyzing touch to the neck—

Just suppose for a minute that Weyland had been brazenly telling the truth all along, counting on her to treat it as a delusion because on the face of it the truth was inconceivable.

Jesus, she thought, *if I'm thinking that way about him, this therapy is more out of control than I thought. What kind of therapist becomes an accomplice to the client's fantasy? A crazy therapist, that's what kind.*

Frustrated and confused by the turmoil in her mind, she wandered into the workroom. By morning the floor was covered with sheets of newsprint, each broadly marked by her felt-tipped pen. Floria sat in the midst of them, gritty-eyed and hungry.

She often approached problems this way, harking back to art training: turn off the thinking, put hand to paper and see what the deeper, less verbally sophisticated parts of the mind have to offer. Now that her dreams had deserted her, this was her only access to those levels. The newsprint sheets were covered with rough representations of Weyland's face and form. Across several of them were scrawled words: "Dear Doug, your vampire is fine, it's your ex-therapist who's off the rails. Warning:

therapy can be dangerous to your health. Especially if you are the therapist. Beautiful vampire, awaken to me. Am I really ready to take on a legendary monster? Give up—refer this one out. Do your job—work is a good doctor."

That last one sounded pretty good, except that doing her job was precisely what she was feeling so shaky about these days.

Here was another message: "How come this attraction to someone so scary?" *Oh ho*, she thought, *is that a real feeling or an aimless reaction out of the body's early-morning hormone peak? You don't want to confuse honest libido with mere biological clockwork.*

Deborah called. Babies cried in the background over the Scotch Symphony. Nick, Deb's husband, was a musicologist with fervent opinions on music and nothing else.

"We'll be in town a little later in the summer," Deborah said, "just for a few days at the end of July. Nicky has this seminar-convention thing. Of course, it won't be easy with the babies . . . I wondered if you might sort of coordinate your vacation so you could spend a little time with them?"

Baby-sit, that meant. Damn. Cute as they were and all that, damn! Floria gritted her teeth. Visits from Deb were difficult. Floria had been so proud of her bright, hard-driving daughter, and then suddenly Deborah had dropped her studies and rushed to embrace all the dangers that Floria had warned her against: a romantic, too-young marriage, instant breeding, no preparation for self-support, the works.

Well, to each her own, but it was so wearing to have Deb around playing the empty-headed *hausfrau*.

"Let me think, Deb. I'd love to see all of you, but I've been considering spending a couple of weeks in Maine with your Aunt Nonnie." *God knows I need a real vacation*, she thought, *though the peace and quiet up there is hard for a city kid like me to take for long.* Still, Nonnie, Floria's younger sister, was good company. "Maybe you could bring the kids up there for a couple of days. There's room in that great barn of a place, and of course Nonnie'd be happy to have you."

"Oh, no, Mom, it's so dead up there, it drives Nick crazy—don't tell Nonnie I said that. Maybe Nonnie could come down to the city instead. You could cancel a date or two and we could all go to Coney Island together, things like that."

Kid things, which would drive Nonnie crazy and Floria too, before long. "I doubt she could manage," Floria said, "but I'll ask. Look, hon, if I do go up there, you and Nick and the kids could stay here at the apartment and save some money."

"We have to be at the hotel for the seminar," Deb said shortly. No doubt she was feeling just as impatient as Floria was by now. "And the kids haven't seen you for a long time—it would be really nice if you could stay in the city just for a few days."

"We'll try to work something out." Always working something out. *Concord never comes naturally—first we have to butt heads and get pissed off. Each time you call I hope it'll be different*, Floria thought.

Somebody shrieked for "oly," jelly that would be, in the background— Floria felt a sudden rush of warmth for them, her grandkids for God's sake. Having been a young mother herself, she was still young enough to really enjoy them (and to fight with Deb about how to bring them up).

Deb was starting an awkward goodbye. Floria replied, put the phone down, and sat with her head back against the flowered kitchen wallpaper, thinking, *Why do I feel so rotten now? Deb and I aren't close, no comfort, seldom friends, though we were once. Have I said everything wrong, made her think I don't want to see her and don't care about her family? What does she want from me that I can't seem to give her? Approval? Maybe she thinks I still hold her marriage against her. Well, I do, sort of. What right have I to be critical, me with my divorce? What terrible things would she say to me, would I say to her, that we take such care not to say anything important at all?*

"I think today we might go into sex," she said.

Weyland responded dryly, "Might we indeed. Does it titillate you to wring confessions of solitary vice from men of mature years?"

Oh no you don't, she thought. *You can't sidestep so easily.* "Under what circumstances do you find yourself sexually aroused?"

"Most usually upon waking from sleep," he said indifferently.

"What do you do about it?"

"The same as others do. I am not a cripple, I have hands."

"Do you have fantasies at these times?"

"No. Women, and men for that matter, appeal to me very little, either in fantasy or reality."

"Ah—what about female vampires?" she said, trying not to sound arch.

"I know of none."

Of course: the neatest out in the book. "They're not needed for reproduction, I suppose, because people who die of vampire bites become vampires themselves."

He said testily, "Nonsense. I am not a communicable disease."

So he had left an enormous hole in his construct. She headed straight for it: "Then how does your kind reproduce?"

"I have no kind, so far as I am aware," he said, "and I do not reproduce. Why should I, when I may live for centuries still, perhaps indefinitely? My sexual equipment is clearly only detailed biological mimicry, a form of protective coloration." *How beautiful, how simple a solution,* she thought, full of admiration in spite of herself.

"Do I occasionally detect a note of prurient interest in your questions, Dr. Landauer? Something akin to stopping at the cage to watch the tigers mate at the zoo?"

"Probably," she said, feeling her face heat. He had a great backhand return shot there. "How do you feel about that?"

He shrugged.

"To return to the point," she said. "Do I hear you saying that you have no urge whatever to engage in sexual intercourse with anyone?"

"Would you mate with your livestock?"

His matter-of-fact arrogance took her breath away. She said weakly, "Men have reportedly done so."

"Driven men. I am not driven in that way. My sex urge is of low frequency and is easily dealt with unaided—although I occasionally engage in copulation out of the necessity to keep up appearances. I am capable, but not—like humans—obsessed."

Was he sinking into lunacy before her eyes? "I think I hear you saying," she said, striving to keep her voice neutral, "that you're not just a man with a unique way of life. I think I hear you saying that you're not human at all."

"I thought that this was already clear."

"And that there are no others like you."

"None that I know of."

"Then—you see yourself as what? Some sort of mutation?"

"Perhaps. Or perhaps your kind are the mutation."

She saw disdain in the curl of his lip. "How does your mouth feel now?"

"The corners are drawn down. The feeling is contempt."

"Can you let the contempt speak?"

He got up and went to stand at the window, positioning himself slightly to one side as if to stay hidden from the street below.

"Edward," she said.

He looked back at her. "Humans are my food. I draw the life out of their veins. Sometimes I kill them. I am greater than they are. Yet I must spend my time thinking about their habits and their drives, scheming to avoid the dangers they pose—I hate them."

She felt the hatred like a dry heat radiating from him. *God, he really lived all this!* She had tapped into a furnace of feeling. And now? The sensation of triumph wavered, and she grabbed at a next move: *hit him with reality now, while he's burning.*

"What about blood banks?" she said. "Your food is commercially available, so why all the complication and danger of the hunt?"

"You mean I might turn my efforts to piling up a fortune and buying blood by the case? That would certainly make for an easier, less risky life in the short run. I could fit quite comfortably into modern society if I became just another consumer.

"However, I prefer to keep the mechanics of my survival firmly in my own hands. After all, I can't afford to lose my hunting skills. In two hundred years there may be no blood banks, but I will still need my food."

Jesus, you set him a hurdle and he just flies over it. Are there no weaknesses in all this, has he no blind spots? Look at his tension—go back to that. Floria said, "What do you feel now in your body?"

"Tightness." He pressed his spread fingers to his abdomen.

"What are you doing with your hands?"

"I put my hands to my stomach."

"Can you speak for your stomach?"

"'Feed me or die,'" he snarled.

Elated again, she closed in: "And for yourself, in answer?"

"'Will you never be satisfied?'" He glared at her. "You shouldn't seduce me into quarreling with the terms of my own existence!"

"Your stomach is your existence," she paraphrased.

"The gut determines," he said harshly. "That first, everything else after."

"Say, 'I resent . . .'"

He held to a tense silence.

"'I resent the power of my gut over my life,'" she said for him.

He stood with an abrupt motion and glanced at his watch, an elegant flash of slim silver on his wrist.

"Enough," he said.

That night at home she began a set of notes that would never enter his file at the office, notes toward the proposed book.

Couldn't do it, couldn't get properly into the sex thing with him. Everything shoots off in all directions. His vampire concept so thoroughly worked out, find myself half believing sometimes—my own childish fantasy-response to his powerful death-avoidance, contact-avoidance fantasy. Lose professional distance every time—is that what scares me about him? Don't really want to shatter his delusion (my life a mess, what right to tear down others' patterns?)—so see it as real? Wonder how much of "vampirism" he acts out, how far, how often. Something attractive in his purely selfish, predatory stance—the lure of the great outlaw.

Told me today quite coolly about a man he killed recently—inadvertently— by drinking too much from him. Is it fantasy? Of course—the victim, he thinks, was a college student. Breathes there a professor who hasn't dreamed of murdering some representative youth, retaliation for years of classroom frustration? Speaks of teaching with acerbic humor—amuses him to work at cultivating the minds of those he regards strictly as bodies, containers of his sustenance. He shows the alienness of full-blown psychopathology, poor bastard, plus clean-cut logic. Suggested he find another job (assuming his delusion at least in part related to pressures at Cayslin); his fantasy-persona, the vampire, more realistic than I about job-switching:

"For a man of my apparent age it's not so easy to make such a change in these tight times. I might have to take a position lower on the ladder of 'success' as you people assess it." Status is important to him? "Certainly. An eccentric professor is one thing; an eccentric pipe-fitter, another. And I like good cars, which are expensive to own and run." Then, thoughtful addition, "Although there are advantages to a simpler, less visible life." He refuses to discuss other "jobs" from former "lives." We are deep into the fantasy—where the hell going? Damn right I don't control the "games"— preplanned therapeutic strategies get whirled away as soon as we begin. Nerve-wracking.

Tried again to have him take the part of his enemy-victim, peasant with torch. Asked if he felt himself rejecting that point of view? Frosty reply: "Naturally. The peasant's point of view is in no way my own. I've been reading in your field, Dr. Landauer. You work from the Gestalt orientation—" Originally yes, I corrected; eclectic now. "But you do proceed from the theory that I am projecting some aspect of my own feelings outward onto others, whom I then treat as my victims. Your purpose then must be to maneuver me into accepting as my own the projected 'victim' aspect of myself. This integration is supposed to effect the freeing of energy previously locked into maintaining the projection. All this is an interesting insight into the nature of ordinary human confusion, but I am not an ordinary human, and I am not confused. I cannot afford confusion." Felt sympathy for him—telling me he's afraid of having own internal confusions exposed in therapy, too threatening. Keep chipping away at delusion, though with what prospect? It's so complex, deep-seated.

Returned to his phrase "my apparent age." He asserts he has lived many human lifetimes, all details forgotten, however, during periods of suspended animation between lives. Perhaps sensing my skepticism at such handy amnesia, grew cool and distant, claimed to know little about the hibernation process itself: "The essence of this state is that I sleep through it—hardly an ideal condition for making scientific observations."

Edward thinks his body synthesizes vitamins, minerals (as all our bodies synthesize vitamin D), even proteins. Describes unique design he deduces in himself: special intestinal microfauna plus superefficient body chemistry extracts enough energy to live on from blood. Damn good mileage per calorie, too. (Recall observable tension, first interview, at question about drinking—my note on possible alcohol problem!)

Speak for blood: "'Lacking me, you have no life. I flow to the heart's soft drumbeat through lightless prisons of flesh. I am rich, I am nourishing, I am difficult to attain.'" Stunned to find him positively lyrical on subject of his "food." Drew attention to whispering voice of blood. "'Yes. I am secret, hidden beneath the surface, patient, silent, steady. I work unnoticed, an unseen thread of vitality running from age to age—beautiful, efficient, self-renewing, self-cleansing, warm, filling—'" Could see him getting worked up. Finally he stood: "My appetite is pressing. I must leave you." And he did.

Sat and trembled for five minutes after.

New development (or new perception?): he sometimes comes across very unsophisticated about own feelings—lets me pursue subjects of extreme intensity and delicacy to him.

Asked him to daydream—a hunt. (Hands—mine—shaking now as I write. God. What a session.) He told of picking up a woman at poetry reading, 92nd Street Y—has NYC all worked out, circulates to avoid too much notice any one spot. Spoke easily, eyes shut without observable strain: chooses from audience a redhead in glasses, dress with drooping neckline (ease of access), no perfume (strong smells bother him). Approaches during intermission, encouraged to see her fanning away smoke of others' cigarettes—meaning she doesn't smoke, health sign. Agreed in not enjoying the reading, they adjourn together to coffee shop.

"She asks whether I'm a teacher," he says, eyes shut, mouth amused. "My clothes, glasses, manner all suggest this, and I emphasize the impression—it reassures. She's a copy editor for a publishing house. We talk about books. The waiter brings her a gummy-looking pastry. As a non-eater, I pay little attention to the quality of restaurants, so I must apologize to her. She waves this away—is engrossed, or pretending to be engrossed, in talk." A longish dialog between interested woman and Edward doing shy-lonesome-scholar act—dead wife, competitive young colleagues who don't understand him, quarrels in professional journals with big shots in his field—a version of what he first told me. She's attracted (of course—lanky, rough-cut elegance plus hints of vulnerability all very alluring, as intended). He offers to take her home.

Tension in his body at this point in narrative—spine clear of chair back, hands braced on thighs. "She settles beside me in the back of the cab, talking about problems of her own career—illegible manuscripts of Biblical length, mulish editors, suicidal authors—and I make comforting comments; I lean nearer and put my arm along the back of the seat, behind her shoulders. Traffic is heavy, we move slowly. There is time to make my meal here in the taxi and avoid a tedious extension of the situation into her apartment—if I move soon."

How do you feel?

"Eager," he says, voice husky. "My hunger is so roused I can scarcely restrain myself. A powerful hunger, not like yours—mine compels. I embrace her shoulders lightly, make kindly uncle remarks, treading that fine line between the game of seduction she perceives and the game of friendly interest I pretend to affect. My real purpose underlies all: what I say, how I look, every gesture is part of the stalk. There is an added excitement, and fear, because I'm doing my hunting in the presence of a third person—behind the cabby's head."

Could scarcely breathe. Studied him—intent face, masklike with closed eyes, nostrils slightly flared; legs tensed, hands clenched on knees. Whispering: "I press the place on her neck. She starts, sighs faintly, silently drops against me. In the stale stench of the cab's interior, with the ticking of the meter in my ears and the mutter of the radio—I take hold here, at the tenderest part of her throat. Sound subsides into the background—I feel the sweet blood beating under her skin, I taste salt at the moment before I—strike. My saliva thins her blood so that it flows out, I draw the blood into my mouth swiftly, swiftly, before she can wake, before we can arrive . . ."

Trailed off, sat back loosely in chair—saw him swallow. "Ah. I feed." Heard him sigh. Managed to ask about physical sensation. His low murmur, "Warm. Heavy, here—" touches his belly "—in a pleasant way. The good taste of blood, tart and rich, in my mouth . . ."

And then? A flicker of movement beneath his closed eyelids: "In time I am aware that the cabby has glanced back once and has taken our—'embrace' for just that. I can feel the cab slowing, hear him move to turn off the meter. I withdraw, I quickly wipe my mouth on my handkerchief. I take her by the shoulders and shake her gently; does she often have these attacks, I inquire, the soul of concern. She comes around, bewildered, weak, thinks she has fainted. I give the driver extra money and ask him to wait. He looks intrigued—'What was that all about?' I can see the question in his face—but as a true New Yorker he won't expose his own ignorance by asking.

"I escort the woman to her front door, supporting her as she staggers. Any suspicion of me that she may entertain, however formless and hazy, is allayed by my stern charging of the doorman to see that she reaches her apartment safely. She grows embarrassed, thinks perhaps that if not put off by her 'illness' I would spend the night with her, which moves her to press upon me, unasked, her telephone number. I bid her a solicitous good night and take the cab back to my hotel, where I sleep."

No sex? No sex.

How did he feel about the victim as a person? "She was food."

This was his "hunting" of last night, he admits afterward, not a made-up dream. No boasting in it, just telling. Telling me! Think: I can go talk to Lucille, Mort, Doug, others about most of what matters to me.

Edward has only me to talk to and that for a fee—what isolation! No wonder the stone, monumental face—only those long, strong lips (his point of contact, verbal and physical-in-fantasy, with world and with "food") are truly expressive. An exciting narration; uncomfortable to find I felt not only empathy but enjoyment. Suppose he picked up and victimized—even in fantasy—Deb or Hilda, how would I feel then?

Later: Truth—I also found this recital sexually stirring. Keep visualizing how he looked finishing this "dream"—he sat very still, head up, look of thoughtful pleasure on his face. Like handsome intellectual listening to music.

Kenny showed up unexpectedly at Floria's office on Monday, bursting with malevolent energy. She happened to be free, so she took him—something was definitely up. He sat on the edge of his chair.

"I know why you're trying to unload me," he accused. "It's that new one, the tall guy with the snooty look—what is he, an old actor or something? Anybody could see he's got you itching for him."

"Kenny, when was it that I first spoke to you about terminating our work together?" she said patiently.

"Don't change the subject. Let me tell you, in case you don't know it: that guy isn't really interested, Doctor, because he's a fruit. A faggot. You want to know how I know?"

Oh Lord, she thought wearily, *he's regressed to age ten*. She could see that she was going to hear the rest whether she wanted to or not. What in God's name was the world like for Kenny, if he clung so fanatically to her despite her failure to help him?

"Listen, I knew right away there was something flaky about him, so I followed him from here to that hotel where he lives. I followed him the other afternoon too. He walked around like he does a lot, and then he went into one of those ritzy movie houses on Third that opens early and shows risqué foreign movies—you know, Japs cutting each other's things off and glop like that. This one was French, though.

"Well, there was a guy came in, a Madison Avenue type carrying his attaché case, taking a work break or something. Your man moved over and sat down behind him and reached out and sort of stroked the guy's neck, and the guy leaned back, and your man leaned forward and started nuzzling at him, you know—kissing him.

"I saw it. They had their heads together and they stayed like that a while. It was disgusting: complete strangers, without even 'hello.' The Madison Avenue guy just sat there with his head back looking zonked, you know, just swept away, and what he was doing with his hands under his raincoat in his lap I couldn't see, but I bet you can guess.

"And then your fruity friend got up and walked out. I did, too, and I hung around a little outside. After a while the Madison Avenue guy came out looking all sleepy and loose, like after you-know-what, and he wandered off on his own someplace.

"What do you think now?" he ended, on a high, triumphant note.

Her impulse was to slap his face the way she would have slapped Deb-as-a-child for tattling. But this was a client, not a kid. *God give me strength*, she thought.

"Kenny, you're fired."

"You can't!" he squealed. "You can't! What will I—who can I—"

She stood up, feeling weak but hardening her voice. "I'm sorry. I absolutely cannot have a client who makes it his business to spy on other clients. You already have a list of replacement therapists from me."

He gaped at her in slack-jawed dismay, his eyes swimmy with tears.

"I'm sorry, Kenny. Call this a dose of reality therapy and try to learn from it. There are some things you simply will not be allowed to do." She felt better: it was done at last.

"I hate you!" He surged out of his chair, knocking it back against the wall. Threateningly, he glared at the fish tank, but, contenting himself with a couple of kicks at the nearest table leg, he stamped out.

Floria buzzed Hilda: "No more appointments for Kenny, Hilda. You can close his file."

"Whoopee," Hilda said.

Poor, horrid Kenny. Impossible to tell what would happen to him, better not to speculate or she might relent, call him back. She had encouraged him, really, by listening instead of shutting him up and throwing him out before any damage was done.

Was it damaging, to know the truth? In her mind's eye she saw a cream-faced young man out of a Black Thumb Vodka ad wander from a movie theater into daylight, yawning and rubbing absently at an irritation on his neck . . .

She didn't even look at the telephone on the table or think about whom to call, now that she believed.

No, she was going to keep quiet about Dr. Edward Lewis Weyland, her vampire.

Hardly alive at staff meeting, clinic, yesterday—people asking what's the matter, fobbed them off. Settled down today. Had to, to face him.

Asked him what he felt were his strengths. He said speed, cunning, ruthlessness. Animal strengths, I said. What about imagination, or is that strictly human? He defended at once: not human only. Lion, waiting at water hole where no zebra yet drinks, thinks "Zebra—eat," therefore performs feat of imagining event-yet-to-come. Self experienced as animal? Yes—reminded me that humans are also animals. Pushed for his early memories; he objected: "Gestalt is here-and-now, not history-taking." I insist, citing anomalous nature of his situation, my own refusal to be bound by any one theoretical framework. He defends tensely: "Suppose I became lost there in memory, distracted from dangers of the present, left unguarded from those dangers."

Speak for memory. He resists, but at length attempts it: "'I am heavy with the multitudes of the past.'" Fingertips to forehead, propping up all that weight of lives. "'So heavy, filling worlds of time laid down eon by eon, I accumulate, I persist, I demand recognition. I am as real as the life around you—more real, weightier, richer.'" His voice sinking, shoulders bowed, head in hands—I begin to feel pressure at the back of my own skull. "'Let me in.'" Only a rough whisper now. "'I offer beauty as well as terror. Let me in.'" Whispering also, I suggest he reply to his memory.

"Memory, you want to crush me," he groans. "You would overwhelm me with the cries of animals, the odor and jostle of bodies, old betrayals, dead joys, filth and anger from other times—I must concentrate on the danger now. Let me be." All I can take of this crazy conflict, I gabble us off onto something else. He looks up—relief?—follows my lead—where? Rest of session a blank.

No wonder sometimes no empathy at all—a species boundary! He has to be utterly self-centered just to keep balance—self-centeredness of an animal. Thought just now of our beginning, me trying to push him to produce material, trying to control him, manipulate—no way, no way; so here we are, someplace else—I feel dazed, in shock, but stick with it—it's real.

Therapy with a dinosaur, a Martian.

"You call me 'Weyland' now, not 'Edward.'" I said first name couldn't mean much to one with no memory of being called by that name as a child, silly to pretend it signifies intimacy where it can't. I think he knows now that I believe him. Without prompting, told me truth of disappearance from Cayslin. No romance; he tried to drink from a woman who worked there, she shot him, stomach and chest. Luckily for him, small-caliber pistol, and he was wearing a lined coat over three-piece suit. Even so, badly hurt. (Midsection stiffness I noted when he first came—he was still in some pain at that time.) He didn't "vanish"—fled, hid, was found by questionable types who caught on to what he was, sold him "like a chattel" to someone here in the city. He was imprisoned, fed, put on exhibition—very privately—for gain. Got away. "Do you believe any of this?" Never asked anything like that before, seems of concern to him now. I said my belief or lack of same was immaterial; remarked on hearing a lot of bitterness.

He steepled his fingers, looked brooding at me over tips: "I nearly died there. No doubt my purchaser and his diabolist friend still search for me. Mind you, I had some reason at first to be glad of the attentions of the people who kept me prisoner. I was in no condition to fend for myself. They brought me food and kept me hidden and sheltered, whatever their motives. There are always advantages . . ."

Silence today started a short session. Hunting poor last night, Weyland still hungry. Much restless movement, watching goldfish darting in tank, scanning bookshelves. Asked him to be books. "'I am old and full of knowledge, well made to last long. You see only the title, the substance is hidden. I am a book that stays closed.'" Malicious twist of the mouth, not quite a smile: "This is a good game." Is he feeling threatened, too—already "opened" too much to me? Too strung out with him to dig when he's skimming surfaces that should be probed. Don't know how to do therapy with Weyland just have to let things happen, hope it's good. But what's "good"? Aristotle? Rousseau? Ask Weyland what's good, he'll say "Blood."

Everything in a spin—these notes too confused, too fragmentary—worthless for a book, just a mess, like me, my life. Tried to call Deb last night, cancel visit. Nobody home, thank God. Can't tell her to stay away—but damn it—do not need complications now!

Floria went down to Broadway with Lucille to get more juice, cheese, and crackers for the clinic fridge. This week it was their turn to do the provisions, a chore that rotated among the staff. Their talk about grant proposals for the support of the clinic trailed off.

"Let's sit a minute," Floria said. They crossed to a traffic island in the middle of the avenue. It was a sunny afternoon, close enough to lunchtime so that the brigade of old people who normally occupied the benches had thinned out. Floria sat down and kicked a crumpled beer can and some greasy fast-food wrappings back under the bench.

"You look like hell, but wide awake at least," Lucille commented.

"Things are still rough," Floria said. "I keep hoping to get my life under control so I'll have some energy left for Deb and Nick and the kids when they arrive, but I can't seem to do it. Group was awful last night—a member accused me afterward of having abandoned them all. I think I have, too. The professional messes and the personal are all related somehow, they run into each other. I should be keeping them apart so I can deal with them separately, but I can't. I can't concentrate; my mind is all over the place. Except with Dracula, who keeps me riveted with astonishment when he's in the office and bemused the rest of the time."

A bus roared by, shaking the pavement and the benches. Lucille waited until the noise faded. "Relax about the group. The others would have defended you if you'd been attacked during the session. They all understand, even if you don't seem to: it's the summer doldrums, people don't want to work, they expect you to do it all for them. But don't push so hard. You're not a shaman who can magic your clients back into health."

Floria tore two cans of juice out of a six-pack and handed one to her. On a street corner opposite, a violent argument broke out in typewriter-fast Spanish between two women. Floria sipped tinny juice and watched. She'd seen a guy last winter straddle another on that same corner and try to smash his brains out on the icy sidewalk. The old question again: what's crazy, what's health?

"It's a good thing you dumped Chubs, anyhow," Lucille said. "I don't know what finally brought that on, but it's definitely a move in the right direction. What about Count Dracula? You don't talk about him much anymore. I thought I diagnosed a yen for his venerable body."

Floria shifted uncomfortably on the bench and didn't answer. If only she could deflect Lucille's sharp-eyed curiosity.

"Oh," Lucille said. "I see. You really are hot—or at least warm. Has he noticed?"

"I don't think so. He's not on the lookout for that kind of response from me. He says sex with other people doesn't interest him, and I think he's telling the truth."

"Weird," Lucille said. "What about Vampire on My Couch? Shaping up all right?"

"It's shaky, like everything else. I'm worried that I don't know how things are going to come out. I mean, Freud's wolf-man case was a success, as therapy goes. Will my vampire case turn out successfully?"

She glanced at Lucille's puzzled face, made up her mind, and plunged ahead. "Luce, think of it this way: suppose, just suppose, that my Dracula is for real, an honest-to-God vampire—"

"Oh *shit*!" Lucille erupted in anguished exasperation. "Damn it, Floria, enough is enough—will you stop futzing around and get some help? Coming to pieces yourself and trying to treat this poor nut with a vampire fixation—how can you do him any good? No wonder you're worried about his therapy!"

"Please, just listen, help me think this out. My purpose can't be to cure him of what he is. Suppose vampirism isn't a defense he has to learn to drop? Suppose it's the core of his identity? Then what do I do?"

Lucille rose abruptly and marched away from her through a gap between the rolling waves of cabs and trucks. Floria caught up with her on the next block.

"Listen, will you? Luce, you see the problem? I don't need to help him see who and what he is, he knows that perfectly well, and he's not crazy, far from it—"

"Maybe not," Lucille said grimly, "but you are. Don't dump this junk on me outside of office hours, Floria. I don't spend my time listening to nut-talk unless I'm getting paid."

"Just tell me if this makes psychological sense to you: he's healthier than most of us because he's always true to his identity, even when he's engaged in deceiving others. A fairly narrow, rigorous set of requirements necessary to his survival—that is his identity, and it commands him completely. Anything extraneous could destroy him. To go on living, he has to act solely out of his own undistorted necessity, and if that isn't authenticity, what is? So he's healthy, isn't he?" She paused, feeling a sudden lightness in herself. "And that's the best sense I've been able to make of this whole business so far."

They were in the middle of the block. Lucille, who could not on her short legs out walk Floria, turned on her suddenly. "What the hell do you think you're doing, calling yourself a therapist? For God's sake, Floria, don't try to rope me into this kind of professional irresponsibility. You're just dipping into your client's fantasies instead of helping him to handle them. That's not therapy; it's collusion. Have some sense! Admit you're over your head in troubles of your own, retreat to firmer ground— go get treatment for yourself!"

Floria angrily shook her head. When Lucille turned away and hurried on up the block toward the clinic, Floria let her go without trying to detain her.

Thought about Lucille's advice. After my divorce going back into therapy for a while did help, but now?

Retreat again to being a client, like old days in training—so young, inadequate, defenseless then. Awful prospect. And I'd have to hand over W. to somebody else—who? I'm not up to handling him, can't cope, too anxious, yet with all that we do good therapy together somehow. I can't control, can only offer; he's free to take, refuse, use as suits, as far as he's willing to go. I serve as resource while he does own therapy—isn't that therapeutic ideal, free of "shoulds," "shouldn'ts"?

Saw ballet with Mort, lovely evening—time out from W.—talking, singing, pirouetting all the way home, feeling safe as anything in the shadow of Mort-mountain; rolled later with that humming (off-key), sun-warm body. Today W. says he saw me at Lincoln Center last night, avoided me because of Mort. W. is ballet fan! Started attending to pick up victims, now also because dance puzzles and pleases.

"When a group dances well, the meaning is easy—the dancers make a visual complement to the music, all their moves necessary, coherent, flowing. When a gifted soloist performs, the pleasure of making the moves is echoed in my own body. The soloist's absorption is total, much like my own in the actions of the hunt. But when a man and a woman dance together, something else happens. Sometimes one is hunter, one is prey, or they shift these roles between them. Yet some other level of significance exists—I suppose to do with sex—and I feel it—a tugging sensation, here—" touched his solar plexus "—but I do not understand it."

Worked with his reactions to ballet. The response he feels to *pas de deux* is a kind of pull, "like hunger but not hunger." Of course he's baffled—Balanchine writes that the *pas de deux* is always a love story between man and woman. W. isn't man, isn't woman, yet the drama connects. His hands hovering as he spoke, fingers spread toward each other. Pointed this out. Body work comes easier to him now; joined his hands, interlaced fingers, spoke for hands without prompting: "'We are similar; we want the comfort of like closing to like.'" How would that be for him, to find—likeness, another of his kind? "Female?" Starts impatiently explaining how unlikely this is—No, forget sex and *pas de deux* for now; just to find your like, another vampire.

He springs up, agitated now. There are none, he insists; adds at once, "But what would it be like? What would happen? I fear it!" Sits again, hands clenched. "I long for it."

Silence. He watches goldfish; I watch him. I withhold fatuous attempt to pin down this insight, if that's what it is—what can I know about his insight? Suddenly he turns, studies me intently till I lose my nerve, react, cravenly suggest that if I make him uncomfortable he might wish to switch to another therapist—

"Certainly not." More follows, all gold: "There is value to me in what we do here, Dr. Landauer, much against my earlier expectations. Although people talk appreciatively of honest speech they generally avoid it, and I myself have found scarcely any use for it at all. Your straightforwardness with me—and the straightforwardness you require in return—this is healthy in a life so dependent on deception as mine."

Sat there, wordless, much moved, thinking of what I don't show him—my upset life, seat-of-pants course with him and attendant strain, attraction to him—I'm holding out on him while he appreciates my honesty.

Hesitation, then lower-voiced, "Also, there are limits on my methods of self-discovery, short of turning myself over to a laboratory for vivisection. I have no others like myself to look at and learn from. Any tools that may help are worth much to me, and these games of yours are—potent." Other stuff besides, not important. Important: he moves me and he draws me and he keeps on coming back. Hang in if he does.

Bad night—Kenny's aunt called: no bill from me this month, so if he's not seeing me who's keeping an eye on him, where's he hanging out? Much implied blame for what might happen. Absurd, but shook me up: I did fail Kenny. Called off group this week also; too much.

No, it was a good night—first dream in months I can recall, contact again with own depths—but disturbing. Dreamed myself in cab with W. in place of the woman from the Y. He put his hand not on my neck but breast—I felt intense sensual response in the dream, also anger and fear so strong they woke me.

Thinking about this: anyone leans toward him sexually, to him a sign his hunting technique has maneuvered prospective victim into range, maybe arouses his appetite for blood. *I don't want that.* "She was food." I am not food, I am a person. No thrill at languishing away in his arms in a taxi while he drinks my blood—that's disfigured sex, masochism. My sex response in dream signaled to me I would be his victim—I rejected that, woke up.

Mention of *Dracula* (novel). W. dislikes: meandering, inaccurate, those absurd fangs. Says he himself has a sort of needle under his tongue, used to pierce skin. No offer to demonstrate, and no request from me. I brightly brought up historical Vlad Dracul—celebrated instance of Turkish envoys who, upon refusing to uncover to Vlad to show respect, were killed by spiking their hats to their skulls. "Nonsense," snorts W. "A clever ruler would use very small thumbtacks and dismiss the envoys to moan about the streets of Varna holding their tacked heads." First spontaneous play he's shown—took head in hands and uttered plaintive groans, "Ow, oh, ooh." I cracked up. W. reverted at once to usual dignified manner: "You can see that this would serve the ruler much more effectively as an object lesson against rash pride."

Later, same light vein: "I know why I'm a vampire; why are you a therapist?" Off balance as usual, said things about helping, mental health, etc. He shook his head: "And people think of a vampire as arrogant! You want to perform cures in a world which exhibits very little health of any kind—and it's the same arrogance with all of you. This one wants to be President or Class Monitor or Department Chairman or Union Boss, another must be first to fly to the stars or to transplant the human brain, and on and on. As for me, I wish only to satisfy my appetite in peace."

And those of us whose appetite is for competence, for effectiveness? Thought of Green, treated eight years ago, went on to be indicted for running a hellish "home" for aged. I had helped him stay functional so he could destroy the helpless for profit.

W. not my first predator, only most honest and direct. Scared; not of attack by W., but of process we're going through. I'm beginning to be up to it (?), but still—utterly unpredictable, impossible to handle or manage. Occasional stirrings of inward choreographer that used to shape my work so surely. Have I been afraid of that, holding it down in myself, choosing mechanical manipulation instead? Not a choice with W.—thinking no good, strategy no good, nothing left but instinct, clear and uncluttered responses if I can find them. Have to be my own authority with him, as he is always his own authority with a world in which he's unique. So work with W. not just exhausting—exhilarating too, along with strain, fear.

Am I growing braver? Not much choice.

Park again today (air-conditioning out at office). Avoiding Lucille's phone calls from clinic (very reassuring that she calls despite quarrel, but don't want to take all this up with her again). Also, meeting W. in open feels saner somehow—wild creatures belong outdoors? Sailboat pond N. of 72nd, lots of kids, garbage, one beautiful tall boat drifting. We walked.

W. maintains he remembers no childhood, no parents. I told him my astonishment, confronted by someone who never had a life of the previous generation (even adopted parent) shielding him from death—how naked we stand when the last shield falls. Got caught in remembering a death dream of mine, dream it now and then—couldn't concentrate, got scared, spoke of it—a dog tumbled under a passing truck, ejected to side of the road where it lay unable to move except to lift head and shriek; couldn't help. Shaking nearly to tears—remembered Mother got into dream somehow—had blocked that at first. Didn't say it now. Tried to rescue situation, show W. how to work with a dream (sitting in vine arbor near band shell, some privacy).

He focused on my obvious shakiness: "The air vibrates constantly with the death cries of countless animals large and small. What is the death of one dog?" Leaned close, speaking quietly, instructing. "Many creatures are dying in ways too dreadful to imagine. I am part of the world; I listen to the pain. You people claim to be above all that. You deafen yourselves with your own noise and pretend there's nothing else to hear. Then these screams enter your dreams, and you have to seek therapy because you have lost the nerve to listen."

Remembered myself, said, Be a dying animal. He refused: "You are the one who dreams this." I had a horrible flash, felt I was the dog—helpless, doomed, hurting—burst into tears. The great therapist, bringing her own hang-ups into session with client! Enraged with self, which did not help stop bawling. W. disconcerted, I think; didn't speak. People walked past, glanced over, ignored us. W. said finally, "What is this?" Nothing, just the fear of death.

"Oh, the fear of death. That's with me all the time. One must simply get used to it." Tears into laughter. Goddamn wisdom of the ages. He got up to go, paused: "And tell that stupid little man who used to precede me at your office to stop following me around. He puts himself in danger that way."

Kenny, damn it! Aunt doesn't know where he is, no answer on his phone. Idiot!

Sketching all night—useless. W. beautiful beyond the scope of line—the beauty of singularity, cohesion, rooted in absolute devotion to demands of his specialized body. In feeding (woman in taxi), utter absorption one wants from a man in sex—no score-keeping, no fantasies, just hot urgency of appetite, of senses, the moment by itself.

His sleeves worn rolled back today to the elbows—strong, sculptural forearms, the long bones curved in slightly, suggest torque, leverage. How old?

Endurance: huge, rich cloak of time flows back from his shoulders like wings of a dark angel. All springs from, elaborates, the single, stark, primary condition: he is a predator who subsists on human blood. Harmony, strength, clarity, magnificence—all from that basic animal integrity. Of course I long for all that, here in the higgledy-piggledy hodgepodge of my life! Of course he draws me!

Wore no perfume today, deference to his keen, easily insulted sense of smell. He noticed at once, said curt thanks. Saw something bothering him, opened my mouth seeking desperately for right thing to say—up rose my inward choreographer, wide awake, and spoke plain from my heart: Thinking on my floundering in some of our sessions—I am aware that you see this confusion of mine. I know you see by your occasional impatient look, sudden disengagement—yet you continue to reveal yourself to me (even shift our course yourself if it needs shifting and I don't do it). I think I know why. Because there's no place for you in world as you truly are. Because beneath your various façades your true self suffers; like all true selves, it wants, needs to be honored as real and valuable through acceptance by another. I try to be that other, but often you are beyond me.

He rose, paced to window, looked back, burning at me. "If I seem sometimes restless or impatient, Dr. Landauer, it's not because of any professional shortcomings of yours. On the contrary—you are all too effective. The seductiveness, the distraction of our—human contact worries me. I fear for the ruthlessness that keeps me alive."

Speak for ruthlessness. He shook his head. Saw tightness in shoulders, feet braced hard against floor.

Felt reflected tension in my own muscles.

Prompted him: "'I resent . . .'"

"I resent your pretension to teach me about myself! What will this work that you do here make of me? A predator paralyzed by an unwanted empathy with his prey? A creature fit only for a cage and keeper?" He was breathing hard, jaw set. I saw suddenly the truth of his fear: his integrity is not human, but my work is specifically human, designed to make humans more human—what if it does that to him? Should have seen it before, should have seen it. No place left to go: had to ask him, in small voice, Speak for my pretension.

"No!" Eyes shut, head turned away.

Had to do it: Speak for me. W. whispered, "As to the unicorn, out of your own legends—'Unicorn, come lay your head in my lap while the hunters close in. You are a wonder, and for love of wonder I will tame you. You are pursued, but forget your pursuers, rest under my hand till they come and destroy you.'" Looked at me like steel: "Do you see? The more you involve yourself in what I am, the more you become the peasant with the torch!"

Two days later Doug came into town and had lunch with Floria.

He was a man of no outstanding beauty who was nevertheless attractive: he didn't have much chin and his ears were too big, but you didn't notice because of his air of confidence. His stability had been earned the hard way—as a gay man facing the straight world. Some of his strength had been attained with effort and pain in a group that Floria had run years earlier. A lasting affection had grown between herself and Doug. She was intensely glad to see him.

They ate near the clinic. "You look a little frayed around the edges," Doug said. "I heard about Jane Fennerman's relapse—too bad."

"I've only been able to bring myself to visit her once since."

"Feeling guilty?"

She hesitated, gnawing on a stale breadstick. The truth was, she hadn't thought of Jane Fennerman in weeks. Finally she said, "I guess I must be."

Sitting back with his hands in his pockets, Doug chided her gently. "It's got to be Jane's fourth or fifth time into the nuthatch, and the others happened when she was in the care of other therapists. Who are you to imagine—to demand—that her cure lay in your hands? God may be a woman, Floria, but She is not you. I thought the whole point was some recognition of individual responsibility—you for yourself, the client for himself or herself."

"That's what we're always saying," Floria agreed. She felt curiously divorced from this conversation. It had an old-fashioned flavor: Before Weyland. She smiled a little.

The waiter ambled over. She ordered bluefish. The serving would be too big for her depressed appetite, but Doug wouldn't be satisfied with his customary order of salad (he never was) and could be persuaded to help out.

He worked his way around to Topic A. "When I called to set up this lunch, Hilda told me she's got a crush on Weyland. How are you and he getting along?"

"My God, Doug, now you're going to tell me this whole thing was to fix me up with an eligible suitor!" She winced at her own rather strained laughter. "How soon are you planning to ask Weyland to work at Cayslin again?"

"I don't know, but probably sooner than I thought a couple of months ago. We hear that he's been exploring an attachment to an anthropology department at a western school, some niche where I guess he feels he can have less responsibility, less visibility, and a chance to collect himself. Naturally, this news is making people at Cayslin suddenly eager to nail him down for us. Have you a recommendation?"

"Yes," she said. "Wait."

He gave her an inquiring look. "What for?"

"Until he works more fully through certain stresses in the situation at Cayslin. Then I'll be ready to commit myself about him." The bluefish came. She pretended distraction: "Good God, that's too much fish for me. Doug, come on and help me out here."

Hilda was crouched over Floria's file drawer. She straightened up, looking grim. "Somebody's been in the office!"

What was this, had someone attacked her? The world took on a cockeyed, dangerous tilt. "Are you okay?"

"Yes, sure, I mean there are records that have been gone through. I can tell. I've started checking and so far it looks as if none of the files themselves are missing. But if any papers were taken out of them, that would be pretty hard to spot without reading through every folder in the place. Your files, Floria. I don't think anybody else's were touched."

Mere burglary; weak with relief, Floria sat down on one of the waiting-room chairs. But only her files?

"Just my stuff, you're sure?"

Hilda nodded. "The clinic got hit, too. I called. They see some new-looking scratches on the lock of your file drawer over there. Listen, you want me to call the cops?"

"First check as much as you can, see if anything obvious is missing."

There was no sign of upset in her office. She found a phone message on her table: Weyland had canceled his next appointment. She knew who had broken into her files.

She buzzed Hilda's desk. "Hilda, let's leave the police out of it for the moment. Keep checking." She stood in the middle of the office, looking at the chair replacing the one he had broken, looking at the window where he had so often watched.

Relax, she told herself. There was nothing for him to find here or at the clinic.

She signaled that she was ready for the first client of the afternoon.

That evening she came back to the office after having dinner with friends. She was supposed to be helping set up a workshop for next month, and she'd been putting off even thinking about it, let alone doing any real work. She set herself to compiling a suggested bibliography for her section.

The phone light blinked.

It was Kenny, sounding muffled and teary. "I'm sorry," he moaned. "The medicine just started to wear off. I've been trying to call you every-place. God, I'm so scared—he was waiting in the alley."

"Who was?" she said, dry-mouthed. She knew.

"Him. The tall one, the faggot—only he goes with women too, I've seen him. He grabbed me. He hurt me. I was lying there a long time. I couldn't do anything. I felt so funny—like floating away. Some kids found me. Their mother called the cops. I was so cold, so scared—"

"Kenny, where are you?"

He told her which hospital. "Listen, I think he's really crazy, you know? And I'm scared he might . . . you live alone . . . I don't know—I didn't mean to make trouble for you. I'm so scared."

God damn you, you meant exactly to make trouble for me, and now you've bloody well made it.

She got him to ring for a nurse. By calling Kenny her patient and using "Dr." in front of her own name without qualifying the title she got some information: two broken ribs, multiple contusions, a badly wrenched shoulder, and a deep cut on the scalp which Dr. Wells thought accounted for the blood loss the patient had sustained. Picked up early today, the patient wouldn't say who had attacked him. You can check with Dr. Wells tomorrow, Dr.—?

Can Weyland think I've somehow sicced Kenny on him? No, he surely knows me better than that.

Kenny must have brought this on himself.

She tried Weyland's number and then the desk at his hotel. He had closed his account and gone, providing no forwarding information other than the address of a university in New Mexico.

Then she remembered: this was the night Deb and Nick and the kids were arriving. Oh, God. Next phone call. The Americana was the hotel Deb had mentioned. Yes, Mr. and Mrs. Nicholas Redpath were registered in room whatnot. Ring, please.

Deb's voice came shakily on the line. "I've been trying to call you." Like Kenny.

"You sound upset," Floria said, steadying herself for whatever calamity had descended: illness, accident, assault in the streets of the dark, degenerate city.

Silence, then a raggedy sob. "Nick's not here. I didn't phone you earlier because I thought he still might come, but I don't think he's coming, Mom." Bitter weeping.

"Oh, Debbie. Debbie, listen, you just sit tight, I'll be right down there."

The cab ride took only a few minutes. Debbie was still crying when Floria stepped into the room.

"I don't know, I don't know," Deb wailed, shaking her head. "What did I do wrong? He went away a week ago, to do some research, he said, and I didn't hear from him, and half the bank money is gone—just half, he left me half. I kept hoping . . . they say most runaways come back in a few days or call up, they get lonely . . . I haven't told anybody—I thought since we were supposed to be here at this convention thing together, I'd better come, maybe he'd show up. But nobody's seen him, and there are no messages, not a word, nothing."

"All right, all right, poor Deb," Floria said, hugging her.

"Oh God, I'm going to wake the kids with all this howling." Deb pulled away, making a frantic gesture toward the door of the adjoining room. "It was so hard to get them to sleep—they were expecting Daddy to be here, I kept telling them he'd be here." She rushed out into the hotel hallway. Floria followed, propping the door open with one of her shoes since she didn't know whether Deb had a key with her or not. They stood out there together, ignoring passersby, huddling over Deb's weeping.

"What's been going on between you and Nick?" Floria said. "Have you two been sleeping together lately?"

Deb let out a squawk of agonized embarrassment, "Mo-*ther*!" and pulled away from her. *Oh, hell, wrong approach.*

"Come on, I'll help you pack. We'll leave word you're at my place. Let Nick come looking for you."

Floria firmly squashed down the miserable inner cry, *How am I going to stand this?*

"Oh, no, I can't move till morning now that I've got the kids settled down. Besides, there's one night's deposit on the rooms. Oh, Mom, what did I do?"

"You didn't do anything, hon," Floria said, patting her shoulder and thinking in some part of her mind, *Oh boy, that's great, is that the best you can come up with in a crisis with all your training and experience? Your touted professional skills are not so hot lately, but this bad?* Another part answered, *Shut up, stupid, only an idiot does therapy on her own family. Deb's come to her mother, not to a shrink, so go ahead and be Mommy. If only Mommy had less pressure on her right now*—but that was always the way: everything at once or nothing at all.

"Look, Deb, suppose I stay the night here with you."

Deb shook the pale, damp-streaked hair out of her eyes with a determined, grown-up gesture. "No, thanks, Mom. I'm so tired I'm just going to fall out now. You'll be getting a bellyful of all this when we move in on you tomorrow anyway. I can manage tonight, and besides—"

And besides, just in case Nick showed up, Deb didn't want Floria around complicating things; of course. Or in case the tooth fairy dropped by.

Floria restrained an impulse to insist on staying; an impulse, she recognized, that came from her own need not to be alone tonight. That was not something to load on Deb's already burdened shoulders.

"Okay," Floria said. "But look, Deb, I'll expect you to call me up first thing in the morning, whatever happens." *And if I'm still alive, I'll answer the phone.*

All the way home in the cab she knew with growing certainty that Weyland would be waiting for her there. *He can't just walk away*, she thought; *he has to finish things with me. So let's get it over.*

In the tiled hallway she hesitated, keys in hand. What about calling the cops to go inside with her? Absurd. You don't set the cops on a unicorn.

She unlocked and opened the door to the apartment and called inside, "Weyland! Where are you?"

Nothing. Of course not—the door was still open, and he would want to be sure she was by herself. She stepped inside, shut the door, and snapped on a lamp as she walked into the living room.

He was sitting quietly on a radiator cover by the street window, his hands on his thighs. His appearance here in a new setting, her setting, this faintly lit room in her home place, was startlingly intimate. She was sharply aware of the whisper of movement—his clothing, his shoe soles against the carpet underfoot—as he shifted his posture.

"What would you have done if I'd brought somebody with me?" she said unsteadily. "Changed yourself into a bat and flown away?"

"Two things I must have from you," he said. "One is the bill of health that we spoke of when we began, though not, after all, for Cayslin College. I've made other plans. The story of my disappearance has of course filtered out along the academic grapevine so that even two thousand miles from here people will want evidence of my mental soundness. Your evidence. I would type it myself and forge your signature, but I want your authentic tone and language. Please prepare a letter to the desired effect, addressed to these people."

He drew something white from an inside pocket and held it out. She advanced and took the envelope from his extended hand. It was from the western anthropology department that Doug had mentioned at lunch.

"Why not Cayslin?" she said. "They want you there."

"Have you forgotten your own suggestion that I find another job? That was a good idea after all. Your reference will serve me best out there—with a copy for my personnel file at Cayslin, naturally."

She put her purse down on the seat of a chair and crossed her arms. She felt reckless—*the effect of stress and weariness*, she thought, but it was an exciting feeling.

"The receptionist at the office does this sort of thing for me," she said.

He pointed. "I've been in your study. You have a typewriter there, you have stationery with your letterhead, you have carbon paper."

"What was the second thing you wanted?"

"Your notes on my case."

"Also at the—"

"You know that I've already searched both your work places, and the very circumspect jottings in your file on me are not what I mean. Others must exist: more detailed."

"What makes you think that?"

"How could you resist?" He mocked her. "You have encountered nothing like me in your entire professional life, and never shall again. Perhaps you hope to produce an article someday, even a book—a memoir of something impossible that happened to you one summer. You're an ambitious woman, Dr. Landauer."

Floria squeezed her crossed arms tighter against herself to quell her shivering. "This is all just supposition," she said.

He took folded papers from his pocket: some of her thrown-aside notes on him, salvaged from the wastebasket. "I found these. I think there must be more. Whatever there is, give it to me, please."

"And if I refuse, what will you do? Beat me up the way you beat up Kenny?"

Weyland said calmly, "I told you he should stop following me. This is serious now. There are pursuers who intend me ill—my former captors, of whom I told you. Who do you think I keep watch for? No records concerning me must fall into their hands. Don't bother protesting to me your devotion to confidentiality. There is a man named Alan Reese who would take what he wants and be damned to your professional ethics. So I must destroy all evidence you have about me before I leave the city."

Floria turned away and sat down by the coffee table, trying to think beyond her fear. She breathed deeply against the fright trembling in her chest.

"I see," he said dryly, "that you won't give me the notes; you don't trust me to take them and go. You see some danger."

"All right, a bargain," she said. "I'll give you whatever I have on your case if in return you promise to go straight out to your new job and keep away from Kenny and my offices and anybody connected with me—"

He was smiling slightly as he rose from the seat and stepped soft-footed toward her over the rug.

"Bargains, promises, negotiations—all foolish, Dr. Landauer. I want what I came for."

She looked up at him. "But then how can I trust you at all? As soon as I give you what you want—"

"What is it that makes you afraid—that you can't render me harmless to you? What a curious concern you show suddenly for your own life and the lives of those around you! You are the one who led me to take chances in our work together—to explore the frightful risks of self-revelation. Didn't you see in the air between us the brilliant shimmer of those hazards? I thought your business was not smoothing the world over but adventuring into it, discovering its true nature, and closing valiantly with everything jagged, cruel, and deadly."

In the midst of her terror the inner choreographer awoke and stretched. Floria rose to face the vampire.

"All right, Weyland, no bargains. I'll give you freely what you want." Of course she couldn't make herself safe from him—or make Kenny or Lucille or Deb or Doug safe—any more than she could protect Jane Fennerman from the common dangers of life. Like Weyland, some dangers were too strong to bind or banish. "My notes are in the workroom—come on, I'll show you. As for the letter you need, I'll type it right now and you can take it away with you."

She sat at the typewriter arranging paper, carbon sheets, and white-out, and feeling the force of his presence. Only a few feet away, just at the margin of the light from the gooseneck lamp by which she worked, he leaned against the edge of the long table that was twin to the table in her office. Open in his large hands was the notebook she had given him from the table drawer. When he moved his head over the notebook's pages, his glasses glinted.

She typed the heading and the date. *How surprising*, she thought, *to find that she had regained her nerve here, and now*. When you dance as the inner choreographer directs, you act without thinking, not in command of events but in harmony with them. You yield control, accepting the chance that a mistake might be part of the design. The inner choreographer is always right but often dangerous: giving up control means accepting the possibility of death. *What I feared I have pursued right here to this moment in this room.*

A sheet of paper fell out of the notebook. Weyland stooped and caught it up, glanced at it. "You had training in art?" Must be a sketch.

"I thought once I might be an artist," she said.

"What you chose to do instead is better," he said. "This making of pictures, plays, all art, is pathetic. The world teems with creation, most of it unnoticed by your kind just as most of the deaths are unnoticed. What can be the point of adding yet another tiny gesture? Even you, these notes—for what, a moment's celebrity?"

"You tried it yourself," Floria said. "The book you edited, *Notes on a Vanished People.*" She typed: ". . . temporary dislocation resulting from a severe personal shock . . ."

"That was professional necessity, not creation," he said in the tone of a lecturer irritated by a question from the audience. With disdain he tossed the drawing on the table. "Remember, I don't share your impulse toward artistic gesture—your absurd frills—"

She looked up sharply. "The ballet, Weyland. Don't lie." She typed: ". . . exhibits a powerful drive toward inner balance and wholeness in a difficult life situation. The steadying influence of an extraordinary basic integrity . . ."

He set the notebook aside. "My feeling for ballet is clearly some sort of aberration. Do you sigh to hear a cow calling in a pasture?"

"There are those who have wept to hear whales singing in the ocean."

He was silent, his eyes averted.

"This is finished," she said. "Do you want to read it?"

He took the letter. "Good," he said at length. "Sign it, please. And type an envelope for it." He stood closer, but out of arm's reach, while she complied. "You seem less frightened."

"I'm terrified but not paralyzed," she said and laughed, but the laugh came out a gasp.

"Fear is useful. It has kept you at your best throughout our association. Have you a stamp?"

Then there was nothing to do but take a deep breath, turn off the gooseneck lamp, and follow him back into the living room. "What now, Weyland?" she said softly. "A carefully arranged suicide so that I have no chance to retract what's in that letter or to reconstruct my notes?"

At the window again, always on watch at the window, he said, "Your doorman was sleeping in the lobby. He didn't see me enter the building. Once inside, I used the stairs, of course. The suicide rate among therapists is notoriously high. I looked it up."

"You have everything all planned?"

The window was open. He reached out and touched the metal grille that guarded it. One end of the grille swung creaking outward into the night air, like a gate opening. She visualized him sitting there waiting for her to come home, his powerful fingers patiently working the bolts at that side of the grille loose from the brick-and-mortar window frame. The hair lifted on the back of her neck.

He turned toward her again. She could see the end of the letter she had given him sticking palely out of his jacket pocket.

"Floria," he said meditatively. "An unusual name—is it after the heroine of Sardou's *Tosca*? At the end, doesn't she throw herself to her death from a high castle wall? People are careless about the names they give their children. I will not drink from you—I hunted today, and I fed. Still, to leave you living . . . is too dangerous."

A fire engine tore past below, siren screaming. When it had gone Floria said, "Listen, Weyland, you said it yourself: I can't make myself safe from you—I'm not strong enough to shove you out the window instead of being shoved out myself. Must you make yourself safe from me? Let me say this to you, without promises, demands, or pleadings: I will not go back on what I wrote in that letter. I will not try to recreate my notes. I mean it. Be content with that."

"You tempt me to it," he murmured after a moment, "to go from here with you still alive behind me for the remainder of your little life—to leave woven into Dr. Landauer's quick mind those threads of my own life that I pulled for her . . . I want to be able sometimes to think of you thinking of me. But the risk is very great."

"Sometimes it's right to let the dangers live, to give them their place," she urged. "Didn't you tell me yourself a little while ago how risk makes us more heroic?"

He looked amused. "Are you instructing me in the virtues of danger? You are brave enough to know something, perhaps, about that, but I have studied danger all my life."

"A long, long life with more to come," she said, desperate to make him understand and believe her. "Not mine to jeopardize. There's no torch-brandishing peasant here; we left that behind long ago. Remember when you spoke for me? You said, 'For love of wonder.' That was true."

He leaned to turn off the lamp near the window. She thought that he had made up his mind, and that when he straightened it would be to spring.

But instead of terror locking her limbs, from the inward choreographer came a rush of warmth and energy into her muscles and an impulse to turn toward him. Out of a harmony of desires she said swiftly, "Weyland, come to bed with me."

She saw his shoulders stiffen against the dim square of the window, his head lift in scorn. "You know I can't be bribed that way," he said contemptuously. "What are you up to? Are you one of those who come into heat at the sight of an upraised fist?"

"My life hasn't twisted me that badly, thank God," she retorted. "And if you've known all along how scared I've been, you must have sensed my attraction to you too, so you know it goes back to—very early in our work. But we're not at work now, and I've given up being 'up to' anything. My feeling is real—not a bribe, or a ploy, or a kink. No 'love me now, kill me later,' nothing like that. Understand me, Weyland: if death is your answer, then let's get right to it—come ahead and try."

Her mouth was dry as paper. He said nothing and made no move; she pressed on. "But if you can let me go, if we can simply part company here, then this is how I would like to mark the ending of our time together. This is the completion I want. Surely you feel something, too—curiosity at least?"

"Granted, your emphasis on the expressiveness of the body has instructed me," he admitted, and then he added lightly, "Isn't it extremely unprofessional to proposition a client?"

"Extremely, and I never do; but this, now, feels right. For you to indulge in courtship that doesn't end in a meal would be unprofessional, too, but how would it feel to indulge anyway—this once? Since we started, you've pushed me light-years beyond my profession. Now I want to travel all the way with you, Weyland. Let's be unprofessional together."

She turned and went into the bedroom, leaving the lights off. There was a reflected light, cool and diffuse, from the glowing night air of the great city. She sat down on the bed and kicked off her shoes. When she looked up, he was in the doorway.

Hesitantly, he halted a few feet from her in the dimness, then came and sat beside her. He would have lain down in his clothes, but she said quietly, "You can undress. The front door's locked and there isn't anyone here but us. You won't have to leap up and flee for your life."

He stood again and began to take off his clothes, which he draped neatly over a chair. He said, "Suppose I am fertile with you; could you conceive?"

By her own choice any such possibility had been closed off after Deb. She said, "No," and that seemed to satisfy him.

She tossed her own clothes onto the dresser.

He sat down next to her again, his body silvery in the reflected light and smooth, lean as a whippet and as roped with muscle. His cool thigh pressed against her own fuller, warmer one as he leaned across her and carefully deposited his glasses on the bed table. Then he turned toward her, and she could just make out two puckerings of tissue on his skin: *bullet scars*, she thought, shivering.

He said, "But why do I wish to do this?"

"Do you?" She had to hold herself back from touching him.

"Yes." He stared at her. "How did you grow so real? The more I spoke to you of myself, the more real you became."

"No more speaking, Weyland," she said gently. "This is body work."

He lay back on the bed.

She wasn't afraid to take the lead. At the very least she could do for him as well as he did for himself, and at the most, much better. Her own skin was darker than his, a shadowy contrast where she browsed over his body with her hands. Along the contours of his ribs she felt knotted places, hollows—old healings, the tracks of time. The tension of his muscles under her touch and the sharp sound of his breathing stirred her. She lived the fantasy of sex with an utter stranger; there was no one in the world so much a stranger as he. Yet there was no one who knew him as well as she did, either. If he was unique, so was she, and so was their confluence here.

The vividness of the moment inflamed her. His body responded. His penis stirred, warmed, and thickened in her hand. He turned on his hip so that they lay facing each other, he on his right side, she on her left. When she moved to kiss him he swiftly averted his face: of course—to him, the mouth was for feeding. She touched her fingers to his lips, signifying her comprehension.

He offered no caresses but closed his arms around her, his hands cradling the back of her head and neck. His shadowed face, deep-hollowed under brow and cheekbone, was very close to hers. From between the parted lips that she must not kiss his quick breath came, roughened by groans of pleasure.

At length he pressed his head against hers, inhaling deeply; taking her scent, she thought, from her hair and skin.

He entered her, hesitant at first, probing slowly and tentatively. She found this searching motion intensely sensuous, and clinging to him all along his sinewy length she rocked with him through two long, swelling waves of sweetness. Still half submerged, she felt him strain tight against her, she heard him gasp through his clenched teeth.

Panting, they subsided and lay loosely interlocked. His head was tilted back; his eyes were closed. She had no desire to stroke him or to speak with him, only to rest spent against his body and absorb the sounds of his breathing, her breathing.

He did not lie long to hold or be held. Without a word he disengaged his body from hers and got up. He moved quietly about the bedroom, gathering his clothing, his shoes, the drawings, the notes from the work-room. He dressed without lights. She listened in silence from the center of a deep repose.

There was no leave-taking. His tall figure passed and repassed the dark rectangle of the doorway, and then he was gone. The latch on the front door clicked shut.

Floria thought of getting up to secure the deadbolt. Instead she turned on her stomach and slept.

She woke as she remembered coming out of sleep as a youngster—peppy and clearheaded.

"Hilda, let's give the police a call about that break-in. If anything ever does come of it, I want to be on record as having reported it. You can tell them we don't have any idea who did it or why. And please make a photocopy of this letter carbon to send to Doug Sharpe up at Cayslin. Then you can put the carbon into Weyland's file and close it."

Hilda sighed. "Well, he was too old anyway."

He wasn't, my dear, but never mind.

In her office Floria picked up the morning's mail from her table. Her glance strayed to the window where Weyland had so often stood. God, she was going to miss him; and God, how good it was to be restored to plain working days.

Only not yet. *Don't let the phone ring, don't let the world push in here now*. She needed to sit alone for a little and let her mind sort through the images left from . . . from the *pas de deux* with Weyland. *It's the notorious morning after, old dear*, she told herself; just where have I been dancing, anyway?

In a clearing in the enchanted forest with the unicorn, of course, but not the way the old legends have it. According to them, hunters set a virgin to attract the unicorn by her chastity so they can catch and kill him. My unicorn was the chaste one, come to think of it, and this lady meant no treachery. No, Weyland and I met hidden from the hunt, to celebrate a private mystery of our own . . . .

Your mind grappled with my mind, my dark leg over your silver one, unlike closing with unlike across whatever likeness may be found: your memory pressing on my thoughts, my words drawing out your words in which you may recognize your life, my smooth palm gliding down your smooth flank . . .

Why, this will make me cry, she thought, blinking. *And for what? Does an afternoon with the unicorn have any meaning for the ordinary days that come later? What has this passage with Weyland left me? Have I anything in my hands now besides the morning's mail?*

What I have in my hands is my own strength because I had to reach deep to find the strength to match him.

She put down the letters, noticing how on the backs of her hands the veins stood, blue shadows, under the thin skin. *How can these hands be strong?* Time was beginning to wear them thin and bring up the fragile inner structure in clear relief. That was the meaning of the last parent's death: that the child's remaining time has a limit of its own.

But not for Weyland. No graveyards of family dead lay behind him, no obvious and implacable ending of his own span threatened him. Time has to be different for a creature of an enchanted forest, as morality has to be different. He was a predator and a killer formed for a life of centuries, not decades; of secret singularity, not the busy hum of the herd. Yet his strength, suited to that nonhuman life, had revived her own strength. Her hands were slim, no longer youthful, but she saw now that they were strong enough.

For what? She flexed her fingers, watching the tendons slide under the skin. *Strong hands don't have to clutch. They can simply open and let go.*

She dialed Lucille's extension at the clinic.

"Luce? Sorry to have missed your calls lately. Listen, I want to start making arrangements to transfer my practice for a while. You were right, I do need a break, just as all my friends have been telling me. Will you pass the word for me to the staff over there today? Good, thanks. Also, there's the workshop coming up next month. . . . Yes. Are you kidding? They'd love to have you in my place. You're not the only one who's noticed that I've been falling apart, you know. It's awfully soon—can you manage, do you think? Luce, you are a brick and a lifesaver and all that stuff that means I'm very, very grateful."

Not so terrible, she thought, *but only a start.* Everything else remained to be dealt with. The glow of euphoria couldn't carry her for long. Already, looking down, she noticed jelly on her blouse, just like old times, and she didn't even remember having breakfast. *If you want to keep the strength you've found in all this, you're going to have to get plenty of practice being strong. Try a tough one now.*

She phoned Deb. "Of course you slept late, so what? I did, too, so I'm glad you didn't call and wake me up. Whenever you're ready—if you need help moving uptown from the hotel, I can cancel here and come down. . . . Well, call if you change your mind. I've left a house key for you with my doorman.

"And listen, hon, I've been thinking—how about all of us going up together to Nonnie's over the weekend? Then when you feel like it, maybe you'd like to talk about what you'll do next. Yes, I've already started setting up some free time for myself. Think about it, love. Talk to you later."

Kenny's turn. "Kenny, I'll come by during visiting hours this afternoon."

"Are you okay?" he squeaked.

"I'm okay. But I'm not your mommy, Ken, and I'm not going to start trying to hold the big bad world off you again. I'll expect you to be ready to settle down seriously and choose a new therapist for yourself. We're going to get that done today once and for all. Have you got that?"

After a short silence he answered in a desolate voice, "All right."

"Kenny, nobody grown up has a mommy around to take care of things for them and keep them safe—not even me. You just have to be tough enough and brave enough yourself. See you this afternoon."

How about Jane Fennerman? No, leave it for now, we are not Wonder Woman, we can't handle that stress today as well.

Too restless to settle down to paperwork before the day's round of appointments began, she got up and fed the goldfish, then drifted to the window and looked out over the city. Same jammed-up traffic down there, same dusty summer park stretching away uptown—yet not the same city, because Weyland no longer hunted there. Nothing like him moved now in those deep, grumbling streets. She would never come upon anyone there as alien as he—and just as well. Let last night stand as the end, unique and inimitable, of their affair. She was glutted with strangeness and looked forward frankly to sharing again in Mort's ordinary human appetite.

And Weyland—how would he do in that new and distant hunting ground he had found for himself? Her own balance had been changed. Suppose his once perfect, solitary equilibrium had been altered too?

Perhaps he had spoiled it by involving himself too intimately with another being—herself. And then he had left her alive—a terrible risk. Was this a sign of his corruption at her hands?

"Oh, no," she whispered fiercely, focusing her vision on her reflection in the smudged window glass. Oh, no, *I am not the temptress. I am not the deadly female out of legends whose touch defiles the hitherto unblemished being, her victim*. If Weyland found some human likeness in himself, that had to be in him to begin with. Who said he was defiled anyway? Newly discovered capacities can be either strengths or weaknesses, depending on how you use them.

Very pretty and reassuring, she thought grimly; *but it's pure cant. Am I going to retreat now into mechanical analysis to make myself feel better?*

She heaved open the window and admitted the sticky summer breath of the city into the office. There's our enchanted forest, my dear, all nitty-gritty and not one flake of fairy dust. You've survived here, which means you can see straight when you have to. Well, you have to now.

Has he been damaged? No telling yet, and you can't stop living while you wait for the answers to come in. I don't know all that was done between us, but I do know who did it: I did it, and he did it, and neither of us withdrew until it was done. We were joined in a rich complicity—he in the wakening of some flicker of humanity in himself, I in keeping and, yes, enjoying the secret of his implacable blood hunger. What that complicity means for each of us can only be discovered by getting on with living and watching for clues from moment to moment. His business is to continue from here, and mine is to do the same, without guilt and without resentment. Doug was right:

the aim is individual responsibility. From that effort, not even the lady and the unicorn are exempt.

Shaken by a fresh upwelling of tears, she thought bitterly, *Moving on is easy enough for Weyland; he's used to it, he's had more practice. What about me? Yes, be selfish, woman—if you haven't learned that, you've learned damn little.*

The Japanese say that in middle age you should leave the claims of family, friends, and work, and go ponder the meaning of the universe while you still have the chance. *Maybe I'll try just existing for a while, and letting grow in its own time my understanding of a universe that includes Weyland—and myself—among its possibilities.*

Is that looking out for myself? Or am I simply no longer fit for living with family, friends, and work? Have I been damaged by him—by my marvelous, murderous monster?

Damn, she thought, *I wish he were here; I wish we could talk about it.* The light on her phone caught her eye; it was blinking the quick flashes that meant Hilda was signaling the imminent arrival of—not Weyland—the day's first client.

We're each on our own now, she thought, shutting the window and turning on the air-conditioner.

But think of me sometimes, Weyland, thinking of you.

THIS TOWN AIN'T BIG ENOUGH

Tanya Huff

Tanya Huff lives in rural Ontario and loves country life. A prolific author, her work includes many short stories, five fantasy series, and a science fiction series. One of these, her Blood Books series, featuring detective Vicki Nelson, was adapted for television under the title *Blood Ties*. A follow-up to the Blood Books, the three Smoke Books, featured Tony Foster as the main character. Her degree in Radio and Television Arts proved handy since Tony works on a show about a vampire detective. Her most recent novel, *The Future Falls*, was published in 2014. When not writing, she practices her guitar and spends too much time online. Her blog is andpuff.livejournal.com.

"This Town Ain't Big Enough" is a Vicki Nelson story. Its mix of detection, the supernatural, a strong female protagonist, and a smattering of romance that might be called "urban fantasy" these days, but the universe of the Blood Books predates that subgenre by a decade . . .

"Ow! Vicki, be careful!"

"Sorry. Sometimes I forget how sharp they are."

"Terrific." He wove his fingers through her hair and pulled just hard enough to make his point. "Don't."

"Don't what?" She grinned up at him, teeth gleaming ivory in the moonlight spilling across the bed. "Don't forget or don't—"

The sudden demand of the telephone for attention buried the last of her question.

Detective-Sergeant Michael Celluci sighed. "Hold that thought," he said, rolled over, and reached for the phone. "Celluci."

"Fifty-two division just called. They've found a body down at Richmond and Peter they think we might want to have a look at."

"Dave, it's . . ." He squinted at the clock. ". . . one twenty-nine in the a.m. and I'm off duty."

On the other end of the line, his partner, theoretically off duty as well, refused to take the hint. "Ask me who the stiff is?"

Celluci sighed again. "Who's the stiff?"

"Mac Eisler."

"Shit."

"Funny, that's exactly what I said." Nothing in Dave Graham's voice indicated he appreciated the joke. "I'll be there in ten."

"Make it fifteen."

"You in the middle of something?"

Celluci watched as Vicki sat up and glared at him. "I was."

"Welcome to the wonderful world of law enforcement."

Vicki's hand shot out and caught Celluci's wrist before he could heave the phone across the room. "Who's Mac Eisler?" she asked as, scowling, he dropped the receiver back in its cradle and swung his legs off the bed.

"You heard that?"

"I can hear the beating of your heart, the movement of your blood, the song of your life." She scratched the back of her leg with one bare foot. "I should think I can overhear a lousy phone conversation."

"Eisler's a pimp." Celluci reached for the light switch, changed his mind, and began pulling on his clothes. Given the full moon riding just outside the window, it wasn't exactly dark and given Vicki's sensitivity to bright light, not to mention her temper, he figured it was safer to cope. "We're pretty sure he offed one of his girls a couple weeks ago."

Vicki scooped her shirt up off the floor. "Irene Macdonald?"

"What? You overheard that too?"

"I get around. How sure's pretty sure?"

"Personally positive. But we had nothing solid to hold him on."

"And now he's dead." Skimming her jeans up over her hips, she dipped her brows in a parody of deep thought. "Golly, I wonder if there's a connection."

"Golly yourself," Celluci snarled. "You're not coming with me."

"Did I ask?"

"I recognized the tone of voice. I know you, Vicki. I knew you when you were a cop, I knew you when you were a P.I. and I don't care how much you've changed physically, I know you now you're a . . . a . . ."

"Vampire." Her pale eyes seemed more silver than gray. "You can say it, Mike. It won't hurt my feelings. Bloodsucker. Nightwalker. Creature of Darkness."

"Pain in the butt." Carefully avoiding her gaze, he shrugged into his shoulder holster and slipped a jacket on over it. "This is police business, Vicki, stay out of it. Please." He didn't wait for a response but crossed the shadows to the bedroom door. Then he paused, one foot over the threshold. "I doubt I'll be back by dawn. Don't wait up."

Vicki Nelson, ex of the Metropolitan Toronto Police Force, ex private investigator, recent vampire, decided to let him go. If he could joke about the change, he accepted it. And besides, it was always more fun to make him pay for smart-ass remarks when he least expected it.

She watched from the darkness as Celluci climbed into Dave Graham's car. Then, with the taillights disappearing in the distance, she dug out his spare set of car keys and proceeded to leave tangled entrails of the Highway Traffic Act strewn from Downsview to the heart of Toronto.

It took no supernatural ability to find the scene of the crime. What with the police, the press, and the morbidly curious, the area seethed with people. Vicki slipped past the constable stationed at the far end of the alley and followed the paths of shadow until she stood just outside the circle of police around the body.

Mac Eisler had been a somewhat attractive, not very tall, white male Caucasian. Eschewing the traditional clothing excesses of his profession, he was dressed simply in designer jeans and an olive-green raw silk jacket. At the moment, he wasn't looking his best. A pair of rusty nails had been shoved through each manicured hand, securing his body upright across the back entrance of a trendy restaurant. Although the pointed toes of his tooled leather cowboy boots indented the wood of the door, Eisler's head had been turned completely around so that he stared, in apparent astonishment, out into the alley.

The smell of death fought with the stink of urine and garbage. Vicki frowned. There was another scent, a pungent predator scent that raised the hair on the back of her neck and drew her lips up off her teeth. Surprised by the strength of her reaction, she stepped silently into a deeper patch of night lest she give herself away.

"Why the hell would I have a comment?"

Preoccupied with an inexplicable rage, she hadn't heard Celluci arrive until he greeted the press. Shifting position slightly, she watched as he and his partner moved in off the street and got their first look at the body.

"Jesus H. Christ."

"On crutches," agreed the younger of the two detectives already on the scene.

"Who found him?"

"Dishwasher, coming out with the trash. He was obviously meant to be found; they nailed the bastard right across the door."

"The kitchen's on the other side and no one heard hammering?"

"I'll go you one better than that. Look at the rust on the head of those nails—they haven't been hammered."

"What? Someone just pushed the nails through Eisler's hands and into solid wood?"

"Looks like."

Celluci snorted. "You trying to tell me that Superman's gone bad?"

Under the cover of their laughter, Vicki bent and picked up a piece of planking. There were four holes in the unbroken end and two remaining three-inch spikes. She pulled a spike out of the wood and pressed it into the wall of the building by her side. A smut of rust marked the ball of her thumb but the nail looked no different.

She remembered the scent.

Vampire.

"... unable to come to the phone. Please leave a message after the long beep."

"Henry? It's Vicki. If you're there, pick up." She stared across the dark kitchen, twisting the phone cord between her fingers. "Come on, Fitzroy, I don't care what you're doing, this is important." Why wasn't he home writing? Or chewing on Tony. Or something. "Look, Henry, I need some information. There's another one of, of us, hunting my territory and I don't know what I should do. I know what I want to do . . ." The rage remained, interlaced with the knowledge of another. ". . . but I'm new at this bloodsucking undead stuff, maybe I'm overreacting. Call me. I'm still at Mike's."

She hung up and sighed. Vampires didn't share territory. Which was why Henry had stayed in Vancouver and she'd come back to Toronto.

Well, all right, it's not the only reason I came back. She tossed Celluci's spare car keys into the drawer in the phone table and wondered if she should write him a note to explain the mysterious emptying of his gas tank. "Nah. He's a detective, let him figure it out."

Sunrise was at five twelve. Vicki didn't need a clock to tell her that it was almost time. She could feel the sun stroking the edges of her awareness.

"It's like that final instant, just before someone hits you from behind, when you know it's going to happen but you can't do a damn thing about it." She crossed her arms on Celluci's chest and pillowed her head on them adding, *"Only it lasts longer."*

"And this happens every morning?"

"Just before dawn."

"And you're going to live forever?"

"That's what they tell me."

Celluci snorted. "You can have it."

Although Celluci had offered to lightproof one of the two unused bedrooms, Vicki had been uneasy about the concept. At four and a half centuries, maybe Henry Fitzroy could afford to be blasé about immolation but Vicki still found the whole idea terrifying and had no intention of being both helpless and exposed. Anyone could walk into a bedroom.

No one would accidentally walk into an enclosed plywood box, covered in a blackout curtain, at the far end of a five-foot-high crawl space—but just to be on the safe side, Vicki dropped two-by-fours into iron brackets over the entrance. Folded nearly in half, she hurried to her sanctuary, feeling the sun drawing closer, closer. Somehow she resisted the urge to turn.

"There's nothing behind me," she muttered, awkwardly stripping off her clothes. Her heart slamming against her ribs, she crawled under the front flap of the box, latched it behind her, and squirmed into her sleeping bag, stretched out ready for the dawn.

"Jesus H. Christ, Vicki," Celluci had said squatting at one end while she'd wrestled the twin bed mattress inside. *"At least a coffin would have a bit of historical dignity."*

"You know where I can get one?"

"I'm not having a coffin in my basement."

"Then quit flapping your mouth."

She wondered, as she lay there waiting for oblivion, where the other was. Did they feel the same near panic knowing that they had no control over the hours from dawn to dusk? Or had they, like Henry, come to accept the daily death that governed an immortal life? There should, she supposed, be a sense of kinship between them but all she could feel was a possessive fury. No one hunted in her territory.

"Pleasant dreams," she said as the sun teetered on the edge of the horizon. "And when I find you, you're toast."

Celluci had been and gone by the time the darkness returned. The note he'd left about the car was profane and to the point. Vicki added a couple of words he'd missed and stuck it under a refrigerator magnet in case he got home before she did.

She'd pick up the scent and follow it, the hunter becoming the hunted and, by dawn, the streets would be hers again.

The yellow police tape still stretched across the mouth of the alley. Vicki ignored it. Wrapping the night around her like a cloak, she stood outside the restaurant door and sifted the air.

Apparently, a pimp crucified over the fire exit hadn't been enough to close the place and TexMex had nearly obliterated the scent of a death not yet twenty-four hours old. Instead of the predator, all she could smell was fajitas.

"God damn it," she muttered, stepping closer and sniffing the wood. "How the hell am I supposed to find . . ."

She sensed his life the moment before he spoke.

"What are you doing?"

Vicki sighed and turned. "I'm sniffing the door frame. What's it look like I'm doing?"

"Let me be more specific," Celluci snarled. "What are you doing here?"

"I'm looking for the person who offed Mac Eisler," Vicki began. She wasn't sure how much more explanation she was willing to offer.

"No, you're not. You are not a cop. You aren't even a P.I. anymore. And how the hell am I going to explain you if Dave sees you?"

Her eyes narrowed. "You don't have to explain me, Mike."

"Yeah? He thinks you're in Vancouver."

"Tell him I came back."

"And do I tell him that you spend your days in a box in my basement? And that you combust in sunlight? And what do I tell him about your eyes?"

Vicki's hand rose to push at the bridge of her glasses but her fingers touched only air. The retinitis pigmentosa that had forced her from the Metro Police and denied her the night had been reversed when Henry'd changed her. The darkness held no secrets from her now. "Tell him they got better."

"RP doesn't get better."

"Mine did."

"Vicki, I know what you're doing." He dragged both hands up through his hair. "You've done it before. You had to quit the force. You were half blind. So what? Your life may have changed but you were still going to prove that you were 'Victory' Nelson. And it wasn't enough to be a private investigator. You threw yourself into stupidly dangerous situations just to prove you were still who you wanted to be. And now your life has changed again and you're playing the same game."

She could hear his heart pounding, see a vein pulsing framed in the white vee of his open collar, feel the blood surging just below the surface in reach of her teeth. The Hunger rose and she had to use every bit of control Henry had taught her to force it back down. This wasn't about that.

Since she'd returned to Toronto, she'd been drifting; feeding, hunting, relearning the night, relearning her relationship with Michael Celluci. The early morning phone call had crystallized a subconscious discontent and, as Celluci pointed out, there was really only one thing she knew how to do.

Part of his diatribe was based on concern. After all their years together playing cops and lovers she knew how he thought; if something as basic as sunlight could kill her, what else waited to strike her down. It was only human nature for him to want to protect the people he loved—for him to want to protect her.

But, that was only the basis for part of the diatribe.

"You can't have been happy with me lazing around your house. I can't cook and I don't do windows." She stepped towards him. "I should think you'd be thrilled that I'm finding my feet again."

"Vicki."

"I wonder," she mused, holding tight to the Hunger, "how you'd feel about me being involved in this if it wasn't your case. I am, after all, better equipped to hunt the night than, oh, detective-sergeants."

"Vicki . . ." Her name had become a nearly inarticulate growl.

She leaned forward until her lips brushed his ear. "Bet you I solve this one first." Then she was gone, moving into shadow too quickly for mortal eyes to track.

"Who you talking to, Mike?" Dave Graham glanced around the empty alley. "I thought I heard . . ." Then he caught sight of the expression on his partner's face. "Never mind."

Vicki couldn't remember the last time she felt so alive. *Which, as I'm now a card-carrying member of the bloodsucking undead, makes for an interesting feeling.* She strode down Queen Street West, almost intoxicated by the lives surrounding her, fully aware of crowds parting to let her through and the admiring glances that traced her path. A connection had been made between her old life and her new one.

"*You must surrender the day,*" Henry had told her, "*but you need not surrender anything else.*"

"*So what you're trying to tell me,*" she'd snarled, "*is that we're just normal people who drink blood?*"

Henry had smiled. "*How many normal people do you know?*"

She hated it when he answered a question with a question but now, she recognized his point. Honesty forced her to admit that Celluci had a point as well. She did need to prove to herself that she was still herself. She always had. The more things changed, the more they stayed the same.

"Well, now we've got that settled . . ." She looked around for a place to sit and think. In her old life, that would have meant a donut shop or the window seat in a cheap restaurant and as many cups of coffee as it took. In this new life, being enclosed with humanity did not encourage contemplation. Besides, coffee, a major component of the old equation, made her violently ill—a fact she deeply resented.

A few years back, CITY TV, a local Toronto station, had renovated a deco building on the corner of Queen and John. They'd done a beautiful job and the six-story, white building with its ornately molded modern windows, had become a focal point of the neighborhood. Vicki slid into the narrow walkway that separated it from its more down-at-the-heels neighbor and swarmed up what effectively amounted to a staircase for one of her kind.

When she reached the roof a few seconds later, she perched on one crenellated corner and looked out over the downtown core. These were her streets; not Celluci's and not some out-of-town bloodsucker's. It was time she took them back. She grinned and fought the urge to strike a dramatic pose.

All things considered, it wasn't likely that the Metropolitan Toronto Police Department—in the person of Detective-Sergeant Michael

Celluci—would be willing to share information. Briefly, she regretted issuing the challenge then she shrugged it off. As Henry said, the night was too long for regrets.

She sat and watched the crowds jostling about on the sidewalks below, clumps of color indicating tourists amongst the Queen Street regulars. On a Friday night in August, this was the place to be as the Toronto artistic community rubbed elbows with wanna-bes and never-woulds.

Vicki frowned. Mac Eisler had been killed before midnight on a Thursday night in an area that never completely slept. Someone had to have seen or heard something. Something they probably didn't believe and were busy denying. Murder was one thing, creatures of the night were something else again.

"Now then," she murmured, "where would a person like that—and considering the time and day we're assuming a regular, not a tourist—where would that person be tonight?"

She found him in the third bar she checked, tucked back in a corner, trying desperately to get drunk, and failing. His eyes darted from side to side, both hands were locked around his glass, and his body language screamed: I'm dealing with some bad shit here, leave me alone.

Vicki sat down beside him and for an instant let the Hunter show. His reaction was everything she could have hoped for.

He stared at her, frozen in terror, his mouth working but no sound coming out.

"Breathe," she suggested.

The ragged intake of air did little to calm him but it did break the paralysis. He shoved his chair back from the table and started to stand.

Vicki closed her fingers around his wrist. "Stay."

He swallowed and sat down again.

His skin was so hot it nearly burned and she could feel his pulse beating against it like a small wild creature struggling to be free. The Hunger clawed at her and her own breathing became a little ragged. "What's your name?"

"Ph . . . Phil."

She caught his gaze with hers and held it. "You saw something last night."

"Yes." Stretched almost to the breaking point, he began to tremble.

"Do you live around here?"

"Yes."

Vicki stood and pulled him to his feet, her tone half command half caress. "Take me there. We have to talk."

Phil stared at her. "Talk?"

She could barely hear the question over the call of his blood. "Well, talk first."

"It was a woman. Dressed all in black. Hair like a thousand strands of shadow, skin like snow, eyes like black ice. She chuckled, deep in her throat, when she saw me and licked her lips. They were painfully red. Then she vanished so quickly that she left an image on the night."

"Did you see what she was doing?"

"No. But then she didn't have to be doing anything to be terrifying. I've spent the last twenty-four hours feeling like I met my death."

Phil had turned out to be a bit of a poet. And a bit of an athlete. All in all, Vicki considered their time together well spent. Working carefully after he fell asleep, she took away his memory of her and muted the meeting in the alley. It was the least she could do for him.

The description sounded like a character freed from a Hammer film: *The Bride of Dracula Kills a Pimp.*

She paused, key in the lock, and cocked her head. Celluci was home, she could feel his life and if she listened very hard, she could hear the regular rhythm of breathing that told her he was asleep. Hardly surprising as it was only three hours to dawn.

There was no reason to wake him as she had no intention of sharing what she'd discovered and no need to feed but, after a long, hot shower, she found herself standing at the door of his room. And then at the side of his bed.

Mike Celluci was thirty-seven. There were strands of gray in his hair and although sleep had smoothed out many of the lines, the deeper creases around his eyes remained. He would grow older. In time, he would die. What would she do then?

She lifted the sheet and tucked herself up close to his side. He sighed and without completely waking scooped her closer still.

"Hair's wet," he muttered.

Vicki twisted, reached up, and brushed the long curl back off his forehead. "I had a shower."

"Where'd you leave the towel?"

"In a sopping pile on the floor."

Celluci grunted inarticulately and surrendered to sleep again.

Vicki smiled and kissed his eyelids. "I love you too."

She stayed beside him until the threat of sunrise drove her away.

"Irene Macdonald."

Vicki lay in the darkness and stared unseeing up at the plywood. The sun was down and she was free to leave her sanctuary but she remained a moment longer, turning over the name that had been on her tongue when she woke. She remembered facetiously wondering if the deaths of Irene Macdonald and her pimp were connected.

Irene had been found beaten nearly to death in the bathroom of her apartment. She'd died two hours later in the hospital.

Celluci said that he was personally certain Mac Eisler was responsible. That was good enough for Vicki.

Eisler could've been unlucky enough to run into a vampire who fed on terror as well as blood—Vicki had tasted terror once or twice during her first year when the Hunger occasionally slipped from her control and she knew how addictive it could be—or he could've been killed in revenge for Irene.

Vicki could think of one sure way to find out.

"Brandon? It's Vicki Nelson."

"Victoria?" Surprise lifted most of the Oxford accent off Dr. Brandon Singh's voice. "I thought you'd relocated to British Columbia."

"Yeah, well, I came back."

"I suppose that might account for the improvement over the last month or so in a certain detective we both know."

She couldn't resist asking. "Was he really bad while I was gone?"

Brandon laughed. "He was unbearable and, as you know, I am able to bear a great deal. So, are you still in the same line of work?"

"Yes, I am." Yes, she was. God, it felt good. "Are you still the Assistant Coroner?"

"Yes, I am. As I think I can safely assume you didn't call me, at home, long after office hours, just to inform me that you're back on the job, what do you want?"

Vicki winced. "I was wondering if you'd had a look at Mac Eisler."

"Yes, Victoria, I have. And I'm wondering why you can't call me during regular business hours. You must know how much I enjoy discussing autopsies in front of my children."

"Oh God, I'm sorry Brandon, but it's important."

"Yes. It always is." His tone was so dry it crumbled. "But since you've already interrupted my evening, try to keep my part of the conversation to a simple yes or no."

"Did you do a blood volume check on Eisler?"

"Yes."

"Was there any missing?"

"No. Fortunately, in spite of the trauma to the neck the integrity of the blood vessels had not been breached."

So much for yes or no; she knew he couldn't keep to it. "You've been a big help, Brandon, thanks."

"I'd say any time, but you'd likely hold me to it." He hung up abruptly.

Vicki replaced the receiver and frowned. She—the other—hadn't fed. The odds moved in favor of Eisler killed because he murdered Irene.

"Well, if it isn't Andrew P." Vicki leaned back against the black Trans Am and adjusted the pair of nonprescription glasses she'd picked up just after sunset. With her hair brushed off her face and the window-glass lenses in front of her eyes, she didn't look much different than she had a year ago. Until she smiled.

The pimp stopped dead in his tracks, bluster fading before he could get the first obscenity out. He swallowed, audibly. "Nelson. I heard you were gone."

Listening to his heart race, Vicki's smile broadened. "I came back. I need some information. I need the name of one of Eisler's other girls."

"I don't know." Unable to look away, he started to shake. "I didn't have anything to do with him. I don't remember."

Vicki straightened and took a slow step towards him. "Try, Andrew."

There was a sudden smell of urine and a darkening stain down the front of the pimp's cotton drawstring pants. "Uh, D . . . D . . . Debbie Ho. That's all I can remember. Really."

"And she works?"

"Middle of the track." His tongue tripped over the words in the rush to spit them at her. "Jarvis and Carlton."

"Thank you." Sweeping a hand towards his car, Vicki stepped aside.

He dove past her and into the driver's seat, jabbing the key into the ignition. The powerful engine roared to life and with one last panicked look into the shadows, he screamed out of the driveway, ground his way through three gear changes, and hit eighty before he reached the corner.

The two cops, quietly sitting in the parking lot of the donut shop on that same corner, hit their siren and took off after him.

Vicki slipped the glasses into the inner pocket of the tweed jacket she'd borrowed from Celluci's closet and grinned. "To paraphrase a certain adolescent crime-fighting amphibian, I love being a vampire."

"I need to talk to you, Debbie."

The young woman started and whirled around, glaring suspiciously at Vicki. "You a cop?"

Vicki sighed. "Not any more." Apparently, it was easier to hide the vampire than the detective. "I'm a private investigator and I want to ask you some questions about Irene Macdonald."

"If you're looking for the shithead who killed her, you're too late. Someone already found him."

"And that's who I'm looking for."

"Why?" Debbie shifted her weight to one hip.

"Maybe I want to give them a medal."

The hooker's laugh held little humor. "You got that right. Mac got everything he deserved."

"Did Irene ever do women?"

Debbie snorted. "Not for free," she said pointedly.

Vicki handed her a twenty.

"Yeah, sometimes. It's safer, medically, you know?"

Editing out Phil's more ornate phrases, Vicki repeated his description of the woman in the alley.

Debbie snorted again. "Who the hell looks at their faces?"

"You'd remember this one if you saw her. She's . . ." Vicki weighed and discarded several possibilities and finally settled on, ". . . powerful."

"Powerful." Debbie hesitated, frowned, and continued in a rush. "There was this person Irene was seeing a lot but she wasn't charging. That's one of the things that set Mac off, not that the shithead needed much encouragement. We knew it was gonna happen, I mean we've all felt Mac's temper, but Irene wouldn't stop. She said that just being with this person was a high better than drugs. I guess it could've been a woman. And since she was sort of the reason Irene died, well, I know they used to meet in this bar on Queen West. Why are you hissing?"

"Hissing?" Vicki quickly yanked a mask of composure down over her rage. The other hadn't come into her territory only to kill Eisler—she was definitely hunting it. "I'm not hissing. I'm just having a little trouble breathing."

"Yeah, tell me about it." Debbie waved a hand ending in three-inch scarlet nails at the traffic on Jarvis. "You should try standing here sucking carbon monoxide all night."

In another mood, Vicki might have reapplied the verb to a different object but she was still too angry. "Do you know which bar?"

"What, now I'm her social director? No, I don't know which bar." Apparently they'd come to the end of the information twenty dollars could buy as Debbie turned her attention to a prospective client in a gray sedan. The interview was clearly over.

Vicki sucked the humid air past her teeth. There weren't that many bars on Queen West. Last night she'd found Phil in one. Tonight; who knew.

Now that she knew enough to search for it, minute traces of the other predator hung in the air—diffused and scattered by the paths of prey. With so many lives masking the trail, it would be impossible to track her. Vicki snarled. A pair of teenagers, noses pierced, heads shaved, and Doc Martens laced to the knee, decided against asking for change and hastily crossed the street.

It was Saturday night, minutes to Sunday. The bars would be closing soon. If the other was hunting, she would have already chosen her prey.

I wish Henry had called back. Maybe over the centuries they've—we've—evolved ways to deal with this. Maybe we're supposed to talk first. Maybe it's considered bad manners to rip her face off and feed it to her if she doesn't agree to leave.

Standing in the shadow of a recessed storefront, just beyond the edge of the artificial safety the streetlight offered to the children of the sun, she extended her senses the way she'd been taught and touched death within the maelstrom of life.

She found Phil, moments later, lying in yet another of the alleys that serviced the business of the day and provided a safe haven for the darker business of the night. His body was still warm but his heart had stopped beating and his blood no longer sang. Vicki touched the tiny, nearly closed wound she'd made in his wrist the night before and then the fresh wound in the bend of his elbow. She didn't know how he had died but she knew who had done it. He stank of the other.

Vicki no longer cared what was traditionally "done" in these instances. There would be no talking. No negotiating. It had gone one life beyond that.

"I rather thought that if I killed him you'd come and save me the trouble of tracking you down. And here you are, charging in without taking the slightest of precautions." Her voice was low, not so much threatening as in itself a threat. "You're hunting in my territory, child."

Still kneeling by Phil's side, Vicki lifted her head. Ten feet away, only her face and hands clearly visible, the other vampire stood. Without thinking—unable to think clearly through the red rage that shrieked for release—Vicki launched herself at the snow-white column of throat, finger hooked to talons, teeth bared.

The Beast Henry had spent a year teaching her to control, was loose. She felt herself lost in its raw power and she reveled in it.

The other made no move until the last possible second then she lithely twisted and slammed Vicki to one side.

Pain eventually brought reason back. Vicki lay panting in the fetid damp at the base of a dumpster, one eye swollen shut, a gash across her forehead still sluggishly bleeding. Her right arm was broken.

"You're strong," the other told her, a contemptuous gaze pinning her to the ground. "In another hundred years you might have stood a chance. But you're an infant. A child. You haven't the experience to control what you are. This will be your only warning. Get out of my territory. If we meet again, I will kill you."

Vicki sagged against the inside of the door and tried to lift her arm. During the two and a half hours it had taken her to get back to Celluci's house, the bone had begun to set. By tomorrow night, provided she fed in the hours remaining until dawn, she should be able use it.

"Vicki?"

She started. Although she'd known he was home, she'd assumed—without checking—that because of the hour he'd be asleep. She squinted as the hall light came on and wondered, listening to him pad down the stairs in bare feet, whether she had the energy to make it into the basement bathroom before he saw her.

He came into the kitchen, tying his bathrobe belt around him, and flicked on the overhead light. "We need to talk," he said grimly as the shadows that might have hidden her fled. "Jesus H. Christ. What the hell happened to you?"

"Nothing much." Eyes squinted nearly shut, Vicki gingerly probed the swelling on her forehead. "You should see the other guy."

Without speaking, Celluci reached over and hit the play button on the telephone answering machine.

"Vicki? Henry. If someone's hunting your territory, whatever you do, don't challenge. Do you hear me? Don't challenge. You can't win. They're going to be older, able to overcome the instinctive rage and remain in full command of their power. If you won't surrender the territory . . ." The sigh the tape played back gave a clear opinion of how likely he thought that was to occur. ". . . you're going to have to negotiate. If you can agree on boundaries there's no reason why you can't share the city." His voice suddenly belonged again to the lover she'd lost with the change. "Call me, please, before you do anything."

It was the only message on the tape.

"Why," Celluci asked as it rewound, his gaze taking in the cuts and the bruising and the filth, "do I get the impression that it's 'the other guy' Fitzroy's talking about?"

Vicki tried to shrug. Her shoulders refused to cooperate. "It's my city, Mike. It always has been. I'm going to take it back."

He stared at her for a long moment then he shook his head. "You heard what Henry said. You can't win. You haven't been . . . what you are, long enough. It's only been fourteen months."

"I know." The rich scent of his life prodded the Hunger and she moved to put a little distance between them.

He closed it up again. "Come on." Laying his hand in the center of her back, he steered her towards the stairs. Put it aside for now, his tone told her. We'll argue about it later. "You need a bath."

"I need . . ."

"I know. But you need a bath first. I just changed the sheets."

The darkness wakes us all in different ways, Henry had told her. We were all human once and we carried our differences through the change.

For Vicki, it was like the flicking of a switch; one moment she wasn't, the next she was. This time, when she returned from the little death of the day, an idea returned with her.

Four hundred and fifty-odd years a vampire, Henry had been seventeen when he changed. The other had walked the night for perhaps as long—her gaze had carried the weight of several lifetimes—but her physical appearance suggested that her mortal life had lasted even less time than Henry's had. Vicki allowed that it made sense. Disaster may have precipitated her change but passion was the usual cause.

And no one does that kind of never-say-die passion like a teenager.

It would be difficult for either Henry or the other to imagine a response that came out of a mortal not a vampiric experience. They'd both had centuries of the latter and not enough of the former to count.

Vicki had been only fourteen months a vampire but she'd been human thirty-two years when Henry'd saved her by drawing her to his blood to feed. During those thirty-two years, she'd been nine years a cop—two accelerated promotions, three citations, and the best arrest record on the force.

There was no chance of negotiation.

She couldn't win if she fought.

She'd be damned if she'd flee.

"Besides . . ." For all she realized where her strength had to lie, Vicki's expression held no humanity. ". . . she owes me for Phil."

Celluci had left her a note on the fridge.

Does this have anything to do with Mac Eisler?

Vicki stared at it for a moment then scribbled her answer underneath.

Not anymore.

It took three weeks to find where the other spent her days. Vicki used old contacts where she could and made new ones where she had to. Any modern Van Helsing could have done the same.

For the next three weeks, Vicki hired someone to watch the other come and go, giving reinforced instructions to stay in the car with the windows closed and the air conditioning running. Life had an infinite number of variations but one piece of machinery smelled pretty much like any other. It irritated her that she couldn't sit stakeout herself but the information she needed would've kept her out after sunrise.

"How the hell did you burn your hand?"

Vicki continued to smear ointment over the blister. Unlike the injuries she'd taken in the alley, this would heal slowly and painfully. "Accident in a tanning salon."

"That's not funny."

She picked the roll of gauze up off the counter. "You're losing your sense of humor, Mike."

Celluci snorted and handed her the scissors. "I never had one."

"Mike, I wanted to warn you, I won't be back by sunrise."

Celluci turned slowly, the TV dinner he'd just taken from the microwave held in both hands. "What do you mean?"

She read the fear in his voice and lifted the edge of the tray so that the gravy didn't pour out and over his shoes. "I mean I'll be spending the day somewhere else."

"Where?"

"I can't tell you."

"Why? Never mind." He raised a hand as her eyes narrowed. "Don't tell me. I don't want to know. You're going after that other vampire, aren't you? The one Fitzroy told you to leave alone."

"I thought you didn't want to know."

"I already know," he grunted. "I can read you like a book. With large type. And pictures."

Vicki pulled the tray from his grip and set it on the counter. "She's killed two people. Eisler was a scumbag who may have deserved it but the other . . ."

"Other?" Celluci exploded. "Jesus H. Christ, Vicki, in case you've forgotten, murder's against the law! Who the hell painted a big vee on your long johns and made you the vampire vigilante?"

"Don't you remember?" Vicki snapped. "You were there. I didn't make this decision, Mike. You and Henry made it for me. You'd just better learn to live with it." She fought her way back to calm. "Look, you can't stop her but I can. I know that galls but that's the way it is."

They glared at each other, toe to toe. Finally Celluci looked away.

"I can't stop you, can I?" he asked bitterly. "I'm only human after all."

"Don't sell yourself short," Vicki snarled. "You're quintessentially human. If you want to stop me, you face me and ask me not to go and then you remember it every time you go into a situation that could get your ass shot off."

After a long moment, he swallowed, lifted his head, and met her eyes. "Don't die. I thought I lost you once and I'm not strong enough to go through that again."

"Are you asking me not to go?"

He snorted. "I'm asking you to be careful. Not that you ever listen."

She took a step forward and rested her head against his shoulder, wrapping herself in the beating of his heart. "This time, I'm listening."

The studios in the converted warehouse on King Street were not supposed to be live-in. A good seventy-five percent of the tenants ignored that. The studio Vicki wanted was at the back on the third floor. The heavy steel door—an obvious upgrade by the occupant—had been secured by the best lock money could buy.

New senses and old skills got through it in record time.

Vicki pushed open the door with her foot and began carrying boxes inside. She had a lot to do before dawn.

"She goes out every night between ten and eleven, then she comes home every morning between four and five. You could set your watch by her."

Vicki handed him an envelope.

He looked inside, thumbed through the money, then grinned up at her. "Pleasure doing business for you. Any time you need my services, you know where to call."

"Forget it," she told him.

And he did.

Because she expected her, Vicki knew the moment the other entered the building. The Beast stirred and she tightened her grip on it. To lose control now would be disaster.

She heard the elevator, then footsteps in the hall.

"You know I'm in here," she said silently, "and you know you can take me. Be overconfident, believe I'm a fool and walk right in."

"I thought you were smarter than this." The other stepped into the apartment then casually turned to lock the door. "I told you when I saw you again I'd kill you."

Vicki shrugged, the motion masking her fight to remain calm. "Don't you even want to know why I'm here?"

"I assume, you've come to negotiate." She raised ivory hands and released thick, black hair from its bindings. "We went past that when you attacked me." Crossing the room, she preened before a large ornate mirror that dominated one wall of the studio.

"I attacked you because you murdered Phil."

"Was that his name?" The other laughed. The sound had razored edges. "I didn't bother to ask it."

"Before you murdered him."

"Murdered? You are a child. They are prey, we are predators—their deaths are ours if we desire them. You'd have learned that in time." She turned, the patina of civilization stripped away. "Too bad you haven't any time left."

Vicki snarled but somehow managed to stop herself from attacking. Years of training whispered, *Not yet.* She had to stay exactly where she was.

"Oh yes." The sibilants flayed the air between them. "I almost forgot. You wanted me to ask you why you came. Very well. Why?"

Given the address and the reason, Celluci could've come to the studio during the day and slammed a stake through the other's heart. The vampire's strongest protection, would be of no use against him. Mike Celluci believed in vampires.

"I came," Vicki told her, "because some things you have to do yourself."

The wire ran up the wall, tucked beside the surface-mounted cable of a cheap renovation, and disappeared into the shadows that clung to a ceiling sixteen feet from the floor. The switch had been stapled down beside her foot. A tiny motion, too small to evoke attack, flipped it.

Vicki had realized from the beginning that there were a number of problems with her plan. The first involved placement. Every living space included an area where the occupant felt secure—a favorite chair, a window . . . a mirror. The second problem was how to mask what she'd done. While the other would not be able to sense the various bits of wiring and equipment, she'd be fully aware of Vicki's scent on the wiring and equipment. Only if Vicki remained in the studio, could that smaller trace be lost in the larger.

The third problem was directly connected with the second. Given that Vicki had to remain, how was she to survive?

Attached to the ceiling by sheer brute strength, positioned so that they shone directly down into the space in front of the mirror, were a double bank of lights cannibalized from a tanning bed. The sun held a double menace for the vampire—its return to the sky brought complete vulnerability and its rays burned.

Henry had a round scar on the back of one hand from too close an encounter with the sun. When her burn healed, Vicki would have a matching one from a deliberate encounter with an imitation.

The other screamed as the lights came on, the sound pure rage and so inhuman that those who heard it would have to deny it for sanity's sake.

Vicki dove forward, ripped the heavy brocade off the back of the couch, and burrowed frantically into its depths. Even that instant of light had bathed her skin in flame and she moaned as for a moment the searing pain became all she was. After a time, when it grew no worse, she managed to open her eyes.

The light couldn't reach her, but neither could she reach the switch to turn it off. She could see it, three feet away, just beyond the shadow of the couch. She shifted her weight and a line of blister rose across one leg. Biting back a shriek, she curled into a fetal position, realizing her refuge was not entirely secure.

Okay, genius, now what?

Moving very, very carefully, Vicki wrapped her hand around the one-by-two that braced the lower edge of the couch. From the tension running along it, she suspected that breaking it off would result in at least a partial collapse of the piece of furniture.

And if it goes, I very well may go with it.

And then she heard the sound of something dragging itself across the floor.

Oh shit! She's not dead!

The wood broke, the couch began to fall in on itself, and Vicki, realizing that luck would have a large part to play in her survival, smacked the switch and rolled clear in the same motion.

The room plunged into darkness.

Vicki froze as her eyes slowly readjusted to the night. Which was when she finally became conscious of the smell. It had been there all along but her senses had refused to acknowledge it until they had to.

Sunlight burned.

Vicki gagged.

The dragging sound continued.

The hell with this! She didn't have time to wait for her eyes to repair the damage they'd obviously taken. She needed to see now. Fortunately, although it hadn't seemed fortunate at the time, she'd learned to maneuver without sight.

She threw herself across the room.

The light switch was where they always were, to the right of the door.

The thing on the floor pushed itself up on fingerless hands and glared at her out of the blackened ruin of a face. Laboriously it turned, hate radiating off it in palpable waves and began to pull itself towards her again.

Vicki stepped forward to meet it.

While the part of her that remembered being human writhed in revulsion, she wrapped her hands around its skull and twisted it in a full circle. The spine snapped. Another full twist and what was left of the head came off in her hands.

She'd been human for thirty-two years but she'd been fourteen months a vampire.

"No one hunts in my territory," she snarled as the other crumbled to dust.

She limped over to the wall and pulled the plug supplying power to the lights. Later, she'd remove them completely—the whole concept of sunlamps gave her the creeps.

When she turned, she was facing the mirror.

The woman who stared out at her through bloodshot eyes, exposed skin blistered and red, was a hunter. Always had been really. The question became, who was she to hunt?

Vicki smiled. Before the sun drove her to use her inherited sanctuary, she had a few quick phone calls to make. The first to Celluci; she owed him the knowledge that she'd survived the night. The second to Henry for much the same reason.

The third call would be to the 800 line that covered the classifieds of Toronto's largest alternative newspaper. This ad was going to be a little different than the one she'd placed upon leaving the force. Back then, she'd been incredibly depressed about leaving a job she loved for a life she saw as only marginally useful. This time, she had no regrets.

Victory Nelson, Investigator: Otherwordly Crimes a Specialty.

VAMPIRE KING OF THE GOTH CHICKS:
A Sonja Blue Story
Nancy A. Collins

Nancy A. Collins is currently the writer of *Vampirella* and co-writer of *Red Sonja: Vulture Circle* comic series. As mentioned in the intro-duction to this volume, she's best known as the creator of punk vampire/vampire slayer Sonja Blue, the protagonist/heroine of a series of novels and short stories that includes Collins' debut novel, *Sunglasses After Dark* (1989) and a comic book series. Although the now-influential character may return someday, the last Sonja Blue novel, *Darkest Heart*, was published in 2002. More recently, Collins has penned three young adult novels, the VAMPS series (2008-2009), and three urban fantasy novels, the Golgotham series (2010-2013).

Here is a taste of the *very* badass Sonja Blue . . .

The Red Raven is a real scum-pit. The only thing marking it as a bar is the vintage Old Crow ad in the front window and a stuttering neon sign that says *lounge*. The johns there are always backing up, and the place perpetually stinks of piss. During the week it's just another neighborhood dive, serving truck drivers and barflies, and not a Bukowski amongst them.

But, because the drinks are cheap and the bartenders never check ID, the Red Raven undergoes a sea of change come Friday night. The clientele grows younger and stranger, at least in physical appearance. The usual suspects that occupy the Red Raven's booths and bar stools are replaced by young men and women tricked out in black leather and so many facial piercings they resemble walking tackle boxes. And there's still not a Bukowski amongst them.

This Friday night is no different from any other. A knot of Goth kids are already gathered outside on the curb as I arrive, plastic go-cups full of piss-warm Rolling Rock clutched in their hands. Amidst all the bad Robert Smith haircuts, heavy mascara, dead-white face powder and black lipstick, I hardly warrant a second look.

Normally I don't bother with joints like this, but I've been hearing a persistent rumor that there's a blood cult operating out of the Red Raven. I make it my business to check out such stories. Most of the time it turns out to be nothing more than urban legend—but occasionally there's something far more sinister going on.

The interior of The Red Raven is crowded with young men and women, all of whom look far more menacing than myself. What with my black motorcycle jacket, ratty jeans, and equally tattered New York Dolls T-shirt, I'm somewhat on the conservative end of the dress code. I wave down the bartender, who doesn't seem to consider it odd I'm sporting sunglasses after dark, and order a beer. It doesn't bother me that the glass he hands me bears visible greasy fingerprints and a smear of lipstick on the rim. After all, it's not like I'm going to drink what's in it.

Now that I have the necessary prop, I settle in and wait. Finding out the low down in places like this isn't that hard. All I've got to do is be patient and keep my ears open. Over the years I've developed a method for listening to dozens of conversations at once—sifting the meaningless ones aside until I find the one I'm looking for. I suspect it's not unlike how sharks can pick out the frenzied splashing of a wounded fish from a hundred miles away.

" *—told him he could kiss my ass goodbye—*"

"*—really liked their last album—*"

"*—bitch acted like I'd done something—*"

"*—until next payday? I promise you'll get it—*"

"*—of the undead. He's the real thing—*"

There. *That* one.

I angle my head in the direction of the voice, trying not to look at them directly. There are three, total—one male and two female—locked in earnest conversation with a young woman. The two females are arche-typical Goth chicks. They look to be in their late teens, early twenties, dressed in a mixture of black leather and lingerie, wearing way too much eye make-up. One is tall and willowy, her heavily-applied death-pale face powder doing little to mask the bloom of acne on her cheeks. Judging from the roots of her boot-black hair, she's a natural dishwater blonde. Her companion is considerably shorter and a little too pudgy for the black satin bustier she's shoehorned into. Her face is painted clown white with tattooed mascara shaped like an ankh at the corner of her left eye, which I've learned is more in imitation of a popular comic book character than a tribute to the Egyptian gods. She's wearing a man's felt top hat draped in a length of black lace that makes her look taller than she really is.

The male member of the group is tall and skinny, outfitted in a pair of leather pants held up by a monstrously ornate silver belt buckle. He isn't wearing a shirt, and his bare, hairless breastbone is visible underneath his leather jacket. He's roughly the same age as the girls, perhaps younger, and constantly nodding in agreement with whatever they say, nervously flipping his lank, burgundy-colored hair out of his face. It doesn't take me long to discern that the tall girl is called Sable, the short one in the hat is Tanith, and that the boy is Serge. The girl they are talking to has close-cropped Raggedy Ann-style red hair and a nose ring, and goes by the name Shawna.

Out of habit, I drop my vision into the Pretender spectrum and scan them for signs of inhuman taint. All four check out clean. This piques my interest even further. I move a little closer to where they are standing, so I can filter out the music blaring out of the nearby jukebox.

Shawna shakes her head and smiles nervously, uncertain as to whether she's being goofed on or not. "C'mon—a *real* vampire?"

"We told him about you, didn't we, Serge?" Tanith looks to the gawky youth hovering at her elbow for confirmation.

Serge nods his head eagerly, which necessitates his flipping his hair out of his face yet again.

"His name is Rhymer. Lord Rhymer. He's three hundred years old," Sable adds breathlessly. "And he said he wanted to meet you!"

Despite her attempts at post-modern chic, Shawna smiles like a flattered schoolgirl."He really said that?

I can tell she's hooked as clean as a six-pound trout and that it won't take much more work on the trio's part to land their catch. The quartet of black-leather clad young rebels quickly leave the Red Raven, scurrying off as fast as their Doc Martens can take them. I give it a couple of beats, and then set out after them.

As I shadow them from a distance, I can't shake the nagging feeling that something isn't adding up. Although I seem to have found what I've come looking for, there's something not quite right about it, but I'll be damned (I know—I'm being redundant) if I can put my finger on it.

In my experience, vampires avoid Goths like a tanning salon. While their adolescent fascination with death and decadence might, at first, seem to make them ideal servitors, their extravagant fashion sense draws far too much attention. Plus, they're huge drama-queens. Vampires prefer their servants far more nondescript and discrete. But perhaps this Lord Rhymer, whoever he may be, is of a more modern temperament than those I've encountered in the past.

I don't know what to make of this trio who seem to be acting as Judas Goats, luring a fresh victim into their master's orbit. Judging by their evident enthusiasm, perhaps they are more converts than servitors. They don't seem to have the predator's gleam in their eyes, nor is there anything resembling a killer's caution in their walk or mannerisms. As they stroll down the darkened streets, their chatter is more like that of mischievous children out on a lark—such as TPing the superintendent's front lawn or soaping the gym teacher's windows. They certainly don't seem aware of the extra shadow that attached itself to them the moment they left the Red Raven.

After a ten-minute walk they arrive at their destination—an abandoned church. Of course. It's hardly Carfax Abbey, but I suppose it will do. It's a two-story wooden structure boasting an old-fashioned spire, stabbing its symbolic finger in the direction of heaven.

The feeling of ill-ease rises in me again. Vampires dislike such obvious lairs. Hell, these aren't the Middle Ages; they don't have to hang out in ruined monasteries and family mausoleums anymore. No, contemporary bloodsuckers prefer to dwell within warehouse lofts or abandoned industrial complexes, even condos. I even tracked one to ground in an inner-city hospital that had been shut down during the Reagan administration. I suspect I'll have to start investigating the various deactivated military bases scattered throughout the country at some point.

As I watch the little group troop inside the church, there is only one thing I know for certain—if I want to know what's going down here, I better get inside. I circle around the building, keeping to the darkest shadows, my senses alert for signs of the usual sentinels that guard a vampire's lair. I reach out with my mind as I climb up the side of the church, trying to pick up the tell-tale dead-air of shielded minds that signifies the presence of renfields, but all I pick up is the excited heat of the foursome from the Red Raven and a slightly more complex signal from deeper inside the church. Curiouser and curiouser.

Turns out the church spire doesn't house a bell—just a rusting Korean War-era public address system dangling from frayed wires. There is barely enough room for a man to stand, much less ring a bell, but at least the trapdoor isn't locked. It opens with a tight squeal of disused hinges, but nothing stirs in the shadows below me. Within seconds I have the best seat in the house, crouched in the rafters spanning the nave.

The interior of the church looks appropriately atmospheric. What pews remain are in disarray, the hymnals tumbled from their racks and spilled across the floor. Saints, apostles, and prophets stare down from the windows, gesturing with upraised shepherd's crooks or hands bent into the sign of benediction. I lift my own mirrored gaze to the mullion window located behind the pulpit. It depicts a snowy lamb kneeling on a field of green against a cloudless sky, in which a shining disc is suspended. The large brass cross just below the sheep-window has been inverted, in keeping with the ever-popular desecration motif.

The only light is provided by a pair of heavy cathedral-style candelabras, each bristling with over a hundred dripping red and black candles, which flank either side of the pulpit. The Goth kids from the Red Raven gather at the chancel rail, their faces turned towards the black-velvet draped altar.

"Where is he?" Shawna whispers, her voice surprisingly loud in the empty church.

"Don't worry," Tanith assures her. "He'll be here."

As if on cue, there is a smell of brimstone and a gout of purplish smoke rises from behind the pulpit. Shawna gives a little squeal of surprise and takes an involuntary step backward, only to find her way blocked by the others.

A deep, cultured masculine voice booms forth. "Good evening, my children! I bid you welcome to my abode, and that you enter gladly and of your own free will."

The smoke clears, revealing a tall man dressed in tight-fitting black satin pants, a black silk poet's shirt, black leather riding boots, and a long black opera cape with a red silk lining. His hair is long and dark, pulled into a loose ponytail by a satin ribbon the color of blood. His skin is as white as milk in a saucer, and his eyes reflect redly in the dim candlelight, like those of a cat. It would seem that Lord Rhymer has finally elected to make his appearance known.

Serge smiles nervously at his demon-lord and steps forward, gesturing to Shawna. "W-we did as you asked, Master. We brought you the girl."

Lord Rhymer smiles slightly, his eyes narrowing at the sight of the new girl.

"Ah, *yesss*. The one called Shawna."

As for Shawna, she stood gaping up at Lord Rhymer as if he was Jim Morrison, Robert Smith, and Danzig all rolled into one. She starts, gasping more in surprise than fright, as the vampire addresses her directly.

"You come before me of your own free will, do you not?"

"Y-yes." Her voice is so tiny it makes her sound like a little girl. But there is nothing child-like in the lust dancing in her eyes.

Lord Rhymer holds out a pale hand to the trembling young woman. His fingernails are long and pointed and lacquered black. He smiles reassuringly, his voice calm and strong, designed to sway those of weaker nature. "Step forward, Shawna. Come to me, so that I might kiss you."

A touch of apprehension crosses the girl's face. She hesitates, glancing at the others, who close in behind her even tighter than before. "I—I—don't know—"

Lord Rhymer narrows his blood-red eyes, intensifying his stare. His voice grows sterner, revealing its cold edge. "*Come* to me, Shawna."

All the tension in her seems to drain away and the Goth chick's eyes grow even more vacant than before, if possible. She moves forward, slowly mounting the stairs to the pulpit, as Rhymer holds his arms out to greet her.

"That's it, my dear. Come closer . . . Just as you have dreamed you would, so many, many times before . . ." He steps forward to meet her, the cape outstretched between his arms like the wings of a giant bat. His smile widens and his mouth opens, exposing pearly white fangs dripping saliva. "Come be my bride . . ." he murmurs in a voice made husky by lust.

Shawna grimaces in pain/pleasure as the fangs penetrate her throat. Even from my shadowy perch above it all I can smell the sharp tang of blood. I feel a dark stirring at the base of my brain, which I quickly push aside. I don't need that kind of trouble—not now. Still, I find it hard to look away from the tableau below me. Rhymer holds Shawna tight against him. She whimpers as if on the verge of orgasm. The blood rolling down her throat and dripping into the pale swell of her cleavage is as dark and slick as spilled molasses.

He draws back, smiling smugly as he wipes the blood off his chin. "It is done. You are now bound to me by the strength of my immortal will."

Shawna's eyelids flutter and she seems to have a little trouble focusing. She touches her bloodied neck and stares at her red-stained finger for a long moment. She steps back, a dazed, post-orgasmic look on her face. She staggers slightly as she moves to rejoin the others, one hand still clamped over her bruised and bleeding throat. Tanith and Sable eagerly step forward to help their new sister, their hands quickly disappearing up her skirt as they steady her, cooing encouragement in soothing voices.

"Welcome to the family, Shawna," Sable whispers, kissing first her cheek before moving on to tongue her earlobe.

"You're one of us, now and forever," Tanith purrs, giving Shawna a probing kiss while scooping her breasts free of their blouse.

Sable presses even closer, licking at the blood smearing Shawna's neck. Serge stands off to one side, nervously chewing a thumbnail and occasionally brushing his forelock out of his face. Every few seconds his eyes flicker from the girls to Lord Rhymer, who stands in the pulpit, smiling and nodding his approval. After a few more moments of groping and gasping, the three women begin undressing one another in earnest, their moans soon mixing with nervous giggles. Black leather and lace drop away, revealing black fish-net stockings and garter belts and crotchless underwear. At the sight of Shawna's pubes—mousy brown, despite her fluorescent red locks—Serge's eyes widen and his nostrils flare. He looks to Rhymer, who nods and gestures languidly with one taloned hand.

Serge fumbles with his ornate silver belt buckle, which hits the wooden floor with a solid *clunk!* I lift an eyebrow in surprise. While the boy may be thin to the point of emaciation, he is hung like a stallion. Sable mutters something into Serge's ear that makes him laugh just before he plants his lips against her own blood-smeared mouth. Tanith, her eyes heavy-lidded and her lips pulled into a lascivious grin, reaches around from behind to stroke him to full erection. Serge breaks free and turns to lift Shawna in his arms, carrying her to the black-draped altar, the other girls trailing after him. There is much biting and raking of exposed flesh with fingernails. Soon they are a mass of writhing naked flesh, giggling and moaning and grunting as the slap of skin against skin fills the silent church. And overseeing it all from his place of power is Lord Rhymer, his crimson eyes twinkling in the candlelight as he watches his followers cavort before him.

To his credit, Serge proves tireless, energetically rutting with all three girls in various combinations for hours on end. It's not until the stained glass windows of the church begin to lighten that it finally comes to an end. The moment Lord Rhymer notices the approaching dawn the smile disappears from his face.

"ENOUGH!" he thunders, causing the others to halt in mid-fuck. "The sun will soon be upon me! It is time for you to leave, my children!"

The Goths pull themselves off and out of each other without a word of complaint and begin to struggle back into their clothes. Once they're dressed they waste no time hurrying off, taking pains to not look one another in the eye. It is all I can do to suppress a groan of relief as the last of the blood cultists lurch out of the building. I thought those losers were *never* going to leave!

I check my own watch against the shadows sliding across the floor below me. Now would be a good time to pay a social call on their so-called "Master." I hope he's in the mood for a little chat before beddy-bye.

Lord Rhymer yawns as he makes his way down the basement stairs. What with the candelabra he's holding and the flowing opera cloak, I'm reminded of Lugosi's Dracula. But Bela Lugosi is dead.

The basement runs the length of the building and has a poured concrete floor. Stacks of old hymnals, folding chairs, and moldering choir robes have been pushed into the corners. A rosewood casket with a maroon velvet lining rests atop a pair of saw-horses in the middle of the room, and an old-fashioned steamer trunk stands nearby.

I watch the vampire set the candelabra down and, still yawning, unhook his cape and carefully drape it atop the trunk. If he senses my presence, here in the shadows, he gives no sign of it.

Smiling crookedly, I deliberately scrape my boot heel against the concrete floor. My smile becomes a grin as he spins around, his eyes bugging with alarm.

"What—? Who's there?"

He blinks, surprised to see me standing to one side of the open casket balanced atop the sawhorse. I had caught the tell-tale smell when I first entered the basement, but a quick glance inside confirms what I already knew: the coffin is lined with earth. I reach inside and lift a handful of dirt, allowing it to spill between my splayed fingers. I look up and meet Rhymer's scarlet gaze.

"Okay, buddy, what the hell are you trying to pull here?"

Rhymer squares his shoulders and pulls himself up to his full height, hissing and exposing his fangs, hooking his fingers into talons. His red eyes glint in the dim light like those of a cornered animal.

I am not impressed.

"Can the Christopher Lee act, asshole! I'm not some Goth chick tripping her brains out!" I kick the saw horses out from under the casket, sending it tumbling to the floor, spilling its layer of soil. Lord Rhymer gasps, his eyes darting from the ruined coffin to me and back again. "Only *humans* think vampires need to sleep on a layer of their home soil," I snarl.

He tries to regain the momentum by pointing a trembling finger at me, doing his best to sound menacing. "You have defiled the resting place of Rhymer, Lord of the Undead! And for that, woman, you will pay with your life!"

"Oh yeah?" I sneer. "Buddy, I *knew* Dracula—and, believe me, you ain't him!"

One moment I'm halfway across the room, the next I'm standing over him, his blood dripping from my knuckles as he lies on the basement floor, wiping at his gushing mouth and nose. A set of dentures, complete with fangs, lies on the floor beside him. I nudge the upper plate with the toe of my boot, shaking my head in disgust.

"Just what I thought: falsies! And the eyes are contact lenses, right? I bet the nails are shaped acrylics, too . . ."

Rhymer tries to scuttle away from me like a crab, but he's much too slow. I grab him by the ruff of his poet's shirt, pulling him to his feet with one quick motion that causes him to yelp like a whipped dog.

"What the fuck are you playing at here?" I snap. "What kind of scam are you running on those Goth kids?"

Rhymer opens his mouth and although his lips are moving there's no sound coming out. At first I think he's so scared he's not able to speak—then I realize he's a serious stutterer when he's not a vampire. "I'm n-not a c-con man, if that's what y-you're thinking. I'm n-not doing it for m-money!"

"If it's not for cash—then why bother?" Not that I didn't know his motivation from the moment I first laid eyes on him. But I want to hear it from his own lips before I make my decision.

"All m-my life I've b-been an outsider. N-no one ever p-paid any attention to m-me. N-not even m-my own p-parents. N-no one ever t-took me seriously. I was a j-joke and everyone k-knew it. The only p-place where I could escape from b-being m-me was at the movies. I really admired the v-vampires in the m-movies. They were d-different, too. But n-no one m-made fun of them or ignored them. They were p-powerful and p-people were afraid of them. They c-could m-make w-women do wh-whatever they w-wanted.

" Wh-when my p-parents died, they left m-me a lot of m-money. So m-much I'd n-never have to w-work again. An hour after their fu-funeral I w-went to a dentist and had all m-my upper teeth removed and the d-dentures m-made.

"I always w-wanted to be a v-vampire—and now c-could to live m-my d-dreams. So I b-bought this old church and s-started hanging out at the R-red Raven, looking for the right type of g-girls.

"T-Tanith was the first. Th-then came S-sable. The rest w-was easy. They w-wanted m-me to b-be real so b-badly, I didn't even have to p-pretend that m-much. B-but then it started to g-get out of hand. They w-wanted m-me t-to—you know—p-put my t-thing in them. So I f-found S-serge. I like to w-watch." Rhymer fixed one of his rapidly blackening eyes on me. His fear was beginning to give way to curiosity. "B-but wh-what difference is any of this to y-you? Are y-you related to one of the g-girls? S-serge's ex-g-girlfriend?"

I can't help but laugh as I let go of him. He flinches at the sound of my laughter as if it was a physical blow. "I knew there was something fishy going on when I spotted the belt buckle on your Goth stud. No dead boy would allow that chunk of silver within a half-mile of his person. And all that hocus-pocus with the smoke and the Black Sabbath folderol? It's a rank amateur's impression of what vampires and vampirism is all about, cobbled together from Hammer films and Anton Levy paperbacks! You really *are* a pathetic little twisted piece of crap, Rhymer—or whatever the hell your real name is! You surround yourself with the icons of darkness and play at damnation—but you don't even recognize the real thing when it steps forward and bloodies your fuckin' nose!"

Rhymer's eyes suddenly widen and he gasps aloud, like a man who has walked into a room and seen someone he has believed long dead reading the newspaper. Clearly overcome, he drops to his knees, his blood-stained lips quivering uncontrollably.

"You're real!"

"Get up," I growl, flashing a glimpse of fang.

But instead of inspiring fear, all this does is cause him to cry out even louder than before. He is now actually groveling, pawing at my boots as he blubbers. "At last! I k-knew if I w-waited long enough, one of y-you w-would finally come!"

"I said *get up*, you little toadeater!" I kick him away, but it does no good. He crawls back on his belly, as fast as a lizard on a hot rock. I was afraid something like this would happen.

"I'll d-do anything you w-want—give you anything you d-desire!" He grabs the cuffs of my jeans, tugging insistently. "B-bite me! Drink my b-blood! *Pleeease!* M-make me like you!"

As I look down at this wretched human who has lived a life so stunted, his one driving passion is to become a walking dead man, my memory slides back across the years, to the night a foolish young girl, made giddy by the excitement that comes with the pursuit of forbidden pleasure and made stupid by the romance of danger, allowed herself to be lured away from the safety of the herd. I remember how she found herself alone with a blood-eyed monster that hid behind the face of a handsome, smooth-talking stranger. I remember how her nude, blood-smeared body was hurled from the speeding car and tossed in the gutter and left for dead. I remember how she was far from dead and yet not living. I remember how she was me.

I am trembling as if in the grips of a high fever. My disgust has given way to anger, something I've never been very good at controlling. Part of me—a dark, dangerous part—has no desire to ever learn. I try hard to keep a grip on myself, but it's not easy. In the past when I've been overwhelmed, I've tried to make sure I only vent my rage on those I consider worthy of attention, such as vampires. Real ones, that is. Ones like myself. But sometimes . . .

Well, sometimes I lose it. Like now.

"You want to be like *me*?!?"

I kick the groveling little turd so hard he flies across the basement floor and collides with the wall. He cries out, but it doesn't exactly sound like pain.

"You stupid bastard—!" I snarl. "*I* don't even want to be like *me*!"

I tear the mirrored sunglasses away from my eyes, and Rhymer's face goes pale. My eyes look nothing like his scarlet-tinted contact lenses. There is no white, no corona—merely seas of solid blood boasting vertical slits that open and close, depending on the light. The church basement is very dark, so my pupils are dilated wide—like those of a shark rising from the sunless depths to savage a luckless swimmer.

Rhymer lifts a hand to block out the sight of me as I advance on him, his trembling delight now replaced by genuine, one-hundred-percent monkey-brain fear. For the first time he seems to realize that he is in the presence of a monster.

"Please don't hurt me, Mistress! Forgive me! Forgive—" For a brief second Rhymer's hands still flutter in a futile attempt to beg my favor, then scarlet spurts from his neck, not unlike that from a spitting fountain, as his still-beating heart sends a stream of blood to where his brain would normally be. I quickly sidestep the gruesome spray without letting go of his head, which I hold between my hands like a basketball.

Turning away from Rhymer's still-twitching corpse, I step over the ruins of the antique coffin and its payload. No doubt the dirt had been imported from the Balkans—perhaps Moldavia or even Transylvania. I shake my head in amazement that such old wives tales are still in circulation and given validity by so many. As I head up the stairs, Rhymer's head tucked under my arm like a trophy, I wonder if Sable and Tanith will make Serge clean up the mess I've left behind.

Rhymer isn't the first vampire wanna-be I've run into, but I've got to admit he had the best set-up. The Goth chicks wanted the real thing and he gave them what they thought it would be, right down to retrofitting the church with theatrical trapdoors and stage magician flashpots. And they bought into the bullshit because it made them feel special, it made them feel real, and—most importantly—it made them feel *alive*. Poor stupid bastards. To them it's all black leather, love bites, and tacky jewelry; where everyone is eternally young and beautiful and no one can ever hurt you again.

Like hell.

As for Rhymer, he wanted the real thing as badly as the Goth chicks. Perhaps even more so. He'd spent his entire life aspiring to monstrosity, hoping his heart-felt mimicry of the damned would eventually turn him into that which he longed to be, or that he would eventually draw the attention of the creatures of the night he worshipped so ardently. As, in the end, it did. I am the real thing all right; big as life and twice as ugly.

But I am hardly the bloodsucking seductress Rhymer had been dreaming of all those years. There was no way he could know that his little trick would not only lure forth not just a vampire—but a vampire-slayer as well.

You see, my unique and unwanted predicament has denied me many things—the ability to age, to love, to feel life quicken within me. And in retaliation against this unwished for transformation, I've spent decades denying the monster inside me; trying—however futilely—to turn my back on the horror that dwells in the darkness of my soul. There is one pleasure, and one alone, I indulge in. And that is killing vampires . . .

And those that would become them.

Dawn is well underway by the time I re-enter the nave. The whitewashed walls are dappled with light dyed blue, green, and red by the stained glass windows. I take a couple of steps backward, then drop-kick Rhymer's head right through the Lamb-of-God window.

The birds chirp happily away in the trees, greeting the coming day with their morning song, as I push open the wide double doors of the church. A stray dog with matted fur and slats for ribs is already sniffing Rhymer's ruined head where it has landed in the high weeds. The cur lifts its muzzle and automatically growls, but as I draw closer it flattens its ears and tucks its tail between its legs and quickly scurries off. Dogs are smart. They know what is and isn't of the natural world—even if humans don't.

The night was a bust, as far as I'm concerned. When I go out hunting, I prefer bringing down actual game, not *faux* predators. Still, I wish I could hang around and see the look on the faces of Rhymer's groupies when they find out what has happened to their "Master." That'd be good for a chuckle or two.

No one can say I don't have a sense of humor about these things.

—from the journals of Sonja Blue

LEARNING CURVE

Kelley Armstrong

New York Times #1 bestseller Kelley Armstrong has been telling stories since before she could write. Her earliest written efforts were disastrous: if asked for a story about girls and dolls, her story would— much to her teachers' dismay—feature undead girls and evil dolls. She grew up and kept writing and now lives in southwest Ontario with a husband and children who do not mind that she continues to spin tales of the supernatural while safely locked away in the basement.

Armstrong is best known for her Otherworld series of urban fantasy (first novel: *Bitten*, 2001; final, and thirteenth, novel: *Thirteen*, 2012). In Armstrong's Otherworld universe, few humans are aware that beings with paranormal powers exist. A female werewolf, witch, half-demon, necromancer, hybrid sorcerer/witch, and a human serve as narrators for the novels; vampires make appearances as supporting characters and are sometimes featured in short stories set in the universe.

Vampire Zoe Takano appears in one book and (so far) three stories. Featured here in "Learning Curve," Zoe shows she can deal handily with human predators as well as misguided vampire hunters . . .

"I'm being stalked."

Rudy, the bartender, stopped scowling at a nearly empty bottle of rye and peered around the dimly lit room.

"No, I wasn't followed inside," I said.

"Good, then get out before you are. I don't need that kind of trouble in here, Zoe."

I looked around at the patrons, most sitting alone at their tables, most passed out, most drooling.

"Looks to me like that's exactly the kind of trouble you need. Short of a fire, that's the only way you're getting those chairs back."

"The only chairs I want back are those ones." He hooked his thumb at a trio of college boys in the corner.

"Oh, but they're cute," I said. "Clean, well-groomed... and totally ruining the ambiance you work so hard to provide. Maybe I can sic my stalker on them."

"Don't even think about it."

"Oh, please. Why do you think I ducked in here? Anyone with the taste to stalk me is not going to set foot past the door."

He pointed to the exit. I leaned over the counter and snagged a beer bottle.

"Down payment on the job," I said, nodding to the boys. "Supernaturals?"

He rolled his eyes, as if to say, "What else?" True, Miller's didn't attract a lot of humans, but every so often one managed to find the place, though they usually didn't make it past a first glance inside.

I strolled toward the boys, who were checking me out, whispering like twelve-year-olds. I sat down at the next table. It took all of five seconds for one to slide into the chair beside mine.

"Haven't I seen you on campus?" he asked.

It was possible. I took courses now and then at the University of Toronto. But I shook my head. "I went to school overseas." I sipped my beer. "Little place outside Sendai, Japan. Class of 1878."

He blinked, then found a laugh. "Is that your way of saying you're too old for me?"

"Definitely too old." I smiled, fangs extending.

He fell back, chair toppling as he scrambled out of it.

I stood and extended my hand. "Zoe Takano."

"You're—you're—"

"Lonely. And hungry. Think you can help?"

As the kid and his friends made for the exit, one of the regulars lifted his head from the bar, bleary eyes peering at me.

"Running from Zoe?" he said. "Those boys must be new in town."

I flipped him off, took my beer to the bar and settled in.

"How about you try that with your stalker instead of hiding out here?" Rudy said.

"That could lead to a confrontation. Better to ignore the problem and hope it resolves itself."

He snorted and shook his head.

The problem did not resolve itself. Which was fine—I was in the mood for some excitement anyway. It was only the confrontation part I preferred to avoid. Confrontations mean fights. Fights mean releasing a part of me that I'm really happier keeping leashed and muzzled. So I avoid temptation, and if that means getting a reputation as a coward, I'm okay with that.

When I got out of Miller's, my stalker was waiting. Not surprising, really. We'd been playing this game for almost two weeks.

As I set out, I sharpened my sixth sense, trying to rely on that instead of listening for the sounds of pursuit. I could sense a living being behind me, that faint pulse of awareness that tells me food is nearby. It would be stronger if I was hungry, but this was better practice.

Miller's exits into an alley—appropriately—so I stuck to the alleys for as long as I could. Eventually, though, they came to an end and I stepped onto the sidewalk. Gravel crunched behind me, booted feet stopping short. I smiled.

I cut across the street and merged with a crowd of college kids heading to a bar. I merge well; even chatted with a cute blond girl for a half-block, and she chatted back, presuming I was part of the group. Then, as we passed a Thai takeout, I excused myself and ducked inside. I zipped through, smiling at the counter guy, ignoring him when he yelled that the washrooms were for paying customers only, and went straight out the back door.

I'd pulled this routine twice before—blend with a crowd and cut through a shop—and my opponent hadn't caught on yet, which was really rather frustrating. This time, though, as I crept out the back door, a shadow stretched from a side alley. I let the door slam behind me. The shadow jerked back. So the pupil was capable of learning. Excellent. Time for the next lesson.

I scampered along the back alley. Around the next corner. Down a delivery lane. Behind a Dumpster.

Footsteps splashed through a puddle I'd avoided. Muttered curses, cut short. Then silence. I closed my eyes, concentrating on picking up that pulse of life. And there it was, coming closer, closer, passing the Dumpster. Stopping. Realizing the prey must have ducked behind this garbage bin. Gold star.

A too-deliberate pair of boot squeaks headed left, so I ran left. Sure enough, my opponent was circling right. I grabbed the side of the Dumpster and swung onto the closed lid.

"Looking for me?" I said, grinning down.

Hands gripped the top edge, then yanked back, as if expecting me to stomp them. That would hardly be sporting. I backed up, took a running leap and grabbed the fire escape overhead. A perfect gymnast's swing and I was on it. A minute later, I was swinging again, this time onto the roof. I took off across it without a backward glance. Then I sat on the other side to wait.

I waited. And I waited some more. Finally, I sighed, got to my feet, made my way across the roof, leapt onto the next and began the journey home.

I was peering over the end of a rooftop into a penthouse apartment, eyeing a particularly fine example of an Edo-period sake bottle, when I sensed someone below. I glimpsed a familiar figure in the alley. Hmmm. Lacking experience, but not tenacity. I could work with this.

I leapt onto the next, lower rooftop. Then I saw a second figure in the alley with my stalker. Backup? I took a closer look. Nope, definitely not. We had a teenage girl and a twenty-something guy, and they were definitely *not* together, given that the guy was sticking to the shadows, creeping along behind the girl.

The girl continued to walk, oblivious. When she paused to adjust her backpack, he started to swoop in. Her head jerked up, as if she'd heard something. He ducked into a doorway.

Yes, you heard footsteps in a dark alley. Time to move your cute little ass and maybe, in future, reconsider the wisdom of strolling through alleys at all.

She peered behind her, then shrugged and continued on. The man waited until she rounded the next corner and slid from his spot. When he reached the corner and peeked around it, I dropped from the fire escape and landed behind him.

He wheeled. He blinked. Then he smiled.

"Thought that might work," I said. "Forget the little girl. I'm much more fun."

He whipped out a knife. I slammed my fist into his forearm, smacking it against the brick wall. Reflexively his hand opened, dropping the knife. He dove for it. I kicked it, then I kicked him. My foot caught him under the jaw. He went up. I kicked again. He went down.

I leapt onto his back, pinning him. "Well, that was fast. Kind of embarrassing, huh? I think you need to work out more."

He tried to buck me off. I sank my fangs into the back of his neck and held on as he got to his feet. He swung backward toward the wall, planning to crush me, I'm sure, but my saliva kicked in before he made it two steps. He teetered, then crashed to the pavement, unconscious.

I knelt to feed. I wasn't particularly hungry, but only a fool turns down a free meal, and maybe waking up with the mother of all hangovers would teach this guy a stalking lesson he wouldn't soon forget.

"Die, vampire!"

I spun as the teenage girl raced toward me, wooden stake on a collision course with my heart. I grabbed the stake and yanked it up, flipping the girl onto her back.

"That's really rude," I said. "I just saved your ass from a scumbag rapist. Is this how you repay me? Almost ruin my favorite shirt?"

She leapt to her feet and sent the stake on a return trip to my chest. Again, I stopped it. I could have pointed out that it really wouldn't do anything *more* than damage my shirt—vampires die by beheading—but I thought it best not to give her any ideas.

She ran at me again. I almost tripped over the unconscious man's arm. As I tugged him out of the way, she rushed me. I grabbed the stake and threw it aside.

She lifted her hands. Her fingertips lit up, glowing red.

"Ah, fire half-demon," I said. "Igneus, Aduro, or Exustio?"

"I won't let you kill him."

"You don't know a lot about vampires, do you? Or about being a vampire hunter. First, you really need to work on your dialogue."

"Don't talk to me, bloodsucker."

"Bloodsucker? What's next? Queen of Darkness? Spawn of Satan? You're running about twenty years behind, sweetie. Where's the clever quip? The snappy repartee?"

She snarled and charged, burning fingers outstretched. I sidestepped and winced as she stumbled over the fallen man.

"See, that's why I moved him."

She spun and came at me again. I grabbed her hand. Her burning fingers sizzled into my skin.

"Fire is useless against a vampire, as you see," I said. "So your special power doesn't do you any good, which means you're going to have to work on your other skills. I'd suggest gymnastics, aikido, and maybe ninjitsu, though it's hard to find outside Japan these days."

She wrenched free and backed up, scowling. "You're mocking me."

"No, I'm helping you. First piece of advice? Next time, don't telegraph your attack."

"Telegraph?"

"Yelling, 'Die, vampire' as you attack from behind may add a nice, if outdated, touch, but it gives you away. Next time, just run and stab. Got it?"

She stared at me. I retrieved her stake and handed it over. Then I started walking away.

"Second piece of advice?" I called back. "Stay out of alleys at night. There are a lot worse things than me out here."

I spun and grabbed the stake just as she was about to stab me in the back.

I smiled. "Much better. Now get on home. It's a school night."

Keeping the stake, I kicked her feet out from under her, then took off. She tried to follow, of course. Tenacious, as I said. But a quick flip onto another fire escape and through an open window left her behind.

I made my way up to the rooftops and headed home, rather pleased with myself. We'd come quite a ways in our two weeks together, and now, having finally made face-to-face contact, I was sure we could speed up the learning curve.

The girl was misguided, but I blamed popular culture for that. She'd eventually learn I wasn't the worst monster out there, and there were others far more deserving of her enthusiasm.

Even if she chose not to pursue such a profession, the supernatural world is a dangerous place for all of us. Self-defense skills are a must, and if I could help her with that, I would. It's the responsibility of everyone to prepare our youth for the future. I was happy to do my part.

THE BETTER HALF

Melanie Tem

Melanie Tem's work has received the Bram Stoker, International Horror Guild, British Fantasy, and World Fantasy awards, and a nomination for the Shirley Jackson Award. She has published numerous short stories, eleven solo novels, two collaborative novels with Nancy Holder, and two collaborative novels and a short story collection with her husband Steve Rasnic Tem. She is also a published poet, an oral storyteller, and a playwright. Solo stories have recently appeared in *Asimov's Science Fiction Magazine*, *Crimewave*, and *Interzone*, and anthologies such as *Black Wings* and *Darke Fantastique*. Her novels *The Yellow Wood* and *Proxy* will soon be published ChiZine Publications.

The Tems live in Denver, CO, where Melanie is executive director of a non-profit independent-living organization. They have four children and six grandchildren.

Her most notable vampire fiction is the novel, *Desmodus* (1995), in which isolated matriarchal vampire clans consider the males of their kind as nearly useless. Her otherwise humanoid vampires are also unusual in that they possess wings and other characteristics of bats.

To say the vampire in "The Better Half" is nothing at all like those in *Desmodus* is probably an understatement . . .

Kelly opened the door before I'd even come close to her house. The opening and closing of the red door in the white house startled me, like a mouth baring teeth. I stopped where I was, halfway down the block. Kelly was wearing a yellow dress and something white around her shoulders. She stepped farther out onto the porch and shaded her eyes against the high July sun.

For some reason, I didn't want her to see me just yet. I stepped behind a thick lilac bush dotted with the nubs of spent flowers. A small brown dog in the yard across the street yapped twice at me, then gave it up and went back to its spot in the shade.

I hadn't seen Kelly in fifteen years. I'd thought I'd forgotten her, but I'd have known her anywhere. In college we'd been very close for a while. Now that I was older and more careful, I'd have expected not to understand the ardor I'd felt for her then; it distressed me that I understood it perfectly, even felt a pulse of it again, like hot blood. Watching her from a distance and through the purple and green filtering of the lilac bush, I found myself a little afraid of her.

Later I learned that it was not Kelly I had reason to fear. But my father had died in the spring, and I was afraid of everything. Afraid of loving. Afraid of not loving. Afraid of coming home or rounding a corner and discovering something terrible that I, by my presence, could have stopped. I cowered behind the lilac bush and wished I could make myself invisible. I wondered why she'd called. I wondered savagely why I'd come. I thought about retreating along the hot bright sidewalk away from her house. I could hardly keep myself from rushing headlong to her.

Slowly I approached her. It was obvious that she still hadn't seen me; she was looking the other way. Looking for me. I was, purposely, a few minutes late. Then she turned, and I knew with a chill that something was terribly wrong.

It wasn't just that she looked alien, although she was elegantly dressed on a Saturday morning in a neighborhood where a business suit on a weekday was an oddity. It wasn't just that I felt invaded, although her house was around the corner from the diner where Daddy and I had often had breakfast, the park where we'd walked sometimes, the apartment where we'd lived. It was more than that. There was something wrong with her. I stopped again and stared.

It was mid-July and high noon. Hot green light through the porch awning flooded her face, the same heavy brows, high cheekbones, slightly aquiline nose. She looked sick. The spots of color high on her cheeks could have been paint or fever. She was breathing hard. Even from here I could see that she was shivering violently. And around her shoulders, in the noonday summer heat, was a white fur jacket.

I have told myself that at that point I nearly left, but I don't think that's true. I stood there looking at her across the neat green of the Kentucky bluegrass in her north Denver lawn. Sprinklers were on, making rainbows. I was drawn to her as I'd always been. Something was wrong, and I was about to be drenched in it, too.

She saw me and smiled, a weak and heart-wrenching grimace. I wished desperately that I'd never come but the impulse toward self-preservation, like others throughout my life, came too late.

"Brenda! Hello!"

I opened the waist-high, filigreed, wrought-iron gate, turned to latch it carefully behind me, turned again to walk between even rows of pin-wheel petunias. "Kelly," I said, with an effort holding out my hand. "It's good to see you."

Her hand was icy cold. I still vividly recall the shock of touching it, the momentary disorientation of having to remind myself that the temperature was nearly a hundred degrees. She leaned toward me over the porch railing, and a tiny hot breeze stirred the half-dozen wind chimes that hung from the eave, making a sweet cacophony. Healthy plants hung thick around her, almost obscuring her face. I could smell both her honeysuckle perfume and the faint sickly odor of her breath. She was smiling cordially; her lips were pale pink, almost colorless, against the yellow-white of her teeth. There were dark circles under her eyes. For a moment I had the terrifying fantasy that she would tumble off the porch into my arms, and that when she hit she would weigh no more than the truncated melodies from the sway of the chimes.

Her voice was much as I remembered it: husky, controlled, well-modulated. But I thought I'd heard it break, as though the two words she'd spoken had been almost too much for her. She took a deep breath, encircled my wrist with the thin icy fingers of her other hand, and said, "Come in."

I had last seen Kelly at her wedding. I'd watched the ceremony from a gauzy distance, wondering how she could bring herself to do such a thing and whether I'd ever get the chance; my father had already been sick and my mother, of course, long gone. Then I had passed through a long reception line to have her press my hand and kiss my cheek as though she'd never seen me before. Or never would again.

Ron, her new husband, had bent to kiss me, too, and I'd made a point to cough at the silly musk of his aftershave. He was tall and very fair, with baby-soft stubble on his cheeks and upper lip. His big pawlike hands cupped my shoulders as he gazed earnestly down at me. "I love her, Brenda." He could have been reciting the Boy Scout pledge. "Already she's my better half."

Later I repeated that comment to my friends; we all laughed and rolled our eyes. Ron was always terribly sincere. He could be making an offhand remark about the weather or the cafeteria food, and from his tone and delivery you'd think he was issuing a proclamation to limit worldwide nuclear arms proliferation.

Ron was simple. Often you could tell he'd missed the punchline of a joke, especially if it was off-color; he'd chuckle good-naturedly anyway. He had a hard time keeping up with our rapid Eastern chatter, but he'd look from one speaker to the next like an alert puppy, as if he were following right along. He was such an easy target that few of us resisted the temptation to make fun of him.

Kelly, who was brilliant, got him through school. At first she literally wrote his papers for him; he was a poli-sci major and she took languages, so it meant double studying for her, but she didn't seem to pull any more all-nighters than the rest of us. Gradually he learned to write first drafts, which she then edited meticulously; you'd see them huddled at a table in the library, Kelly looking grim, Ron looking earnest and genial and bewildered.

She taught him everything. How to write a simple sentence. How to study for an exam. How to read a paragraph from beginning to end and catch the drift. How to eat without grossing everybody out. How to behave during fraternity rush. At a time when the entire Greek system was the object of much derision on our liberal little campus, Ron became a proud and busy Delt; senior year he was elected president, and Kelly, demure in gold chiffon, clung to his arm.

We gossiped that she taught him everything he knew about sex, too. That first year, before the mores and the rules loosened to allow men and women in each other's rooms, everybody made out in the courtyard of the freshman women's dorm. Because Kelly said they had too much work to do, they weren't there as often as some of the rest of us; for a while that winter and spring, I spent most of my waking hours, and a few asleep, in the courtyard with a handsome and knowledgeable young man from New Jersey named Jan.

But Ron and Kelly were there often enough for us to observe them and comment on their form. His back would be hard against the wall and his arms stiffly down around her waist. She'd be stretched up to nuzzle in his neck—or, we speculated unkindly, to whisper instructions. At first, if you said hello on your way past—and we would, just to be perverse—Ron's innate politeness would have him nodding and passing the time of day. Kelly didn't acknowledge anything but Ron; she was totally absorbed in him. Before long, he had also learned to ignore us, or to seem to.

Kelly was moody, intense, determined. Absolutely focused. I knew her before she met Ron; they assigned us as roommates freshman year. There was something about her—besides our age, the sense that we were standing on a frontier—that made me tell her things I hadn't told anybody, hadn't even thought of before. And made me listen to her self-revelations with bated breath, as though I were witness to the birth of fine music or ferreting out the inkling of a mystery.

In those days Kelly was already fascinated by women who had died for something they believed in, like Joan of Arc about whom she read in lyrical French, or for something they were and couldn't help, like Anne Frank whose diary she read in deceptively robust German. I didn't understand the words—I was a sociology major—but I knew the stories, and I loved the way Kelly looked and sounded when she read. When she stopped, there would be a rapturous silence, and then one or both of us would breathe, "Oh, that was beautiful!"

After she met Ron, things between Kelly and me changed. At first all she talked about was him, and I understood that; I talked about Jan a lot, too. But gradually she quit talking to me at all, and when she listened it was politely, her pen poised over the essay whose editing I had interrupted.

Ron seemed as open and expansive and featureless as the prairies of his native Nebraska. I was convinced she was wasting her life. He wasn't good enough for her. I could not imagine what she saw in him.

Unless it was the unlimited opportunity to play puppeteer, sculptor, inventor. I said that to her one night when we were both lying awake, trying not to be disturbed by the party down the hall. She was my best friend, and I thought I owed it to her to tell her what I thought.

"What is it between you and Ron anyway?" I demanded, somewhat abruptly. We'd been complaining desultorily to each other about the noise and making derogatory comments about some people's study habits, and in my own ears I sounded suddenly angry and hurt, which was not what I'd intended. But I went on anyway. "What is this, a role-reversed Pygmalion, or what?"

She was silent for such a long time that I thought either she'd fallen asleep or she was completely ignoring me this time I was just about to pose my challenge again, maybe even get out of bed and cross the room and shake her by the shoulders until she paid attention to me, when she answered calmly. "There are worse things."

"Kelly, you're beautiful and brilliant. You could have any man on this campus. Ron is just so ordinary."

"Ron is good for me, Brenda. I don't expect you to understand." But then she assuaged my hurt feelings by trying to explain. "He takes me out of myself."

That was the last time Kelly and I talked about anything important. It was practically the last time we talked at all. For the rest of freshman year I might have had a single room, except for intimate, hurtful evidence of her—stockings hung like empty skin on the closet doorknob to dry, bottles of perfume and makeup like a string of amulets across her nightstand— all of it carefully on her side of the room. The next year she roomed with a sorority sister, somebody whom I didn't know and whom I didn't think Kelly knew very well, either.

I was surprised and a little offended to get a wedding invitation. I told myself I had no obligation to go. I went anyway, and cried, and pressed her hand. To this day I'm not sure she knew who I was when I went through the reception line. I spent most of the reception making conversation with Kelly's parents, a gaunt pale woman who looked very much like Kelly and a tall fair robust man. They were proud of their daughter; Ron was a fine young man who would go far in this world. Her father was jocular and verbose; he danced with all the young women, several times with me. Her mother barely said a word, seldom got out of her chair; her smile was like the winter sun.

At the time I didn't know that I'd noticed all that about Kelly's parents. I hadn't thought about them in years, probably had never thought about them directly. But the impressions were all there, ready for the taking. If I'd just paid attention, I might have been warned. And then I don't know what I would have done.

Since college, Kelly and I had barely kept in touch. For a while I had kept approximate track of her through mutual friends and the alumni newsletter. I moved out West because the dry climate might be better for Daddy's health, got a graduate degree in planning and a job with the Aurora city government. Left Daddy alone too much, then hired a stranger to nurse him so I could live my own life. As if there was such a thing.

From sporadic Christmas cards, I knew that Kelly and her family had lived in various parts of Europe; Ron was an attorney specializing in international law and a high-ranking officer in the military, and his job had something to do with intelligence, maybe the CIA. I knew that they had two sons. In every communication, no matter how brief, Kelly mentioned that she had never worked a day outside the home, that when Ron was away she sometimes went for days without talking to an adult, that her languages were getting rusty except for the language of the country she happened to be living in at the time. It seemed to me that even her English was awkward, childlike, although it was hard to tell from the few sentences she wrote.

Last year I'd received a copy of a form Christmas letter on pale green paper with wreaths along the margin, ostensibly composed by Ron. It was so eloquent and interesting and grammatically sophisticated that at first I was a little shocked. Then I decided—with distaste, but also with a measure of relief that should have been a clue if I'd been paying attention—that Kelly must still be ghostwriting.

For some reason, I'd kept that letter, though as far as I could remember I hadn't answered it. After Kelly's call, I'd pulled it out and re-read it. The letter described the family's travels in the Alps; though it read like a travel brochure, the prose was competent and there were vivid images. It outlined the boys' many activities and commented, "Without Kelly, of course, none of this would be possible." It mentioned that Kelly had been ill lately, tired: "The gray wet winters of northern Europe really don't agree with her. We're hoping that some of her sparkle will return when we move back home."

I'd thought there was nothing significant in that slick, chatty, green-edged letter. I'd been wrong.

Kelly's house was very orderly and close and clean. She led me down a short hallway lined with murky photographs of people I didn't think I knew, into a living room where a fire crackled in a plain brick fireplace and not a speck of ash marred the dappled marble surface of the hearth. Heavy maroon drapes were pulled shut floor to ceiling, and all the lights were on; the room was stifling.

Startled and confused, I paused in the arched doorway while Kelly went on ahead of me. I saw her pull the white fur jacket closer around her, as if she were cold.

"We haven't lived here very long," she said over her shoulder. She was apologizing, but I didn't know what for.

"It's nice," I said, and followed her into the nightlike, winterlike room. She gestured toward a rocker-recliner. "Make yourself at home."

I sat down. Though the chair was across the room, the part of my body which faced the fire grew hot in a matter of seconds, and I had started to sweat. Kelly pulled an ottoman nearly onto the hearth and huddled onto it, hugging her knees.

I was quickly discomfited by the silence between us, through which I could hear her labored breathing and the spitting of the fire. "How long have you lived here?" I asked, to have something to say.

"Just a few months. Since the first of April." So she was aware it was summer.

"How long will you be here?" I knew it was sounding like an interrogation, but I desperately needed to ground myself in time and space. That was not a new impulse, though I hadn't been so acutely aware of it before. I was shaking, and the heat was making my head swim. It seemed to me that I had been floating for a long time.

I understand now, of course, how misguided it was to look to Kelly for ballast. She had almost no weight herself by that time, no substance of her own, so she couldn't have held anybody down.

Abruptly, as often happened to me when I was invaded by even a hint of strong emotion—fear, pleasure, grief—I could feel the slight weight of my father's body in my arms, the web of his baby-fine hair across my lips. I closed my eyes against the pain and curled my arms into my chest as though to keep from dropping him.

Almost tonelessly Kelly asked, "What's wrong, Brenda?" and I realized I'd covered my face with my empty hands.

"You remind me of somebody," I said. That surprised me. I wasn't even sure what it meant. Self-stimulating like an autistic child, I was rocking furiously in the cumbersome chair. I forced myself to press my palms flat against its nubby arms, stopping the motion. "Somebody else who left me," I added.

She didn't ask me what I meant. She didn't defend against my interpretation of what had happened between us. She just cocked her head in a quizzical gesture so familiar to me that I caught my breath, although I wouldn't have guessed that I remembered anything significant about her.

Absently she picked two bits of lint off the brown carpet, which had looked spotless to me, and deposited them into her other palm, closing her fingers protectively. I noticed her silver-pink nails. I noticed that her mauve stockings were opaque, thicker than standard nylons, and that the stylish high-heeled boots she wore were fur-lined. I wanted to go sit beside her, have her hug me to warm us both. I was sweating profusely.

I think I was on the verge of telling her about my father. I think I might have said things to her that I hadn't yet said to myself. I'm still haunted by the suspicion that, if I'd spoken up at that moment, subsequent events might have turned out very differently. The thought makes my blood run cold.

But I didn't say anything, for at that moment Kelly's sons came home. I flinched as I heard a screen door slam, heard children's voices laughing and squabbling. It was as if their liveliness tore at something.

Daddy had died while I was out. He hadn't wanted me to go, though he would never have said so. He hadn't liked the man, any man, I was with. When I came home—earlier than I'd intended though not early enough, determined not to see that man again—I'd found my father dead on the floor. If I'd been there I could have saved him, or at least held him while he died. I owed him. He gave me life.

Struggling to stay in focus when the boys burst in, I kept my eyes on Kelly. The transformation was remarkable. Many times after that I saw it happen to her, and I was always astounded, but that first time was like witnessing a miracle, or the results of a spectacular compact with the devil.

She filled out like an inflatable doll. Color flooded into her cheeks. Her shoulders squared and she sat up straight. By the time her boys found us and rushed into the living room, bringing with them like sirens their light and fresh air and energy, she was holding out her arms to them and beaming and the white fur jacket had slipped from her shoulders onto the hearth behind her, where I thought it might burn.

I stayed at Kelly's house for a long time that first day, though I hadn't intended to. When Kelly introduced me as an old friend from college, Joshua, the younger child, stared at me solemn-eyed and demanded, "Do you know my daddy, too?" I admitted that I did, or used to. He nodded. He was very serious.

We had a picnic lunch outside on the patio. I watched the children splash in the sprinkler and bounce on the backyard trampoline, watched

Kelly bask like a chameleon in the sunshine. She was a nervous hostess. She fluttered and fussed to make sure the boys and I were served, persistently inquired whether the lemonade was sweet enough and whether the sandwiches had too much mayonnaise, was visibly worried whenever any of us stopped eating. She herself didn't eat at all, as if she wasn't entitled to. She didn't swat at flies or fan herself or complain about the heat. She hardly talked to me; her interactions with the children were impatient. She watched us eat and play, and the look on her face was near-panic, as if she couldn't be sure she was getting it right.

I was restless. I wasn't used to sitting still for so long without something to occupy me—television, a newspaper, knitting. At one point I got up and went over to join the boys. I tossed the new yellow frisbee, spotted Clay on the tramp, squirted Joshua with the sprinkler. I was clumsy and they didn't like it; my intrusion altered the rhythms of their play. "Quit it!" Josh shrieked when the water hit him, and Clay simply slid off the end of the trampoline and stalked away when he discovered I'd taken up position at the side.

Somewhat aimlessly, I strolled around the yard. Red and salmon late roses climbed the privacy fence; I touched their petals and thorns, bent to sniff their fragrance. "Ron likes roses," Kelly said from behind me, and I jumped; I hadn't realized how close she was. "That's why we planted all those bushes. They're hard to take care of, though. I'm still learning. Ron buys me books."

"They're beautiful," I said.

"They're a lot of care. He's never here to do any of it. It's part of my job."

Clay appeared at my elbow. He was carrying a framed and glass-covered family portrait big enough that he had to hold it with both hands.

"Clay!" his mother remonstrated, much more sharply than I'd have expected from her. "Don't drop that!"

"I'll put it back," he said lightly, dismissing her. "See," he said earnestly to me. "That's my dad."

I didn't know what I was supposed to say, what acknowledgment would be satisfactory. I looked at him, at his brother across the yard, at the portrait. It had been taken several years ago; the boys looked much younger. Kelly was pale and lovely, clinging to her husband's arm even though the photographer had no doubt posed her standing up straight. The uniformed man at the hub of the family grouping was taller, ruddier, and possessed of much more presence than I remembered. "You look like him." I finally said to Clay. "You both do." He grinned and nodded and took the heavy picture back into the house.

I sat on the kids' swing and watched a gray bird sitting in the apple tree. It was the wrong time of the season, between blossom and fruit, to tell whether there would be a good crop; I wondered idly whether Kelly made applesauce, whether Ron and the boys liked apple pie. "My dad put up those swings for us!" Joshua shouted from the wading pool, sounding angry. I took the lemonade pitcher inside for more ice, although no one who lived there had suggested it.

Being alone in Kelly's kitchen gave me a sense of just-missed intimacy. I guessed that she spent a good deal of time here, cooking and cleaning, but there seemed to be nothing personal about her in the room. I looked around.

The pictures on the wall above the microwave were standard, square, factory-painted representations of vegetables, a tomato and a carrot and an ear of corn, pleasant enough. On the single-shelf spice rack above the dishwasher were two red-and-white cans and two undistinguished glass bottles: cinnamon, onion powder, salt, and pepper. Nothing idiosyncratic or identifying. No dishes soaked in the sink; no meat was thawing on the counter for dinner.

I remember thinking that, if I looked through the cupboards and drawers and into the back shelves of the refrigerator, I'd surely find something about Kelly, but I couldn't quite bring myself to make such a deliberate search. Now, of course, I know there wouldn't have been anything anyway. No favorite snacks of hers secreted away. No dishes that meant anything special to her. No special recipes. In the freezer I'd probably have found Fudgsicles for Clay and Eskimo Pies for Josh, and no doubt there was a six-pack of Coors Lite on the top shelf of the refrigerator for Ron. But, no matter how deeply I looked or how broadly I interpreted, I wouldn't have found anything personal about Kelly, except in what she'd made sure was there for the others.

I set the pitcher on the counter and moved so that I was standing in the middle of the floor with my hands at my sides and my eyes closed. I held my breath. It was like being trapped in a flotation tank. I could hear the boys squealing and shouting outside, the hum of a lawnmower farther away and the ticking of a clock nearby, but the sounds were outside of me, not touching. I could smell whiffs and layers of homey kitchen odors—coffee, cinnamon, onions—but I had never been fed in this room.

I opened my eyes and was dizzy. Without knowing it, I had turned, so that now I was facing a little alcove that opened off the main kitchen. A breakfast nook, maybe, or a pantry. I rounded the multicolored Plexiglas partition and caught my breath.

The place was a shrine. On all three walls, from the waist-high wainscoting nearly to the ceiling, were photographs of Ron and Clay and Joshua. Black-and-white photos on a plain white background, unlike the busy kitchen wallpaper in the rest of the room. Pictures of them singly and in various combinations: Ron in uniform, looking stoic and sensible; Clay doing a flip on the trampoline; Joshua in his Cub Scout uniform; the three of them in a formal pose, each boy with his hand on his father's shoulder; the boys by a Christmas tree. I counted; there were forty-three photographs.

I couldn't bring myself to go into the alcove. I think I was afraid I'd hear voices. And there was not a single likeness of Kelly anywhere on the open white walls.

Later, a grim and wonderful thought occurred to me: it would have been virtually impossible for a detective to find out anything useful about Kelly. Or for a voodoo practitioner to fashion an efficacious doll. There was little essence of her left. There were few details. By the end, it would have been easy to say that she had no soul.

For the rest of that summer and into the fall, I spent a great deal of time at Kelly's house. It started with lunch on Saturdays, always a picnic lunch with the boys on the patio, sandwiches and lemonade and chips. She never let me bring anything; she seemed to take offense when I tried to insist.

"Why don't you and I go somewhere for lunch, Kelly? Get a sitter for the boys or take them to the pool or something."

"The pool isn't safe. I don't like the kind of kids who go there. And I would never leave them with a sitter."

Kelly and I never seemed to be alone together. Her sons were always there, in the same room or within earshot or about to rush in and demand something of her. I chafed. I didn't much like the boys anyway; I found them mouthy and rude, to me but especially to their mother, and altogether too high-spirited for my taste.

"It's nice to see a mother spend as much time with her kids as you do," I said once, lying, trying to understand, trying to get her to talk to me about something.

"We've always been—close," she said, a little hesitantly. "They both nursed until they were almost two. Sometimes Josh will still try to nip my breast. In play, you know."

Somewhat taken aback, I said, "You seem to enjoy their company." I didn't know whether that was true or not.

She shrugged and laughed a little. "I think I've inherited my father's attitudes toward children. They'd be fine if you could teach them and train them and mold them into what you want. Otherwise, they're mostly irritating." She laughed again and shivered, hugged herself, passed a hand over her eyes. "But I don't have to like my kids in order to be a good mother, do I?"

For a long time, I didn't see Ron. He was always at work when I was there, and, no matter how late I stayed, he worked later.

"Come with me to see this movie. I've been wanting to see it for a long time, and it's about to leave town, and I don't want to go alone."

"There's a movie that the boys want to see. One of those kung fu things. I promised I'd take them this weekend."

Kelly's roses faded, and the marigolds and petunias and then chrysanthemums came into their own. The apple tree bore nicely, tiny fruit clustered all on the south side of the tree because, Kelly speculated, the blossoms on the north side had been frozen early in the spring. That distressed her enormously; her eyes shone with tears when she talked about it. The boys went back to school.

"Now you have lots of free time. Let's go to the art museum one morning next week. I can take a few hours off."

"Oh, Brenda, the work around here is endless. Really. I have fall housecleaning to do. I'm redecorating Clay's room. There must be a dozen layers of wallpaper on those walls. My first responsibility is to Ron and the children. You're welcome to come here, though. I could fix you lunch."

One crisp Wednesday in late September I had a meeting over on her side of town, and I didn't have to be back at the office until my two o'clock staff meeting. Impulsively, I turned off onto a side street toward her house.

I had never been to Kelly's house on a weekday before. I had never dropped in on her unexpectedly. I had seldom dropped in on anybody unexpectedly; I liked to have time to prepare, and was keenly aware of the differences between people in private and people when they met the world, even the small and confused part of the world represented by me. My heart was skittering uneasily, and I felt a little feverish, chilled, though the sun was warm and the sky brilliant. The houses and trees and fence rows along these old blocks had taken on that sharp-edged quality that autumn sometimes imparts to a city; every brick seemed outlined, every flower and leaf a jewel.

I parked by the side of her house, across the street. I opened and shut the gate as quietly as I could. I stood for a while on her porch, listening to the wind chimes, catching stray rainbows from the lopsided paper leaf Josh had made in school and hung in the front window. She had moved the plants inside for the winter, and the porch seemed bare. Finally I pushed the button for the doorbell and waited. A few cars went by behind me. I touched the doorbell button again, listened for any sound inside the house, could hear none.

When I tried the door, it opened easily. I went in quickly and shut the door behind me, thinking to keep out the light and dust. I was nearly through the front hall and to the kitchen before I called her name.

"In here, Brenda," she answered, as though she'd been expecting me. I stopped for a moment, bewildered; maybe I'd somehow forgotten that I had called ahead, or maybe we'd had plans for today that I hadn't written in my appointment book.

"Where?"

"In here."

I found her, finally, in the master bedroom. She was in bed, under the covers; she wore a scarf and a stocking cap on her head, mittens on the hands that pulled the covers up to her chin. Around her neck I could see the collar of the white fur jacket. Her teeth were chattering, and her skin was so pale that it was almost green. I stood in the doorway and stared. The shaft of light through the blinded window looked wintry. "Kelly, what's wrong? Are you sick?" It was a question I could have asked months before; now it seemed impossible to avoid.

"I'm cold," she said weakly. "I—don't seem to have any energy."

"Should I call somebody?"

"No, it's all right. Usually if I stay in bed all day I'm all right by the time the boys get home from school."

"How often does this happen?"

"Oh, I don't know. Every other day or so now, I guess."

I had advanced into the room, stood by the side of the bed. I was reluctant to touch her. I now know that the contagion had nothing to do with physical contact with Kelly, that I was safer alone in that house with her than I've been at any time since. But that morning all I knew was cold fear, and alarm for my friend, and an intense, exhilarating curiosity. "Where's Ron?" I demanded. "Is he still out of town? Does he know about this?"

"He came home late last night," she told me, and I had no way of appreciating the significance of what she'd said.

"What shall I do? Should I call him at work? Or call a doctor?"

"No." With a great sigh and much tremulous effort, she lifted her feet over the side of the bed and sat up. I could feel her dizziness; I put my hand flat against the wall and lowered my head to let it clear. Kelly stood up. "Take me out somewhere," she said. "I'm hungry. Let's go to lunch."

Without my help, she made it out of the house, down the walk, and into the car. The sun had been shining in the passenger window, so it would be warm for her there. There was definitely a fall chill in the air, I decided, as I found myself shivering a little. "Where do you want to go?" I asked her.

"Someplace fast."

In Denver I have always been delighted, personally and professionally, by contrasts, one of which is the proximity of quiet residential neighborhoods like Kelly's to bustling commercial strips. We were five minutes from half a dozen fast-food places. Kelly said she didn't care which one, so I drove somewhat randomly and found the one with the least-crowded parking lot. She wanted to go inside.

The place was bright, warm, cacophonous. I saw Kelly wrap herself more tightly in the fur jacket, saw people glance at her and then glance away. She went to find a seat, as far away from the windows and the doors as she could, and I ordered for both of us, not knowing what she wanted, taking a chance. There was a very long line. When I finally got to her, she was staring with a stricken look on her face at the middle-aged woman in the ridiculous uniform who was clearing the tables and sweeping the floor. "I talked to her," Kelly whispered as I set the laden tray down. "She has a master's degree."

"In what?" I asked, making conversation. It seemed important to keep her engaged, though I didn't know what she was talking about. "Here's your shake. I hope chocolate's all right. They were out of strawberry."

When she didn't answer right away I looked at her more closely. The expression of horror on her face made my stomach turn. Her eyes were bloodshot and bulging. She was breathing heavily through her mouth. Her gloved hands on the tabletop were clawed, as if trying to find in the

Formica something to cling to. "That could be me a few years from now," she said hoarsely. "Working in a fast-food place, for a little extra money and something to do. Alone. That could be me."

"Don't be silly," I snapped. "You have a lot more going for you than that woman does."

Suddenly she was shrieking at me. "How do you know that? How can you know? I've let everybody down! Everybody! All my teachers and professors who said I had so much potential! My father! Everybody! You don't know what you're talking about!" Then, to my own horror, she struggled to her feet and hobbled out the door. For a moment, I really thought she'd disappeared, vanished somehow into the air that wasn't much thinner than she was. I told myself that was crazy and followed her.

The lunchtime crowd had filled in behind Kelly and was all of a piece again. I pushed through it and through the door, which framed the busy street scene as though it were a poor photograph, flat and without meaning to me until I entered it. I looked around. Kelly had collapsed on the hot sidewalk against the building. Her knees were drawn up, her head was down so that the stringy dark hair fell over her face, the collar of the jacket stood up around her ears. Two women in shorts and halter tops crouched beside her. I hurried, as though to save her from them, although, of course, by then Kelly wasn't the one who needed protecting.

I met Ron at the hospital. From the ambulance stretcher, in a flat high voice that almost seemed part of the siren, Kelly had told me how to reach him. I hadn't wanted to; I hadn't wanted him with us. By the time I made it through all the layers and synapses of the bureaucracy he worked in and heard his official voice on the other end of the line, I was furious. But I hadn't missed anything; Kelly was still waiting in the emergency room, slumped in a chair. Ron did not sound especially alarmed; I told myself it was his training. He said he'd be there in fifteen minutes, and he was.

They had just taken Kelly to be examined when he got there. I was standing at the counter looking after her, feeling bereft; they wouldn't let me go back behind the curtain with her, and she was too weak to ask for me. When the tall blond uniformed man strode by me, I didn't try to speak to him, and no one else did, either. I doubt that Kelly asked for him, or gave permission, or even recognized him when he came. None of that was necessary. He was her husband. She was part of him. He had the right.

My father and I had been bound like that, too. If I'd asserted the right to be part of him, welcomed and treasured it, I could have been. Instead, I'd thought it was necessary for me to grow up, to separate. And so I'd lost him. Lost us both, I thought then, for without him I had no idea who I was.

I felt Ron's presence approaching me before I opened my eyes and saw him. "She's unconscious," he said. "They don't know yet what's wrong. You don't look very good yourself. Come and sit down."

I didn't let him touch me then, but I preceded him to a pair of orange plastic bucket chairs attached to a metal bar against the wall. We were then sitting squarely side-by-side, and the chairs didn't move; I didn't make the effort to face him. He was friendly and solemn, as befitted the occasion. He took my hand in both of his, swallowing it. "Brenda." He made my name sound far more significant than I'd ever thought it was, and—despite myself, despite the circumstances, despite what I'd have mistakenly called my better judgment—something inside me stirred gratefully. "It's nice to see you again after all these years. I'm sorry our reunion turned out to be like this. Kelly has talked a great deal about you over the past few months."

I nodded. I didn't know what to say.

"What happened?" Ron asked. He let go of my hand and it was cold. I put both hands in my pockets.

"She—collapsed," I told him. The more I told him, the angrier I became, and the closer to the kind of emptying, wracking sobs I'd been so afraid of. Now I know there's nothing to fear in being emptied; Kelly simply hadn't taken it far enough. To the end, some part of her fought it. I don't fight at all anymore.

"What do you mean? Tell me what happened. The details." He was moving in, assuming command. It crossed my mind to resist him, but from the instant he'd walked into the room I'd felt exhausted.

"I dropped by to see her. I was in the neighborhood. When I got there she was sick. She asked me to take her out to lunch. So we—"

"Out?" His blond eyebrows rose and then furrowed disapprovingly. "Out of the house? With you?"

I mustered a little indignation. "What's wrong with that?"

"It's—unusual, that's all. Go on."

I told him the rest of what I knew. It seemed to take an enormous amount of time to say it all, though I wouldn't have thought I had that much to say. I stumbled over words. There were long silences. Ron listened attentively. At one point he rested his hand on my shoulder in a comradely way, and I was too tired and disoriented to pull free. When I finished, he nodded, and then someone came for him from behind the curtains and lights, and I was left alone again, knowing I hadn't said enough.

Kelly never came home from the hospital. She died without regaining consciousness. Many times since then I've wondered what she would have said to me if she'd awakened, what advice she would have given, what warning, how she would have passed the torch.

I wasn't there when she died. Ron was. He called me early the next morning to tell me. He sounded drained; his voice was flat and thin. "Oh, Ron," I said, foolishly, and then waited for him to tell me what to do.

"I'd like you to come over," he said. "The boys are having a hard time."

I haven't left since. I haven't been back to my apartment even to pick up my things; none of my former possessions seems worth retrieval. I had no animals to feed, no plants to water, no books or clothes or furniture or photographs that mean anything to me now.

Kelly kept her house orderly. From the first day, I could find things. The boys' schedules were predictable, although very busy; names and phone numbers of their friends' parents, Scout leaders, piano teachers were on a laminated list on the kitchen bulletin board. In her half of the master bedroom closet, I found clothes of various sizes, and the larger ones, from before she lost so much weight, fit fine.

The first week I took personal leave from work. Since then I've been calling in sick, when I think of it; most recently I haven't called in at all and, of course, they don't know where I am.

Ron is away a good deal. The work he does is important and mysterious; I don't know exactly what it is, but I'm proud to be able to help him do it.

But he was home that first week, and we got used to each other. "You're very different from the man I knew in college," I told him. We were sitting in the darkened living room. We'd been talking about Kelly. We'd both been crying.

He was sitting beside me on the couch. I saw him nod and slightly smile. "Kelly used to say I'd developed my potential beyond her wildest dreams," he admitted, "and she'd lost hers."

I felt a flash of anger against her. She was dead. "She had a choice," I pointed out. "Nobody forced her to do anything. She could have done other things with her life."

"Don't be too sure of that." His sharp tone surprised and hurt me. I glanced at him through the shadows, saw him lean forward to set his drink on the coffee table. He took my empty glass from my hands and put it down, too, then swiftly lowered his face to my neck.

There was a small pain and, afterwards, a small stinging wound. When he was finished he stood up, wiped his mouth with his breast pocket handkerchief, and went upstairs to bed. I sat up for a long time, amazed, touched, frightened. No longer lonely. No longer having decisions to be made or protection to construct. That first night, that first time, I did not feel tired or cold; the sickness has since begun, but the exhilaration has heightened, too.

Ron says he loves me. He says he and the boys need me, couldn't get along without me. I like to hear that. I know what he means.

SELLING HOUSES

Laurell K. Hamilton

As mentioned in the introduction, Laurell K. Hamilton is the bestselling author of the Anita Blake, Vampire Hunter novels—the twenty-first of which will be published in 2015. She also authors the Merry Gentry series about a Princess of Faerie who must cope with the intrigues of her own kind while dealing with life in a world where humans know faeries exist. Hamilton lives in Missouri, with her husband and her daughter.

Hamilton sets "Selling Houses" in Anita Blake's world, but it has nothing to do with the novels' characters. Instead, the author considers what more mundane folks do now that vampires are legally alive. What if, for instance, you sold real estate?

The house sat in its small yard looking sullen. It seemed to squat close to the ground as if it had been beaten down. Abbie shook her head to clear such strange notions from her mind. The house looked just like all the other houses in the subdivision. Oh, certainly it had type-A elevation. Which meant it had a peaked roof, and it had two skylights in the living room and a fireplace. The Garners had wanted some of the extra features. It was a nice house with its deluxe cedar board siding and half-brick front. Its small lot was no smaller than any of the other houses, except for some of the corner lots. And yet…

Abbie walked briskly up the sidewalk that led through the yard. Daffodils waved bravely all along the porch. They were a brilliant burst of color against the dark-red house. Abbie swallowed quickly, her breath short. She had only talked to Marion Garner on the phone maybe twice, but in those conversations Marion had been full of gardening ideas for their new home.

It had been Sandra who had handled the sell, but she wouldn't touch the house again. Sandra's imagination was a little too thorough to allow her to go back to the place where her clients were slaughtered.

Abbie had been given the job because she specialized in the hard-to-sell. Hadn't she sold that monstrous rundown Victorian to that young couple who wanted to fix it up, and that awful filthy Peterson house? Why, she had spent her days off cleaning it out so it would sell, and it had sold, for more than they expected. And Abbie was determined that she would sell this house as well.

She admitted that mass murder was a very black mark against a house. And mass murder with an official cause of demon possession was about as black a mark as any.

The house had been exorcised, but even Abbie, who was no psychic, could feel it. Evil was here like a stain that wouldn't come completely up. And if the second owners of this house fell to demons, then Abbie and her Realtor company would be liable. So Abbie would see that the house was cleansed correctly. It would be as pure and lily-white as a virgin at her wedding. It would have to be.

The real problem was that the newspapers had made a horrendous scandal of it all. There wasn't a soul for miles around that didn't know about it. And any prospective buyer would have to be told. No, Abbie would not try to keep it a secret from buyers, but at the same time she wouldn't volunteer the full information too early in the sales pitch either.

She hesitated outside the door and said half aloud, "Come on, it's just a house. There's nothing in there to hurt you." The words rang hollow somehow, but she put the key in the lock and the door swung inward.

It looked so much like all the other houses that it startled her. Somehow she had thought that there would be a difference. Something to mark it apart from any other house. But the living room was small with the extra vaulted ceiling and brick fireplace. The carpet had been a beige-tan color that went with almost any décor. She'd seen pictures of the room before. There was bare subflooring, stretching naked and unfinished.

The flooring was discolored, pale and faded, almost like a coffee stain, but it covered a huge area. Here was where they had found Marion Garner. The papers said she had been stabbed over twenty times with a butcher knife.

New carpeting would hide the stain.

The afternoon sunlight streamed in the west-facing window and illuminated a hole in the wall. It was about the size of a fist and stood like a gaping reminder in the center of the off-white wall. As she walked closer, Abbie could see splatters along the wall. The cleanup crew usually got up all the visible mess. This looked like they hadn't even tried. Abbie would demand that they either finish the job, or give back some of the deposit.

The stains were pale brown shadows of their former selves, but no family would move in with such stains. New paint, new carpeting; the price of the house would need to go up. And Abbie wasn't sure she could get anyone to pay the original price.

She spoke softly to herself, "Now what kind of defeatist talk is that? You will sell this house." And she would, one way or another.

The kitchen/dining room area was cheerful with its skylight and back door. There was a smudge on the white door near the knob but not on it. Abbie stooped to examine it and quickly straightened. She wasn't ure if the cleanup crew had missed it or just left it. Maybe it was time to hire a new cleaning crew. Nothing excused leaving this behind.

It was a tiny handprint made of dried blood. It had to belong to the little boy; he had been almost five. Had he come running in here to escape? Had he tried to open the door and failed?

Abbie leaned over the sink and opened the kitchen window. It seemed stuffy in here suddenly. The cool spring breeze riffled the white curtains. They were embroidered with autumn leaves in rusts and shades of gold. They went well with the brown and ivory floor tiles.

She had a choice now, about where to go next. The door leading to the adjoining garage was just to her right. And the stairs leading down to the basement next to that. The garage was fairly safe. She opened the door and stepped onto the single step. The garage was cooler than the house, like a cave. Another back door led from the garage to the backyard. The only stains here were oil stains.

She stepped back in and closed the door, leaning against it for a moment. Her eyes glanced down the stairs to the closed door of the basement. Little Brian Garner's last trip had been down those stairs. Had he been chased? Had he hidden there and been discovered?

She would leave the basement until later.

The bedrooms and bath stretched down the long hallway to the left. The first bedroom had been the nursery. Someone had painted circus animals along the walls. They marched bright and cheerful round the empty walls. Jessica Garner had missed her second birthday by only two weeks. Or that's what Sandra said.

The bathroom was across the hall. It was good-sized, done mostly in white with some browns here and there. The mirror over the sink was gone. The cleanup crew had carted away the broken glass and left the black emptiness in the silver frame. Why replace anything until they knew for sure the house wasn't being torn down? Other houses had been torn down for less.

The wallpaper was pretty and looked undamaged. It was ivory with a pattern of pale pink stripes and brown flowers done small. Abbie ran her hand down it and found slash marks. There were at least six holes in the wall, as if a knife had been thrust into it. But there was no blood. There was no telling what Phillip Garner thought he was doing driving a knife into his bathroom wall.

The master bedroom was next with its half bath and ceiling fan. The wallpaper in here was beige with a brown oriental design done tasteful and small. There was a stain in the middle of the carpet, smaller than the living room's blood. No one knew why the baby had been in here, but it was here that he killed her.

The papers were vague about exactly how she had died, which meant it was too gruesome to print much of it. Which meant that Jessica Garner had glimpsed hell before she died. There was a pattern of small smudges low along one wall. It looked like tiny bloody handprints struggling. But at least here the cleanup crew had tried to wash them away. Why hadn't they done the same in the kitchen area?

The more Abbie thought about it, the madder she got. With something this awful, why leave blatant reminders?

The little bathroom was in stainless white and silver, except for something dark between the tiles in front of the sink. Abbie started to bend down to look, but she knew what it was. It was blood. They had gotten most of it up, but it clung in the grooves between the tiles like dirt under a fingernail. She'd never seen the cleanup crew so careless.

The boy's bedroom was in the front corner of the house. The wallpaper was a pale blue with racing cars streaking across it. Red, green, yellow, dark blue, the cars with their miniature drivers raced around the empty walls. This was the only carpeting in the house that had some real color to it; it was a rich blue.

Perhaps it had been the boy's favorite color. The sliding doors to the closet were torn, ripped. The white scars of naked wood showed under the varnish. One door had been ripped from its groove and leaned against the far wall. Had Brian Garner hidden here and been flushed out by his father?

Or had Phillip Garner only thought his son was in here? For it was certain the boy had not died here.

There were no bloodstains, no helpless handprints.

Abbie walked out into the hallway. She had walked into hundreds of empty houses over the years, but she had never felt anything quite like this. The very walls seemed to be holding their breath, waiting, but waiting for what? It had not felt this way a moment before, of that Abbie was sure. She tried to shake the feeling but it would not leave. The best thing to do was finish the inspection quickly and get out of the house.

Unfortunately, all that was left was the basement.

She had been reluctant to go down there before, but with the air riding with expectation she didn't want to go down. But if she couldn't even stand to inspect the house, how could she possibly sell it?

She walked purposefully through the house, ignoring the bloodstained carpet and the hand-printed door.

But by ignoring them she became more aware of them. Death, especially violent death, was not easily dismissed.

Rust-brown carpet led down the steps to the closed door. And for some reason Abbie found the closed door menacing. She went down.

She hesitated with her hand almost over the doorknob and then opened it quickly. The cool dampness of the basement was unchanged. It was like any other basement except this one had no windows. Mr. Garner had requested that, no one knew why.

The bare concrete floor stretched gray and unbroken to the gray concrete walls. Pipes from upstairs hung from the ceiling and plunged out of sight under the floor. The sump pump in one corner was still in working order. The water heater was cold and waiting for someone to light it.

Abbie pulled on all three of the hanging chains and illuminated all the shadows away. But the bare lightbulbs cast shadows of their own as they gently swung, disturbed by her passing. And there in the far corner was the first stain.

The stain was small, but considering it had been a five-year-old boy, it was big enough.

There was a trail of stains leading round the back of the staircase. They were smeared and oddly shaped as if he had bled and someone dragged him along.

The last stain was in the shape of a bloody pentagram, rough, but recognizable. A sacrifice then.

There was a spattering on one wall, high up without a lower source. Probably where Phillip Garner had put a gun to his head and pulled the trigger.

Abbie turned off two of the lights and then stood there with her hand on the last cord, the one nearest the door. That air of expectation had left. She would have thought that the basement where the boy was brutalized would have felt worse, but it didn't. It seemed emptier and more normal than upstairs. Abbie didn't know why but made a note of it. She would tell the psychic who would be visiting the house.

She turned off the light and left, closing the door quietly behind her. The stairs were just stairs like so many other houses had. And the kitchen looked cheerful with its off-white walls. Abbie closed the window over the sink; it wouldn't do to have rain come in.

She had actually stepped into the living room when she turned back. The handprint on the back door bothered her. It seemed such a mute appeal for help, safety, escape.

She whispered to the sun-warmed silence, "Oh, I can't stand to leave it." She fished Kleenex from her pocket and dampened them in the sink. She knelt by the door and wiped across the brownish stain.

It smeared fresh and bloody, crimson as new blood. Abbie gasped and half-fell away from the door. The Kleenex was soaked with blood. She dropped it to the floor.

The handprint bled, slowly, down the white door.

She whispered, "Brian." There was a sound of small feet running. The sound hushed down the carpeted stairs to the basement. And Abbie heard the door swing open and close with a small click.

There was a silence so heavy that she couldn't breathe. And then it was gone, whatever it was. She got to her feet and walked to the living room. *So there's a ghost*, she told herself, *you've sold houses with ghosts before*. But she didn't pick up the soggy Kleenex and she didn't look back to see how far down the blood would go before it stopped.

She was out the door and locking it as fast as she could and still maintain some decorum. It wouldn't help things at all if the neighbors saw the real estate agent running from the house. She forced herself to walk down the steps between the yellow flowers. But there was a spot in the middle of her back that itched as if someone were staring at it.

Abbie didn't look back, she wouldn't run, but she had no desire to see Brian Garner's face pressed against the window glass. Maybe the cleanup crew had done the best they could. She'd have to find out if all the marks bled fresh.

The house would have to be re-blessed. And probably a medium brought in to tell the ghost that it was dead. A lot of people took it as a status symbol to have a ghost in their house. Certain kinds of ghosts, though. No one liked a poltergeist, no one liked bleeding walls, or hideous apparitions, or screams at odd times in the night. But a light that haunted only one hallway, or a phantom that walked in the library in eighteenth-century costume, well, those were call for a party. The latest craze was ghost parties. All those that did not have a ghost could come and watch one while everyone drank and had snacks.

But somehow Abbie didn't think that anyone would want Brian's ghost in their house. It was romantic to have a murdered sixteenth-century explorer roaming about, but recent victims and a child at that…. Well, historic victims are one thing, but a ghost out of your morning newspaper—that was something else entirely.

Abbie just hoped that Brian Garner would be laid to rest easily. Sometimes the ghost just needed someone to tell it that it was dead. But other times it took more stringent measures, especially with violent ends. Strangely, there were a lot of child ghosts running around. Abbie had read an article in the Sunday magazine about it. The theory was that children didn't have a concept of death yet, so they became ghosts. They were still trying to live.

Abbie left such thinking up to the experts. She just sold houses. As soon as the car started Abbie turned on the radio. She wanted noise.

The news was on and the carefully enunciated words filled the car as she pulled away from the house.

"The Supreme Court reached their verdict today, upholding a New Jersey court ruling that Mitchell Davies, well-known banker and real estate investor, is still legally alive even though he is a vampire. This supports the so-called Bill of Life, which came out last year, widening the definition of life to include some forms of the living dead. Now on to sports…"

Abbie changed the station. She wasn't in the mood for sports scores or news of any kind. She had had her own dose of reality today and just wanted to go home. But first she had to stop by her office.

It was late when she arrived and even the receptionist had gone home. Three rows of desks stretched catty-corner from one end of the room to the other. Most of the overhead lights had been turned off, leaving the room in afternoon shadows. A thin strip of white light wound down the center and passed over Sandra's desk. Sandra sat waiting, hands folded in front of her. She had stopped even pretending to work.

Her blue eyes flashed upward when she saw Abbie come in. The relief was plain on her face and in the sudden slump of her shoulders.

Abbie smiled at her.

Sandra made a half smile in return. She asked, "How was it?"

Abbie walked to her desk, which put her to Sandra's left, and two desks over. She started sorting papers while she considered how best to answer. "It's going to need some work before we can show it."

Sandra's high heels clicked on the floor, and Abbie could feel her standing behind her. "That isn't what I mean, and you know it."

Abbie turned and faced her. Sandra's eyes were too bright, her face too intense. "Sandra, please, it's over, let it go."

Sandra gripped her arm, fingers biting deep. "Tell me what it was like."

"You're hurting me."

Her hand dropped numbly to her side and she almost whispered, "Please, I need to know."

"You didn't do anything wrong. It wasn't your fault."

"But I sold them that house."

"But Phillip Garner played with the Ouija board. He opened the way to what happened."

"But I should have seen it. I should have realized something was wrong. I did notice things when Marion contacted me. I should have done something."

"What, what could you have done?"

"I could have called the police."

"And told them that you had a bad feeling about one of your clients? You aren't a registered psychic, they would have ignored you. And Sandra, you didn't have any premonitions. You've convinced yourself you knew beforehand, but it isn't true. You never mentioned it to anyone in the office." Abbie tried to get her to smile. "And get real, girl, if you had news that important, you couldn't keep it to yourself. You are the original gossip. A kind gossip, but still a gossip."

Sandra didn't smile, but she nodded. "True, I don't keep secrets very well."

Abbie put her arm around her and hugged her. "Stop beating yourself up over something you had nothing to do with. Cut the guilt off; it isn't your guilt to deal with."

Sandra leaned into her and began to cry.

They stayed there like that until it was full dark and Sandra was hoarse from crying.

Sandra said, "I've made you late getting home."

"Charles will understand."

"You sure?"

"Yes, I have a very understanding husband."

She nodded and snuffled into the last Kleenex in the room. "Thanks."

"It's what friends are for, Sandra. Now go home and feel good about yourself, you deserve it."

Abbie called her husband before locking up the office, to assure him that she was coming home. He was very understanding, but he tended to worry about her. Then she escorted Sandra to her car and made sure she drove away.

It was weeks later before Abbie stood in the newly carpeted living room. Fresh hex signs had been painted over the doors and windows. A priest had blessed the house. A medium had come and told Brian Garner's ghost that it was dead. Abbie did not know, or want to know, if the ghost had been stubborn about leaving.

The house felt clean and new, as if it had just been built. Perhaps a registered psychic could have picked up some lingering traces of evil and horror, but Abbie couldn't.

The kitchen door stood white and pure. There were no stains today, everything had been fixed, everything had been hidden. And wonder of wonders, she had a client coming to see it.

The client knew all about the house and its history. But then Mr. Channing and his family had been having difficulties of their own. No one wanted to sell them a house.

But Abbie had no problem with selling to them. They were people, after all; the law said so.

She had turned the lights in the living room and kitchen on. Their yellow glow chased back the night.

Charles had been unhappy about her meeting the clients alone, at night. But Abbie knew you couldn't sell to people if they didn't think you trusted and liked them. So she waited alone in the artificial light, trying not to think too much about old superstitions. As a show of great good faith, she had no protection on her.

At exactly ten o'clock the doorbell rang. She had not heard a car drive up.

Abbie opened the door with her best professional smile on her face. And it wasn't hard to keep the smile because they looked like a very normal family. Mr. and Mrs. Channing were a young handsome couple. He was well over six feet with thick chestnut hair and clear blue eyes. She was only slightly shorter and blond. But they did not smile. It was the boy who smiled. He was perhaps fourteen and had his father's chestnut hair, but his eyes were dark brown, and Abbie found herself staring into those eyes. They were the most perfect color she had ever seen, solid, without a trace . . . she was falling. A hand steadied her, and when she looked, it was the boy who touched her, but he did not meet her eyes.

The three stood waiting for something as Abbie held the door. Finally, she asked them in. "Won't you please come inside?"

They seemed to relax and stepped through the door with the boy a little in front.

She smiled again and put a hand out to Mr. Channing and said, "It's a pleasure to meet you, Mr. Channing."

The three exchanged glances and then polite laughter.

The man said, "I'm not Channing; call me Rick."

"Oh, of course." Abbie tried to cover her confusion as the woman introduced herself simply as "Isabel."

It left Abbie with only one other client, but she offered her hand and her smile. "Mr. Channing."

He took it in a surprisingly strong grip and said, "I have looked forward to meeting you, Ms. McDonnell. And please, it's just Channing, no Mr."

"As you like, Channing. Then you must call me Abbie."

"Well then, Abbie, shall we see the house?" His face was so frank and open, so adult. It was disconcerting to see such intelligence and confidence in the eyes of a fourteen-year-old body.

He said, "I am much older than I appear, Abbie."

"Yes, I am sorry, I didn't mean to stare."

"That's quite all right. It is better that you stare than refuse to see us."

"Yes, well, let me show you the house." Abbie turned off the lights and showed the moon shining through the skylights. The brick fireplace was an unexpected hit. Somewhere Abbie had gotten the idea that vampires didn't like fire.

She did turn on the lights to show them the bedrooms and baths. They might be able to see in the dark, but Abbie didn't think it would impress them if she tripped in the dark.

The female, Isabel, spun round the master bedroom and said, "Oh, it will make a wonderful office."

Abbie inquired, "What do you do?"

The woman turned and said, "I'm an artist, I work mostly in oils."

Abbie said, "I've always wished I could paint, but I can't even draw."

The woman seemed not to have heard. Abbie had learned long ago that you didn't make conversation if the client didn't want to talk. So they viewed the house in comparative silence.

There was one point in the master bathroom, when the three had to crowd in to see, that Abbie turned and bumped into the man. She stepped away as if struck and to cover her almost-fear she turned around and nearly gasped. They had reflections. She could see them in the mirror just as clearly as herself. Abbie recovered from the shock and went on. But she knew that at least Channing had noticed. There was a special smile on his face that said it all.

Since they had reflections, Abbie showed them the kitchen more thoroughly than she had been intending.

After all, if one myth was untrue, perhaps others were; perhaps they could eat.

The basement she saved for last, as she did in most of her houses. She led the way down and groped for the light pull cord but did not turn on the lights until she heard them shuffle in next to her. She said, "You'll notice there are no windows. You will have absolute privacy down here." She did not add that no sunlight would be coming down because after the mirror she wasn't sure if it was pertinent.

Channing's voice came soft and low out of the velvet dark. "It is quite adequate."

It wasn't exactly unbridled enthusiasm, but Abbie had done her best. She pulled on the light and showed them the water heater and the sump pump. "And the washer and dryer hookups are all set. All you need are the machines."

Channing nodded and said, "Very good."

"Would you like me to leave you alone for a few moments to discuss things?"

"Yes, if you would."

"Certainly." Abbie walked up the stairs but left the door open. She went into the living room so they would be sure she wasn't eavesdropping. She wondered what the neighbors would think about vampires living next door. But that wasn't her concern; she just sold the house.

She did not hear them come up, but they stood suddenly in the living room. She swallowed past the beating of her heart and said, "What do you think of the house?"

Channing smiled, exposing fangs. "I think we'll take it."

The smile was very genuine on Abbie's part as she walked forward and shook their hands. "And how soon will you want to move in?"

"Next week, if possible. We have had our down payment for several months, and our bank is ready to approve our loan."

"Excellent. The house is yours as soon as the papers are signed."

Isabel ran a possessive hand down the wall. "Ours," she said.

Abbie smiled and said, "And if any of your friends need a house, just let me know. I'm sure I can meet their needs."

Channing grinned broadly at her and put his cool hand in hers. "I'm sure you can, Abbie, I'm sure you can."

After all, everyone needs a house to call their own. And Abbie sold houses.

GREEDY CHOKE PUPPY

Nalo Hopkinson

Nalo Hopkinson, born in Jamaica, has lived in Jamaica, Trinidad and
Guyana, and for the past thirty-five years in Canada. She is currently a
professor of creative writing at the University of California, Riverside,
USA. The author of six novels, a short story collection, and a chapbook.
Hopkinson is a recipient of the Warner Aspect First Novel Award, the
Ontario Arts Council Foundation Award for emerging writers, the John
W. Campbell Award for Best New Writer, the Locus Award for Best New
Writer, the World Fantasy Award, the Sunburst Award for Canadian Liter-
ature of the Fantastic (twice), the Aurora Award, the Gaylactic Spectrum
Award, and the Norton Award. A new short story collection, *Falling in
Love With Hominids*, will be a 2015 release from Tachyon Publications.

In "Greedy Choke Puppy" we meet a supernatural being based on
Afro-Caribbean folklore: the soucouyant. Hopkinson's debut novel *Brown
Girl in the Ring* (1998) also features a soucouyant . . .

"I see a Lagahoo last night. In the back of the house, behind the pigeon peas."

"Yes, Granny." Sitting cross-legged on the floor, Jacky leaned back
against her grandmother's knees and closed her eyes in bliss against the
gentle tug of Granny's hands braiding her hair. Jacky still enjoyed this
evening ritual, even though she was a big hard-back woman, thirty-two
years next month.

The moon was shining in through the open jalousie windows, bringing
the sweet smell of Ladies-of-the-Night flowers with it. The ceiling fan beat
its soothing rhythm.

"How you mean, 'Yes, Granny'? You even know what a Lagahoo is?"

"Don't you been frightening me with jumby story from since I small?
Is a donkey with gold teeth, wearing a waistcoat with a pocket watch and
two pair of tennis shoes on the hooves."

"Washekong, you mean. I never teach you to say 'tennis shoes.'"

Jacky smiled. "Yes, Granny. So, what the Lagahoo was doing in the pigeon peas patch?"

"Just standing, looking at my window. Then he pull out he watch chain from out he waistcoat pocket, and he look at the time, and he put the watch back, and he bite off some pigeon peas from off one bush, and he walk away."

Jacky laughed, shaking so hard that her head pulled free of Granny's hands. "You mean to tell me that a Lagahoo come all the way to we little house in Diego Martin, just to sample we so-so pigeon peas?" Still chuckling, she settled back against Granny's knees. Granny tugged at a hank of Jacky's hair, just a little harder than necessary.

Jacky could hear the smile in the old woman's voice. "Don't get fresh with me. You turn big woman now, Ph.D. student and thing, but is still your old nen-nen who does plait up your hair every evening, oui?"

"Yes, Granny. You know I does love to make mako 'pon you, to tease you a little."

"This ain't no joke, child. My mammy used to say that a Lagahoo is God horse, and when you see one, somebody go dead. The last time I see one is just before your mother dead." The two women fell silent. The memory hung in the air between them, of the badly burned body retrieved from the wreckage of the car that had gone off the road. Jacky knew that her grandmother would soon change the subject. She blamed herself for the argument that had sent Jacky's mother raging from the house in the first place. And whatever Granny didn't want to think about, she certainly wasn't going to talk about.

Granny sighed. "Well, don't fret, doux-doux. Just be careful when you go out so late at night. I couldn't stand to lose you, too." She finished off the last braid and gently stroked Jacky's head. "All right. I finish now. Go and wrap up your head in a scarf, so the plaits will stay nice while you sleeping."

"Thank you, Granny. What I would do without you to help me make myself pretty for the gentlemen, eh?"

Granny smiled, but with a worried look on her face. "You just mind your studies. It have plenty of time to catch man."

Jacky stood and gave the old woman a kiss on one cool, soft cheek and headed toward her bedroom in search of a scarf. Behind her, she could hear Granny settling back into the faded wicker armchair, muttering distractedly to herself, "Why this Lagahoo come to bother me again, eh?"

The first time, I ain't know what was happening to me. I was younger them times there, and sweet for so, you see? Sweet like julie mango, with two ripe tot-tot on the front of my body and two ripe maami-apple behind. I only had was to walk down the street, twitching that maami-apple behind, and all the boys-them on the street corner would watch at me like them was starving, and I was food.

But I get to find out know how it is when the boys stop making sweet eye at you so much, and start watching after a next younger thing. I get to find out that when you pass you prime, and you ain't catch no man eye, nothing ain't left for you but to get old and dry-up like cane leaf in the fire. Is just so I was feeling that night. Like something wither-up. Like something that once used to drink in the feel of the sun on it skin, but now it dead and dry, and the sun only drying it out more. And the feeling make a burning in me belly, and the burning spread out to my skin, till I couldn't take it no more. I jump up from my little bed just so in the middle of the night, and snatch off my nightie. And when I do so, my skin come with it, and drop off on the floor. Inside my skin I was just one big ball of fire, and Lord, the night air feel nice and cool on the flame! I know then I was a soucouyant, a hag-woman. I know what I had to do. When your youth start to leave you, you have to steal more from somebody who still have plenty. I fly out the window and start to search, search for a newborn baby.

"Lagahoo? You know where that word come from, ain't, Jacky?" asked Carmen Lewis, the librarian in the humanities section of the Library of the University of the West Indies. Carmen leaned back in her chair behind the information desk, legs sprawled under the bulge of her advanced pregnancy.

Carmen was a little older than Jacky. They had known each other since they were girls together at Saint Alban's Primary School. Carmen was always very interested in Jacky's research. "Is French creole for werewolf. Only we could come up with something as jokey as a were-donkey, oui? And as far as I know, it doesn't change into a human being. Why does your Granny think she saw one in the backyard?"

"You know Granny, Carmen. She sees all kinds of things, duppy and jumby and things like that. Remember the duppy stories she used to tell us when we were small, so we would be scared and mind what she said?"

Carmen laughed. "And the soucouyant, don't forget that." She smiled a strange smile. "It didn't really frighten me, though. I always wondered what it would be like to take your skin off, leave your worries behind, and fly so free."

"Well, you sit there so and wonder. I have to keep researching this paper. The back issues come in yet?"

"Right here." Sighing with the effort of bending over, Carmen reached under the desk and pulled out a stack of slim bound volumes of *Huracan*, a Caribbean literary journal that was now out of print. A smell of wormwood and age rose from them. In the 1940s, *Huracan* had published a series of issues on folktales. Jacky hoped that these would provide her with more research material.

"Thanks, Carmen." She picked up the volumes and looked around for somewhere to sit. There was an empty private carrel, but there was also a free space at one of the large study tables. Terry was sitting there, head bent over a fat textbook. The navy blue of his shirt suited his skin, made it glow like a newly unwrapped chocolate. Jacky smiled. She went over to the desk, tapped Terry on the shoulder. "I could sit beside you, Terry?"

Startled, he looked up to see who had interrupted him. His handsome face brightened with welcome. "Uh, sure, no problem. Let me get . . ." He leapt to pull out the chair for her, overturning his own in the process. At the crash, everyone in the library looked up. "Shit." He bent over to pick up the chair. His glasses fell from his face. Pens and pencils rained from his shirt pocket.

Jacky giggled. She put her books down, retrieved Terry's glasses just before he would have stepped on them. "Here." She put the spectacles onto his face, let the warmth of her fingertips linger briefly at his temples.

Terry stepped back, sat quickly in the chair, even though it was still at an odd angle from the table. He crossed one leg over the other.

"Sorry," he muttered bashfully. He bent over, reaching awkwardly for the scattered pens and pencils.

"Don't fret, Terry. You just collect yourself and come and sit back down next to me." Jacky glowed with the feeling of triumph. Half an hour of studying beside him, and she knew she'd have a date for lunch.

She sat, opened a copy of *Huracan*, and read:

SOUCOUYANT/OL' HIGUE (Trinidad/Guyana)
Caribbean equivalent of the vampire myth. "Soucouyant," or "blood-sucker," derives from the French verb "sucer," to suck. "Ol' Higue" is the Guyanese creole expression for an

old hag, or witch woman. The soucouyant is usually an old, evil-tempered woman who removes her skin at night, hides it, and then changes into a ball of fire. She flies through the air, searching for homes in which there are babies. She then enters the house through an open window or a keyhole, goes into the child's room, and sucks the life from its body. She may visit one child's bedside a number of times, draining a little more life each time, as the frantic parents search for a cure, and the child gets progressively weaker and finally dies. Or she may kill all at once.

The smell of the soup Granny was cooking made Jacky's mouth water. She sat at Granny's wobbly old kitchen table, tracing her fingers along a familiar burn, the one shaped like a handprint. The wooden table had been Granny's as long as Jacky could remember. Grandpa had made the table for Granny long before Jacky was born. Diabetes had finally been the death of him. Granny had brought only the kitchen table and her clothing with her when she moved in with Jacky and her mother.

Granny looked up from the cornmeal and flour dough she was kneading. "Like you idle, doux-doux," she said. She slid the bowl of dough over to Jacky. "Make the dumplings, then, nuh?"

Jacky took the bowl over to the stove, started pulling off pieces of dough and forming it into little cakes.

"Andrew make this table for me with he own two hand," Granny said.

"I know. You tell me already."

Granny ignored her. "Forty-two years we married, and every Sunday, I chop up the cabbage for the saltfish on this same table. Forty-two years we eat Sunday morning breakfast right here so. Saltfish and cabbage with a little small-leaf thyme from the back garden, and fry dumpling and cocoa-tea. I miss he too bad. You grandaddy did full up me life, make me feel young."

Jacky kept forming the dumplings for the soup. Granny came over to the stove and stirred the large pot with her wooden spoon. She blew on the spoon, cautiously tasted some of the liquid in it, and carefully floated a whole ripe Scotch bonnet pepper on top of the bubbling mixture.

"Jacky, when you put the dumpling-them in, don't break the pepper, all right? Otherwise this soup going to make we bawl tonight for pepper."

"Mm. Ain't Mummy used to help you make soup like this on a Saturday?"

"Yes, doux-doux. Just like this." Granny hobbled back to sit at the kitchen table. Tiny graying braids were escaping the confinement of her stiff black wig. Her knobby legs looked frail in their too-beige stockings. Like so many of the old women that Jacky knew, Granny always wore stockings rolled down below the hems of her worn flower-print shifts. "I thought you was going out tonight," Granny said. "With Terry."

"We break up," Jacky replied bitterly. "He say he not ready to settle down." She dipped the spoon into the soup, raised it to her mouth, spat it out when it burned her mouth. "Backside!"

Granny watched, frowning. "Greedy puppy does choke. You mother did always taste straight from the hot stove, too. I was forever telling she to take time. You come in just like she, always in a hurry. Your eyes bigger than your stomach."

Jacky sucked in an irritable breath. "Granny, Carmen have a baby boy last night. Eight pounds, four ounces. Carmen make she first baby already. I past thirty years old, and I ain't find nobody yet."

"You will find, Jacky. But you can't hurry people so. Is how long you and Terry did stepping out?"

Jacky didn't respond.

"Eh, Jacky? How long?"

"Almost a month."

"Is scarcely two weeks, Jacky, don't lie to me. The boy barely learn where to find your house, and you was pestering he to settle down already. Me and your grandfather court for two years before we went to Parson to marry we."

When Granny started like this, she could go on for hours. Sullenly, Jacky began to drop the raw dumplings one by one into the fragrant, boiling soup.

"Child, you pretty, you have flirty ways, boys always coming and looking for you. You could pick and choose until you find the right one. Love will come. But take time. Love your studies, look out for your friends-them. Love your old Granny," she ended softly.

Hot tears rolled down Jacky's cheeks. She watched the dumplings bobbing back to the surface as they cooked; little warm, yellow suns.

"A new baby," Granny mused. "I must go and visit Carmen, take she some crab and callaloo to strengthen she blood. Hospital food does make you weak, oui."

I need more time, more life. I need a baby breath. Must wait till people sleeping, though. Nobody awake to see a fireball flying up from the bedroom window.

The skin only confining me. I could feel it getting old, binding me up inside it. Sometimes I does just feel to take it off and never put it back on again, oui? Three a.m. 'Fore day morning. Only me and the duppies going to be out this late. Up from out of the narrow bed, slip off the nightie, slip off the skin.

Oh, God, I does be so free like this! Hide the skin under the bed, and fly out the jalousie window. The night air cool, and I flying so high. I know how many people it have in each house, and who sleeping. I could feel them, skinbag people, breathing out their life, one-one breath. I know where it have a new one, too: down on Vanderpool Lane. Yes, over here. Feel it, the new one, the baby. So much life in that little body.

Fly down low now, right against the ground. Every door have a crack, no matter how small.

Right here. Slip into the house. Turn back into a woman. Is a nasty feeling, walking around with no skin, wet flesh dripping onto the floor, but I get used to it after so many years.

Here. The baby bedroom. Hear the young breath heating up in he lungs, blowing out, wasting away. He ain't know how to use it; I go take it.

Nice baby boy, so fat. Drink, soucouyant. Suck in he warm, warm life.

God, it sweet. It sweet can't done. It sweet.

No more? I drink all already? But what a way this baby dead fast!

Childbirth was once a risky thing for both mother and child. Even when they both survived the birth process, there were many unknown infectious diseases to which newborns were susceptible.

Oliphant theorizes that the soucouyant lore was created in an attempt to explain infant deaths that would have seemed mysterious in more primitive times. Grieving parents could blame their loss on people who wished them ill. Women tend to have longer life spans than men, but in a superstitious age where life was hard and brief, old women in a community could seem sinister. It must have been easy to believe that the women were using sorcerous means to prolong their lives, and how better to do that than to steal the lifeblood of those who were very young?

Dozing, Jacky leaned against Granny's knees. Outside, the leaves of the julie mango tree rustled and sighed in the evening breeze. Granny tapped on Jacky's shoulder, passed her a folded section of newspaper with a column circled. *Births/Deaths*. Granny took a bitter pleasure in keeping track of who she'd outlived each week. Sleepily, Jacky focused on the words on the page:

Deceased: Raymond George Lewis, 5 days old, of natural causes. Son of Michael and Carmen, Diego Martin, Port of Spain. Funeral service 5:00 p.m. November 14, Church of the Holy Redeemer.

Sunlight is fatal to the soucouyant. She must be back in her skin before daylight. In fact, the best way to discover a soucouyant is to find her skin, rub the raw side with hot pepper, and replace it in its hiding place. When she tries to put it back on, the pain of the burning pepper will cause the demon to cry out and reveal herself.

Me fire belly full, oui. When a new breath fueling the fire, I does feel good, like I could never die. And then I does fly and fly, high like the moon. Time to go back home now, though.

Eh-eh! Why she leave the back door cotch open? Never mind; she does be preoccupied sometimes. Maybe she just forget. Just fly in the bedroom window. I go close the door after I put on my skin again.

Ai! What itching me so? Is what happen to me skin? Ai! Lord, Lord, it burning, it burning too bad. It scratching me all over, like it have fire ants inside there. I can't stand it!

Hissing with pain, the soucouyant threw off her burning skin and stood flayed, dripping.

Calmly, Granny entered Jacky's room. Before Jacky could react, Granny picked up the Jacky-skin. She held it close to her body, threatening the skin with the sharp, wicked kitchen knife she held in her other hand. Her look was sorrowful.

"I know it was you, doux-doux. When I see the Lagahoo, I know what I have to do."

Jacky cursed and flared to fireball form. She rushed at Granny, but backed off as Granny made a feint at the skin with her knife.

"You stay right there and listen to me, Jacky. The soucouyant blood in all of we, all the women in we family."

You, too?

"Even me. We blood hot: hot for life, hot for youth. Loving does cool we down. Making life does cool we down."

Jacky raged. The ceiling blackened, began to smoke.

"I know how it go, doux-doux. When we lives empty, the hunger does turn to blood hunger. But it have plenty other kinds of loving, Jacky. Ain't I been telling you so? Love your work. Love people close to you. Love your life."

The fireball surged toward Granny. "No. Stay right there, you hear? Or I go chop this skin for you."

Granny backed out through the living room. The hissing ball of fire followed close, drawn by the precious skin in the old woman's hands.

"You never had no patience. Doux-doux, you is my life, but you can't kill so. That little child you drink, you don't hear it spirit when night come, bawling for Carmen and Michael? I does weep to hear it. I try to tell you, like I try to tell you mother: Don't be greedy."

Granny had reached the back door. The open back door. The soucouyant made a desperate feint at Granny's knife arm, searing her right side from elbow to scalp. The smell of burnt flesh and hair filled the little kitchen, but though the old lady cried out, she wouldn't drop the knife. The pain in her voice was more than physical.

"You devil!" She backed out the door into the cobalt light of early morning. Gritting her teeth, she slashed the Jacky-skin into two ragged halves and flung it into the pigeon peas patch. Jacky shrieked and turned back into her flayed self. Numbly, she picked up her skin, tried with oozing fingers to put the torn edges back together.

"You and me is the last two," Granny said. "Your mami woulda make three, but I had to kill she, too, send my own flesh and blood into the sun. Is time, doux-doux. The Lagahoo calling you."

My skin! Granny, how you could do me so? Oh, God, morning coming already? Yes, could feel it, the sun calling to the fire in me.

Jacky threw the skin down again, leapt as a fireball into the brightening air. *I going, going, where I could burn clean, burn bright, and all you could go to the Devil, oui!*

Fireball flying high to the sun, and oh, God, it burning, it burning, it burning!

Granny hobbled to the pigeon peas patch, wincing as she cradled her burnt right side. Tears trickled down her wrinkled face. She sobbed, "Why all you must break my heart so?"

Painfully, she got down to her knees beside the ruined pieces of skin and placed one hand on them. She made her hand glow red hot, igniting her granddaughter's skin. It began to burn, crinkling and curling back on itself like bacon in a pan. Granny wrinkled her nose against the smell, but kept her hand on the smoking mass until there was nothing but ashes. Her hand faded back to its normal cocoa brown. Clambering to her feet again, she looked about her in the pigeon peas patch.

"I live to see the Lagahoo two time. Next time, God horse, you better be coming for me."

TACKY

Charlaine Harris

Charlaine Harris, a native of Mississippi, wrote the lighthearted Aurora Teagarden mystery books and the much edgier Lily Bard series. Now she's working on a series about a lightning-struck young woman named Harper Connelly. But the thirteen novels featuring Sookie Stackhouse (which blend mystery, humor, romance, and the supernatural) became an international phenomenon when Alan Ball based the HBO series *True Blood* on them.

Although she appears only briefly in the novels, the petite and beautiful vampire Dahlia Lynley-Chivers is featured in a computer game and a growing number of short stories set in the "Sookieverse." "Tacky" is the first story in which Dahlia played the leading role. She's been a favorite of the author (and this editor) ever since . . .

"I'm going because I can't believe I've lived to see it," Dahlia said. "Also, I'm a bridesmaid, which is an honor. I have an obligation." She widened her eyes at her companion, to emphasize the point. She had big green eyes, so it was a vivid effect.

Glenda Shore choked on her sip of synthetic blood. "You're kidding," she said faintly. "You think this is an honor? Well, bite me. Being a bridesmaid means we have to mingle with the nasty things. Like that party tonight, at the Were bar. Taffy called me specially, but I put her off. I won't do it! It's bad enough, all the teasing I've gotten. Maisie called me 'Fur Lover'; Thomas Pickens gives wolf howls whenever he sees me. It's just humiliating."

Dahlia gave her head a practiced toss to flip her long wavy black hair back over her shoulders. She glanced down to make sure her strapless burgundy cocktail dress was still in place. There was a line between being adorably provocative and simply tacky. Dahlia was an expert at treading that line.

"I've known Taffy for maybe a couple hundred years," Dahlia said quietly. "I feel that I have to go through with this." She kept her voice casual; she didn't want to sound smugly superior. Glenda hadn't even been alive that long—or dead, rather. Neither had the other two females Taffy had asked to act as bridesmaids.

Glenda was a very young vampire, a flat-chested flapper who'd been turned during the Al Capone era in Chicago. To Dahlia's distaste, Glenda still liked wearing clothes reminiscent of the ones she'd worn while she was living. Tonight she was wearing a cloche hat. Conspicuous.

Oh, sure, it was legal to be a vampire now that the synthetic blood marketed by the Japanese had proven to satisfy the nutritional needs of the undead. But there was more to surviving as a vamp than slugging down TrueBlood or Red Stuff in all-night bars that catered strictly to vamps, like this one. There were pockets of humans who snatched vamps off the streets and drained their blood to sell on the black market.

There were other cults who simply wanted vamps dead because they'd decided vamps were evil blood-sucking fiends.

You had to learn discretion.

Besides various fringe groups of humans, you had to add to the list of vampire haters the Werewolves, whose ongoing feud with the undead occasionally flared into out-and-out war. Thinking of Weres brought Dahlia back to the subject at hand, her friend Taffy's wedding.

"Taffy and I nested together for a decade in Mexico," Dahlia said. "We were quite close. We went through the War of 1812 together; nothing cements a relationship like going through a war. And we've nested together at Cedric's for the past, oh, twenty years?"

"Where could Taffy have met such a creature?" Glenda asked, fingering the long, long string of pearls that dangled to her waist. Her eyes glinted with relish. This was as much fun as discussing a previously unencountered sexual perversion.

Dahlia beckoned to the bartender. "Taffy was always . . . adventurous. She lived with a regular human for ten years, once."

Glenda looked pleasurably horrified. "Do you think she'll wear white?" Glenda asked. "And our bridesmaid dresses . . . I bet we'll have pink ruffles."

"Why would it be pink ruffles?" Dahlia's mouth was suddenly pressed in a grim line. Dahlia took her clothes very, very seriously.

"You know what they say about bridesmaid dresses!" Glenda laughed out loud.

"I do not," said Dahlia, her voice cold enough to goose an icicle. "I was turned before there was such a thing as a designated attendant for the bride."

"Oh, my goodness!" The younger vampire was shocked. And then delighted at the prospect of introducing her superior friend to the certainty of an unpleasant ordeal. "Then let's go find a church and watch a wedding. Well, maybe not a church," she added nervously. Glenda had been a Christian in life, and churches made her mighty twitchy. "Maybe we'll check out a country club, or find a garden wedding."

Glenda actually had a sensible idea, Dahlia decided. It would help to know the worst. And though all the bridesmaids were due at a party in honor of the happy couple, if she and Glenda hurried, they wouldn't be late.

"The big mansions on the lakeside," she suggested. "It's a June weekend. Isn't that a prime time for weddings in America?" Dahlia had a vague recollection of seeing bridal magazines on the shelves at newspaper kiosks when she'd been buying her monthly copy of *Fang*.

"That's a keen idea. Let's go!" Glenda was eager. The worst enemy of a vampire was ennui. Any new diversion was worth its weight in gold.

Since they were both gifted with flight (not all vampires possessed this skill), the two were able to reach the most imposing mansions in the city quickly. Glenda and Dahlia hovered over them to detect an outside celebration that might prove to be a wedding. At the VanTreeve place, they struck nuptial pay dirt. Tiffany VanTreeve was marrying Brendan Blaine Buffington that very night. The two vamps landed unobtrusively behind a tent set up on the grounds.

Dahlia eyed the scene critically, taking mental notes. The vampire sheriff of her area in the city of Rhodes, Cedric Deeming, was worried about giving a proper wedding in such a hurry. Though lazy and lax in many respects, Cedric was a stickler for protocol. He'd urged all the vampires who nested with him to bring home details of modern wedding proceedings.

Dahlia obediently began making mental notes. Close to the house, there were two long tables loaded with food and a huge cake, though the food was discreetly covered with drapes for the moment. There was a cage full of doves, with an attendant in coveralls. Perhaps these were intended for a ritual sacrifice? There were two phalanxes of white chairs on the lawn, arranged facing a large white dais adorned with banks of pink flowers. A long red carpet ran between the two sections of chairs, right up the steps of the dais, where a minister in a sober black robe stood waiting.

Note to self: Find some kind of priest. Wasn't Harry Oakheart some kind of Druid? Maybe he knew a ceremony.

A string quartet was playing Handel. (*Note to self: Find musicians.*) Not only were all the seats full, but there was a standing crowd at the back.

"What a swell spread," Glenda whispered, eyeing the buffet tables. "I guess the wolves'll need food. Looks like we're expected to feed them. The sheriff won't like that. You know what a tightwad he is. At least Cedric won't have to provide food for half the guests." She winked at Dahlia, as if it were very funny that vampires didn't eat food. "And we'll need liquor for the Weres, and we'll need a big stock of blood. Maybe we could nip off the guests?"

Dahlia looked daggers at Glenda. "Don't even say it as a joke," she told the younger vampire. "You know what'll happen if we even suggest that to a breather. Follow the rules. Only from a willing adult!"

"Spoilsport," Glenda muttered.

"Cedric has already hired a caterer, a man who says he can do the whole thing, flowers and all. Cedric is so cheap, he took the lowest bid. No sit-down dinner, just . . . finger food." Even Dahlia could not suppress her smile at the term, and Glenda laughed out loud. A few of the guests turned to see who was so being so boisterous, and Dahlia slammed Glenda in the ribs with a sharp elbow. Everyone else present was being properly solemn. "But we have to do it properly," Dahlia said, in a whisper inaudible to the humans around her. "We can't be found wanting. It would shame Taffy, and the nest."

Glenda gave it as her opinion that the Weres should be grateful they were even being allowed in Cedric's mansion. "I'm surprised Cedric will acknowledge the wedding," she said.

The music gave a final flourish, and the guests rustled expectantly.

The two vampires watched the ceremony unfold: Glenda with a sentimental tear or two (tinged red) and Dahlia with fascinated horror. The groom, looking as though he'd been hit over the head with something large, took his place in front of the minister and stared down the strip of red carpet rolling between the two fields of white chairs. His groomsmen lined up on his side of the dais. At a signal that was invisible to Dahlia, who was stretching up on her tiptoes to see, the traditional music began.

"Here's the most interesting part," Glenda whispered.

One by one, the bridesmaids emerged from the white tent. Some were tall and some were small; some were buxom and some were slim as reeds. But the seven girls were all united in costume. Dahlia, the most elegant and particular of women, closed her eyes in appalled horror.

All the bridesmaids were wearing matching floor-length lime-green silk sheaths. *If you could strip the dress down to its basic essentials, it wouldn't be too bad*, Dahlia thought. But the dresses were accessorized with lace gloves and tiny veiled hats pinned to each lacquered head. Worst of all, there was a gigantic bow perched atop each girlish butt. The waggle of each passing lime-green rear end made Dahlia feel like weeping, too, along with some of the female guests—though Dahlia assumed they were crying for a different reason.

Glenda gave an audible snigger, and Dahlia despaired of ever teaching the girl manners. Dahlia herself was maintaining an appropriately pleasant wedding guest face despite the dreadful possibility that she'd have to wear such a monstrous ensemble. Though the prospect was a blow, Dahlia conscientiously remained to note the entire procedure. She was disappointed when the doves were simply released into the sky at the climax of the ceremony.

Long after Glenda had lost interest, Dahlia traced all the events of the wedding back to their human director, who was hovering at the rear of the gathering. Though the poor wedding planner was quite busy, Dahlia was ruthless (in a charming way) in getting the answers to several astute questions. She garnered information that made her feel that (if it had been beating at all) her heart would now burst.

"The groomsmen—those men up there on the husband's side—they'll be from among the groom's friends," Dahlia said, her hand gripping Glenda's shoulder.

"Well, sure, Dally," Glenda said. "Really, you! Didn't you know that?"

Dahlia shook her raven head back and forth. "Werewolves," she moaned. "They'll all be Werewolves."

"Ewww," said Glenda. "We'll have to let one *touch* us, Dally. Did you see that each bridesmaid took the arm of a groomsman on their way out of the . . . the . . . designated wedding area?"

And for the first time in her long, long life, Dahlia Lynley-Chivers said, "Ewww."

To cover her shame, she added quickly, "If you call me Dally again, I'll tear your throat out."

When Dahlia said something like that, it was smart to assume she meant it. Glenda said, "Well, I'm sure not going to any stupid Were party with you *now*."

Dahlia had to back down, something she was unused to doing. "Glenda," she said stiffly, "neither Cassie nor Fortunata will go, and I was relying on you. It's your duty as a bridesmaid to attend this party. Taffy said so."

"If you think we'll be greeted with open arms by a bunch of stupid Weres, you can think again, Miss Perfect. Open jaws is what they'll have." Glenda disappeared behind the tent to conceal her liftoff, and Dahlia watched her companion disappear. No doubt, Glenda would describe the bridesmaid dresses to any vamp who would listen.

With her little jaw set grimly, Dahlia Lynley-Chivers made her way to a part of Rhodes she seldom visited. This time, she took a cab. Humans became very upset when they saw her fly, and she was determined to do her best by her friend Taffy. Taffy had been born Taphronia, daughter of Leonidas, centuries ago. She'd been calling herself Taffy for the past forty years. Taffy and her fiancé, Don Swift-foot (of course that was his pack name—his human name was Don Swinton), were celebrating their forthcoming nuptials at a bar in the Werewolf part of town. The whole wedding party would be there; at least, the whole wedding party was supposed to be there. Since the other bridesmaids had dropped the baton, Dahlia feared she'd be the only vampire in attendance. She had a wide range of curses at her disposal since she'd lived so long, and she voiced a few of them on the drive through the city. Luckily, the cabdriver spoke none of the languages she used.

Dahlia got out of the cab a block away from the bar. This area of Rhodes was a bit run-down, a bit seedy. The sidewalks were crowded, even this late at night, with bar-hopping humans who didn't realize they were just on the safe side of the moon cycle. Of course, no one who lived in Rhodes realized they were partying in an area that had a high concentration of Werewolves. Humans didn't know about Werewolves yet. The two-natured had to retain their human faces on their nights out.

The bar, called Moonshine, was practically buzzing with energy and magic. Any humans who wandered in uninvited developed severe headaches, and went home early, as a rule. Moonshine was closed three nights out of the month.

Dahlia made sure her cocktail dress was smooth over her hips. Since she was representing her nest, she put on a little lipstick and brushed her rippling hair before she entered the bar. It was marked by a blinking neon sign formed in a white circle—representing the moon, if you had a lot of imagination.

"Tacky," Dahlia muttered. She read the notice taped to the door: *Closed tonight for private party.* Because she was a little anxious about entering a Werewolf-infested bar, she stood a little straighter on her spike heels—which brought her height all the way up to five foot one—held her head proudly, tucked her tiny flat purse under her bare arm, and marched inside, her haughtiest expression fixed on her heart-shaped face.

A chorus of so-called wolf whistles met her entrance. Of course, in their wolf forms, these guys couldn't whistle for diddly-squat; but they managed just fine in their human guise. Dahlia pretended to be deaf as she scanned the tiny bar for Taffy.

Really, you can't expect any better, she told herself. After all, true Weres were generally guys and gals with a keen interest in motorcycles and monster trucks. All the Weres in this bar were pure Weres, with two full-blooded parents. (Even Taffy wouldn't expose her friends to mongrels.)

Dahlia couldn't spy Taffy among the people, mostly male, crowding the bar, so she began to make her way to the only doorway not marked: *Restroom.*

A very tall and very athletically built male stepped in front of her. "Sorry, lady, this bar is closed tonight for a private party."

"Yes, I read the sign on the door."

"Then you're pretty slow taking a hint."

Dahlia looked up (and up) at the bright blue eyes in the broad face. This Were had thick, curling brown hair pulled back into a ponytail, and he was clean-shaven. He was wearing gold-rimmed glasses, a bit to her surprise, and a tight T-shirt and jeans . . . the jeans, now that she came to take a look, were pretty damn tight, too. And boots. He had on big boots.

Dahlia shook herself (mentally, of course). The rude jerk was waiting for her reply. "I am here seeking my friend Taffy," she said coldly, meeting his eyes squarely.

They stood stock-still for a long minute.

"A vamp," he said, loathing replacing the admiration in his voice. "Damn, I knew we shoulda put some new lightbulbs in this place. Then I woulda noticed how pale you are. What do you want with Taff? You gonna try to talk her out of marrying Don, too?"

If it was possible to get any stiffer, Dahlia did. "I am going to . . . actually, what I want with Taffy is none of your business, Were. I require an audience with her." Dahlia was so rattled by the Were's anger that she became colder and stiffer and caught herself reverting to former speech patterns.

"Oh yeah, and we're supposed to bow and scrape for the little madam?" he said. "You should get that stick out of your ass and behave more like Taffy. She doesn't act so snooty and superior. After all, what you got on us? We live longer than humans, and we're stronger than humans, and we can do all kinds of things that humans can't do."

"Excuse me," Dahlia said frigidly. "I am so not interested."

"I'll show you interested," the huge monster growled, reaching down as if he was actually going to pick Dahlia up and give her a shake. The next instant, he was looking up at her from the floor and his friends had leaped to their feet, their eyes glowing. Snarls issued from several male throats and one or two female ones.

"No," called the man from the floor, just as Dahlia prepared to free her hands for fighting by tucking her tiny evening purse into the gartered top of her hose (a process that distracted the males for a few long seconds), "she's in the right, guys."

"What?" asked a blond man built like a fire hydrant. "You gonna let a vamp get away with putting you on the floor?"

"Yeah, Richie," said the man, getting up. "She did it fair and square after I provoked her."

The rest of the Weres seemed disconcerted, but they backed away a foot or two. Dahlia felt a mixture of relief and regret. Her fangs had extended as she readied to fight, and she would have enjoyed relieving the tension by ripping off a few limbs.

"Come on, little highness," Brown Ponytail said. "I'll take you to Taffy."

She nodded curtly. He turned to lead the way, and she followed right behind him. The crowd parted along the way rather reluctantly.

"Cold-blooded creep," said one Were woman. She was built like an Amazon, broad shouldered. Dahlia would have loved to flash out a hand

and bury it in the Were's abdomen, but ladies didn't do such things—not if they wanted the truce to hold.

Dahlia was proud of herself when she didn't meet the woman's eyes in challenge. Instead, Dahlia kept her gaze focused forward. *Which is no hardship*, she had to admit to herself, as she examined the curve of the butt moving in front of her. It certainly was a prime one, packed into the worn Levi's in a most attractive way

Dahlia winced, realizing that she'd actually caught herself admiring a Were.

Her guide stepped aside, and Dahlia was relieved beyond measure to see Taffy sitting in a padded booth behind a round table with Don cuddling close to her right and another Were to her left. Dahlia barely kept her upper lip from drawing back in distaste. It was like seeing a racehorse cavorting with zebras.

"Dahlia!" shrieked Taffy. Her auburn curls were piled up on top of her head, and she was wearing a halter-top and blue jeans, as far as Dahlia could tell. Oh, *really*, Dahlia thought, exasperated, remembering the care she'd taken to dress correctly. *Taffy looks like a real human.* Probably trying to blend in. As if she could.

"Taffy," Dahlia said, thrown seriously off track, "can we have a talk?" She didn't even want to acknowledge Don. He was as redheaded as Taffy, but his hair was short and rough looking, like the coat of a terrier.

"Hey, beautiful!" Don said expansively.

Dahlia gave Don a stiff nod of greeting. She was no barbarian.

Don had a beard, and bright filaments of red stuck out from the neck of his golf shirt. Dahlia shuddered. She was glad to look back at Taffy.

"You still got that cold bitch thing goin' on," Don observed. "Doesn't she, Todd?"

"She's got it down pat," agreed her guide. "Didn't even bother to introduce herself." Dahlia realized, with a pang, that the Were was correct. "She's a brave little thing, though," the Were went on. "Knocked me ass-backward."

Don grinned approvingly. "People should do that more often, Todd. It seems to soften you up."

While Dahlia tried to estimate how long it would take her to kill them all, Taffy was extricating herself from the booth, which seemed to involve a lot of unnecessary brushing against Don, with wriggling and kisses strewn in for good measure. This was the source of many teasing comments and much laughter from the assembled Weres.

I seem to be the only one who's in a bad mood, Dahlia thought, and then without meaning to, her eyes met the tall Were's again. Nope, Todd was less than happy, too. Dahlia wondered whether it was the engagement between Don and Taffy or her own intrusion that had triggered Todd's irritation.

"This is my friend Dahlia Lynley-Chivers," Taffy announced to the crowd of Weres. "She's my maid of honor."

There was a smattering of polite response. Dahlia inclined her head civilly. She couldn't force a smile.

"Snotty-nose bitch," muttered the other Were sitting in the booth. He had dark curly hair and a pugnacious attitude. "Having one in the bar at a time is enough."

Dahlia's tiny hand darted out and dug into the Were's throat.

He gagged, his eyes going wide with shock and fear, and the atmosphere of the bar went into high gear.

"Dahlia!" said Taffy. "He didn't know what he was saying, Dahlia. Please, for me."

Dahlia released the dark-haired Were, and he collapsed against the wood of the booth, breathing heavily. There was an uneasy stirring among the denizens of the crowded bar.

"Thanks, honey," Taffy murmured. "Let's take this out on the sidewalk, okay?"

Her back as straight and her head as high as ever, Dahlia followed Taffy out of the bar, looking neither to the right nor to the left, ignoring the growing chorus of growls that surged in her wake.

"Smooth move, Dahlia," Taffy said, the words bursting out as soon as they were on the sidewalk.

"You were the one who invited me! If you weren't the one engaged to that . . . that dog man . . . do you think I'd go inside such a place?"

"Where are the others?" Taffy lost her anger and looked a bit lost. Maybe she hadn't been quite as comfortable as she'd seemed, being the only vamp in a crowd of Weres.

"Ah, they couldn't make it." Dahlia couldn't think of any way to cushion the rudeness of Taffy's other bridesmaids and her sheriff, Cedric.

Taffy sighed. "I didn't think it was too much to ask, coming to a party in our honor to wish me well." Dahlia's cheeks would have flushed if they could have; she was embarrassed at the poor manners of her sisters. "I guess it's a measure of our friendship that you came inside to see me," Taffy admitted. "I know we're buddies. Please, help me get through this wedding with peace between our people. I want you there on my wedding day, and I want my other friends there, too, and the last thing I want is a bloodbath between the two tribes, us and the Weres, right there in Cedric's garden."

Cedric had offered the garden of his mansion as the locale for the wedding, to everyone's surprise. Cedric had told Dahlia, in his languid way, that he had been sure Taffy would cry off before the day actually arrived. Now that the wedding was fast approaching and still a reality, the notably lazy Cedric was scrambling to get the grounds ready and also calling in markers in an effort to assemble some of the more levelheaded vamps to act as security for the big night, which was shaping up to be the scandalous social event of the season in the supernatural world.

Ignoring the Weres who were peering out of the bar, Dahlia and Taffy began to stroll down the street, arm in arm, an old-fashioned habit that drew a few stares.

"Taffy, I'm worried."

"What about, Dahlia?" Taffy asked gently.

"You know that Cedric's mansion is in a turmoil of preparation," Dahlia began, trying to think of the best way to voice her concerns without sounding like a complete alarmist.

"I heard." Taffy laughed, her throat tilted back. "That old bastard! Serves Cedric right for making a promise he had no intention of keeping."

"Taffy, you've been with the Weres too much. Don't disrespect the sheriff so boldly."

"You're right," Taffy said, sobering quickly enough to satisfy even the worried Dahlia. "So, Cedric's in an uproar. What of it?"

"The Weres and the vampires aren't the only ones who may have heard of this wedding," Dahlia said. She was voicing something she'd not told anyone else, and her voice wasn't completely steady. "Since the Weres haven't come out yet, to the world it must look as though you're illegally marrying a human."

Vampires didn't have the legal right to marry in the United States, not yet anyway. Dahlia couldn't have cared less about her legal rights, since she knew how transitory governments were, but there was no denying it was sweet to be able to walk the streets openly, admitting her true nature, and to know that if she was killed, her death would be state-avenged.

Well, maybe, under certain circumstances.

The point was, society was moving in the right direction, and the backlash from this affair might knock all of them sideways.

"Who in the mundane world knows?"

"It won't make a difference if humans know it afterward; we can explain it wasn't a true wedding at all. Cedric can get reporters to believe anything. But if it becomes common knowledge beforehand, there'll be human reporters all over the place, and protesters, and who knows what else."

"Cedric's gardeners are human," Taffy said slowly. "The florist is human." Her face was utterly serious now, and she looked like a true vampire. They turned back to return to the bar.

Dahlia nodded, silently, knowing her point had been taken. She was thrilled to see Taffy looking like her former self, until she realized that though the familiar calculation had returned to Taffy's face, something had been taken away: the lighthearted joy that made the ancient vampire look so renewed.

"So, you're saying that we might need more security than Cedric's thinking of providing," Taffy continued.

Dahlia cursed inside. Her point had been that Taffy should call off this insane ceremony. But Taffy had simply not considered it for a moment. "Sister," Dahlia said, calling on the bond of the nest-mate. "You must not go through with this wedding. It will bring trouble on the nest, and . . . and . . ." Dahlia had a flash of inspiration. "It may bring the Weres out into the open before they are ready to be known," Dahlia said, confident she was playing a trump card.

"This is a big secret," Taffy whispered, and not even a gnat could have heard her whisper, "but in the next month, the Weres are voting at their council about that very issue."

It had taken years of worldwide secret negotiations to pick the moment for the vampires: months of coordination, selection, and a carefully composed text that had been translated into a myriad of languages. The Weres would probably slouch in front of the television cameras with beers in their paws and dare the world to deny them citizenship.

"Then delay the wedding until then," Dahlia urged, trying to ignore all these side issues and stick to the main point.

"Sorry, no can do," Taffy said.

It took Dahlia a minute to grasp the meaning of Taffy's words. "Why not?" she asked. She made her lips manufacture a smile. "I know you're not pregnant." Dead bodies, however animated they looked, could not produce live children.

"No, but Don's ex is." Taffy's face was grim as she looked down at Dahlia's stunned face. "We have to get hitched before she has the baby, or she can appear before the Were council and demand they reinstate her marriage. Don hasn't had a child with anyone else, and you know how the Weres are about the purebloods reproducing with each other."

Dahlia could not do something so gauche as gape, but she came close. "I've never heard of such a thing," she said weakly.

"None of us knows much about the Were culture," Taffy said. "Our arrogance keeps us ignorant." The two stepped off the curb to cross the mouth of the alley. The bright lights of the bar were only half a block away.

Dahlia brightened. "I'll kill her," she said. There, she'd solved the problem. "Then you can hold off on your marriage, or cancel it altogether. No need to get married, right? What does this bitch look like?"

"Like this," said a sweet voice from the shadows, and a young woman leaped out, the knife in her hand glinting in the streetlight. But as fast as the Were stabbed at Taffy, Dahlia jumped to intercept it. She deflected the knife with her bare hands, but not quickly enough. It lodged between Dahlia's ribs, and the strong Were woman began to twist the blade. Just in time, Dahlia gripped the Were's wrist, and neatly broke it before the gesture could be completed.

The woman's screams drew an outrush of Weres from the bar. They circled Dahlia, growling and snapping, sure that the vampire had attacked first. Dahlia herself was standing very still, trying to keep from shrieking. That would have been unseemly, in Dahlia's opinion, and she was a vampire who lived by a code.

Taffy was so shocked that she didn't react with the speed one expected of a vampire. Between trying to explain to her fiancé what had happened and positioning herself to slap away the hands that would have struck Dahlia, Taffy was too occupied to evaluate Dahlia's plight. Oddly enough, it was Todd who calmed things down by silencing the crowd with a yell that was perilously close to a howl.

Into the hush he said, "Keep all humans away, first of all." There was a flurry of activity as the few humans who'd been drawn by the ruckus were hustled off, diverted with some story that would hardly make sense when it was reconsidered.

"What happened?" Don asked Taffy. Several female Weres were kneeling on the ground around the moaning ex-wife. The Amazonian Were called, "The vamp bitch attacked Amber and broke her arm!" A chorus of growls swelled the throats of the werewolves.

Dahlia concentrated on her breathing. Though vamps healed with amazing speed, the initial injury hurt just as much as it would any other being. The blood dripped from her hands, but it was slowing. She held them out in the light, and the crowd murmured. Taffy exclaimed, "She did this for me!" and then became quite still. Her voice shaking with a very unvamplike quiver, Taffy said, "Dahlia protected me with her life. Not exactly in the bridesmaid description."

Don was clearly conflicted between the woman on the ground (whom Dahlia could see now was what she thought of as medium pregnant), his distraught fiancée, and Dahlia.

"Dahlia, what do you say?" he asked harshly.

"I say, the fucking bitch stabbed me," Dahlia said clearly. "And would someone please pull out this damn knife before I heal around it? I mean, just any old time will do, unless you want to moan some more over Little Miss Homicide there." It was convenient that none of them had heard Dahlia offer to take care of Don's ex a few moments earlier. It gave her the definite moral high ground. Pregnant women, after all, were revered by almost everyone, both supernatural and human, and Dahlia needed all the leverage she could get. Without moving, because the pain was so intense she might fall down, Dahlia scanned the ring of Weres blocking the group from the view of passersby. "Todd, would you do the honors?" she asked, biting her lips with the pain. "You might even enjoy it."

Todd looked like there was nothing he'd enjoy less.

He bent down to look into Dahlia's green eyes, narrowed with the effort of sustaining her dignity. "I salute your courage," he said, and then he put one hand against her abdomen and yanked out the knife with the other.

Dahlia would have collapsed to her knees (terribly embarrassing) if the big Were hadn't caught her.

The next few minutes were a dim blur for Dahlia. She heard Don's stern voice, even deeper than usual, ordering Amber to tell the truth. Amber, a medium-sized blonde with a large bosom, wept copious tears and told her own jumbled version of events. In this version, she just happened to have a knife with her, in fact, ready in her hand, when Dahlia had jumped her. As to why Amber happened to be there in the first place, she whined that she'd just wanted to catch a glimpse of Don. Even the Weres didn't believe that.

"An attack on the packmaster's wife is an attack on the packmaster himself," Todd said.

"Then this vampire is as much at fault for breaking Amber's arm as Amber is for trying to kill Taffy," said the Amazon, trying very hard not to smile. "Since Amber is Don's wife."

"*Was* Don's wife," the packmaster himself corrected. "Before the state and the pack, I divorced Amber. Her attack on Taffy counts as an attack against me."

"Does not," argued the Amazon. "You haven't married Taffy, yet."

"Oh, for goodness' sake," Dahlia muttered. "Bore me to death, why don't you."

She felt Todd's chest shaking, and realized he was laughing silently. The wound in her side was almost healed, but she took her time pushing away from the Were's support. He was warm, and he smelled good.

She looked down at herself, taking stock. Her dress was ruined. Ruined! And she'd just paid off her credit card bill! "My dress," she said sadly. "At least make her pay for my dress. Did blood get on my shoes?" She hobbled over to a streetlight and held out a foot in an attempt to survey the damage. "Yes!" she said, going from grief to outrage in an undead minute. The shoes were brand-new and had cost more than the dress. "Okay, that does it." Her head snapped up and she glared at Don. "Amber pays for my dress and my shoes, and she doesn't come within five miles of Taffy for a year."

She was speaking into a chasm of silence. At the sound of her crisp voice, all conversation had ceased. Everyone was staring at her, even the whimpering Amber.

Don blinked. "Ah, that sounds fair," he said. "Honey?"

There was another embarrassing moment when both Amber and Taffy believed this appellation referred to them and began to respond simultaneously. Don gave Amber a look of withering contempt, which prompted a fresh burst of noisy tears.

Taffy said, "That seems a very moderate sentence, to me."

Dahlia knew from her friend's mild tone that Taffy thought Amber should be drawn and quartered, no matter what her condition.

"Amber, do you agree?" Don asked.

"What about her paying my hospital bill? I have to get this wrist set, after all."

"That's stupid, even for you," Todd said, into the general silence. "Amber, one more offense and the whole pack will abjure you."

Dahlia didn't know what being abjured consisted of, but the mere threat was an effective deterrent. Amber was shocked silent.

Two of the Were women loaded Amber into a car and headed off, presumably for the hospital. The rest of the crowd dispersed, leaving Todd, Dahlia, Don, and Taffy on the sidewalk.

Dahlia held up a hand to examine in the light. The slash across the palm had completely healed, and when she touched the wound in her ribs, she only felt a slight tenderness. "I'll take my leave," she said. She wanted to divest herself of her ruined clothes, shower, and knock back a few pints of synthetic blood before dawn.

"I'll walk you home," Todd said. It would be hard to say who in the little crowd was the most surprised by this statement.

"That's not necessary," Dahlia said, after a moment's recovery.

"I know you can carry me over your shoulder like a sack of potatoes," Todd said. He looked down at Dahlia. "And I'm not saying I'm happy about my packleader marrying a vamp, legal or not. But I'm gonna walk you home, unless you fly away."

Dahlia's brows drew together.

"After all," he said, "I'm in charge of security for the wedding, and I'm the best man. Since you're the maid of honor, I understand, you'll be responsible for security on your side? We should talk."

Dahlia turned to Don and Taffy, who were standing hand in hand, looking shell-shocked. "I will see you tomorrow night, Taffy," the vampire said formally. "Don." She nodded at the packleader, still not able to think of a formal pleasantry that would suit the unsuitable alliance.

The big Were and the little vampire walked side by side for a few blocks. Everyone they met stepped off the sidewalk to give them room, and the odd pair never even noticed.

"You're quite articulate for a Were." Dahlia's voice was cool and steady.

"Hey, some of us have even graduated from high school," he said easily. "Myself, I made it through college without tearing up one single coed."

"I shared my brother's tutor until my parents decided that, as a girl, I didn't need to learn any more," Dahlia said, to her own surprise. To cover her confession, Dahlia launched into a discussion of the security measures for the wedding. The vampires would guard the doors to the mansion; the only people on the premises should be the invited guests and the catering staff.

"Are all the vampires living in the mansion invited to the wedding?" Todd asked, trying to sound casual.

"Yes," Dahlia said, after a moment's consideration. "We're all nest-mates, after all."

"How's that work?"

"Well, we live together under Cedric's rule, since he's the sheriff of this area. As long as we're nest-mates, we protect each other and come to each other's aid."

"And contribute to Cedric's purse?"

"Well, yes. If we stayed in a hotel, we'd pay for lodging, so that's fair."

"And do his bidding?"

"Yes, that, too."

"A lot like the pack does for the packleader."

"I had assumed so. What part will the Weres play in security?" Dahlia asked. Todd was asking entirely too many questions.

"There should be a Were at every door, too, along with a vamp. We need to make sure that one or the other knows everyone who comes into the mansion that day. This wedding isn't popular with anyone, vamps or Weres, and though Don is totally not worried, I am."

"None of the vampires are worried, except me," Dahlia confessed. They'd arrived at a side door to the huge house on a street in the heart of the haughtiest section of the city. Cedric had had centuries of savings to use in purchasing this prime piece of Rhodes real estate, and though having a vampire among them hadn't made the wealthy neighbors happy, the city's Freedom of Housing ordinance had reinforced the vampires' right to live where they chose.

Todd said, "Good night, dead lady."

"Good night, hairball," she said. But just before the door closed behind her, she turned to smile at him.

The day of the wedding closed clear and warm, ideal for the outside ceremony. Acting uneasily in tandem, the Were and vamp security teams had admitted the catering staff, scanning their ID cards quickly. The teams paid more careful attention to the invitations presented by their own kind.

When Dahlia checked out the garden, the fountain of synthetic blood was flowing beautifully, champagne glasses arranged in a tier on a table beside it. It was a pretty touch, and Dahlia was proud she'd arranged it with the caterer, along with a groaning buffet for the Weres and a bar with drinks both alcoholic and nonalcoholic. Dahlia walked down the buffet, checking the stainless-steel eating utensils and the napkins and heated containers full of food. It seemed sufficient, though Dahlia was not much of a judge. The two servers stood stiffly behind the buffet, eyeing her passage with unhappy eyes.

Every human on the catering staff was tense. *They've never served vampires*, she thought, *and maybe the Weres are giving off some kind of vibration, too.*

She wasn't a bit surprised to encounter Todd, who was making a circuit of the high brick wall that guarded the large backyard of the mansion.

"Where's your dress?" he asked. "I'm panting to see it." Dahlia was in a black robe, modestly tied at her waist. Todd was already in his tuxedo. Dahlia had to blink.

"You look good," she said, her voice almost as calm as usual, though her fangs were sliding out. "Good" was a definite understatement. "Like a life-size Ken doll."

"I can't believe you even know what a Ken doll is," he said, laughing. "If I'm a big Ken, you're a miniature vampire Barbie." She'd been called worse things. She'd always admired Barbie's wardrobe and fashion sense.

"See you in a few minutes," she said, and went to get dressed.

Hanging over the door to the closet in Dahlia's little room was the bridesmaid dress. After a prolonged struggle with Taffy, Dahlia had talked her out of ordering pale pink with ruffles or pale blue with artificial roses sewn across the bodice. And no big bow on the butt. And no hat with veil. In fact, her nest-mate Fortunata came in just as Dahlia shimmied into the gown. Fortunata smiled at Dahlia's cautious look down the length of her body.

Taffy, despite her strange lack of judgment about this marriage, had finally had the sense to realize vampires would look ridiculous in innocent ruffles, girlish flounces, and insipid colors. The bridesmaids, four of them, were wearing dark blue square-necked long dresses that were form-fitting but not sleazily tight, and the spaghetti straps ensured that no one would lose whatever modesty she might possess.

There were a few glittery sequins strewn across the chest to give the dress a little sparkle, and they were all wearing black high heels and carrying bouquets of pale pink and creamy white roses. Fortunata had just come from adding a little extra item to the bouquets, at Dahlia's request.

"Mission accomplished. Now I'm ready to fix your hair," Fortunata said, finding Dahlia's brush in the clutter on the dressing table.

Fortunata had had a way with hair for centuries, and she brushed and pulled and twisted until Dahlia's black tresses were a model of sophisticated simplicity, with a couple of ringlets trailing here and there carelessly, to add just that touch of sensuous abandon.

"Not too shabby," was Fortunata's verdict when she and Dahlia stood side by side, and Dahlia had to agree. She felt a pleasurable tingle when she thought of Todd seeing her in the complete ensemble, and she hurriedly suppressed the reaction. Every time she viewed herself in a mirror, she felt a thrill of pleasure that the old canard about vamps having no reflection simply wasn't true.

The two bridesmaids united with the rest of the bride's side of the wedding party in the large common room at the back of the mansion. Taffy was in full wedding regalia, a pale redhead dripping in ivory lace. "She looks like a big white cake covered in icing," Fortunata muttered, and Dahlia, who actually agreed, said, "Hush. She looks beautiful." The long sleeves, the lace, the veil, the coronet of pearls . . . "We're lucky we're bridesmaids," Dahlia muttered. She drifted across the enormous, opulent room to gaze out the French doors at the scene outside. The French doors led out onto the flagstoned terrace, and from the terrace down onto the lawn. The scene looked very familiar, with white chairs in two groups of orderly lines, with a red carpet bisecting the groups. Either the catering company Cedric had hired was the same one that had had the concession at the wedding Dahlia attended a couple of weeks before or the arrangement was standard operating procedure. Dahlia had dispensed with the doves, fearing some of the Weres would eat the birds before they could be released.

A fairy or two mingled with the crowd, carefully staying over on the groom's side. Fairies were notoriously delicious to vampires, and though everyone was sure to be on his or her best behavior, not every vamp had the same threshold of self-control. Dahlia recognized a goblin or two that Cedric did business with and assorted shape-shifters, including one dark exotic who changed into a cobra. (That had been a memorable sight on a memorable night. Dahlia smiled reminiscently.)

Just then, a chorus of howls outside announced the arrival of the groomsmen, all decked out in their tuxes. Dahlia could distinguish Todd even at a distance. His burnished head was shining in the torches that had been set at intervals up and down the lawn. His glasses glinted. Dahlia sighed.

The music, provided by a Were rock band that was a favorite of the groom's, was surprisingly pleasant. The lead singer had a wonderfully tender voice that wrapped itself around love songs in an affecting way. He began to sing a number that she knew was called simply "The Wedding Song," because Taffy had dragged her along when she picked out the music.

Of course, the words weren't altogether pertinent since the subjects getting married weren't human. Don wasn't going to leave his mother, and Taffy wasn't going to leave her home. Taffy's home had slid into the ocean a couple of centuries before, and Don's mother was now pregnant by another member of the pack. But the sentiment, that the two would cleave together, was timely.

Just as Dahlia's eyes began to feel a little watery, Cedric appeared to give Taffy away. This was his right as sheriff, and Dahlia was proud that Cedric had stirred himself enough to be fitted for a traditional tuxedo. (He'd threatened to appear in an elaboration of his court costume from the time of Henry VIII.) The scene outside seemed to be boiling with activity, lots of the caterer's minions milling around. They needed to be more unobtrusive, Dahlia thought, and frowned.

The music changed, and Dahlia recognized the signal. She snapped her fingers. The bridesmaids grew still, and Taffy stared around her, looking as though she was going to panic. Cedric was searching around in his pocket for a handkerchief, since he was prone to tears at weddings, he'd said. Though he was perhaps a foot shorter than Taffy, he looked quite dapper in his black-and-white. His gleaming skin and dark Van Dyke beard and mustache made him appear quite distinguished, and if it hadn't been for a few niggling worries, Dahlia would have been very satisfied with the showing the vampires were providing. Cedric might not be a ball of energy, but he was handsome and had a polished turn of phrase that would come in handy at the wedding banquet.

"What's happening out there?" Taffy asked. "Do I look all right?"

"Don has come to stand by his friend the minister," Dahlia reported. She had to stand on her tiptoes, even though she was at a slight elevation, to see what was happening. Don's friend, who'd been chosen over Harry the Druid, was a mail-order minister who happened to have a wonderfully solemn voice and an appropriate black robe. The marriage wouldn't exactly be legal anyway, so appearance was more important than religious preference. "He's looking toward the house, waiting for you!" Dahlia tried her best to sound excited, and the other bridesmaids twittered obligingly.

"Here's Todd, coming for me," she said, making sure she sounded quite emotionless. This was the way they'd agreed to do it, each bridesmaid going down the aisle paired with a Were, echoing the bridal couple.

"That sucks," Glenda had said frankly, but Dahlia had given the other bridesmaids her big-eyed gaze, and they'd buckled.

Dahlia held her bouquet in the correct grip, and as Fortunata opened the door, Dahlia stepped out to meet the approaching Todd, who offered his arm at the right moment. The assembled guests gasped and murmured in a gratifying way at Dahlia's beauty, but Dahlia wanted to record only one reaction. Todd's eyes flared wide in the response Dahlia had long recognized as signaling sure attraction. Dahlia suppressed a grin and tried her best to look sweet and demure as she reached up to take Todd's brawny arm.

He bent down to tell her something confidential, and she waited with the faintest of smiles as they walked slowly down the red carpet.

"The caterers," he whispered. "There are too many of them."

"I wondered," she said, keeping her face arranged in a smile with some effort. "How'd they get in?"

"The caterer's in on it. They all had ID cards."

"This may be more fun that we'd counted on," she said, looking up at him for the first time.

He caught his breath. "Woman, you stir my blood," he said sincerely.

She put her own feelings into her eyes and felt his pulse quicken in response. She murmured, "Armed?"

"Don't think we need to be," he said. "Tomorrow night's the full moon. We can change tonight, if we throw ourselves into it."

"When do you think it'll happen?"

"When the bride comes out," he said.

"Of course." The fanatics would want Taffy most of all. What a triumph for them if they could destroy the dead thing that wanted to marry a living man!

"If you change . . . there can't be any survivors," she observed, her soft voice audible only to his sharp ears.

He smiled down at her. "Not a problem."

They'd reached the front of the assemblage now. Dahlia was close enough to notice that the waiting groom was trembling with nerves, though Todd's arm under her hand felt rock-steady. They were due to split up here, Dahlia going to the bride's side and Todd to the groom's. "Don't separate," she said at the last minute, and they turned to face the guests together, but no longer arm in arm. The pair following in their wake, Fortunata and the stubby blond Were named Richie, were quick enough on the uptake to follow suit, as did the other two couples.

Now they formed a wall in front of the groom, and all Dahlia's hopes for her friend's safety depended on Taffy getting down the aisle and gaining safety behind the phalanx formed by the wedding party.

The men and women in white jackets—who'd been setting up tables and ferrying food from the kitchen and setting up the blood bar and the alcohol bar were now trying to subtly position themselves in a loose circle around the guests and the wedding party.

All Dahlia's suspicions were confirmed.

It didn't take the crowd long to smell something odd. A confused murmur had just begun to spread through the guests when an apparently unsuspecting Taffy stepped out of the French doors. Cedric followed right behind her, giving her room to emerge in her full bridal splendor.

The caterers drew their weapons from under their white jackets and opened fire. Lots of the bullets were aimed at the bride.

But Taffy wasn't there. She had jumped five feet up in the air, and she was hurling her bridal bouquet at the nearest shooter hard enough to knock him down. Her eyes were blazing. Her red hair came loose from its elaborate arrangement, and she looked magnificent, every inch a vampire: a vampire totally pissed off that her wedding plans were being ruined.

Dahlia was proud enough to burst. But there wasn't any time to revel in her pleasure, because just as Todd bent to the ground and began to turn furry, Richie's chest exploded in a spray of red and Fortunata gasped with pain as a shot penetrated her arm.

From her own bouquet Dahlia extracted the wicked dagger she'd gotten Fortunata to conceal in its center, and with a bloodcurdling battle yell, she laid into the nearest server, a pie-faced young woman who hadn't mastered the art of close combat.

Dahlia and the other vamps mowed through the white-coated gun-slingers like scythes, and the huge bronze wolf by her side was just as effective.

Though they may have been heavily briefed on the evil and vicious nature of vampires, the attackers certainly hadn't counted on such an instantaneous and drastic counterattack. And they didn't know anything about Werewolves. The shock value of seeing many of the guests turn into animals rendered some of the gun toters simply paralytic with astonishment, during which moment the wolves rendered them—well, literally rendered them.

One fanatical young man faced Dahlia's approach and held open his arms to either side, proclaiming, "I am ready to die for my faith!"

"Good," Dahlia said, somewhat startled that he was being so obliging. She separated him from his head with a quick swipe of the knife.

When the fighting was over, Dahlia and Todd found themselves back-to-back on a pile of rather objectionable corpses, looking around for any further opposition. But the only live people around them were those of their own kind. Dahlia turned to her companion.

"It appears there are no more objections to the marriage," she said.

From the expression on his muzzle Dahlia could tell that she'd never looked so beautiful to the big Were—even covered in blood, her dress ruined. Todd changed from a wolf into an equally blood-dappled man wearing no clothes at all. "Oh," Dahlia said, happily. "Oh, *bravo!*"

Dahlia had paused to take some gulps of the real thing (to hell with the synthetic blood fountain) during the slaughter, and now she was rosy cheeked and feeling quite invigorated.

"The knives were your idea, weren't they?" Todd said admiringly.

Dahlia nodded, trying to look shy.

"It's a human tradition that the best man and the maid of honor have a fling at the wedding," Todd said.

"Is that right?" Dahlia looked up at him. "But you know, there hasn't been a wedding yet."

They looked around them as they made their way to the terrace.

Cedric and Glenda were sipping from cups they'd filled with blood that wasn't synthetic at all. Ever the gracious host, Cedric had uncorked some champagne and offered the bottle to Don. Taffy, hanging on to Don's bare arm, was laughing breathlessly. Her pearl coronet was still straight, but her dress was ripped in several places.

She didn't seem to care.

Richie, the sole serious casualty on the supernatural side, was being tended ably by a little doctor who looked suspiciously like a hobbit.

"I now pronounce you man and wife!" called the Were friend who'd been the "minister" at the ceremony. He was as naked as Todd. He had his arms wrapped around the Amazonian Were woman, who was equally bereft of clothing. They seemed quite happy, but not as happy as Don and Taffy as they kissed each other.

The wedding was pronounced a great success. In fact, though it had been termed scandalous before it occurred, Taffy and Don's wedding turned out to be the social event of the Rhodes summer season, in certain supernatural circles.

The disappearance of the Lucky Caterer's entire staff was a nine-day wonder in Rhodes law enforcement circles. Luckily for the vampires and the Weres, owner Lucky Jones had kept the wedding off the books because she expected the humans would kill all the guests.

And it's true that, as Dahlia had told Glenda, going through a war together breeds comradeship; less than a year later, the same Were minister was officiating at Todd and Dahlia's nuptials.

The couple wisely opted to have a less formal wedding—in fact, a potluck. Dahlia had decided that, contrary to all social indicators, caterers were simply tacky.

NEEDLES

Elizabeth Bear

Elizabeth Bear was born on the same day as Frodo and Bilbo Baggins, but in a different year. When coupled with a childhood tendency to read the dictionary for fun, this led her inevitably to penury, intransigence, and the writing of speculative fiction. She is the Hugo, Sturgeon, Locus, and Campbell Award winning author of more than twenty-five novels— the most recent is *Karen Memory*, from Tor—and almost a hundred short stories. Her dog lives in Massachusetts; her partner, writer Scott Lynch, lives in Wisconsin. (She spends a lot of time on planes.)

When Bear dabbles in the vampiric, you can always expect a fresh twist. Her collection of linked supernatural mystery stories, *New Amsterdam* (2007), and its sequel novellas *The White City* (2010) and *Ad Eternum* (2012) feature Don Sebastien de Ulloa, a thousand-year-old wampyr, in an alternative history/steampunkish setting. In her novel *One-Eyed Jack*, a pivotal character is a vampire named Tribute, who bears a striking resemblance to a certain long-lost icon of popular music. Bear's short story "Needles" mixes standard vampire themes and Mesopotamian mythology for a darkly memorable story . . .

The vampires rolled into Needles about three hours before dawn on a Tuesday in April, when the nights still chilled between each scorching day. They sat as far apart from each other as they could get, jammed up against the doors of a '67 Impala hardtop the color of dried blood, which made for *acres* of bench seat between them. Billy, immune to irony, rested his fingertips on the steering wheel, the other bad boy arm draped out the open window. Mahasti let her right hand trail in the slipstream behind a passenger mirror like a cherub's stunted wing.

Mahasti had driven until the sun set. After that, she'd let Billy out of the trunk and they had burned highway all night south from Vegas through

CalNevAri, over the California border until they passed from the Mojave Desert to the Mohave Valley. Somewhere in there the 95 blurred into cohabitation with Interstate 40 and then they found themselves cruising the Mother Road.

"Get your kicks," Billy said, "on Route 66."

Mahasti ignored him.

They had been able to smell the Colorado from miles out, the river and the broad green fields that wrapped the tiny desert town like a hippie skirt blown north by prevailing winds. Most of the agriculture clung along the Arizona side, the point of Nevada following the Colorado down until it ended in a chisel tip like a ninja sword pointed straight at the heart of Needles.

"Bad feng shui," Billy said, trying again. "Nevada's gonna stab California right in the balls."

"More like right in the water supply," Mahasti said, after a pause long enough to indicate that she'd thought about leaving him hanging but chosen, after due consideration, to take pity. Sometimes it was good to have somebody to kick around a little. She was mad at him, but he was still her partner.

She ran her left hand through her hair, finger-combing, but even at full arm's stretch, fingertips brushing the windshield, she didn't reach the end of the locks. "If they thought they could get away with it."

She curled in the seat to glance over her shoulder, as if something might be following. But the highway behind them was as empty as the desert had been. "We should have killed them."

"Aww," Billy said. "You kill every little vampire hunter who comes along, pretty soon no vampire hunters. And then what would we do for fun?"

She smiled in spite of herself. It had been a lot of lonely centuries before she found Billy. And Billy knew he wasn't in charge.

He feathered the gas; the big engine growled. He guided the Impala towards an off ramp. "Does this remind you of home?"

"Because every fucking desert looks alike? There's no yucca in Baghdad." She tucked a thick strand of mahogany-black hair behind one rose-petal ear. "Like I even know what Baghdad looks like anymore."

The door leaned into her arm as the car turned, pressing lines into the flesh. The dry desert wind stroked dry dead skin. As they rolled up to a traffic signal, she tilted her head back and scented it, curling her lip up delicately, like a dog checking for traces of another dog.

"They show it on TV," Billy said.

"They show it blown up on TV," she answered. "Who the fuck wants to look at that? Find me a fucking tattoo parlor."

"Like that'll change you." He reached across the vast emptiness of the bench seat and brushed her arm with the backs of his fingers. "Like anything will change you. You're dead, darlin'. The world doesn't touch you."

When you were one way for a long time, it got comfortable. But every so often, you had to try something new. "You never know until you try."

"Like it'll be open." The Impala ghosted forward with pantherine power, so smooth it seemed that the wheels had never quite stopped turning. "It's three in the morning. Even the bars are closed. You'll be lucky to find an all-night truck stop."

She looked out the window, turning away. The soft wind caught her voice and blew it back into the car with her hair. "You wanna try to make L.A. by sunup? It's all the same to me, but I know you don't like the trunk."

"Hey," Billy said. "There's a Denny's. Maybe one of the waitresses is knocked up. That'd be okay for both of us."

"They don't serve vampires." Mahasti pulled her arm back inside, turned to face front. With rhythmic push-pull motions, she cranked the window up. "Shut up already and drive."

Colorado River Florist. Spike's Bar-B-Que. Jack in the Box. Dimond and Sons Needles Mortuary. Spike's Saguaro Sunrise Breakfast. First Southern Baptist Church (Billy hissed at it on principle) and the Desert Mirage Inn. A Peanuts cartoon crudely copied on the sign over a tavern. Historic Route 66 ("The Mother Load Road," Billy muttered) didn't look much as it had when the Impala was young, but the motel signs were making an effort.

Of Needles itself, there wasn't much *there* there, which was a good thing for the vampires: they crisscrossed the whole downtown in the hollow dark before Billy pulled over to a curb and pointed, but it took them less than a hour.

Mahasti leaned over to follow the line of his finger. A gray corner-lot house with white trim and a yard overrun by Bermuda grass and mallow huddled in the darkness. It was doing a pretty good impression of a private residence, except for the turned-off neon "open" sign in the window and the painted shingle hanging over the door.

"Spike's Tattoo," she said. "Pun unintended?"

As they exited the car, heavy swinging doors glossy in the street-lit darkness, Billy cupped his hands and lit a cigarette. It flared bright between streetlights. "Why is everything in this damned town named after some Spike guy?"

Mahasti tugged her brown babydoll tee smooth from the hem. An octopus clutching a blue teddy bear stretched across her insignificant breasts. Billy liked Frye boots and black dusters. Mahasti kicked at a clod with fuchsia Crocs, the frayed hems of her jeans swaying around skinny ankles. "Because he lives in the desert near here."

Billy gave her a dour look over the ember of the cigarette. He took a drag. It frosted his face in orange.

"*Peanuts*?" she tried, but the blank look deepened. "Snoopy's brother? It's their claim to fame."

Billy didn't read the newspapers. It wasn't even worth a shrug. He flipped the cigarette into the road.

He was dead anyway. He hadn't been getting much good out of it.

"Come on." Gravel crunched on the dirty road as he strode forward. "Let's go ruin somebody's morning."

Mahasti steepled her fingers. "I'll be right back. I'm just going to walk around the block."

Spike's Tattoo bulwarked the boundary between the commercial and the residential neighborhoods. Mahasti turned her back on Billy and walked away, up a quiet side street lined on either side by low block houses with tar-shingled roofs that wouldn't last a third of a Minnesota winter.

They didn't have to.

Mahasti moved through the night as if she were following a scent, head tilted to one side or the other, nostrils flaring, the indrawn air hissing through her arched, constricted throat.

Billy came up behind her. "You smell anything?"

She shot him with a look. "Your fucking menthol Camels."

He smiled. She jerked her chin at the gravel side drive that gave access to the gate into the backyard of Spike's. "I'm taking that one. You better go roll a wino or something."

"Bitch," he said without heat. "I'll wait at the front door, then."

He spun on the scarred ball of his cowboy boot. He was lean, not too tall, stalking down the street as if the ghosts of his spurs should be jingling. The black duster flared behind him like a mourning peacock's tail, but for once he hadn't shot the collar. A strip of brown skin with all the blood red dropped out showed between his coarse black hair and the plaid band of his cowboy shirt. Even as short as that, the hair was too straight to show any kind of curl.

She sighed and shook her head and turned away.

"Tucson was fucking prettier." Mahasti could bitch all she wanted. There was no one to hear.

The houses here had block walls around the back, water-fat stretches of grass in the front. The newer neighborhoods might be xeriscaped, but in the nineteen-forties a nice lawn was a man's God-given American right, and no mere inconvenience like the hottest desert in North America was going to stop him from having one. She walked up a cement sidewalk between stubby California fan palms on the street side and fruitless mulberry in the yards, still pausing every few feet to cast left and right and sniff the air.

She finished her stroll around the block and found herself back at Spike's Tattoo. A sunbeat gray house, paint peeling on the south side, it wore its untrimmed pomegranate hedge like a madman's fishy beard. The side door sunk, uninviting, between shaggy columns of leaves and branches. A rust-stained motorboat, vinyl canopy tattered, blocked the black steel gate that guarded the passage between the side drive and the back yard.

Mahasti, who'd been sticking to the outside sidewalks on the block she was walking, looked both ways down the street and crossed, fetching up in the streetlight shadow of one of those stubby palms. She eyed the house as she walked into the side yard. It eyed her back—rheumy, snaggled, discontented.

She looked away. Then she stepped out of her squishy plastic shoes ("What will they think of next?" Billy had said, when she'd pulled them from a dead girl's feet outside of Winnemucca) and lofted from ground to boat-deck to balanced atop the eight-foot gate in a fluid pair of leaps, pausing only for a moment to let her vulture shadow fall into the gravel of the yard.

She spread her arms and stepped down lightly, stony gravel silent under her brown bare foot, the canopy of her hair trailing like a comet tail before swinging forward heavily and cloaking her crouched body to the ankles. It could trap no warmth against her, but it whisked roughly on the denim of her jeans.

Hair, it turned out, actually *did* keep growing after you were dead.

She tilted her head back, sniffing again, eyes closed to savor. When she smiled, it showed white, even, perfectly human teeth. When she uncoiled and glided forward it was one motion, smooth as any dancer. "Everything we need."

There was a dog in the yard, stretched out slumbering on a pallet made of heaped carpet squares. The third security window—long, narrow, and a foot over her head—she tried with palms pressed flat against the glass slid open left to right. There were no screens.

Hands on the window ledge, she chinned herself. In a cloak of red-black hair robbed of color by the darkness, she slid inside.

It was a cold space of tile illuminated by a yellow nightlight: the bathroom. Mahasti's bare dead feet were too dry to stick to the linoleum, her movements too light to echo. The door to the hall stood ajar. She slipped sideways through it without touching and paused just outside. The rasp of human breathing, human heartbeat, was stentorian. Their scent saturated the place.

Three. Infant, woman, and man.

Mahasti slithered around the open bedroom door, past the crib, one more shadow among shadows. The little boy slept on his stomach, knees drawn up under him, butt a round crooked mountain under the cheap acrylic blanket.

When Mahasti picked him up, he woke confused and began to cry. The parents roused an instant after, their heat crystal-edged against the dimness, fumbling in the dark. "Your turn," the man said, and rolled over, while the woman slapped at her nightstand until her fingers brushed against her eyeglass frames.

"You probably have a gun in the nightstand." Mahasti hooked the hem of the octopus shirt and rucked it up over her gaunt, cold belly, revealing taut flesh and stretch marks. She slung the baby against her shoulder with her left hand. "I don't think you want to do that."

The woman froze; the man catapulted upright, revealing a torso streaked with convoluted lines of ink. *His* feet made a moist noise on the floor.

"Lady," the man said, "who the hell are you? No wetback fucking junkie is gonna come in my house . . . ."

"You shouldn't put a child to sleep on his stomach."

The baby's wails came peacock-sharp, peacock-painful. She cupped him close, feeling the hammering of his tiny heart. She freed her breast one-handed and plugged him on to the nipple with the deftness of practice.

He made smacking sounds at first, then settled down contented as her milk let down. Warmth spread through her, or perhaps the chill drained from her dead flesh to his living.

The vampire didn't take her eyes off the man, and he didn't move towards the nightstand. The mother—a thick-shouldered woman bare-legged in an oversized shirt—stayed frozen, her hands clawed at her sides, her head cocked like a bird's. An angry mother falcon, contemplating which eye to go after first.

Mahasti moved. She closed, lifted the woman up one-handed, and tossed her across the room. Trivial, and done in the space of a blink; the mother had more hang-time than it took Mahasti to return to her original place by the door. The man jumped back, involuntarily, as the mother hit the wall beside him. "Shit," he said, crouching beside her. "Shit, shit, shit."

The woman pushed herself up the wall, blood smearing from a swollen lip, a cheek split over the bone.

"What's your son's name?" Mahasti said, threat implicit in her tone. The babe had not shifted.

The mother settled back on her heels, but the stretched tension in the tendons of her hands did not ease. "Alan." She gulped air. "Please don't hurt him. We have a little money. We don't have any drugs—"

Mahasti stood away from the door. "We're going out front," she said to the man. "And then you're going to open the front door."

It took thirty seconds and a glare from the woman before the man decided to comply. Once he had, though, he moved quickly around the bed and past Mahasti. He was lean as a vampire himself, faded tattoos winding down the ropy stretched-rubber architecture of his torso to vanish into striped cotton pajamas.

He paused in the doorway and glanced back once at the nightstand. Mahasti coughed.

He stepped into the hall. The woman made a noise low in the back of her throat, as involuntary as an abandoned dog.

"You too." Mahasti snuggled the baby closer to her breast. "Go with him. Do what I say and you won't get hurt."

She made them precede her down the short hall to the front of the house, which had been converted into the two rooms of the tattoo parlor. A counter constructed of two-by-fours and paneling divided the living room. Cheaply framed flash covered every wall.

Bullet-headed as a polar bear, sparing Mahasti frequent testing glances, the man went to the door. He turned the lock and pulled it open, revealing Billy with his hat pulled low, on the other side of the security door. A muscle jumped in his jaw as the man opened that lock, too, and stepped back, as if he could make himself flip the lever but not—quite—turn the handle.

"Invite him in," Mahasti said.

She came from another land, where the rules were different. But unfair as it was, Billy was cursed to play the game of the invader.

"Miss—" the woman said, pleading. "Please. I'll give you anything we have."

"Invite," Mahasti said, "him in."

"Come in," the man said, in a low voice, but perfectly audible to a vampire's ears.

Billy's hat tilted up. In the shadow of the brim, his irises glittered violet with eyeshine.

He opened the security door—it creaked rustily—stepped over the threshold and tossed Mahasti's Crocs at her feet. "Your shoes."

"Thanks."

He shut the security door behind him. The woman jerked in sympathy to the metallic scrape of the lock. An hour still lacked to dawn, but that didn't concern the rooster that crowed outside, greeting the first translucency of the indigo sky. Dawn would come soon, but for now all that light was good for was silhouetting the shark-tooth range of mountains that gave Needles its name

The man drew back beside the woman, against the counter. "What do you want?"

The baby, cool and soft, had fallen asleep on Mahasti's warm breast. She gently disconnected him and tugged her shirt down. "I want you to change me. Change me forever. I want a tattoo."

She told him to freehand whatever he liked. He studied her face while she gave him her left arm. Billy held the kid for insurance, grumbling about the delay. The mother went around hanging blankets over the windows and turning on all the lights.

"What are you?" he asked.

"A 'wetback fucking junkie,'" she mimicked, cruelly accurate. "Do you think if you talk to me you'll build a connection, and it will keep you safe?"

He looked down at his tools, at the transfer paper on the book propped on his lap. "You don't have much accent for a wetback."

He glanced up at Billy and the baby, lips thin.

Mahasti held out her right hand. "Give me Alan, please. He needs to suckle."

"Ma'am." The woman pinned the last corner of a blanket and stepped back from the window. "Please. I'm his mother—"

Billy glared her still and silent, though even the force of his stare could not hush the sobs of her breath. He slid the baby into the crook of Mahasti's arm, supporting its head until the transfer was complete.

"When I learned what would become your language—" Mahasti spoke to the man as if none of the drama had occurred "—it was across a crusader's saddle. I was too young, and the child the bastard got on me killed me coming out." She smiled, liver-dark lips drawn fine. "And when I was dead I rose up and I returned the favor, to both of them."

He drew back from her needle teeth when she smiled. His hands shook badly enough that he lifted his pencil from the paper and pulled in a steadying breath. Without meeting her eyes, he went back to what he had been drawing once more.

At Mahasti's other breast, the child suckled. The touch still warmed her.

"Somebody will notice when we don't open," the woman said. "Someone will know there's something wrong."

"Maybe," Mahasti said. "In a week or two. You people never want to get involved in a goddamned thing. So shut up and let him fucking draw."

He drew, and he showed her. A lotus, petals like a crown, petals embracing the form of a newborn child. "White," he said. "Stained with pink at the heart."

"White ink." She held up her brown arm for inspection. "You can do that?"

He nodded.

If a child changed her once, maybe a child could change her again. She said, "You've got through the daylight to make me happy. When the sun goes down we're moving on."

He didn't ask "and?" Neither did the mother.

As if they had anyway, Billy said, "And there's two ways we can leave you when we go."

"I'll get clean needles," said the man.

Billy paced while the man worked on Mahasti's arm and the baby dozed off against her breast once more. Dimly, Mahasti heard the flutter of a heart. The woman finally sat down on the couch in the waiting area and pulled her knees up to her chest. The man kept wanting to talk. The dog barked forlornly in the yard.

After several conversational false starts, while the ink traced the arched outlines of petals across Mahasti's skin and the at-first-insistently ringing phone went both unanswered and more frequently quiet, he said, "So if she was a kidnapped Persian princess, what were you?"

Billy skipped a bootheel off the floor and turned, folding his arms. "Maybe I was Billy the Kid."

Mahasti snorted. "Billy the Kid wasn't an Indian."

"Yeah? You think anybody would have written it down if he was? What if I was an iron-fingered demon? I wouldn't need *you* to get me invited in."

With a cautious, sidelong glance at Mahasti, the man said, "What's an iron-fingered demon?"

"If I were an iron-fingered demon, I could eat livers, cause consumption, get on with my life. Unlife. But no, *you* get to be a *lamashtu*. And *I* had to catch the white man's bloodsucker disease."

Mahasti spoke without lifting her head, or her gaze from the man's meticulous work. The lotus taking shape on her skin was a thing of beauty. Depth and texture. No blood pricked from her skin to mar the colors, which were dense and rich. "You *could* be an iron-fingered demon. If you were a Cherokee. Which you aren't."

"Details," he said. "Details. First I'm too Indian, then I'm not the right kind of Indian? Fuck you very much."

"Billy," Mahasti said, "Shut up and let the man work or we won't be ready to go when the sun sets."

She was a desert demon, the sun no concern. It was on Billy's behalf that they stalled.

The dog's barking has escalated to something regular and frantic. A twig cracked in the yard.

Mahasti looked at the man, at the cold baby curled sleeping in the corner of her arm. She lifted her chin and stared directly, unsettlingly, at the woman. "Mommy?"

The mother must have been crying silently, curled in her corner of the couch, because she stammered over a sob. "Yes?"

"You've been such a good girl, I'm going to give you Alan back. You and Billy can take him in the back. I know you're not going to try anything silly."

The woman's hands came up, clutched at air, and settled again to clench on the sofa beside her bare legs. "No."

Mahasti looked at the man. "And you won't do anything dumb either, will you?"

He shook his head. Under the lights, his scrawny shoulders had broken out in a gloss of sweat. "That's good, Cathy," he said. The eye contact between him and the woman was full of unspoken communication. "You take Alan and put him to bed."

"Here," Mahasti said, offering him up, his heartbeat barely thrumming against her fingertips. She tingled, warm and full of life. "He's already sleeping."

Billy sat crosslegged on the unmade bed, his bootheels denting the mattress. The woman pulled all the toys and pillows from the crib and lay the baby on his back atop taut bedding. She moved tightly, elbows pinned to her ribcage, spine stiff. He slouched, relaxed.

Until the front door slammed open.

"Fucking vampire hunters." He was in the hall before the words finished leaving his mouth, the woman behind him bewildered by the fury of his passage. A spill of sunlight cut the floor ahead, but the corner of the wall kept it from flooding down the corridor.

Billy paused in the shadow of the hall.

Three men burst into the front room—one weedy, one meaty, and one perfectly average in every way except the scars. Mahasti moved from the chair, the disregarded needle blurring a line of white across her wrist, destroying the elegance of the artist's design. The artist threw himself into a corner behind the counter. By the time he got there and got his back against the wall, the fight was over.

The perfectly average man was fast enough to meet her there, in the sunlight, and twist her un-inked right arm up behind her in a bind.

The silver knife in his left hand pricked her throat. An image of a Persian demon, inscribed on the blade, flashed sunlight into Mahasti's eyes.

"Well, fuck," she said.

The meaty one grabbed her free hand and slapped a silver cuff around it.

"Silence, *lamashtu*," the vampire hunter growled, shaking her by her twisted arm. "Call the other out, so I can burn him too. You'll terrorize no more innocents."

She rolled her eyes. "He's not coming out when there's daylight in the room."

"Really?" he laughed. "Your protector thinks so little of you?"

"I'm my own protector, asshole," she said, and kicked back to break the bone of his thigh like a fried chicken-wing.

She threw the meaty one down the hall to Billy, and ripped the throat out of the weedy one while the perfectly average one was still screaming his way to the floor.

She shut the door before she killed him. The noise was going to bring the neighbors around. Then she went to help Billy drag the third body up to the pile, and make sure the woman hadn't run out the back in the confusion.

She was still crouched by the crib. Mahasti left her there and met Billy in the hall. "See?" he said. "More fun if you don't use 'em up all at once."

Mahasti said, "He had a knife with an image of Pazazu etched on it. That could have been the end of *all* our fun."

"He got prepared before he followed us here." Billy grimaced. "They're getting smarter."

"Not smart enough to use it before asking questions, though."

Mahasti jerked her thumb over her shoulder, towards the rear of the house. The white lotus and babe, blurred on her wrist, shone in the dark. She felt different. Maybe. She thought she felt different now.

She said, "What about them? If there are any more hunters they will be able to answer questions."

"We could take them with us. Hostages. The Impala's got a six-body trunk. It's cozy, but it's doable."

"Fuck it," Mahasti said. "They'll be a load. It'll be a long fucking drive. Leave them."

"Fine," Billy said. "But you got what you needed from the kid. *I* still have to get a snack first."

He met her on the concrete stoop two minutes later, licking a split lip. Smoke curled from his fingers as he pulled his hat down hard, shading his face from the last crepuscular light of the sun. "Cutting it close."

"The car has tinted windows," she said. "Come on."

Traffic thinned as the night wore on, and the stark, starlit landscape grew more elaborately beautiful. Mahasti read a book by Steinbeck, the lotus flashing every time she turned a page. Billy drove and chewed his thumb.

When the sky was gray, without turning, she said, "Pity about the kid."

"What do you care? He was just gonna die anyway." He paused. "Just like we don't."

She sighed into the palm of her hand, feeling her own skin chilling like age-browned bone. There was no pain where the needles had worked her skin—but there *was* pain in her empty arms, in her breasts taut with milk again already. "Mommy's going to miss him."

Billy's shrug traveled the length of his arms from his shoulders to where his wrists draped the wheel. "Not for as long as I'd miss you."

They drove a while in silence. Without looking, she reached out to touch him.

A thin line of palest gold shivered along the edge of the world. Billy made a sound of discontent. Mahasti squinted at the incipient sunrise.

"Pull over. It's time for you to get in the trunk."

He obeyed wordlessly, and wordlessly got out, leaving the parking brake set and the door standing open. She popped the trunk lid. He lay back and settled himself on the carpet, arms folded behind his head. She closed the lid on him and settled back into the car.

Her unmarred brown left arm trailed out the window in the sun. Tonight, somewhere new, they'd do it all over again.

Once in a while, Billy was right. Nothing changed them. She could touch the world, but the world never touched her.

The Impala purred as she pulled off the shoulder and onto the road. Empty, and for another hour it would remain so.

FROM THE TEETH OF
STRANGE CHILDREN

Lisa L. Hannett

Lisa L. Hannett has had over fifty-five short stories appear in venues including *Clarkesworld*, *Fantasy*, *Weird Tales*, *ChiZine*, the *Year's Best Australian Fantasy and Horror* (2010, 2011, and 2012), and *Imaginarium: Best Canadian Speculative Writing* (2012 and 2013). She has won three Aurealis Awards, including Best Collection 2011 for her first book, *Bluegrass Symphony*, which was also nominated for a World Fantasy Award. She coauthored themed collections *Midnight and Moonshine* (2012) and *The Female Factory* (2014) with Angela Slatter. Her first novel, *Lament for the Afterlife*, is being published by CZP in 2015. You can find her online at lisahannett.com and on Twitter @LisaLHannett.

Hannett's Mister Pérouse is, like the archetypal vampire, an evil creature—but he and his not-at-all-merry band are also quite original . . .

What do ghosts look like?

The whisper cracks my voice, but I know he's heard me. He takes a hesitant step forward and drops his rucksack inside the entrance. Dust lifts off the bag, settles onto the scuffed floorboards. Then he stands there, half in the daylight, half in the dark of our lampless, curtained sitting room. He clears his throat and fingers the house key like he's amazed it still works. As though Ma was the one who'd left, not him, and changed the locks on her way. I couldn't have been more than nine when his pack last disappeared, leaving nothing but a few scratches in the doorframe to show where he'd dragged it out behind him. Eight years later, he's got a truck to carry most of his things, more white in his hair, and an expression so downcast I can't yet tell whose father he is. Mine or Harley's.

"Ada," he says, nothing more. No questioning lilt to the way he pronounces my name—he recognizes me even though I look nothing like the little girl he once protected. And hearing the rumble of his coffee-and-cigarette voice, I know him in return. In a familiar, unconscious gesture, Banjo runs his hand over his stubbly beard. Harley's dad always was a fidgety one, never could sit still for more than a minute. A need to see the world beyond our farm, to do things the way city folk might, set his muscles twitching and kept his feet planted on the trail. I reckon he's much like his twin in that sense; Ma once said neither he nor Jez, my father, ever had it in them to stay put for long. And as long as they didn't mind other men keeping the chill from her bed, she didn't begrudge them their freedom.

Again, Banjo coughs. Too many excuses, too many overdue answers fight their way up his throat. A lifetime of words glue his mouth shut.

I don't get up from the couch, so I have to crane my neck to the right to see him. "That's what Harley asked me," I explain, motioning Banjo to come all the way in and close the door. The summer months have scrubbed the sunlight thin over the fields but it's still too bright for Ma. She's curled up on the cushions beside me, skin clammy with sweat though she's stripped to her petticoat, mouth clamped on wads of cotton and gore. I pull the afghan up to cover her shoulders, wipe the blood from her cheek. "The first time we saw Mister Pérouse at one of Ma's parties, Harl asked—almost hissing, so Ma wouldn't catch us sneaking—he asked, 'What do ghosts look like? Ain't that one?' Peering through the slats in the pantry door where we were hiding, Harl's eyes stretched wide enough to swallow the night. His hand shook, clutching mine, but a smile tickled his lips as we stared. A mix of dread and awe—but that's just like our Harl, isn't it? Always mistaking fear for excitement. Then again, seeing that man, so pale he was more blue than white, so skinny he seemed to float while the rest of us clung heavy to our footsteps, for once I knew how Harl felt."

My gaze drifts to Ma's face as I speak. Anxiety lines her forehead, even in sleep. Each breath she takes is shallow; her exhalations are thick wheezes of air.

"I've thought about this a lot," I say. "Spent years doing little but."

Banjo's fingers worry at his chin, *scritch-scritching* over his bristles.

"I can't stop hearing his voice," I continue. "Even now I'm back here. 'Cause, far as I can tell, that was it: the parties, those outfits, that ghost of a man. His dreams. His high notions of what made proper living. Everything that changed us; right there, dancing on the other side of the pantry door.

"Of course, how could we know that then? Harl always was young for his age—you said so yourself, remember? And Ma thought I was too sweet for fourteen, too innocent to wear such a grown-up face." I feel the color rising in my cheeks. Outside, Banjo's truck cools, settles with a series of metallic pings. There's no wind to shake the trees ringing our twenty-acre lot, no harvest for revving tractors to tend. Crickets hum pure white noise, thrumming beyond register in the heat. Silence plods into the room, sits like a boulder between me and Banjo.

I can see he wants to ask more about Harl.

Instead, he shifts from foot to foot, still hanging back. "Where are the girls?"

"With their brother." I swallow hard; there's no time for tears. "It's rude to linger in doorways, you know."

Harl's dad squints and takes a good look at me, but doesn't show any sign of moving.

"I'm fine," I say, sighing. Baring my teeth, I run my tongue across their blunt edges. "See? Harmless as Ma."

He releases a pent-up breath and finally lets the door swing shut. My eyes take a minute to adjust to the returned gloom. Outdoor scents waft from him as he sits in the worn recliner across from me: maple and pine and a rich hint of hot earth. He brushes invisible dirt from his jeans. Smooths out the lifelines they've collected over the years; exhausted white wrinkles like the ones on the backs of his hands.

"I'd offer you a drink." I look down at Ma, then back at Banjo. "I don't know if she's got any. And after this morning . . . She couldn't even tell me if she'd change for the phone box. I hunted for her purse and she kept crying the whole time; crying and pulling at my arms, telling me not to go. When I found it I had to lock her in the cellar—don't look at me like that! It's the only way I knew, to keep her from chasing me to the truck stop . . .

"She's only just dozed off. She might not even remember telling me to call you." I hesitate before admitting, "You and Jez."

Banjo nods once. Doesn't ask who I called first—he's never been much of a talker. I think that's why Ma got together with him in the first place, why she kept taking him back though she kept the door closed on his brother. After a while, my father's opinions were just too vocal, too hard for her to handle. *You call this living?* Jez'd said, on more than one occasion. *Scouring dirt for scraps what ain't fit for eating, guzzling potato wine, pumping out babies what ain't got no hope of leaving this heap?* Even when she made an effort, took a job in town, it wasn't enough for my dad. The costume shop embarrassed him—as did the parties Ma threw. Our closest neighbors happily traveled the five miles between their places and here, just to come dressed in Ma's wares. The stitching on her pieces proved so fine, she started getting mail orders from all over the country—her boss even gave her a raise! All that only seemed to make things worse with Jez.

Ain't no old-fashion time we's living in, Wendy, he'd say, looking at her fine silks and brocades like they were sewn from pig-hide and dung. *This here's the future, fer fuck's sakes—even them radio jockeys says so. Why don't y'all give them a listen, since you clearly ain't gots the sense to hear me?*

Guilt trips didn't work so well on Ma. Day after day, she frocked up in skirts with bustles, whalebone corsets and elaborate jackets. Jez hollered like a good thing when she stopped taking us to the church ladies' bazaars to buy our clothes, and started making everything but the hard leather boots she selected from Roebuck catalogues. He split her lip when she cancelled the electricity, opting to use candles and a woodstove. An old icebox and the house's root cellar kept our goats' milk fresh and veggies from our garden cool. And when she sold the car for thirteen bales of cotton, Jez grabbed a bag from the linen cupboard. Shouldered it and said he needed to check out a breach in our property's fence.

We loved Ma for all of it; more so after Jez left. Even Harley, who kicked up a stink fighting for costumes much plainer than us girls'—even he never said our way of living was odd. Chopping and carrying wood to heat the house, drawing water from a pump out back, shitting in a flea-bitten outhouse. Anyone who came 'round our place played their part in Ma's old style life, right up until it was time for them to go home.

Ain't it just a lark, Ada? They'd ask, buttoning themselves back into overalls and faded work shirts, putting on their regular life suits. *Ain't it grand playing the regal lady like yer Ma?*

And I'd smile, knowing how lucky we were to have her, how special. Knowing it wasn't just play. *Ain't goin'ta deny it,* I'd reply—that's how I spoke then, all *ain'ts* and *y'alls* and *none of yer never minds,* uttered without the slightest shame—*Bring them fiddles and guitars with y'all next time, and we'll have ourselves a regular honky-tonk!*

Their music burned like fireweed down the hall to our bedroom at night; in the morning, fast jigs and slow reels echoed through our day-dreams. While Ma worked her shifts in town, Harley and I stayed home and explored our land's twenty acres, learned the ins and outs of its crazed wheat fields and dry river gullies. Sometimes we spent hours, days, searching the flat land for Panagonquin treasure. Empty-handed we ran as far from the highway as our short legs could take us; took shelter in copses of birch and sycamore; made bracelets from wisps of white bark. Around us Chinook winds whistled through parched branches, told us our fortunes in the language of dried autumn leaves.

As the oldest, it was only right that I'd watch the kids, keep them from climbing too high or falling off edges. Feed them when they were hungry, bandage their skinned knees. I didn't mind. Most of the time, it was no more trouble than caring for puppies.

On burning summer days, when the sky stretched along with the hours and scalded air leached clouds from the endless blue, we'd stay inside. Harl hated being cooped up—his skin was baked brown as clay from all his time outdoors—but even he'd settle down if it meant Ma would tell us tales of our seafaring ancestors, folk whose ships had led them astray, stranding us in this landlocked county. He loved those ones most, Banjo's son. Stories of heroes and betrayals. Of men thriving against all odds.

The way I remember it, Banjo mostly observed all this without comment. He wasn't fussed about what we wore, or that we didn't go to school—said he reckoned a lady with Ma's talents was well suited for teaching her own children. With Banjo, Ma never had to worry about being contradicted or criticized. Not so she could hear it, anyway. He was easy to smile when the mood struck, open with his affections—even with me, his brother's daughter. Even with Bethany, who was born a year after he and Ma split the first time. And so too with Miah, who followed her sister into this world ten months after Banjo's boots found their way back to our porch. Yes, even Miah got her share of his love, though her black hair and tawny coloring screamed she wasn't of his stock. Dandling the brown babe on his knee, Banjo never said a word: the grins she and Ma wore all his doing.

Sometimes, that was enough.

When it wasn't, his opinions were no louder than the front door hinges squeaking open. Quiet as footfalls receding down the gravel path to the highway.

"Wendy's dress fits you pretty nice," he says now, trying small talk.

It doesn't. The collar is too high for my neck. I have to wear it open, ruining the aesthetic of having a long line of buttons up the front. The bodice and sleeves hang loose, emphasizing the swell of my belly, the sag in my bust, the scrawniness of my arms. And I'm swimming in heavy red drapery, skirts swinging too low around my distended waist. With her curves and her deep brown hair, Ma could pull this dress off. But after so long with Mister Pérouse, I know I'll never again wear her creations comfortably.

"She seemed so upset . . . I thought it might help her relax." As if, after three years, I could've zipped back into her life like nothing had happened between costume changes. I look down and shrug. "And you don't notice her blood as much on this fabric."

He raises his eyebrows. I tell him Ma wore this dress when she revealed what it was to be a woman in our family. Fabric red as the moon bloods she told me to tuck away where no one could touch them. *Don't tell a soul where you hid them,* she'd said, handing me rags for the task. *Out here, blood is power. It ain't just a bond. Ain't just what gave you my eyes and Harl that great cleft in his chin.* Leaning so close I could smell her lavender soap, she took my hand, pressed until I felt the throb of her pulse. *There's folk out to take advantage of that red tide, baby. Wrong folk and cold. Keep them rags safe, like you do yer kin. Yer blood carries our secrets, our stories. Our future. Believe you me; it's gonna hold our memories long after my body is dust.*

"Well," Banjo says, shifting in his seat. His eyes trace the mess of Ma's mouth. His hands clench to keep from wringing the blood-soaked cotton stuffed between her gums, to keep from wiping and wiping until her face is clean. "I s'pose I should take her. Keep her from turning to dust too soon, hey?"

He doesn't smile though his tone is friendly. I hold his gaze, lock onto it.

"Not yet," I say, getting my thoughts in order, my voice under control. "I need to tell you this. My tongue—my lips need to shape these words, need to push them out. I can't send it in a letter. Paper is too flimsy to carry the weight of Ma's head in my lap, the history in my belly." I tear open the useless buttons on my bodice, lift my camisole to reveal scars dotting my swollen abdomen. Dozens of puncture wounds scabbed over, raised in tiny red welts. Anyone can see the nape of my neck is unblemished, smooth as a pearl. My stomach tells a different story.

One shaped by the teeth of strange children.

"For three years I've told you what's happened. You, Ma, and Jez. In my head I've rehearsed, imagined how I'd explain where I've been, what I've done. What's been done to me." I wish I had that drink now. My mouth is so dry, my voice already breaking. "And now you're here. Bethany and Miah—and Harl, poor stupid Harl—they may never get a chance like this. So you'll wait, and maybe you'll judge."

Again, I take in the sight of Ma nestled against my pregnant belly and I almost can't say, "But no matter what, you won't end up like us."

He opens his mouth and I cut him off.

"Stop. Before you take or lay blame, sit here a spell and listen."

Listen.

They came for us at night.

Mister Pérouse shook me from a dream. The light from his candle obscured my vision. My head was bleary with sleep, so what I saw after I'd rubbed my eyes didn't make much sense. Strangers, two men and an old woman, were leaning over the children's beds. They were pressing their faces too close to Harl's; to Bethany's; to Miah's. Each adult paired with one child, as though whispering secrets into their ears, or nuzzling their necks so they'd laugh. But there was no laughter, no talking. More like a snuffling, a smacking, accompanied by the kids' night-time sighs.

"How are you feeling, *chérie*?" Mister Pérouse's voice ruffled like pages in a book. His breath smelled of roast lamb.

"What?"

"Are you well?" He brushed my forehead with his fingertips. I flinched from the cold of his hand, not from his touch. It felt like months and months had passed since Harl and I'd first seen him from our hidey-hole in the pantry; in that time he'd become Ma's favorite evening visitor. With his wan coloring and milkweed hair, he was a hit at her parties—he had no need for makeup or wigs. He wasn't stingy with the grog either, though he rarely drank. And while he always left in the wee hours of night, more than one morning greeted us with a gold-toothed smile when we found the coins he'd left behind for our trouble.

"Leave it to an out-of-towner to show us locals how to treat a host," Ma had said, the only time she commented on Mister Pérouse's contributions. "Ain't no hick 'round these parts would spare a crust for a starving man unless he were kin."

That didn't stop her from inviting these hicks to her shindigs, of course. But from then on she kept the newest and best apparel aside for Mister Pérouse: a square-cut velvet waistcoat belted with a fringed sash, tied in a drooping bow; ribbed leggings tucked into high boots; a lacy cravat spilling from his collar; a floor-length, hoodless mantle worn open on the shoulders. All of which, apart from the blue-black cloak, were the fine gray of sodden ash.

Mister Pérouse fired questions at me. "Does your head hurt? *Mal au ventre?* Can you sit up?" He stroked my cheeks with the back of his hand, then took hold of my chin and forced me to look directly at him. His irises were pink in the candlelight, his lashes long and white. Over his costume he wore the rancher's coat Ma had made for him when she learned he dealt in livestock.

"Ma?" The strangers were lifting my brother and sisters from their beds, carrying them like sacks of spuds over their shoulders. I tried to turn my head to see where they were being taken, but Mister Pérouse's fingers were bands of iron around my jaw.

"*Elle est malade, chérie*—she has come down very sick," he said. And then I heard her groans through the wall between our rooms. Her head knocking against the plaster. The bedsprings squeaking as she thrashed. Her cries, muffled, turning to whimpers. A man's rumbling voice, deep and close, strained as though struggling to speak. "*Attends,*" I think he said, I think he growled. "Hold still and take it," he said, and other things I couldn't quite understand.

My confusion must have been obvious. "I've summoned a doctor to inspect her," Mister Pérouse said. "He'll see to her, *ne t'inquiète pas.*"

The words didn't sound right, but he was so earnest I couldn't *not* believe him.

"It's a miracle you haven't fallen ill, Ada." He released my chin, pulled back the covers. Immediately I started shivering. "The children are all afflicted, though nowhere near as badly as your mother." I straightened my thin cotton shift while he smiled down at me. His gaze lingered as I searched for my slippers. "There's hope for them yet, but I'll need your help."

"I gots to piss," I said, though it wasn't strictly true. My bloods were coming; I could feel their arrival as a pain in my lower back, a warm ache in my belly. I wanted to check they hadn't started yet.

"No time," he replied. "Come along, quickly."

I followed him past Ma's room—dead quiet now—to the lounge. Weird light streamed through the windows and the open front door, casting odd shadows across the room, tricking my eyes into seeing headstones instead of dining chairs, coffins instead of empty couches. Most times I'd find at least one or two of the neighbors snoring there come morning, sleeping off the bourbon and gin I could still smell in the air. But maybe they'd had less to drink, or they'd been called home early; either way, the only ones left that evening were Mister Pérouse and his gang.

"I'm gonna fetch my coat," I said. Mister Pérouse shook his head. "Take nothing with you, *ma chère*. We don't know what's contaminated." He pulled me behind him, offering reassurances that things would be better tomorrow. Outside, the high-beams of his black four-wheel drive, his companions' sedans and pickup trucks, illuminated the house in a way I hadn't seen before. My home looked so small, so forlorn in that artificial glare. Crouched in the spotlight, it cowered from menacing night.

If only Harl was awake, I thought, watching as he was buckled into the vehicle's back seat. *He always talks about riding in cars.*

"Get in the front," Mister Pérouse said, opening the door for me. The seats were leather, so cold they felt slimy, and the interior smelled of smoke and plastic. The odor was suffocating. I wanted to open a window but couldn't figure out how to work the controls. Mister Pérouse walked around to the driver's side while giving his friends orders, strobing the headlights with his movements.

"He's not a ghost," I said to Harl, who couldn't care less, wrapped as he was in the ignorance of sleep. Directly behind me, Nellie and Ike Porter were huddled beneath a blanket, their rosy-cheeked faces now blank with illness. Like Harl, the flax farmer's kids were unconscious, their necks smeared with red.

Mister Pérouse slid into the cab beside me and closed the door. "Ain't no one healthy no more?" I asked. He ignored the question, rolled down his window with ease, and spoke to the tall splotchy-faced man waiting in the driveway.

"Jacques, drop by the farmstead two kilometers north. See who's there then meet Théo at—" He turned to me, "What is the name of that couple, Ada? The ones who dip the *chandelles* for your mother?"

"Allambee."

"*Ah, oui.*" He directed his attention back out the window and pointed at the squat, bald man who still cradled Bethany in his arms. "Join Théo at the Allambee farm. I'll see you back at the Haven before dawn."

Without a word, they accepted his directions and got into their cars. "Arianne," Mister Pérouse continued, "go inside and collect the doctor. He's done all he can for tonight."

The old woman nodded. As her head bobbed up and down, the light played across her features: one moment she was wrinkled, the next smooth. A half-smirking, half-frowning Janus face that gave me chills as it glared first at me, then at Miah in the sedan's passenger seat.

"Can't we say goodbye 'fore we go? Ma'll flip her top if she don't know where we gone."

"*Non.*" Mister Pérouse rolled up his window, cutting off the fresh breeze that was helping to clear my head. Reaching over, he patted my knee. My stomach cramped, and I felt a dampness, a slickness in my knickers. "It's best if we leave her alone. But tomorrow." He stopped, sniffed the air, stared at my legs, my hands fidgeting in my lap. "Tomorrow," he repeated, "things will be different."

Tears welled in my eyes as the pain in my belly increased. I looked down and two salty drops plinked onto my nightie. I hoped I hadn't stained the seat with my blood—how could I hide leather upholstery? I hoped it hadn't spread beyond my shift, beyond my skin. Ma would be so disappointed.

"I'm sorry," I mumbled.

Again, Mister Pérouse patted my knee. Patted and patted, the motion fervent and hypnotic. He licked his lips, and tore his gaze away with visible effort.

Things changed the next morning, but not for the better.

The sun was inching over the horizon by the time we arrived at Mister Pérouse's compound. There were no houses around, no farmsteads. The land here was untilled, untenable: skeletons of crops long gone to seed stretched as far as I could see, dotted here and there with sentinel trees and shacks even hobos would disdain. Anyone with a mind for survival long ago followed the highway, arrow-straight and pointing the only way out of here. A wall rose ten meters high and ran a jagged loop around the property, too long for me to judge its distance at this early hour. Layers of grime outlined its rough sandstone surface, the lower half shadowed further with soot. The gatehouse, smooth white plaster cornered with chunky yellow bricks, was dingy with dirt. Rows of barred and blackened windows perforated the walls, bracketing a tall set of arched double doors.

I knuckled my eyes as Mister Pérouse hefted Harley over his shoulder, leaving the Porter kids in the backseat for the moment. Grit and sleep blurred my sight as I followed him into the dark gatehouse, then beyond into a courtyard that smelled dank with an undertone of manure. Inside, peak-roofed walkways connected a series of wooden buildings, all bleached pale gray and pocked with patches of silver-green lichen. I could see the bottom half of an old barn, empty of horses, slumping close on our left; three large pens to our right, in which dozens of hogs lolled, grunting as they slept; five or six little shacks a few hundred meters away, their windows dark and chimneys cold. Pigeons cooed from the rafters overhead, dropping feathers and dead spiders as we passed beneath. I kept my head low, and prayed we wouldn't emerge covered in droppings. At the far end of the promenade down which Mister Pérouse led us, the first story of the largest mansion—or warehouse? I couldn't tell which—I had ever seen blocked my view of anything else.

I stepped off the path and into the yard as dawn licked red streaks across the building. Caught a glimpse of three or four more hulking stories; rectangular windows boarded up; a crooked weathervane squeaking a slow circle above a gable—then Mister Pérouse hauled me back into the shadows.

"I weren't dallying," I said, but he silenced me with a glance. Behind us, the gatehouse door opened and I could hear that Arianne-woman as she spoke to the doctor; her voice grating across my soul. I was almost overwhelmed by an urge to hide behind Mister Pérouse's thick cloak. Instead, I patted Harley's back to reassure him everything was fine; straightened my shoulders as the great door clanged shut. The sound of iron bolts shunting into place rang across the courtyard.

I swallowed tears and dust. My neck was stiff from sleeping upright, my heart stiffer at the thought of Ma sick and alone at home.

"It's rude to linger in doorways," Mister Pérouse said, striding past. "Come."

Eventually I got used to the command in his tone, but right then it came as a surprise. As long as I'd known him he'd always been, if not jolly, at least pleasant. Friendly in that way adults are with children who aren't their own: familiar and a little bit fake. His presence used to set us at ease—we knew he'd make Ma happy.

But this Mister Pérouse was different. This version showed an interest that demanded attention. He made my stomach roil.

Inside the hallway stretched from left to right, describing the Haven's perimeter instead of plunging straight into its heart. We crossed it in no more than ten steps, the sound of our footfalls petering out before reaching its ends. Mister Pérouse took me by the hand. Led me into a room resounding with the whisperings of children.

Large enough to house at least three barns end to end, it nevertheless felt claustrophobic as soon as Mister Pérouse closed the doors behind us. Columns ran in arches around its border, dividing the space into cloisters. Single beds with woolen blankets and plain pillows were tucked behind these pillars, placed in orderly lines against the chocolate brown walls, leaving the larger, central part of the room free. All around us snippets of sound murmured up to the ceiling, four stories above our heads. Shuttered galleries climbed the walls, gazed blindly down on two long refectory tables running lengthwise down the center of a hardwood floor. Skylights perforating the ceiling would have brightened the place enormously had they not been covered in cardboard. Instead, dim light issued from oil lamps dangling from chains and dotting the tabletops.

At the back, three groups of school desks, a dozen at least, were arranged in rough circles. A stern-looking man slipped into the room, and with a nod from Mister Pérouse locked the door. He crossed to consult a young girl who'd obviously been supervising the students in his absence; his tweed jacket, matching pants, and bowler hat could've easily been rented at Ma's shop. One by one, the kids sitting or standing there noticed our entrance. Conversations hushed. Pencils and books hung forgotten in hands that had stopped tidying up. Pink irises shone as they all openly stared.

"Good morning, children." Mister Pérouse waited until he had everyone's attention. "How go the lessons? Diction? Vocabulary? Memory-drills? I trust you've all had a productive night."

A babble of replies, all positive, filled our ears. At the sound of so many voices, Harley lifted his head, and looked blearily at our surroundings.

"Ma?" he croaked.

I reached up and absentmindedly patted my brother's cheek while trying not to goggle at the other kids. Bright eyes ringed with dark circles were worn all around; hair slicked colorless with grease; skin the hue of old lard. To someone accustomed to unique outfits, bright fabrics, elaborate headwear, the *sameness* of their features, the sloppiness of their clothes, was breathtaking. Here it was dull tartan dresses for the girls, short pants and collared shirts for the boys. On the far wall, boxy jackets hung neglected on hooks, dust lying thick across their shoulders. No jewelry to speak of. No hats.

"Good," Mister Pérouse continued, his breath fogging in the chill air. "We've been blessed with six new souls today—and if all goes well Jacques and Théo should return with more. For now, Doctor Jeffries, I'll trust you to amend your lessons to accommodate five extra pupils. Initiate them quickly: these children have been unschooled for far too long."

"I know what I'm doing, Anton."

Mister Pérouse conceded the point with a tilt of his head, but still proceeded with his instructions. "No field trips until they are made familiar with the curriculum, *d'accord*? *Bon*. Now, as for the rest of you, allow me to introduce Harold *et* Adelaide."

My heart stopped at the names. I was sure he knew us better than that.

"Excuse me, sir," I said, shivering with more than cold. Ma taught me always to be polite, especially when correcting someone's mistake. "That's *Harley* and I'm *Ada*."

Mister Pérouse's only reaction was to adjust his hold on Harl, and place a heavy hand on my shoulder. "The sun is well up, children. Help get Harold ready for bed. The Haven is his home now: make him welcome. Adelaide, this way."

My feet were rooted to the floor as Harl was passed from Mister Pérouse to a boy a year or two older than me. Everything about him was lanky: limbs, earlobes, unkempt fringe. He carried my brother in arms that looked like bone sheathed in tissue, too weak even for such a light burden. But when he smiled his teeth were overly long. Sharp and white. The cleanest things in the room.

A panel stood open in the far wall, not so much a door as a breach in the room's symmetry. Mister Pérouse drew me through it, then I was led down a narrow hallway. Small electric lights nestled in wall sconces, illuminating little but a series of old photographs—all depicting my guide standing proudly beside class after class of the Haven's students. His steps were assured even in the darkness between lamps; I knew he could run these corridors blindfolded, if necessary. I stumbled in the black, and was pathetically grateful for the bulbs' small haloes. I needed their comfort.

It's weird how, in moments of panic, our minds focus on absurdities. Though my pulse raced and my throat cramped from holding back tears, I found myself wondering why they'd used plastic lights shaped like candlesticks; why they'd topped them with glass flames. Why not use real candles? And if they could see fine without them, why turn the things on? Except to allow black-and-white children, their faces so like the ones

I'd just met they could have been one and the same, to follow me with their eyes as we sped past. They watched, expressionless, organized and catalogued in their wooden frames, as my feet were dragged along grooves their soles had worn in the floor.

Mister Pérouse's apartments were at the far end of the manse. Up three flights of stairs, along the hall, and back down so many steps we might have ended up in the basement. My legs were shaking by the time we arrived; blood dripped down my thighs. A receiving room, a study, a chambermaid's cupboard, and a master bedroom with modern en suite were all barricaded behind a thick oak door, secured with a brass deadbolt. The costumes he'd worn to Ma's parties spilled from a wardrobe, littered his bed. Their fine fabric chafed my skin when he threw me upon them. When he showed me, in no uncertain terms, what my role was to be in this household.

I flailed and kicked. My screams, half-formed and breathless; wrists trapped in the vice of his hands. I butted my head against his until my skull ached, but he simply leaned back, waited for me to tire. He used the advantage years of practice had given him, pinning me down with his torso. Hungry saliva dripped on my cheek, trickled down my neck.

"Mama, Mama, Mama," I cried, as he shoved my nightie up, pulled my drawers down, revealed the mess of blood between my legs. He wriggled more firmly on top of me, pressed my arcing back flat with his weight, then slid down my body until his face was in line with my crotch.

"Your mother is dead," he said, matter-of-factly. His tongue, rough as a cat's, began to rasp along my inner thighs.

No. The fight, the life went out of me. *She can't be.* I'd squeezed my eyes shut, but now they flew open. My mind was blank, my mind raced. I looked up, not down. Ma's voice rang in my ears, telling Harley tales. The cinnamon smell of her breakfast oatmeal filled my nostrils—not sweat, not blood, not Mister Pérouse's lamb-carcass breath. In my mouth, raspberry cordial laced with brandy; the drink Ma gave me the first time I'd hidden my blood-soaked rags. *No, no, no.* I looked up, *stared* up. A watermark shaped like our state stained the ceiling. I tried to pinpoint the county where I grew up—a splotch of mold covered it. Covered Ma. I cried out—

Not dead.

I didn't look down; wouldn't. In my mind I saw Mister Pérouse's chin drip with my blood. Saw his teeth lengthen, glistening and red. Felt them pierce. The prod of his tongue. Sucking, drinking deep. Taking his fill.

Everything was silent.

A tornado howled through the room.

Face contorted, mouth shaped words. Expression evangelical, like Bible-bashers Ma sent from our door each Sunday. Still wearing the cowboy coat she'd made, he slithered back on top. Nicked the tip of his penis. Smeared his blood. Mixed it with mine.

Searing pain to dull throb. Breath whooshed out. In and out.

In and out.

His body preached at mine: I didn't hear a thing. I looked at the county lines overhead, traced their borders with my eyes.

No.

He grew stronger, stronger. Licked my jugular. Moaned. Didn't bite.

Numb, I watched us from the settee on the opposite side of the room. Looked at the spectacle we made on my mother's costumes. My legs like slabs of ham on the mattress. His hips twitching, plunging. My hands clenching, unclenching, clenching. Intent and inert.

Waited for him to finish. Waited for my spirit to return. Waited to feel.

Not dead.

I didn't see Harley or the girls for days afterwards. By then I was too tired to be scared for any of us.

Mister Pérouse kept me in his bedroom until my menses stopped flowing. Nightmares plagued me all day, then came to life at dusk. For five nights he drank his fill, reopened the thin cut on his cock, climbed on top of me. Humming all the while about a child born of blood. He rubbed my belly before pulling out, for luck or to mark his territory, or both.

Though they came knocking, claiming their turns with the "live one," Mister Pérouse wouldn't let Théo or Jacques in. "*Mais, monsieur,*" they'd protest, their voices muffled through the door. "Arianne hasn't bled for decades—"

My master wouldn't hear a word against her. "Patience, *les gars.* I won us three *filles* this time, *non?* The two youngest are yours—take them as gifts. *Pour vous remerciez.*"

The men said nothing.

"Aha," said Mister Pérouse, sighing, rolling off me. "You've opted for the weakling's fare—sucking a few hours' of youth from babes—and now you're here to challenge me? *Mais c'est drôle!* You want the Prime's share? You haven't the patience. *Mon dieu,* our houseful of little changed ones prove *you have not the patience.* A few short human years—what is that to us? A blink, no more—and Adelaide's sisters could have been yours for breeding. To start your own empires, *peut-être?* They've many years of blood in them, these girls; many chances of bearing true kin. Can't you see the benefit in that? Our numbers increased with children *born,* not simply *made?* Reinvigorating our bloodlines, *les gars.* Extending it, drawing power direct from the fountainhead. From our newborns right back to Adam's kin, *comprends?* Linked all the way back to the *source."*

I didn't hear the men's responses. My eyelids drooped; I pulled a chenille blanket up to still my shivering. If the past few evenings were any indication, Mister Pérouse would want another round with me before morning. I needed sleep more than information.

By the end of the week my master looked healthier, stronger. Ten years younger, more than fit to squash Jacques and Théo if they razzed him without the protection of three inches of oak. His back was straight, step springy, as he set me in the chambermaid's closet, and told me to get cleaned up for school.

"You must learn to speak properly, Adelaide, if you are to raise our child to prominence. I will not have my heir speaking like a *pécore* for all his mother's failings. Fine soaps will only scrub so much of the yokel from you, *chèrie."*

I didn't want to wash, I wanted to go home. But the windows were blocked, the outer doors bolted; my freedom subject to Mister Pérouse's whim. And for the first time since my arrival he fancied I could be let out. I could see other people. So I rubbed myself raw with the soap and sponge he provided, then slipped on a uniform so misshapen a hundred other girls might've worn it before. I folded my nightie and stuffed it beneath the low pallet I'd sleep on when my master had no other use for me. The shift was soiled and smelled rotten, but it was my last tie with Ma. I didn't want to look at it, couldn't bear to throw it away.

I don't know what happened to Harley's clothes. Like me, he was now dressed in a drab copy of the other children's outfits. Unlike me, he looked content to be so.

"You okay?" His neck was swaddled with bandages, and the sun was fading from his skin. Veins were visible in his eyelids and temples and he smelled of sour milk. I brushed my hand through his hair, trying to ignore the hints of grease I found there, and pulled him close. He returned my embrace quickly then stepped away, too embarrassed to be seen hugging his sister with so many eyes watching. The other children were too occupied with their tasks to notice. Some recited poems in my master's language; some tidied the beds, then arranged folding screens to separate sleep and work areas; some clambered high up the walls, scaling the bricks from gallery to gallery under Doctor Jeffries' watchful eye. No matter how hard I tried, I couldn't see any ropes. Catching my perplexed gaze, Harley shrugged and rubbed his hand along his jaw, so much like his father it hurt.

"Mister told us about Ma," he said. "Beth and Miah ain't took it so good—Miss Arianne gave them medicines so's they'd calm down. They're a lot better now, though."

"And you?" I asked.

Again, that shrug. Who was this boy? The Harl I knew got fired up if he didn't get his way; if he thought Ma spent more time with us girls than with him. And now that she's dead? A shrug. It didn't make sense.

"My gums is sore," he said, almost sheepishly.

"Give us a look." To my surprise, he peeled back his lips and opened his mouth. I couldn't trust what I saw: it wasn't bright enough where we were standing. I drew Harl over to the first long dining table, sat him close to the lamp. The results were the same.

His incisors, top and bottom, were more than twice their usual length. I explored their rough edges, hoping touch would prove their appearance a trick of the light.

Gently, I positioned my forefinger behind the tooth and pulled towards me. It had grown far too sharp, far too long. I tried again, just to be sure it was real, and as I did so a pearl of creamy liquid, like snake venom or dandelion milk, beaded on my fingertip.

"That hurt?" I asked, tugging, watching the drop grow fat and heavy. The syrup spilled over, soon began marbling with red. Harley's blood oozed down the length of my finger and pooled, ghosted with white fluid, in my palm.

"Nuh." He shook his head, unintentionally snicking my digit in the process.

"Watch it," I said, snatching my hand away, sucking to stem the flow—

—*being leached from my neck. No: Harley's neck. Energy sapping from my body, pulsating. Teeth stinging like horseflies in the dip beside my collarbone, the crook of my elbow. Smiling faces, kissing, drinking. "He tastes like swimming," a high voice says. That's Nellie Porter, maybe. Or Ike. No: Ike's at my feet, draining the webbing between my toes. They like me, I think—Harl thinks: and, They need me. I'm warm, so warm the room is fuzzy. I'm sleepy, so sleepy. I can hardly feel the table beneath my back. My plate is broken; rare beef from dinner squelches under my hip. "He tastes like sunshine," says Alistair. I giggle. My friend is giving me a hickey, and now there's a fire in my belly. A hunger. I sit up, nip him on the shoulder. Barely break the skin. "That's enough." Doctor Jeffries claps, whistles till the tingling stops. "End of lesson." The small mouths pull away, melt into the room's dim corners. The doctor keeps Ike and Alistair back. "What have I told you? Stun with the jus; drink only enough to make you feel strong; bite hard to inject your charge. Don't be greedy: no killings within the Haven." My head is woozy, I can't lift it to see where they've gone. Too heavy. "No killings in the family—"*

"When did this happen?"

Harley looked at me like I'd gone crazy. "What?"

"This—" I licked the last trace of Harley's venom-laced blood from my finger. "*This.*" I yawned, felt a prickling in my lips. "The biting, them other kids—"

"Oh, that." Harl crossed his arms, flicked a lock of hair from his eyes. "Ain't nothing. You know, it happens."

I wasn't convinced by his cool demeanor. Again, I tasted the blood and milk from Harl's tooth, and it hit me like a kick to the ribs. The scent of cedar and hot dirt. Bullfrogs at the bottom of gullies on our land like croaking men clearing their throats. Ma's chamomile shampoo. Her soft singing lifted on bathroom steam. Pure, unrefined memories of home. The other children had tasted these moments. Ingested them. And Harl hadn't stopped them.

"I can't believe you'd let them do that to you," I hissed, emphasizing the word *let*. "You ain't even tried to stop them—not even a little bit!"

Harl sighed, and for the third time his shoulders rose and fell noncommittally. He looked empty. Emptier. "I can't always fight, Ada. Not always."

Beth kicked me in the shins when I took her face in my hands, drew her mouth to mine, and sucked blood and venom from her teeth. Where Harl's fangs had grown close together, adding a rat's angular profile to his already narrow features, Beth's had sprouted from her canines. Blunt but strong. When the hanging lights reflected in her dark eyes, she was no longer a seven-year-old girl but a feral cat.

I dragged her behind a folding screen, checked that no one could see us, and sat her down on the foot of a cot.

"This ain't—*isn't*—my bed, Ada. I mean, Adelaide. Mine's over there—"

"Quiet," I hissed, grabbing her face again and drinking. I stopped the instant the flavor of her memories shifted from ash to honey, when the liquid was more red than clear. My mouth was numb from her poison; it itched down my throat, made me woozy. Beth bit my lip as I pulled away—then immediately asked what had happened, why was there blood on my chin? Exhaling, I swallowed visions of her and Miah smothered in a swarm of grabbing hands; suckling at Arianne's shriveled neck and breasts. Something was missing, and it wasn't just my sister's memory of the past thirty seconds.

There was no essence of fear. Not in Beth, not in Harl. Tinges of sorrow seasoned the cloudy blood I drank, yet it wasn't overwhelming. It wasn't purely their own. They felt Ma's loss, I could taste it. But not acutely, not like I did. That sadness was buried in them, beneath dozens of other, foreign sadnesses. Those they'd adopted from their new playmates.

For a few moments Beth was bright and happy, the way she'd always been at home, and I knew it was because of me. When she sat on my lap, wrapping her scrawny arms around my waist, the hug she gave was genuine. Threading her fingers through my hair, she seemed content. Harley loitered by the closest pillar and watched us for a while, not joining in but not discouraging. I wanted to ask him to come sit with us, to hide beneath the blankets, to help keep the ghosts at bay.

But at that moment Arianne strode past a gap between the screens concealing us from the common room, leading by the hand the boy who'd carried Harley the day we'd arrived. His eyes were glazed, a silly smile plastered on his face. His feet scuffled along the floor as though too heavy to lift.

Four steps later, the clunking of Arianne's heels stopped. Four more steps brought her back, her glare so sharp I winced. She released her companion's hand, then pushed the screen away, sending it clattering to the floor.

"*Va t'en!*" she growled at Beth, her gaze never leaving mine.

She wrenched Beth from my lap, slapped her bottom. "Go!"

Harley shrank from Arianne's wrath, inched away to avoid drawing her attention. As it was, he could have tap-danced and she wouldn't have noticed: her crimson-eyed stare was reserved for me.

"Stay away, you *espèce de salope*! You'll have your own soon enough—these are not for you."

I rose clumsily. "Arianne—"

She held up her hand to silence me. "*Non*—not a word, *petite bête*. The classroom, you can enter. Do not come behind here again."

As though on cue, Doctor Jeffries called us to our lessons. Diction and composition first; then while the other children climbed, learned techniques of stealth, and practiced bleeding each other on the table, I was isolated from the group. Taught to pore over books tracing the history of Mister Pérouse's people. By the time the tutorials were over, I was shaken—and Beth's posture had stiffened. When I crossed to her circle of desks, she looked at me as she would a stranger. Her mouth twitched, barely suppressing a hiss.

Harl had drifted away to join Alistair and the other boys. His footsteps already more like floating than walking.

For the next two years I did what I could for Harley and the girls. I'd milk them whenever they let me; whenever Arianne was away; whenever Mister Pérouse released me from our rooms. I dreaded the coming of my bloods, not because it meant I'd have to endure my master's attentions—these moon-time visits were exercises in stamina on his part, and I'd become expert at *being* and *not being* there while they lasted—but because it meant I was kept away from the kids.

Twice it seemed Mister Pérouse's work had paid off: my periods stopped, the second time for twelve weeks. My master, already confident in his role as Prime, now strutted like a peacock as he gave Théo and Jacques their instructions; directing them to tackle Tapekwa County next, to find themselves suitable mates in Napanee. To steal farmers' young, the more isolated the better, to become pupils of Mister Pérouse's *school*. Fatherhood, it seemed, made him benevolent.

He let me wander wherever I wanted, the child in my womb almost as good as a skeleton key. Whispers followed me as I roamed the hallways, or dropped in on Doctor Jeffries' classes. "Breeder," the children would say, perhaps at Arianne's bidding. Perhaps not: often the jealousy in their words rang too true to be second-hand. "Breeding *enculeuse*." They taunted me for doing what they couldn't yet do—their metabolisms so slow now fifty years would pass before they hit puberty. Sometimes I think Harley joined in, just to be one of the crowd. But with Mister Pérouse's spawn in my belly, none of them could do more than jeer. Even Arianne was compelled to leave me alone. And when her back was turned, I'd inevitably make my way to one of two places: the front doors, to test the locks; or the dormitory behind the screens, to draw poison from my sisters' mouths.

In these quiet moments, the girls would become themselves again; all smiles, crass jokes, and innocence. Hearing them giggle, anxiety would seep from my body and I'd weep with relief.

At the Haven, joys like these were always short-lived.

Soon it became clear that my understanding of the girls' happiness didn't quite match their reality. Though he wouldn't admit it, Harley could remember our other life: Ma and her friends, the itch of newly sewn garments, the brush of wind on our sunburnt faces. But Miah? She was three when we came here. Now five, she'd spent nearly half her life in this place. *This* was what she knew, *this* was her home. No doubt she'd be as fond of the fields and the sun as she would a stake through her heart. She thought it a game when I drew sap from her baby teeth, a romp like the ones she enjoyed with the other kids. She didn't know any different: she'd snap at my cheeks, then wait for my reaction, just as she would when seeking her classmates' approval. None of the children looked more than a week or two older than when we first arrived, while I continued to grow up as well as out. Beth and Miah laughed at the changes in my height and figure—and when they did, I'd pluck at their fangs until my fingers were thick with scratches. Always, I came away from these meetings coughing up dust.

I didn't realize I could give something back, return parts of their memories, until I miscarried the second time. Arianne had sniffed the truth of my loss before I was aware of it myself—her knowing laugh was triumphant and bitter. Her teeth were so sharp; her hunger was sharper. The scent of my baby's death beguiled her. She followed me so close, waiting for the blood to flow, that Mister Pérouse sequestered me in his rooms three days early.

The pain of expelling the fetus kept me bedridden that whole time.

My master's old mattress had long ago conformed to my shape. I aligned my back with the contour earlier versions of me had made, and tried to ignore the sound of his jaw cracking as he devoured the remnants of our failure. I imagined it was all the same to him; he benefitted whether the child stayed in my belly or was digested in his. I convinced myself he wouldn't be angry for something beyond my control. And for a moment, I almost believed it.

Sucking the blood off his fingers, Mister Pérouse's face was pure joy, almost handsome. He actually smiled as he leaned back. I didn't know how to react. Then he exhaled, and disappeared.

Disappeared.

Two years ago, I'd have leapt from the bed right then. Tried my hand at the door, tried anything to get free. Now I was smarter—I knew this wasn't the right time. He'd never done this before, never just dropped out of sight, but he wouldn't have left me this way. I froze while my gaze darted like a frightened goldfish. *That's it.*

Body tense, I sat up, suddenly gasping. *He's not gone.*

I can still hear him breathing.

I felt his weight on the mattress before I saw his shadow reappear, growing from pale gray to charcoal across the floor, his youthful features brightening back into view.

"*Merveilleux,*" he whispered, actually grinning. "See what we can do, Adelaide? The two of us together?"

I tried to smile, I honestly did. But if devouring the hint of a child meant he could vanish at will, what would happen when I carried one to term...

My master's expression darkened at my silence. He fingered the puck-ered wounds his teeth had left; two deep blots of red, oozing far below my navel. In that instant, he looked so much like Arianne I gasped.

"Stay away from those children," he said, remnants of my milkings rancid on his breath.

"I wi—" He crushed the lie from my mouth, his kiss a punishment not a reward. Out of habit, I ran my tongue up and down sharp fangs, sucked. He gouged at the insides of my lip, pierced the soft palate, scraped until blood from my shredded gums mingled with that from my womb. Blended with the potent serum stretching like cobwebs from the tips of his teeth.

Oh, what a feast of visions.

In his mouth I tasted incoherent feathers of our unborn baby's thoughts. I sampled my agony, distilled in his venom. But there was more, much more: Miah's giggles as Ma tickled her feet; Beth's disappoint-ment when the birthday cake she'd baked for me sank in the middle, a cool draught from the chimney flue ruining her hard work; and Harley, confident as only ten-year-old boys can be, leaping from high rocks into the black waters of a quarry on the edge of our property. Their joy, their recollections, trapped in Mister Pérouse's bloodstream.

He's bitten them, I thought, and in the same instant, *I've tasted these moments in their teeth.*

Which did he get from their necks? Which from the depths of my belly?

My head spun with the power of his sedative, but I lapped at his fangs until my jaw ached. I swallowed all the memories he'd stolen. Kept drinking until their tone changed, deepened. Aged with Mister Pérouse's years. I gulped his love for Arianne, as a mother or wife I couldn't tell; slurped the certainty that Théo—his own cousin!—was kept close for enmity more than friendship; savored all the small vipers in Doctor Jeffries' schoolroom, now knowing they were offspring he had *made* not *fathered*. Just like Harley, me and the girls, they all came from poor families, single mothers—humans my master deigned unworthy of raising children. I drank it all in, this and more, until I was too drowsy to move. Until all I could feel was a weight like lead in my guts.

I did as my master bid for several weeks, though I would've rebelled given the chance. If Mister Pérouse could leach the children's blood and *jus* from my stomach, I realized, they could do the same. I could rescue their memories, I knew it.

I could return them. *Re-turn them.*

So I kissed Mister Pérouse, devoured him whenever he came close enough to bite. Let him take my interest as affection, as enthusiasm, as a gesture of reconciliation; let him think I was grateful for being his brood mare. I didn't care, so long as his mouth was on mine and my family's history trickling down my throat.

In those moments, I closed my eyes and imagined the sensation of Beth and Miah's tiny bites as they drank down forgotten stories. But no matter how hard I tried, I couldn't picture Harley joining in.

That image of my sisters sustained me for five months. I tried reading to pass the time but the books cluttering Mister Pérouse's apartments were failed distractions; their plots like snowflakes melting in my fevered mind. I hardly remembered a word. Always I thought of the girls as the days turned to weeks, refined my plan until the flutter of kicks in my womb drove me to act. I needed fresh air if this third baby was to survive; I needed to move. More than anything, I needed to see if I was right.

When Théo delivered my food tray, as he had morning after morning, I stopped him before he went to bed.

Lifting my hand from his sleeve as though it were infected, he sneered at my belly. "You think to keep this one, *non*?"

"She'll survive," I agreed, positive my child was a girl. I straightened into every inch of my height, a head taller than Théo. Looking down, I met his gaze and held it. A shadow fell across his face. He tilted his bald head, stared up at me with magpie eyes. If I'd flinched then, the moment would've been broken, my opportunity lost. But though I spoke quickly, my voice was steady. "I can barely breathe in here—" Carefully timed pause. "You don't know what it's like to be trapped, Théo."

He didn't blink. A slight frown furrowed his forehead. Of course he knew what it was to be held unwillingly. He'd been here three times longer than I'd lived. Was that enough to poison his mind? Enough to convince him to let me out? Maybe not, but I was willing to risk it. Even those whose hearts have stopped beating must *feel*, sometimes. Loneliness isn't governed by the warmth in our veins.

"I just need to see my family," I said. "I'll come right back—I just want to kiss them goodnight."

Théo snorted. "*Sensiblerie*. Stupid girl, what do I care for family?"

Silently, I wrapped my arms around myself and hunched. Tried to make myself look small and vulnerable. Again, Théo blew air from his lips; half laugh, half derision. I didn't respond, but sank to the edge of Mister Pérouse's bed as his cousin left the room. The door closed with a hollow clunk.

Floorboards creaked as he paused on the other side. The key slid in, scraped out.

There was no sound of bolts shifting home.

I waited a heartbeat, two; then sprang to my feet, crept to the door. Pressing my ear to the wood, I could hear the diminishing scuff of Théo's boots as he moved down the corridor. Away from me.

My pulse was so loud in my ears I couldn't tell if he'd actually gone or if it was a trick. Taking deep breaths, I steadied myself—or tried to. Of its own volition, my shaking hand moved to the doorknob, turned. Spots whirled in front of my eyes; the excitement was almost too much. Exhaling, I flung open the door.

I sped toward my sisters as though I were being chased.

They showed no delight in seeing me, not until I guided them away from Harley and the boys to the private corner where Beth's bed resided. Harl watched us pass but pretended not to: his back was too stiff, his laugh too loud to be natural. The girls didn't spare him a second look. Frantically, I pulled the screens to; quickly, so quickly. When I thought we were out of his sight, I raised my pinafore and urged my sisters to drink. Then, finally, they were all smiles. Voracious and thirsty.

Stretched out on Beth's quilt, I closed my eyes. Mister Pérouse rarely lifted my skirts higher than necessary; so unless they marred my neck or cleft, he wouldn't see any marks they made. I bit my tongue when their fangs perforated my belly. Again and again, their heads bobbed as they sought the sweetest blood I had to offer. I directed them around the places I thought my daughter lay curled—soon a double band of dripping holes was scratched beneath my ribcage. Time slowed. I floated on their quiet slurping, the musk of unwashed skin and blankets. I didn't have to force them off me; satiated, they stopped on their own. Looking at the mess of red pooled beneath me, soaked into mattress and clothes, I hoped they'd guzzled enough to remember.

For a moment, none of us spoke. Miah sniffed, went back for seconds. My heart sank. I couldn't bear to look at her, or at Beth. Couldn't see the forgetful glimmer in their eyes, the dew on their lips.

I'd done it for nothing. Risked everything for nothing.

"I've got to go." I swallowed the lump in my throat, and gently pushed to dislodge Miah. Tried to muster sufficient energy to stand. "Dawn's breaking: time for night creatures to go to sleep."

Warm tears spilled over my cheeks as Beth wriggled up beside me until her head was parallel with mine. Flinging an arm across my chest, she squeezed and said, "Tell us a story before you go. The one Ma always told. You know, with the crazy bird in the gumdrop tree? The one who cried and cried instead of laughed and laughed?"

"Okay," I said, though I could hardly speak for crying, hardly breathe for hugging. Beth's eyes had gone from pink to blue. Focused. Clearer than I'd seen them in two and a half years. A giggle burst from my throat, and its echo came from Beth's. Neither of us had heard that story since Miah was smaller than the baby inside me. My laughter died off as I looked at my youngest sister. When I began the tale, the pressure of her mouth at my waist increased. Nothing more.

"Once upon a time—"

"*Qu'est ce que tu fait?*"

Mister Pérouse's voice whipped me upright. In a blur he was upon me. His fingernails pierced the soft flesh in my upper arm; yanking me from the bed, he knocked the girls to the floor like ragdolls. Neither of them cried out: already the memories were fading from Beth's eyes. "It isn't enough!" My face hot with tears. "I need more time." But there was none to be had.

A fist slammed into my cheek. I stumbled, skinned my knees. He pulled me up, tearing my hair, my dress. Théo shook his head, pretended not to hear the commotion as he skittered up the far wall, taking refuge in a fourth-floor balcony. Arianne nodded at my master; with a lift of her eyebrow, beckoned him to visit her chamber after punishments had been meted. Few of Mister Pérouse's young flunkies paid any attention, no matter how hard I sobbed, nor how loudly I begged as he dragged me down the hallway. Except, that is, for Harley. Shuffling from foot to foot, he loitered just outside the *grande salle*. Like a puppy waiting to be let in after he'd done his business.

Like a messenger just returned from an errand.

Harl averted his eyes as we screamed past. Back to Mister Pérouse's apartments; back to thick musty draperies; back to stagnant air. I cried out and clawed at the wallpaper, at the doorframes, until my nails were split and bleeding. Harley followed, staring at his toes. My stomach churned with lava. Rage, not fear, filled my mouth. I spat at my brother, a big shining gob of hate.

The least I could do, the most I could do, was ruin the traitor's boots.

Rats crawled all over me.

Claws scritching, scratching; jaws squeaking like door hinges. Skittering across the storage room's cold concrete floor, they spoke with my brother's voice.

"Get up," they said. Thump, thump; a herd of them landed on my shoulder. Jump, jump; they urged me awake.

"Get up," they repeated. I didn't want to. My head was heavy, my lashes stuck together with the glue of dried tears. The bites on my stomach itched, already healing; the bruises Mister Pérouse had left on my face, thighs and buttocks throbbed. My ears rang with the sound of his blows, the echo of his words.

"*You think I've hidden you for my sake?*" Whack. "*Imbécile.*" Whack. "*Idiot.*" Pause. "*I've done this for you,*" whack, "*not me.*" Whack, whack. "*For the baby.*" Whack. Whack. Whack. "*He'll not be born for years if you're turned.*" Whack. Pause. "*We don't need another Arianne!*"

My cheeks grew hot with shame. They stung like someone was slapping me. I rolled over, but the feeling persisted.

Someone was slapping me.

"I'm sorry," I said to the baby.

"Get up, hurry! It's almost dusk—he'll be awake soon."

I peeled my eyelids apart; it hardly made a difference. Harley's silhouette blocked most of the light sneaking in from the corridor. Eyes open or closed, the space was dark, and so small it hardly deserved to be called a room. It was barely a cupboard, just outside my master's quarters; no more than a few meters deep, half again as wide. Bare shelves lined the walls and a rusted bed frame was crammed in at the back. Three of its legs were twisted. One was snapped off at the base.

I sat up, my back and joints aching. The baby turned and kicked, as unhappy to sleep on the floor as her mother. Harley put down the pail and broom he carried, then pulled at my hand, "Come on. You don't have much time and this—" he gestured at the cleaning supplies "—won't fool anyone for long."

It took me a second to realize what his presence meant. "You have a key?"

The question was redundant: I could see it clutched in his fist. I stared at him, mouth agape. My hand rose to my belly, and Harl read the gesture for what it was: *Why haven't you used it before now?*

"I don't want any trouble. Just go. You're ruining everything, Adelaide." Adelaide, not Ada. "It was all fine—everything is *fine*. We're happy here. I'm happy. We're *happy*." He dragged me to my feet. The door was open, yet I couldn't go through it.

"Harl—"

He shook his head. "See? That's what I mean. My name is Harold—get used to it." His voice went up an octave, and for a second he was the little boy I chased snakes with. The boy who leaped from quarry ridges, a coconut oil sheen on his skin. "But you can't, can you?"

I thought I'd wept myself dry on the storage room floor, but my sight blurred as I looked at this young man who'd taken over my little brother's body.

"No," I said. "No."

Emotions streamed across Harley's face; I couldn't catch all of them. Confusion? Maybe. Disappointment? Certainly. And resolution. Yes, that most of all.

I looked for love, for remorse.

Kept looking.

"Go," he said, firm as the key he pressed into my palm. "Go home. Now."

"Oh, Harl." My voice cracked as I squeezed his hand. "I'll get Bethany, you get Miah—"

He pulled away. "No, Ada. Just you."

I stopped halfway out the door. Miah might be lost, but there was still hope for Beth. "It won't take long, I'll just—"

"No." Every line in Harley's face read, *Don't make me regret this.* "'Just' nothing. Leave."

Ma would be so upset if I left them alone. *There's so many dangerous critters in this land*, she'd reminded me, almost every day, before she went to work. Then she'd tickle me until I squirmed, adding a witch's cackle to her voice. *And ain't they all got a hankering for children's sweet meat!*

Irrational, unbidden thoughts. I stamped them out. "Who'll look after you?"

"Go," he repeated. No reassuring smile, no farewell embrace. "We're fine. We've been doing just fine."

"I can't," I begin to say, but my daughter kicked me into action. *You can*, she assured me with a jab to the ribs. *You will.*

"You sure he's asleep?"

Harley shrugged.

Without another word I slipped from the room, the key warm and slippery with sweat. I *can't thank you*, I wanted to finish, but didn't. Such thanks would be too much for what Harl hadn't done. Too little for what he had.

That evening, I watched the sun set.

Its vibrant colors reduced my eyes to slits. The ochres and golds mirrored the late summer fields; the highway's black line the only sign of what was ground, what sky. I ran towards the road, towards the light. Tried to shake away the darkness. Tried to stop looking over my shoulder, to stop imagining Mister Pérouse appearing, disappearing, appearing. Tried to erase images of Harley luring Jacques away from the front door, and Arianne to his bed. His manipulation, their hunger: a whiff of his lukewarm skin all the bait he needed to secure my escape.

Headlights in the distance spurred me on. I moved as fast as I could, forced to stop and catch my breath too frequently. Even I knew the highway belonged to truckers at night: if I missed this one, another would be along sooner or later. I couldn't afford it to be later.

Dry air scraped in and out of my lungs as I ran. Every tuft of chickweed, every patch of wild wheat seemed to hide my master. I didn't stop at the freeway's edge—lifting a thumb was too subtle for my needs. I staggered onto the road, waited on the painted division between lanes. Solid white double lines: *no passing*. A good omen, I hoped.

The hiss of hydraulic brakes accompanied by blinding headlights. I scurried to the driver's side, knelt like a supplicant. Wasn't refused.

"Where you headed, darlin'?" The trucker nodded as I mentioned the crossroads between our acreage and Kaintuck town. "I know it," he said, lending me a hand getting into the cab, squeezing my fingers as though making sure I was solid. "Buckle up."

He turned the radio on, whistled through tobacco-stained teeth along with four hours of country and western tunes. Once, he offered me water and half an egg salad sandwich, both of which I gratefully accepted. Otherwise, the bulge of my belly, the dried blood on my dress, or the anxious scowl on my face kept his eyes on the road, hands firmly on the wheel. When we reached my stop, I had no payment to give him but a smile. He took it kindly then returned it twofold.

"Take care now," he said. "And good luck."

"Thanks." The croak of my voice was lost in the drone of bullfrogs and crickets; the chorus of my childhood. The adrenaline that had sustained me all night left my body in a rush, and exhaustion flooded in. As the truck's taillights winked out over the horizon, I stumbled into a ditch by the roadside, immersed in familiar, foreign sounds. Five kilometers separated me from my family's doorstep, but it might as well have been a million. Every part of me cried out for rest.

I slumped to the ground. With both feet plunged in murky water pooling in the dip of the trench, my face and arms scratched to bits by thistles and long grass, and my back twisted on hard soil, I slept.

I woke hot and thirsty. The sun was a half a hand's width above the hills; the dried grass waving above me scant protection from its harsh rays. I was too exposed: the top of my head felt like it was on fire. Already the water at my feet had dwindled to muck—I scooped up as much as I could, coated my face and hair in it. More mud than liquid, it wasn't fit for drinking. So with a sandpaper tongue and black slop dripping down my back, I started the final leg of my journey home, wishing I had one of Ma's bonnets.

My thoughts wandered as I walked. Would raccoons have infested the house? What if it had burned down? Would there be anything left for me to return to? Would Mister Pérouse have beaten me there? Most of all, would my blood-rags, hidden in jars all these years, still be safe? The urge to destroy them quickened my pace.

In and out, I thought. *Break all blood-ties. Don't let master sniff them out...*

I knew I couldn't stay. But it was important I see the place, see that something had remained. That all wasn't lost.

The baby was restless. My stomach didn't stop churning until I got to the familiar wooden fence. Until I followed it to the open gate, rusted but still intact. Until I saw the birches and cedars unscathed by axe or fire. Until I reached the yard and the house. Both worse for years of neglect, but both whole. Both there.

I released a pent-up breath.

Home.

The front lock held, which surprised me. I rattled at the doorknob, but the noise only inspired a scurrying inside. A stir of scrabbling feet.

Raccoons, I thought, relieved. *Or squirrels.* I could handle vermin and I could handle a barred door. These were the least of all evils I'd envisaged. At the back of the house, my bedroom window was slightly ajar. I had no praise for useless gods, just gratitude to the carpenter who'd constructed frames prone to contracting in the heat. After jimmying it with a stick, the glass slid easily in its tracks. The casement was low—any higher and I don't think I could've managed it. My entrance wasn't graceful, but it did the job.

Inside, the air was close and rich with decay. Fluorescent orange splotches of possum piss dotted the sheets and area rugs; brown pellets covered every flat surface and led like a breadcrumb trail out of the room. Slumbering and still, the house wrapped me in its embrace. I walked down the hall carefully, quietly, lest I wake it. The living room was darker than whiskey dregs. My feet crunched across the floorboards, snapping and popping on unseen twigs. At the far side, I stubbed my toe on the corner of the woodstove—it never felt so good letting loose a blue streak of curses.

Heavy woolen curtains, three layers deep, were draped in front of the windows. These were . . . new? I fumbled at the unexpected fabric, trying to recognize it, trying to situate it in my memory of this room. *Light streamed in through the windows the night they came.* I searched for the split between panels. *Light streamed in through the windows the night Ma died.* In the end, I felt my way to the edge: the material was fastened to the wall with staples or pins. Furious, I dug through the layers, through the metal. *How dare they?* I thought, tearing to unveil Ma's picture window. *How dare they.*

"The light! Close it, close it!"

Her voice was a hot poker up my spine. I jumped and spun to see Ma cowering on the couch. She crab-walked into the shadows, looking at me between strands of lank hair. Her figure was wizened beyond recognition. Bones protruded from her chest and shoulders, visible through her threadbare gown. The curve of her stomach was the inverse of mine, despite the litter of rabbit and cat bones on the floor. She continued to plead that I cover the windows—I responded by standing and staring. Her mouth, double-fanged like a panther's, stretched wide; it unleashed a wail of illness and starvation that sent me scaling a rickety chair. Hooking darkness and silence back into place.

Despite my efforts thin shafts of light oozed in, sluggish with dust. Ma's eyes were glassy as she moaned, "Stop haunting me." Knees pulled to her chest, she rocked back and forth mumbling, "Oh Ada, oh my Ada. Jesus Christ, stop haunting me."

Ice water ran through my veins. "I'm here, Ma." She continued her mantra, her rocking. "Ma, I'm here." I hurried to her, arms outstretched. "I'm home. Look: I'm home. I'm home."

"Liar!" The force of her anger was enough to give me whiplash. "That's what you always say—and it just ain't true, Ada. It ain't true…"

My knees buckled and I dropped to the couch. "No, Ma." I spoke softly to keep the tremble from my voice. She looked at me sideways, sniffed and tasted the air. *"Liar."*

"That's the hunger talking, not you." I inched closer, gently laid my hand on her shoulder. I wanted to pull her to me, to fill the gaps between her bones with my tears. But I recognized the look on her face: Mister Pérouse wore it each time my bloods drew near. "Look at me."

She turned away.

"Look at me." I cradled her chin in my hand, not pressing too hard for fear of breaking her. Forced her to see me. To accept me as real. Thinking of the jars I'd kept stacked beneath the front porch, I repeated, "I'm here, Ma. I'm here, and I'll feed you."

Her hallucinations must've never made such an offer. She blinked slowly, focusing her gaze.

"Ada," she croaked. When she frowned the tips of her teeth caught on her bottom lip, distorting her mouth in a maniac's grimace. I wondered which of her fangs would produce the milk, the blood. Which ones I should drain first. She looked down, stared at my belly—her expression frozen between joy and horror. Saliva wet on her lips.

"Oh, Ada." She got up, searched for something on the coffee table, on the armchair, the dining hutch. "Oh, Ada. My baby."

"I kept my blood-rags safe, like you said." I twisted in my seat, followed her bewildering progress from room to room. "You can have them—might not be fresh, but—they're yours. You'll feel better once you've eaten."

Dishes smashed in the kitchen, pots and pans clanging as Ma pushed them aside.

"I remember exactly where I hid them," I continued, clearing a path to the front door. "Just outside—"

"No!" Ma raced over, clasping a hammer. "Don't leave." Her eyes were wild, her breathing frantic. "I swear I ain't never gonna touch a drop from you—from neither of y'all. Them bloods ain't mine, baby. They's yers. All I ask is for you to stay. I swear to God."

And before I could stop her, she kept her promise. Twice the hammer connected with her mouth, an unholy collision of flesh and iron. "Don't leave me alone."

Her words bubbled red as she spat shards of teeth on the floor.

Banjo gathers Ma's few belongings, I collect mine. There's nothing more for us to say: no apologies, no forgiveness. One's not his to give, the other's not mine to request. For now, that's enough.

We wait until nightfall to bundle Ma into Banjo's truck, swaddled in the first cloak she ever sewed: hooded black felt, fringed in elaborate lace. The iron tang of her injury follows us outside. I brush it away with the flies.

"Keep safe," Banjo says, handing me a shotgun and a pouch of ammunition. From its heft, it's filled with enough lead to last until doomsday. Messy bullets, these. The thought of testing them on Mister

Pérouse makes me smile. I keep one eye on the horizon, but neither my master nor my father show by the time we say our goodbyes. I check Ma's seatbelt, kiss her forehead, and swear I'll visit soon.

Her words are muffled but I can hear the smile behind them. "That's what you always say, Ada."

No point in waiting until morning; I've grown accustomed to night. Before I leave, I take one last tour of the house. I don't take anything more than I can carry: a sleeping bag and tarp, a good coat, one of Banjo's old packs. A sackful of Ma's finer creations to sell or to cherish—at this stage, I'm not sure which.

Her boots, good as new. Comfortable on my swollen feet.

I tip the candles we lit in the sitting room, wait to make sure they catch. The carpets, curtains, couches wick the eager fire, spread it rumor-fast. Soon the whole house is ablaze. Walking out, I leave the door open.

My lungs stretch full with fresh air.

Flames gnaw at the veranda, chew away the front porch. As I hike down the driveway, I can hear jars shattering, popping. I smile. None will find them now. The heat of my past is warm on my back; before me is only darkness. Gusts of fiery wind urge me forward and I comply. It's time to move. I won't go far; just far enough to be both here and away. To stay alive and reacquaint myself with this land; its lore and its language. Maybe I'll study Ma's pieces, teach myself to sew. And when my daughter is born and can wield the right tools, maybe I'll teach her too. With each stitch she'll discover our history: Ma's and mine. Hers. A child made for darkness, she'll be my shadow as I walk across fields drenched in sun. Wherever we end up, when she's draped in suits of our making, my girl will know where she belongs.

And when it's time, be it a dozen years from now or sixty, she'll know where to bury her blood.

FATHER PEÑA'S LAST DANCE

Hannah Strom-Martin

Hannah Strom-Martin's fiction has appeared in *Realms of Fantasy, Beneath Ceaseless Skies, OnSpec, Andromeda Spaceways Inflight Magazine*, and the anthology *Amazons: Sexy Tales of Strong Women*. With Erin Underwood she is the co-editor of *Futuredaze: An Anthology of YA Science Fiction*. She currently resides in Northern California and attempts to blog at www. nocommonplace.wordpress.com.

The Argentine tango is a sensuous, passionate dance; to combine it with vampires is understandable. There is ardor in "Father Peña's Last Dance," but that does not always guarantee romance . . .

The woman finally approached me across from La Recoleta Cemetery, following me to my table at Munich—the least tourist-infested café on Restaurant Row. I fancied her a *porteno*. Her hair, red as lipstick, was wound in perfect, bushy coils about her face. Her clothes had come from the best shops. Her sunglasses made an insect of her, but also a movie star: Audrey Hepburn without the softness. As she approached it seemed the mad sounds of Sunday tourism faded. Suddenly I was Mr. Bogart, watching my latest deadly siren approach through the wisps of cigarette smoke, the endless strains of tango music. The tango never stops in Buenos Aires. It goes on and on and we all dance to it in our time, helplessly drawn when fate initiates the *cabezazo*.

For as long as I knew her, she wore red. Not always a bright, traffic-light hue, though on that first day it was indeed the blood-colored flash of her linen dress which alerted me to her presence among the tombs. She wore pale pink once, like the stain left on butcher's wrap. Later she wore a sleek maroon sweater, fine and soft, covering her from throat to wrist against the encroaching gulf winds. Secretly, I called her Pandora, for hers was a red of unlocking. Of drive and of searching. You don't understand me yet, but you will.

"*Mate´*," she told the waitress, and sat across from me as if we were old friends. I knew she was a tourist, then. And American. But she had none of a tourist's awkwardness. She looked at me directly, her gaze discernable even through her enormous glasses. I folded my hands and smiled at her, but for a moment my old heart fluttered beneath its fat. It was noon. She could not have been one of *them*, yet she had their stillness. I imagined her ears beneath the gorgeous fall of hair perking like a listening dog's.

"Father Peña," she said.

Cautiously, I nodded.

"I'm sorry for haunting you," she said. "However, you of all people must know it takes a long time to trust."

"What can I do for you, señora?"

She smiled: red and nearly mocking.

"Have you seen the lights in the cemetery, Father?" she asked.

I grew dizzy for a moment. Had the record player skipped? No. People didn't use records any more. The disc, then? Perhaps I'd simply aged ten years, finally lost my hearing along with my sanity. Sixty-four years in the city and no one had ever mentioned the lights. How could this woman, this outsider, know of them?

I nearly rose to go.

The woman's hard, hungry face softened abruptly into something like pity.

"I'm sorry," she said.

I laughed. Words failed.

"I'm Cole," she said. She extended her hand and her nails were also hard and red. "We have some friends in common."

"Friends?"

"Or enemies. But such things are not safe to speak of in the open."

I looked at my coffee, feeling suddenly I was being sucked down into a whirlpool. When had I become so old, so frightened? Thirty years since Maria, and only now did I feel I was truly slipping into darkness. "Safe," I whispered. "No, señora. Not safe."

Her red-tipped hand descended on mine, her flesh warm and dry as sunbaked stone.

"I understand," she said.

On their wedding night Cole's husband was taken by a vampire.

Cole and Ash were making love, the doors of their balcony open upon a summer night. The vampire drifted in from the terrace, a silent, slow-motion horror. Cole watched the gauzy curtains grow pregnant with its shape, wondering how the cloth could swell without a breeze. Then the vampire emerged. Before Cole could reconcile its floating figure, her new husband's unawareness, and the scream, half pleasure, half fear, building in her throat, the creature—a woman—descended on Ash's back.

Ash's eyes widened. The last sound Cole had of him was a gasp that might have been the sound his body made as he disappeared out the window. Cole tried to follow but the vampire had done something to the room. Trying to get out of bed, Cole fell into a black fog, only waking when the afternoon sun began to burn her skin the following day.

Though his shirts and razor, trouser socks and shoes, remained in his conspicuously present suitcases, the police said Ash had run away. Their questions were ceaseless: Had he angered the government? Had he faked his own death? (This man who had spoken of children. This man who had picked out the plot where he and Cole would build their home.)

No, Cole said. No, no, no. Someone had been in the room that night. Ash had been kidnapped.

Later, when she had numbed herself with wine and marijuana, Cole remembered Ash's last business trip. From a hotel room in Buenos Aires he had written her a message on his computer:

The city doesn't sleep until dawn. The clubs and bars only really begin to pump around 3 a.m. Our hotel is in La Recoleta—near the "City of the Dead." I roam there with Kevin all night while he tries to buy drinks for the girls on their mopeds.

The women are stunning, but never as stunning as you, chula. One tried to get me to tango with her two nights ago. I passed her on to Kevin but she kept smiling at me.

Buenos Aires. It was the last stumbling block in his smoothly paved life. A girl. A cemetery. It didn't bode well.

"So you came here," I said, the café and afternoon far behind us. Cole drank gin straight from a glass and chewed the ice. We sat on the sidewalk that served as my front lawn, resting on warm cement as the multi-colored sidings of La Boca gleamed with deceptive cheer above us. After Maria I had thought to move somewhere festive. Yet the shadows were lengthening now. Mothers called children to supper and the boys with their soccer balls vanished from the streets. I could smell meat and spices, hear the beef sizzling when the traffic lulled. The breeze came in from Canal Sur, stinking of oil. A salsa band began to tune in the distance, the trumpet mewling, lost in amongst the bright and dirty dwellings. Another colored night coming now. Another night.

"I've got a jealous nature," Cole said, blowing smoke from her cigarette. "I won't let another woman have him. Even if she *is* a vampire."

When I winced she quirked the side of her mouth.

"Shall I speak more softly?" she asked.

"Perhaps you should," I said. "No one speaks that word. Other people would think you were . . ." Why was it so hard? I had acquired *more* caution in my old age, instead of less.

"*Loco*?" Cole asked.

I spread my hands, nodded.

"Vampire," Cole whispered. "Wampyre. El Vampiro." She laughed in her low, rough way and blew the names of the demons out in clouds of nicotine. "I'm not afraid, Father," she said.

I sighed. "Perhaps you should be."

Cole was the only person I'd ever met who knew about them. My fellow *portenos* had to have seen things, but even in this city it was hard to acknowledge magic greater than the peace brought you by the Virgin's effigy, or the hell of too many nights in drink. This was still the modern world. Even Cole and I had only been able to believe after they stole our hearts: Cole's from a hotel room, mine from a courtyard café.

"Maria," Cole said. "Your priest friends told me about her. I think they miss you at that little church."

I laughed. My turn for gin now. We sat sweating in my flat, the bottle nearly empty between us. Passing cars provided the only light. I kept the ceiling fan on but would not touch the lamp. Cole seemed to understand. We sat and smoked, growing drunker. This is what lonely lovers do without their other half. It doesn't matter if two years have passed or twenty.

"You still wear the collar," Cole said.

I touched my throat: its white-starch band. She noticed so much, enough even to mark the stir in the air when one of *them* appeared. Is that how she had traced them, I wondered? To ask in churches until she found rumors and then stories and finally the local legends that brought her to me?

"I was told to retire," I said. I was drunk enough to sound bitter. "They wouldn't like it if they knew Father Peña still fancies himself a priest. But I never left them—they left *me*."

"You aren't a priest though, are you? Not anymore?"

"My religion is Maria. Father Adelmo and Father Sanchez—they knew it, even before she vanished. My heart had not been God's for some time."

"What happened, Father?" I could hardly see her in the dark. Just the outline of her hair.

"A girl of seventeen won the love of a priest twice her age." I said it calmly, as if I had told the story before. "On the night they would consummate their love the priest arrived late to a tango and a man in a black suit was standing with the girl. The dance was held outside amongst the garden lamps and torches, but the man cast no shadow. When I . . . When the priest looked at the suited man, his eyes slid away, as if the place where the man stood was somehow unfit for human sight. The priest no longer believed in God, but he knew enough to recognize His opposite.

"The priest froze, not understanding how the devil could look like a mortal man. Even the girl, who had only begun to understand about God and Satan, seemed to sense the man in black was dangerous. She tried to pull away, but he pulled her close, into a dance.

"Something in their dancing woke the priest. He could sense something terrible had been set in motion.

"He pressed forward, pushing against the bodies of other dancers. It was difficult, because everyone who saw the dance of the girl and the man in black became awed. They crowded in around them, blocking the way. At last, frantic and afraid, the priest bulled through them, calling the girl's name. But as if God Himself had planned it, a fire pit lay directly in his path. Still calling her, he fell into the flames, scorching his hand. And as he lay writhing in the spilled coals, the man in black began to laugh.

"The priest knew then that he had been right: the man in black was a demon. Even now, his laughter was sucking out the priest's soul.

"There was nothing the priest could do. Before he could get to his feet, a dark wind rose. When it cleared, the man in black and the girl who carried the priest's heart were gone.

"Maria…"

I let my voice die and finished my gin. I had never told the story before. I had raved to Father Sanchez of demons. I had given a sermon that frightened the faithful from the pews. But I had never sat as I did now, calmly, with another person, and simply talked.

"At first I thought God was punishing me," I said, my voice distant to my own ears. "But that *thing* . . . God would have been offended by its very existence."

"I never had much use for God," Cole said. "What people call God is just love."

"It has been thirty years, snora," I said. "I haven't seen Maria again. Sometimes I don't know if I want to."

"You want to," Cole said. "Even if the worst is true and she and Ash are demons, living in hell, don't you at least want to save them?"

I laughed. "Me? A faithless priest? If you think to use me as a talisman, I'm afraid you've come to the wrong man."

Though no light shone on her, I could sense her smile.

"I didn't come looking for you because of your religion," she said. "I came looking for you because the *portenos* say you can dance."

Even now, I don't know how she figured it out: about the vampires and the tango. At times I still wondered if she were one of *them*, so preternatural were her instincts.

I hardly paid attention to where she led me the next morning, my head aching with gin. Too much for an old man. Too much. My dreams had been of fire and redheaded women.

The courtyard had been closed for years, hidden behind a wooden gate. Yellow and green paint still clung, stubborn and faded, to the insect-eaten boards. Pale weeds bent with a crackle as Cole pushed it open.

I followed her, my head down. Slowly the worn stones of the courtyard came into focus. My heart throbbed a warning even before I recognized the dilapidated remains of the café sagging on my right.

"No," I said. Brown leaves skittered across the yard, fetching up against the stone wall that circled the property. Mr. Pepe (he'd refused to let us call him "Señor") had built the barbeque pit into the wall so he could roast an endless supply of suckling pigs. Long before I fell in love with Maria, I came to Pepe's to eat and watch the dancing. The pit was full of leaves now. They dropped from a withered banyan, rustling as they fell.

Sweat ran wet fingers down my neck. The trees trapped the heat, coaxed the smell of mildew from the café's swollen walls. A strand of triangular plastic flags still hung above the courtyard where Mr. Pepe had strung them, their beer advertisements melted by thirty years of rain. They pointed down at the stones like fingers at a ghost.

"Why?" I said, rounding on Cole. My body shook.

Cole lit her second cigarette of the morning.

"Your friends like to tango," she said. "If we dance, they'll take an interest."

"Why here?" My voice drove unseen birds from the trees.

Cole pursed her hard, American mouth, redder than any red on God's earth, around her cigarette. I hated her, I thought. I hated her rigidity.

"It's reverse psychology, Father," she said. "If you can dance *here*, you'll be able to dance anywhere—even in front of your friends."

"Don't call them that!" I said. I approached her, clenching my fists in front of me. "They are no *friends* of mine, señora. They took her. Right under those flags. She stood right *there*—"

Abruptly, the ball of anger melted in my throat. Heat swept through me, wrapping aching coils about my heart. I dashed towards the place where Maria had stood, not knowing if the sickness that surged within me was bile or tears.

Then I was on my knees, the stones hurting even through my clumsy padding of flesh. I placed a hand against the stones, thinking perhaps this would be like touching her, across the years. Only stone met my fingertips. Cupped over my mouth, my other hand felt the watery release of an old man's tears.

"Well," Cole said behind me. "That's one hurdle down."

"*Cabezazo*, right?"

We stood across from each other, on either side of the courtyard, my back to the café, hers to the bordering trees.

"Yes," I said, no longer resisting her. Whether through age or expenditure of grief, I felt oddly detached from this. She wanted me to teach her the tango so she could impress the vampires. What else was there to do on a Wednesday afternoon?

"The *cabezazo*," I said, continuing the lesson "is the moment when the man and woman first make eye contact."

"Across a smoky room." She hoisted her cigarette. "Then what?"

"We approach one another. Only professionals really trouble with this part anymore. The laymen go right to the embrace."

"Let's do it right," she said. She sauntered towards me, holding her cigarette in her right hand, her wrist at a ninety-degree angle.

"No," I said. "No, no, no."

"What?" She smiled insolently. "Do we need to hire an accordion?"

A wave of anger disrupted my apathy. I hadn't felt angry in a long time and now I realized I had missed it: missed feeling *anything*, whatever the cause. When my blood stirred I did not shy away from it. The señora wanted a dance, did she? Father Peña could oblige her.

I stepped into anger.

"First," I said, drawing close enough to hiss the word in her face, "only whores carry this." I knocked the cigarette away with the back of my hand. Señora Cole began to protest but I drew her into the starting position: my offending hand in the small of her back, my other hand joined to hers above our waists.

"Hold on to me," I ordered. "No. Only our upper bodies touch. You lean into me and I guide you, like so." Her chest was flat and hard, but her back felt good beneath my hand. I showed her the basic step. In tango, the man leads, the woman must always be on the point of resistance. My left foot went forward while her right went back: *el paseo*.

"Keep your upper body erect and pressed to mine," I said. "Our hearts always touch but never our feet. This is the Argentine Tango, señora."

She learned quickly, incorporating her desire to pull away into the dance. We progressed to *la cuinta*, the rocking step, and *la chasse*: the chase.

"Now," I told her, "backwards eights!" and she complied. Slow, slow, quick, quick, slow. Slow, slow, quick, quick. After an hour I could smell my own musk and her clean, soapy perfume. She wanted to keep going, her face flushed, two honest points of red pricking her cheek.

"And, *salida*," I said, at last. I needed a drink of water. More gin. A beer.

Abruptly she fell into me, the tension in her neck relaxing, her strong, thin arms coming about my stoutness.

"Thank you, Father," she said. Her fingernails caught the short hairs at the back of my neck. "I knew you'd help me. You still dance like a young man."

"A young man is what *they* will want," I said. My anger had faded. My heart beat now with a strange peacefulness. "I don't know why you think I can bring you closer to them. They thrive on youth and beauty—you must know this if you've been close enough to see them dance."

"I've seen them," she said. "It isn't the youth they want, though."

"You mean they take old women with blue hair?"

"No," she said. "But you don't have to be young. They feed off emotion. They got you when you were going to bed Maria, right? And me on my wedding night, with Ash . . ." She trailed off a moment, raised her hand to her mouth as if anticipating the cigarette that wasn't there. "They'll get us," she said, quietly. "We have too much circling us—all that bad history. They'd be nuts not to go for it, don't you think?"

"Your guess is as good as mine, señora."

She released me and stepped away. I thought she would go for the purse she had left near the gate—for her smoking. But she hugged herself, rubbing her arms as though she were cold.

"The tango is like life," she said. "Struggle, struggle, struggle and then—what did you call it?"

"*Salida*," I said. "The end."

She nodded. "Yeah," she said. "*Salida*."

That afternoon we went to La Recoleta and walked among the tombs. Cole ate a *dolce de leche* cone in ravenous little bites that made me question her age. I had placed her at thirty, yet now she seemed younger. Her step even bounced a little as she walked past the marble sarcophagi, immune to the flocks of tourists. She had more energy since we'd danced.

"You're younger than I think you are, aren't you?" I asked.

Her eyes narrowed above the rims of her sunglasses.

"I thought you were part of the generation who thinks those sorts of questions are rude," she said.

I waited, but she said no more. We walked in silence, enjoying the sun, staying clear of Evita's mausoleum. She was happy to be doing something, I decided. It explained her sudden lightness.

After I left my church, I had only felt alive when I followed one of *them* to an assignation. I took a pathetic thrill knowing I could recognize one, shadow it while it prowled, unaware. Such delights, however, faded when I began to notice them everywhere. After dark they haunted the restaurants, lurking, never eating. I'd seen one in a barber's shop once, reading a newspaper. Some had passed the little hall where, for a few months, I had taught the tango to old folks and tourists. They'd never liked my clientele. Their paths always ended with the abduction of another young beauty. Another Maria.

I thought of Cole's theory: were they drawn to emotion, somehow? To love? It could be. But why here, in this city? The vast streets and close-knit barrios were a beating heart upon which they preyed.

"The lights start about midnight," Cole said around the last bite of her cone.

I nodded. "You can see them from the street."

"We should come back after dinner," she said. "Hide until the guards leave."

"What? You mean watch from inside?"

She pushed the sunglasses down her nose. "You've never done that?"

I shook my head. I'd always seen the lights from a distance, circling the cemetery on foot. It had never occurred to me to get closer.

"Well," Cole said. "We can fix that. Come with me tonight. I'll take the first watch—Jesus!"

If she had still had her cone she would have dropped it, bowled over by a pair of speckled cats who came charging from between the tombs. They vanished into the shadow of a large mausoleum, hissing and spitting as they fought.

"Tonight," Cole said, firmly, straightening her skirt.

When her back was turned, I crossed myself.

Nothing happened that night, save that she grew even younger to me. We took turns sleeping, crammed into a nook of broken stone where the backside of an enormous tomb had crumbled. No watchmen came near. My only company as I fell asleep, too tired to care if my cheek pressed into her hard young shoulder, was the distant howling of cats.

In the middle of the night I jolted awake. Cole put her hand on my shoulder and together we watched the silver-blue light bloom over La Recoleta. Beyond the boundaries of the cemetery the nightlife would carry on, the neon glare masking the glow to the casual eye, but I heard no motorcycles rev, no horns or voices, not a single strain of music. The light hummed, casting moon colored shadows on the cemetery paths.

"God," I said.

Cole nodded. I could smell the new-washed sweetness of the sweatshirt she had used as a pillow and wanted suddenly to burrow into it. Her grip tightened on my shoulder.

"I want to go to them," she whispered. "But we aren't ready. Have you ever thought that they might be different when they're at home?"

I shook my head. They were terrible enough when they roamed the streets, pretending to be human.

"Not ready," Cole said again. "Not yet. But we will be."

I remember her at our first dance: tight mouthed, determined not to falter. Her dress was scarlet, a color far different from simple red. How deeply the vanished Ash must have loved her.

Nervously, we waited for the evening to begin. My burned hand tingled, my dreams the night before all of fire. Cole crossed her arms under her small, apple-like breasts, watching as the unholy materialized among the tables.

It had been years since I'd paid attention to the individual aspects of a vampire. At first I had scanned their ranks, looking for Maria. When she never appeared the rest of them took on a kind of uniformity. Male or female all were slender, all beautiful, all surrounded by subtle darkness. You would mistake them for *portenos* if your eyes didn't slip across them when you tried to stare.

Five sat in the crowd that night: three women, two men. I recognized a cruel faced boy who had only appeared in the last decade. The others were strangers. Their ranks kept growing, new faces every year. They were making their own *portenos* now: a whole city, perhaps, lying beneath our feet. Did Maria live there too—hidden away all these years? She would no longer be the girl in the modest white dress, but something unholy and refined.

The music began. In the clubs, couples are expected to dance with strangers. After the first dance, Cole and I would be expected to switch partners. We had one chance. We waited for our song.

It came at last with accordion and bass: an Argentine Tango. No one bothered with the slow seduction of the *cabezazo* anymore, so we took to the floor, beginning our routine with the *entrada*.

I had started to dance on my slow fall from the priesthood, sneaking to Mr. Pepe's during the week. Cole had taken ballet and yoga. The greatest trick we could pull off—her with her inexperience, I with my age, was the *volcada*—the falling step. Even then, it was only my years that made the feat memorable, for I looked incapable of performing it.

Cole danced stiffly at first, her teeth set. As she began her first *firuletes*—a small kick with her back foot as she turned, a quick hook to my leg before going into her backwards-eights—the vampires perked up. Over the heads of the other dancers I saw them rise, drifting towards one another. Their heads tossed back and forth, scanning the crowd.

"Shit," Cole whispered. She grew even stiffer, faltering. I fought the urge to run. I could see them coming, their sleek, gleaming heads bobbing as they waded towards us.

"Shit!" Cole said again. It would all be for nothing if she lost heart now.

I could think of one thing to do.

"Surrender," I whispered. I pressed, my leg on hers, driving her deeper into the crowd. She resisted. Her eyes flashed to mine:

Are you crazy, old man?

"Surrender," I said. Another push. "Dance."

At last, she did.

I remember the smoke of that night. The smell of her fear. Other couples were prettier, evenly matched, young. None danced more earnestly. None as if their heart and soul hung in the balance. A sheen of sweat bejeweled Cole's forehead, snaring wisps of red hair. For the first time I thought her beautiful. For the first time we moved with a single purpose, no longer at odds—*porteno* and American, man and woman. We moved like two determined martyrs, knowing the danger and plunging ahead to the end: *volcada*. The fall.

Salida.

When the music stopped the laughter took me by surprise. The couples stood about, applauding one another, some already drifting back to their tables. Yet the room pulsed with raucous laughter. Cole shuddered, clambering up from out finishing pose.

Two vampires stood beside us: a man and a woman. They had been there all along.

I realized their laughter was in my head.

"Touching!" the female said. "How lost and tragic you are!" She bent towards me and sniffed, once, like an animal. The points of her teeth flashed.

"Sad, sad," said the male. "As if we would take such as you."

"You're here now, aren't you?" I flinched as Cole spoke. She stepped away from me, straight-backed and angry, her teeth very white as she matched the woman's aggressive expression. "I know who you are, *puta*," she said. "I recognize your disgusting hair."

The female smiled too widely for humanity. "Ash's wife," she said.

Cole nodded. "Tell me where he is."

"I will tell you nothing, *chula*. Only the worthy may speak to us." Abruptly she turned to me: a movement so fast I was shocked to find her face in mine.

"Ave Maria, Father," she whispered, bringing sharp-tipped nails to brush my cheek. The air she stirred smelled of decay. Her touch felt like the wriggling of a grave worm. I gagged.

"No!" I said. Another tango was beginning, people flocking to the floor, yet they all veered away from us, sensing not to come near. A woman knocked against me, then slipped away as if I'd passed right through her.

"I'm going to kill you," Cole said.

The vampires laughed. *Oh, such passion!* Were they speaking, or were their voices in my head again?

"I won't live in a world with you in it." Cole said. "One of us is going to die."

We shall see.

Their scorn filled my head, driving out their laughter. A familiar black mist descended.

Maria, I thought. *Maria.*

The image of Cole's red stiletto followed me into a place of darkness and fire.

Cole brought a single bag with her to Argentina. The night of our humiliation I woke on my couch to find her rummaging in the corner. From the bag, she took something I had only seen in monster movies at the Sunday matinee.

"Show me again," she said.

She'd dragged my back to Mr. Pepe's, demanding more lessons. She had another plan.

"No," I said. "Damn you. It's over."

"I don't accept that."

"They won't take us. Besides: why would you go there, knowing he's one of them? You will die horribly or else end up the same!"

"I love him, Father," Cole said. "I'm going to save him. Don't you need to save *her*? Are you just going to give up now—thirty years later—and never find Maria?"

I was livid. "How dare you speak her name?" I said. "You know nothing of us. Nothing! I wake up in the night, sweating because she is gone. In my dreams I am consumed by the fires of hell!"

"You don't believe in hell!" Cole screamed at me. "You don't believe in God, or even love! You only believe in your own fear! Coward!"

I hit her. She tripped backwards in her flame-red heels, holding a hand to her cheek. For a moment, we faced each other. Then something kindled in her eyes. She came back at me, her fingernails splayed like talons.

"You've betrayed her!" she shrieked. "You stupid man! You've betrayed us all! My Ash! My husband! Maria!"

We fought, dancing back and forth across the stones. Her nails clung to my shirt, jerking me. My feeble bulk strained against her. Late August heat blew around us and it began to rain. Soon we were both wet and exhausted. She slapped at me and I fought her off, trying to ignore the tears which streamed down her face, smearing her makeup, revealing how frightened and pale she really was.

Eventually she collapsed on my chest, sobbing. The hands with which she had shaken me with clung fast to keep herself from falling.

My heart broke so suddenly I feared a stroke. But no. My heart still beat. But it ached now. A deeper ache than I had ever known.

We slipped down upon the rain-slicked stones, holding one another like children. The names of our lovers fell from our lips and we embraced fiercely, trying not to let the world take us, the storm spin us up into the sky.

Eventually the rain stopped. A muggy sun emerged, making the stones steam. I rested my old, foolish head on hers and patted her bedraggled hair.

"Do you ever think," she said, "that the flames in your dreams aren't really from hell? That maybe they're simply the love you never had, burning you from the inside?"

When I failed to respond she rested her head on my shoulder.

"Please help me, Father," she said. "I don't want to burn."

"All right," I said. "All right."

On that last day, some months later, we hid in La Recoleta until the silver light bloomed over the tops of the graves. Then we ventured forth into the true City of the Dead.

Between tangos, Cole had theorized that we could simply follow the light to its source. We were only two mortals, after all. Why would *they* stop us?

We came to the center of the cemetery, where the monuments towered above us like great houses. Stone angels wept into fountains. A rose window glittered in the corpse-light. Here was the source: blinding. Immense. We approached resolutely. Cole had her bag over one arm.

I had resigned myself to whatever fate awaited me. I very much doubted we would walk away from this. They would drain us, leave us stranded on the shores of death, or else resurrect us to their soulless life. I seldom thought of this. Cole took up my days. In six months I hadn't been alone for more than a few hours at a time.

We stood a moment, contemplating the tomb, just visible beyond the glaring light. A watchman, had he passed, might have seen an unexplained blur as we shifted in place. We were invisible now. I knew it as I knew vampires.

"So this is the mouth of hell," I said.

Cole laughed. Her hand brushed mine.

"Thank you, Father," she said.

I nodded.

We stepped into the light.

A great, basalt tomb yawned before us, a long staircase descending into the dark.

"Listen," Cole whispered.

From the mouth came the high-pitched whine of a violin. Had I never seen a vampire, I would have known a dead man sawed those strings.

"Come on," Cole said. She gripped the strap of her bag with one hand and pulled me after with the other. Before I lost sight of her in the darkness, she set her jaw, light sparking in her eyes. I wondered where the source of that light was. The flash had been the color of flame.

Stone surrounded us. We stumbled downward, following the music. It stank of must, here. Iron. Old bones. Other tunnels crossed ours. Other staircases branched away. The music lay straight ahead, always.

Slowly, a light grew, illuminating green veins in the ancient stone. I grit my teeth, swallowing as we passed, imbedded in the stone itself, the skulls of men and women interred here in forgotten times.

We came to a landing with a corroding granite balustrade. A great torch-lit chamber lay below us, swarming with figures. On the other side, directly facing us a labyrinth of cloisters, niches, and stairways branched and tunneled across an endless expanse of stone.

"Ant hive," Cole whispered.

Helplessly, I tiptoed to the balustrade, seduced by the warren of strange shapes and stairs that led nowhere. The music swelled around us, majestic and insane, drifting up from the chamber. The dark clad bodies, writhing and tossing beneath me, cast no shadows, their actions stark in the light of the torches they had set on all sides of their hall.

Not a hive, I thought. *A kingdom.*

I started as Cole touched me.

"Come on," she said. "I've found a way down."

A set of craggy steps let us in at the back of the hall. The vampires remained oblivious as Cole and I clambered down. I hardly had the sense to feel afraid anymore, so intent was I on the details of their strange dwelling. Broken statues of the Virgin lay in a pile beneath a fallen arch. Cole's high heel caught in the eye-socket of a skull.

We made it halfway across the chamber before they noticed us. A man bending his partner over in a *volcada*, bared his teeth. The couple next to him stopped in the middle of *la chasse*. One by one they all grew still. The hellish fantasia died. Only the fires stirred.

You are unworthy, they told us, voices cold within my mind. *Why have you come?*

Cole stepped forward.

"Ash Marcus," she told them. "You will give him back to me."

As one, they smiled. Lips slid audibly across teeth.

The unworthy are not permitted here.

"We are not unworthy," Cole said.

Laughter. This time, they spoke with their minds but laughed with their mouths. I sweat as a waft of rotting breath swept over me. Cole had taken my hand and her grip was steel.

"Let us dance!" she shouted over them. "Kill us if we displease you!"

The laughter ceased as they pondered. Then their shoulders relaxed. The women slumped, leaning against their partners. Some of the men nodded in tandem.

Proceed.

"Music," Cole said. "A tango Argentine."

An unseen band swept bows across strings and we began.

Months ago, we had decided it was no longer enough to simply dance. If Cole was to rescue Ash, we would have to *live* our trials.

So our tango was not sophisticated or soft or beautiful. I hadn't even been able to practice all the *firuletes* because I knew I could only give most of them once. What we lacked in refinement, we made up for in terror.

This was a tense dance, but isn't it always? The tango is life, they say. And life is a pull and withdrawal, a tug and a rebound. Life, lived correctly, is love. So Cole and I tried to live in the music. We tried to make our last act in this or any world, one of love.

At some point, I sensed the pricking of vampiric ears, the rustle of their clothing as we drew them in. The sounds unnerved me, filling me with images of rot. But it wasn't them I remembered: the sense of bodies closing in around me. I remembered Cole: her face, bone white and desperate, but so brave.

I knelt, let her kick a leg over my head before grabbing her ankle. Flesh had never felt so real to me. Her skin burned through her stockings, burrowed into my sweating palms. When we clung or fell or rocked in place, our fingernails left dents in one another's flesh. She tore my shirt, circling me, slashing with her nails as she re-lived her loss. I could hardly contain my sob as my hands ran down her body, relating how I had loved in my youth. Across the uneven floor, strewn with the bones of fools, we fought and danced and loved back and forth. And finished: my head pressed to her belly as the strings swept to a halt.

"I love you," I whispered. The words simply fell out of me. Her body pulsed against my cheek, her hand caught painfully in my thin hair. In this place of death, I felt more alive than I had in thirty years.

"It's all right," she said. "Get up, Father."

I rose, aching all over. I had sacrificed the last of my elasticity for her. I had knelt on that floor an old man. I rose decrepit.

Cole placed her hands on my shoulders, squeezing as she looked at me. Her face glowed, flushed and beaded with sweat. I knew we had made a terrible mistake coming here. Yet only here could I have realized: what I had whispered to her belly was true.

"Cole," I said. Strange bodies were pressing near, heated and barely restrained. Their breath dragged at us, sucking bits of us away.

"It's all right," she said again. A tear coursed down her cheek, moving quickly as it merged with her sweat. "He's coming now," she said. "We won."

"What?" I wanted her to keep looking at me. I would never live if she looked away: this light of love on her face. This euphoria. Her whole body trembled: alive. Alive.

But not for me.

Ash's wife. The crowd, hovering around us, parted ranks. From a Moorish arch, three figures approached. I recognized the woman who led them.

"Cole," I whispered. The heat of our dancing faded rapidly, my heartbeat speeding from exertion to fear. I tried to hold on as she pulled away, heading for the woman. She'd taken the object from her bag.

A man followed the vampire woman, and a smaller figure, but I had no time for them. The man, tall and pale, his dark hair slicked to the side, was beautiful as a sculpture. I was sure he had been even more glorious when he was alive.

"Cole!" I cried, trotting painfully after her. She gave no heed, unaware of anyone but herself and the woman. And Ash.

"*Cole,*" the vampire mocked. She held up her hand and Cole froze, grimacing.

"No, Cole! No!" I forced myself to reach her, tugged at her arm. "It isn't him anymore," I said. "It isn't him. Don't do this."

"I said I would kill you," Cole told the woman. "I meant it."

"Maybe you should listen to your friend," the woman said. "Ash is ours now. Once we have taken someone, they are ours forever. Isn't that right, Father?"

As she spoke, the little figure behind her came forward. A dirty veil covered its face—swath after swath of yellowed net. The bridal gown might have been fashionable in my youth.

I trembled, knowing somehow what would happen. Then the vampire flipped the veil aside and I saw a face I had not seen in thirty years.

Earth bit my knees. I did not remember falling. The vampire led Maria towards me and she came with the tentative steps of a girl at her first communion. Her face was blank and beautiful and cold, her dark, liquid eyes taking me in without recognition.

As I bent beneath my grief, the vampire moved towards Cole.

"You see?" she said. "She is ours. Ash is ours. There is nothing you can do."

"There are ways," Cole said again.

I looked up just in time to see her stab the object from her purse into the woman's empty heart.

A gasp went through the hall. The vampire stumbled back almost comically, examining the stake in her breast with an expression of disbelief. Black blood coursed between her breasts, slicking the earth as she wavered and fell.

"You are unworthy of my husband," Cole told her. "And of me." While the vampire struggled to die, Cole stepped over her and approached the still, watchful figure of Ash. She placed her hands on either side of his face.

"No," I groaned. For I knew what she would do. It was what I longed to do as Maria stood over me in her sweet, corrupted beauty. How easy to beg the one you love to save you. For thirty years I had wanted Maria to come back from hell and end mine. I had put such trust in love, ascribed more power to it than to that of God. But love was dead now. It stood over me, reeking of decay.

"Cole!" I scrambled to my feet, away from the slight form of the bride who I had once wanted more than salvation or breath. Cole stood murmuring to Ash, rubbing her radiant hair against his neck. They welcomed me with a calm look. His fingers wound greedily in her hair.

"No, Cole," I begged her. "Don't do this. Don't let him make you like *them*."

She smiled sadly. "This is what I came for, Father. For this very thing." Something rustled behind me. White skirts trailing on the earthen floor. I wouldn't look.

"You found Maria," Cole said.

"It isn't her."

"I know. Your love is different from mine. I'm not like you, Father. I want to be where Ash is. To be at his side whatever form he takes."

"Even death?"

"What else is life without love?" That light was in her eyes again—the gleam with no source. This had been her plan, I realized. The whole time. Every moment.

"Cole," I said, forcing myself to sound reasonable, "come with me now. You were meant to be alive—to love in the sunlight."

"This is the purest form of love I know," she said. "And someone must stay here, Father. Or they'll never let you go."

As she spoke I felt a prickling at my back. They were behind me. The entire hall. One of their own was dead and they were filled with hunger, and rage.

"I've fallen in love with you, señora," I said, my heart dropping away from me.

"I know. That is why I won't let them hurt you. But you must get out, Father. Go far away." Abruptly she addressed the hall: "Do you hear me? Let the Father go. He is unworthy of this hall—you shall not sully yourself with him!" A murmur greeted her words. I cannot say if it was agreement. Their energy was like nothing human or animal, and she had made herself its center.

"Go now," she said. She touched my cheek and I seized her fingers, kissing them.

"Señora, please!"

"The dance is over, Father," she said. She dropped my hand, caressing Ash's gleaming face. As she offered up her long, white neck, I bolted. The crowd, held back for so long, broke and rushed past me like a flood.

I ran. Back to the other end of the chamber. Back up the stairs. Back into the tunnel. I fled the roar of voices. I fled the blistering Argentine tango that burst suddenly to life at my back, mocking everything Cole and I had shared. My breath shuddered in and out, phlegm creeping up my throat. My bones felt they would tear away from one another as I forced myself towards the surface.

Just once, before I came to the mouth of the tomb, I thought I head the scrape of slippers on stone, the whisper of a woman's elaborate train. But I forced myself to grow deaf, to block out the cries and moans and tipsy drumbeats which emanated from the depths of that subterranean hell.

When I broke from the tomb, tumbling out into a morning terrible and wondrous in its blue-skied beauty my tears were flowing uncontrollably, blinding me as sobs wracked my breast.

I fell, scrabbling at the dusty path between the mausoleums, breathing sweet air, beside myself with feelings, horrible and otherwise, which I am not sure I have resolved within myself even to this day.

I knew only two things for certain as I lay on the path, the sun warming me back from what seemed an eternity of chill: My name was Antonio Peña and I would never dance the tango again.

Salida.

The End.

SUN FALLS

Angela Slatter

Angela Slatter is the author of the Aurealis Award-winning *The Girl with No Hands and Other Tales*, the World Fantasy Award finalist *Sourdough and Other Stories*, Aurealis finalist *Midnight and Moonshine* (with Lisa L. Hannett), as well as the 2014 releases *Black-Winged Angels*, *The Bitterwood Bible and Other Recountings*, and *The Female Factory* (again with Lisa L. Hannett). Her short stories have appeared in periodical such as *Fantasy*, *Nightmare*, *Lightspeed*, and *Lady Churchill's Rosebud Wristlet*, and anthologies including *Fearie Tales*, *A Book of Horrors*, and Australian, UK, and U.S. "best of" anthologies. She is the first Australian to win a British Fantasy Award (for "The Coffin-Maker's Daughter"). Slatter blogs at www.angelaslatter.com about shiny things that catch her eye.

Perhaps not surprisingly—since she is Australian—Slatter's take on a contemporary or near-future vampire is distinctly and delightfully set Down Under.

I tap the fingers of one hand against the steering wheel, beating out a rhythm to replace the one that went missing when we got beyond the reach of any radio reception. It helps me to ignore the noises from the back seat.

The window is down so I can blow away the smoke from a hand-rolled ciggie. Barry hates it when I smoke in his car. Few things in the world Barry loves more than this old Holden, with its mag wheels, racing stripes, flames painted on the bonnet, and the fluffy dice dangling from the rear view mirror like a pair of square, furry testicles. He adores it better than any woman. I wouldn't be allowed to drive if it weren't an emergency of the most urgent kind.

Me? I think he looks like an idiot driving it, like some clueless pimp. But I'm not stupid enough to tell Barry that. Nope, not stupid enough at all. And it's not as if I'm paid for my opinion. In fact, I'm not paid. Just here to shut up and earn my keep, as Barry says. Just like my Mum did before me and her mum before that, all serving Barry for as long as we can remember.

Two hundred years give or take. It's a long time to be a slave.

Outside it's cooling down, which is a blessing because the air-con died a few hours back. The sky is splashed garish pink by the setting sun and now it's low enough to not hurt my eyes. I push the cheap sunnies to the top of my head, hook the earpieces into my hair so they stay put. I enjoy the rush of the breeze moving in and out of the car. In those brief moments when the engine doesn't howl, I can hear the sounds of the night: cicadas, possums, snakes, lizards, hares, wallabies. All manner of nasties that don't come out in the sunlight.

Kinda like Barry.

I can't hear the words he's shouting, but he knows the dark's come and he wants out. I've got a fair idea what he's saying. *Terry, open the fucking box.* There'll be that for a few more k, then *Teresa, love, sweetie, please open the box. Please let me get some fresh air. It's cold in here.*

I leave it just until I sense he's about to move to threats, then I reach behind, keeping my eyes on the road, feel around on the back seat, find the cooler and flip the lid off. It lands on the floor with the sort of noise only falling polystyrene can make, both offended and humble, a sort of squeal like it's not happy but doesn't want to bother you.

"Thank fuck for that!" Barry's got quite a voice on him for someone currently without lungs. "Are you deaf?"

"Couldn't hear you, Barry. Engine's too noisy." And the machine doesn't make a liar of me—it rumbles and protests like an old man with emphysema. It's been a long trip.

"Well, this thing better keep going, I can't afford to get stuck out in the middle of nowhere in this state."

Barry's "state" has been a cause of concern for a couple of days now. There have been gang fights on the streets of Sydney—not the usual sorts, not the drug peddlers or the slave traders, not the gunrunners or the money launderers. Not this time anyway. Rival gangs of bloodsuckers, all trying to survive, to reach the top of the tree. All trying to be the big dog and negotiate with the breeders, those few Warm who are in the know (even with the current state of societal decay, there are some things you don't want the general populace to find out). But there are those who understand the night isn't a safe place, never has been, not since the First Fleet came and nicked the nation from under the nose of the indigenous population. That even on those ships, the greatest enemy wasn't scurvy or the lash, it was the things, just one or two, that roamed the lonely hours picking off the weak so as not to draw attention to themselves. Those who slept nestled in hidden compartments until the daylight passed.

Barry was one of them. Nasty bastard by all accounts (I've read the diaries my grandmothers kept). Didn't make too many of his own kind initially, just found a thin girl, none too bright, pregnant and fearful, someone he could bully and boss, someone who could do what was needed when the sun ruled the sky and who thought his protection worth the price of her liberty. Minnie: my ever-so-great-grandmother, a silly little pickpocket too slow to not get caught, who sold all our freedoms with her one stupid decision.

She couldn't read or write, but her daughter could, so Minnie told the story and her girl wrote it down. And so on and so on—we've all kept notes of some kind, some more literary than others. The Singleton women have quite a collected work now.

After Minnie's dimness, Barry decided we'd be more useful if educated, so fancy schools for his girls, university if you wanted it (I have a science degree for all the good it did me). He never turned any of us, just keeps us, generation after generation, like family retainers . . . or pets. We don't run. I asked my Mum why, but she just gave me that sleepy junkie smile. In her own way she did run—she just found her escape at the pointy end of a needle.

I've thought about it a lot in the years since and I reckon we stay put because we're told from the cradle there's nowhere else to go. How do you outrun the night? How do you go on living when closing your eyes means you might wake with a weight on your chest that doesn't go away? It's easier to live in the eye of the storm than to try and outrun it. And, ashamed as I am to say it, the protection of the devil you know is preferable to being meat to something else. There are worse things in the dark than Barry.

Of course there's always the theory that girls without fathers will attach themselves quite willingly to father-figures. Barry's a bad dad if ever there was one, but he's always looked after us. Can't argue with that.

So we shut up, do what's expected or find a way out. I'm never quite sure if Mum intended things to go the way they did. The drugs numbed her, but she could function, and Barry turned a blind eye. I guess I always thought it would go on like that forever until I got the call to say Barry had found her one night, stiff and cold under the pergola, propped against the BBQ with the little silver happy stick still in her arm. So, the big recall for me. Goodbye, uni; goodbye, honors degree; goodbye, normal life.

But I digress.

Barry and his state.

He thought himself safe; thought himself well-protected. He'd built up his empire and believed himself king of the vampires. Didn't occur to him that his bodyguard—not me, I'm just a kind of housekeeper—might not be content with the status quo. That Jerzy might want a change of pace, of lifestyle, of regime. That Jerzy might take the great big Japanese sword Barry liked to keep hanging on the wall of his study and use it to separate Barry's head from the rest of his body before the other bodyguards had a chance to tear Jerzy up like a hunk of shredded pork. Then, untethered, they all bolted out of the big house with its Greek columns and stamped concrete driveway, its seldom-used-in-daytime swimming pool, blackout blinds, and luxuriously appointed cellar, leaving the wrought iron gates open and me to wander in from the kitchen to find all the excitement had passed.

What should I see but Barry's head still intact? His body nothing but a pile of cinders and ash, but the head was all in one piece. And talking. Well, less talking than screaming and yelling obscenities. That's when I went to find the cooler, as much ice as I could, and Barry's car keys.

And here we are, heading towards the arse-end of nowhere because Barry says so. Because he says there's a place he can find help, a place where life begins again.

The road is more dirt than black stuff now and it's starting to rise, just a little. Around each bend, the incline gets steeper and the car protests more loudly. Soon, I should imagine, it will make its wishes known with the mechanical equivalent of a big *fuck you.*

"So, tell me how this is going to go again, Boss."

Dawn is starting to gray the sky and Barry's gotten lethargic as you might expect. He's quietened down and I should probably put the lid back on his box—the last of the ice I'd dumped in the esky turned to warmish water hours ago, but I don't guess he'll drown. Looks like he's immortal, if not invulnerable.

"It'll all be sweet, Terry. I'll be good as new," his voice is low and sleepy.

"Fine and dandy, Barry, but what are the details? What about me?"

"What about you? This isn't about you, you dopey bitch." More awake now.

"Never said it was, Barry, but: point of order. We're walking into this place. What's out there? More of your brethren? You're not really in a position to protect me, are you? I'm a canapé on legs. So, *what's out there*?"

"Nah, Terry," he says but he doesn't sound very sure. "It'll be okay, nothing there, no one. Nothing to worry about."

And for the first time in my life I don't believe Barry. I don't trust him to look after me and it gives me a funny feeling in the pit of my stomach. Of course, that could be hunger—that last apple was three hours ago and I'm down to a packet of muesli bars and a tube of Pringles. "Sure, Barry. Sure."

No one, my arse. I know enough about bumps in the night and deserted dead hearts to know nothing's ever really empty. If Barry knows about this place, so does someone else. *You're not king of the vampires here, Bazza, you're just a talking head.* I pull over to the shoulder of the road, reach back and put the lid on Barry and his polystyrene swimming pool. I get out of the car and look around, stretching my long body as my back protests and my worn-too-long cargos and tee stick to my skin. I can smell my own sweat and the determined stink of the cigarettes that ran out not far out of Sydney. I stare into the bush. It's changing as we head up the mountains, getting greener, darker, denser, wetter. More like a rainforest. Not sure what I expect to see . . . nothing there, no movement, not even the twitch of a leaf in the breeze. I feel weird though; I feel watched. *Imagination*, I tell myself. *Bullshit*, I tell myself.

I slide back into the driver's seat and turn the key in the ignition.

The only answer I get is the exhausted metallic grinding of a thing that's gone as far as it can go. I lean forward and rest my head against the steering wheel, smelling the stale-sour scent of hands gripped too long about the leather cover. My spidey senses tell me this road trip will not end well.

I've got Barry's box in one hand and in the other is the long Japanese sword that parted him from his body. It seemed like a good idea to bring it along—just made sure Barry didn't see it, sore point and all that. The water bottle hanging at my waist is making sad little wishy-washy sounds. Not much more than a mouthful left and I'm thirsty. The need for nicotine is dancing under my skin.

The air is cool and damp, the clouds are sitting on the road and it's hard to see too much in front of me. The condensation is plastering the fringe to my forehead. It's mid-afternoon and I don't know where I'm going, I'm just following the road. Can't open the box to ask Barry; he's been in deep sleep for hours now. I just keep walking, although my boots have rubbed blisters onto my soles and the outer edges of my little toes.

Up ahead I can hear a sound, sweet and clear. Running water.

I pick up my pace and stumble off the road, down a slight slope to find a clearing, a little creek running through it. There's a fire pit that looks like it hasn't been used in a long, long time. I refill the water bottle, drink deeply, then peel off my boots and socks and plunge my feet in. It's icy and hurts only for a little while before the numbing cold makes everything seem okay. I lean back, raise my face to where the sun should be and imagine it on my skin. Problem with being in service with a night crawler is that you don't tend to see too much daylight. Oh, you have to run errands and some of those are unavoidably day-oriented. But mostly, you become as nocturnal as your master. Feels like shift-work. Do it long enough you either get used to it or go nuts. Or a bit of both.

Behind me there's a sound; behind me, where I dropped Barry's box (the katana I kept close). There's that distinct polystyrene noise and I turn to see the biggest freaking possum I've ever seen in my life. It looks like a large dog, a Labrador maybe, on its hind legs and it's got the lid off the cooler and one paw buried deep inside. It pulls Barry's head out by the messy black hair.

There it dangles at the end of possum claws, eyes closed, lips slack and a little open, the neck so cleanly severed you could almost admire it as a nice tidy job. I stand slowly. The possum sniffs at Barry's nose, licks it, then opens its mouth and sinks sharp white teeth into the substance of Barry's pert little snoz.

I take a good few fast steps and bring the katana sweeping upward and the possum paw drops to the ground, which leaves Barry hanging briefly by his nose in the grip of the teeth of a very unhappy marsupial. Possum spits out its meal and gives me a look that makes me think twice about getting any closer. Then I remember that I've got the sword and about four feet in height on the thing. But it's fast and the remaining claws sharp; my cargos and the leg underneath get a nasty gash before I manage to take the stinking thing's head off.

I have a rest, bent over, hands on knees, breathing hard while I watch blood dribble out of my injured flesh. There's a yell and I fear a possum support column may have arrived. But it's only Barry, waking up.

"What the fuck happened to my nose? Do you have any idea how much this hurts? What the hell did you do to me?"

"Oh, Barry, you don't want to know. Now, which way? There are no signs for Sun Falls."

"Just keep following the road." The he pitches his eyes downwards, trying to get a good look at the state of his nose. I manage not to laugh as he goes a little cross-eyed. "Fuck this hurts."

A bonfire and five figures gathered around it: a woman, an old man, two young men, and a teenage girl. Raggedy stragglers, left out here with orders to guard the place, I guess. They're vampires, though, so it doesn't matter if there are five or a hundred. The rush and roar of water is clear from somewhere in the darkness. I can feel a damp spray I think might come from the falls.

I washed the wound and wrapped my leg up tight, but I know they can smell it before I step into the circle of light. There's a collective growl that must be something like a gazelle hears before a pride of lions brings it down. I might be able to take out a couple before they get to me. The fire catches the edge of the katana and pinwheels in Barry-unboxed's wide open eyes. The pack stays back, however. I must look as though I know what I'm doing—well, you can fool some of the vampires some of the time, I guess.

The woman stands and takes a few steps towards me.

"Hello, dinner," she says. "How obliging of you to turn up."

"You might want to re-think that," I say, and raise my boss's head.

Barry pipes up, "Lynda, keep your hands off her. She's no one's meal."

"Is that you, Barry?" The woman squints. Her hair is wound into filthy dreads, not all of her teeth remain and the breeze tells me she's not washed in some time. Hillbilly vamps, who'd have thought it? Feeding on the occasional lost tourist, stray cattle, giant possums. "Aw, Barry. What the fuck happened?"

"Long fucking story. I need to use the pool," he says shortly.

"The pool? No one's done that in a hundred years—you dunno what's gonna happen." She gets a cunning look in her eye. "What's it worth to ya?"

"How about a snack?"

Told you Barry was a nasty piece of work. But you know what, I'm less afraid of him than I am of them. One thing I do know is this: no matter how much he lies to everyone else, he's always kept his word to my family. He said I would be safe. He's also the only thing protecting me from the cast of a bloodsucking *Deliverance*.

I'm flanked by two underfed youths with straggly beards and, if I didn't know better, a look that says "Inbreeding keeps it in the family." One of them carries a torch plucked flaming from the fire. They don't need it to see, hell, they don't need fire at all, but I recognize in the building of the bonfire a remnant of their warm days, a little thing to hang onto. A memory of *back when*, of kids playing at grown-ups, of a time when heat meant comfort, meant life. Creatures pretending one day there might be light.

The falls are a couple of minutes walk away, down a path strewn with sticks and pebbles, occasionally hidden by touchy-feely ferns. When we reach the bottom, there's a shallow pool and a whole lot of spray where the water crashes down. One of my escorts points to a break in the foliage, right next to the cataract; the other pushes me roughly forward. My Docs slip and slide on the damp rocks. I keep my balance though; with a head in one hand, a sword in the other, and Barry cursing me the whole while it's no mean feat. I walk around behind the curtain of wet and see an entrance, a glow coming from inside it like a jack-o'-lantern.

There are no torches here, I notice, but the walls glow. Phosphorous? I wait until we're far enough down the tunnel for my guard of honor to not hear.

"Barry, you ungrateful bastard. I carry your sorry metaphorical arse all the way here, nearly get eaten by a mutant possum, and this is the thanks I get?" I shake him by the hair and glare into his blue eyes. "You think I'm an *hors d'oeuvre*?"

"Calm down. Wait—possum? Is that what happened to my nose? You let a possum eat my fucking nose?"

"Focus, Barry. Seriously, do you think I'm going to drop you in the all-healing, all-fixing pond so you can serve me up to that lot?" I shake him again and he winces. "Or are you gonna snack on me yourself?"

"Don't worry about it. Once I'm whole again, no one's going to mess with you."

"You didn't answer me!"

"I might need a little blood when I'm done," he admits. I give his head a good rattle and a few choice profanities, and he yells, "Not much! Not much! Just a little to top up. I promise!"

"What are we talking? A thimbleful? A shot glass?"

"Just a—bit. Terry, I promise I won't drain you, I won't turn you."

What choice do I have? The devil I know or the ones I don't.

The pool is at the bottom of the slope, in roughly the center of a small cavern. The liquid in it is milky-white with the same sheen as mother-of-pearl, and the smell is a little like household cleaner. A bit bleachy—more *Domestos* than *Dettol*.

"What's that?" I ask, trying not to breathe too deeply.

"Stuff. You know—stuff."

"You knew about this how?"

"Stories, Chinese whispers, old diaries—your lot aren't the only ones who keep records, you know. Nothing precise, nothing exact, just hints."

"You *read* our diaries?" I shouldn't be surprised.

"Yeah, yeah, yeah, I'm a bad person. Throw me in."

"But what if it doesn't work?"

"Not really in a position to be picky, am I? Fountain of youth, a wellspring, a cauldron of plenty. There are legends and they all say it brings life."

I don't point out to Barry that strictly speaking he has been for some time well and truly beyond the usual span of any creature. Well and truly outside the spectrum of what we call "life."

"So," I say, "life?"

"Life. Now hurry the fuck up and toss me in."

I walk around the edge. It's about five meters across and bubbling enthusiastically. If I drop him, maybe he'll just drown—this is a bit deeper than the esky—which still leaves me with a problem.

"Here's the deal, Barry: I'll put you in but in return you let me go. I'm no one's lunch, I'm no one's slave, I'm gone. I'm out. I do whatever I want."

"Terry . . ."

"You want life or not?"

"Yes, fuck it!" He gives a growl of frustration. "Alright. Agreed. I can find better than you at the local whorehouse anyway."

"Touché."

I kneel beside the pond and lower Barry in, resisting the impulse to drop him from a height to see how much of a splash he'll make. Some of the fluid leaps up like a nipping fish and lands on my fingers. It stings like ice. I grit my teeth and keep going, don't release the head until he is thoroughly submerged.

I try to straighten up, withdraw my arm, but I feel sharp teeth in my wrist. Barry, you bastard. That, however, is the least of my problems: the water has me. Blood spurts from my nose and turns pink as it hits the milky pond. It's like I'm in the grip of an electrical current. It tugs at me and tugs at me until I over-balance and it pulls me beneath the surface.

I feel as if I'm dying forever.

My last sight before I'm overwhelmed is Barry's head tossed and churned, jumping about like popping corn. Angry fingers of fluid force their way into my mouth and race down my throat, filling my lungs like inhaled fire. My skin seems to peel off, each hair follicle is a tiny pin in my scalp. Surely my eyes burst.

When it stops hurting, the water lets me go.

I crawl out and lie on the surprisingly warm rock. I'm whole, intact if somewhat soaked. I rub a hand against my shin, right where the possum bite was and feel . . .

And feel . . .

Nothing.

I roll up the leg of my cargos and strip away the bandage. There's just a pink mark that might have been a scar but fades as I watch. The katana is where I left it, and I pick it up, prick at my finger with its sharpness. Something silver oozes out from the cut and just as quickly the opening closes over.

A great spout of water comes from the pool and a body lands not far from me, gives a displeased groan.

Barry, whole again, tall and handsome and muscular and . . .

And no longer pale as if he tries to tan beneath the moon.

He rolls on his back, coughing, making a noise like an espresso machine. He breathes. I poke at him with the katana. A tiny drop of blood blossoms on his skin and he swears. Rich, fresh, oxygenated, *living* blood.

"Oh, Barry," I say. "You were right."

He sits up, runs his hands over his arms and legs, wondering, not understanding. "But. . ."

"It does give life, Barry. You've been dead a long time." I can't keep the laughter out of my voice.

"But . . . Fuck!" He stands up, pacing. "Okay. I don't have to outrun them, I just have to outrun you."

"Here's the thing, Baz, I don't think they're going to be interested in me anymore." I rise, do the thing with the poking and the quick silvery bleed. "Close as I can figure it, nature abhors a vacuum. The pond finished what you started, taking my blood and all, then . . . replaced it."

I start up the path, cast a look behind, "Long time since you've been meat. How's it feel?"

MAGDALA AMYGDALA

Lucy A. Snyder

Lucy A. Snyder is the Bram Stoker Award-winning author of the dark urban fantasy novels *Spellbent, Shotgun Sorceress, Switchblade Goddess,* and the collections *Orchid Carousals, Sparks and Shadows, Chimeric Machines,* and *Installing Linux on a Dead Badger.* Her most recent books are *Shooting Yourself in the Head for Fun and Profit: A Writer's Survival Guide* (Post Mortem Press) and *Soft Apocalypses* (Raw Dog Screaming Press). Her writing has been translated into French, Russian, and Japanese and has appeared in publications such as *Apex, Nightmare, Strange Horizons,* and *Weird Tales,* as well as anthologies *Hellbound Hearts, Dark Faith, Chiaroscuro, GUD, Chiral Mad 2, Best Horror of the Year, Volume 5,* and others. You can learn more about her at www.lucysnyder.com.

With "Magdala Amygdala" Snyder takes us into a near future in which a form of vampirism has "gone viral" . . .

> "I was bound, though I have not bound. I was not recognized. But I have recognized that the All is being dissolved, both the earthly and the heavenly."
>   —*The Gospel of Mary Magdalene*

"So how are you feeling?" Dr. Shapiro's pencil hovers over the CDC risk evaluation form clamped to her clipboard.

"Pretty good." When I talk, I make sure my tongue stays tucked out of sight. I smile at her in a way that I hope looks friendly, and not like I'm baring my teeth. The exam-room mirror reflects the back of the good doctor's head. Part of me wishes the silvered glass were angled so I could check my expression; the rest of me is relieved that I can't see myself.

Nothing existed before this. The present and recent past keep blurring together in my mind, but I've learned to take a moment before I

reply to questions, speak a little more slowly to give myself the chance
to sort things out before I utter something that might sound abnormal.
My waking world seems to have been taken apart and put back together
so that everything is just slightly off, the geometries of reality deranged.

Most of my memories before the virus are as insubstantial as dreams;
the strongest of them feel like borrowed clothing. The sweet snap of peas
fresh from my garden. The crush of hot perfumed bodies against mine
at the club and the thud of the bass from the huge speakers. The pleasant
twin burns of the sun on my shoulders and the exertion in my legs as I
pedal my bike up the mountainside.

The life I had in those memories is gone forever. I don't know why
this is happening to humanity. To me. I'd like to think there's some greater
purpose, some meaning in all this, but God help me, I just can't see it.

"So is the new job going well? Are you able to sleep?" My doctor
shines a penlight in my eyes and nostrils and marks off a couple of boxes.
Thankfully, she doesn't ask to see my tongue. It's the same set of questions
every week; I'd have to be pretty far gone to answer badly and get myself
quarantined. The endless doctor-visits wear down other Type Threes, but I
hang onto the belief that someday there might be actual help for me here.

I nod. "It's fine. I have blackout curtains; sleep's not a problem. They
seem pretty happy with my work."

My new supervisor is a friendly guy, but he always has an excuse for
why he can't meet with me in person, preferring to call me on his cell
phone for our weekly chats. I used to bounce from building to building,
repairing computers, spending equal amounts of time swapping gossip
and hardware. After I got out of the hospital, I went on the graveyard shift
in the company's cold network operations center. These nights, I'm mostly
raising processes from the dead, watching endless scrolling green text on
cryptic black screens. I'm pretty sure the company discreetly advised my
quiet coworkers to carry tasers and mace just in case.

"Do you feel that you're able to see your old friends and family often
enough?" Dr. Shapiro asks.

"Sure," I lie. "We meet online for games and we talk in Vent. It's fun."

For the sake of his own health, my boyfriend took a job and apartment
in another state; we speak less and less on the phone. What is there to say
to him now? We can't even chat about anything as simple as food or wine;
I must subsist on bananas, rice, apple juice, and my meager allotment of
six Bovellum capsules per day. The law says I can't go to crowded places

428 • LUCY A. SNYDER

like theaters and concerts. I only glimpse the sun when I'm hurrying from the shelter of my car's darkly tinted windows to monthly 8:00 a.m. appointments with my court-ordered physician.

So I'm striding up the street to Dr. Shapiro's office, my head down, squinting behind sunglasses, when suddenly I hear a man in the park across the street shouting violent nonsense. Or he used to be a man, anyhow; he's wearing construction boots, ragged Carhartt work overalls, and a dirty gray T-shirt, all freshly spattered with the blood of the woman whose head he is enthusiastically cracking open against the curb. He howls at the sky, and I can see he's missing some teeth. Probably whatever he did for a living didn't pay him enough to see a dentist. But his skin looks flush and smooth, so much healthier than mine, and for a moment I envy him.

He stops howling and meets my shadowed stare, breaking into a gory, gap-toothed smile. The kind of grin you give an old, dear friend. I've never laid eyes on this wreck before, and the woman beneath him is beyond anyone's help. They both are. I don't want to be outed, not here, not like this, so I pretend I don't even see him and stride on.

A few seconds later, I hear the spat of rifle fire and the thud of a meaty body hitting the pavement, and I know that the SWAT team just took out Ragged Carhartts. They're never far away, not in this part of town. And once they've taken out one Type Three, they don't need much excuse to kill another, even if you're just trying to see your doctor like a good citizen.

"Oh, God," a lady says. She and another fortyish woman are standing in the doorway of an art gallery, staring horrified at the scene behind me. They're both wearing batik dresses and lots of handmade jewelry. "That's the third one this month."

"If this keeps up, we'll have to close." The other woman shakes her head, looking gray-faced. "Nobody will want to come here. The whole downtown will die. Not just us. The theaters, the museums, churches—everything."

"I heard something on NPR about a new kind of gel to keep the virus from spreading," the first woman replies, sounding hopeful.

I keep moving. Her voice fades away. People still talk about contagion control as if it matters, as if masks and sanitizers and prayers can stop the future.

The truth is, unless you've been living in some isolated Tibetan monastery, you've already been exposed to Polymorphic Viral Gastroencephalitis. Maybe it gave you a bit of a headache and some nausea, but after a few days' bed rest you were going out for Thai again. Congratulations! You're Type One and you probably don't even know it.

But maybe the headache turned into the worst you've ever had, and you started vomiting up blood and then your stomach lining, and when you came out of the hospital you'd lost the ability to digest most foods and to make certain proteins. And in the absence of those proteins, your body has trouble growing and healing. The enzymes your DNA uses to repair itself don't work very well anymore.

Sunlight is no longer your friend. Neither are X-rays. Even if you quit smoking and keep yourself covered up like a virgin in the Rub' Al Khali, your skin cracks and your body sprouts tumors. Your brain begins to degenerate; you start talking to yourself in second person. Sooner or later, you develop lesions on your frontal lobe and hippocampus that cause a variety of behaviors which will lead to your friendly neighborhood SWAT team putting a .308 bullet through your skull. That means you're a Type Two, or maybe a Type Three, like me.

If you're Type Four, we aren't having this conversation. Unless you're a ghost. You aren't a ghost, are you? I don't think I believe in them. But if you were a Type Four, your whole GI tract got stripped. I hope you were lucky and had a massive brain bleed right when it got really bad, and you never woke up.

I'm pretty sure I woke up.

"Do you find yourself having any unwanted thoughts or violent fantasies?" Dr. Shapiro asks.

"Of course not." I try to sound mildly indignant.

There's one upside, if it can be called that. If you lived past all the pain and vomiting, the symptoms of your chronic disease can be alleviated, if you consume sufficient daily quantities of one of a couple of raw protein sources.

If the best protein source for you is fresh human blood, congratulations, you are a Type Two! Provided you have a fat bank account, or decent health insurance, or are quick with a razor and fast on your feet, you can resume puberty or your athletic career. Watch out for HIV; it's a killer.

If, however, the best source for you comes from sweet, custard-like brains . . . you are a Type Three. Your situation is much more problematic. And expensive. You better have a wealthy family or truly excellent insurance. Or mob connections. Otherwise, sooner or later, you'll end up trying to crack open someone's skull in public. The only question then is if you'll get that one moment of true gustatory bliss right before you die.

I have excellent health insurance. There's no bliss for me. What I and every other upstanding, gainfully employed, fully-covered Type Three citizen gets is an allotment of refrigerated capsules containing an unappetizing gray paste. Mostly it's cow brains and antioxidant vitamins with just the barest hint of pureed cadaver white matter. It's enough to keep your skin and brains from ulcerating. It's enough to keep your nose from rotting off. It's enough to help you think clearly enough to function at your average white-collar job.

It is not enough to keep you from constantly wishing you could taste the real thing.

"I was wondering about something," I say, as Dr. Shapiro begins to copy the contents of her survey into the exam room computer.

She stops typing and gives me a wary smile. "Yes, what is it?"

"My medication. I feel okay, you know? But I think I could feel . . . better. If I could have a little more?" I'm choosing my words as carefully as possible. My tongue feels thick, twitchy.

I can't talk about the cravings I'm feeling. I can't mention wanting more energy, because nobody in charge wants someone like me feeling energetic.

I wonder if there's a sniper watching from behind the mirror on the wall; has he tightened his grip on his rifle? Are gas canisters waiting to blow in the air conditioner vent above me? My skin itches in dread anticipation.

Dr. Shapiro hedges. "Well, I know there's been a shortage of raw materials these days."

I swallow down my impatience and worry. The capsules are ninety-eight percent cow brains, for God's sake. Probably they can squeeze a single human brain for thousands of doses. I can't imagine the pharmaceutical companies are running short of anything.

"Could you check, just the same? Could you ask for me?" I sound meek. Pathetic. The opposite of hostile. That's good.

She gives me a pitying look and sighs. The mirror doesn't explode in gunfire. Gas doesn't burst from the vents.

"I'll see what I can do," my doctor says.

I try to believe she'll come through for me.

I go home. I take my capsules with some Mott's apple juice. I rinse my mouth out with peroxide and don't look at my tongue. I rub salve on the places my clothes have rubbed raw, and I climb naked into my bed.

Sometime later, the alarm goes off, and I rise, shower, dress, and drive to work in darkness.

My shift is dull-clockwork, until just after gray drizzling dawn, when one of the new tech leads comes in to talk to my coworker George about some of the emergency server protocols. I haven't seen this young man before; he's wearing snug jeans and the sleeves of his black polo shirt are tight over biceps tattooed with angels and devils. His blond hair is cut close over a smooth, high-browed skull. He starts talking about database errors, but he's thinking about a gig he has with his band on Friday night, and it suddenly hits me not just that I know what he's thinking but that I know because I can smell the sweet chemicals shifting inside his brain. The chemicals tell me his name is Devin.

I am filled with Want in the marrow of my bones. I am filled with Need from eyeballs to soles. I excuse myself and hurry out into the mutagenic morning and punch Betty's number into my cell. Soon after we met, she made me promise not to save her details in my phone, just in case anything went wrong.

It's early for her. But she answers on the third ring. Speaking in the casual code we've used since we met online, we agree to meet that evening. It's her turn to host.

I sleep fitfully. When my alarm goes off, I call in sick, shower, dress, and check my phone. Betty's texted a cryptic string of letters and numbers for my directions. And so I drive out to a hotel we've never visited before, drinking Aquafinas the whole way. It's a dark old place, once grand, now crumbling away in a forgotten corner of downtown. I wonder if she's running short of money or if the extra anonymity of the place was crucial to her.

Still, as I get out my car and double-check my locks in the pouring rain, I can't help but peer out into the oppressive black spaces in the parking lot, trying to figure out if any of the shadows between the other vehicles could be lurking cops or CDC agents. The darkness doesn't move, so I hurry to the front door, head down, hands jammed in my raincoat pockets, my stomach roiling with worry and anticipation. I avoid making eye contact with any of the damp, tired-looking prostitutes smoking outside the hotel's front doors. None of them pay any attention to me.

My phone chimes as Betty texts me the room number. I take the creaking, urine-stinking elevator up four floors. My pace slows as I walk down the stained hallway carpet, and I pause for a moment before I knock on the door of Room 512. What if the watchers tapped Betty's phone? What if she's not here at all? My poised hand quivers as my heart seems to pound out "A trap—a trap—a trap."

I swallow. Knock twice. Step back. A moment later, Betty answers the door, wearing her Audrey Hepburn wig and a black cocktail dress that hangs limply from her skeletal shoulders. It's appalling how much weight she's lost; her eyes have turned entirely black, the whites permanently stained by repeated hemorrhages.

But she smiles at me, and I find myself smiling back, warmed by the first spark of real human feeling I've had in months. I have to believe that we're still human. I *have* to.

"You ready?" Her question creaks like the hinge of a forgotten gate.

"Absolutely." My own voice is the dry fluttering of moth wings.

She locks the door behind me. "I'm sorry this place is such a pit, but the guy at the Holiday Inn started asking all kinds of questions, and this was the best I could do on short notice."

"It's okay." The room isn't as seedy as the lobby and exterior led me to expect it to be, and it's got a couch in addition to the queen-sized bed. Betty has already covered the couch and the carpet in front of it with a green plastic tarpaulin. Her stainless steel spritzer bottle leans against a couch arm.

"Want some wine?" She gestures toward an unopened bottle of Yellow Tail Shiraz on the dresser.

"Thanks, but no . . . I couldn't drink it right now. Maybe after."

She nods. "There's a really good Italian restaurant around the corner. Kind of a Goodfellas hangout, but everything's homemade. Great garlic bread."

Betty pulls off the wig. Before she got the virus, she could grow her thick chestnut hair clear down to her waist. I've never seen it except in pictures; her bare scalp gleams pale in the yellow light from the chandelier.

The scar circumscribing her skull looks red, inflamed; I wonder if she's been seeing other Type Threes. I quickly tamp down my pang of jealousy. We never agreed to an exclusive arrangement. And maybe she just had to go to the hospital instead; she told me she's got some kind of massive tumor on her pituitary.

She looks so frail. I can't possibly begrudge her what comfort she can get. I should just be grateful that she agrees to see me when I need her.

And, oh sweet Lord, do I need her tonight.

Betty pulls me down to her for a kiss. Her hands are icy, but her lips are warm. She slips her tongue into my mouth, and I can taste sweet cerebrospinal fluid mingled in her saliva. The tumor must have cracked the bony barriers in her skull. Before I have a chance to try to pull away, my own tongue is swelling, toothed pores opening and nipping at her slippery flesh.

She squeaks in pain and we separate.

"Sorry," I try to whisper. But my tongue is continuing to engorge and lengthen, curling back on itself and slithering down my own throat; I can feel the tiny maws rasping against my adenoids.

"It's okay." Her wan smile is smeared with blood. "We better get started."

She kisses the palm of my hand and begins to take my clothes off. I stare up at the tawdry chandelier, watching a fly buzz among the dusty baubles and bulbs. When I'm naked, she slips off her cocktail dress and leads me to the tarp-covered couch.

"Be gentle." She presses a short oyster knife into my hand and sits me down, the plastic crackling beneath me. I nod, barely keeping my lips closed over my shuddering tongue, and spread my legs.

With slow exhalation, Betty settles between my thighs, her back to me. She's a tiny woman, her head barely clearing my chin when we're seated, so this position works best. Her skin is already covered in goose bumps. The anticipation is killing both of us.

I carefully run the tip of the sharp oyster knife through the red scar around her skull; there's relatively little blood as I cut through the tissue. Betty gives a little gasp and grips my knees, her whole body tensed. The bone has only stitched back together in a few places; I use the side-to-side motion she showed me to gently pry the lid of her skull free.

She moans when I expose her brain; it's the most beautiful thing I could hope to see. Her dura mater glistens with a half-inch slick of golden jelly. Brain honey. When I breathe in the smell of her, I feel my blood pressure rise hard and fast.

I set the bowl of skin and bone aside and present the knife to her in my outstretched left hand. With a flick of her wrist, she slits the vein in the crook of my arm and presses her mouth against my bleeding flesh. I wrap my cut arm around her head and pull her tight to my breast.

I open my mouth and let my tongue unwind like an eel into her brain-pan. It wriggles there, purple and gnarled, the tiny maw sucking down her golden jelly. It's delicious, better than caviar, better than ice cream, better than anything I've had in my mouth before. Sweet and salty and tangy and perfect.

The jelly gives me flashes of her memories and dreams; she's been with other Type Threes. She's helped them murder people. I don't care. I keep drinking her in, my tongue probing all the corners of her skull and sheathed wrinkles of her brain to get every last gooey drop.

I can control my tongue, but just barely. It's hard to keep it from doing the one thing I'd dearly love, which is to drive it through her membrane deep between her slippery lobes. But that would be the end of her. The end of us. No more, all over, bye-bye.

A little of what my body and soul craves is better than nothing at all. Isn't it?

My arm aches, and I'm starting to feel lightheaded on top of the high. We're both running dry. I release her, spritz her brain with saline and carefully put the top of her head back into place. She's full of my blood, and already her scalp is sealing back together. We've done well; we spilled hardly anything on the tarp this time. But my face feels sticky, and I've probably even gotten her in my hair.

She daintily wipes my blood from the corners of her mouth and smiles at me. Her skin is pink and practically glowing, and her boniness seems chic rather than diseased. "Want to go to that Italian place after we get cleaned up?"

"Sure." I'm probably glowing, too. My stomach feels strong enough for pepperoncinis.

I head to the bathroom to wash my face, but when I push open the door—

—I find myself in Dr. Shapiro's office. She's staring down at an MRI scan of somebody's chest. The monochrome bones look strange, distorted.

"There's definitely a mass behind your ribs and spine. It's growing fast, but I can't definitely say it's cancer."

I'm dizzy with terror. How did I get here? What mass? How long have I had a mass?

"What should we do?" I stammer.

She looks up at me with eyes as solidly black as Betty's. "I think we should wait and see."

I back away, turn, push through her office door—

—and I'm back in a rented room. But not the downtown dive with the dusty chandelier. It's a suburban motel someplace. Have I been here before?

The green tarp on the king-sized bed is covered in blood and bits of skull. There's a body wrapped in black trash bags, stuffed between the bed and the writing desk. Did I do that? What have I done?

Oh, God, please make this stop. I have to lean against the wall to keep myself from tumbling backward.

Betty comes out of the bathroom, dressed in a spattered silk negligee. I think it used to be white. There's gore in her wig. Her eyes go wide.

"I told you not to come here!" She grabs me by my arm, surprising me with her strength. In the distance, I can hear sirens. "They'll be here any minute—get away from here, fast as you can!"

She presses a set of rental car keys into my palm, hauls me to the door and pushes me out into the hallway—

—and I'm stepping into the elevator at work.

Handsome blond Devin is in there. A look of surprised fear crosses his face, and I know the very sight of me repels him. His hand goes to his jeans pocket. I see the outline of something that's probably a canister of pepper spray. It's too small to be a taser.

But then he pauses, smiles at me. "Hey, you going up to that training class?"

I nod mechanically, and try to say "Sure," but my lungs spasm and suddenly I'm doubled over, coughing into my hands. When did simply breathing start hurting this much?

"You okay?" Devin asks.

I try to nod, but there's bright blood on my palms. A long-forgotten Bible verse surfaces in the swamp of my memory: *Behold, I am vile; what shall I answer thee? I will lay mine hand upon my mouth.*

I look up and see my reflection in the chromed elevator walls—my face is gaunt, but my body is grotesquely swollen. I've turned into some kind of hunchback. How long have I had the mass?

Instead of the pepper spray, Devin's pulled his cell phone out. I can smell his mind. He's torn between wanting to run away and wanting to help. "Should I call someone? Should I call nine-one-one?"

The elevator is filled with the scent of him. Despite my pain and sickness, the Want returns with a vengeance. Adrenaline rises along with my blood pressure. My tongue is twitching, and something in my back, too. I can feel it tearing my ribs away from my spine. It hurts more than I can remember anything ever hurting. Maybe childbirth would be like this.

Betty. I need Betty. How long has it been since I've seen her? Oh God.

"Call nine-one-one," I try to say, but I can't take a breath, can't speak around the tongue writhing backward down my throat.

"What can I do?" Devin touches my shoulder.

And the feel of his hand against my bony flesh is far too much for me to bear.

I rise up under him, grab him by the sides of his head, kissing him. My tongue goes straight down his throat, choking him. He hits me, trying to shake me off, but as strong as he is, my Want is stronger.

When he's unconscious, I let him fall and hit the emergency stop button. The Want has me wrapped tightly in its ardor, burning away all my human qualms. The alarm is an annoyance, and I know I don't have as much time as I want. Still. As I lift his left eyelid, I take a moment to admire his perfect bluebonnet iris.

And then I plunge my tongue into his eye. The ball squirts off to the side as my organ drills deeper, the tiny mouths rasping through the thin socket bone into his sweet frontal lobe. After the first wash of cerebral fluid I'm into the creamy white meat of him, and—

—Oh, God. This is more beautiful than I imagined.

I'm devouring his will. Devouring his memories. Living him, through and through. His first taste of wine. His first taste of a woman. The first time he stood onstage. He's at the prime of his life, and oh, it's been a wonderful life, and I am memorizing every second of it as I swallow down the contents of his lovely skull.

When he's empty, I rise from his shell and feel my new wings break free from the cage of my back. As I spread them wide in the elevator, I realize I can hear the old gods whispering to me from their thrones in the dark spaces between the stars.

I smile at myself in the distorted chrome walls. Everything is clear to me now. I have been chosen. I have a purpose. Through the virus, the old gods tested me, and deemed me worthy of this holiest of duties. There are others like me; I can hear them gathering in the caves outside the city. Some died, yes, like the ragged man, but my Becoming is almost complete. Nothing as simple as a bullet will stop me then.

The Earth is ripe, human civilization at its peak. I and the other archivists will preserve the memories of the best and brightest as we devour them. We will use the blood of this world to write dark, beautiful poetry across the walls of the universe.

For the first time in my life, I don't need faith. I know what I am supposed to do in every atom in every cell of my body. I will record thousands of souls before my masters allow me to join them in the star-shadows, and I will love every moment of my mission.

I can hear the SWAT team rush into the foyer three stories below. Angry ants. I can hear Betty and the others calling to me from the hollow hills. Smiling, I open the hatch in the top of the elevator and prepare to fly.

THE COLDEST GIRL IN COLDTOWN

Holly Black

Holly Black is the author of bestselling contemporary fantasy books for kids and teens. Some of her titles include The Spiderwick Chronicles (with Tony DiTerlizzi), The Modern Faerie Tale series, The Good Neighbors graphic novel trilogy (with Ted Naifeh), the Curse Workers series, and *Doll Bones*. Her most recent novels are *The Darkest Part of the Forest* and (with Cassandra Clare) *The Iron Trial (Magisterium #1)*. She has been a finalist for the Mythopoeic Award and Eisner Award, and the recipient of the Andre Norton Award and a Newbery Honor. She currently lives in New England with her husband and son in a house with a secret door.

Her dark fantasy novel, *The Coldest Girl in Coldtown*—it grew out of the following story—was named an Amazon Best Teen Book of the Year and a School Library Journal Best Book of the Year as well as to the YALSA Best Fiction for Young Adults and Kirkus Best YA Books lists. But I don't feel it is necessarily just for teens: I've reprinted it before and present it here again because I feel it is one of the most chilling interpretations of the vampiric life ever imagined . . .

Matilda was drunk, but then she was always drunk anymore. Dizzy drunk. Stumbling drunk. Stupid drunk. Whatever kind of drunk she could get.

The man she stood with snaked his hand around her back, warm fingers digging into her side as he pulled her closer. He and his friend with the open-necked shirt grinned down at her like underage equaled dumb, and dumb equaled gullible enough to sleep with them.

She thought they might just be right.

"You want to have a party back at my place?" the man asked. He'd told her his name was Mark, but his friend kept slipping up and calling him by a

438

name that started with a D. Maybe Dan or Dave. They had been smuggling her drinks from the bar whenever they went outside to smoke—drinks mixed sickly sweet that dripped down her throat like candy.

"Sure," she said, grinding her cigarette against the brick wall. She missed the hot ash in her hand, but concentrated on the alcoholic numbness turning her limbs to lead. Smiled. "Can we pick up more beer?"

They exchanged an obnoxious glance she pretended not to notice. The friend—he called himself Ben—looked at her glassy eyes and her cold-flushed cheeks. Her sloppy hair. He probably made guesses about a troubled home life. She hoped so.

"You're not going to get sick on us?" he asked. Just out of the hot bar, beads of sweat had collected in the hollow of his throat. The skin shimmered with each swallow.

She shook her head to stop staring. "I'm barely tipsy," she lied.

"I've got plenty of stuff back at my place," said MarkDanDave. *Mardave*, Matilda thought and giggled.

"Buy me a 40," she said. She knew it was stupid to go with them, but it was even stupider if she sobered up. "One of those wine coolers. They have them at the bodega on the corner. Otherwise, no party."

Both of the guys laughed. She tried to laugh with them even though she knew she wasn't included in the joke. She was the joke. The trashy little slut. The girl who can be bought for a big fat wine cooler and three cranberry-and-vodkas.

"Okay, okay," said Mardave.

They walked down the street and she found herself leaning easily into the heat of their bodies, inhaling the sweat and iron scent. It would be easy for her to close her eyes and pretend Mardave was someone else, someone she wanted to be touched by, but she wouldn't let herself soil her memories of Julian.

They passed by a store with flat-screens in the window, each one showing different channels. One streamed video from Coldtown—a girl who went by the name Demonia made some kind of deal with one of the stations to show what it was really like behind the gates. She filmed the Eternal Ball, a party that started in 1998 and had gone on ceaselessly ever since. In the background, girls and boys in rubber harnesses swung through the air. They stopped occasionally, opening what looked like a modded hospital tube stuck on the inside of their arms just below the crook of the elbow. They twisted a knob and spilled blood into little paper cups for the partygoers. A boy who looked to be about nine, wearing a string of glowing beads around his neck, gulped down the contents of one of the cups and then licked the paper with a tongue as red as his eyes. The camera angle changed suddenly, veering up, and the viewers saw the domed top of the hall, full of cracked windows through which you could glimpse the stars.

"I know where they are," Mardave said. "I can see that building from my apartment."

"Aren't you scared of living so close to the vampires?" she asked, a small smile pulling at the corners of her mouth.

"We'll protect you," said Ben, smiling back at her.

"We should do what other countries do and blow those corpses sky high," Mardave said.

Matilda bit her tongue not to point out that Europe's vampire hunting led to the highest levels of infection in the world. So many of Belgium's citizens were vampires that shops barely opened their doors until nightfall. The truce with Coldtown worked. Mostly.

She didn't care if Mardave hated vampires. She hated them too.

When they got to the store, she waited outside to avoid getting carded and lit another cigarette with Julian's silver lighter—the one she was going to give back to him in thirty-one days. Sitting down on the curb, she let the chill of the pavement deaden the backs of her thighs. Let it freeze her belly and frost her throat with ice that even liquor couldn't melt.

Hunger turned her stomach. She couldn't remember the last time she'd eaten anything solid without throwing it back up. Her mouth hungered for dark, rich feasts; her skin felt tight, like a seed thirsting to bloom. All she could trust herself to eat was smoke.

When she was a little girl, vampires had been costumes for Halloween. They were the bad guys in movies, plastic fangs and polyester capes. They were Muppets on television, endlessly counting.

Now she was the one who was counting. Fifty-seven days. Eighty-eight days. Eighty-eight nights.

"Matilda?"

She looked up and saw Dante saunter up to her, earbuds dangling out of his ears like he needed a soundtrack for everything he did. He wore a pair of skintight jeans and smoked a cigarette out of one of those long, movie-star holders. He looked pretentious as hell. "I'd almost given up on finding you."

"You should have started with the gutter," she said, gesturing to the wet, clogged tide beneath her feet. "I take my gutter-dwelling very seriously."

"*Seriously.*" He pointed at her with the cigarette holder. "Even your mother thinks you're dead. Julian's crying over you."

Maltilda looked down and picked at the thread of her jeans. It hurt to think about Julian while waiting for Mardave and Ben. She was disgusted with herself, and she could only guess how disgusted he'd be. "I got Cold," she said. "One of them bit me."

Dante nodded his head.

That's what they'd started calling it when the infection kicked in— Cold—because of how cold people's skin became after they were bitten. And because of the way the poison in their veins caused them to crave heat and blood. One taste of human blood and the infection mutated. It killed the host and then raised it back up again, colder than before. Cold through and through, forever and ever.

"I didn't think you'd be alive," he said.

She hadn't thought she'd make it this long either without giving in. But going it alone on the street was better than forcing her mother to choose between chaining her up in the basement or shipping her off to Coldtown. It was better, too, than taking the chance Matilda might get loose from the chains and attack people she loved. Stories like that were in the news all the time; almost as frequent as the ones about people who let vampires into their homes because they seemed so nice and clean-cut.

"Then what are you doing looking for me?" she asked. Dante had lived down the street from her family for years, but they didn't hang out. She'd wave to him as she mowed the lawn while he loaded his panel van with DJ equipment. He shouldn't have been here.

She looked back at the store window. Mardave and Ben were at the counter with a case of beer and her wine cooler. They were getting change from a clerk.

"I was hoping you, er, *wouldn't* be alive," Dante said. "You'd be more help if you were dead."

She stood up, stumbling slightly. "Well, screw you too."

It took eighty-eight days for the venom to sweat out a person's pores. She only had thirty-seven to go. Thirty-seven days to stay so drunk that she could ignore the buzz in her head that made her want to bite, rend, devour.

442 • HOLLY BLACK

"That came out wrong," he said, taking a step toward her. Close enough that she felt the warmth of him radiating off him like licking tongues of flame. She shivered. Her veins sang with need.

"I can't help you," said Matilda. "Look, I can barely help myself. Whatever it is, I'm sorry. I can't. You have to get out of here."

"My sister Lydia and your boyfriend Julian are gone," Dante said. "Together. She's looking to get bitten. I don't know what he's looking for . . . but he's going to get hurt."

Matilda gaped at him as Mardave and Ben walked out of the store. Ben carried a box on his shoulder and a bag on his arm. "That guy bothering you?" he asked her.

"No," she said, then turned to Dante. "You better go."

"Wait," said Dante.

Matilda's stomach hurt. She was sobering up. The smell of blood seemed to float up from underneath their skin.

She reached into Ben's bag and grabbed a beer. She popped the top, licked off the foam. If she didn't get a lot drunker, she was going to attack someone.

"Jesus," Mardave said. "Slow down. What if someone sees you?"

She drank it in huge gulps, right there on the street. Ben laughed, but it wasn't a good laugh. He was laughing at the drunk.

"She's infected," Dante said.

Matilda whirled toward him, chucking the mostly empty can in his direction automatically. "Shut up, asshole."

"Feel her skin," Dante said. "Cold. She ran away from home when it happened, and no one's seen her since."

"I'm cold because it's cold out," she said.

She saw Ben's evaluation of her change from *damaged enough to sleep with strangers* to *dangerous enough to attack strangers*.

Mardave touched his hand gently to her arm. "Hey," he said.

She almost hissed with delight at the press of his hot fingers. She smiled up at him and hoped her eyes weren't as hungry as her skin. "I really like you."

He flinched. "Look, it's late. Maybe we could meet up another time." Then he backed away, which made her so angry that she bit the inside of her own cheek.

Her mouth flooded with the taste of copper and a red haze floated in front of her eyes.

Fifty-seven days ago, Matilda had been sober. She'd had a boyfriend named Julian, and they would dress up together in her bedroom. He liked to wear skinny ties and glittery eye shadow. She liked to wear vintage rock T-shirts and boots that laced up so high that they would constantly be late because they were busy tying them.

Matilda and Julian would dress up and prowl the streets and party at lockdown clubs that barred the doors from dusk to dawn. Matilda wasn't particularly careless; she was just careless enough.

She'd been at a friend's party. It had been stiflingly hot, and she was mad because Julian and Lydia were doing some dance thing from the musical they were in at school. Matilda just wanted to get some air. She opened a window and climbed out under the bobbing garland of garlic.

Another girl was already on the lawn. Matilda should have noticed that the girl's breath didn't crystallize in the air, but she didn't.

"Do you have a light?" the girl had asked.

Matilda did. She reached for Julian's lighter when the girl caught her arm and bent her backwards. Matilda's scream turned into a shocked cry when she felt the girl's cold mouth against her neck, the girl's cold fingers holding her off balance.

Then it was as though someone slid two shards of ice into her skin.

The spread of vampirism could be traced to one person—Caspar Morales. Films and books and television had started romanticizing vampires, and maybe it was only a matter of time before a vampire started romanticizing *himself*.

Crazy, romantic Caspar decided that he wouldn't kill his victims. He'd just drink a little blood and then move on, city to city. By the time other vampires caught up with him and ripped him to pieces, he'd infected hundreds of people. And those new vampires, with no idea how to prevent the spread, infected thousands.

When the first outbreak happened in Tokyo, it seemed like a journalist's prank. Then there was another outbreak in Hong Kong and another in San Francisco.

The military put up barricades around the area where the infection broke out. That was the way the first Coldtown was founded.

Matilda's body twitched involuntarily. She could feel the spasm start in the muscles of her back and move to her face. She wrapped her arms around herself to try and stop it, but her hands were shaking pretty hard. "You want my help, you better get me some booze."

"You're killing yourself," Dante said, shaking his head.

"I just need another drink," she said. "Then I'll be fine."

He shook his head. "You can't keep going like this. You can't just stay drunk to avoid your problems. I know, people do. It's a classic move, even, but I didn't figure you for fetishizing your own doom."

She started laughing. "You don't understand. When I'm wasted I don't crave blood. It's the only thing keeping me human."

"What?" He looked at Matilda like he couldn't quite make sense of her words.

"Let me spell it out: if you don't get me some alcohol, I am going to bite you."

"Oh." He fumbled for his wallet. "Oh. Okay."

Matilda had spent all the cash she'd brought with her in the first few weeks, so it'd been a long time since she could simply overpay some homeless guy to go into a liquor store and get her a fifth of vodka. She gulped gratefully from the bottle Dante gave her in a nearby alley.

A few moments later, warmth started to creep up from her belly, and her mouth felt like it was full of needles and Novocain.

"You okay?" he asked her.

"Better now," she said, her words slurring slightly. "But I still don't understand. Why do you need me to help you find Lydia and Julian?

"Lydia got obsessed with becoming a vampire," Dante said, irritably brushing back the stray hair that fell across his face.

"Why?"

He shrugged. "She used to be really scared of vampires. When we were kids, she begged Mom to let her camp in the hallway because she wanted to sleep where there were no windows. But then I guess she started to be fascinated instead. She thinks that human annihilation is coming. She says that we all have to choose sides and she's already chosen."

"I'm not a vampire," Matilda said.

Dante gestured irritably with his cigarette holder. The cigarette had long burned out. He didn't look like his usual contemptuous self; he looked lost. "I know. I thought you would be. And—I don't know—you're on the street. Maybe you know more than the video feeds do about where someone might go to get themselves bitten."

Matilda thought about lying on the floor of Julian's parents' living room. They had been sweaty from dancing and kissed languidly. On the television, a list of missing people flashed. She had closed her eyes and kissed him again.

She nodded slowly. "I know a couple of places. Have you heard from her at all?"

He shook his head. "She won't take any of my calls, but she's been updating her blog. I'll show you."

He loaded it on his phone. The latest entry was titled: *I Need a Vampire.* Matilda scrolled down and read. Basically, it was Lydia's plea to be bitten. She wanted any vampires looking for victims to contact her. In the comments, someone suggested Coldtown and then another person commented in ALL CAPS to say that everyone knew that the vampires in Coldtown were careful to keep their food sources alive.

It was impossible to know which comments Lydia had read and which ones she believed.

Runaways went to Coldtown all the time, along with the sick, the sad, and the maudlin. There was supposed to be a constant party, theirs for the price of blood. But once they went inside, humans—even human children, even babies born in Coldtown—weren't be allowed to leave. The National Guard patrolled the barbed wire–wrapped and garlic-covered walls to make sure that Coldtown stayed contained.

People said that vampires found ways through the walls to the outside world. Maybe that was just a rumor, although Matilda remembered reading something online about a documentary that proved the truth. She hadn't seen it.

But everyone knew there was only one way to get out of Coldtown if you were still human. Your family had to be rich enough to hire a vampire hunter. Vampire hunters got money from the government for each vampire they put in Coldtown, but they could give up the cash reward in favor of a voucher for a single human's release. One vampire in, one human out.

There was a popular reality television series about one of the hunters, called *Hemlok*. Girls hung posters of him on the insides of their lockers, often right next to pictures of the vampires he hunted.

Most people didn't have the money to outbid the government for a hunter's services. Matilda didn't think that Dante's family did and knew

Julian's didn't. Her only chance was to catch Lydia and Julian before they crossed over.

"What's with Julian?" Matilda asked. She'd been avoiding the question for hours as they walked through the alleys that grew progressively more empty the closer they got to the gates.

"What do you mean?" Dante was hunched over against the wind, his long skinny frame offering little protection against the chill. Still, she knew he was warm underneath. Inside.

"Why did Julian go with her?" She tried to keep the hurt out of her voice. She didn't think Dante would understand. He DJed at a club in town and was rumored to see a different boy or girl every day of the week. The only person he actually seemed to care about was his sister.

Dante shrugged slim shoulders. "Maybe he was looking for you."

That was the answer she wanted to hear. She smiled and let herself imagine saving Julian right before he could enter Coldtown. He would tell her that he'd been coming to save her and then they'd laugh and she wouldn't bite him, no matter how warm his skin felt.

Dante snapped his fingers in front of Matilda and she stumbled.

"Hey," she said. "Drunk girl here. No messing with me."

He chuckled.

Melinda and Dante checked all the places she knew, all the places she'd slept on cardboard near runaways and begged for change. Dante had a picture of Lydia in his wallet, but no one who looked at it remembered her.

Finally, outside a bar, they bumped into a girl who said she'd seen Lydia and Julian. Dante traded her the rest of his pack of cigarettes for her story.

"They were headed for Coldtown," she said, lighting up. In the flickering flame of her lighter, Melinda noticed the shallow cuts along her wrists. "Said she was tired of waiting."

"What about the guy?" Matilda asked. She stared at the girl's dried garnet scabs. They looked like crusts of sugar, like the lines of salt left on the beach when the tide goes out. She wanted to lick them.

"He said his girlfriend was a vampire," said the girl, inhaling deeply. She blew out smoke and then started to cough.

"When was that?" Dante asked.

The girl shrugged her shoulders. "Just a couple of hours ago."

Dante took out his phone and pressed some buttons. "Load," he muttered. "Come on, *load*."

"What happened to your arms?" Matilda asked.

The girl shrugged again. "They bought some blood off me. Said that they might need it inside. They had a real professional set-up too. Sharp razor and one of those glass bowls with the plastic lids."

Matilda's stomach clenched with hunger. She turned against the wall and breathed slowly. She needed a drink.

"Is something wrong with her?" the girl asked.

"Matilda," Dante said, and Matilda half-turned. He was holding out his phone. There was a new entry up on Lydia's blog, entitled: *One-Way Ticket to Coldtown.*

"You should post about it," Dante said. "On the message boards."

Matilda was sitting on the ground, picking at the brick wall to give her fingers something to do. Dante had massively overpaid for another bottle of vodka and was cradling it in a crinkled paper bag.

She frowned. "Post about what?"

"About the alcohol. About it helping you keep from turning."

"Where would I post about that?"

Dante twisted off the cap. The heat seemed to radiate off his skin as he swigged from the bottle. "There are forums for people who have to restrain someone for eighty-eight days. They hang out and exchange tips on straps and dealing with the begging for blood. Haven't you seen them?"

She shook her head. "I bet sedation's already a hot topic of discussion. I doubt I'd be telling them anything they don't already know."

He laughed, but it was a bitter laugh. "Then there's all the people who want to be vampires. The websites reminding all the corpsebait out there that being bitten by an infected person isn't enough; it has to be a vampire. The ones listing gimmicks to get vampires to notice you."

"Like what?"

"I dated a girl who cut thin lines on her thighs before she went out dancing so if there was a vampire in the club, it'd be drawn to her scent." Dante didn't look extravagant or affected anymore. He looked defeated.

Matilda smiled at him. "She was probably a better bet than me for getting you into Coldtown."

He returned the smile wanly. "The worst part is that Lydia's not going to get what she wants. She's become the human servant of some vampire who's going to make her a whole bunch of promises and never turn her. The last thing they need in Coldtown is new vampires."

Matilda imagined Lydia and Julian dancing at the endless Eternal Ball. She pictured them on the streets she'd seen in pictures uploaded to Facebook and Flickr, trying to trade a bowl full of blood for their own deaths.

When Dante passed the bottle to her, she pretended to swig. On the eve of her fifty-eighth day of being infected, Matilda started sobering up.

Crawling over, she straddled Dante's waist before he had a chance to shift positions. His mouth tasted like tobacco. When she pulled back from him, his eyes were wide with surprise, his pupils blown and black even in the dim streetlight.

"Matilda," he said and there was nothing in his voice but longing.

"If you really want your sister, I am going to need one more thing from you," she said.

His blood tasted like tears.

Matilda's skin felt like it had caught fire. She'd turned into lit paper, burning up. Curling into black ash.

She licked his neck over and over and over.

The gates of Coldtown were large and made of consecrated wood, barbed wire covering them like heavy, thorny vines. The guards slouched at their posts, guns over their shoulders, sharing a cigarette. The smell of percolating coffee wafted out of the guardhouse.

"Um, hello," Matilda said. Blood was still sticky where it half-dried around her mouth and on her neck. It had dribbled down her shirt, stiffening it nearly to cracking when she moved. Her body felt strange now that she was dying. Hot. More alive than it had in weeks.

Dante would be all right; she wasn't contagious and she didn't think she'd hurt him too badly. She hoped she hadn't hurt him too badly. She touched the phone in her pocket, his phone, the one she'd used to call 911 after she'd left him.

"Hello," she called to the guards again.

One turned. "Oh my god," he said and reached for his rifle.

"I'm here to turn in a vampire. For a voucher. I want to turn in a vampire in exchange for letting a human out of Coldtown."

"What vampire?" asked the other guard. He'd dropped the cigarette, but not stepped on the filter so that it just smoked on the asphalt.

"Me," said Matilda. "I want to turn in me."

They made her wait as her pulse thrummed slower and slower. She wasn't a vampire yet, and after a few phone calls, they discovered that technically she could only have the voucher after undeath. They did let her wash her face in the bathroom of the guardhouse and wring the thin cloth of her shirt until the water ran down the drain clear, instead of murky with blood.

When she looked into the mirror, her skin had unfamiliar purple shadows, like bruises. She was still staring at them when she stopped being able to catch her breath. The hollow feeling in her chest expanded and she found herself panicked, falling to her knees on the filthy tile floor. She died there, a moment later.

It didn't hurt as much as she'd worried it would. Like most things, the surprise was the worst part.

The guards released Matilda into Coldtown just a little before dawn. The world looked strange—everything had taken on a smudgy, silvery cast, like she was watching an old movie. Sometimes people's heads seemed to blur into black smears. Only one color was distinct—a pulsing, oozing color that seemed to glow from beneath skin.

Red.

Her teeth ached to look at it.

There was a silence inside her. No longer did she move to the rhythmic drumming of her heart. Her body felt strange, hard as marble, free of pain. She'd never realized how many small agonies were alive in the creak of her bones, the pull of muscle. Now, free of them, she felt like she was floating.

Matilda looked around with her strange new eyes. Everything was beautiful. And the light at the edge of the sky was the most beautiful thing of all.

"What are you doing?" a girl called from a doorway. She had long black hair, but her roots were growing in blonde. "Get in here! Are you crazy?"

In a daze, Matilda did as she was told. Everything smeared as she moved, like the world was painted in watercolors. The girl's pinkish-red face swirled along with it.

It was obvious the house had once been grand, but it looked like it'd been abandoned for a long time. Graffiti covered the peeling wallpaper and couches had been pushed up against the walls. A boy wearing jeans but no shirt was painting make-up onto a girl with stiff pink pigtails, while another girl in a retro polka-dotted dress pulled on mesh stockings.

In a corner, another boy—this one with glossy brown hair that fell to his waist—stacked jars of creamed corn into a precarious pyramid.

"What is this place?" Matilda asked.

The boy stacking the jars turned. "Look at her eyes. She's a vampire!" He didn't seem afraid, though; he seemed delighted.

"Get her into the cellar," one of the other girls said.

"Come on," said the black-haired girl and pulled Matilda toward a doorway. "You're fresh-made, right?"

"Yeah," Matilda said. Her tongue swept over her own sharp teeth. "I guess that's pretty obvious."

"Don't you know that vampires can't go outside in the daylight?" the girl asked, shaking her head. "The guards try that trick with every new vampire, but I never saw one almost fall for it."

"Oh, right," Matilda said. They went down the rickety steps to a filthy basement with a mattress on the floor underneath a single bulb. Crates of foodstuffs were shoved against the walls, and the high, small windows had been painted over with a tarry substance that let no light through.

The black-haired girl who'd waved her inside smiled. "We trade with the border guards. Black-market food, clothes, little luxuries like chocolate and cigarettes for some ass. Vampires don't own everything."

"And you're going to owe us for letting you stay the night," the boy said from the top of the stairs.

"I don't have anything," Matilda said. "I didn't bring any cans of food or whatever."

"You have to bite us."

"What?" Matilda asked.

"One of us," the girl said. "How about one of us? You can even pick which one."

"Why would you want me to do that?"

The girl's expression clearly said that Matilda was stupid. "Who doesn't want to live forever?"

I don't, Matilda wanted to say, but she swallowed the words. She could tell they already thought she didn't deserve to be a vampire. Besides, she wanted to taste blood. She wanted to taste the red, throbbing, pulsing insides of the girl in front of her. It wasn't the pain she'd felt when she was infected, the hunger that made her stomach clench, the craving for warmth. It was heady, greedy desire.

"Tomorrow," Matilda said. "When it's night again."

"Okay," the girl said, "but you promise, right? You'll turn one of us?"

"Yeah," said Matilda, numbly. It was hard to even wait that long.

She was relieved when they went upstairs, but less relieved when she heard something heavy slide in front of the basement door. She told herself that didn't matter. The only thing that mattered was getting through the day so that she could find Julian and Lydia.

She shook her head to clear it of thoughts of blood and turned on Dante's phone. Although she didn't expect it, a text message was waiting: *I cant tell if I luv u or if I want to kill u.*

Relief washed over her. Her mouth twisted into a smile and her newly sharp canines cut her lip. She winced. Dante was okay.

She opened up Lydia's blog and posted an anonymous message: *Tell Julian his girlfriend wants to see him . . . and you.*

Matilda made herself comfortable on the dirty mattress. She looked up at the rotted boards of the ceiling and thought of Julian. She had a single ticket out of Coldtown and two humans to rescue with it, but it was easy to picture herself saving Lydia as Julian valiantly offered to stay with her, even promised her his eternal devotion.

She licked her lips at the image. When she closed her eyes, all her imaginings drowned in a sea of red.

Waking at dusk, Matilda checked Lydia's blog. Lydia had posted a reply: *Meet us at the Festival of Sinners.*

Five kids sat at the top of the stairs, watching her with liquid eyes.

"Are you awake?" the black-haired girl asked. She seemed to pulse with color. Her moving mouth was hypnotic.

"Come here," Matilda said to her in a voice that seemed so distant that she was surprised to find it was her own. She hadn't meant to speak, hadn't meant to beckon the girl over to her.

"That's not fair," one of the boys called. "I was the one who said she owed us something. It should be me. You should pick me."

Matilda ignored him as the girl knelt down on the dirty mattress and swept aside her hair, baring a long, unmarked neck. She seemed dazzling, this creature of blood and breath, a fragile manikin as brittle as sticks.

Tiny golden hairs tickled Matilda's nose as she bit down.

And gulped.

Blood was heat and heart running-thrumming-beating through the fat roots of veins to drip syrup slow, spurting molten hot across tongue, mouth, teeth, chin.

Dimly, Matilda felt someone shoving her and someone else screaming, but it seemed distant and unimportant. Eventually the words became clearer.

"Stop," someone was screaming. "Stop!"

Hands dragged Matilda off the girl. Her neck was a glistening red mess. Gore stained the mattress and covered Matilda's hands and hair. The girl coughed, blood bubbles frothing on her lip, and then went abruptly silent.

"What did you do?" the boy wailed, cradling the girl's body. "She's dead. She's dead. You killed her."

Matilda backed away from the body. Her hand went automatically to her mouth, covering it. "I didn't mean to," she said.

"Maybe she'll be okay," said the other boy, his voice cracking. "We have to get bandages."

"She's *dead*," the boy holding the girl's body moaned.

A thin wail came from deep inside Matilda as she backed toward the stairs. Her belly felt full, distended. She wanted to be sick.

Another girl grabbed Matilda's arm. "Wait," the girl said, eyes wide and imploring. "You have to bite me next. You're full now so you won't have to hurt me—"

With a cry, Matilda tore herself free and ran up the stairs—if she went fast enough, maybe she could escape from herself.

By the time Matilda got to the Festival of Sinners, her mouth tasted metallic and she was numb with fear. She wasn't human, wasn't good, and wasn't sure what she might do next. She kept pawing at her shirt, as if that much blood could ever be wiped off, as if it hadn't already soaked down into her skin and her soiled insides.

The Festival was easy to find, even as confused as she was. People were happy to give her directions, apparently not bothered that she was drenched in blood. Their casual demeanor was horrifying, but not as horrifying as how much she already wanted to feed again.

On the way, she passed the Eternal Ball. Strobe lights lit up the remains of the windows along the dome, and a girl with blue hair in a dozen braids held up a video camera to interview three men dressed all in white with gleaming red eyes.

Vampires.

A ripple of fear passed through her. She reminded herself that there was nothing they could do to her. She was already like them. Already dead.

The Festival of Sinners was being held at a church with stained-glass windows painted black on the inside. The door, papered with pink-stenciled posters, was painted the same thick tarry black. Music thrummed from within and a few people sat on the steps, smoking and talking.

Matilda went inside.

A doorman pulled aside a velvet rope for her, letting her past a small line of people waiting to pay the cover charge. The rules were different for vampires, perhaps especially for vampires accessorizing their grungy attire with so much blood.

Matilda scanned the room. She didn't see Julian or Lydia, just a throng of dancers and a bar that served alcohol from vast copper distilling vats. It spilled into mismatched mugs. Then one of the people near the bar moved and Matilda saw Lydia and Julian. He was bending over her, shouting into her ear.

Matilda pushed her way through the crowd, until she was close enough to touch Julian's arm. She reached out, but couldn't quite bring herself to brush his skin with her foulness.

Julian looked up, startled. "Tilda?"

She snatched back her hand like she'd been about to touch fire.

"Tilda," he said. "What happened to you? Are you hurt?"

Matilda flinched, looking down at herself. "I . . ."

Lydia laughed. "She ate someone, moron."

"Tilda?" Julian asked.

"I'm sorry," Matilda said. There was so much she had to be sorry for, but at least he was here now. Julian would tell her what to do and how to turn herself back into something decent again. She would save Lydia and Julian would save her.

He touched her shoulder, let his hand rest gingerly on her blood-stiffened shirt. "We were looking for you everywhere." His gentle expression was tinged with terror; fear pulled his smile into something closer to a grimace.

"I wasn't in Coldtown," Matilda said. "I came here so that Lydia could leave. I have a pass."

"But I don't want to leave," said Lydia. "You understand that, right? I want what you have—eternal life."

"You're not infected," Matilda said. "You have to go. You can still be okay. Please, I need you to go."

"One pass?" Julian said, his eyes going to Lydia. Matilda saw the truth in the weight of that gaze—Julian had not come to Coldtown for Matilda. Even though she knew she didn't deserve him to think of her as anything but a monster, it hurt savagely.

"I'm not leaving," Lydia said, turning to Julian, pouting. "You said she wouldn't be like this."

"*I killed a girl*," Matilda said. "I killed her. Do you understand that?"

"Who cares about some mortal girl?" Lydia tossed back her hair. In that moment, she reminded Matilda of her brother, pretentious Dante who'd turned out to be an actual nice guy. Just like sweet Lydia had turned out cruel.

"You're a girl," Matilda said. "You're mortal."

"I know that!" Lydia rolled her eyes. "I just mean that we don't care who you killed. Turn us and then we can kill lots of people."

"No," Matilda said, swallowing. She looked down, not wanting to hear what she was about to say. There was still a chance. "Look, I have the pass. If you don't want it, then Julian should take it and go. But I'm not turning you. I'm never turning you, understand."

"Julian doesn't want to leave," Lydia said. Her eyes looked bright and two feverish spots appeared on her cheeks. "Who are you to judge me anyway? You're the murderer."

Matilda took a step back. She desperately wanted Julian to say something in her defense or even to look at her, but his gaze remained steadfastly on Lydia.

"So neither one of you want the pass," Matilda said.

"Fuck you," spat Lydia.

Matilda turned away.

"Wait," Julian said. His voice sounded weak.

Matilda spun, unable to keep the hope off her face, and saw why Julian had called to her. Lydia stood behind him, a long knife to his throat.

"Turn me," Lydia said. "Turn me, or I'm going to kill him."

Julian's eyes were wide. He started to protest or beg or something and Lydia pressed the knife harder, silencing him.

People had stopped dancing nearby, backing away. One girl with red-glazed eyes stared hungrily at the knife.

"Turn me!" Lydia shouted. "I'm tired of waiting! I want my life to begin!"

"You won't be alive—" Matilda started.

"I'll be alive—more alive than ever. Just like you are."

"Okay," Matilda said softly. "Give me your wrist."

The crowd seemed to close in tighter, watching as Lydia held out her arm. Matilda crouched low, bending down over it.

"Take the knife away from his throat," Matilda said.

Lydia, all her attention on Matilda, let Julian go. He stumbled a little and pressed his fingers to his neck.

"I loved you," Julian shouted.

Matilda looked up to see that he wasn't speaking to her. She gave him a glittering smile and bit down on Lydia's wrist.

The girl screamed, but the scream was lost in Matilda's ears. Lost in the pulse of blood, the tide of gluttonous pleasure and the music throbbing around them like Lydia's slowing heartbeat.

Matilda sat on the blood-soaked mattress and turned on the video camera to check that the live feed was working.

Julian was gone. She'd given him the pass after stripping him of all his cash and credit cards; there was no point in trying to force Lydia to leave since she'd just come right back in. He'd made stammering apologies that Matilda ignored; then he fled for the gate. She didn't miss him. Her fantasy of Julian felt as ephemeral as her old life.

"It's working," one of the boys—Michael—said from the stairs, a computer cradled on his lap. Even though she'd killed one of them, they welcomed her back, eager enough for eternal life to risk more deaths. "You're streaming live video."

Matilda set the camera on the stack of crates, pointed toward her and the wall where she'd tied a gagged Lydia. The girl thrashed and kicked, but Matilda ignored her. She stepped in front of the camera and smiled.

My name is Matilda Green. I was born on April 10, 1997. I died on September 3, 2013. Please tell my mother I'm okay. And Dante, if you're watching this, I'm sorry.

You've probably seen lots of video feeds from inside Coldtown. I saw them too. Pictures of girls and boys grinding together in clubs or bleeding elegantly for their celebrity vampire masters. Here's what you never see. What I'm going to show you.

For eighty-eight days you are going to watch someone sweat out the infection. You are going to watch her beg and scream and cry. You're going to watch her throw up food and piss her pants and pass out. You're going to watch me feed her can after can of creamed corn. It's not going to be pretty.

You're going to watch me, too. I'm the kind of vampire that you'd be, one who's new at this and basically out of control. I've already killed someone and I can't guarantee I'm not going to do it again. I'm the one who infected this girl.

This is the real Coldtown.

I'm the real Coldtown.

You still want in?

IN THE FUTURE WHEN ALL'S WELL

Catherynne M. Valente

Catherynne M. Valente is the *New York Times* bestselling author of over a dozen works of fiction and poetry, including *Palimpsest*, the Orphan's Tales series, *Deathless*, and the crowdfunded phenomenon *The Girl Who Circumnavigated Fairyland in a Ship of Own Making*. She is the winner of the Andre Norton, Tiptree, Mythopoeic, Rhysling, Lambda, Locus, and Hugo awards. Valente has been a finalist for the Nebula and World Fantasy awards. She lives on an island off the coast of Maine with a small but growing menagerie of beasts, some of which are human.

Valente's near-future "In the Future When All's Well" has been called (by *SFRevu*) "the most original vampire story written in the last ten years." Whether you agree or not, is up to you. But there *is* something particularly unnerving about vampirism viewed as something unremarkable that "just happens" . . .

These days, pretty much anything will turn you into a vampire.

We have these stupid safety and hygiene seminars at school. Like, before, it was D.A.R.E. and *oh my god if you even look crosswise at a bus that goes to that part of town you will be hit with a firehose blast full of PCP and there is nothing you can even do about it so just stay in your room and don't think about beer.* Do you even know what PCP looks like? I have no idea.

I remember they used to say PCP made you think you could fly. That seems kind of funny, now.

Anyway, there's lists. Two of them, actually. On the first day of S/H class, the teacher hands them out. They're always the same, I practically have them memorized. One says: *Most Common Causes.* The other says:

High-Risk Groups. So here, just in case you ditched that day so you could go down to *that part of town* and suck on the firehose, you fucking slacker.

Most Common Causes:
Immoral Conduct
Depression
Black Cat Crossing the Path of Pregnant or Nursing Mother
Improper Burial
Animal (Most Often Black) Jumping Over Grave, Corpse
Bird (Most Often Black) Flying Over Grave, Corpse
Butterfly Alighting on Tombstone
Ingestion of Meat from Animal Killed by a Wolf
Death Before Baptism
Burying Corpse at Crossroads
Failing to Bury Corpse at Crossroads
Direct Infection
Blood Transfusions Received 2011–2013

High Risk Groups (HR):
Persons Born With Extra Nipple, Vestigial Tail, Excess Hair, Teeth, Breech
Persons Whose Mothers Encountered Black Cats While Pregnant
Persons Whose Mothers Did Not Ingest Sufficient Salt While Pregnant
Seventh Children, Either Sex
Children Conceived on Saturday
Children Born Out of Wedlock
Children Vaccinated for Polio 1999-2002
Children Diagnosed Autistic/OCD
Promiscuous Youngsters
Persons Possessing Unkempt Eyebrows
Persons Bearing Unusual Moles or Birthmarks
Redheads with Blue Eyes

I swear to god you cannot even walk down the *street* without getting turned. That list doesn't even get into your standard jump-out-of-the-shadows schtick. Like, half the graduating class have to get their diploma indoors, you know? Plus, I think they just put in that shit about promiscuous youngsters because it's like their duty as teachers to make sure no one ever has sex. Who says *youngsters*, anyway? The problem with S/H class is that, just like the big scary PCP, we all know where to get it if we want it, so the whole thing is just . . . kill me now so I can go get a freaking milkshake.

My dad says this is all because of the immigrants coming in from Romania, Ukraine, Bulgaria. I don't know. I read *Dracula* and whatever. Doesn't seem very realistic to me. Vampires are sort of something that just *happens* to you, like finals. I know people used to think they were all lords of the night and stuff, and they are, I guess. But it's like, my friend Emmy got turned last week because a black dog walked around her house the wrong way. Sometimes things just get fucked up and it's not because there was a revolution in Bulgaria.

But I guess the point is I'm going to graduate soon and I'm just sort of waiting for it to happen to me. There's this whole summer before college and it's like a million years long and I have red hair and blue eyes so, you know, eventually something big and black is just going to come sit on my chest till I die. I told Emmy: *it's not your fault. It's not because you're a bad person. It's just random. It doesn't mean anything. It's like a raffle.*

So my name is Scout—yeah, my mom read *To Kill a Mockingbird*. Leave it to her to think fifth-grade required-reading is totally deep. She also has a heart thing where she's had to be on a low-sodium diet since she was my age, which means while she was pregnant with me, so *thanks*, mom. With high-risk groups, birds don't even have to fly over your own grave. It can be, like, anyone's grave, if you're nearby. It's like a shockwave. I heard about this one HR guy like two towns over who was a seventh son with a unibrow *and* red hair *and* was born backwards, and he just turned *by himself.* Just sitting there in English class and *bang*. That's what scares me the most. Like it's something that's inside you already, and you can't stop it or even know it's there, but there's a little clock and it's always counting down to English class.

The other night I was hanging out with Emmy, trying to be supportive friend like you're supposed to be. In S/H class they say high-risk kids should cut off their friends if they get turned. Like it's one of those movies about how brutal high school is and we're all going to shun Emmy on Monday if she's wearing a little more black than usual. As if I would ever.

"What's it like?" I said. Because that's what they don't tell you. What it feels like. *PCP is bad, it'll make you jump off buildings. Yeah, but before that.* What's it like? Before you crave blood and stalk the night. What's it like?

"It's stupid. My hair's turning black. I have to go to this doctor every two weeks for tests. And, I don't know… it's like, I want to sleep in the dirt? When I get tired, my whole head fills up with this idea of how nice it would be to dig up the yard and snuggle down and sleep in there. The way I used to think about bubble baths."

"Have you… done it yet?"

"Oh, blood? Yeah. Ethan let me right away. He's good like that." Emmy shoved her bangs back. She had a lot of makeup on. Naturally Sunkissed was a big color that year. Keeps the pallor down but it doesn't make you all Oompa-Loompa. "What? What do you want to hear? That it's gross or that it's awesome?"

"I don't know. Whatever it is."

"It's… like eating dinner, Scout. When somebody goes to a little effort to make something nice for you, it's great. When they eat healthy and wash really good but don't taste like soap. When they let you. But sometimes it just gets you through the night." She lit a cigarette and looked at me like: *why shouldn't I, now?* "Did you hear about Kimberly? She got turned the old fashioned way, by this gnarly weird guy from Zagreb, and she can *fly*. It's so fucking unfair."

Emmy wasn't very different as a vampire. We had this same conversation after she lost her virginity—Ethan again—and she was all *it is what it is* then, too, with an extra helping of *I am part of a sacred sisterhood now*. Emmy has always been kind of crap as a friend, but I've known her since Barbies and kiddie soccer, so, whatever, right?

I don't know, I suppose it was dumb, but things can get weird between girls who've known each other that long. Like this one time when we were thirteen we did that whole practice kissing on each other thing. We'd been hanging out in my room for hours and hours and rooms get all whacked out when you lock yourselves in like that. We sat cross-legged on my lame pink bedspread and kissed because we were lonely and we didn't know anything except that we wanted to be older and have boyfriends because our sisters had them and her lips were really soft. I didn't even know you were supposed to use tongue, that's how thirteen I was. Her, too. We never told anyone about it, because, well, you just don't. But I guess I'm talking about it now because I let Emmy feed off of me that night, even though I'm HR, and it was kind of like the same thing.

I didn't see her much, though, after that. It was just awkward. I guess that sort of thing happens after senior year. People drift.

Back in seventh grade, right after the first ones started showing up, like every freaking book they assigned in school was a vampire book. That's when I read *Dracula. Carmilla* and *The Bride of Corinth*, too. *The Vampyre, The Land Beyond the Forest. Varney the Freaking Vampire.* Classics, you know—they said all the modern stuff was agitprop, whatever that means. It's weird, though, because back then there were maybe twenty or thirty vampires in the whole world, and people just wrote and wrote about them, even though there's like statistically *no way* that Stoker guy ever met one. And now there's vampires all over. Google says there's almost as many as there are people. They have a widget. But nobody's written a vampire book in years.

So I've been hanging out in cemeteries a lot lately. I know, right? I mean, before? I would *never*. Have you seen how much it costs to get up in black fingernail polish and fishnets? And now, for an HR like me, it's pretty much like slitting your wrists in the bathtub with a baby blue razor for sensitive skin. Everyone knows you're not serious, but there's a slim chance you'll fuck up and off yourself anyway. If you want to get turned you don't have to go chasing it. Not when some bad steak will do you for about $12.50, and a guy down on Bellefleur Street will do it for less than that.

So, I'm one of those girls. Like we didn't know that already. Like you never did anything embarrassing. Anyway, it's kind of peaceful. Not peaceful, really. Just kind of flat. I don't do anything. I sit there on the hill and think about how like half my family is buried down there. Any second, a black bird could fly out over one of them. I wonder if you can see it when it happens, the affinity wave. What color it is. That's what Miss Kinnelly calls it. An affinity wave. She leads an after-school group for HRs that my dad says I have to go to now. He picked Miss Kinnelly because she's a racist bitch, or as he would put it, "has a strict policy against Eastern Europeans attending." I was all: *duh, we're Jewish, and isn't Gram from like Latvia or wherever?* And he was all: *Jews aren't Slavic, it's the Slavs that are the problem, why do you think they knew about all the HR vectors before we did?* And I was like: *what the hell do you know about HR vectors? Your eyebrows are fucking perfect!*

Anyway, group is deeply pointless. Mostly we talk about who we know that got turned that week, and how it happened. And how scared we all are, even though if you keep talking about how scared you are eventually you stop really being scared, which I thought was the point of having a group, but apparently not, because being scared is like what these people do for fun. All anyone wants to talk about is how it happened to their friend or their brother. It's like someone gets a prize for the most random way. Some girl goes: "Oh my god, my cousin totally drank three bottles of vodka and passed out at the Stop & Rob and woke up a vampire!" And even though that is *highly* retarded, and it probably doesn't work that way, at least, it doesn't work that way yet, everyone goes *oooooh* like she just recited *The Rime of the Ancient Mariner*. Oh, yeah. We had to read that one, too. It's not even about vampires, it's about zombies, which is totally not the same thing, but apparently it falls under supplementary materials or something. Anyway, Miss Kinnelly then lectures for a hundred years about how immoral conduct is the most pernicious of all the causation scenarios, because you can never know where that "moral line" lies. By the time she gets to the part about abstinence is the only sensible choice, I want to stick her fake nails through her eyes. Once I said: "I hear you can totally get it from drinking from a glass one of them drank from." And they all gasped like I was serious. God. Before, I wouldn't have spent three seconds after school with those people. But the sports program is basically over.

This one time Aidan from my geometry class started talking about staking them, like in old movies. Everyone got real quiet. Thing is, it's not like those movies. A vampire's body doesn't go anywhere if you mess with it. It doesn't go *poof*. It just lies there, and it's a dead person, and you have to bury it, and god, burying things by yourself is practically a crime these days. There's hazmat teams at every funeral. It's the law, for like three years now. Plus, it's not that big a town. Everyone knows everyone, and you try stabbing the kid you used to play softball with in the heart. I couldn't do it. They're still the same kids. They still play softball. We're the ones who've stopped.

Sometimes, when I'm sitting up on the hill by the Greenbaum mausoleum, I think about Emmy. I wonder if she's still going to State in the fall.

Probably not, I guess.

I dated this guy for a while during junior year. His name was Noah. He was okay, I guess. He was super tall, played center for basketball, one of the few sports we still played back then. Indoors, right? I remember when the soccer teams moved indoors. It was horrible, your shoes squeak on the floor because it's shellacked within an inch of its life. The way it used to be, soccer was the only thing I really liked to do. Run around in the grass, in the sun. There's something really satisfying about kicking the ball perfectly so it just flies up, the feeling of nailing it just on the right part of your foot. I've played since I was like four. Every league. And then, finally, they just called it off. Too dangerous, not enough girls anymore. You can't just go running around outside like that now. You could fall down. Get cut. Scrape your knee. So now instead of running drills I have to read *The Land Beyond the Forest* for the millionth time and stay inside. God, I'm turning into one of those snotty brainy hipster chicks.

Oh, right, Noah. See, the soccer girls date basketball boys. We're the second tier. Baseballers are somewhere below us, and then there's like archery and modern dance circling the drain. And then all the people who cry into their lockers because they can't hit a ball. Football and cheerleaders are up at the top, still, even though it's not exactly 1957 and not exactly the Midwest where they still play football. But some things stick. I think maybe it's because all the TV shows still have regular high school. It's a network thing. No one wants to show vampires integrating, dating chess geeks, whatever would be jam-packed with soap opera hilarity. TV is strictly *pre*. So we keep acting like what we did in sixth grade matters, even though no one actually plays football or cheers at all. It's like we all froze how we were three or four years ago and we'll never get any older.

Anyway, I remember Noah drank like two jumbo bottles of Diet Coke every day. He'd bring his bottle into class and park it next to his desk. When we kissed, he always tasted like Coke. Everyone thought we were sleeping together, but really, we weren't. It's not that I didn't think I was ready or whatever. Sex just doesn't really seem like that big a deal anymore. I guess it should. My dad says it definitely qualifies as immoral conduct. I just don't think about it, though. Like, what does it matter if Alexis let the yearbook editor go down on her in the darkroom if she found out like not even a week later that the Hep A vac she got for the senior trip to Spain was tainted and now she freaks out if the teacher drops chalk because she has to count the pieces of dust? It's just not that important. Plus, this couple Noah and I hung with sometimes, Dylan and Bethany, turned while they were doing it, just, not even any warning, straight from third base to teeth out in zero point five. We broke up a little after that. Just didn't see much point. I don't watch TV anymore, either.

But lately, I've been seeing him around. He turned during midterms. I think he even dated Emmy for a while, which, fine. I get it. They had a lot in common. I just didn't really want to know. Anyway, it wasn't any big plan. One minute I barely thought about him anymore and the next we're sitting on the swing set in Narragansett Park way past midnight, kicking the gravel and talking about how he still drinks Diet Coke, it just tastes really funny now.

"It's like, before it was just Coke. But now all I can taste is the aspartame. And not really the aspartame, but like, the chemicals that make up aspartame. I taste what aspartame is like on the inside. I still get the shakes, though. So I'm down to a can a day."

Noah isn't exactly cute. The basketball guys usually aren't, not like the football guys. He's extra-lanky and skinny, and the whole vampire thing pretty much comes free with black hair and pale skin. He used to have really nice green eyes.

"How did it happen to you?" I hated saying it like that. But it was the only think I could think of. How it happens to you. Like a car accident. "You don't have to tell me if you don't want to. If it's, you know, private."

Noah was counting the bits of gravel. He didn't want me to know he was doing it, but he moved his lips when he counted. That's why OCD is on the high-risk list. Because vampires compulsively count everything. I think it's the other way, though. You don't turn because you're OCD. You're OCD because you turned.

"Yeah, no, it's not private. It's just not that interesting. Remember when the HR list first came out and I was so freaked because I was conceived on a Saturday and I have that mole on my hip? I was so sure I'd get it before everyone else. But it didn't happen like I thought, like when that third grader just flipped one day and the CDC guys figured out it was because her mom is a crazy cat lady and she doesn't even have a path to cross without a black cat there to cross it for her. Ana Cruz. I thought it would be like that. Like Ana. I couldn't *stop* thinking about how it would be. Just walking down the street, and *bang*. But it wasn't. I woke up one night and this woman was looking in my window. She was older. Pretty, though. She looked… kind, I guess."

"How old was she?"

"One of the oldest ones in California, it turned out, so about six? Her name was Maria. She used to be an anesthesiologist, down at the hospital."

"Were you guys… together? Or something?"

"No, Scout, you just kind of get to talking eventually. Afterward, there's not that much to do but wait, and she was nice. She stayed with me. Held my hand. She didn't have to. Anyway, I opened the window, but I didn't let her in. I'm not an idiot. I just sat there looking back at her. You know how they look after they're past the first couple of years. All wolfy and hard and stuff. And finally she said: 'why wait?' And I thought, shit, she's right. It's gonna happen, sooner or later. I might as well get on with it. If I do it now, at least I can stop *thinking* about it. So I climbed out." He laughed shortly, like a bark. "I didn't invite her in. She invited me out. I guess that's sort of funny. Anyway, you know how it works. I don't want to get all porny on you. It was really gross at first. Blood just tastes like blood, you know? Like hot syrup. But then, it sort of changes, and it was like I could hear her singing, even though she was totally silent the whole time. Anyway. It hurts when you wake up the next night. Like when your arm falls asleep but all over. My mom was really mad."

I picked at the peeling paint on the side of the swingset. "I think about it."

"Oh! Do you want me to...?" God, Noah was always so fucking eager to please. He's like a puppy.

It took me a long time to answer. I totally get him. Why wait. But finally, I just sighed. "I don't think so. I have a bio test tomorrow."

"Okay." Noah lit a cigarette, just like Emmy. He looked like a total tool. Like he's the vampire Marlboro Man or whatever.

"What does blood taste like now?" I asked. I can't help it. I still want to know. I always want to know.

"Singing," he mumbled around the cigarette, and puffed out the smoke without inhaling.

The other week, my Uncle Jack came to visit. He lives in Chicago and works for some big advertising company. He did that one billboard with the American Apparel kids all wrapped up in biohazard tape. My mom cooked, which means no salt, and Uncle Jack just wasn't having that. He travels with his own can of Morton's and made sure my steak tasted like beef jerky.

"Kids in your condition have to be extra careful," he said.

"Yeah, I'm not pregnant, Uncle Jack."

"You really can't afford to take the risk, Scout. You have to think about your future. There's so much bleed these days."

That should pretty much tell you everything you need to know about what a bag of smarm my uncle is. He'll use a terrible pun to talk about something that'll probably kill me. He was talking about how that list of common causes is actually kind of out of date. Like how kids used to use textbooks that said: *maybe someday man will walk on the moon*. About a year ago, some of the causes started having baby causes. Like, it doesn't have to be meat killed by a wolf anymore, it can be any predator, so hunting game is right out. Even for non-HRs. We've always kept kosher, so it's not really an issue for us, but plenty of other ones are. They've acted like sex was on the no-no list since the beginning, but I don't think it was. I think that was recent. If sex could turn you into a vampire way back in ancient Hungary, we'd all be sucking moonlight by now. Some people, who are assholes, call this *bleed*. But never in front of an HR. It's just flat out rude.

My Uncle Jack is an asshole. I mean, I said he was in advertising, right?

"My firm is sponsoring a clean camp up in Wisconsin. Totally safe environment, absolutely scrubbed. For HRs, it's the safest place to be. God, the only place to be, if I were HR! You should think about it."

"I don't really want to move to Wisconsin."

"We wouldn't feel right about that, Jack," said my mother quietly. "We'd rather have her close. We take precautions, we take her in for shots."

Uncle Jack made a fake-sympathetic face and started babbling the way old people do when they want to sound like they care but they don't really. "My heart just breaks for you, Scout, honey. You, especially. You must be so scared, poor thing! I feel like if we could just get a handle on the risk vectors, we could gain some ground with this thing. It's pretty obvious the European embargo isn't doing any good."

"Probably because it's not the like it's the Romanian flu, Uncle Jack. You can't blockade *air*. I don't even think it really started there. Practically every culture has vampire legends."

Mom quirked her eyebrow at me.

"Come on, Mom. There's like *nothing* left to do but read. I'm not stupid."

"Well, Scout," continued Uncle Jack in a skeevy isn't-it-cute-how-you-can-talk-like-a-grown-up voice. "You don't see people here detaching their heads and flying around with their spines hanging out, or eating nail clippings with iron teeth, so I think it's safe to say the Slavic regions are the most likely source."

"And AIDS comes from Africa, right? Isn't it funny how nothing ever comes from us? Nothing's ever our fault, we're just *victims*."

Uncle Jack put down his fork quietly and folded his hands in his lap. He looked up at me, scowling. His was face scary-calm.

"I think that kind of back-talk qualifies as immoral conduct, young lady."

My mother froze, with her glass halfway up to her mouth. I just got up and left. Fuck that and fuck you, you know? But I could hear him as I stomped off. He wanted me to hear him. That's fine, I wanted him to hear me stomping.

"Carol, I know it's hard, but you can't get so attached. These days, kids like her are a lost cause. HRs, well, they're pretty much vampires already."

The problem is they live forever and they can't have kids. That's it, right there. That's the problem. They don't play nice with the American dream. They won't do the monkey-dance. They don't care about what kind of car they drive. They don't care about what's on TV—they know for damn sure *they're* not on TV, so why bother? Guys like Uncle Jack can't sell them anything. I mean, yeah, there's the blood thing, too, but it's not like nobody was getting killed or disappearing before they came along. Anyway, Noah says they mostly feed off each other when they're new. Blood is blood. Cow, human, deer.

They all think I don't get it, that I'm just a dumb kid who thinks vampires are cool because they all grew up reading those stupid books where some girl goes swooning over a boy vampire because he's so *deep* and *dreamy* and he lived through centuries waiting for *her*. Gag. I guess that's why that crap is banned now. No one wants their daughters getting the idea that all this could ever be hot. But guess what? They don't have body fluids. They only have blood. You do the math. And then come back when you're done throwing up. No one dates vampires.

Anyway, I'm not dumb. It's hard to be dumb when half your friends only come out at night. I get it. Pretty soon they'll outnumber us.

And then, pretty soon after that, it'll be all of us.

Noah and I went to the park most nights. Nobody gave us any shit there— no kids play in parks anymore, anyway. It's just empty. And it was so hot that summer, I couldn't stand being inside. Even at night, I could hardly breathe.

One time Noah brought Emmy along. I wasn't freaked or anything. I knew they weren't dating anymore. Gossip knows no species, you know?

I guess it must be pretty lonely to hang out with a human girl all the time and explain your business to her. They sat in the tire swing together and kind of draped their arms and legs all over each other. They didn't make out or anything, they just sat there, touching.

"Do… you guys need some time alone?" I asked. Okay, I was a little freaked.

"It's just something we do, Scout," sighed Emmy. "Share ambient heat. It's cold."

"Are you kidding? It's like ninety degrees."

"Not for us," Emmy said patiently.

"It's not just that, you know," added Noah. "Ever seen pictures of wolf pups? How they all pile together? Well, you know, some days, a bunch of us just sleep that way. It's… comforting."

I plunked down on one of those plastic dragons that bounce back and forth on a big spring. I bounced it a couple of times. I didn't know what to say.

"So what are you guys gonna do in the fall?"

They just looked at each other, kind of sheepish.

Noah moved his leg over Emmy's. It was just about the least sexual thing I've ever seen. "We were thinking we might go to Canada. Lots of us are going. There's jobs up there. On, like, fishing boats and stuff. In Hudson Bay. The nights… are really long. It's safer. There's whole towns that are just ours. Communities. And, well. You probably heard, about Aidan?"

Aidan's the kid from group who thinks he's Van Helsing. Emmy sniffed a little and sucked on her cigarette.

"Well, you know, he was kind of seeing Bethany?"

"*What?* Bethany turned like a year ago! Why would he even touch her?"

They shrugged, identically.

"So they were messing around in back of his truck and all of the sudden he just fucking killed her," Noah whispered, like he didn't really believe it. "She trusted him. I mean god, he let her *feed* off him! That's like… I don't know how to explain it so you'll understand, Scout. That's serious shit with us. It's way more intimate than screwing. It's a *pact*. A promise."

Emmy and I glanced at each other, but we didn't say anything. Some things you don't want to say.

Noah's voice cracked. "And he put a piece of his dad's fence through her heart. And they're not even going to arrest him, Scout. He got a *fine*. Disposal of Hazardous Materials Without Supervision."

"It seems like a good time to clear out," said Emmy softly. Her eyes flashed a little in the dark, like a cat's.

"You could come with us," Noah said, trying to sound nonchalant. "I bet you've never even seen snow."

Well, you know what he meant by that.

"I have a scholarship. I'm gonna be a teacher. Teach little kids to do math and stuff."

Noah sighed. "Scout, why?"

"Because I have to do something."

Whenever people have more than five seconds to talk about this, they always come around to the same thing.

Why did it happen? Where did it start?

You know that TV show you used to like? And somewhere around the third season something so awesome and fucked up happened and you just had to know the answer to the mystery, who killed sorority girl whoever or how that guy could come back from the dead? You stayed up all night online looking for clues and spoilers, and still, you had to wait all summer to find out? And you were pretty sure the solution would be disappointing, but you wanted it *so bad* anyway? And, oh, man, *everyone* had a theory.

It's like that. They all want to act like it's a matter of national security and we all *have* to know, but seriously, we're way past it mattering. It's just... wanting the whole story. Wanting to flip to the end and know everything.

You want to know what I think? There were always vampires. We know that, now. There's still about ten of them who've been around since before Napoleon or whatever. They're in this facility in Nebraska and sometimes somebody gets worked up about their civil rights, but not so much anymore. But something happened and all of the sudden, there were HRs and lists of common causes and clean camps and Uncle Jack's billboards everywhere and Bethany lying dead in the back of a truck and oh, god, they always told us PCP makes you think you can fly, and I'll never play soccer again and at the bottom of it all there's always Emmy's mouth on me in the dark, and the sound of her jaw moving. All of the sudden. One day to the next, and everything changes. Like puberty. One day you're playing with an EZ Bake and the next day you have breasts and everyone's looking at you differently and you're bleeding, but it's a secret you can't tell anyone. You didn't know it was coming. You didn't know there was another world on the other side of that bloody fucking mess between your legs just waiting to happen to you.

You want to know what I think? I think I aced my bio test. I think in any sufficiently diverse population, mutation always occurs. And if the new adaptation is more viable, well, all those white butterflies swimming in the London soot, they start turning black, one by one by one.

See? I'm not dumb. Maybe I used to be. Maybe before, when it couldn't hurt you to be dumb. Because I know I used to be someone else. I remember her. I used to be someone pretty. Someone good with kids. Someone who knew how to kick a ball really well and that was just about it. But I adapted. That's what you do, when you're a monkey and the tree branches are just a little further off this season than they were last. Anyway, it doesn't really matter. If it makes you feel better to think God hates us or that some mutation of porphyria went airborne or that in the quantum sense our own cultural memes were always just echoes of alternate matrices and sometimes, just sometimes, there's some pretty deranged crossover or that the Bulgarian revolution flooded other countries with infected refugees? Knock yourself out. But there's no reason. Why did little Ana Cruz turn as fast as you could look twice at her and I've been waiting all summer and hanging out in the dark with Emmy and Noah and I'm fine, when I have way more factors than she did? Doesn't matter. It's all random. It doesn't mean you're a bad person or a good person. It just means you're quick or you're slow.

I went down to Narragansett Park after sunset. The sky was still a little light, all messy red smeary clouds. I'd say it was the color of blood, but you know, everything makes me think of blood these days. Anyway, it was light enough that I could see them before I even turned into the parking lot. Noah and Emmy, shadows on the swing set. I walked up and Noah disentangled himself from her.

"I brought you a present," he said. He reached down into his backpack and pulled out a soccer ball.

I smiled something *huge*. He dropped it between us and kicked it over. I slapped it back, lightly, with the side of my foot, towards Emmy. She grinned and shoved her bangs out of her face. It felt really nice to kick that stupid ball. My throat got all thick, just looking at it shine under the streetlight. Emmy knocked it hard, up over my head, out onto the wet grass and we all took off after it, laughing. We booted it back and forth, that awesome sound, that *amazing* sound of the ball smacking against a sneaker thumping between us like a heartbeat and the grass all long and uncut under our feet and the bleeding, bleeding sky and I thought: *this is it. This is my last night alive.*

I kicked the ball as hard as I could. It soared up into the air and Noah caught it, in his hands, like a goalie. He looked at me, still holding up the ball like an idiot, and he was crying. They cry blood. It doesn't look nice. They look like monsters when they cry.

"So," I said. "Hudson Bay."

ACKNOWLEDGMENTS

"Learning Curve" © 2010 Kelley Armstrong. First publication: *Evolve: Vampire Stories of the New Undead*, ed. Nancy Kilpatrick (Edge Science Fiction & Fantasy Publishing, 2010.)

"Needles" © 2011 Elizabeth Bear. First publication: *Blood and Other Cravings*, ed. Ellen Datlow (Tor, 2011).

"The Coldest Girl in Coldtown" © 2009 Holly Black. First publication: *The Eternal Kiss: 13 Vampire Tales of Blood and Desire*, ed. Trisha Telep (Running Press Kids).

"The Power and the Passion" © 1989 Pat Cadigan. First publication: *Patterns* (Ursus Imprints).

"Vampire King of the Goth Chicks" © 1998 Nancy A. Collins. First publication:. *Cemetery Dance #28*, May 1998.

"Where the Vampires Live" © 2010 Storm Constantine. First publication: *The Bitten Word*, ed. Ian Whates (NewCon Press, 2010).

"Chicago 1927" © 2000 Jewelle Gomez. First publication: *Dark Matter: A Century of Speculative Fiction from the African Diaspora*, ed. Sheree R. Thomas (Warner Books, 2000).

"Selling Houses" © 2006 Laurell K. Hamilton. First publication: *Strange Candy* (Berkley Books, 2006).

"From the Teeth of Strange Children" © 2011 Lisa L. Hannett. First publication: *Bluegrass Symphony* (Ticonderoga Publications, 2011).

"Tacky" © 2006 Charlaine Harris. First publication: *My Big Fat Supernatural Wedding*, ed. P. N. Elrod (St. Martins Griffin, 2006).

"Blood Freak" © 1997 Nancy Holder. First publication: *The Mammoth Book of Dracula:Vampire Tales for the New Millennium*, ed. Stephen Jones (Robinson, 1997).

ABOUT THE EDITOR

Paula Guran edits the annual Year's Best Dark Fantasy and Horror series as well as a growing number of other anthologies. She is senior editor for Prime Books and earlier edited the Juno fantasy imprint from its small press inception through its incarnation as an imprint of Pocket Books. In an previous life she produced weekly email newsletter *DarkEcho* (winning two Stokers, an IHG award, and a World Fantasy Award nomination), edited magazine *Horror Garage* (earning another IHG and a second World Fantasy nomination), and has contributed reviews, interviews, and articles to numerous professional publications. It is easy to find her online through paulaguran.com, Twitter, Facebook, and elsewhere. The mother of four, mother-in-law of two, and grandmother of one, Guran lives in Akron, Ohio. She has, to her knowledge, never met a vampire.